alone in
the dark

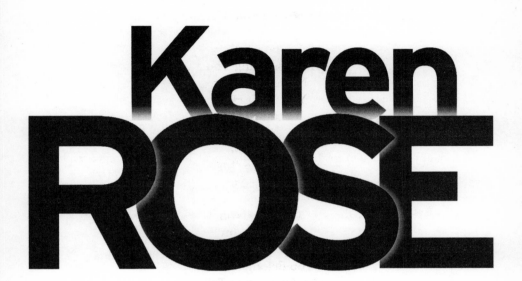

Karen ROSE

alone in the dark

headline

First published in 2015 by
HEADLINE PUBLISHING GROUP

1

Cataloguing in Publication Data is available from the British Library

Hardback ISBN 978 0 7553 9000 7
Trade Paperback ISBN 978 0 7553 9001 4

Typeset in Palatino by Avon DataSet Ltd, Bidford-on-Avon, Warwickshire

Printed and bound in Great Britain by Clays Ltd, St Ives plc

MIX
Paper from
responsible sources
FSC
www.fsc.org   FSC® C104740

Headline's policy is to use papers that are natural, renewable and recyclable
products and made from well-managed forests and other controlled sources.
The logging and manufacturing processes are expected to conform to the
environmental regulations of the country of origin.

HEADLINE PUBLISHING GROUP
An Hachette UK Company
Carmelite House
50 Victoria Embankment
London EC4Y 0DZ

www.headline.co.uk
www.hachette.co.uk

To the Starfish – Cheryl, Chris, Kathy, Susan, and Sheila. Thank you for the hours and hours of friendship, support, and – of course – the word counts!

And to Martin. I love you.

Acknowledgments

Linda Hurtado for insight into the character of my journalist hero. (Batman lives.)

Dr. Marc Conterato for always having an answer when I say, 'I need an injury that does [fill in the blank].'

Kay Conterato, Mandy Kersey, Sonie Lasker, Terri Bolyard, and my husband, Martin, for always being there when I get stuck.

The Starfish for keeping me disciplined and on track!

Mike Magowan for answering my questions about firearms.

Tory and Kirk Smith for providing the most comfortable working environment I could ask for! The words simply poured out.

Caitlin Ellis for keeping me stocked with jugs of tea and microwave meals. And cookies.

The Urban Institute for their in-depth and startling exposé on the victimization process of human trafficking in the United States. I will be forever changed having read this report.

As always, all mistakes are my own.

Prologue

Cincinnati, Ohio
Tuesday 4 August, 2.45 A.M.

Where is he? He promised he'd be here.

Controlling her panic, Tala looked around, quick, furtive glances. All she saw were the neighborhood residents, going about their business. Of course, at this time of night, very little of their business was good.

Nobody noticed her. Nobody had followed her. She hoped.

She shrank back into the shadows, deciding to give him another minute. She had to get back before they discovered she'd slipped away. If they hadn't already.

And if they had . . . her life was over. Maybe literally. And not only *her* life. She'd risked the lives of every member of her family too. If she were caught, all of their lives would be forfeit. Yet she'd risked it. Because of the baby.

Everything she did was for that little bundle, who smiled and cooed because she wasn't yet old enough to know how bad the world really was. Tala would sell her soul to keep the baby safe, to keep her from being sucked into this hell – as Tala had been when she was only fourteen years old. That had been three years ago. Three years that had aged her a lifetime. Three years that had stolen the light from her mother's eyes and turned her proud father into a shell of a man. Her parents were frozen, powerless, because they feared for their children. Tala understood that. But she also understood that things couldn't continue as they were. So she'd bided her time, waiting for the perfect moment.

This was about as perfect a moment as she was going to get. *Please come. Please.*

If he didn't come, it would all have been for nothing.

A footstep had her spinning around, her eyes frantically searching the darkness as her pounding heart began to race. A man approached, a large

1

man. Tala's fists tightened and she shifted her weight, preparing to flee in the event it was not the man she expected.

His step was slow. Careful. His hands lifted, palms out. 'It's me. I won't hurt you.'

Her heart settled. He had the most beautiful voice. It had been what had drawn her to begin with. She'd heard him singing quietly, sitting by the pond in the park where she was allowed to walk the ridiculous dog whose diamond-studded collar would have fed her family for a year. His voice had been so sweet, it had made her want to weep.

And she had. She'd stood that day listening, the tears streaming down her cheeks. Later, she'd paid for that stolen concert. She'd paid dearly. Still, she'd stopped to listen again when she walked the dog and saw him at the pond. She'd stopped every night for a week. Because that, like this, had been worth the risk. She'd been caught a second time a few nights before. Punished even more viciously.

Still . . . she hadn't been able to help herself. His song had drawn her, making her reckless. But even as her heart sang mournfully along with him, even when he'd turned to see her standing there, tightly clenching the ridiculous dog's leash in her fist, even when he'd asked her why she cried . . .

She hadn't said a word. Not until today.

She hoped she wasn't making the biggest mistake of her life. Because she was putting her life and the lives of everyone she loved in his hands.

'Yes,' she whispered. 'I'm here.'

He came closer, his face still in the shadows. 'I'm Marcus,' he said simply. 'Tell me why you cry.'

Marcus. She liked his name. Trusted his voice. But now that she was with him, her tongue seemed to be tied in knots. The secret she'd kept for so long . . . it was stuck deep within her. The words would not come. She backed away. 'I'm sorry. I . . . can't.'

'Don't go. Please.' He took a step closer, keeping his hands in front of him where she could see them. 'What's your name?'

She swallowed hard. 'Tala.'

His lips curved encouragingly. 'It's a pretty name. Why do you cry, Tala?'

'Why do you?' Because he had been. She'd seen his tears when he thought no one was watching.

His faint smile faded. 'I lost my brother. He was murdered. He was only seventeen.'

She swallowed hard. 'My age.'

He nodded. 'Will you let me help you, Tala?'

2

'I . . . I can't pay you.'

He shook his head. 'I don't need your money. I don't want it.'

Oh, she thought, suddenly realizing what he did want. Dread overwhelmed her and she took another step back. Then she stopped, lifted her chin. Made her lips curve in what she knew to be a sensuous way. She reached for the waistband of his black jeans, steeling her voice to be as sexy as she could make it. 'I understand,' she purred. 'I can make you feel good.'

He blinked, looking shocked. Then horrified. *'No.'* He took a giant step back. 'Stop. You don't understand. That's not what I want. I don't want anything from you. I just want to help you.'

Tala's hands dropped to her sides. 'Why? Why would you help me? I'm no one.'

He shook his head again, slowly. Sadly. 'Everyone is someone,' he murmured, then exhaled. 'Why do you cry, Tala?'

His voice dipped deep, touched her soul. Made her eyes fill with hot tears. 'It's dangerous,' she whispered. 'They're dangerous. My family will die if I'm found here.'

His dark brows knit together. 'Who are you afraid of?'

'The man. His wife. They . . .' She averted her eyes, ashamed. 'They own us.'

Marcus shifted, jaw clenching, eyes narrowing. 'How? Who?'

At the edge of her vision she saw the glint of moonlight on metal – but she was a split second too late. The flash of fire, the boom of thunder, the burning agony in her stomach, the scrape of asphalt on her face . . .

'Tala!' Marcus was shouting, but his voice was far away. So far away. 'Don't die, dammit. Don't you dare die.'

She didn't want to die. She hadn't yet lived. Her family . . . She needed him to save her family. She opened her mouth to tell him so. 'Help Mala . . .' Her mouth moved, but no sound came out. There was not enough air to carry her voice. *Say it. Tell him.* She forced herself to inhale, forced the word out in an agonized huff. 'Malaya.'

And then a second burst of thunder tore the air, followed by the shock of a great weight crushing her. *Marcus.* He'd been shot too. Suddenly she could no longer draw even the shallowest breath.

I'm going to die. Her family was going to die. And the man called Marcus . . . he'd only wanted to help her. But now he was going to die too.

One

Cincinnati, Ohio
Tuesday 4 August, 2.49 A.M.

Detective Scarlett Bishop left her jacket in her car on purpose. Partly because it was too damned hot and sticky to even consider wearing a stitch more clothing than was absolutely necessary. But mostly so that the weapon holstered under her arm – the Glock she normally kept concealed under a jacket – would be readily seen.

She wasn't in the mood for any shit tonight.

Taking a look around, she frowned at the sight of the nearly deserted street. On any given night, this was where dealers and prostitutes peddled their wares. But nobody was peddling anything tonight, which made Scarlett uneasy. Something had sent them scurrying into their hidey-holes, and whatever that something had been, it wasn't likely to have been good.

There was no evidence of the man who'd called her here – asking her to come alone. Normally she would have been suspicious enough to bring backup. But the man's voice . . . She would admit this to no one but herself, but hearing his voice again after so many months had shaken her soundly. The number on her cell phone's caller ID was unfamiliar, but she'd never forget his voice, no matter how long she lived. When she'd heard it again on the phone tonight, it had stirred her from a sound sleep to full alertness. Nine months had passed without a single spoken word between them. And why would there have been? Her presence would bring him and his family only pain, remind them of their loss.

But tonight he'd said, 'Can you meet me? Alone? Please. As soon as humanly possible.'

'Why?' she'd asked.

'It's . . . important.'

'All right,' she'd said. 'Where?' But he'd already hung up. A second later, a text had popped up, specifying this street corner.

The last time he'd called her out of the blue, his information had led her to four dead bodies. So, without hesitation, she'd done as he'd asked. But now he wasn't here.

The only visible signs of life on the street were the two homeless people eyeing her with unabashed interest from their spot on the stoop of the boarded-up building nearest to where she stood. She took two bottles of water from the trunk of her car, conscious of three other people peeking out from the windows of the building across the street. She handed a bottle to each of the two elderly people tucked up against the building for the night, their belongings in a shared shopping cart. Tommy and Edna were regulars on this corner. She'd known them for years.

'It's hot,' Scarlett said quietly.

'A real scorcher,' Tommy agreed, his teeth flashing white against his dark skin as he struggled with the bottle's cap, crowing when he twisted it off. 'Whatchu doin' here this time of night, Miss Scarlett?' he asked, exaggerating his deep drawl as he said her name.

'Tommy,' Scarlett chided gently, glancing up and down the street. Still no sign of her caller. 'Whatchu doin' out here in this heat? You know it's not good for your heart.'

Tommy sighed dramatically. 'My heart's done for already. It got all trampled on by you, Miss Scarlett, when I asked you to marry me for the very last time.'

Scarlett's lips curved. Tommy was a rascal, but she genuinely liked him. 'If I'd said yes, that really would be bad for your heart. You couldn't handle me.'

Tommy's laugh was raspy from a lifetime of smoking. 'You're right 'bout that.' He lifted a finger in warning. 'And don't be telling me to go to the Meadow. I been there three times this week. That pretty Dr Dani says I'm right as rain.'

The seventy-year-old woman next to him snorted. Edna had lived on the streets of Cincinnati for as long as Scarlett had been a cop. 'He's full of shit, that one is, but he's telling the truth about the Meadow. He did go this week. Once.'

Scarlett lifted her brows. 'And did Dr Dani say he was right as rain?'

Edna shrugged. 'Acid rain, maybe.'

The Meadow was the local shelter, and 'that pretty Dr Dani' was Danika Novak, ER doc and sister of Scarlett's partner, Deacon. Dani volunteered most of her free hours to the shelter, and had roped most of their circle of friends into helping her, Scarlett included.

Scarlett shook her head, but didn't push. It wouldn't do any good. She'd found permanent housing for both Edna and Tommy a couple of times over the years, but they always came back to the street. Which was bad for their health but, at times, beneficial to Scarlett's investigations. The two were a reliable source of information about the neighborhood.

She looked around again, but there was still no sign of the man she'd come to meet. 'Have you two heard any trouble tonight?'

Edna hid her water bottle in the deep pocket of the smock she never seemed to be without, then pointed to her left. 'You wanna look maybe three alleys down that way, honey. Gunshots. Three of 'em.'

Scarlett's heart stuttered. 'Why didn't you say so before?' she demanded.

'Because you didn't ask,' Edna said with a shrug.

'Gunshots happen 'round here,' Tommy added. 'We got to the point where we don't pay them no nevermind unless they're shootin' at us.'

Scarlett shoved her temper down. 'When was this?'

'A few minutes ago,' Tommy said, 'but I don't know 'xactly when. Don't got no watch,' he added in a yell, because Scarlett had already started to run, her dread building.

Her phone had rung thirteen minutes ago. If he'd been shot, he could be dead by now. He couldn't be dead. *Please don't let him be dead.*

She skidded to a stop when she got to the alley, her vision drawn first to the motionless body on the ground. *It isn't him.* The victim was far too small to be him.

She drew her weapon with one hand, holding her Maglite in the other as she cautiously approached. She swept the beam of her light over the victim, a female who appeared to be of Asian descent. Who was she? And where was *he*? Another sweep of her light up and down the alley revealed no one else.

Scarlett crouched next to the body, her heart sinking. The victim, who appeared to be in her late teens, lay on her back, dark brown eyes staring up at the sky, wide and unseeing. *So young,* she thought. Setting the Maglite on the asphalt so that it illuminated the victim's face, she pulled a glove on to her left hand, keeping her weapon firmly gripped in her right.

Pressing her fingers to the victim's throat, Scarlett found no pulse, which was no surprise. But the young woman hadn't been dead long. Her skin was still warm.

Her lower torso was bare, her white polo shirt cut away to just below her breasts.

A bullet had entered three inches below her sternum, but based on the amount of blood on and around the body, it had probably not been immediately fatal. Cause of death was far more likely to have been the small hole in the victim's left temple. The exit wound behind her right ear was the size of Scarlett's fist.

The girl had been pretty before someone had taken out a chunk of her head.

Not him. It couldn't have been him. Scarlett couldn't believe it. *You just don't want to believe it.* Which was fair enough, she supposed. Where was he?

Picking up the flashlight, she ran the beam over the body. Blood had been wiped from the exposed skin of the victim's midriff, the balled-up and blood-soaked remnant of her torn shirt lying on the ground next to her hip. Someone had attempted first aid.

'He tried to save you,' Scarlett murmured aloud.

'Tried. Failed.'

Her head jerked up. He was here. The man who'd dominated her thoughts, her dreams. For months. The man who once again had called her out of the blue to the scene of a homicide.

Marcus O'Bannion.

The voice she remembered so well had come from behind her, deep in the shadows. Holding her weapon at her side, she rose, turned and aimed the Maglite at the alley wall, illuminating long legs, a broad torso and wide shoulders, all clad in black. He leaned against the brick, shoulder to the wall, arms crossed over his chest. He was looking down, his face obscured by a dark baseball cap.

He lifted his head and her heart stuttered again. His skin was ashen, his expression grim. He didn't blink at the bright light.

She hadn't heard him approach, wouldn't even have known he was there had he not spoken. He'd been quiet in a way that few men could manage. He'd been army at one time, she knew. Now she also knew that whatever he'd done for Uncle Sam, he'd been very well trained.

'Where did you come from?' Scarlett managed to ask calmly, despite the fact that her pulse pounded wildly in her throat.

'The street,' he said, indicating the way she'd come with a jerk of his head.

'Why?'

'I was chasing the guy who did that,' he said flatly, nodding at the body with another jerking motion.

He hadn't moved his arms, not once. Scarlett crossed the alley, stopping a foot from where he stood. Now she could see that his shoulders were hunched, his back curved unnaturally. She could also see the little lines bracketing his mouth. He was in pain. 'Were you hit too?' she asked.

'No. Not like her.'

'What happened?'

He still didn't blink. Kept his gaze fixed on the broken young body. 'You got here fast.'

'I don't live far.'

He met her gaze then and she drew a breath, instantly riveted. Just like the first time she'd seen him. He'd been on a stretcher that day, his wounds nearly fatal. Wounds he'd received saving the life of a woman he didn't even know. But his eyes – and his voice – had made everything inside her wake up and take notice. Tonight it was the same.

'I know,' he said quietly.

She blinked, surprised. They'd never discussed anything as personal as her home address during their brief conversations in his hospital room all those months ago. 'What happened, Marcus? Who is she?'

'I don't know, exactly. Her name is Tala.'

'Tala what?'

'I don't know. We didn't get that far.' He tilted his head, listening as the sound of sirens filled the air. 'Finally,' he muttered.

'You called them?'

'Five minutes ago. She was still alive then.' Pushing away from the wall, he straightened carefully, and Scarlett was surprised once again. At five-ten in her bare feet, she rarely had to look up to meet a man's eyes, but she had to lift her chin to meet his.

She realized that she'd never seen him standing. She'd seen him lying down, first on a stretcher and then in a hospital bed – and then sitting in a wheelchair at his brother's funeral.

The sirens were getting louder. 'Quickly,' she said. 'Tell me what happened.'

'She asked me to meet her.'

Scarlett's brows shot up. 'She asked you to meet her? In the middle of the night? *Here?*'

His nod was curt. 'I was surprised too. This isn't where I'd met her in the past.'

Okay . . . 'Where had you been meeting her, Marcus?' she asked softly. Warily.

His eyes narrowed dangerously, his jaw clenching. 'It wasn't like that.'

She'd angered him with her insinuation. Too damn bad. He was a grown man meeting a young woman in the dead of night. A young woman who was now dead. 'Then tell me what it *was* like.'

'I'd see her when she walked her dog in the park near my place. She was always crying. I asked her what was wrong – several times – but she never said a single word, even though I could tell she desperately wanted to. Then tonight I got a text, asking me to meet her at the same corner I texted to you. I called you because I thought she might need . . . protection. I knew you would help her.'

She struggled not to let his words affect her. 'But things obviously went very wrong.'

'Obviously,' he said bitterly. 'She wasn't at the corner, but I saw her peeking out from this alley, so I followed her here. As soon as she started talking, the first bullet hit her.'

'The one in her gut.'

'Yes. I ran to the end of the alley.' He pointed to the end opposite from where Scarlett had entered. 'But the shooter was gone. I called 911, then ran back to her and tried to stop the bleeding.' His jaw clenched harder, a muscle twitching in his cheek. 'I hoped you'd get here before the cops. I was going to tell you what I knew and then leave her with you.' He hesitated. 'I figured everyone would jump to the same conclusion you just did.'

'Was she a prostitute, Marcus?' she asked levelly.

He looked her in the eye. 'I don't know. I only knew she was in trouble of some kind.'

That was the truth, Scarlett thought. But not the whole truth. He was holding something back. Something important. She wasn't sure how she knew. She just did. 'How did she know how to reach you?'

'I left her my card on the park bench. Stuck it between the wood and the iron frame.'

She frowned. 'Why did you leave it for her? Why not just give it to her?'

'Because she never came close enough. Not once. She always stayed at least twenty-five feet away.' His mouth tightened, his eyes growing dark with fury. 'And because the last time I saw her, she was limping. She was wearing sunglasses – with big frames. But not big enough to hide the bruise on her cheek.'

Scarlett got the picture. 'She was being terrorized by someone.'

'That was my take. The last time I saw her, I didn't say a word. I just held up my card, then stuck it in the bench and walked away.'

'When was that?'

'Yesterday afternoon. Around three.'

'All right. After she was shot in the stomach, you started first aid. What happened then?'

He looked away. 'I didn't hear him. He must have circled around. Came up behind me. I was talking to her, telling her to hold on, not to die. That help was coming. I wasn't paying attention.' His throat worked as he swallowed hard. 'I should have been paying attention. He shot me, then . . . her. In the head.'

Scarlett drew a careful breath. 'He shot you? Where?'

'In the back.' His lower lip curled in disdain that seemed self-targeted. 'But I'm wearing a vest.'

'A vest? Why?' she asked coolly, even as her heart thumped in relief. The size of the exit wound in the victim's head indicated a very large-caliber weapon fired at close proximity. Had Marcus not been wearing a vest, Scarlett knew she'd have come across a very different scene. 'Did you expect violence?'

'No. Not like this. Never like this. But I always wear the vest now.'

'Why?' she asked again, watching in wary fascination as twin flags of color stained his cheekbones.

'My mother made me promise.'

That Scarlett could believe. Marcus's mother had lost her youngest son nine months before and had very nearly lost Marcus too. Scarlett could understand a mother's demand for that promise.

Except . . . why would his mother believe that Marcus would be targeted again? Instincts prickling to alertness, Scarlett left the question for later. 'And then?'

'The hit knocked me flat. On top of her.' He touched his finger to his chest, then held the finger up for Scarlett's inspection. It was dark red. The black fabric of his shirt had hidden the stain. 'Hers. When I got my breath back, I pushed off her. Then I saw . . . I saw what he'd done. I tried to go after him, but by the time I got out of the alley, he was gone again. I circled the block, but everyone had scattered, including the shooter.'

'So then you came back to meet me?'

A one-shouldered shrug. 'To meet someone. Either you or the first responders.'

Who'd now arrived, a cruiser coming to a screeching halt at the far end of the alley.

Scarlett glanced at the cruiser, then looked back at Marcus's face, needing the answer to one last question before the officers arrived. 'You said you were going to leave once I got here, when she was still alive. Once she was dead, why did you come back? There was no need to continue first aid, and the shooter might have come back again. Might have realized you were still alive. Might have tried to shoot you again. Why did you come back?'

He looked down at the dead girl, his expression stark. 'I couldn't leave her alone in the dark.'

Cincinnati, Ohio
Tuesday 4 August, 2.52 A.M.

Chest heaving, he took a quick look over his shoulder, then slid into the passenger seat of the waiting car and slammed the door. *'Drive.'* He leaned into the cold air coming out of the AC vent, took in huge lungfuls as he tried to slow his breathing. If he'd run that fast on the track last year, he'd have a roomful of trophies.

Frowning, Stephanie pulled away from the curb. 'Where is she? And why are you so sweaty?'

They were moving at a damn crawl. 'Just *drive*, for God's sake.' Gripping Stephanie's knee, he shoved it down, sending the Mercedes lurching forward in a squeal of tires.

'Fuck!' Stephanie slammed on the brakes, taking them back to a crawl. 'You want to get us arrested? Where is she?'

He focused on the side mirror, watching for flashing blue lights. *I should have shot them both when I first saw them. Together.* His gut still twisted with fury. 'Back in the alley.'

'So I was right,' Stephanie said with contempt. 'I knew something was up. The bitch was two-timing us. You shouldn't have left her there all alone. God only knows what she's doing with Styx. He's butt-ugly but he's got the best shit around. He's probably got her on her back right now.'

She was on her back all right, he thought grimly. And it served her right. 'Yeah. Probably.'

Putting on the left blinker, Stephanie shot him a wary glance. 'I'd have thought you'd be more worried. Styx can't be clean. I'm betting he has every disease in the book. If she's doing him for free party Chex, he's polluting our pool as we speak.'

'We'll just have to find another place to swim,' he ground out through clenched teeth. He grabbed the wheel when Stephanie started to turn left. 'Just where the hell do you think you're going?'

Stephanie blinked. 'Back to get her. We can't just leave her here.'

'I said drive, goddammit.' He could hear the sirens now. 'The cops are coming. Get us out of here.'

Stephanie hit the brakes so hard they both pitched forward. 'The cops? What did you do?'

He met her frightened eyes with a cold, hard stare. 'She's dead. So if you don't want to go to prison, you will drive like a bat outta goddamn hell.'

'Dead?' Stephanie's mouth opened and closed like a fish. 'You killed her? You killed Tala?'

'I never said that.' He had, but he was never admitting it to anyone. 'But we'll be blamed. So get us home or so help me God, you'll end up just like her.'

Hands shaking, Stephanie obeyed, heading out of the city. 'Why did you kill her?'

'I didn't say I did.'

'So you found her there? Dead?'

'Yeah,' he lied tonelessly.

'Did Styx kill her?'

'It's possible, I suppose.'

'Oh my God. This is terrible. This is just . . . Oh God. Mom and Dad. They'll know. I'm gonna be . . . Hell. They're gonna know I took her out.' Stephanie was breathing hard, nearly hyperventilating. 'They're gonna find out. They're gonna kill me.'

'They're not going to kill you, because you are going to pull yourself together. Nobody's going to find out anything.'

'Because you say so?' Stephanie cried. 'Don't be a fool. She'll be on the news. They'll report a body on the news. My parents watch the news.'

In her current hysterical state, Stephanie was a neon sign screaming GUILTY. *Calm her down*, he thought. *Take a breath. Take the tension down.*

'So?' he asked, his tone now level. Reassuring. Convincing, even. He shrugged carelessly. 'She got out. How can they possibly know you took her unless you tell them? She was an addict. She wanted to score some blow. She crossed the wrong dealer and he blew her and her boyfriend away.'

Stephanie went still. 'Her what?'

'Her boyfriend. She was with someone, there in the alley.'

A shuddered-out breath. 'Who?'

'I don't know. Some old guy.'

'A cop?'

'Don't think so. Doesn't matter now anyway. They're both dead. Neither of them is going to say a word.'

'But what . . . ?' It was barely a whisper. 'What if he *was* a cop? If she was talking to a cop . . . maybe she was telling him everything. Maybe the cop told his partner. Maybe she told them about my family. Maybe the cops will—'

'Maybe you'd better concentrate on driving,' he interrupted, his tone still calm. Still smoothly menacing. 'We wouldn't want to have an accident.'

'No,' Stephanie whispered, and she seemed almost dazed. 'We wouldn't want that.'

She was blowing it all out of proportion. It was more likely that Tala was turning tricks in that alley and the guy was a simple john. Or maybe even a pimp. Tala was far too scared to say a word to anyone. But just in case Stephanie was even a little right . . .

Even if the dead guy wasn't a cop, if he'd told anyone about Tala there could be trouble. He needed to find out who the guy was, how the asshole had met Tala, and who he'd talked to about her.

Cincinnati, Ohio
Tuesday 4 August, 3.35 A.M.

Scarlett Bishop was watching him.

Under normal circumstances, Marcus O'Bannion might have welcomed the openly appreciative stare of a beautiful woman as he lounged, shirtless and sweaty. But these were not normal circumstances and Scarlett Bishop was no ordinary beautiful woman. She was a homicide detective.

Sitting in the back of an ambulance having his vitals taken by a paramedic was about as far from lounging as a man could get. And the detective's stare was not appreciative. It was watchful. Worried. Wary.

Because Scarlett was smart. *She should be a lot more than worried*, he thought. *She should be scared. Because I am.* Not of the fact that the bullet could very well have ended him, but because, for just a moment, he wished it had.

I'm tired. Tired of the greed and the violence and the twisted perversion going on all around him. He was tired of seeing the hopelessness in the eyes of the victims. He was tired of being too late. Because even if he could save every victim, he couldn't erase what had been done to them. Tonight he hadn't even saved the victim.

Tala was on her way to the ER, where they'd pronounce her DOA. Because she'd reached out to him for help. *I should have been paying attention. I should have kept her safe.*

He'd known she was being abused. The fear in the young woman's eyes had been real, tonight and every time he'd seen her in the park. *She trusted me. And I let her down.*

'Your pressure is normal,' the paramedic said, removing the cuff from his bare upper arm. 'So's your pulse.'

Marcus had told them that would be the case, but they hadn't listened to him, insisting on checking him out. He knew his body. Knew what it felt like when its functions weren't normal. But they were only doing their job, so he mustered a nod and a rusty 'Thanks.'

14

'You really should go in for an X-ray,' the paramedic continued. 'Just because the vest kept the bullet from piercing your skin doesn't mean it didn't do serious damage. You may have a broken rib or two.'

'I don't,' Marcus replied quietly, his focus on Bishop, who'd finally turned back to the crime scene. Starting where Tala's body had lain, she was slowly walking an outwardly spiraling circle, taking in every detail with eyes that he knew missed very little.

Abruptly she dropped into a crouch, leaning forward to check out what looked like a pile of trash swept into a crevice along the alley wall – until her black braid slid over her shoulder. Impatiently she stripped off her gloves and coiled the braid into a figure eight, fixing it to the back of her head with some elastic gizmo she pulled from the pocket of her jeans. Her movements were quick and practiced, which came as no surprise. Unpinned, the tip of her braid nearly reached the small of her back. It likely got in her way often.

It would have been more practical – not to mention safer – to have cut it long ago. It would be a major vulnerability in a hand-to-hand fight, giving her opponent an easy way to immobilize her.

It would also give her lover something to hold on to as he . . . *No. Not going there. Not today.* But his mind already had, just as it had many, many times over the past nine months.

Ruthlessly corralling his thoughts, Marcus watched her motion to the CSU photographer, pointing to the asphalt, then pull on a new pair of gloves as the man snapped a picture.

She reached into the trash and drew out something that glinted in the beam of her Maglite. A bullet casing. A big-ass bullet casing. *No wonder my back hurts so much.*

She dropped the casing into an evidence bag, then rose fluidly to continue her search of the crime scene. She was, he thought, everything he remembered. Tall and proud. Lithe and graceful. Strong, yet compassionate. *Too compassionate for her own good.* Her job was eating her alive. There were shadows in her eyes that had nothing to do with lack of sleep. He knew this because he saw the same haunted expression in the mirror.

She was haunted too. Still, she'd come when he called. Just as she'd done before.

And just as before, he'd sensed a . . . connection between them, something more than the physical attraction he hadn't even tried to deny – not in his waking thoughts or in his dreams. He wasn't sure exactly what the connection was, but he knew deep down that Scarlett Bishop would understand.

15

Understand what? he demanded bitterly. *Me. She would understand me.* The choices he'd made. The secrets he kept. The razor-fine edge that he walked. The darkness that drew him ever closer. She would understand. She might even help him.

Which was why he'd left her alone, and would continue to do so. Because as much as he yearned for the solace she might provide, he refused to drag her down with him.

Her gaze shifted from the crime scene to the man with a shock of bright white hair who'd just joined her in the alley – FBI Special Agent Deacon Novak, Scarlett's partner on the Major Case task force. Marcus actually knew Deacon better than he knew Scarlett, having met the man at a handful of social gatherings co-engineered by Marcus's stepfather and his cousin, Faith, most recently the party celebrating Faith and Deacon's engagement. Marcus had been happy for them. Deacon seemed to be a decent man.

Too decent, he thought. He couldn't see Novak approving of any of the blood-soaked fantasies of revenge that flooded his mind as a crime-scene tech placed markers on the asphalt, next to the mess that had been Tala's blood and brains.

She was only seventeen. And she'd been gunned down like an animal.

A sheet of white paper attached to a clipboard appeared in his vision, blocking his view of the carnage. 'If you're not going to let us transport you to the ER,' the paramedic said in a disapproving tone, 'you need to sign this form.'

'I've had broken ribs before. I'm just bruised,' Marcus said, glancing at the form long enough to sign it before returning his attention to Bishop. She was now walking toward him, Deacon Novak at her side.

Marcus pushed to his feet, biting back a grimace. His back throbbed like a bitch, but he had his pride. It was bad enough that he was shirtless while Scarlett and her partner were fully clothed – Deacon in a suit and tie, no less. Talking to them from a sitting position was simply not going to happen.

Scarlett met his eyes for a brief moment before turning to the paramedic. 'Well?' she asked crisply. 'What's the verdict?'

'Contusions,' the paramedic said. 'Possible broken ribs.'

She frowned. 'So why isn't he en route to the ER?'

The paramedic shrugged. 'He's refused transport.'

'Because it's only a bad bruise,' Marcus muttered. 'Can I have my shirt back?'

Her glance flicked down to his bare chest, then shot back up to his face like a rocket. 'I'm sorry. Your shirt is evidence now, along with the Kevlar vest, but my partner brought you something to wear,' she said, her tone coolly efficient.

'Marcus,' Deacon said pleasantly.

Marcus nodded once. 'Deacon,' he said in the same pleasant tone.

Deacon held out a plain black T-shirt. 'Good to see you're not dead.'

Marcus clenched his teeth against the memory of the shots fired at close range. 'Yeah,' he said bitterly. 'That would have left an even bigger mess.' He tugged the shirt over his head, managing to swallow most of a groan as fire streaked across his shoulders and down his back.

'I heard that. You need to go to the hospital,' Scarlett said firmly.

'No. I don't.' Marcus took an experimental deep breath, happy when both his lungs inflated properly. 'I've had enough of hospitals to last me a lifetime. Nothing they can do for broken ribs anyway.' He gave the medic a nod. 'But thanks for checking me out.'

'Whatever,' the paramedic said, shaking his head as he slammed the ambulance doors closed and drove away.

Then it was just the three of them at the end of the alley, standing in a little bubble of silence as CSU processed the scene fifty feet away. Scarlett and Deacon were waiting for his statement, he knew. Suddenly wearier than he'd been in months, Marcus straightened his spine, his gaze arrowing in on the patch of bloodstained asphalt. He had to be careful. He was tired, he was in pain. But most of all, he was filled with cold rage. In this state he could easily reveal more than he should.

Clear your mind. Tell them only what is relevant to catching Tala's killer. Everything else was not their business.

He cleared his throat. 'Her name was Tala. She was only seventeen.'

Cincinnati, Ohio
Tuesday 4 August, 3.45 A.M.

'Tala what?' Scarlett asked evenly, thanking God that the man had put a shirt on. Not staring at his chest had taken a sizeable portion of her concentration. Now she could focus on his words. *Now I can do my damn job.* A girl was dead. The victim deserved justice, not the half-assed efforts of a homicide detective who couldn't keep her hormones in check.

Scarlett was glad Deacon had arrived. In the moments she'd stood in the alley alone with Marcus O'Bannion, she'd lost her professional perspective. Her emotions had taken over – and a few of those emotions hadn't left her feeling proud of herself. She'd felt jealous of the dead girl, for God's sake, because he'd been meeting her. Then disappointment that he'd been

17

meeting her. All combined with a nearly obsessive refusal to believe that whatever Marcus was up to could be wrong in any way.

She believed too deeply, too blindly, that he was a good man. That he was a hero.

'She never said her last name.' Marcus didn't look at them as he spoke. He was staring at the crime scene, at the spot where the girl had died. 'I didn't get the chance to ask.'

Because the girl had been shot. As had Marcus.

'What *did* she get the chance to say?' Scarlett asked.

Marcus clenched his jaw. 'That her family was in danger. When I asked from who, she said, "The man and his wife, they own us."'

Scarlett's heart sank.

Deacon muttered a curse. 'Owned exactly how?' he asked.

'I started to ask, but that's when the first shot was fired and she collapsed. The only other words she said were "Help" and "Malaya". Then she was gone.'

'*Malaya.*' Deacon was already typing on his phone. 'She could have been talking about a place. A reference to modern-day Malaysia.'

'Or it could have been a word,' Marcus added quietly. 'Tagalog for "freedom".'

'Tagalog,' Scarlett murmured. 'A dialect of Filipino, right?' Which would make sense. The girl's ethnicity was Southeast Asian. That included the Philippines.

Marcus nodded once. 'Yes.'

Deacon glanced at him with interest. 'You speak Tagalog?'

'No. It's also a newspaper based out of Manila,' Marcus answered.

'How do you know that?' Deacon asked, more curious than suspicious.

Marcus shrugged. 'My family is in the newspaper business. My grandfather read five papers before breakfast every morning when I was a boy. He collected the front pages of papers with famous headlines. One was from the *Malaya,* on the day Marcos was exiled. I asked him what it was all about, and he told me that *malaya* meant freedom.'

'You remembered that, after all this time?' Scarlett asked. 'That was nearly thirty years ago. You couldn't have been more than four or five years old.'

Another shrug. 'I remember nearly everything he ever said. This one word was very important to him, though. He'd been in the Philippines during the war, made friends with some of the locals. They were prisoners together. In Bataan.'

As one, Scarlett and Deacon winced. 'Rough,' Scarlett murmured.

'Yeah. *Malaya* was one of the first words my grandfather learned there.'

'So what do you think Tala meant?' Scarlett asked.

'I think she wanted me to help free her family. Trouble is, I don't know where she came from. I don't know where her family is being kept.'

'Detective Bishop said you met Tala at the park,' Deacon said.

'Not exactly. I never actually *met* her until tonight. I'd only *see* her at the park. Up until tonight, it's been me asking her questions and her running away without answering.'

'Where is this park, and when did you first see her?' Deacon asked.

'Near my house. Two weeks ago. About one A.M.'

Scarlett lifted her brows in surprise. 'You go to the park at one in the morning?'

'Not normally. Normally I go mid-afternoon, but it's been so hot lately that I've been going after dark, around eleven.'

'You're a runner?' Deacon asked him.

'I was. Haven't done any running in the last nine months.'

Not since he'd nearly been killed, Scarlett thought, the events of that day seared into her memory. A bullet had pierced his lung as he'd protected an innocent young woman who'd been targeted by a sociopath. They'd nearly lost Marcus that day.

Marcus returned his attention to the crime scene. 'I have an older dog with a heavy coat,' he went on quietly. 'She has a bad heart and doesn't do well in the heat, so I walk her after dark. Two weeks ago I got tied up on a project at work and it was after one when I got home, but BB needed to be walked, so we went to the park. It was deserted, so I . . .' He hesitated, shrugged uncomfortably. 'I was sitting on a bench letting her sniff the grass when Tala came down the path with a standard poodle, all groomed in that frou-frou show-dog style. The dog's collar caught my eye before Tala did.'

'The dog had a reflective collar?' Deacon asked.

Scarlett was stuck back on 'It was deserted'. *It was deserted, so you what?* she wanted to ask. Because he was blushing again, just like he had when he admitted he'd promised his mother he'd wear Kevlar. She tabled the question for later.

Marcus shook his head. 'No. The collar was diamond-studded.'

Both Scarlett and Deacon blinked. 'Diamonds?' she repeated. 'Are you sure they weren't rhinestones? Or CZ?'

'Pretty sure. The collar had a brand tag sewn in to it – one of the exclusive jewelers in Chicago.' He gave them the name. 'When I called the store to inquire, the jeweler told me they haven't sold that model in a while. He suggested that I check eBay.'

19

Scarlett frowned. 'Why am I not surprised that you already called?'

Marcus shrugged. 'I was hoping to identify her later. At first, I was just appalled. I mean, who'd put that kind of collar on a dog? And what was a girl her age doing walking the dog at one A.M.? Alarm bells started ringing in my head, so I stood up and started to walk in the opposite direction, but . . .' He sighed. 'She was crying.'

'So you stayed?' Deacon asked carefully.

Marcus leveled him a sharp glare. 'Only long enough to ask her why she was crying and if she needed help. She just turned and ran away. I started to follow her, but BB can't run anymore. By the time I picked up the dog, the girl was gone.'

'When did you see her again?' Scarlett asked, her mind suddenly filled with the image of him cradling an old dog in his arms.

'The next night, but not as close up. I went back at one in the morning, sat on the bench and waited, but she stayed back so far that I didn't see her. But I did see her dog. She wore black, but the poodle is white, so he showed up through the trees. I called out to her, but she ran again. Then the third night, she came close enough that I could see she was crying again.'

Scarlett studied Marcus's face. He was holding something back. 'What made her come close the third night?'

He hesitated, then rolled his eyes. 'I'm not sure. Maybe because I was singing.'

Again she and Deacon blinked. 'You were singing?' she echoed. 'As in . . . a song?'

He scowled at her. 'Yes, as in a song. I was all alone the first night. Or thought I was. I sometimes sing when I'm alone. I thought if I sang again she might come closer.'

Fascinating. His blush had deepened, his shoulders hunching defensively. He thought she was going to laugh at him. Nothing could be further from the truth. She was drawn by his voice too. When he spoke, she heard music. The saddest music she'd ever heard, she'd thought the very first time she'd heard him speak. That he used that voice to make actual music was no surprise.

'I sing when I'm alone too,' she said quietly. 'Mostly because nobody wants to hear me. I take it that Tala wanted to hear you.'

The stiffness in his shoulders melted a bit. 'Yeah. I guess she did.'

'What were you singing?' Deacon asked.

His jaw tightened. 'Vince Gill. "Go Rest High On That Mountain".'

Scarlett sucked in a breath, the ache in her chest sudden and sharp. She'd

20

heard that song too many times, at too many funerals. The first funeral at which she'd heard it still haunted her nightmares.

That the most recent one still haunted Marcus was evident from the pain on his face.

'I understand,' she whispered. He met her eyes, and she could see that he believed her.

Deacon was looking at them, confused. 'I don't. What is that song?'

'It's a country song,' Scarlett said, holding Marcus's gaze. 'Vince Gill wrote it for his brother, after his brother's death. It's often played at funerals. It was played at Marcus's brother's funeral.' Her throat grew thick and she swallowed hard. 'It was a good choice.'

Marcus's eyes flickered, gratitude mixing with the pain.

Deacon let out a quiet breath. Critically wounded while taking down Marcus's brother's killer, he hadn't attended the seventeen-year-old's funeral, but he had seen the boy's dead body in its shallow grave. As had Scarlett.

As had Marcus. Scarlett wished she could have kept him from having that picture in his mind. He was clearly still grieving. Seeing his brother's body tossed into a grave like so much trash would make healing that much harder. This Scarlett knew from experience.

'I see,' Deacon said quietly. 'So Tala was drawn by the song that night. Did she speak to you then?'

Marcus shifted his body, staring at the crime scene once again, breaking their connection. 'No. She never spoke until tonight. I kept going back to the park at one A.M., hoping she'd tell me why she was so afraid. After the first few nights, I brought my guitar with me. I thought maybe she'd find me less threatening if my hands were full, but that wasn't the case. She let the dog approach close enough for me to pet it, but the closest Tala came to me was twenty-six feet.'

Twenty-six feet? Scarlett frowned, then nodded when the detail clicked in her mind. 'The length of the poodle's retractable leash.' She glanced at Deacon. 'It's the size for large dogs. I have one that I use when I walk Zat.' She returned her attention to Marcus. 'Did you see the poodle's ID tags when you petted it?'

'There was only a name tag attached to the collar – no rabies or license tags. The name tag said "Coco". Tala came to the park for seven straight nights and would stay long enough to hear me sing a song or two. On the eighth night she didn't show up, or the two nights after that, so I started going to the park during the day, all different times. We finally crossed paths again late yesterday afternoon. About twelve hours ago.'

21

'When she was bruised and limping,' Scarlett murmured.

An angry nod. 'Yeah. Someone had roughed her up. At the time, I didn't think it had anything to do with me, because I never saw anyone following her when she walked the dog. Now I think it must have been because someone knew she was meeting me. She'd be alive otherwise,' he added bitterly.

'You told Detective Bishop that you left your card on the bench,' Deacon said, 'and that Tala texted you to meet her here. Can we get the number she called from?'

Marcus handed Deacon his phone. 'She asked me not to call her, told me she was deleting the texts so she wouldn't get caught. I didn't call the number, but I did run it. It's disposable.'

Deacon frowned. 'How did you run the phone number?'

'I run my family's newspaper, Deacon,' he said mildly. 'I have all kinds of ways to get information.'

Deacon narrowed his eyes in annoyance. 'None of which you plan to tell me.'

'Of course not.'

Deacon looked like he'd argue, but decided against it. 'Fine. What else can you tell us?'

Marcus looked at Scarlett, his expression suddenly grimly uncomfortable. 'You asked me if she was a prostitute and I said I didn't know. That's true. But she was accustomed to . . . pleasing men.' He sighed. 'When I offered to help her, she said she couldn't pay me. I told her I didn't want her money. She got this desperate, revolted look on her face. Then in the blink of an eye she changed into this sultry temptress. Went for the button of my jeans. Said she could make me feel good.' His jaw hardened. 'I told her no, that I didn't want that either.'

'And then?' Scarlett asked quietly.

'She looked hopeless. Asked why I would help her. Said she was "nobody".' His shoulders sagged. 'She believed that. She also believed her family was in danger.'

'Did she mention sisters or friends?' Deacon asked. 'Do we know what kind of family she wants us to help? Are they blood relatives or simply other captives?'

Marcus shook his head. 'She only said "my family". My first thought was that the man and his wife used her for the sex trade.'

Scarlett pulled up a photo of the victim that she'd taken with her phone, showing it to Deacon. 'My first thought too,' she said.

'Young and pretty,' Deacon agreed. 'Just the type sexual slavery operations go for. How was she dressed when she walked the dog in the park? What I mean is, did it look like she was dressed for seduction? Was she on the clock, just taking a break during business hours?'

'She was wearing a polo shirt and old jeans,' he said. 'She looked like any other high-school kid.'

'Walking a dog with a diamond-studded collar,' Deacon murmured. 'Well, whoever she was protecting, whatever their relationship, they had to have been very important to her. Her "owners" trusted their hold on her enough to let her walk their dog, knowing she'd come back.'

'Did she have an accent?' Scarlett asked. 'How was her English? Did she sound like she'd been in this country for a while?'

'Her English was flawless, but she did have an accent.' Reaching behind him, Marcus pulled a dark baseball cap from the back pocket of his jeans. 'You can judge for yourself. I recorded the conversation.' A hesitant pause, followed by a shrug. 'I recorded every interaction after that first night.'

Scarlett stared at the cap, then up at his face. 'You have a microphone in your hat?'

'A camera, actually. It's hidden on the edge of the bill.'

Deacon's eyes narrowed. 'Why?'

Marcus's jaw set. 'I wanted to be able to protect myself in case I was being set up.'

Deacon took the cap, his eyes narrowing further. 'And exactly who would be setting you up, Marcus?' he asked softly.

Marcus's spine straightened, his face taking on the stony expression of a soldier preparing for an interrogation. 'I don't know.'

There was frustration in his tone, she thought. And honesty. Or maybe that was just what she wanted to hear. 'The same people that made you promise your mother you'd wear Kevlar?'

Two

*T*he same people that made you promise your mother you'd wear Kevlar?

Startled, Marcus stiffened, then one side of his mouth quirked up as he glanced down at her, grudging respect in his eyes. Scarlett Bishop didn't miss a detail. *So tread carefully here.* For her sake as well as his own. 'Maybe. And before you ask – no, I don't know who "they" are.'

'But "they" are threatening you?' Deacon asked. 'Why?'

The Fed didn't miss much either. Over the months, Marcus had come to respect the sharp eye and quick mind of his cousin Faith's fiancé. As a team, Scarlett and Deacon were scary-good investigators. Which was one of the reasons Marcus had consciously and consistently avoided them both whenever possible. 'I don't know,' he said again.

'Who else knew you would be here tonight?' Deacon asked.

Marcus frowned, startled once again. 'You think *I* was the target?'

'You were wearing Kevlar and a camera,' Deacon pointed out dryly. 'You tell me.'

Marcus hadn't even considered it, but he did now. It certainly wouldn't be the first time someone had taken a shot at him. That the bullets he'd taken last November were the first to actually require a hospital stay was pretty damn close to a miracle. He had a few projects brewing, but none were at a flashpoint, none hot enough to warrant such a physical retaliation. Past projects . . . It was possible. He'd stepped on an awful lot of toes.

'I'm a newspaper publisher,' he finally said carefully. 'My staff break stories that make people unhappy. Sometimes there are threats. Most of them are nothing to worry about. I can't think of anything right now that especially would be. I don't think I was the target tonight.'

'Unfortunately, we're going to have to be the judges of that,' Scarlett said, the softness gone from her tone. She was a cop again, her jaw hard, her eyes sharp. 'A girl is dead. If one of your "threats" is responsible, we need to know. And don't even consider telling me that you won't reveal your sources,' she snapped, interrupting him before he could do exactly that. 'You called me because you knew I'd help that girl. Don't stand in my way now.'

She was right, he had to admit. He had called her. He had involved her. 'I'll have it to you within the hour.'

'What will I get?' she asked warily.

'A list of the threats I've received.' Those he was willing to share, anyway. Some of the threats were not credible. Others had already been dealt with. Others would be far too revealing, especially to this pair of investigators. He'd pick and choose the ones that would do him no damage. 'How far back do you want me to go? Six months? A year? Five years?'

She blinked once. 'You keep a list?'

'My office manager does. Just in case.'

She glanced at Deacon. 'How far back do you think? Three years?'

Deacon shrugged. 'It's as good a place to start as any.' He turned his odd bi-colored eyes on Marcus in a cool stare. 'I'll need your gun.'

Marcus was glad he'd had the opportunity to get used to Deacon's eyes in the less stressful, more social environment of their family get-togethers. Otherwise he might have been startled into making an admission he'd regret later. They were half brown, half blue, each iris split down the middle. At first glance, the sight was unsettling. A little mesmerizing. Marcus was certain that Deacon used his eyes to the greatest advantage during interrogations.

Now, Marcus simply returned Deacon's stare without a blink. 'What makes you think I have a gun?'

Deacon rolled those odd eyes. 'Because you're wearing Kevlar and a damn camera,' he said once again. 'You're wasting my time, Marcus.'

Yes, he was, Marcus realized, and was suddenly ashamed of himself. Because as soon as he gave them his gun, they'd let him go. Scarlett would walk away to do her job. And he'd be alone again. Which was even more pathetic than it sounded in his head.

'You're right.' He dropped to one knee and removed the pocket-sized Sig from its ankle holster, then straightened his spine and placed the gun in Deacon's outstretched palm.

Deacon sniffed the barrel. 'You didn't fire tonight.'

'No. I drew my weapon, but the shooter was gone. It was fired two days ago, at the range. Your CSU guy did a gun residue test before you got here. It was negative.'

Deacon didn't blink. 'You could have worn gloves.'

'I didn't.' He ventured a glance at Scarlett, found her gaze watchful. And aware of him in a way that she probably shouldn't be. In a way that made his skin heat. In a way that had nothing to do with fury and everything to do with . . . want.

'What about your knife?' she asked, her cool tone at odds with the look in her eyes.

Caught off guard, he blinked, his brain backtracking quickly. 'My knife?'

'You cut her shirt,' she said quietly, 'when you tried to stop her bleeding. The knife you used will have her blood on it. Where is it?'

Annoyed for allowing himself to be surprised, he dug in his pocket and pulled out the folding knife he never left home without. 'I want it back,' he muttered as he dropped it into the evidence bag she held out.

She tilted the bag toward the crime-scene unit's spotlights so that she could examine the knife's hilt. 'This is very nice.' She glanced at him again. 'Army issue?'

If she knew he'd been army, she'd been checking up on him. He wondered how deep she'd dug, how much she'd learned. 'Surplus store,' he said, uttering the half-truth smoothly. The knife he'd handed over to Bishop was the same one he'd carried through combat. It had saved his life more times than he wanted to count, and he'd found himself curiously unable to part with it when his tour was up. When the time had come to turn in his gear, he'd bought a replacement of the same make to give back to the army. He'd carried the knife since the day he'd come home from the Gulf . . . just because. *Okay, fine.* It was a security blanket. He was man enough to admit that. Just barely.

He hadn't started carrying the gun until after he'd worked at the newspaper for a few months – and made a few enemies right here in Cinci. The list had grown considerably over the years, but he wouldn't undo a single deed he'd done.

Except . . . Damn, he hoped Tala had been the target. He didn't want to consider that she'd been killed because of him. He looked up, troubled. 'She was just a kid.'

Scarlett's shoulders sagged, softening her almost military stance. 'Your brother Mikhail's age,' she murmured, compassion darkening her eyes. 'I'm so sorry, Marcus.'

Meeting her gaze, he felt it again. That spark between them. That connection. 'Thank you.'

Discomfort flickered across her features a split second before her shoulders straightened and her expression grew cold and piercing. In the blink of an eye she was back to being a cop. 'We don't have any reason to hold you,' she said brusquely, 'but we're sure to have more questions. You don't have any upcoming travel planned, do you?'

Well, he thought sourly. Her allotted moment of compassion was evidently over. He opened his mouth to reply with something sarcastic, but stopped himself. He wasn't being fair. Her compassion was still there. It had always been there. He'd seen it the day she'd stood beside his hospital bed, then again at his brother's grave, even though she'd kept to the very back of the gathered crowd. He could see it now, lurking behind the piercing focus of her eyes.

She didn't want it to show and he could respect that. For now. 'No,' he answered quietly. 'I'm not planning to go anywhere.'

She gave him an assessing look. 'Because you're going to search for Tala's killer.'

He lifted a shoulder. 'I make my living digging for news, Detective.'

'Don't,' she said sharply. 'Don't go looking for the shooter or anyone else. Send me that list of people you've annoyed, and any other recordings you made of Tala in the park – as quickly as you can.' She handed him her card. 'My email is at the bottom.'

He already knew her email. He already knew almost everything about her – everything he could dig up legally from afar, that was. Well, he allowed, mostly legally. And mostly from afar. Because he'd been way too curious about this woman since he'd opened his eyes to find her standing over his hospital gurney, her gaze dark and wary. And full of respect.

He'd seen it again tonight, he realized. Respect. When he'd come back to make sure Tala's body was properly cared for. When he hadn't left the girl alone in the dark. It had been too long since he'd felt true respect for himself. He'd once done the right thing simply because it was the right thing to do. His self-respect had kept him from giving in to the ever-growing temptation to deliver his own brand of justice to the slimy, perverted sons-of-bitches responsible for making the news he dug up for a living. But his self-respect dwindled every time the slimy SOBs won, every time he failed to remove a threat from the community. Every time a child went to bed afraid because the slimy SOB still slept in the next room.

Now the only thing that stayed his hand was his fear of falling so deep into the abyss that he could never pull himself out. Delivering one's own brand of justice was a slippery slope. Marcus O'Bannion knew this from experience.

But tonight he'd seen respect in Scarlett Bishop's eyes, and suddenly he wanted to see that again. Desperately. He'd been too curious about this woman from afar for far too long. Maybe fate had finally done him a favor. Maybe Scarlett had crossed his path for a reason. Maybe she was his way back into the light. Or maybe he was just so pathetically lonely that he'd believe anything that allowed him to spend a little more time with her. *I'm okay with that too.*

'I'll go to my office straight from here.' Marcus lifted his brows, watching her face. 'If you're done with me,' he added, just mildly enough that she could take his words as either an invitation or a challenge. Either would work, for now.

Her eyes flickered for the briefest of moments before control returned. She'd drawn a breath, slow and deep, and he wondered which of the two she'd chosen. Invitation or challenge?

'You didn't say you wouldn't go looking for Tala's killer,' she stated flatly.

No, he hadn't. Nor would he make that promise, because it would be a lie. 'So . . . you're done with me?' he asked, then watched in fascination as the color rose in her cheeks.

'Goddammit,' she hissed. 'You're going to get yourself killed for real this time.'

It was possible, he supposed. It had always been possible. He turned to Deacon Novak. 'Am I free to go?' he asked formally.

Deacon blew out an annoyed sigh. 'Yes, you are free to go. Just don't get yourself killed. Faith likes your family, and I'm finally starting to feel like they might not totally hate me.'

Marcus nearly smiled. 'Maybe not totally.' Not at all, really. Deacon Novak had a charm that had thrown his family off balance, making them laugh in the midst of their grief. He had a way of making Marcus's mother, brother, and sister smile even on their very worst days, and for that Marcus would be forever grateful. Faith had been a tireless source of emotional support after Mikhail's murder, blending into the O'Bannion clan so seamlessly that it almost seemed she'd always been around. Getting close to the cousin they'd never known was the only good thing to come from the last nine months.

That, and meeting Scarlett Bishop, who was still scowling at him. 'Seeing as how you make your living digging for news, should we expect to see Tala's murder in the headline of today's *Ledger*?' she asked.

'No. Today's printed edition has already gone to press.'

'What about the online edition?' Scarlett asked, her disapproval clear.

It made him wish he could promise her anything she wanted, just to erase that look from her face. But he wouldn't lie to her. 'I guarantee

28

someone else will run with the story as soon as Tala's body hits the morgue. Wouldn't you rather we publish the truth first?'

She tilted her head slightly, her eyes gone speculative. 'How much of the truth do you intend to tell?'

'Are you asking me to hold back details, Detective?'

'Would you, if I asked?'

He should be offended. Conceptually, her request went against everything a newspaperman believed in, but Marcus was no ordinary newspaperman. He'd used the *Ledger* to punish evil ever since he'd taken the helm five years before. His investigative team followed normal news leads, but often took on special projects – exposing the lies of abusive men and women who'd managed to evade punishment by Children's Services or the courts. Men and women who'd hurt their families and would go on hurting them unless they were stopped.

His team didn't always play fair, and from time to time they'd acquired information in ways that crossed the legal lines. But they did so to protect victims. They knew they couldn't save the world, but they could positively impact their little corner of it.

Honoring Scarlett Bishop's request wouldn't be that different from his status quo. But he didn't want her to know that, so he shook his head. 'It's unlikely. It would depend on what you wanted me to hold back. I want that girl's killer found too, but I do have a responsibility to report all of the news. Not just the news you approve. What detail were you wanting to withhold?'

'The location of the park where you met, the shell casing we found, and her last words.'

It was exactly what he'd expected her to say and exactly the details he'd already planned to omit. 'That's three details.'

She ignored him. 'You may print her photo and where she was killed.'

'All that?' he drawled. 'Am I allowed to quote myself as an eyewitness?'

'That's up to you,' she said. 'I thought you might want to keep your involvement on the down-low.'

He did, but he knew it was too late for that. 'That'll be hard to do, given that I'll end up in your police report. I'll end up front-page news in my competitors' papers.'

'I can't keep you out of the report. Sorry.' She did look a little regretful, actually. 'I could lock it down, but too many people saw you here.'

'Then it's already out there,' he said mildly. 'I'll do no harm by including it.'

Regret vanished, annoyance taking its place. 'Then please make sure the photo of Tala that you use is from the portion of the video you took in the park – where she's still alive.'

Marcus frowned at her. Now he was offended. 'Do you really think I'd use a photo of her dead body, Scarlett? What kind of man do you take me for?'

'A man who makes his living selling newspapers,' she said quietly.

Touché. He glanced at Deacon. 'Give my best to Faith, will you?' He dipped his head in a nod to Scarlett. 'Detective. You'll get those files within the hour.'

Cincinnati, Ohio
Tuesday 4 August, 4.05 A.M.

Scarlett frowned as Marcus O'Bannion disappeared from view. 'Do you think he'll withhold the details?'

'I don't know,' Deacon murmured. 'Marcus is hard to read.'

That was an understatement, she thought. Just when she'd started to figure him out, he'd gone all newspaperman on her. 'He has another gun somewhere.'

Beside her, Deacon's snow-white brows lifted in a way that told her that he'd come to the same conclusion. 'Why do you think so?'

'Because there's no way he'd bring only a knife to a gunfight.'

'He had the Sig.'

'In an ankle holster that he couldn't get to that easily. The man wore Kevlar and a spy camera, for God's sake. He expected trouble. He would have brought a bigger gun that he could have had instant access to.'

'I agree, although it's only important if he fired it.'

'No GSR on his hands,' she murmured. 'But like you said, he could have worn gloves.'

'Either way, it's our word against his. Do you think he fired his other gun?'

'I don't think he shot Tala. If I did, I never would have let him walk away. But he could have fired on the shooter.' She bit at her lip. 'I don't like that he hid another gun from us.'

'Agree again.' Deacon tilted his head, watching her a little too carefully. 'Why would he?'

She glanced up at him sharply. 'You ask me like I know him. I can count on one hand the number of times I've talked to him and still have fingers left. You know him a hell of a lot better than I do.'

'But he called you tonight. Not me. Not us.'

That was true. *I knew you would help her*, he'd said. But Deacon could have helped her too. *He* could *have called us both. But he called me. Only me.* That the knowledge left her feeling warm to her toes annoyed the hell out of her. 'Because he was meeting a seventeen-year-old girl,' she snapped. 'He didn't want it to look any worse than it already did. He said he knew I'd come to help her. That's all there is.'

'All right,' Deacon said in his soothing voice, the one that grated like nails on a chalkboard. 'Whatever you say, partner.'

She gritted her teeth. 'Dammit, you know I hate it when you talk like that.'

'I know.' His sudden grin cut through her irritation. Deacon had a way of defusing her temper, helping her think more clearly. Initially it had annoyed her, but after nine months of working together, she'd come to appreciate his rare gift.

'I'm sorry,' she said, and meant it. It wasn't Deacon's fault she was out of sorts. She laid that firmly at her own feet. Being around Marcus O'Bannion never failed to leave her unsettled and . . . anxious. Scarlett hated being anxious. She drew a breath, found her center. None of this was about her anyway. This was about a seventeen-year-old girl on her way to the morgue. 'I haven't been sleeping well lately. It's left me a bit tight.'

'Uh-huh.' Deacon's expression said that she was fooling no one. 'So why did he lie about his gun?'

She replayed Marcus's words in her mind. 'He didn't lie. He said, "I drew my weapon." He never said he drew the baby gun. But if he recorded the whole thing . . .'

'His gun would be caught on his cap-cam.' Deacon shook his head. 'Although I doubt he'd have been so free with offering us the video if it had anything incriminating on it. That he didn't tell us about the other gun has me wondering why.'

She reached for the ball cap that Deacon had dropped into an evidence bag, inspecting it from all angles. *Clever little thing.* 'Does this store the video in the camera or does it feed to a drive somewhere else?' she asked, all too familiar with Deacon's penchant for gadgets.

'If the camera has storage, it's probably not big enough for more than a minute or two of video. I'd bet he sent the feed to an external drive, wirelessly.'

'What's the range?'

'Depends on how much Marcus spent on the camera. With his bucks, I'm sure it's top of the line, so maybe a few hundred feet. But he lives a couple miles away and . . .' He let the thought trail, then rolled his eyes. 'Sneaky sonofabitch had the hard drive in his car. He could have handed the whole thing over to us before he walked away, but he didn't.'

Sneaky sonofabitch indeed. Any residual warmth from Marcus's earlier trust dissipated like mist. 'He'll delete the gun part before he sends over the video, won't he?'

'Most likely. Unless he stopped recording when the bullets started flying.'

She lifted the cap so that it was level with her line of sight, squinting at the camera in the edge of the bill. 'How would he have turned this thing on and off?'

'Through his phone. But not the one he showed us. That was a throw-away.'

'I figured that one out for myself.' She sighed. 'What's your take on Marcus?'

'I don't think he shot the girl either, if that's what you're asking. I think we'll find the footage from this camera supports every word of his story about Tala. But he wasn't telling the whole truth about the enemies who'd want him dead. He was startled when I asked him if he could be the target.'

Yes, she thought, Marcus had looked startled. And dismayed. And maybe even guilty at the notion that he'd inadvertently caused the girl's death. 'That was good intuition on your part.'

Deacon shrugged. 'Reporters tend to make a lot of enemies. I know I don't like them.'

Scarlett's lips curved. Deacon had very good reasons not to like the press. His snow-white hair and the wraparound shades he wore during the daylight hours made him easy fodder for the media. The heat of the summer meant he wasn't wearing his signature black leather overcoat, but every reporter in town had captured him on film wearing the thing during the winter, so the damage was long done. Deacon Novak was larger than life, which meant the cameras were trained on him.

Better you than me. She'd been quoted by reporters in her role as a cop plenty of times. That was part of the job. But she'd once been personally involved in a news story and didn't care to repeat the experience. The very memory was enough to tie her stomach into knots.

'He's listed as the paper's publisher,' she said. 'The *Ledger* used to be second in town, after the *Enquirer*, but he's built up the readership substantially since he took over five years ago, when he came back from Iraq. Yet I've never seen his name as a byline. He's not one of the reporters going out and pestering people for a story.'

Deacon tilted his head. 'So you've checked him out pretty thoroughly, huh?'

Scarlett felt her cheeks heat. 'Yes, last year when we were looking at the O'Bannions as suspects.' Nine months ago, when they'd been trying to catch a killer. Marcus had saved a girl's life and Scarlett had desperately wanted to believe him to be the good guy he appeared. 'I wanted to know what kind of man he was.'

'And?'

'I think he's basically good, but the media do disrupt lives while they're getting the story. And rarely do they care.'

Deacon was watching her too closely, with that look in his eye that meant he was seeing far more than she wanted him to see. 'That sounds like the voice of experience talking.'

'It is.' And it would be a shame Scarlett would carry for the rest of her life. 'I had a friend back in college who died because a reporter broke a story that should have been dealt with privately. He got the big byline and my friend got a pretty angel to stand over her grave.'

'You blame the reporter for her death?'

'Partially, yes.' And partially Scarlett blamed herself. 'But ultimately I blame the sick, sadistic sonofabitch who murdered her.'

'Oh. I thought you meant she'd committed suicide.'

'No. She was killed by her ex-boyfriend, but she might have survived had that damned reporter kept his mouth shut.' *And you too, Scarlett.* She'd trusted that damned reporter, told him things far better left unsaid. *Because I was a million kinds of stupid.* 'I've wanted to see her killer pay for more than ten years, but I have to admit there were times I wanted to make the reporter pay too. His callous disregard for the consequences of his actions led to the death of an innocent woman.'

'You don't want to believe that Marcus is that kind of journalist.'

No, she didn't want to, but she wouldn't trust so blindly. Never again. Of course the proof would be in the article he printed about Tala's murder. He had the power to withhold the facts the police wouldn't have told the public. She knew his paper had cooperated in the past, but she'd never interacted with Marcus directly. 'Like I said before, Marcus isn't credited as a reporter with his paper. He owns the paper and is listed as the publisher. That opens the field to anyone impacted by any story he allowed to be printed. He is responsible for the actions of the reporters on his staff who break stories that make people unhappy.'

'So our suspect list could be anyone who blames any reporter Marcus has ever employed. That could be a big list. Luckily he keeps track of the specific threats.'

'True, but I don't think he wanted to admit that the threats to his life were credible – to us or to himself. Yet his mother made him promise to wear Kevlar, so they must have been credible to her. Which means his family – or at least his mother – knows about them too.'

'I agree. So if the killer was someone Marcus pissed off through his paper, then Marcus was the target and Tala was simply collateral damage.'

Scarlett turned, her gaze dropping to the asphalt where Tala had bled out. 'But my gut tells me this is more about Tala than Marcus. She asked him to meet her here. She was shot first. And the killer doubled back to make sure she was dead. It's more probable that Tala was the target and Marcus was collateral damage. Or a loose end. In which case, all we have to go on is her body, her first name, her last words, a shell casing, the general vicinity of where she lived, and the name of a poodle with a diamond-studded collar.'

'And the fact that a man and his wife "owned" her,' Deacon said grimly.

Scarlett considered it. 'We've closed cases starting with far less. If we're dealing with human trafficking, we'll need your Bureau contacts.' Deacon was officially on loan from the FBI to Cincinnati PD's Major Case Enforcement Squad, but he'd integrated into the group so completely that most days she forgot he was still a federal agent.

He nodded. 'I'll check with my SAC and find out who's trafficking people in this area.'

'I'll get a cleaned-up copy of Tala's face and a photo of the dog from Marcus's video files once he sends them to us. We'll start canvassing the area around the park where she and Marcus met, see if anyone remembers seeing her.'

'If she mainly walked the dog at night, that could be a problem.'

'Or a blessing. She'll be more memorable. We can also check with the area vets. A fancy dog like that will have been well cared for.'

'What about eyewitnesses on this block?'

'The dealers and hookers may have seen something, but they all scattered before I got here.' Scarlett checked her watch. 'It'll be sunrise soon, so none of them will be back till sundown tonight. Tommy and Edna may have seen something. They knew the shooting had happened in this alley. They didn't mention seeing anyone fleeing, but I didn't stick around long enough to ask that question.'

'Tommy and Edna?'

'The homeless man and woman sitting on the stoop three blocks up. I've known them for years. I'll ask them on my way out. I'll tackle ID-ing the girl as soon as I get to the office.'

'And I'll get started with the Bureau's trafficking team. Call me when Marcus sends you the video files and the list of threats.'

'As soon as they hit my inbox. See you in the office.'

Cincinnati, Ohio
Tuesday, August 4, 4.35 A.M.

'Motherfucker,' Marcus muttered as he eased his body into the chair behind his desk, glad that it was too early for anyone else to be in the office yet. The paper had gone to press at two A.M., which meant that Diesel and Cal were home snoring, and Gayle and the rest of the day shift wouldn't be in till nine.

His staff would fret, especially Gayle, his office manager. She'd been his mother's social secretary when Marcus was born, then later she'd become his nanny – his and his brothers' and sister's. She'd retired from her nanny position when Mikhail, the youngest, had hit middle school, coming to work for Marcus at the paper. But her retirement from nanny-hood never really took. Gayle tended to hover, more so even than his mother.

Both women had been driving him crazy, watching him like a hawk ever since he'd been released from the hospital nine months ago. They'd do so again when the story broke. Mentally he prepared for the hovering to commence.

He unlocked his desk drawer and pulled out the laptop he used for confidential matters. If there was anything on the Tala video – for example, the fact that he'd had another gun whose serial number had been filed off – he'd save the original on this laptop, then send a modified version to the cops.

He hadn't minded turning the Sig backup over to Scarlett this morning. It was so new he'd only fired it at the range, so even if they ran it through Ballistics, they'd come up with nothing. He didn't even mind if she knew he'd had another gun. But he had no intention of handing over his PK380. He'd had the gun for too many years. Besides, though he didn't think a ballistics check would turn up anything incriminating, he was taking no chances.

If he had to turn over a PK380, he had several others, most of which were properly registered. He'd give her one of those.

Marcus believed in keeping his privacy. Which was why he actually had several 'confidential' laptops. No one laptop held all the data on any given project, so if one happened to fall into the wrong hands, the project would be only partially compromised. And because none of his confidential laptops were listed as company assets, they couldn't be subpoenaed should he or his staff ever draw the attention of law enforcement.

Like he had this morning.

It wasn't supposed to have gone down like that. He was supposed to have handed Tala over to Scarlett Bishop and walked away, having done a good deed. Instead . . .

His hands stilled on the keyboard. Instead, an innocent young woman was dead and he had plunked himself on the cops' radar, front and center.

Why did you come back? Scarlett had asked. Why had he? Why hadn't he gotten away while the getting was good?

I couldn't leave her alone in the dark. No, he couldn't have. Even if it meant having the cops on his tail for a while. That Scarlett Bishop was one of those cops would be either boon or bane. Time would tell. Either way, he'd handle it.

So handle it. Give her the files you promised so that she can do her job.

The video of Tala would be more valuable to Scarlett's investigation than the threat list, so he connected the laptop to the hard drive he'd stored in the back of his Subaru, hoping he hadn't moved out of range during the events of the night. The camera hidden in the bill of his cap transmitted about five hundred feet, but Marcus had run around the block looking for the shooter. He found the file and clicked it open, crossing his fingers. Hopefully the camera had captured something worthwhile, something he hadn't seen with his eyes.

'What a fucking waste,' he muttered in the quiet of his office as he stared grimly at Tala's terrified face on his laptop screen, knowing that in a few seconds he'd see her die. He listened once again as she worried about her family.

He heard himself demand who she was afraid of. Heard her whispered reply: 'The man. His wife. They own us.'

And then – a split second before he heard the shot – he saw it. A flicker in her eyes. Terrified recognition.

Not only had she seen who shot her, *she'd known the shooter*.

'Sonofabitch,' he snarled, ignoring the short stab of pain in his back as he leaned forward too quickly, his gaze locked on the screen. *Please, please, let the camera have gotten something.*

The video lurched, the camera on the bill of the ball cap sweeping across the bricks of the alley in a blur as Marcus had spun to see behind him. When the picture refocused, the entrance to the alley was empty, just as he remembered. He'd begun running then, the camera jumping all over the place as he looked for the gunman – or woman – but when he got to the end of the alley, the shooter was gone.

The camera spun again as he'd turned back to see Tala lying on the asphalt, her polo shirt already soaked with blood.

'Sonofa*fucking*bitch.' The oath cracked out of the speaker as he watched himself run back to start first aid. *'Tala!'*

Marcus sat back with a sigh. The camera had picked up nothing more than his eyes had. The video would be of no use to Scarlett Bishop.

Still, he rewound and watched again, this time focusing on Tala's mouth, turning up the volume at the point where he'd started first aid, hoping the camera's microphone had picked up more words than those he'd relayed to the police.

But once again, there was nothing new. Tala hadn't said anything else, at least not loudly enough to be recorded. He disconnected the hard drive from his confidential laptop, hooked it up to his official, on-the-books office computer, and sent the video files to Scarlett Bishop as he'd promised.

He glanced at the clock. Plenty of time before Gayle arrived. He needed to check the list of threats she'd been compiling for the past few years. He didn't believe there was any chance that he'd been the target, but if Gayle found him looking at the list, she'd know something was up. More importantly, if he was still here when she arrived, she'd take one look at him and know he'd been hurt. She'd make a fuss and then the whole staff would be in his business. Worse still, she would tell his mother.

He'd always trusted Gayle to keep his secrets and she'd never betrayed him, not even once in all the years he'd known her. And he'd asked her to keep some very big secrets. But she'd made it clear from the beginning that his physical health was one area that she would not keep from his mother.

Marcus wasn't sure his mother could stand the shock of hearing he'd been shot again. She seemed to be holding on by the slimmest of threads since Mikhail's murder. Hell, even his sister Audrey had been minding her Ps and Qs. She hadn't been arrested once in nine months.

Marcus would not be the one to upset the family apple cart. Not right now. He needed a few hours' sleep, a hot shower, and an ice pack for his back before he let any of them see him. But he'd promised Scarlett Bishop the list of threats, and Marcus O'Bannion kept his promises.

Once he'd sent her the list, he'd focus on the story. He'd give it to Stone. His brother was currently between the assignments he did for the magazine he worked for – probably because he didn't want to leave the country while their mother was still so fragile. Whatever Stone's reasons for remaining local, he was available to write the story of Tala's murder.

And importantly, Stone was one of the few people Marcus trusted with all of the details. He'd make sure that Stone omitted the facts that Scarlett had requested, but his brother was a hell of an investigator. Marcus had a better chance of finding Tala's family with Stone's help.

He picked up his phone and speed-dialed Stone's cell. Not surprisingly, Stone answered on the first ring. His brother didn't sleep any more than Marcus did.

'What's up?' Stone asked, the television in the background going mute.

'I have a story I need you to cover.'

'Where? When?'

'Now. Here in the office. On your way, can you stop by my place and pick me up some clean clothes?' He didn't want to be seen going into his apartment wearing bloody jeans. 'And walk BB for me?' He shifted, the bruise on his back a reminder. 'And get the Kevlar vest from my bureau drawer. Should be second from the bottom.'

Stone was quiet for a moment. 'Um . . . why?'

'I'll tell you when you get here.' He brought up the threat list on his computer and sighed. 'You should wear a vest too. Just to be safe.'

Another pause. 'Safe from what?'

'I'll tell you when you get here,' he repeated. 'Thanks,' he added, and hung up before Stone could ask any more questions.

Marcus skimmed Gayle's list, his eyes going a little blurry, his lack of sleep starting to catch up with him. *Coffee, stat.* His brain needed to be alert so that he could catch all the threats he didn't want Scarlett or Deacon to see. If they saw certain information on this list, the two were smart enough to put two and two together and realize he was doing far more than reporting the news. He didn't want to leave any breadcrumbs leading back to him or his core staff, the handful of men and women he'd trusted enough to bring into his real business – the real reason he'd kept this newspaper alive for years after it should have died a natural death like most other city dailies across the country.

He had a feeling Scarlett would respect his real business on a conceptual level. She might not agree with his tactics, however, and her disapproval could risk the livelihood – and the freedom – of the people who trusted him as much as he trusted them.

Unfortunately, not one of those trusted people was here to make the damn coffee. He pushed to his feet to make it himself, so that he could focus on keeping his promises.

Cincinnati, Ohio
Tuesday 4 August, 4.45 A.M.

That Marcus had another gun was a given in Scarlett's mind, and the fact of it had gnawed at her all the way home from the crime scene. He'd handed over his knife and his backup pistol, but not his main gun. What else was he hiding? And why?

He makes his living with the news. That explained it all. The press was made up of a bunch of slippery weasels, lying as easily as they breathed, always angling for the big story. She'd never met a newsman or woman who cared who they hurt. Still, she found herself hoping that Marcus was different. That he was the hero she wanted him to be.

You're setting yourself up for a major disappointment. More than likely he would run Tala's story, then go on to the next, never looking back.

Scarlett downshifted as she turned on to the narrow road that ended in front of her house, creating a T with her own street. The downside of living at the top of one of the city's steepest hills was that skilled driving and a four-wheel-drive vehicle were required to make it to the top during the winter. But snow and ice were months away and her little Audi, while rather elderly, was more than ready to take on the climb.

On those rare blizzardy days, she drove her ancient Land Cruiser. Twenty-five years old and affectionately called the Tank by her and her brothers, it had been bequeathed to Scarlett by their late Grandpa Al. Too big to fit in her garage, it sat in her driveway most of the year, unused. It was a pain in the ass to park anywhere in the city and gas mileage was practically zero, but it had plowed straight through six-foot drifts in the past and Scarlett planned to keep it for another twenty-five years. Being unaffected by even the worst weather left her free to fully enjoy the benefits of living at the top of the hill – the most obvious being the killer views of both the city and the river from her upstairs windows.

That those upstairs windows enabled her to see anyone approaching by car or foot was an advantage that hadn't originally attracted her to the house but that had become something on which she relied. Being able to identify who'd come calling gave her time to transform herself into whichever Scarlett Bishop she needed to be by the time she answered the door – calm, loving, patient Scarlett-Anne for her mother, professional, not-about-to-lose-it Detective Bishop for her father, just-one-of-the-guys Scar for her brothers, or let's-drink-wine-and-gossip Scarlett for any of the very small circle of girlfriends she'd trusted with her address.

Her mother, of course, presented the most critical challenge. Scarlett had to find a way to hide the aggression and violence that churned within her, shoving it down deep so that she could maintain the calm, collected persona she'd adopted for her mom for nearly a decade. Seeing who her daughter had truly become would break her mother's heart, and Scarlett would walk over hot coals before she allowed that to happen. Jackie Bishop had suffered enough loss already. Scarlett would be damned before she added to her mother's pain.

Greeting her father required the same burying of her aggression and rage, but for a very different reason. Her dad, a decorated Cincinnati PD cop, would report her state of mind to her superiors, getting her grounded so fast her head would spin. It would kill him to do it, but he would without hesitation. *To protect me from myself. Because I'm not strong enough for the job.* Her father had once said that she wasn't tough enough to survive the stresses of the police force. That she was too emotional, her heart too tender.

So she'd spent the last ten years proving him wrong.

Only to realize that he was right. She *was* too emotional. She'd been too angry for too long. She was a powder keg ready to blow, a danger to herself and others. Which made her unfit to serve. She knew this, but she didn't know any other life. So she protected the one she'd built.

Unfortunately her entire family was very perceptive, so Scarlett had spent the last ten years hiding her true self without completely disengaging. It was an exhausting tightrope to walk. But her brother Phin had broken relations with them all, and it was killing her parents, so Scarlett walked the line.

She was a good daughter. A good sister. The favorite auntie. She was even relearning to be a good friend.

Deacon's sister, Dani, and his fiancée, Faith, had drawn Scarlett in to their circle of friends. Dani was a doctor and Faith a psychologist, and both women saw too much. Spending time with them would have been threatening enough, but their circle also included Meredith Fallon, another shrink – one of the most perceptive Scarlett had ever known.

Girls' nights were difficult, because they required Scarlett to share confidences and have actual fun while keeping up her guard. Her fledgling friendships with these women often felt like a minefield, but she had not been able to make herself back away. It had been ten long years since she'd had a true friend. Her heart seemed to soak it up, like rain falling on parched earth. She had a sudden urge to call them now and tell them that Marcus had called her tonight.

But I won't, of course. She'd kept her obsession with Marcus O'Bannion to herself for nine long months. That he'd called tonight meant nothing without that context. *It only means something if he's been obsessing about me too.* That the thought made her heart beat faster was pathetic. If he'd been interested, he would have done something about it. He would have called.

But he did call.

Scarlett frowned. Tonight's call didn't count. Tonight's call was about helping Tala. *If he'd been interested at all in* me, *he would have called months ago.*

Like you called him? the little voice in her mind asked sarcastically.

'Shut up,' she muttered aloud. But it was true. She could have called him at any time over the last nine months. Why hadn't she?

Because you're scared.

Not entirely true. 'I'm cautious,' she said, intending it to come out firmly, but she could hear the defensiveness in her own voice. *So? So what?* 'Anyone would be under the circum—'

Halfway up the hill her thoughts scattered, a weary groan escaping her lips. Another advantage to living on a steep hill was being able to see her own driveway as she approached. It should hold only the Tank, but right now it didn't. The sleek black Jag parked next to her battered old Land Cruiser filled her with a guilty dread. What the hell was he doing here anyway? It wasn't even dawn.

Like you don't know. Why does he ever come by? And how many times would she have to tell him that it was over before he stopped? She sighed heavily. She didn't want to deal with Bryan right now. It had been a long, long time since she'd wanted to deal with Bryan.

Unfortunately, she couldn't hide behind her window curtains this time. *You're going to have to talk to him.*

The last few times Bryan had stopped by uninvited in the middle of the night, she'd been home. Which he hadn't known because, after spying his Jag struggling up the hill, she'd decided against coming to the door. Having no energy to rehash the same arguments again, she'd gone back to bed and pulled the covers over her head, leaving him to sit in the driveway.

The first time he'd stayed only a few minutes. But the periods of waiting had grown longer each time. Three nights ago he'd arrived a little after two A.M. and stayed almost an hour, getting out of his car at the end to pound on her door, demanding she let him in. She hadn't fooled him. He'd known she was home. She'd been halfway down the stairs when her neighbor opened her window and shouted that she'd call the cops if Bryan didn't stop making such a racket. A minute later his engine had roared and he'd sped away, making Scarlett feel like a worm.

You are a coward, Scarlett. It was true. She'd rather deal with a psycho killer hopped up on meth than hurt the feelings of an old friend.

She made it to the top of the hill and parked behind her Land Cruiser, careful not to block the Jag's exit. She didn't want to give him any excuse to linger. She got out of her car and quietly closed the door. Her neighbor still had amazing hearing despite being eighty-five years old. Not only would Mrs Pepper wake up, but the little old lady would make sure to catch every word. By dawn's early light, the entire neighborhood would know. Her neighbors were good people, but nosy as hell. And everyone would have advice.

Still in his car, Bryan pointed at her front door, but she shook her head. The last time she'd let him in 'just for coffee', he'd refused to leave. It had been super-awkward.

Bryan got out of the Jag, slamming his door hard enough to make Scarlett's teeth clench. Staying on his side of the car, he glared at her over the car's low roof. 'Where have you—' he started, way too loudly.

'Sshh!' Scarlett pointed to the surrounding houses, all of the windows still dark. 'Do you mind?' she whispered fiercely. 'You'll wake the whole neighborhood.'

He blew out a frustrated breath. 'I'm sorry,' he whispered back. 'I was just worried.'

No, she thought. *He was just horny.* Just like every other time he stopped by. If he was here, it meant that he was 'between relationships', as he termed it, but Scarlett knew better.

Bryan Richardson was a total womanizer, moving from woman to woman with ease. He made no promises, so he told no lies. Most people thought he should have settled down long before now, but most people didn't know what Bryan had been through.

Scarlett knew, though. Because she'd gone through it right along with him. Their shared nightmare had fused them in a way that was utterly unhealthy, creating an on-again, off-again thing they'd had since college. Friends with benefits. A way to take off the edge when her physical need began to cloud her rational mind. Someone to turn to when the loneliness grew too big to bear.

That Bryan would never be her happily-ever-after any more than she would be his had never bothered Scarlett at all. Not until nine months ago, when she'd heard Marcus O'Bannion's voice for the first time, when she'd stood at his bedside in the hospital watching him fight for his life after he'd been shot while saving the life of a woman he'd never seen before.

Why? she'd asked Marcus then.

Because it was the right thing to do, he'd whispered back.

It had changed everything. And nothing at all. She was still alone and might always be. But now what she had – or had never had – with Bryan bothered her a great deal. She'd told him that they were done, that he needed to find another port in the storm, but obviously not firmly enough.

End this now. For both of your sakes.

'I'm a cop, Bryan,' she said quietly. 'Just like I've been for the past ten years. You've never worried about me in the past.'

He slowly walked around the Jag, coming to a stop an uncomfortable six inches from where she stood. 'I've worried about you every day of my life since the day I met you, but I didn't think you'd be too happy to hear it so I kept it to myself,' he said, his voice carrying a thread of tension that went beyond sexual frustration.

Something was wrong. But then again, something was always wrong with Bryan. He had issues. Jagged scars, deep inside where no one could see. *As do I.* Their shared issues had been the glue that had held their relationship together. But the glue had lost some of its stick.

'So why tell me tonight?' she asked.

He lifted his hand to stroke her cheek, but she flinched, shifting so that he touched only air. His hand dropped to his side and his mouth curved bitterly. 'Because I feel you moving away from me and I don't know why. It's been almost a year since we—'

'Hooked up,' Scarlett said flatly, because that was all it had been. 'And it's been more than a year. It's been eighteen months.' His confused frown made her sigh. 'The last time was before Julie,' she supplied dryly.

'Oh yeah.' His lips curved, but his eyes remained oddly distant. 'We had a good run, Julie and I.' His slight smile faded. 'When it was over, I came to you, but you said you weren't in the mood.'

That had been a month after she'd met Marcus. 'No, what I said was that I didn't want to hook up anymore.' Her cheeks heated at the memory of the times she'd given in and had casual sex with him. At how little she'd expected for herself. At how very reckless she'd been. 'I still don't, Bryan.'

Scarlett had turned him away that night and all the other nights he'd shown up at her door thereafter. When Bryan had tried to cajole her into changing her mind, all she could hear was Marcus's deep voice in her mind. *Because it was the right thing to do.*

Bryan's gaze dropped abruptly, then winged back up a moment later, troubled. Wounded. 'Did I do something wrong? Something to hurt you?'

Pity pricked at her heart. 'No, Bryan. You haven't done anything wrong and you haven't hurt me. You're exactly who you've always been.'

His tension draining away, he leaned in far enough to press his face into the curve of her shoulder while taking care to touch her nowhere else. He breathed in deeply, drawing in her scent. 'Then let's go upstairs,' he whispered. 'I need you tonight. It's been too long.'

She took a step back, coming up short when her ass hit her car door. Bryan remained frozen in place, his back bent, his shoulders hunched.

'I'm sorry, Bryan,' she whispered. 'I can't. I've told you this, over and over.'

'Can't or won't?' he asked harshly.

'Either. Both.'

'Why?' he asked, his whisper barely audible.

'Because even though you haven't changed, I have.'

He exhaled, dropped his chin to his chest. 'Is there someone else?'

'No,' she said honestly. *Not yet. Maybe not ever.* She drew a deep breath. 'But maybe I want there to be.'

He looked up then, eyes narrowed. 'But that isn't me.'

'No.' She smiled to soften her words. 'We both know that you're not forever material.'

'True,' he murmured. That it hadn't even seemed to occur to him to deny it made her want to cry. He straightened slowly, studying her. 'Are *you* forever material?'

Tears rose to burn her eyes, because she knew exactly what he was asking. Was she even capable of being some guy's happily-ever-after? Importantly, could she be *Marcus's* happily-ever-after? 'I don't know. I'm just as messed up as you are.'

He was quiet for a long moment and she instinctively knew he was thinking about that day, that horrible, horrible day. The day that had changed their lives so irrevocably. It might as well have been yesterday, the memory was so vividly clear. *So much blood.* In all the years she'd been a cop, she'd never yet seen another crime scene with so much blood.

She blinked, startled out of the memory by the feeling of soft fabric touching her face. Bryan held a cotton handkerchief and was using it to dry her wet cheeks. The tears in her eyes had spilled without her realizing it.

'I'm sorry,' he whispered.

She made herself smile. 'For what?'

'For not being forever material. I wish I could be. But I can't. Not even for you.'

Touched, she cupped his cheek. 'Maybe when you meet the right person it'll seem easy.'

Again his eyes narrowed, this time in discovery. 'You've met that person.' He crossed his arms over his chest, going from wistful to menacing in a heartbeat. 'Did he hurt you?'

'No. It's not like that. He's just . . .' She sighed. 'He doesn't know.'

'Then he's blind and stupid,' Bryan declared, and the wicked gleam she knew so well was back in his eyes. 'I could help you forget him,' he suggested slyly.

Scarlett shook her head, more than a little glad that the moment was over. 'I appreciate your offer to make the sacrifice,' she said. 'But the answer is still no.'

'Coffee then?' he said.

'Sorry, not now. I have a body on its way to the morgue.'

He frowned, lightly lifting the thin strap of her tank top with his pinkie before letting it snap back against her shoulder. 'You dress like this while you're on duty?'

Her cheeks heated. It was on the skimpy side as tank tops went, baring her shoulders and hugging her curves. Neither her top nor her low-riding jeans were the proper attire of a law enforcement professional. *But I didn't get dressed for work.* She'd dressed for Marcus. She thought now about the way his dark eyes had followed her as she'd processed the crime scene. He'd noticed.

'I have a jacket in the car.' A jacket she'd deliberately left off at the crime scene.

Bryan's frown didn't falter. 'I thought you were off duty today.'

Scarlett blinked, then set her jaw. 'How did you know that?'

'I called your mother last night and asked her,' he said unapologetically.

'You asked my mother?' she asked, incredulous at first, then resigned. Her mother had always had a soft spot for Bryan. 'How did my mother know?'

'She asked your father.'

Scarlett sighed. 'And of course he knew.' Her father knew nearly everything that went on in CPD, especially when it concerned the three of his seven children who'd followed in his footsteps to join the force. She tilted her head to one side, studying Bryan's face in the harsh glare of the streetlights. 'Why did you call my mom looking for me, Bryan?'

His shrug was careless. 'You'd been pushing me away. And I was . . . lonely.'

'What about Sylvia?'

'Ancient history. We broke up six months ago. Kathy followed Syl, and then there was Wendy.'

'What happened to Wendy?'

A one-shouldered shrug. 'We broke up two weeks ago.'

Scarlett lifted a brow. This was the Bryan she'd known since their

45

freshman year of college. His slew of recent visits now made sense. Had he and Wendy still been a thing, he would not be standing in Scarlett's driveway. 'So you came to me,' she said.

At least he had the good grace to look ashamed. For a second, anyway. Then he lifted his chin, his jaw taut. 'I came by a few other times last week, but you weren't home.'

The accusing way he said it made her wonder if he knew she really had been home those times too. It made her wonder how he'd known she was home the last time, when he'd banged on her front door with his fists. Because she didn't want to admit she'd been hiding under her bedcovers, she didn't ask that question. 'I work odd hours, Bryan. You know this.'

He gave her a pointed look. 'I also know when your car is parked in your garage. It smells like dirty socks.'

She let out a breath. *Damn diesel fuel.* 'I'm sorry, okay? I didn't want to hurt you.'

'Well I'm about to hurt you,' he said flatly. 'So brace yourself. I saw Trent Bracken downtown last week, eating lunch with the senior partner of Langston and Vollmer.'

Scarlett flinched, feeling like she'd been physically slapped. Then the fury hit and she had to take a deep breath to keep it contained. Trent Bracken should be on death row, not lunching with the most powerful law firm in town. 'Why?' she asked hoarsely.

Bryan's mouth twisted. 'Because they just brought him in as a junior partner. His win record in the courtroom is "legendary". That was the word the partners used in the memo they sent out to everybody in the firm.'

'Fucking bastards.' Scarlett had to take another breath, this one to keep from throwing up. 'They'd hire a murderer?'

'They would and they did,' Bryan said bitterly. 'They said his "horrific experience with the justice system" had given him a passion for "defending the rights of the innocent".'

Scarlett's knees wobbled and she leaned against her car for support. 'The innocent,' she whispered. 'Michelle was innocent. Don't they care that he killed her?' Huffing a bitter laugh, she answered her own question. 'Of course they don't. They're just like the animals who got Bracken off in the first place.' Defense attorneys looking for any possible loophole, not caring that they pushed a killer back on the streets. 'Of course they'd hire scum like him. They *are* scum like him.'

'I thought you should know in case you met him in court. I didn't want you blindsided.'

New tears had risen to burn her eyes and she blinked them away. 'So that's why you've been coming to see me? To tell me about Bracken?'

He nodded, then shrugged. 'And for sex,' he admitted.

Her chuckle was unsteady at best. 'Hell, Bryan. Go home, get some rest. Maybe you'll meet someone new tomorrow.'

'Maybe,' he said sadly. 'Who is he, Scarlett? At least tell me that.'

She frowned, still in enough shock over Bracken's new mockery of justice that it took her a second to process Bryan's question. *Oh*, she thought, and then the memory of Marcus's voice was filling her mind, soothing the frayed edges.

She wasn't willing to tell anyone yet. Not when it could, quite literally, be all in her mind. 'There isn't a "he". Not until one of us makes a move. Assuming one of us ever does.'

'If he's not dead, he'll make a move,' Bryan predicted grimly, then turned and walked back to his car. 'I guess I'll see you . . . when I see you. Next month for sure.'

Scarlett nodded, still feeling sick. 'For sure.' When Michelle's friends would gather by her grave on the anniversary of her death and remember the woman whose loss had scarred them all. She stepped out of the way as he slammed the door of his Jag and revved the engine loud enough to wake everyone on the street. Peeling out of her driveway with a squeal of tires, he set off down the hill at a speed far too high to be safe. Scarlett might have whispered a prayer for his safety . . . if she still believed in prayer. Which she had not since the moment she'd found Michelle's body in that alley, covered in blood.

The thought of bodies and alleys jerked her out of the past. *Tala*. Michelle had never gotten her justice, but Tala sure as hell would. Digging deep for the anger that had kept her going for ten long years, Scarlett straightened her spine, marched up her front steps, unlocked the door and stepped inside. As she locked it behind her, the sob she'd been holding back barreled up from her gut like a tornado, stealing her breath. Slumping against the foyer wall, she slid to the floor, burying her face against her bent knees as she rocked herself for comfort, her keening cries echoing in the empty space.

The uneven patter of claws on her newly laid hardwood floor cut through her tears, giving her a moment's warning before a sandpapery tongue licked her cheek. Choking on a wet laugh, she threw her arm around the three-legged bulldog whose life she'd saved the day she'd brought him home from the shelter. 'Hey, Zat,' she whispered, still surprised at how quickly he'd wormed his way into her heart.

She sat there with the dog for several minutes, then pushed herself to her feet and climbed the stairs to the one bathroom she'd finished remodeling. A shower, clean clothes and some coffee, and she'd be ready to start searching for Tala's identity. And her killer.

That the search might include more interactions with Marcus O'Bannion shouldn't seem like a silver lining, but it did. 'And who knows,' she murmured as she turned on the shower. 'Maybe I'll be the one to make the first move.'

Three

Cincinnati, Ohio
Tuesday 4 August, 5.15 A.M.

'You're here awful early, boss.'

Shock had Marcus jerking his gaze from his laptop to frown at the woman who leaned against his office doorframe looking sleep-rumpled, her curly hair all over the place and her clothes crushed and wrinkled.

Jill Ennis was not supposed to be here by herself. She was not one of his trusted staff. Not yet. And maybe not ever.

She'd never done anything overtly untrustworthy, and her work was impeccable, but she gave off an odd vibe that made Marcus uncomfortable, though he wasn't sure why. He would have fired her months ago, except that she was Gayle's niece, which put him in one hell of a bind. Jill's parents had died five years before, and she'd moved in with Gayle. She had graduated from high school a year ago, and Gayle had asked Marcus if he would give her a job while the girl decided what to do with her life.

Marcus had never been able to deny Gayle anything, so he'd said yes. Jill had been tasked with updating their website, and she did good work. But recently she'd started college and had taken to coming in after hours to finish her work, often having to be almost kicked out when the others went home at two A.M., when the paper went to press.

'Why are you here?' he asked, wondering what Jill had overheard.

'I was working on an ad layout for a new client and couldn't get it quite right. I fell asleep at my desk. I dreamed someone was cursing, then woke up and realized it was you. What's going on?'

Ignoring her question, Marcus refocused his attention on the list of threats that filled his computer screen. The last time he'd seen the list was more than nine months ago, and it was far longer than he remembered – with too many totally capable of taking a shot at him. Or at someone standing next to him. He couldn't give this entire list to Scarlett Bishop. She was smart enough to see patterns. To figure out that he was

49

doing a lot more than simply publishing the news.

'You wouldn't keep falling asleep at your desk if you weren't burning the candle at both ends,' he grumbled. 'I pay you well enough that you shouldn't need to go to school after working here all day.'

'You pay me far too well,' Jill said mildly. 'That's never been an issue.'

He looked up from the list. 'Then what *is* the issue? Why are you killing yourself like this? You know I don't care about any stinkin' degrees.'

Her lips curved, but it was nowhere close to a smile. 'You don't really want to know the answer to that question, Marcus.'

Startled at the anger behind her words, Marcus shoved his own irritation back down, made his voice civil. 'Try me.'

'Okay, fine.' Jill crossed her arms loosely over her chest and gave him a look that reminded him of Gayle when she'd scolded them as children.

'Your aunt could freeze me with that look when I was a kid,' he commented, leaning back in his chair, wondering what could have put that expression on Jill's face.

'I know. She said that Stone was always able to charm her out of it and into giving him cookies, but that you would always confess whatever "misdeed" you'd done.'

'That's pretty accurate,' he said. Of course there was one childhood misdeed that Marcus had never confessed to Gayle or to anyone else, partly because he was ashamed. Partly because he was worried about the impact the truth would have on his mother and Stone. But mostly because he'd only been eight years old at the time, a traumatized little boy in a situation no child should ever need to face.

He hadn't needed to confess to Gayle. She'd seen the whole thing and had kept his secret for the past twenty-seven years. Her love and care had ensured that his eight-year-old self hadn't fallen into the abyss that called to his adult self. He sat here today because Gayle had never given up on him.

Now he faced her furious niece calmly. 'But I'm not a kid, Jill, and you're not Gayle. I'm your boss.' He let the sentence hang, hoping to see some respect in her eyes. When she continued the staring contest, he sharpened his tone. 'Why don't you tell me exactly what it is that I don't want to know?'

Jill squared her shoulders. 'You're looking at the threat list. Why?'

Marcus stiffened in shock, the anger he'd been controlling for hours suddenly collapsing into an icy ball in his gut. How had she known that? He hadn't trusted her with the true mission of the paper, so he'd kept her access to sensitive information to a minimum. 'How do you even know that such a list exists?' he asked quietly.

'My aunt told me.'

Impossible. 'No, she didn't tell you, I'm sure of that.'

Gayle was the only person Marcus would ever have trusted with the task of cataloguing the threats to his life. She would never have told anyone outside their specific small circle.

'Okay, fine, Aunt Gayle didn't tell me. I hacked into her computer and figured it out for myself.' Her jaw jutted out, her gaze daring him to condemn her.

The hairs lifted on the back of his neck. Something was very wrong here. And considering he'd just witnessed a seventeen-year-old girl being gunned down in front of him, that was saying something. Jill's mild manner a few minutes before had been a facade. She was furious with him. He wondered how long she'd carried her rage.

'When?' he asked.

'The day Mikhail died.'

'Was murdered,' Marcus corrected, his words clipped. 'Mikhail was murdered.'

'Fine.' Her tone was as cold as his. 'The day Mikhail was *murdered*, I came into the office and found Aunt Gayle pale as a ghost, clutching her chest. It was her heart.'

Marcus sat straight up in his chair, his bruised back protesting the movement. But he barely felt the pain because panic had gripped him. 'What? Gayle had a heart attack?'

'Yeah. A "little" one. Not that she'd ever admit it to any of you,' she added bitterly.

Marcus closed his eyes. Gayle hadn't come to see him in the hospital the first week. He hadn't seen her until Mikhail's funeral. He hadn't asked why because he figured she'd been grieving too. She'd raised Mikhail from infancy. His murder must have cut her in two. But he'd never suspected, never even thought that she could have . . .

'Gayle had a heart attack,' he whispered, unable to find any other words.

'I believe that's what I just told you.' Jill blew out an annoyed breath. 'This is where you're supposed to say, "Why didn't she tell me?"'

He opened his eyes, met her angry gaze. Figured that on some level he deserved it. 'I don't have to ask. I already know why. Gayle puts everyone else's needs first. She always has. If you think I don't know that, you're wrong. And if you wanted me to feel guilty for not knowing she'd been sick, for expecting her to come in and work in the office afterward, then you hit the jackpot. I knew she'd be devastated by Mickey's murder, but I never once suspected it had pushed her heart over the edge.'

'It wasn't Mickey's death that pushed her over the edge. She hadn't even heard about that yet. It was you, Marcus.'

His eyebrows shot up. 'Me? She heard I'd been shot and that caused her attack?'

'No. She had her heart attack that morning, hours before you were shot. I found her clutching her chest with one hand and a piece of paper with the other. I called 911 as soon as I realized what was happening, told her to try to relax, to be still, but while I was on the phone with the operator, she closed the document she was working on and hid the piece of paper she'd been holding. All while she was gasping for breath.'

He could see it happening, which just made him feel even worse. 'So you wanted to see what she'd been working on that got her so upset. I guess I can understand that. I take it that she'd been updating this threat list.' He glanced at the screen, searching for a threat credible enough, terrible enough to send a fifty-five-year-old woman into heart failure.

'Yeah,' Jill said flatly. 'She'd been cataloguing the threats to your life, Marcus. For years.'

'I know. I asked her to.'

'I figured you must have. That's why I'm angry with you.'

'I suppose that's fair.' Because he was now angry with himself. 'I shouldn't have put that responsibility on her shoulders.'

Jill's glare could slice through steel. 'No, Marcus, you really shouldn't have. Aunt Gayle is too old to be worrying about you.'

Marcus frowned. 'Wait just a minute. Gayle isn't old. I agree that she doesn't need to be worrying about me, but she's only fifty-five. She's always been healthy.'

'Not anymore, she's not.'

New panic slithered down his spine. 'Just how bad was this heart attack?'

'Bad enough. The doctor told her that she should be retiring soon.'

'She only has to ask. She knows I'll take care of her.' He heard a note of desperation in his own voice, but he didn't care. Gayle was family, his second mother since he was old enough to remember. 'A house in Florida, a nurse to live with her . . . Whatever she wants.'

New ire sparked in Jill's eyes. 'She won't retire. She's too devoted to you and your family. And now that Mickey's gone, she doesn't feel like she can leave your mother.'

'Then I'll *tell* her that she's retiring.'

'No. You're not supposed to know, and if Gayle finds out that I told you, she'll be angry with me.'

Frustrated, Marcus looked back at his screen. 'She didn't log anything on that day, and none of the threats since then have been serious enough to worry about. Certainly nothing so dire that she had a heart attack. Did you find the paper she was holding?'

'No.'

'And she never mentioned it? If it was so terrifying that it caused her heart to jump its track, I would have thought she would have warned me at least.'

Jill shrugged. 'Maybe in all the chaos of Mickey's funeral and your hospitalization, she forgot.'

'She wouldn't just forget. Not something like that.'

Another icy glare. 'What part of *heart attack* didn't you hear, Marcus? Heaven forbid that she think about something besides you and your precious family for once – like her health.'

The temptation to snap that he was still Jill's boss burned on the tip of his tongue, but he bit it back. Because she was right. He swallowed hard. 'How long was she in the hospital?'

'Four days.'

Three of those days he'd been in ICU. 'Where?'

'Luckily not at County. With you and Stone ending up there, it would have been difficult to keep the news of Mikhail's murder from her. When I heard what had happened to Mickey, hell, what happened to all of you . . .'

'You were afraid that she'd have another heart attack.'

'Yeah, and her doctor agreed. We were able to keep her away from the news – not an easy feat with Aunt Gayle. I broke it to her three days later, with her doctor present. By then Stone was okay and you were at least out of ICU. I could assure her that you two were going to be all right, so that it wasn't all bad news.'

'She loved Mikhail,' Marcus murmured.

'I know,' Jill said, her tone softer. 'She was devastated when I told her. But her heart didn't fail again, so I was relieved.'

'Didn't she wonder why we didn't come to visit her in those first few days?'

Jill's tone hardened again. 'No. She didn't want me to tell any of you that she was ill. She made me promise to tell your mother that she'd taken a little vacation. But by the time she was stabilized, I'd gotten the news about Mikhail's murder and that you and Stone were hurt, so I didn't say anything to anyone. Nobody even asked where she was.'

'My mother did.' The words came out in an accusatory tone, which was okay because Marcus was now pissed off with Jill, and to some extent with Gayle too.

Gayle had mothered him when his own mother had fallen into such a deep depression that she hadn't been able to care for him and Stone herself. It was Gayle who'd put Band-Aids on his skinned knees and elbows, helping him with his homework and teaching him to ride a bike.

And when he was eight years old, it was Gayle who'd sat beside his bed night after night when the nightmares would wake him up – men with cold eyes and big guns, the terrified sobs of his brothers, the gunshots that somehow sounded even louder than they'd actually been. He'd woken scared and screaming for months and months to find Gayle sitting beside him, crooning soft promises of safety. Until he'd told her he'd grown out of the dreams. In reality, he'd just learned how to lie quietly in his bed, pretending to sleep. But he'd always had the assurance that if he called out to her, she would come.

She'd been there for him for almost as long as he could remember. But he hadn't been there when she'd needed him. He'd been in the hospital, true, but Gayle hadn't known that. She had denied him the opportunity to take care of her, and that stung. But he was far more upset on his mother's behalf than his own.

'My mother called her phone, looking for her,' he added harshly. 'When Gayle didn't answer, Mother sent someone to her house to find her, but there was no one home.'

Jill's chin lifted, her lips pursed thin. 'Sorry, but that wasn't my problem. Your mother had lots of people waiting on her hand and foot. She didn't need Aunt Gayle fetching and carrying for her too.'

Wow. This – Jill's contempt for his family – was the bad vibe he'd felt all along.

'My mother didn't try to find her because she needed her to fetch and carry,' he said evenly. 'She did it because she didn't want Gayle to hear about Mikhail on the news. From a stranger. She was worried because Gayle had simply vanished. Because Gayle is her friend, despite what you seem to think.'

Jill glared at him a moment longer, then looked away, her jaw still squared and angry. 'I'm sorry,' she said stiffly. 'I was trying to do right by my aunt. Working for your family has required her to sacrifice her own needs and wants too many times. Certainly more than you all deserv—' She drew a deep breath. 'More than she should have,' she amended.

More than we deserved? Marcus had never looked at it like that before. Gayle had always been there. She'd never complained, never behaved like it was a burden or a sacrifice, and he'd never questioned her presence or her motivation. She loved them. That was all he'd needed to know. But now he wondered . . .

Shit. I do not need this right now. He'd promised Scarlett Bishop the list of the people who'd made threats on his life. He owed it to Tala to find out who she'd been and where she'd been living, because despite what Deacon and Scarlett had theorized – and everything he'd just learned about his threat list – he still didn't believe the shooter had been targeting him.

The man and his wife, they own us. Discovering where Tala had lived would likely lead to her killer. *Help. Malaya.* Malaya. Freedom. She'd feared for her family. Marcus hoped it wasn't already too late to save them.

But this thing with Jill, this simmering contempt, it was important too. The young woman obviously did not like him or his family, which made Marcus wonder why she'd wanted to work for him to start with. Which made him remember how all this had begun.

Jill had known about the threat list.

'How did you know I was looking at the threat list, Jill?'

She blinked at the subject change, surprise displacing the anger in her eyes for the briefest of moments. But the surprise was quickly quashed and the anger was back. Anger and defiance . . . and fear. She was afraid of him. Yet she stood steadfast, her body language that of a soldier prepared to defend to the death.

What the hell? What the hell did she think he was going to do to her? What did she think they'd done to Gayle all these years?

'I put an alarm on the file,' she said. 'Whenever anyone opens it, I get an alert sent right to my phone. The buzz from the alert woke me up.'

He regarded her cautiously. 'You're handier with a computer than you let on when I hired you.' It made him wonder what else she'd seen in the year she'd worked for him.

She shrugged. 'I wasn't expecting you to access the file, if that makes you feel better. I was watching over my aunt. She had a heart attack when she was looking at that file. She hasn't had any issues since, but if she did, I needed to know. I caught the first heart attack in time out of sheer luck. I can't count on being that lucky twice.'

That made a certain kind of sense. 'I guess I can respect your reason.'

Her lip curled in a slight sneer. 'But?'

But . . . he didn't believe her. She was too quiet. Too careful. She'd had access to Gayle's files for nine months.

And if she's seen too much?

Gayle's niece could be a real problem.

Offering to pay her to keep her silence didn't seem like the best of ideas. He already paid her far more than the going rate for graphic designers.

You pay me too well. That's never been the issue.

So they were back to why she burned the candle at both ends, working for him all day and taking classes for her degree at night. Then sometimes, like tonight, coming back to work through the night, just to make a deadline. *Why?*

'But,' he said, 'I now realize that there is much that I don't know about you.'

She rolled her eyes. 'Jeez. Y'think?'

He ignored her sarcasm. 'I asked you why you were killing yourself for a degree and you answered by asking me why I was looking at the threat list. I don't get the connection.'

'No, I don't suppose you do. Why did you ask my aunt to catalog the threats?'

He was getting tired of her answering his questions with her own. 'I needed to keep track of them.'

'That's not a good enough reason.'

'It's all the reason I feel compelled to give you,' he said. 'I am your boss, after all.'

'Yes, you are. For now.'

He lifted a brow. 'You plan to quit?'

Anger flashed in her eyes once again. 'No, *boss*. I plan to have to find a new job when you're murdered by one of the many people you've pissed off, and most employers *do* care about "stinkin' degrees".'

Ah. The pieces fell into place, relief settling over him. 'You're worried someone on that list will kill me.'

'So are you,' she challenged. 'Otherwise you wouldn't be here looking at it and cursing. Here.' She tossed him a flash drive. 'The most recent, *complete* list.'

Reflex had him reaching out to catch the small drive, the movement sending a spear of pain through the bruise on his back.

Her eyes narrowed at the grimace he hadn't been able to control. 'Somebody got to you, didn't they?' she asked. 'You're hurt.'

Fuck. 'I'm not hurt. What do you mean, this is the most complete list?' He pointed at his screen. 'This one isn't complete?'

'No. The file you're looking at is stored on the *Ledger*'s server. That's the one that Aunt Gayle works on. She believes it's complete, for what it's worth.'

Marcus rubbed his eyes. 'What have you done, Jill?' he asked, suddenly exhausted.

'I've been intercepting the mail for the past nine months. Any letter that's just a garden-variety-I-hate-your-guts-and-you-need-to-die, I let go through. Aunt Gayle logs it in. The really vicious ones, I move to that flash drive so she doesn't see.'

His head was starting to throb. 'Why?'

'Because she loves you too much to be reading all that vitriol. It terrifies her that people want to kill you. I love *her* too much to let her sacrifice her health, so I took . . . liberties.'

'What other liberties have you taken?'

'I pay the bills and sort your mail.'

Both things Gayle was supposed to do. That didn't sound like the Gayle he knew. But the Gayle he knew had had a heart attack without telling him too. 'What did you leave for her to do?'

'She keeps your calendar, answers the phones, schedules all those fancy meetings that you hate so much, and tracks the threats against you and your team – minus the ones I remove first, of course.'

'Gayle knows about the duties you've taken on?'

'Everything but the threats. She didn't want to let me do it, but it was the only way I'd allow her to come back to work after her heart attack. She should have stayed home, but she said you needed her here since you were still recuperating from being shot.'

He closed his fist around the flash drive, not sure who he was angriest with – Gayle for keeping this from him, Jill for aiding and abetting, or himself for being so blind. 'I've been back for six months. She could have retired or quit or, heaven forbid, even told me the truth. What did she think I'd do? Fire her?' *Like that could ever happen.* 'I'd cut out my own tongue before I'd even raise my voice to her.'

Jill's lips curved, the small smile seeming genuine. 'I know that. That's why I've let this go on so long. She believes that you still need her. That you're still "not yourself" since Mikhail died. Maybe that's true, maybe it's not. I don't know. But I do know that Aunt Gayle needs to be needed. And I give her what she needs.'

Marcus found his anger draining away. Jill was right about Gayle. The woman did need to be needed, and he and his family had probably taken advantage of that more times than he wanted to consider over the years, without even realizing it.

Opening his fist, he glanced down at the flash drive before lifting his eyes to Jill's face. 'Gayle always told me about the worst threats, so that I could be prepared,' he said, watching for any sign that Gayle's niece knew more than she should.

Jill's head tilted to one side, her eyes narrowing. 'So that you could be prepared, or so that you could eliminate the threat?'

She didn't know, Marcus thought. But she suspected, and that was troubling enough. He chilled his tone. 'Perhaps you should define "eliminate".'

The pulse fluttered at the base of her throat, the color rising in her cheeks. She was afraid, but she didn't blink. That could be very good or very, very bad. 'You were a Ranger, Marcus. You own every gun known to man, and very few of them are registered.'

How she knew about his army background and his gun collection would be a question he'd table for later. 'Yet you stay.'

She lifted a shoulder. 'Like I said before, you pay me well. And Aunt Gayle won't leave you. I can't tell her what I think. She won't believe you are capable of doing any wrong. She thinks you walk on water.'

Because Gayle loved him. Of that, Marcus had never had a single doubt. 'You didn't answer my question, Jill,' he said, letting menace creep into the words. 'Define "eliminate".'

She swallowed hard. 'I saw the patterns in the threats that came in before I took over. Some were just . . . noise. People spouting off. But others were serious. They got bad, then worse, then . . . they stopped.'

Marcus stared at her as the seconds ticked by. He'd admit to nothing, not until she made an accusation. Finally, she dropped her gaze, focusing on her feet. 'Did you kill them?'

He had to admire her guts. 'No,' he said quietly. At least he hadn't killed any of them yet. But he'd been tempted so many times. 'I have other means.'

Her swallow was audible this time, and his admiration grew when she lifted her chin, locking stares once again. 'Legal means?'

Damn, the girl really did have a spine. He smiled at her, very nearly amused. 'Mostly.'

'That's all you're going to say?' she asked, her voice rising an octave. 'Mostly?'

'That's all you asked.'

She drew a breath. 'All right, if that's the way the game is played. If you're caught doing something that falls outside of "mostly", will my aunt be in trouble with the law?'

He regarded her carefully. 'Aren't you worried about yourself?'

'Of course, but I'm more worried about Aunt Gayle. If she gets arrested . . . Her heart couldn't take that.'

'You assume Gayle knows about any activities that are less than "mostly".'

'I *assume* nothing,' she said stiffly. 'I *know* there are parts of Gayle's hard drive that I couldn't access. I also *know* that she has a separate, secret email account that I couldn't break into. She clearly has something to hide. I just want her safe. And alive.'

That Jill hadn't been able to hack into their protected, encrypted files made him feel a little better. Unless she was lying to buy his confidence. Always a possibility.

He tossed the flash drive in the air and caught it again. 'You said you were worried that one of these threats could be real, that I'd get killed, and that you'd lose your job. But you didn't think to warn me?"

'No. I figured you couldn't be too worried. You never checked the file yourself.'

'I thought you didn't set out to monitor me.'

'I didn't. It was merely a side benefit. Are . . . are you going to fire me?'

He probably should. She was too smart and knew a little too much. But he'd keep her close for now so that he could monitor her. 'No. You love your aunt, as do I. You acted to protect her. You shouldn't have needed to. I should have realized I was asking too much of her, long ago. I won't make that mistake again.'

'Thank you.' Her rigid shoulders relaxed and she drew a deep breath, as if she were bracing herself. As it turned out, she had been. 'So, are you going to tell me what's in the secret files that my aunt keeps for you?'

He gave her a cutting glance. 'Don't push your luck, kid.'

Her shoulders went rigid again. 'You don't trust me.'

'You're damn right I don't.' He pulled an ancient laptop from his desk drawer. This old beast wasn't connected to any network, so if there were any viruses or Trojans on Jill's drive, they'd do no damage. 'Trust is earned. You haven't earned mine yet.'

'But I still can?'

'That's totally up to you.' He powered up the laptop, plugged in the flash drive, then gave her a cold look. 'Your initial instincts were good, Jill. I'm not a gentle man. I'm not always a nice man. But I try to do the right thing and I am loyal to those who have earned my trust and respect. I hired you because Gayle asked me to, but make no mistake – if you fuck with me, being Gayle's niece won't help you. Do you understand me?'

She swallowed audibly again. 'I understand. Do you plan to tell my aunt?'

'No. But I will find a way to "discover" her heart attack and make sure she takes it easy.' He'd also make sure that he limited Jill's access to his business. He'd get one of his other staff members – someone he truly trusted – to intercept the mail from now on.

'Thank you,' she said on a shuddered exhale.

'You're welcome. You should go home, get some rest.' The ancient laptop had finally opened the file on the flash drive, and he shifted his attention from Jill to his screen, dismissing her. The list she'd compiled was several steps up in vitriol compared to the sanitized list Gayle had been keeping, but he saw pretty quickly that none of the threats could plausibly be behind the shooting this morning. He'd choose the ones that were most likely to set Detective Bishop's mind at ease about him having been the target.

'Why now?' Jill asked.

His head jerked up, his brow furrowing when he saw her still standing in the doorway. 'I thought you were going home.'

She crossed the room to stand at the edge of his desk. 'Why did you check the list now, when you haven't looked at it for the past nine months?'

He gritted his teeth. 'None of your business, Jill. Now go home.'

'It is my business if it affects my aunt,' she insisted. 'You came to check the list because you got hurt tonight. I don't see any blood, so I guess you'll be okay. But if you think someone on Gayle's list or on that flash drive is trying to hurt you, they might hurt her too.'

He met her eyes, held her gaze, made his own as threatening as he could. But even though she trembled, she didn't stand down. This girl did have courage. Whether she had honor remained to be seen.

Again she swallowed audibly. 'Who is Tala? I heard you say her name.'

He started to swear, but hesitated, unsure of what to do. Obviously she'd heard the tape he'd been listening to. He didn't want to tell her anything, but he knew she would figure it out. Even if he didn't have Stone write the story of Tala's murder, some other news source would report it, together with Marcus's presence at the scene. She'd put two and two together.

He wanted to fire her, but he knew it was too late for that.

The front door to the office suite opened. 'Marcus?' Stone called from the lobby.

Jill jerked in surprise, glancing at the clock on the wall. 'What's he doing here?'

'I asked him to come,' Marcus said, and suddenly the solution was clear. 'You want to earn my trust?'

Her expression faltered. 'Yes,' she said slowly, uncertainly. 'How?'

Stone's heavy footsteps got louder, then he stopped abruptly in the doorway, filling it easily. He blinked in surprise. 'Jill? What are you doing here so early?' He lifted his brows at her appearance. 'Or should I say late?' He gave Marcus a questioning look.

'I want Jill to assist you in investigating the story I called you about.'

Stone's eyes grew huge and displeased. 'What the hell?'

Jill's eyes grew even larger. 'Me?'

'Yeah, you. You said you wanted to be trusted. Do you still?'

Her eyes narrowed. Smart girl. 'I don't know.'

Marcus pointed at the door. 'Go get us some breakfast while you're thinking about it. When you come back, Stone can bring you up to speed.'

Jill skirted around Stone, who looked stunned and annoyed. 'I'll be back,' she promised.

'I figured you would,' Marcus said pleasantly. When she was gone, he lowered his voice to Stone. 'Watch to make sure she actually leaves, then lock the door. We need to talk.'

Cincinnati, Ohio
Tuesday 4 August, 5.50 A.M.

The ringing of the phone pulled Kenneth Sweeney out of a very nice dream. Scowling at the abrupt loss of the quiet beach and the beautiful, faceless woman who'd been servicing him quite nicely, he patted the nightstand, searching for his cell phone. He squinted at the caller ID, then sat upright in bed, fully awake now. The security office was only to contact the CEO directly when there was an emergency. Since an emergency usually involved a police raid of some kind, he braced himself for the worst. 'Yes? What is it?'

A hesitation on the other end. 'Mr Sweeney? This is Gene Decker.'

Ken blinked hard, recognizing the voice. Gene had been one of his bodyguards until the younger man had been injured on the job the month before. He'd performed admirably in the line of duty, taking a bullet in the leg while saving Ken's ass from a trigger-happy wannabe competitor – a small-time hood who'd wanted a slice of Ken's OxyContin clientele. It turned out that Decker had studied to be an accountant in college, so they'd placed him in the business office while he recuperated.

Gene Decker had proven himself a damn fine accountant in the interim, but that didn't come close to explaining why he was calling now – and from security's command central.

'Why are you calling, Decker?' Ken asked harshly.

'There's some kind of alarm going off on the computer here in the security office.'

'Where's the security man on duty?'

A slight hesitation. 'He appears to be asleep, sir.'

Ken's temper blew, sending his blood pressure skyrocketing until he could feel the pulse in the top of his skull. 'Asleep?' he asked, very quietly.

'There appears to be alcohol on his breath.'

Ken counted backward from ten. 'All right. First, where is Reuben Blackwell?'

'I already called him at home, sir. I got his voicemail, so I left a message for him to call back, that it was an emergency. I hope that was okay.'

No, it was not okay. His chief of security was supposed to be on call 24/7. *So where the fuck is he?* 'Tell me what happened, Decker, starting with why you are in the office before normal business hours.'

'It's fiscal year close, sir. We submit our financials on the fifteenth. I've been working through the night for the last week.'

'Where is your boss?'

'I assume Joel's at home, asleep.'

Leaving the junior guy to crunch numbers, Ken thought, which made sense. But Joel Whipple was responsible for *all* of Ken's accounts, most of which Gene Decker had not been authorized to see. Ken knew that Joel was most likely not home asleep, but crunching numbers himself. 'So what about this alarm?' he asked.

'I took a break, took a walk through the hallways to clear my head. I heard the alarm through the door to the security office. I knocked hard, but nobody answered, so I went in.'

'The door was unlocked?' Holy shit, Reuben was going to have hell to pay for this.

'Uh . . . well, yes, sir. I found the man on duty on the floor. I shook him, asked him what I should do, who I should call. He woke up and seemed like he was lucid for a few seconds. He told me to dial "one", then went back to sleep. "One" was Reuben Blackwell's voicemail. When he didn't answer, I decided to take a chance and dial "two". That was you, sir.'

'All right. But I don't hear any alarm.'

'I muted the computer so I could hear what the security man on the floor was trying to tell me. Do you want to hear it? It was just a klaxon. The screen says "501 in progress".'

Shit. One of the trackers had been tampered with. This was definitely not anything that Gene Decker needed to know about. 'I'll take care of it, Decker. Leave the man you found on the floor. Go back to your area and do whatever that thing was that you were doing before.'

'Fiscal year close, sir.'

'Yeah, that. And, Decker? I expect discretion on your part.'

'Lips are sealed, sir.'

Ken hung up, then dialed Reuben's cell. His security chief answered on the first ring. 'Ken, what's wrong?'

Ken had known Reuben for fifteen years – ever since the former Knoxville cop had caught him with a trunk full of Oxy that he'd been moving up I-75 from Florida. Ken had thought his goose was cooked that day, but Reuben had let him go, wanting only a piece of the action. After gaining their trust, Reuben had become the fourth partner in the business, eventually moving his wife up from Tennessee to Cincinnati.

Ken had known his other two partners – accountant Joel and purchasing manager Demetrius – since their freshman year in college, thirty very long years ago. Only Reuben had a wife anymore, the rest of them divorced at least once. Wives were a distraction at best. A vulnerability at worst, especially if they got too curious about the business side of things.

Which Ken's second wife had done. She'd actually tried to blackmail him with what her curious self had learned. Now Ken was a widower, sleeping alone in his big bed, having shown his late wife the error of her ways by taking a knife to her throat.

It had been Reuben's quick eye that had caught Ken's ex-wife hatching her plot, Reuben who'd regretfully shown him the proof. Reuben who'd helped Ken get rid of her body after they'd eliminated her as a problem. Ken trusted Reuben as much as he trusted anyone – which wasn't a hell of a lot.

'Where are you, Reuben?' he asked evenly. He used his CEO voice and not his let's-grab-a-beer voice so that Reuben would know this wasn't a social call.

Reuben's answer was cautious. 'On my way into the office. What do you need?'

'Did you get a call from the security office?'

'Yes, but I was in the shower at the time, and when I tried calling back, no one answered. Which is why I'm headed in. Why?'

'I also got a call.' As Ken explained the situation, Reuben swore under his breath.

'Jackson isn't a drinker. I don't know what happened, but I'll get to the bottom of this.'

'See that you do. I'll be in the office at my normal time. I want a full report when I arrive. On both your staff and the tracker alarm.'

'Yes, sir.'

Four

Scarlett sat down at her desk and fired up her computer, grateful that the squad room was relatively deserted. She'd showered and even put on makeup, but her eyes were still puffy from her crying jag. She needed another cup of coffee. Hell, she needed a whole pot. But what she really needed was never to have heard that Michelle's killer had scored a job with the most successful defense firm in the city. *No*, she told herself firmly, *you need to do your job*. Michelle's killer had escaped justice. Tala's killer could not be allowed to do the same.

Footsteps behind her had her tensing. 'Morning, Scar,' a male voice said.

Scarlett fought the urge to hide her swollen eyes as Detective Adam Kimble dropped into his desk chair, right next to hers. 'Good morning, Adam.' The detective had recently returned from personal leave after a particularly difficult case had emotionally wiped him out.

Just seeing Adam was enough of a motivation to keep her own emotions locked down. She didn't want to be forced into taking a mental-health leave. Couldn't stand the thought of her family knowing she'd cracked from the strain. 'You're here early,' she offered.

Adam gave her an annoyed look. 'Yeah. I got called to a crime scene this morning and was halfway there when Dispatch said, "Never mind." Another detective had taken over.'

Scarlett winced. 'Sorry about that.'

'You should be. I put on a tie and everything.' He studied her face. 'You okay, kid?'

They'd known each other for years and she genuinely liked him. That he was Deacon's first cousin meant she and Deacon had been able to stay in touch with him while he'd been on leave. Adam had seemed relaxed, but there were still shadows in his eyes.

'Yeah. I'm okay,' she said. 'You?'

'Just peachy. Came in and did some paperwork since I was all dressed up anyway.'

Scarlett made herself smile. 'You can't let a tie like that go to waste.'

'Exactly. Now I'm gonna take my mother to breakfast.' Rising, he hesitated, then squeezed her shoulder. 'This morning was a rough one, huh?'

'Yeah.' She'd let him think that because she didn't want to admit to anyone that she'd lost it, sobbing in her own foyer as she thought about Michelle. Besides, any case involving the discovery of a body in an alley was a rough one. 'But I'll be fine, thanks. Say hi to your mom.'

Waiting until he was gone, she logged into her email account and felt her shoulders relax. The top email in her inbox was from Marcus O'Bannion. The newsman had come through.

There was no attachment, but there was a link followed by a short note.

Detective Bishop,

At this link you can download the video files we discussed earlier.

Please do not hesitate to call if you have any further questions.

M. O'Bannion

Publisher and CEO, *The Ledger*, Inc.

There was no mention of the list of those who'd threatened him either in the email or the link he'd provided. There were, however, eleven video files, each labeled with a date. The first file was dated two weeks before, the last with today's date. That would be the murder in the alley.

Still raw from her conversation with Bryan, Scarlett decided to put the murder video off for a little while. Just until the memories of Michelle's crime scene receded a bit more. She didn't want to taint her first impressions of Tala's murder with memories of Michelle's. That was simply good investigative procedure. At least that was what she told herself.

She downloaded the first video and hit PLAY. It was in color, but the quality was grainy, the angle odd. It was Marcus's visual perspective, she realized, the camera planted on the edge of the bill of his cap.

'Easy, old girl.' Marcus's voice came out of her speakers, rich and lovely, sending a shiver down Scarlett's spine and licking across her skin. He looked down, bringing into view his feet, the sidewalk, and a slightly limping Sheltie on a leash. 'Come, BB. Let's sit here.'

His dog, she thought. He'd said the dog was elderly and couldn't run fast, that he'd gathered her in his arms when he'd run after Tala the first time, but that incident had not been recorded. On the screen, the dog curled up at his feet and blew out an exhausted sigh before resting her muzzle on her front paws.

'I know,' he murmured. 'I miss him too.' Then he switched to a companionable tone. 'So, BB, do you think the girl will show up tonight? The one with the prissy dog? I sat here and waited last night and the night before, but she didn't come.' The camera slowly panned in a circle as Marcus checked the woods all around him. 'I'm going to try one more time, and if she doesn't come back, I'm going to have to drop it. I can't help her if she won't come close enough for me to find out what's wrong.'

Nearly two minutes passed with no activity except for the few times Marcus leaned down to scratch BB behind the ears. 'Maybe it was the singing,' he murmured to the dog. 'I suppose it can't hurt to try.'

Scarlett had expected the Vince Gill ballad, had braced herself for the memory, but what came out of the speakers hit her far harder. 'Ave Maria'. Her heart stuttered, her breath backing up in her lungs. The last time she'd heard it had been at her nephew's christening, which was the last time she'd set foot in a church. She could only hope that none of her single brothers would get married and that the married brothers would have no more children who had to be christened, because weddings, christenings and funerals were the only times she forced herself to enter a church. To kneel. To grit her teeth while everyone around her prayed.

Marcus's 'Ave Maria' was the most beautiful rendition she'd ever heard – clear and pure and strong. Still, she was relieved when he suddenly broke off, the camera on his cap swinging in a wide arc as he twisted to look behind him.

There Tala stood, barely visible behind the line of trees where she waited, poised to flee. She wore a white polo shirt and jeans, just as she'd worn today. At her side was a tall white standard poodle, cut the fancy way, with rosettes on its hindquarters, puffy pompons around its ankles and a topknot on its head. It was groomed like the dogs she'd seen on that famous dog show that came on TV on Thanksgiving Day, right after the Macy's Parade.

Putting 'Ave Maria' from her mind, she focused on the dog. A dog that fancy would have to be groomed frequently, she thought – and had an *aha* moment. Groomers would probably be more inclined to answer questions than vets would. Asking a vet about an animal's owner was an interrogation. Asking a groomer for the names of owners of poodles he or she had groomed – that was getting a reference. She'd written 'groomer' on the notepad on her desk when Marcus began to sing again, and all thought fled.

This time he did choose Vince Gill's 'Go Rest High On That Mountain', catching her unprepared. Her stuttering heart rose to fill her throat and tears flooded her eyes as the memory of funeral after funeral flashed through her mind. Michelle's. Then the one for the best friend of her oldest brother, killed in Iraq. A colleague, shot in the line of duty. A firefighter she'd grown up with, killed in a blaze. So many others that it hurt to recall. And, of course, the funeral of Marcus's brother. Whoever had planned Mikhail's funeral had hired the star tenor with the Cincinnati Opera to sing the song, and he'd done a commendable job. But Marcus's version . . .

It broke her heart, but it also soothed it.

Tala, too, had been drawn to Marcus's song. On the video, she moved slowly but carefully through the trees until she came to a path that met the small clearing where Marcus remained seated on the bench, turning only his head to follow her progress. Tears ran down the young woman's face unchecked, one hand pressed to her mouth, muffling the sobs that shook her slim shoulders. Her other hand stayed fisted around the dog's leash.

She stood like that until he'd sung the last note. Marcus's microphone picked up his very audible swallow, then his cleared throat.

'Why are you crying?' he asked so gently that Scarlett found herself pressing the heel of her hand to her heart to alleviate the ache there.

The camera jostled as he started to rise, but an instant later Tala took off through the trees, the white of her polo shirt and the white of the dog visible until she turned a corner, taking a path out of the park.

At least we know which way she ran. It would give Scarlett a place to direct the uniforms who were gathering at this very moment to canvass the neighborhoods around the park, showing Tala's photo to the residents. *And the dog's too.* That dog was so distinctive that it must be well known in the neighborhood where it lived.

She backed up the video to the point where Tala and the dog appeared, then went frame by frame until she found the clearest image from which to pull the still photo. Zooming in, she checked out the shiny stones on the poodle's pink collar – she counted at least six that were so large they had to be rhinestones. But if Marcus was right and they really were diamonds? The very notion made Scarlett's blood boil. *How dare they?* The couple who owned Tala and her family threw away hundreds, even thousands of dollars on a damn collar for a dog.

Still, it was a feature most people would remember. That would be a plus in identifying the dog, which should then lead them to the dog's owner – and hopefully to Tala's killer.

Needing a break before starting the next video, Scarlett opened the contact list on her phone to the Ks. Delores Kaminsky. Shot by a madman and left for dead under a van in a grocery store parking lot nine months before, Delores was a medical marvel. She'd taken a bullet in the back of the head at point-blank range, but she'd survived against all odds.

Before being shot, Delores ran an animal shelter and operated a brisk mobile grooming business. Now, post-incident, she had restarted her shelter services. Once she was further along with her therapy, she'd resume her grooming business as well. That was her plan, anyway. None of her friends had any doubt she'd succeed. Scarlett had met her only a few times, but she believed in Delores too.

It was coming up on six thirty, but Delores had told Scarlett that she was an early riser. She'd probably be feeding the dogs by now. Scarlett dialed, hoping to at least leave a message if Delores was still asleep. But the phone was answered on the second ring by a voice that sounded surprisingly wary.

'Patrick's Place Animal Shelter. How can I help you?'

'Delores, this is Scarlett Bishop.'

'Scarlett,' the woman replied on an exhale. 'I saw Cincinnati Police on the caller ID and I thought . . . Well, I'm just glad it's you.'

Scarlett frowned. 'I called from the office. My cell only gets two bars here and I didn't want to lose you. I didn't mean to scare you.' It had been nine months since Delores's assault, and while her body's rehab was coming along, Scarlett questioned how well she was dealing with the emotional trauma of being left for dead.

'You didn't really scare me. I mean, the guy who attacked me is dead, so what can happen, right? I was just . . . Never mind. I'm just being foolish. So what can I do for you this morning? I hope Zat's working out all right for you?'

Scarlett wanted to press for more details about what had scared Delores, because clearly something had. But the woman deserved her privacy, so Scarlett simply answered her question. 'Zat is wonderful,' she assured her. 'He seems to have made himself at home.'

'No shoe-chewing?' Delores asked, amused.

'Not even one. That's Deacon's complaint, not mine. I was smart enough not to choose a puppy.' *Choose, nothing.* Scarlett hadn't chosen Zat. The three-legged bulldog had chosen her. 'I'm actually calling to pick your brain about—' Scarlett stopped herself, wincing at her poor choice of words. Delores had been shot in the head, and while the bullet hadn't pierced her brain, her skull had suffered trauma when her attacker had thrown her to

68

the pavement, kicking her under a parked van to hide her body. The woman's brain had been badly bruised. 'I'm sorry, Delores. I can't believe I said that.'

The snicker on the other end untangled the knots in Scarlett's gut. 'It's okay. Really. It's actually pretty funny. So you want to pick my poor addled brain about what?'

'Groomers,' Scarlett said, relieved.

'I'm not doing any grooming yet. I haven't built up enough strength.'

'I don't need you to groom an animal, but I do need to know about the area groomers, especially those that might cater to wealthy clients with expensive dogs.'

'Okay,' Delores said slowly. 'I don't know everyone, of course, but I have lots of friends in the business who might be able to help you. Any specific breed?'

'Standard poodles.'

'I know several groomers who do standards. But . . .' A hint of fear edged into her voice. 'They won't know I gave you their names, right?'

'No, they will not know. But listen, if you don't feel comfortable working with me, I can find another groomer. It's okay.'

'No, no. I'm just being silly.' She laughed self-consciously. 'If you tell me what you're looking for, I may be able to help you. I've groomed quite a few standards in the past. I had three who went Best in Show.'

Scarlett's ears perked up. 'Would you know if a dog was a show dog by looking at a picture of it?'

'It depends on the quality of the photo. I could certainly tell you if it's not. Did a standard poodle commit a homicide?' The lightness of the question was a bit forced. Delores was nervous, but still willing to help them. Scarlett respected that.

'No,' Scarlett said, keeping her tone equally light, then let her seriousness return. 'But I need to find its owner.'

'I've taken hundreds of pictures of dogs at shows. You can take a look through them, if you think it will help. Kind of like a mug-shot book.'

Excitement had Scarlett's heart thumping. 'Do you have time to meet with me this morning?'

'I can after eleven. I have a PT appointment this morning and won't be back till then. If it's urgent, I can cancel my appointment.'

'Tell you what. You keep your appointment, but also keep your phone with you. If I need your help earlier, I'll call you.'

'Sounds perfect. Take care, Scarlett.'

'Delores, wait. Did you have a chance to call that friend of mine?

Meredith.' Her new friend Meredith Fallon counseled mostly children and adolescents, but occasionally took on adults.

I should know. She's taken me on, whether I like it or not. But Meredith did it in a way that made Scarlett know it was because she cared. Scarlett wasn't sure Meredith even knew how to flip her therapist off-switch, even in a casual setting. So Scarlett watched what she said, not ready to reveal the full extent of her inner turmoil. *Not yet anyway. Maybe not ever.* The risk to her career was too high.

A small pause. 'Not yet,' Delores admitted. 'I'm not ready yet. I'm sorry.'

'Don't be sorry. I can respect not being ready.' Scarlett had to, or she'd be a total hypocrite. 'When you are, she'll be waiting. For now, you do what you need to do to make it through each day.'

A long, long pause. So long that Scarlett thought the connection had been lost. 'Delores? You still there?'

'Yeah. I guess I was just wondering if . . . I mean if you . . .' A sigh of frustration. 'You just sounded like you understood. I was wondering if you'd ever been, you know, a victim?'

Scarlett's lungs began to burn and she realized she'd been holding her breath. She didn't want to answer that, but Delores had been through hell and deserved an honest response. 'No. I've never been assaulted. I've been smacked around from time to time, but that's in the line of duty and the smackers usually ended up in cuffs with my knee in the small of their back. I've guess I've just seen too much.' *Way too much.* 'Contact me when you get back from PT, and I'll meet you at your shelter at eleven.'

She hung up and stared at her screen, still frozen on the enlarged still of the poodle. She needed to go through all of these videos. Starting with the one in the alley.

But I don't want to. Which was ridiculous, wasn't it? She was a homicide detective and saw death every day. But seeing a victim already dead was far different from seeing her die. And sometimes one victim's pain cut more deeply than others. She had the feeling that Tala was going to be one of the hard ones. The girl's pain had hurt Marcus too, even before he'd been shot. She knew that about him.

So do your job. Get her justice. Knowing that Tala's killer had been punished wouldn't ease her pain, or Marcus's, today, but eventually it might.

But Scarlett's hand guiding the mouse didn't cooperate, switching to her email instead of opening the video file. There were no new emails from Marcus. No sign of the list of threats that he had promised. *Maybe he forgot. Or he said his assistant kept the list. Maybe she hasn't sent it to him yet.* But he did say he'd have the list to her within the hour. *Maybe he sent it and it got lost in the ether somewhere.*

Okay, that last one was reaching.

Why don't you just ask him? Her phone's two bars would be enough to send a text.

Scarlett Bishop here, she typed. *Just wondering if you've sent the file with the list of threats against you. I got the video files but haven't received the list.* She stared at the message for a moment. She should probably have said 'Detective' instead of using her first name. It would be more proper. But she didn't want to be proper. She'd had Marcus O'Bannion on her mind for nine months. He may have been making the first move when he'd called her, or he might just have been asking for her help. She'd never know unless she made the next move. Without overthinking it any more than she already had, she pressed SEND.

Now do your damn job.

She returned to the list of video files, resolutely clicked on the one taken in the alley, and prepared herself to watch Tala die.

Cincinnati, Ohio
Tuesday 4 August, 6.20 A.M.

Deacon Novak took a tentative breath as he entered his house, then huffed it out in relief. Not only had the new puppy not had an accident on the kitchen floor, cause for celebration in and of itself, but the air was full of the aroma of breakfast. Standing at the stove, looking all soft and sleep-rumpled, was the woman who still made his heart stop each time he saw her.

Two dogs sat on the floor at her feet. One was a full-grown Lab they'd named Zeus, the other a golden-mix puppy with enormous paws that they'd named Goliath. Both dogs were rescues from an animal shelter, and Deacon was glad they were there, even if the puppy routinely chewed his shoes. He didn't like leaving his woman alone when he was called away to crime scenes in the middle of the night, but knowing she had protection made him feel a bit better.

Both dogs got to their feet when the door opened, Zeus growling impressively until he saw who it was. Then he curled back up at Faith's feet while Goliath loped clumsily across the floor. Deacon dropped to a crouch to scratch the puppy's ears. He might grumble about his shoes, but he really liked the dogs.

Faith looked over her shoulder, her mouth curved into a smile of welcome even as her eyes gave him a quick head-to-toe assessment. She worried about him every time he left the house, but she never said a word.

Straightening, Deacon held out his arms obligingly. 'Look, Ma, no blood.'

She laughed, shaking her head. 'Always a good way to start the day. Hungry?'

He waggled his brows with an evil chuckle. 'Yes, but we don't have time for that.'

She blushed prettily, and he didn't think he'd ever get tired of the sight. 'Wash up, sit down and hush.' She put two plates filled with eggs and bacon on the table, then sat next to him. 'What happened? Was Scarlett okay?'

He'd left the house knowing only that his partner had discovered a body in an alley, not knowing how she'd come to be there. 'Yeah. So was Marcus.'

Faith's brows shot up, her green eyes widening. 'Marcus? You mean our Marcus?'

'Your cousin,' he said with a nod. 'One and the same.' He told her the basic details and watched her lips droop in sympathy.

'That poor young woman. Marcus isn't hurt?'

'He was wearing Kevlar, but he was still lucky that he's only bruised. Fool wouldn't go to the ER.'

'Of course not,' she said with an eye roll. 'Neither would you unless you were too unconscious to refuse. Damned hard-headed men. You guys aren't really bulletproof, you know.'

'This isn't about your damned hard-headed fiancé,' he said lightly. 'This is about your damned hard-headed cousin.'

Her lips quirked up briefly before bending into a worried frown. 'This is not going to improve the situation with his mother. Ever since she lost Mikhail, Della worries that something's going to happen to the rest of her kids. When she's sober. Or even awake. Which between the booze and the pills isn't too often anymore. I'll go out and see her today.'

Faith hadn't met her extended family until nine months before, but she'd quickly become an honorary O'Bannion. They loved her, nearly as much as Deacon did. He'd leaned in to kiss the frown off her mouth when his cell rang.

'It's Zimmerman,' he told her. 'I gotta take it.' He answered the call from his boss, the special agent in charge of the Bureau's Cincinnati field office. Deacon was part of the Major Crimes Enforcement Squad, a CPD/FBI joint task force, and CPD's Lieutenant Lynda Isenberg was his direct boss. But he officially belonged to the FBI, so SAC Zimmerman was also his boss. He didn't tell Zimmerman everything about every case, but for this one he needed Bureau resources. 'Morning, Andy. Thanks for calling me back so early.'

'What's up?' Zimmerman asked.

'We may have a case of human trafficking.'

'Labor or sex or both?'

'Not sure yet.' He relayed what Tala had told Marcus, watching Faith's eyes narrow in silent anger. She'd counseled victims of sexual assault for years, guarding her clients like a mother bear. Tala would have been in good hands with his Faith, had the young woman survived. 'Detective Bishop is tracking down her identity.'

'We have a task force investigating trafficking at the local and state levels,' Zimmerman said. 'Special Agent Troy is lead investigator and we're transferring in another agent to partner with him. That person isn't slated to start for another few weeks, but I'll try to move that up. In the meantime, I'll contact Troy and get him down here ASAP. He's been working a case in Cleveland that will hopefully close today.'

'I'll keep you up to date with what we find,' Deacon promised, and hung up.

Faith covered his hand with hers and squeezed softly. 'We used to get a lot of victims of trafficking through our office in Miami. We expected it there. Nobody really expects it here in Ohio. But I know it's here. Unfortunately, it's everywhere.'

Deacon thought of Tala, on her way to the morgue. 'Unfortunately, you're right.'

Cincinnati, Ohio
Tuesday 4 August, 6.20 A.M.

'Holy shit, Marcus.' Stone's big hands dragged down his face, a weary gesture. 'You could have been killed.'

Marcus had told his brother everything that had happened that morning – or almost everything. His fascination with Scarlett Bishop he'd keep to himself. 'But I wasn't.'

Stone sat back in his chair and closed his eyes. 'I can't bury another brother,' he said hoarsely. 'Please don't make me do that.'

'What would you have me do?' Marcus asked, careful not to keep any sign of anger or criticism out of his tone. Stone didn't respond well to anger, and Marcus's criticism could cut his brother off at the knees when very few other things could.

'Just let it go. For once in your life, don't be a goddamn hero. Let. It. Go.'

Marcus tamped down his irritation and shoved at the defensive wall that sprang up reflexively. 'So I should hide in this office for the rest of my life?'

Stone's eyes opened slowly, his jaw tight from gritting his teeth as Marcus had told his tale. 'No. But that doesn't mean you have to charge to the rescue every damn time somebody gets in trouble.' He slapped the arm of the chair in frustration. 'Goddammit, Marcus. Mom needs you. Audrey needs you. So does Jeremy.' He swallowed hard. 'And so do I.'

Marcus's temper drained away. His mother and stepfather had been nearly destroyed by Mikhail's murder, and Audrey . . . His sister had grown up overnight, both grieving their brother and terrified at their mother's fragile state. And Audrey wasn't the only one.

He and Stone had also been walking around their mother on eggshells, neither of them wanting to distress her further. Marcus had seen her like this before. He knew exactly how bad it could get.

However, out of all them, Marcus worried about Stone the most. Stone was a pressure cooker waiting to blow, never admitting how ravaged Mikhail's death had left him. Marcus had been preparing himself for the worst for nine months. But he wasn't prepared to change who he was. He wasn't prepared to stop helping people who had nowhere else to turn.

'I know,' he murmured. 'But we have each other. Who did Tala have?'

For a long moment there was silence between them. Then Stone exhaled. 'You're going to get yourself killed someday.'

'But not today,' Marcus replied evenly.

Stone narrowed his eyes, his anger unhidden. 'The day is still young.'

Marcus's temper sparked. 'I wore a damn vest! Just like I promised I would.'

'Then I guess you're just lucky that he only shot you in the back.' Stone flung the words back sarcastically. 'What if he'd decided to finish the job like he did with the girl? A vest ain't gonna protect your fool hard head from a bullet. You think you're charmed or something? That you're invincible? Unkillable?' His voice had grown louder with each word, until he was shouting. 'Are you really that fucking stupid?'

Marcus winced. No, he was not that stupid. He weighed the risks, considered the odds. And he always decided that the victim he was saving was worth whatever it took.

Stone sucked in a startled breath. 'You want to die,' he whispered. 'You sonofabitch.'

Marcus shook his head. 'No. It's not like that.'

Stone straightened in his chair, his gaze growing coldly furious. 'Then what *is* it like? Tell me so that your slow brother can understand.'

Marcus rubbed his temples, where a headache was now in full force. Stone only pulled the 'slow' card when he was really upset, a throwback to the childhood that neither of them ever wanted to remember, but that neither of them could ever seem to forget. The same events, the same loss, had touched them so differently, forming them into the men they were today.

'I didn't ask you to come in this morning so that we could fight,' Marcus murmured.

Stone set his jaw, his hands clenching into fists. 'That's just too damn bad. 'Cause we're gonna.'

'Oh for God's sake. I don't want to die, Stone,' Marcus said, suddenly too exhausted to argue, much less fight. 'But I see people like Tala and . . . they deserve to have a life.'

'More than you do?' Stone demanded.

Again Marcus let his silence speak, and Stone shoved his hands through his hair, yanking on the ends like a man at the edge of his sanity.

Which was far too close to the truth. For both of them.

'And they said I was the slow one,' Stone snarled, releasing his hair. Roughly he smoothed it back, dropping his chin to his chest in defeat. 'You're a goddamn stubborn idiot.'

Under the circumstances, Marcus supposed that was fair. 'Will you help me anyway?' he asked quietly.

Stone's eyes flew up, their gazes clashing like swords. 'Help you kill yourself? No. No fucking way in fucking hell.'

'I don't want to die,' Marcus repeated, more forcefully this time. 'I'm asking you to help me deal with this whole Tala situation, and with Jill. Sooner or later some other paper or news crew will see my name in the police report. They'll know I was with a seventeen-year-old girl in an alley when she was shot to death. I'd like to get the real story out there before I'm turned into a sadistic pedophile.'

Stone paled. 'Shit. I'm sorry. I didn't think past you being shot.'

'Well I need you to think a little further out now.'

Stone squared his shoulders. 'What do you want me to do?'

Finally, Marcus thought. He'd expected a little anger from his brother, but not the shit storm he'd just sailed through. Mikhail's death had them all riding too close to the edge, Stone most of all.

'I want an article with your byline on the *Ledger*'s home page ASAP, and in tomorrow's edition on the front page, above the fold. I want you to report that I had been approached by the victim in the park and that she asked me to meet her so that I could help her escape an abusive household. That we were meeting a CPD cop, but that the victim was shot minutes before the cop arrived.'

'Abusive household,' Stone repeated. 'Not the fact that she'd been "owned".'

'No. That's for the cops to follow up on.' *And for me as well*, he thought, but he wasn't going there with Stone right now. His brother had been far too shaken by what had already happened.

'Okay,' Stone said, his eyes narrowing suspiciously, and Marcus knew he had not been fooled. 'How do you want me to explain the fact that you were in an alley in a shitty part of town?'

'Say that Tala didn't want to be picked up in her neighborhood because she was afraid word would get back to her abuser. Just don't make it sound like a quote. A quote could be challenged by anyone who has access to all the evidence.'

'Specifically the video you handed over to Bishop.' Stone grimaced, as if merely saying Scarlett Bishop's name left a bad taste in his mouth. 'Why the hell did you do that, anyway? You didn't have to reveal the video files, much less give them away.'

Yes I did. I really did. If for no other reason than to obliterate the mistrust that had suddenly shadowed her dark eyes. He had grown accustomed to that look from others in the five years since he'd taken the *Ledger*'s reins. People – especially cops – tended to despise newspapermen, and Marcus could live with that. Because at the end of the day he knew that whatever he'd done, whatever he'd had to do, it had been the right thing for those too helpless to defend themselves.

But seeing that look in Scarlett Bishop's eyes . . . It stung. And it made him angry. Because alongside the mistrust had been a bruised fury that had seemed far more personal than the normal contempt cops had for the press. Some reporter at some point had crossed a line and hurt her.

Marcus would do whatever it took so that she never had cause to look at him that way again. Even if it meant trusting her with his own pain. She had to have viewed the videos by now. She'd seen his visceral, personal reaction to Tala's murder. He'd allowed her to see his heart.

'Marcus?' Stone leaned forward, snapping his fingers in front of his brother's face. 'You still in there?'

Marcus blinked, bringing Stone's worried face back into focus. 'Yeah, I'm here.'

Stone leaned back, worry becoming wary regard. 'You got all glassy-eyed there for a second. Maybe you should see a doctor.'

'I got checked out by the paramedics. I'm fine.'

Stone was unconvinced. 'They told you to go to the hospital, didn't they?'

'Yeah, but I'm okay.' Actually he felt a little queasy, but he always did at the mere thought of entering a hospital. He swallowed hard and cleared his throat. 'I gave Detective Bishop the files because someone murdered a young woman right in front of me. It was the—'

'Right thing to do,' Stone interrupted, rolling his eyes. 'Yeah, yeah, yeah. I got it.'

Marcus wondered sometimes. Stone could be shown the right thing, but his brother didn't always get it on his own.

'It also takes me out of the suspect pool,' Marcus said quietly. *I hope.*

'Let me see it too.'

'I don't think you really want to.'

Stone's expression hardened. 'No, I don't, but I need to know what I'm up against in case Bishop decides to release the video to the rest of the press. Show me. Now.'

Marcus didn't think Scarlett would do such a thing, but he kept that opinion to himself as he turned his monitor around so that Stone could view the screen. Stone watched in silence, flinching at the gunshots, his face going positively gray after the second bullet knocked Marcus flat on his face. And then, when Tala's splintered skull came back into view, his breathing became hard and choppy.

'You okay?' Marcus murmured.

Stone jerked a trembling nod and kept watching. When the video ended, he drew a deep breath, let it out in a shuddering exhale. 'You gave her . . .' he started, his voice rusty. And breaking. He cleared his throat hard. 'You gave her this exact file?'

'Yeah.'

Stone lifted his eyes, and for a moment Marcus could see the boy his brother had been. So young, so scared. So vulnerable. Looking for comfort.

'Okay. I get it now. You had to do what you did,' Stone said.

'Which thing? Helping Tala, or giving Detective Bishop the file?'

Stone closed his eyes. 'Either,' he whispered. 'Both.' When his eyes opened, the vulnerability was gone, replaced by his usual confident facade. It was Stone's armor, his last line of emotional defense. When that broke down, he lost control and . . . well, that was never good. But Marcus would never share that with anyone.

But you did. You told Scarlett. Yes, he had. Kind of. He'd been lying in a hospital bed with a punctured lung, and Scarlett had come to see him. She'd been so angry with Stone because his brother had withheld information that had been vital to saving the lives of a woman and a little girl. Scarlett hadn't understood. Hadn't had a clue about what made Stone tick.

Marcus had lashed out. Shouted at her. *Until you've walked a mile in Stone's shoes, don't you dare criticize him.* She still hadn't understood what made Stone tick, because Marcus hadn't given her any additional details. But she'd backed off, hadn't pushed for more like a lot of people might have done. She'd accepted his word. Respected his privacy. And then she'd stood guard over him until another cop came to relieve her. *She made sure I was safe.*

Marcus had trusted her then. He trusted her now. 'I don't think the detective will share that video with anyone who doesn't need to see it, but if she does, my conversation with Tala will be documented publicly. Make sure that anything you print can't be disproven by the video. Do not disclose the location of the park or her last words.'

'You want a photo of the girl?'

'Yes. You'll have to grab a frame from one of the videos I took in the park. I'll send you the same link to the files that I sent to Bishop. Also add that I've helped victims in the past. Pick two that don't show up on the threat list.'

Back in control of his emotions, Stone's eyes narrowed again. 'Why? What does it matter if they are or aren't on that damn list? The girl – Tala – she was the target, not you.'

'That's where Jill comes in. She's seen the list.'

Stone sat up straighter, fire in his eyes. 'How? Gayle never would have shown it to her.'

Marcus studied his brother, hoping he was stable enough for the next part. 'Did you know Gayle had a heart attack?'

Stone's jaw dropped. 'What the fuck?'

'Yeah, that's pretty much what I said.' Marcus told his brother what Jill had told him.

'So the kid's been doing Gayle's job all this time?'

'A lot of it, yeah.'

Stone sat back in his chair, frowning. 'I guess we can't really blame her. If Gayle was my aunt, I'd have done the same.' His frown grew troubled. 'But I never knew Gayle felt that way about us.'

'I don't think Gayle does. I think Jill thinks Gayle should. Anyway, the kid's seen the list and has catalogued every threat since. She noticed that many of the threats start out vicious and abruptly go away.' Marcus rolled his eyes. 'She thinks I'm bumping them off.'

Stone snorted. 'Yeah, you're a regular Don Corleone. Why didn't you tell her the truth?'

'Because I don't trust her and I don't fully understand why, so don't ask.

78

Maybe what I've sensed all this time is her resentment of us for the relationship we have with Gayle.' *Or maybe it's more. Or maybe I'm just being paranoid.*

'Did she threaten to expose us?'

'It wouldn't have been us. It would have only been me, because she doesn't know you know about it. But she never made a threat of her own. She only asked whether what we'd involved Gayle in could land her aunt in jail. I think she believed me when I told her no, but she's going to dig just the same, especially now that I've been injured. She's worried that whoever got to me will come after Gayle next.'

'Again, we can't really blame her for that, especially since she thinks we're selfish bastards who don't appreciate her aunt enough. But if she's told that Tala was the target, she won't worry about Gayle getting caught in the crossfire.' He gave Marcus a single nod. 'By coming forward, you kill two birds with one stone. You nip any speculation of your involvement in Tala's murder in the bud, and Jill backs off. Not bad. Not bad at all.'

'If she believed me. I'm still not sure she did.'

'All right,' Stone said slowly. 'So . . . short of bumping her off, what are we going to do about her?'

'I want the two of you to investigate each threat on that list together, and I want you to show her that they were all made by angry people just blowing off steam. That nothing's ever come of any of them in the past and it's highly likely that nothing ever will.'

Stone raised an eyebrow. 'You mean you want me to lie.'

Marcus sighed. 'No, I just want you to convince her that Gayle is safe.'

'Then what about the threats we made go away? If I don't tell her the truth on those, she'll go on thinking you're some kind of Mafia boss.'

'I'd almost prefer that,' Marcus muttered. 'I could tell her to leave it alone or she'll be taking a swim in the Ohio wearing concrete galoshes.' Rubbing his temples, he tried to think, but his brain was starting to stumble around in his skull. It had been too many nights since he'd truly slept. 'Find a way to explain why those people stopped sending threats. Hell, tell her we sent our lawyer after them and counter-threatened them with legal action.'

'And if she cross-checks with Rex?'

The *Ledger*'s attorney was one of Marcus's oldest friends, but he'd kept him out of the loop to protect him from any ethical dilemmas. 'He'll tell her he's bound by client confidentiality. And then he'll come over here and lecture me on all the reasons I shouldn't be doing whatever it is that I'm doing. After which,' Marcus continued lightly, 'I'll promise him I'll stop all my shenanigans and walk the straight and narrow for the rest of my days.'

Stone snorted. 'As if.'

'And then Rex will roll his eyes and go away, muttering under his breath that I'm going to get myself in "Big Trouble" some day.' Marcus shrugged. 'Same old, same old.'

Stone shook his head. 'All right, if that's how you want to play this thing, I've got your back.'

'You always have,' Marcus murmured. In his own way, Stone was the most loyal man on the planet. 'Thank you.'

Cheeks darkening, Stone dismissed the thanks with an embarrassed flip of his hand. 'So what are you going to do now?'

'Edit the list, then send it to Bishop.'

Stone's eyes nearly popped out of his head. 'Why in God's green earth would you do that?'

'Because I promised her I would.'

'You told her? About the list? What the fuck, Marcus? You swore us all to secrecy and then you go handing it off to her without a blink?'

'She and Novak asked if I'd been threatened. To categorically deny it seemed unwise, so I told them that my office manager kept a list. I never planned to send her the *real* list.' Stone was still staring like Marcus had three heads. 'They were suggesting that I might have been the target. It seemed like the right thing to do.'

Closing his eyes, Stone pinched the bridge of his nose. 'Shit, boy. You and your right thing are gonna get us a lot of unwanted attention from that detective. We need a plan to get her off your ass.'

Marcus thought of Scarlett Bishop looking up at him in that alley right before the medics arrived, her eyes filled with approval. Respect. Desire. He drew a deep breath, fighting to let it out on an even exhale rather than a shuddering one. Any attention she gave him was about as far from unwanted as anything could get. 'Don't worry about the detective.' The words came out a husky rumble. 'I'll deal with her.'

Stone's eyes popped open to lock on his in disbelief. 'You *like* her. Oh my *God*. You have got to be freaking *kidding* me.'

For a split second Marcus considered denying it, but realized he didn't want to. 'Why? Because she's a cop?'

'Because she's *Bishop*. She eats men for breakfast, spits out their bones, then grinds them up to make her bread. She's a fucking praying mantis.'

Marcus's lips twitched. He was feeling true amusement for the first time in a long while. 'Where do you get this stuff? She grinds their bones to make her bread? Really?'

'She's a hardass,' Stone insisted. 'A real ball-buster.'

Stone and Scarlett Bishop had not met under ideal circumstances. Deacon and Scarlett had been investigating an abduction, and Stone had been withholding evidence. To be fair, Stone had just found Mikhail's body buried in a shallow grave, so his emotions had been unstable at best.

'You lied to her, Stone,' Marcus said mildly. 'Did you honestly expect her to be okay with that?'

Stone stared, dumbfounded. 'Did the medics give you hallucinogenic drugs? Because that's the only way this is making any sense to me. I mean, okay, she's built. I'll give you that. Really built.' He held his hands out lewdly, as if squeezing a woman's breasts. 'Under the circumstances, I guess I can understand your momentary lapse of sanity, because the bitch has an impressive rack. Take her out for a spin if you have to, just to get her out of your system. But guard your nuts while you do, because if you don't, she'll add 'em to her personal collection. And once you've taken her around the block, park her somewhere and, for the love of God, walk away.'

Marcus's amusement had evaporated as soon as Stone started with the crude commentary on Scarlett's physical appearance. 'That's enough,' he snapped. 'You don't like her. I get it. I can even accept it. But I won't accept you talking about her that way. You don't like the way she does her job, that's your opinion, but the rest . . .' He trailed off, stopped in his tracks by the bewildered look on his brother's face.

'Whoa, whoa, whoa. Let me get this straight.' Stone's forehead bunched as he considered it. 'You really *like* her? As in someone you might even . . .' He grimaced. 'Date?'

'I don't really know her,' Marcus said truthfully. 'Not yet, anyway. I may never get to know her.'

'But you'd like to?'

Marcus shrugged. 'Maybe. I may never see her again, but if I do, I don't intend for it to be a single spin around the block.'

Stone sighed. 'No, I guess not. You're just not built that way. Okay, Mr Right-thing-to-do, give her the damn list. Just give me copies of everything you give her. I need to know where you're vulnerable.'

'That's fair. I can do that.' Marcus glanced at the security monitor on his desk. From here he could see every entrance and exit to the building. 'Jill's in the lobby and she's got her arms full of breakfast. She could use a hand with the boxes.'

Stone stood up. 'I'll let her in and then get started on the story about Tala.'

'I don't want Jill poking around here unattended.'

Stone's eyes widened. 'I'm her babysitter?'

'Until I can find someone else to do it, yes.'

Stone was not pleased. 'If she's smart enough to hack into Gayle's email, I'm sure she's able to access the computers remotely. I'm not going to watch her 24/7.'

'I'll change all the passwords on the servers,' Marcus said. 'And I'll get Diesel to add a few firewalls or something.' Diesel was their resident computer nerd. Marcus could manage around the computers, and had even hacked into a system or two, but Diesel was a fucking artist. 'Just watch her for the next few hours. I want to know what she tries to do.'

'You think she knows more than she's letting on?'

'I think she's a lot more curious than is safe. For her or for us. Just watch her, at least until morning meeting. Then we'll figure out what to do about her.'

'Okay,' Stone said with a shake of his head. 'You're the boss.'

Marcus waited until the door was closed before muttering, 'Yay me.'

He leaned back in his chair to fish his phone from the pocket of his jeans. It had vibrated with an incoming text while he and Stone had been talking. He read the text, then, his heart hammering, read it again. Especially the greeting. *Scarlett Bishop here*. Not 'Detective Bishop', but 'Scarlett'. It was warmer. Inviting, even. *And you're a fool, O'Bannion*.

It wasn't an invitation. It was her name, clear and simple. *So don't read in shit that isn't there, and focus on the actual message*.

The prompt for the list in and of itself came as no surprise, as he was overdue on delivering it, but he had hoped that after seeing this morning's video, she'd realize the list wasn't necessary. Clearly Tala had been the target.

However, he'd met enough cops to know that once they got an idea in their heads, they wouldn't let up until they had evidence in hand. He just needed to find a few names that would satisfy her while not piquing her curiosity so much that she started to dig. Because what she'd find probably wouldn't end well for either of them.

Five

'What is this?' Lieutenant Lynda Isenberg asked sharply as she leaned against the side of Scarlett's desk. 'I thought you were watching the O'Bannion footage of the victim.'

The note of disapproval in her boss's voice startled Scarlett to attention. Lynda rarely used that tone on anyone, and almost never with Scarlett. Scarlett had never given her reason to.

Surreptitiously wiping her eyes, Scarlett muted her computer before pausing the video she'd been watching. And listening to. Which, admittedly, had perhaps involved getting a little too lost in the beauty of Marcus's music. His singing voice was exactly as she'd expected – rich and smooth, soothing the hurts in her heart even as it drew a new kind of pain to the surface.

'I *am* watching the victim,' she said, relieved that her own voice was steady. 'She's right there.' She pointed at the edge of her screen, where Tala stood, tentative and wary, barely visible through the trees bordering the clearing where Marcus had recorded the scene with his cap-cam.

'She looks like she's about to bolt,' Lynda observed, her voice oddly cold. Something was wrong, but Scarlett respected Lynda enough not to pry. Her boss would share if she so chose. Thankfully Lynda extended the same respect to her people. If she'd noticed Scarlett's eyes were still a little red from crying, she gave no indication of it.

'But she doesn't bolt,' Scarlett said. 'Not until he stops singing. I've watched five of the ten video clips from the park. When Marcus finishes his song, she leaves, but not before.'

Lynda's gray brows snapped up to the edge of her hairline, her eyes going wide in a rare display of shock. 'That was Marcus O'Bannion singing? Really?'

'It was. That's how he got Tala's attention the first time. He said that he'd

83

been singing because it was the middle of the night and he thought he was alone. He looked up and saw her in the trees with the dog.' That had been the ballad, the one he'd sung for his dead brother. Scarlett hadn't expected to hear it, since Marcus hadn't recorded that first meeting, but she'd heard it on every one of the park video files she'd watched so far. Sometimes he sang three or four other songs first, but he'd always switch to the ballad as soon as Tala came into view.

The first time Scarlett had heard it, she'd been as stunned as Lynda was right now. Every time thereafter, Scarlett's throat had closed and her eyes had filled, memories of Michelle blasting through her mind. Always ending with the worst one, of course. *So much blood.*

This was why she didn't let herself truly remember Michelle very often. Doing so left her raw and far too vulnerable until she was able to shove the memories back down. Or until she could reaffix her usual calm, cool, collected expression to her face. An expression just like Lynda usually wore. But neither woman looked like that now. It was strangely comforting.

Lynda drew a breath, exhaling unsteadily. 'They played that song at my husband's funeral,' she murmured, almost as if to herself.

Stunned, Scarlett could only stare. She'd reported to Lynda for five years, yet she'd never known her boss had been married. 'I'm sorry,' she finally said, so softly that only Lynda could hear. 'I didn't know.'

Lynda blinked, a quick, embarrassed flush spreading across her cheeks, then shook her head hard and fast as if to clear it. A heartbeat later, her expression had returned to normal – alert, brusque, and all business. 'It was fifteen years ago,' she said, flicking her hand through the air, dismissing the emotion. 'Nothing to do with this case.'

'They say that songs take you back faster and harder than any other reminder,' Scarlett murmured. Now that she'd seen her boss's vulnerability, she didn't want to see the real Lynda to disappear behind her hard shell. Not until Scarlett herself was able to do the same. 'We played that song at my best friend's funeral too. So . . . yeah.' She shrugged fitfully. 'It's hard.'

They were silent for a long minute, neither looking at the other. Then Lynda cleared her throat, pointed to the computer screen. 'Does she ever come out of the woods?'

'Not that I've seen so far. Marcus said that she let the dog come close enough to be petted, but she stayed back. I haven't gotten to that file yet, but everything I've seen on these videos has corroborated his story.'

'I didn't expect that he'd voluntarily give you anything that wouldn't,' Lynda said carefully.

Her tone had Scarlett glancing up once again. This time Lynda's eyes were shadowed with concern. 'What?' Scarlett demanded, hearing her own belligerence.

'You're personally connected with this man. He's a witness now, but he could become a suspect. A murder suspect, Scarlett. I am, quite frankly, concerned.'

Scarlett didn't think Marcus would ever become a suspect, but she wasn't going to argue the point, not wanting to give Lynda any reason to kick her off this case. Not because of Marcus, but because of Tala.

'I'm not connected,' she replied, not looking away. 'Not like you're thinking, anyway. I've interacted with Marcus O'Bannion five times.' She held up her hand, counting on her fingers. 'When he was wounded saving a woman's life, twice in the hospital afterward, then at his brother's funeral, and now tonight. We have no relationship beyond that.'

She didn't have to count all the nights she'd lain awake wishing that they did, right? *Best to keep that little jewel to myself.*

Lynda did not look convinced. 'Then how *are* you connected, if it's not the way I'm thinking?'

'I think we're testing each other's preconceptions. He doesn't trust many cops, but he believed he could trust me to help Tala. I don't trust newsmen, but I'm hoping he's different. I do hope you're planning to have this same conversation with Deacon,' she added coolly. 'He's more connected than I am, what with Marcus being his future cousin-in-law.'

Lynda gave her a long, probing look before pointing back at the screen, where Tala was still frozen in place at the forest's edge. 'What more can you tell me about her?'

'Seventeen, possibly an immigrant. I've already watched today's file. I couldn't see her face that clearly because there was very little light in the alley, but the audio was clear as a bell. Her English is flawless, but she has a definite accent. I'm thinking Filipino.' Marcus had suggested that first. *Again, keeping that to myself.* Scarlett brought up the video Marcus had taken that morning in the alley, cranked up the sound and hit PLAY.

Scarlett turned her screen so that Lynda had a better viewing angle, then sat back in her chair, watching the events unfold for the fifth time – Tala's hesitant greeting, Marcus's careful, gentle questions.

Why do you cry, Tala?

Why do you? the girl pushed back.

That Marcus hadn't denied it made Scarlett's throat hurt, just as it had all the other times she'd watched. It wasn't just that he still grieved for the brother he'd lost. It was that he wasn't ashamed to admit it. Still, he'd cried when he'd thought himself alone. It made Scarlett wonder about the face he showed his family and the rest of the world.

It made her wonder if he'd ever show his grief to her.

Then she realized that he just had. By turning over the videos without any coercion, he'd effectively bared his soul not only to Scarlett, but to anyone she allowed to watch. He'd trusted her. Thrown suddenly off balance, she decided that these videos would be locked up and she'd do whatever she had to do to ensure that as few people as possible viewed them.

Will you let me help you, Tala?

I . . . I can't pay you.

The picture shifted side to side as Marcus shook his head hard.

I don't need your money. I don't want it.

A second of heavy silence followed, Tala's shoulders sagging, her head hanging in defeat. Then she lifted her chin, her young face having transformed from frightened to sensuously inviting. She reached for the waistband of Marcus's jeans, her husky whisper intended to entice.

I understand. I can make you feel good.

The picture jolted abruptly as Marcus took a giant step back, his hands shoving into the frame, palms out. His response was panicked. Horrified.

No. Stop. You don't understand. That's not what I want. I don't want anything from you. I just want to help you.

Why? Why would you help me? I'm no one.

Scarlett's throat hurt again. For Tala and for all the victims she'd ever met who believed they were no one.

Everyone is someone, Marcus said sadly. *Why do you cry, Tala?*

Tala's expression was a jumble of fear and hope that made Scarlett's heart twist. Help had been so damn close, but in the next minute it would be brutally ripped away.

It's dangerous. They're dangerous. My family will die if I'm found here.

Marcus's voice became icy. Brittle. Furious. *Who are you afraid of?*

The man. His wife. They . . . Tala looked away. *They own us.*

How? Marcus demanded. *Who?*

Scarlett braced herself, knowing what was coming, but still she flinched at the gunshot.

Tala crumpled to the pavement, her face filling the screen as Marcus dropped to one knee beside her. *Tala? Shit. You're hit.* His hands were trembling as he cut a piece of her shirt and packed the wound, then sprang to his feet.

Lynda made a sound of disapproval. 'He's leaving her alone.'

86

'For just a minute,' Scarlett murmured. 'He's calling 911 and securing the scene.'

'Not a soul in sight,' Lynda said, her jaw taut as they watched him run. 'It would have been too much to expect that he'd catch a glimpse of the shooter.'

'He didn't know it then,' Scarlett said, 'but the shooter was circling the block, coming back to take two more shots. He made the 911 call at 2.47.'

Tala's face was filling the screen once again as Marcus resumed his first aid.

Tala! he was shouting at her now. *Don't die, dammit. Don't you dare die.*

Tala's lips moved on the word *Help*, but no sound came out. She forced the next word out in an agonized huff. *Malaya*.

Lynda grabbed the mouse and paused the video. 'Help and *malaya*.' She glanced at Scarlett. 'What does *malaya* mean?'

'According to Google, it means "free" in both Tagalog and Malay,' Scarlett supplied, once more keeping the original source of the information to herself. She'd double-checked the definition, and determined that Marcus had been correct.

'She was asking him to free her family,' Lynda murmured, then lined up the frozen frame of Tala at the edge of the trees with that of the young woman as she lay dying on the asphalt. 'Same clothes.'

Scarlett nodded. 'I noticed that. She wears the same exact thing in every video I've seen so far. A white polo shirt and faded blue jeans.'

'A uniform of some kind?'

'I thought that,' Scarlett said. 'I didn't see any logo on the shirt she was wearing when she was shot, but there was a lot of blood on it. The CSU tech working the crime scene said that Vince would call me if the lab found any identifying marks on her clothes, but I haven't heard from him yet.'

If there was anything to find, Sergeant Vince Tanaka would find it. The head of CSU ran a tight ship, and his people were well trained and meticulous.

'There don't appear to be any visible logos on the shirts she wore to the park, either,' Scarlett went on, 'although the video quality is grainy. The lab is checking that too.' Reaching for the mouse, she rewound the alley video to a point about two thirds through. 'There are two other things I can tell you. One, Tala knew who shot her.'

She advanced the video frame by frame, stopping at the moment the young woman's eyes flared wide in terror. And recognition.

Lynda's sigh was quiet. 'You're right. So much for a random shooting.'

'Or for wondering which of them was the target,' Scarlett said grimly.

'You thought O'Bannion was the target?'

A half-shrug. 'He does make his living digging up news. It stood to reason that he might have pissed off somebody enough to want to shut him down. He was supposed to have already sent me a list of the threats he's received over the last few years, but I haven't seen that yet.'

'I'm sure he viewed this video before he sent it to you. Maybe he assumed the same thing we have and decided you didn't need the list after all.'

'Maybe.' Highly likely, actually. 'I still want the list, though, just in case.'

'I agree. If you have to, get a warrant.'

'I'll give him another hour before I ask him for it again. If he balks, I'll get the warrant, but if he doesn't want me to see the list, he's probably already deleted it. For now, I'm moving forward with Tala being the target. We'll canvass the neighbors with photos of her and the dog, and interview all the visitors to the park. Folks in the park may be more likely to remember seeing the fancy dog than the girl, though, so I'll also work on the dog's ID.'

'You'll canvass the veterinarians, too?'

'Definitely, but I started thinking that I might have better luck with high-end pet groomers. This dog had a fancy haircut, so I'm assuming it has a regular appointment at the salon.'

'Do you know any groomers?'

'As a matter of fact, I do. Do you remember Delores Kaminsky?'

At first Lynda frowned, but then her expression perked up. 'Of course! The woman who lived? She's a groomer? I thought she ran an animal shelter.'

'She did both before the shooting, and her goal is to reopen both.'

Lynda tilted her head, her eyes assessing. 'I didn't know you kept up with the victims.'

Scarlett shrugged her embarrassment away. 'I don't,' she lied. The truth was that she kept an eye on all of them from afar. Especially the young ones. They'd already survived one trauma. She hated to see that experience screw up the rest of their lives. She'd made more than one call to area outreaches, giving them a heads-up when one of the victims started down a wrong road. Sometimes they were able to drag the kids back to the straight and narrow. More often they failed, and the kids fell into the black hole of the criminal justice system.

But she'd tried, and she'd keep trying. Not that she wanted anyone to know it.

Lynda said nothing, waiting with a knowing look that made Scarlett's cheeks burn hotter.

'I got dragged to the shelter by Dani and Faith,' Scarlett said with an exasperated huff. Deacon's sister and his fiancée had pretended to need Scarlett's Land Cruiser to transport their newly adopted animals, but she knew they were trying to include her in their girl group. Damned if she hadn't been sucked right in. 'They visited Delores after she woke up in the hospital. Her friends had been taking care of the animals, placing the ones they could. But there were a lot of dogs.'

'Faith got two dogs, as I recall,' Lynda said, her lips starting to twitch. 'A three-year-old shepherd mix and a golden-mix puppy.'

'I know. Deacon's always muttering about his shoes being chewed up.' Lynda's gray brows lifted in startled delight. 'Don't tell me you got one too.'

Scarlett rolled her eyes. 'Yeah. They guilted me into it.'

Lynda's expression softened. 'You have a good heart. Don't be ashamed of that.'

'I'm not.' Which was a total lie. 'I just have a reputation to protect.'

'Well, your secret's safe with me. What kind of dog did you get?'

Another roll of her eyes. 'A bulldog. He's . . . missing a leg. Nobody else wanted him.'

Lynda stared at her for a long moment. 'And? How has he adapted?'

Scarlett thought of the way Zat had comforted her this morning when her emotions had dragged her under. Despite living through conditions of abuse for most of his life, he was sweet-natured and loving. And if Scarlett had anything to say about it, he'd live like a king for all the years he had left.

'Okay, I guess,' she said briskly. 'He doesn't eat as much as I thought. Anyway, I'm meeting Delores later to show her a photo of the poodle. See if she can narrow my groomer search at all.'

Lynda turned her attention back to the screen, still frozen on Tala's frightened eyes. 'You said there were two things you knew about Tala. What was the second?'

Grateful to be out of the emotional quicksand, Scarlett reached for her mouse. 'That you can take Marcus O'Bannion off your potential suspect list. He didn't shoot her.' She forwarded the video to the point where Marcus was on his knees doing first aid. 'Here's the second shot – it came from behind Marcus. It hits him in the back and he's knocked flat.' On the screen, the picture pitched as Marcus was thrown forward from the force of the bullet, then the screen went dark.

'The camera broke?' Lynda asked.

'No, it's pointing at the concrete. He landed across her body. Her blood was soaking his shirt when I got there. The third shot is also fired from behind him.'

Thirty seconds elapsed, then, on a groan of pain, Marcus slowly lifted his head.

Tala, he muttered. *Oh God*. The lurch of the camera was punctuated by another, quieter groan as he shoved himself back up to kneel beside Tala's lifeless body, freezing on the bullet hole in her head. And then the picture began to tremble, because Marcus had begun to tremble.

No, he whispered hoarsely. *Goddammit, no*. Slowly he leaned forward, reaching one hand to grip the girl's chin with a gentleness that made Scarlett's eyes sting. He turned Tala's head with the same slow deliberation, bringing the exit wound into view.

'Oh no,' Lynda whispered. 'That poor girl.'

Scarlett said nothing, her throat too thick for any words to get through, because she knew what was coming.

He rolled Tala's head back to its original position with the same gentleness. Then his hands clenched into fists and slowly lowered to rest on his thighs. All while his body shook like a leaf.

Scarlett clenched her jaw, steeling herself for the low cry of pain that sounded like it came from a wounded animal rather than a man. He'd been so in control by the time she'd arrived. So . . . unmovable. Invincible. Seeing him – hearing him – had left Scarlett shaken as well, every time she'd watched the video.

Lynda sighed quietly. 'His brother Mikhail was also shot in the head, wasn't he?' she murmured.

Scarlett nodded. 'Marcus and his brother Stone found him.' Buried in a shallow grave. 'Mikhail was only seventeen.'

'Just like Tala.'

On the screen, he knelt beside Tala's body for another fifteen seconds, panting like he'd sprinted a mile, then pushed to his feet with a groan of pain. He looked behind him, but the lens picked up nothing, the shooter long gone.

Scarlett stopped the video. 'He went to look for the shooter, but there was no one there. I'll have the lab check to be sure there isn't something in the background that I'm missing. Marcus voluntarily surrendered a small pistol he'd holstered at his ankle,' she added.

'Deacon said that you both think O'Bannion had a gun that he didn't surrender.'

That Deacon had called Lynda with his initial report was no surprise. Scarlett had done the same after she'd showered and cleared her throat about a million times, not wanting her boss to notice that she'd been crying.

'Yes,' Scarlett said. 'And before you ask me – yes, that bothers me a helluva lot. Marcus O'Bannion is definitely hiding something, but that something isn't involved in Tala's murder.'

'Find out what it is,' Lynda said. 'I don't want any surprises coming out in court if he does prove to be our star witness.'

'Yes, ma'am.' Scarlett wasn't keen on surprises either. She'd dig until she discovered exactly what he hadn't told them, then she'd decide if he was the kind of man she could even consider trusting.

She checked her email, saw that she had no new messages from Marcus O'Bannion, so still no list of threats. She didn't think he was holding on to the list just to be difficult, or because he was embarrassed or ashamed. He'd given up the video files so easily, so quickly, with no demand for discretion, even though they revealed severe cracks in his emotional armor.

The list was probably irrelevant with regard to finding Tala's killer, but it just might give Scarlett insight into the man himself. Either way, it gave her an excuse to talk to him again.

So that I can start looking for whatever it is that he's hiding, she told herself sternly.

That she'd hear his voice again was simply a bonus.

Six

The buzzing of his cell phone drew Drake's attention from the TV in his bedroom. Ever since Stephanie had dropped him off at home, he'd been channel-surfing the news while periodically searching online for any mention of what had gone down this morning. So far, nothing more than a few vague reports of shots fired in the ghetto downtown. Of course the reporter would never call it 'the ghetto'. That wasn't PC.

He rolled his eyes. The media was overrun by liberals with their heads up their asses, where it was so dark that they couldn't see what was really happening in the world, or – luckily for Drake – even in their own city. They'd mumbled about 'unidentified victims' whose status was 'still undetermined'. Idiots. Their status was dead. D-E-A-D, dead.

There had been no mention of Tala or the man she'd been with. Not yet, anyway.

He rolled his eyes again when he saw the caller ID on his cell phone. Stephanie. Probably wanting to be reassured. Picking up his phone, he frowned, annoyed that his hand still trembled. The adrenaline high had crashed hours before, leaving him a little on the shaky side. He needed some food, but there hadn't been anything in the fridge except beer.

The phone in his hand stopped buzzing. He'd stared at it too long, and Stephanie's call had gone to voicemail. He considered calling her back, but knew there was no need. Too OCD for words, Stephanie would try him again in a few minutes.

Drake's stomach churned, bile bubbling up to burn his throat. *Dammit. I really need some food*. Especially since he'd gone ahead and drunk all the beer. His older sister was gonna shit a ring when she came home tonight to the empty fridge. *So I'd better refill it before she gets home*. Not because he was afraid of her, but just so he didn't have to hear her bitch.

Stephanie would give him the money for more beer. He wasn't worried about that.

What did worry him was that he'd drunk the entire six-pack and his hand still trembled. Both hands, actually. Okay, fine. He was shaking all over, like a damn leaf.

You're rattled. It's okay. It's not every day you kill someone. Someones, actually.

It still didn't seem quite real. *I killed two people.*

He hadn't really planned to – especially not the guy. The big dude dressed in black had moved like a cop, but he hadn't been arresting Tala. He'd been talking to her, a serious expression on his face.

Probably just trying to convince the bitch to give him a blow job.

But Drake knew it was a helluva lot more likely that Tala had planned to tell. Now he'd never know – nor would anyone else. The only thing he knew for sure was that she'd arranged to meet the guy, whoever he was, because she'd used Drake's cell phone to send him a text. She'd thought she'd been so clever, slipping the phone from the pocket of the jacket he'd left on Stephanie's living-room sofa. Of course he had left it there on purpose, just to see what she'd do.

Served her right for thinking she could keep secrets. He'd felt the business card through her bra when he'd come up behind her, grabbing a breast in each hand. He would have had the card out of her bra a second later had Stephanie's father not picked that moment to walk into the room.

Drake huffed a chuckle. Stupid bastard. Stephanie's old man actually thought he could keep Tala all to himself. Drake had lost count of the number of times he and Stephanie had proved the old man wrong. But Stephanie didn't want to piss her father off, so they played along when Papa was in the room. Which meant that by the time Drake caught up with Tala again, she'd hidden the card and neither he nor Stephanie had been able to find it. So he'd set her up and Tala had taken the bait just like he'd known she would, thinking she'd pulled something over on him by borrowing his phone.

Stupid backward bitch. He and Stephanie had set the trap by telling Tala that they'd be going out that night to get Steph some coke. Tala had texted someone to meet her a few blocks from the homeless shelter where Drake and Stephanie always bought their blow. Tala's text was no longer on his phone. She had immediately deleted it, thinking she was safe.

Well, tonight she'd been educated, hadn't she? Drake had simply used his laptop to open the app that synced his phone, tablet and computer.

He only wished he'd been able to stay to watch her bleed, but he hadn't had the luxury of time. He'd made sure that he'd finished the job by putting a bullet in her skull before running like hell. And not a second too soon. He'd escaped those sirens by five seconds. Ten tops. Way too close for his liking.

But at least Tala wasn't a problem anymore. And even if she had told the guy everything, it didn't matter. They were both dead and wouldn't be talking to anyone else.

His phone buzzed again, startling him, sending his pulse rocketing up. *It's just Stephanie.* Who would freak if Drake wasn't calm and in control. *So calm the fuck down so she doesn't freak. Answer the phone like it's nothin' special.*

'Yeah?' He injected a note of bored impatience into his voice. Like he had a million things better to do. 'What is it now?'

'He knows.' Stephanie's whisper was harsh.

Drake's heart gave a little stutter. Stephanie's father shouldn't know anything yet. 'There's nothing on the news,' he said smoothly. 'So how did he find out?'

'I didn't tell him. I swear. The alarm went off.' Stephanie was talking way too fast. 'The ankle tracker had a tamper alarm. I thought we'd disabled it on my dad's computer when we hacked into his system, but we didn't. He had it set so that the alarm went to his phone and the house alarm. It went off hours ago. This is the first chance I've had to call.'

Drake closed his eyes. How the fucking hell had they forgotten about the damn tracker strapped to Tala's ankle? They were always so careful when they took her out to play, disabling the old man's tracking software on the household's server so that the girl's temporary absence wouldn't be detected. Stephanie's father would only notice if he specifically went into the logs to check Tala's position, and there had been no need to do so as long as they returned her to her pallet on the floor before the other servants woke up.

'I didn't know it triggered the house alarm. It was loud enough to wake the . . .' Stephanie faltered. 'It was really loud.'

'Somebody had to have cut the tracker off her body,' Drake said quietly. Damn. He hadn't thought of that when he'd left her body behind. But taking her with him had never been an option. 'What did he say to you?'

'He only asked me if I knew where Tala was. I told him no. I don't think he believed me, though. He gave me the look.'

Drake rolled his eyes. 'He always has that look. Like he swallowed a lemon.'

'No, this was different. He knew I was lying.'

94

'So what are you going to do?' he asked smoothly.

A slight pause. 'What am *I* going to do?' she asked quietly. Too quietly, actually. 'You're the one who killed her. What are *you* going to do?'

Her calm rattled him a little. She was supposed to be terrified. Girls always got terrified when there was trouble. They squealed and begged him for direction. Stephanie would too. She just didn't know it yet.

'What *we're* going to do is hang loose and pretend like we don't have a care in the world. And what we're going to do is remember that *we* were in that car *together*.' He hardened his tone, made it menacing. 'Right?'

'Right.' A deep breath and a decidedly less aggressive tone. 'Right. Whatever you say.'

'Good answer.' And if Stephanie folded? Drake might just have to up his killing tally to three.

Somehow the idea didn't bother him as much as it probably should have.

Besides, Drake was not afraid of Stephanie's father. He had insurance. He had the flash drive in his underwear drawer. On it, he'd burned a copy of Stephanie's father's files every time he accessed the man's computer. Every time they took Tala out to play.

When the old man saw what Drake had on him, he would never bother them again.

Cincinnati, Ohio
Tuesday 4 August, 7.45 A.M.

'Mr Sweeney? Do you have a minute?' Ken's secretary's voice came through the intercom. At the office, Alice Newman always called him Mr Sweeney. Any other place, he was simply Dad. Alice had never been a Sweeney – mostly for her own protection, especially when she was a child. Ken made too many enemies to allow either of his children to be made into targets by association. Then again, Ken hadn't been born a Sweeney either. None of his team used the names they'd been born with. It was tidier that way.

His daughter with his first wife, Alice had graduated with honors from the University of Kentucky's law school and was learning the business from the ground up. Ken hoped she'd take over soon so that he could meet his goal of retirement to a sunny beach by the time he was fifty. Luckily Alice was a quick study, because Ken had only two years to go. 'One of your employees would like to talk with you,' she added professionally.

Ken looked up from the P&L statements he was reviewing. The profits were lower and the losses were higher than they'd been a year ago.

Combined with the morning surprise from security and the fact that Reuben had as of yet failed to report, he was not in a good mood.

'Who is it, Alice?' he asked impatiently.

'Gene Decker. He, um, says it's important.'

Ken frowned. *What the hell?* 'Tell Decker to route any accounting concerns through his boss. And tell Joel that he needs to keep his people busier so they don't have time to bother me. And where the fuck is Reuben?'

'Mr Blackwell hasn't called in yet. And Mr Decker says it's not about accounting. It's related to the call he made to you this morning.'

Fuck. Decker was supposed to have gone back to the accounting office and minded his own business. 'Send him in,' Ken said coldly.

'Thank you, Mr Sweeney,' Gene said respectfully a minute later as he came in and closed Ken's office door. He didn't come in any farther, taking a military stance – staring straight ahead, his feet spread wide, his hands clasped behind his back. 'I appreciate your time, sir. I know you're busy.'

Ken blew out a breath, trying not to snap. 'Come the hell in and sit down,' he said, pointing to one of the leather wingback chairs on the other side of his desk. He silently observed the man's fluid movements as he obeyed.

'It looks like your injury's healed,' he remarked. 'Your limp is gone.'

'Yes, sir. Mostly, anyway.' Decker lowered himself into the wing chair gingerly, as if afraid his weight might break it. Had the chair been of lesser quality, he might have been right. Built like a linebacker, he'd surprised them early on by demonstrating the speed of a sprinter and the footwork of a boxer. The combination had made him one hell of a bodyguard, a fact to which Ken could personally attest. Ken wouldn't be sitting at his desk today if Gene Decker hadn't been so fast on his feet. Unfortunately the accident had robbed Decker of some of his speed and agility. He wouldn't be returning to personal security anytime soon.

Decker's loss had been the company's gain, though. Skilled bodyguards were a dime a dozen, but a man with Decker's creative accounting skills? The young man had quite a future ahead of him.

Decker shifted in the chair that dwarfed most men, but his shoulders were simply too wide for a comfortable fit. Giving up, he leaned forward, resting his elbows on his knees. His expression was troubled. 'We have a problem, sir.'

'I take it that this is regarding the computer alarm from last night?'

Decker nodded. 'Sean in IT says a 501 is a tracker tamper alert.'

Ken did not allow his expression to change, but inside he was seething.

He went to IT? After I expressly told him to drop it? 'I told you to go back to accounting and to leave the alarm to Mr Blackwell. Why didn't you?'

'I did, sir. I stayed at my desk for an hour thinking Mr Blackwell would come to me to get my statement about what had happened with the alarm and the guy on duty. But he never showed up, so I went looking for him.'

'There was no need for Reuben Blackwell to get your statement. He was fully aware of the situation because I spoke with him – after I told you to go back to accounting.'

Decker didn't flinch. 'But he never came in at all, sir. When I went up to the security office to find him, Jason Jackson was still lying on the floor, asleep. The 501 warning was still flashing on the computer screen.'

Ken couldn't mask his disbelief. 'Excuse me?'

'I know, sir. But that's what happened. I imagine the security office is wired, so there should be a video to prove what I'm saying.'

And Ken would be watching that video as soon as Decker had gone back to his office. 'What did you do next?'

'I helped Jackson to his feet, but he . . . well, he threw up.' A slight grimace. 'He had a fever and I wasn't sure what to do with him, so I dialed "one" to get Mr Blackwell's cell phone, but all I got was voicemail again. So I left a message with Blackwell, cleaned Jackson up, called him a cab, and sent him home. When I was cleaning him up, I found a bottle of cough syrup in his pocket. That could have been the alcohol I smelled on his breath. I saved the bottle in case you wanted to see it.'

Ken let out a slow breath, counting to ten. 'And you just . . . sent him home.'

'Yes, sir. In a cab, sir.' A slight hesitation, then Decker barreled forward. 'Jackson is a good man, Mr Sweeney. He's loyal. I worked a few shifts with him when I was in personal security. We weren't exactly friends, but we did share a few meals. I didn't think he'd drink on the job. I was glad to find the cough syrup. Maybe it reacted with another medication he'd taken, I don't know.'

'I'll send someone to check on him.' And someone else to check on Blackwell. 'I take it that you took it upon yourself to go to IT?'

A single nod, no regret on Decker's face. 'Like I said, the computer was still blinking with the 501 code. I assumed no one had taken care of it, and you'd made it clear you didn't want to be called back, so I went to IT to find out what was going on. I was part of security before I got hurt. I didn't think this was a huge issue.'

And that was where Decker was wrong. He'd been part of the legitimate security arm. The tracker wasn't. But he had been right about one thing –

the tracker alarm needed to be attended to, and quickly. Someone had escaped and could even now be revealing all to the police.

The escapee could not identify Ken, but he or she would probably report their owner. While the vast majority of the owners knew better than to identify Ken as their distributor, sometimes a customer tended to be less discreet when questioned by the authorities. Sometimes those customers needed a little reminder to keep their mouths shut. Some reminders needed to be stronger – and more permanent – than others.

'All right,' Ken said calmly. 'What did you learn in IT?'

'Not much. As I said, Sean told me that the 501 code meant tracker tampering. He brought the tracking map up on his computer and swore when he saw the tracker's last location.'

'Last location?'

'Apparently the battery died, sir, at the corner of Fourteenth and Race.'

That was two blocks from CPD headquarters. Ken's gut convulsed, but he managed to suppress his agitation. 'I see. Did Sean identify the tracking unit?'

'No, but the number on his screen was 3942139-13.'

Ken's brows lifted. 'You have a good memory.'

'Not really. I wrote it down.' Decker held up his left hand, showing the number he'd scrawled on his palm with a black Sharpie.

Ken unlocked his desk drawer and ran his finger over the spines of the notebooks stored there, checking the dates. These notebooks held all his most personal notes and records. As much as he loved gadgets, he did not trust any computer system to keep his personal data secure. The only way anyone was getting access to his notebooks was by taking the key from his cold, dead fingers.

He chose the notebook he'd used three years before, found the tracker's serial number in the index, then flipped to the correct page. The tracker had been assigned to Charles 'Chip' Anders, who lived with his wife and daughter in Hyde Park.

I remember him. Anders was a tall, thin man who'd made his first million honestly enough, but for whom a merely comfortable lifestyle had not been enough. He'd been spurred to earn more by his brash wife, who'd grown up solidly middle class. Mrs Anders had wanted diamonds and furs, a vacation home in France. Servants. She'd wanted to hobnob with the rich and famous.

Ken inwardly winced. Her words. Certainly not his own.

Anders himself had craved the power he could broker among that same crowd. So he'd expanded his businesses, riding a swell of prosperity, until the market tanked and Anders's factories were no longer churning out the profits he required to support his new lifestyle.

Which was when Ken had stepped in, offering him a way to keep it all. To have his cake and eat it too.

Anders personal fortune had rebounded and he'd returned to giving his wife and daughter everything their greedy little hearts had desired. The daughter drove a luxury car and attended an Ivy League school. Anders and his wife had bought a house in an exclusive Cincinnati community where they'd partied with the wealthy elite, "hobnobbing" until the cows had come home.

There had been costs involved, of course. And responsibilities. And consequences for carelessness.

'The customer received five trackers,' Ken said. He had the serial numbers for all of them recorded in this notebook. 'Did Sean in IT tell you which wearer had triggered the alert?'

Gene shook his head. 'I don't even know . . .' He pursed his lips, apparently having edited himself. 'No, sir. He didn't tell me. I only saw the number.'

Ken's brows lifted. 'You don't even know what?'

'What you're tracking.'

'Didn't you ask Sean?'

'I did. He told me I should ask you.'

'Just like that?'

'Well, no, sir. He looked a little alarmed, then looked me up on his computer. Apparently I do not have clearance to view this information. I supposed that by asking, I revealed my position on the need-to-know totem pole.'

Score one for Sean in IT, Ken thought, satisfied. Ken's son with wife number two shouldn't have talked to Decker to begin with, but unlike Alice, Sean didn't spend much time with the employees, preferring to stay holed up with the computers. Most of the employees weren't even aware that he and Ken were related, as Sean had kept his mother's last name, which had also been an alias. Sean's mother had been no angel herself.

Decker hadn't been cleared to see or know anything other than the legitimate side of the business. That he had even known about the alert had only been because the man on duty – who *had* had top clearance – had been derelict in his responsibilities.

Jason Jackson better be sick. He'd better be so sick that he was dead, or close to it. Otherwise he would be punished accordingly.

Perhaps it was time to reward Decker's creative accounting and initiative with a bit more responsibility.

Ken filed the notebook, then locked the drawer. He looked up to find Decker watching his every move. 'Do you want to know what we're tracking?'

Decker didn't even blink. 'Yes.'

Ken's lips curved. 'If I tell you, I might have to kill you,' he said lightly, but Decker's gaze didn't waver.

'I figured that,' he said quietly. 'I've figured that for some time.'

Ken tilted his head, genuinely intrigued. 'How?'

Decker's chin lifted a fraction, just enough to be assertive without being arrogant. 'Because I see the books and I'm not stupid.' One of those big shoulders shrugged. 'You sell children's toys. You make a respectable amount of money with it. But your organization is far too big to exist on what you bring in from video games and stuffed animals.'

Ken wasn't sure if he should be angry or more intrigued. The video games covered their illegal porn distribution, and stuffed animals were one of the best ways to hide the pills that, even though not as big a business as they'd been a decade ago, were still one of the company's biggest money-makers. 'I see.'

'Do you?' Decker asked, his expression intensely serious. 'Do you really? If *I* can see that the legit profits don't balance with the visible spending, don't you think others can?'

Ken drew a quiet breath. 'Others . . . like who?'

'Competitors. Law enforcement.' Decker exaggerated a grimace. 'And even worse, the IRS. Trust me, you do *not* want the IRS noticing you.'

Ken suppressed a shudder. No, he certainly did not. 'I suppose you have a solution?'

'Yeah. I do. But you're going to have to let me see more than I see now.'

'You must know I'm not going to give you full access right away.'

'Like I said, I'm not stupid.'

'I never thought you were.' Leaning back in his chair, Ken crossed his legs and flicked a piece of lint off the knee of his trousers. 'People.'

Decker blinked once as Ken's meaning sank in. A few seconds ticked by, during which Ken could almost see the wheels turning in Decker's mind.

'Sex, labor or both?' Decker finally asked, as if inquiring as to what Ken wanted for breakfast.

'Labor. Mostly.' Some of their choicest acquisitions went to the sex trade. Some went to the production of the porn they distributed illegally. But most did go to labor.

'Sales and distribution territory?'

'Large.' Which was all he'd say on the matter until Decker had proved himself further.

'Fair enough. Sourcing? Domestic, international or both?'

'Both.' Ken didn't feel he'd revealed too much with that answer. The man was smart enough to guess that on his own.

'Okay. I'll need to see the accounts so that I can recommend actions to make your legit books less of a flare to the IRS.'

'Of course. But first I have another task.'

Decker's jaw tightened and his eyes flashed with something stronger than annoyance but not quite anger. When he spoke, it was with tempered restraint. 'You're testing me?'

'Shouldn't I? Wouldn't you in my place?'

Decker exhaled quietly. 'Yes. Yes, I would. What's the task?'

'I want you to deal with the tracker issue. Go back to IT and find out which wearer's tracker was tampered with, and where. Retrace the tracker's last movements. And check the tapes. Report back ASAP.'

Decker rose to his feet, but didn't immediately turn to leave. 'Can I assume Sean will be informed of this before I get to his office? Otherwise he'll just tell me to go away again.'

'You may assume this. Any other questions?'

'What tapes am I supposed to check?'

'We get an audio feed from each tracker. All conversations are recorded. I don't think they're actually on tapes anymore,' he added with a self-deprecating eye roll. 'But they are recorded, and the recordings are stored.'

'For how long?'

'You don't need to know that. They're stored far back enough for you to determine what happened this morning. Obviously there's no need to check the tapes made before the alarm went off. It could be that the wearer of the tracker escaped and has since been recaptured. If that turns out to be the case, I'd expect a call from the customer to whom the tracker was assigned, requesting a replacement. I would provide one once I knew how the wearer managed to escape and what has been done to ensure that doesn't happen again. If the wearer is dead, I want to know how and when. The customer to whom the tracker is assigned is required to inform me, but they don't always do so in a timely fashion. I'd expect you to deal with that.'

Decker nodded grimly. 'I understand.'

'You also understand that you'll be under very close scrutiny.'

Another nod. 'That's a given. I'll get to work.'

Ken waited until Decker had closed the door behind him, then punched

'1' on his speed dial. His chief of security did not pick up and the call went to voicemail.

Shit. Where the fuck are you, Reuben? he thought, dialing the next number. Demetrius, the director of purchasing, picked up on the first ring, his smooth, deep bass booming over the car noise in the background. 'This is Demetrius.'

'Demetrius, it's me. Have you seen Reuben?'

'No, I was about to call you to ask the same thing. He and I had a meeting scheduled with a supplier for nine thirty, and Rube never showed. I ended up closing the deal myself. That boy's got some serious ass-kissin' to do to make this up to me. He was supposed to keep Morticia occupied while I negotiated terms with Gomez, but noooo. I had to concentrate on the contract and keep that damn little bitch's hands off my privates at the same time, without breaking any of her bones. Which I really wanted to do,' he finished in a growl.

Ken glared at the speaker phone on his desk, totally confused. 'What the fuck are you talking about, Demetrius? Who the fuck are Gomez and Morticia?'

'You know. The Barbosas. They run shipments up from Rio. The wife sits next to the negotiator from the other team and pets him under the table, messing with his lower brain so that her husband can sneak all kinds of shit into the contract. But if you're rude to the wife and tell her to get her mitts off your junk, she cries and the husband up and leaves. They're a coupla scam artists. Well, duh, of course they are. But their shipments are really nice quality and Reuben doesn't mind the petting, so he takes one for the team so that I can get through the negotiations – except for today he didn't show. I am so gonna kick him into—'

Ken cut off the diatribe. 'He's missing.'

'What? Reuben? Since when?'

'I talked to him just before six this morning. He was on his way to the office but he never showed up.' Ken quickly filled Demetrius in on the situation. 'I don't know where he is or what the hell's going on.'

'What about this Decker? Can he be trusted?'

'I don't know. I want him watched, but I wanted to be sure that Reuben wasn't with you before I brought anyone else into this. Get back here just in case we have to do damage control.'

'On my way.'

'I'm texting you the address for Jason Jackson, the man Decker sent home. Stop there first and find out what the hell's going on with him. He better have fucking Ebola or his ass is fried for sleeping on the damn job.

We've had an unaccounted-for tracker floating around out there for three hours.'

'I'll call you from Jackson's house.'

Ken hung up and called Sean in the IT office. 'Decker is headed your way. I'm bringing him in on this missing tracker. Give him access to the audio feed for the last twelve hours. While he's listening to that, I want you to map the tracker's path for the last twenty-four hours and give that to him too.'

'You're just going to give it to him, boss?' Sean was always careful to call Ken 'boss' while they were on the job. Rarely, if ever, did he call him Dad, even when they were alone, but Ken didn't let that bother him. Sean had always been a weird kid, always tinkering with some gadget or other. He'd already been working to bring their operation into the twenty-first century when Ken had been forced to eliminate the boy's mother a few years before.

Sean believed his mother had run away with her yoga instructor, which was what Ken and Reuben had made sure everyone believed, including their business partners, Demetrius and Joel. It didn't pay to allow too many people to know the details of an execution.

'Yes, but I'll assign someone from Security to watch him. Make sure Decker doesn't have any recording devices on him. Call me if you see anything squirrelly.'

'Will do.'

Seven

'I fucking love Tuesdays.'

Marcus glanced up at the growled greeting, halting the coffee pot in his hand mid-pour. Diesel shuffled in and flopped into one of the padded swivel chairs surrounding the mahogany conference table that had been Marcus's grandfather's pride and joy. At six-six and a muscled two-seventy-five, Diesel made the long table look like a little girl's tea party.

Marcus finished pouring the coffee and gave the first cup to Diesel, who guzzled it down without a flinch, despite the beverage being scalding hot. After the life Diesel Kennedy had lived, he probably didn't have any taste buds left on his tongue, and the lining of his esophagus had most likely petrified years before. God only knew what the man's stomach looked like, because Diesel hadn't seen a doctor in more than ten years.

Marcus knew exactly when that had been, because he'd been with him at the time. Moral support, he'd thought back then. But Diesel hadn't needed it, leaving the doctor's office with no emotion on his face, not a flicker of recognition that he'd just been handed a death sentence. Instead, he had taken to drinking booze, smoking like a chimney, driving his motorcycle like a bat out of hell, and drinking coffee by the pot . . . and no one said a word to him. It wasn't like any of those vices was likely to kill him any faster than the bullet that hovered millimeters from his heart. Too delicately placed to remove, and able to kill him at any moment.

Diesel lifted the mug, wordlessly requesting a refill. The man was all about the caffeine, because he never slept, always working hard or playing harder. And it showed.

Pot still in hand, Marcus refilled the mug and waited while Diesel downed it just as fast as he had the first. Marcus poured him a third cup, then poured himself his first and sat down. 'Why?' he asked, and Diesel stared blankly back at him.

'Why what?'

'Why do you fucking love Tuesdays?'

Diesel's mouth curved, reminding Marcus a little of the Grinch as he'd contemplated cleaning out Whoville on Christmas Eve. 'It's Cal's day to bring the doughnuts. He brings the best ones.'

Marcus snorted. 'And I thought it would be something a lot more, oh, I don't know. Profound, maybe.'

'You want profound, go to church,' Diesel drawled lazily.

'As if,' Marcus muttered, then decided to take advantage of the fact that they were the only ones who'd shown up for the morning meeting so far. 'You were here last night, right?'

'Closed up shop at two, just like always.' Diesel's eyes narrowed. 'Why?'

'Because Jill was here when I came in this morning at 4.35. She never left last night.'

Diesel's eyes widened. 'What the hell? I did a sweep.'

'Of the ladies' room too?' Marcus asked, and watched Diesel flinch.

'Hell, Marcus,' he muttered like a little kid, his face turning a dark red that women found charming – if they were lucky enough to see it. Diesel was not a man to romantically entangle himself. 'I can't go in there. I opened the door and said, "Hey, anybody in here?" and nobody answered.' He shuddered. 'I can't go in there,' he said again. 'There's . . . women stuff in there.'

Incredulous, Marcus just looked at him. 'Are you kidding me? You have stormed enemy bunkers with bullets flying all over the damn place.' Marcus should know – he'd been shoulder-to-shoulder with Diesel every time. 'Are you seriously trying to tell me you're scared of "women stuff"? What the hell, Diesel? Just . . . what the hell?'

Diesel's glare promised retribution. 'Why would Jill not answer me?'

Marcus sighed. 'As it turns out, she's been secretly intercepting incoming threats and keeping the worst of them from Gayle.'

Diesel's expression turned glum. 'Because of Gayle's heart attack.'

Marcus's eyes popped wide. 'You *knew*?'

'You didn't?'

'No!' Marcus cried, exasperated. 'I was slightly *hospitalized* at the time.'

'Oh.' Diesel frowned. 'Yeah. I forgot about that.'

Marcus leaned over the table to slug Diesel's shoulder. 'You asshole. I almost died.'

'Ow.' Diesel rubbed his shoulder, scowling. 'For real, I thought you knew. I figured she'd told you. I thought we were all being discreet for Gayle's sake.'

Marcus scrubbed his palms over his face. Diesel's social skills were less than polished. 'How did *you* know?' he asked.

Diesel shrugged. 'I was here when it happened. Down in the basement. When I heard all the ruckus upstairs, I came up and had a look. Medics looked like they had everything under control.' Something flickered behind his eyes. 'So I left them alone to do their job.'

Marcus sighed, reading between the lines. Diesel had had an 'episode', which meant he'd gone into a panicked shutdown mode at the sight of paramedics. Diesel was a poster child for PTSD. 'All right,' Marcus murmured. 'The issue is, Jill has read the threat list. She's been fielding all the new threats, and Gayle hasn't seen them.'

'That could be bad,' Diesel mumbled.

'Yeah, it could be. Especially if she puts two and two together.'

Diesel slumped in his chair. 'Oh, shit.' He met Marcus's eyes. 'Just tell her, man. She's okay for a kid.'

'I can't. Not until I know for sure.'

'What's that going to take?' Diesel drained his third cup of coffee and slammed the mug back on the table. 'A fucking blood oath?'

Marcus rolled his eyes. 'No. But . . . I don't know. She bothers me.'

'Well, you've always been a better judge of people than me,' Diesel conceded. 'How are you going to keep her contained?'

'Stone's watching her.'

Diesel stared a second, then snorted, then threw back his head and laughed so hard that he nearly knocked his chair over. When Stone walked into the conference room, Diesel only laughed harder, until tears streamed down his cheeks.

'What,' Stone asked when Diesel stopped to gasp for breath, 'is so damn funny?'

Wiping his cheeks, Diesel started laughing again, this time more quietly. 'You,' he said with a snicker, 'babysitting Miss Lush-n-Lusty.'

Marcus's eyes widened again when Stone just huffed out an angry breath and went to get his own coffee. 'Miss Lush-n-Lusty?' Marcus repeated. 'Diesel, you can't say that here. Even if it wasn't inappropriate and just plain . . . disrespectful, it's legally sexual harassment, and you know I won't tolerate that.'

Diesel shrugged his shoulders, wider even than Stone's. 'Whatever you say, boss.' He sat up straight, cleared his throat and, folding his hands on the table in front of him, tamed his natural growl into a sophisticated tone any butler would envy. 'I merely found it humorous that Mr *Montgomery* O'Bannion would have to babysit Miss Jill Ennis.'

Stone's glare turned glacial. He hated his given name. He'd earned the nickname Stone when he'd fallen on his head as a toddler and been pronounced unhurt by a doctor who'd proclaimed his head to be harder than a stone. The nickname had stuck, because Stone was also as stubborn as a rock. 'Call me that one more time . . .'

Diesel's veneer cracked, his grin delighted. 'You're on, *Montgomery*. Just name the time and place. I'll be there.'

'Stop it,' Marcus snapped when Stone opened his mouth to reply. 'Good God, are you both five-year-olds?'

'Ten-year-olds,' Diesel allowed, not insulted.

'Asshole,' Stone grunted as he sat down with his coffee. 'I left Jill with Bridget in Accounting while we're in morning meeting. They're running budgets. Even Jill can't hurt anything when they're running budgets. Where's Cal with the damn doughnuts? It's Tuesday, for God's sake.'

'I'm here.' Cal trudged in and set the box of doughnuts on the table with an eye roll. 'Here. Devour. Use napkins.'

Calvin Booker had been at the *Ledger* since the mid-sixties, working his way up from the mailroom to become Marcus's grandfather's right-hand man and the paper's editor-in-chief. Cal should have retired years ago, but kept pushing the date out further and further. He said he would just be bored at home, but Marcus knew the old man had stayed on to help him. He wasn't sure where he'd be without Cal.

'Save a jelly for me.' Lisette Cauldwell entered the room, followed closely by her brother, Phillip. The managing editor, Lisette was Marcus's age. Phillip, who managed all the advertising, was in his late twenties, although he could pass for far younger. Marcus had known Lisette since high school, and her father had been a *Ledger* editor until the day he died. Lisette had earned Marcus's trust long ago, and both she and Cal had vouched for Phillip, which had been good enough for the rest of them.

Both Lisette and Phillip had started out as reporters and would still pinch-hit from time to time when the newsroom got busy. Or when the story was so big that Marcus needed all hands on deck.

'Close the door,' Marcus said, and waited until everyone had coffee and the box of doughnuts had been emptied.

'Where's Gayle?' Stone asked.

'At the doc— Oof.' Phillip cut himself off with a wince, glancing at his sister, who glared at him. 'Don't kick me,' he whined. 'That hurt.'

Stone huffed in annoyance. 'Those two knew about Gayle?' he asked Marcus.

'I suppose so. So did Diesel.' Marcus met Cal's eyes. 'Did you know too?'

107

Cal sighed. 'Not till last week. We've used the same doctor for years, and I ran into her at his office. She made me promise not to tell you two or your mom.'

Marcus folded his arms over his chest, grinding his teeth. 'What were you doing at the doctor's office, Cal?'

Cal met his gaze unblinkingly. 'My annual checkup.'

Marcus shook his head, pushing his anger down deep where it could explode without damaging his team. 'You do know that I have won every damn hand of poker we've ever played, don't you? Your "tell" is that look. The one on your face right there. The one you *think* makes you look like you're *not* lying.'

Cal rolled his eyes. 'And all this time I thought you were just cheating. Shit, Marcus.'

Stone fumed. 'Did you have a heart attack too, Cal?'

'No. Just a stent. I have an arrhythmia. I'm fine.'

For the second time in fifteen minutes, Marcus scrubbed his palms down his face. 'This is fucking insane,' he said tightly. 'What is *wrong* with this picture? Does anyone else have secrets they're keeping from us?'

Phillip shook his head hard and fast.

Diesel just looked at him.

Lisette sighed. 'Things haven't been . . . comfortable around here lately. Nobody wants to add to your stress, Marcus. Or yours, Stone. Nothing's suffered on the business side or on the *special* business side. We've got your back. You know that.'

Everyone around the table nodded, and Marcus's shoulders sagged wearily. 'Thank you. But you don't have to treat us with kid gloves. We need to know what's going on around here. And that means what's going on with all of you. We're not going to break. No more secrets. Right, Stone?'

'Right.' His brother raised a brow in challenge. 'So on that note, tell them the secret *you're* keeping, Marcus.'

All eyes turned his way. With a sigh, Marcus retold the story, from the first time he'd seen Tala in the park, all the way up to finding Jill alone in the building that morning and assigning Stone to watch her. When he was finished, they were all twitching in anger, but it was directed squarely at him.

'You have the *nerve* to get pissy with us?' Lisette said from behind clenched teeth. 'You nearly get yourself *killed* and you're pissy at *us*?'

'I'm not pissy,' Marcus said. 'I've never been pissy once in my life.'

'No,' Diesel drawled, his eyes angry. 'Not you.'

Marcus ignored him for now. He'd deal with Diesel's temper later. He was more worried about Cal, who'd paled, his hands trembling. 'Cal, are you all right?'

'Yeah. I'm fine. Absolutely peachy. I'll order you another vest.'

'I'm okay,' Marcus assured him. 'I had the paramedics on the scene check me out, but you can look at my back yourself if you want.' Cal had changed his diapers, as the old man often reminded him. Marcus supposed he owed it to him to at least offer.

Cal shook his head. 'No. If the medics checked you out, I don't need to. You're a grown man now. You're going to do whatever you want to do, and what I say doesn't matter.'

Marcus frowned. 'Of course it matters. And I was going to tell you this morning. I was going to tell everyone in the world. I had Stone write up an article for the website.'

Stone slid a printed sheet across the table. 'Make sure I didn't leave anything out.'

Marcus dropped his eyes to Stone's story, grateful for the momentary respite from the accusatory stares around the table. 'It's complete,' he said after scanning it twice. 'Thank you. Put it up online.'

Lisette reached for it, her own hand trembling. 'You do so get pissy,' she muttered. 'Who is this Bishop woman? Can she be trusted?'

'No,' Stone said.

'Yes,' Marcus said at the same time.

Diesel resettled himself in his chair. 'Now this just got interesting.'

Marcus rolled his eyes. 'God help me,' he murmured. 'She's a good cop,' he told Lisette. 'She and Stone have history, so you have to take his opinion with a grain of salt.'

'I remember her,' Phillip said, looking up from his phone. He held it up so that everyone could see the photo of Scarlett he'd pulled off Google. 'She was at Mikhail's funeral. I'm not ashamed to say that she scared the livin' shit out of me.'

Lisette studied Scarlett's photo on Phillip's phone. 'Why?' she asked her brother.

'Because she looked . . . cold. Like she'd freeze a guy's balls with a single look.'

'Told you so,' Stone muttered under his breath.

'I'd like to let her try,' Diesel said, speaking to Phillip, but his curious gaze never left Marcus's face.

Marcus sighed. 'If you're expecting me to go all jealous caveman, you'll be disappointed,' he said to Diesel, then turned to Cal. 'I'd like you to find a consultant who does training in sexual harassment in the workplace. Schedule a session for Monday at the latest. Everyone attends. Everyone.'

Everyone except Cal groaned.

'I don't need no training on that,' Diesel said.

'He's plenty good at it already,' Lisette said. 'They all are.'

'Which is why we're having it,' Marcus said firmly. 'Phillip, you know you shouldn't talk like that. I don't care if you're talking about a cop or a hooker or the lady who makes the damn doughnuts. And if you say it about a woman like Scarlett Bishop, be prepared for unpleasant consequences if she finds out, because she's every bit as tough as you think she is. And Diesel, no more comments like "Miss Lush-n-Lusty". What the hell was that about anyway?'

Diesel just smiled his curly-mouthed Grinch smile. 'She has been snuggling up to Stone ever since she started working here. Even a blind man could have seen it. Oh, wait. Sorry. Was I supposed to filter stuff about disabled people too? And minorities, too, I bet. Damn. What's left to say?'

'You're an asshole, Diesel,' Stone said, shaking his head. But he was biting back a smile.

'Thank you,' Diesel said with a magnanimous nod. 'I strive for perfection in all things.'

Lisette sighed loudly. 'Back to the Jill issue. She's been angling for Stone even before she started working here. I really can't believe you didn't notice, Marcus. Even I feel sorry for Stone. The child is relentless.'

Marcus turned to Stone, who looked uncomfortable. 'Is this true? Why didn't you say something? I wouldn't have put you with her if I'd known.'

'She's had a crush on me since forever,' Stone said. 'She's just a kid and I didn't want to hurt her. I was always able to hide from her because I was off on assignment, but the past nine months since I've been home have been increasingly . . . difficult. I had to confront her about it sooner or later, so I did it this morning, since we'd be spending time together on this list project you gave me.'

'How'd she take that?' Cal asked quietly.

Stone's answer was terse. 'She cried. I feel like shit. We both decided we should complete this task and never speak of it again. So please don't tease her.'

Lisette rose and gave Stone a hug. 'You did the right thing.'

'Thanks.' Stone sighed, patting her shoulder. 'Though every time anyone says that, they sound so damn surprised. Anyway, we're going over the old list and the one Jill had been keeping from Gayle. There are some pretty explicit threats on it. I don't think Jill understood all of them, but at least she doesn't think you're a mob boss anymore, Marcus.'

Lisette took her seat, eyes wide. 'She thought you were a mob boss?'

Marcus nodded dryly. 'She thought I was rubbing out my detractors, which was why they stopped threatening me.'

'Now *there's* an idea,' Diesel said.

'Shut up, Diesel,' everyone said together.

Diesel shrugged. 'I'm just sayin'.'

'Well stop sayin',' Cal said. 'What kind of threats are we talking about this time?'

'Mostly more of the same,' Stone said, ticking them off in an affected bored voice that fooled no one. Stone took these threats as seriously as any of them did. 'I'm going to gut you, shoot you, slit your throat, ruin you. About half are targeted at Lisette, Phillip and me for reporting the stories. But the worst ones were targeted at Marcus as the publisher of "that rag".'

'Same old, same old,' Marcus said, playing it down like he always did. Play it down and never go anywhere unarmed was pretty much his motto. 'Any escalations?'

'Just one – a woman who said she was going to stake "that lying reporter" down, pour honey on him and leave him for the fire ants for even suggesting that her "innocent" husband – "the real victim here" – could have molested young girls. The "lying reporter" was you, Phillip.'

'I guess the fire ants are a nice touch,' Phillip said lightly.

'I bet that came from the drama coach,' Lisette said. 'The one whose husband had recorded said molestations with his iPhone and uploaded them to the cloud.'

'Breaking into his account was child's play,' Diesel said with disgust. 'His password was the name of his dog.'

'At least the wife is consistent,' Stone said. 'There's drama in her threat just like there was in her denial, even though the police showed her the evidence in full color. We didn't address the first threat, because we didn't see it – because Jill was sitting on it – and this woman ended up making others, the most recent just last week. Said she was going to make you suffer by hitting you where it really hurts. That she was losing her house because her husband had lost his job after being arrested and the bank is foreclosing on them. She says she's planning to sue the paper and you personally, Marcus, for slander.'

'She's not suing me,' Phillip said, tongue in cheek, 'because I have nothing of any value for her to win. Sucks to be the rich boss.'

'Let Rex deal with that one,' Marcus said. 'A week's gone by since she threatened to sue. He can find out if she's retained an attorney in the meantime and do that lawyer-to-lawyer thing that he does so well.'

Cal got up to refill his coffee cup. 'This doesn't worry me at all. When they start talking money, a lot of the unpredictable emotional responses disappear. If they're truly after cold, hard cash, they'll refrain from doing anything violent that jeopardizes that.'

'Hopefully it is just about money,' Stone said, 'because if the woman truly intends to follow through, we may not be able to tie the threats to her.' He scowled. 'Because Jill moved them from the corporate server to her own laptop. Hopefully she didn't destroy the electronic trail.'

'Stupid kid,' Diesel muttered, then glanced at Marcus from the corner of his eye. 'Can I at least call her "stupid"?'

'Yes, you can. Even though you were just saying that I should trust her.'

'And then I said you were better at judging people than I am,' Diesel fired back. 'I need Jill's laptop. Tell her it is not negotiable. That if she refuses, you will fire her ass. May I say "ass", boss, in this context?' he asked sarcastically.

'Only if I can tell you to shut up,' Marcus said. 'Stone, if she gives you any problems, tell her I will terminate her. Make me the bad guy if you want. She already thinks the worst of me. Until Diesel tracks this threat, we all take precautions, especially at night.' Nods around the table. 'Okay, what actual business do we have? Special business,' he clarified.

As opposed to their legit business, which they saved for the end.

Lisette opened her file. 'Two investigations ongoing. One's domestic violence and the other is suspected foster family molestation. The domestic violence came through our friend.'

Their 'friend' was officially an anonymous source, but was in reality a woman in the hierarchy of Children's Services. Only Lisette knew her true identity. Marcus didn't want to know, for their informant's protection. He couldn't tell what he didn't know.

Their first case had come five years ago. Since then, the social worker had sent a number of very unofficial referrals their way, cases in which Children's Services suspected abuse but hadn't been able to prove it. Just like the one Lisette now summarized.

'This started out as a suspected child abuse, called in to the hotline,' she said. 'A neighbor saw that one of the children had a friction burn on his arm. He said he got it playing with his friends, but she didn't believe that and called it in. The kid's dad is some corporate VP and had a high-priced

112

attorney. None of the other neighbors would comment, but a couple of the neighbors' maids did – all under condition of anonymity. Nobody wanted to get any of the people in this neighborhood angry with them. The child confided in his social worker that his father hit him and his mother, but later recanted. The father's attorneys claimed the social worker coerced the child to speak against his father. That she bribed him with candy. And now the social worker is under investigation, suspended without pay.'

'Why does that tactic still hold any water?' Cal murmured.

'Good question,' Lisette said grimly. 'Our friend doesn't like being forced to walk away from a child because the parent has enough money to buy his way out of the legal system. She also doesn't like that the other employees are going to be gun-shy around any accused parent with influence, financial or political. She's asked us to find out what we can.'

'Sounds like he didn't even get close to the legal system,' Marcus said.

'Exactly. So what's the plan?'

Everyone went quiet, thinking of their next steps. This was what they did. When the legal way didn't work, Marcus's team skirted the accepted rules.

They all had reasons for what they did, but not the reasons one might think. Only Diesel had been knocked around as a kid. Phillip and Lisette joined the team because Phillip's childhood friend had been killed by an abusive father. Lisette had been the child's babysitter, and both siblings had tried to tell their parents that something was not right in that home, but the Cauldwells had been convinced that the friend's parents were good church-going people and that Lisette and Phillip had been watching too much television. When the child died from a beating at the hands of his father, Lisette's parents had become two of the city's leading advocates for children.

Marcus's grandfather had contributed a significant chunk of his own millions to child-rescue charities, instructing Cal to ensure they had free advertising space in the *Ledger* for fund-raising. Cal had continued that work after Marcus's grandfather had died. Cal's reasons had always been his own, and even Marcus had never learned what they were. But Marcus knew exactly why his grandfather had become a supporter of child advocates.

Because of what happened to us, he thought now. But those were words he and Stone never spoke aloud. They were too painful, and simply . . . not available. Marcus always panicked and froze, unable to make the words exit his mouth when the subject arose – which was thankfully infrequently. Stone coped by getting mad and hitting things. And people. It hadn't been a problem when he was a scrawny kid who no one could tempt with food. But later . . . he had grown so large that he could make grown men piss themselves with a single angry look. Underneath the rage, he was a decent, kind man. But the rage ran really, really deep.

'The tried-and-true income tax evasion won't work this time,' Cal said. 'This guy probably has expensive accountants who cover his ass six ways to Sunday.'

They'd used that approach a few times, with Diesel creatively accessing the suspects' personal computers to see expenses versus what had been declared to the IRS. The tax fraud had to be excessive for it to result in any jail time for the abusers, but when it worked, it got the abuser out of the home, which was their team's ultimate goal.

These abusers weren't being punished for beating their children, but they were being punished – and most people were more terrified of the IRS than they were of the cops. Marcus figured if it had been good enough for *The People v. Al Capone*, it was good enough for them.

'You're probably right, Cal,' he said. 'This guy is too smart to openly cheat on his taxes, but let's let Diesel take a look anyway. He's had too many easy cases recently. Too much low-hanging fruit. We need to keep his skills sharp.'

'I'm sitting right here, asshole,' Diesel snarled, but his eyes were bright with the challenge. 'If I don't find any tax irregularities, I might find something else we can use. This guy may have a secret porn collection he doesn't want anyone to know about, or he may be having an affair he wants to keep secret. I'll need to know more about him to guess his passwords – hobbies, friends, old lovers. This'll be too much fun.'

Lisette's lips curved even as she shook her head. 'Be careful, big guy. Don't get so excited that you trip any alarms.'

Diesel gave her an injured look. 'You wound me, Lissy.'

'I will totally wound you if you expose us,' she warned, but it was without heat. 'I was wondering if this prince has assaulted anyone outside his immediate family. Maybe someone who works for him. His household staff wouldn't talk, but one of his employees might.'

'How were you planning to get his corporate staff list?' Stone asked.

She waggled her brows. 'I was thinking of sending someone in with a delivery. You can get a lot of info from mailroom clerks. But it would need to be someone young – or who looks young. Someone who could pull off being a courier. Someone who hasn't had any photos of himself in the press, unlike Stone, and who doesn't scare small children with his tattoos, unlike Diesel.' She gave her brother a beaming smile, and Phillip sighed.

'Give me the address. I'll go home and get my courier uniform and my bike.'

'Start with the ladies' names,' Lisette said, sobering. 'Guys like this pick on people they think are weaker than they are.'

'I know what to do,' Phillip reminded her. 'I've done this before.'

He had, and successfully. Phillip had a youthful face that people simply trusted.

'And if we can't get any legit goods on him?' Stone asked, and the table again fell silent, everyone turning to Marcus.

'Then we find a way to create a situation he can't resist,' Marcus said. They had used entrapment only once, when the suspect was a child predator who'd been too smart to get caught by police chat-room stings. Because they weren't cops, they weren't bound by the same anti-entrapment rules. And that perp was now serving eight-to-twenty-five in the state pen. Life without rules could be a beautiful thing.

'What about the foster family situation?' Cal asked.

'That one came from a contact at the high school,' Marcus said. 'One of Mikhail's friends.' A wave of emotion hit him like a brick and he had to clear his throat. 'He called to tell me goodbye because he's headed off to college. He was, um, missing Mickey.' The room went still as Marcus focused on filling his lungs with air. Just saying Mikhail's name could still suck all the oxygen from a room. 'They were always supposed to go to college together, the two of them and another boy. Best friends, you know.'

'John,' Stone murmured. 'Those boys were joined at the hip. I always forget we aren't the only ones to miss him.'

Marcus swallowed hard when Lisette leaned against Stone, resting her head on his shoulder, trying to give him comfort.

There was no romance, not among any of them. But they all loved one another just the same. In many ways, he and Stone had ended up far better than Marcus had ever hoped. He liked to think his grandfather would be happy to see this. And maybe a little proud.

He cleared his throat again. 'Anyway, John and I got to talking. He was sad because, of the three of them, only he was going away to the college they'd picked. The third boy got accepted and would have been a scholarship student, but right before graduation, he "went all zombie". John's words. He said it was like the lights went out overnight. The boy failed his finals, his GPA dropped and he lost his scholarship. John's afraid to go away to school now, worried that his friend might do something stupid, like kill himself.'

'Hell of a burden for an eighteen-year-old boy to carry,' Cal said gruffly.

'The kid was molested,' Stone said flatly. 'He was in foster care?'

Marcus nodded. 'Yeah. John said he tried to get him to go to the authorities, but the boy wouldn't – and made John promise he wouldn't call the hotline. Apparently there are other kids there who would suffer. Kids this boy was protecting. John thought that he could get around his promise by asking me to call, but I told him to give me a few days. That I'd see what could be done so that all the kids would be protected.' He turned to Diesel, who looked ready to kill. 'You want a shot at this foster scum's computer before I go to Children's Services?'

Diesel huffed. 'Try to stop me.'

'D,' Lisette murmured, 'be careful.'

Diesel bared his teeth in a parody of a smile. 'You always say that, Lissy. And I'm always careful. No way I'm letting some sick sonofabitch off the hook because I got careless.'

She nodded, still wary. 'You're already tracing the emails for Marcus and digging into Mr Rich and Arrogant. Let me help you. You don't have to carry this one alone.'

'Yeah, sweetie, I do,' Diesel said grimly. No one ever talked about Diesel's background, but everyone knew that child rapists were his temper's trigger. It didn't take a genius to connect the dots. 'I'll back-burner Rich and Arrogant for a day or two. If I haven't found anything to nail Foster Dick, then I'll come to you for help.'

'All right,' Marcus said. 'What about legit business? What stories are we covering today?'

'Well, the girl in the alley is our lead,' Lisette said. 'There were a few minor stories that showed up in the police reports this morning. Nothing as big as yours.' She briefly went through each one, detailing which of her small group of reporters she planned to send, and it started to sound like a normal staff meeting.

Lisette glanced over at Diesel, who was already on his laptop, his expression too intense, then back at her brother. 'I'd like you to do the groundwork for Diesel on Mr Rich and Arrogant. His plate is full.'

'I'm fine,' Diesel growled.

Phillip nodded at Lisette, ignoring Diesel. 'Will do.'

They spent another twenty minutes discussing the more routine business – sports, the arts, all subjects that were unlikely to get any of them threatened or shot at.

'If no one has anything else, then we're done,' Marcus said. 'Keep me informed.'

The team filed out of the conference room, Cal bringing up the rear. The old man paused at the door, looking over his shoulder. 'Have you told your mother what happened this morning?'

Marcus shook his head, feeling nauseated at the thought. 'No, but I will. She needs to hear it from me and not from Stone's story.'

Cal gave him a nod and closed the door behind him, leaving Marcus sitting alone, dreading the conversation with his mother. Either way he cut it, she'd be devastated. That he'd been protecting 'a stranger', as she'd put it, would make it worse. Protecting 'a stranger' was how she'd nearly lost him nine months ago. She couldn't see past that point.

His mother had buried Mikhail. And Matty, so long ago. They never spoke of the third of her five children. No one wanted to hurt her. But Marcus had hurt her again by getting injured that day nine months ago. He'd hurt her when he joined the army, too. He would hurt her again when he told her about this morning. *Hell, maybe Stone was right. Maybe I do have a death wish.* But he wouldn't change anything he'd done. Not even that one most despicable thing that haunted him more than all the others put together. But none of that was relevant. Those mental images flashing through his mind had nothing to do with the reality of what he had to do today, so he pushed the memories from his mind and focused.

He still had a list to compile for Scarlett Bishop – one that wouldn't arouse any undue curiosity. And he still had to figure out what to do about Jill. And Gayle. And of course there was Tala. As soon as he was done with the damn list, he'd go to the park and start looking for anyone who could ID that poodle.

But first he'd call his mother. Straightening his spine, he prepared himself for her anger. Prepared to apologize without agreeing to change his behavior. Because he planned to continue protecting 'strangers' – as often and as long as he was able to, whether his mother liked it or not.

Eight

Cincinnati, Ohio
Tuesday 4 August, 8.15 A.M.

W hen Scarlett arrived at the morgue, she found Deacon waiting for her outside the door to the autopsy suite.

'Did Carrie tell you anything when she called to tell us to come over here?' he asked.

'Only that she had something to show us.' Dr Carrie Washington, the ME, was not a chatty woman. 'Your buddies at the Bureau any help?'

'Maybe. The Bureau's watching several suspected trafficking operations in the Midwest, most of them here in Ohio. The Cincinnati Field Office has the lead, so all of the data flows through here. That should work in our favor.'

Scarlett shook her head. 'You know, I've read the Bureau's reports on trafficking and I've been trained to spot the victims, but every time I hear that Ohio has one of the highest rates in the whole country, I think it's got to be some kind of mistake.' But she knew it wasn't. The most recent stats had Ohio in the top ten, closely trailing the 'usual suspects' of California, New York, Florida and Texas. Hell, Toledo alone was the third worst city in the entire country for sex trafficking. Which was damn hard to believe. 'I mean, *Ohio*? Seriously?'

'Location, location,' Deacon said grimly.

'I know, but still . . .' Sitting just a hop-step from Canada, with the I-75 corridor running straight through the state, Ohio was an ideal distribution route for all kinds of illegal activity. That Cincinnati was the I-75 gatekeeper at the southern end of the state meant that local law enforcement had always needed to be vigilant when it came to catching drug runners. Every rookie knew what to look for. But this . . . The trafficking of humans through the state was still new to law enforcement. *At least our awareness of it is.* 'I wonder how long it's been going on right under our noses,' she murmured.

'Far longer than we think, I'm sure. Most of the information I saw at the

118

field office this morning dealt with the sex trade, so we might find a connection to Tala.'

'You're assuming she was forced into prostitution?'

'Aren't you?'

'Yeah,' she admitted. 'Especially with the way she tried to pay Marcus back for his help. Besides, dog walking can't be her only job.'

'Exactly. The agent heading the investigation is checking to see which, if any, of the suspected operators deal in Filipino women. He's supposed to get back to me by lunchtime. What about you? Did the two homeless people see anything valuable?'

'Edna and Tommy were gone when I walked back to my car. They may have gotten nervous with all the sirens and taken off. I swung by Dani's shelter to see if they'd gone there. They hadn't yet, but they might still. If I can't find them at the shelter, they'll be back at their stoop later tonight.'

'Have you heard from Marcus?'

She nodded. 'He sent the video files of the park and the alley like he promised. I got a few decent quality stills of both Tala and Coco the poodle from them. I ran copies of the stills for the uniforms to show the homeowners around the park. But my biggest takeaway was that Tala appeared to know the person who shot her.' And that Marcus had been literally shaking at the sight of the bullet hole in her skull. But sharing that felt too much like a betrayal. Which was ridiculous, as she owed the man nothing. Still, it wasn't relevant, so she kept it to herself.

'Interesting. Marcus didn't mention that.'

'He may not have realized it himself.'

'I imagine he knows now. I don't guess he'd have sent us video files he hadn't personally reviewed.'

'I'm sure you're right about that,' she murmured, still stunned that Marcus had allowed her to see his pain. 'The dog may be our best lead out of the video. Very fancy schmancy. So I talked to Delores Kaminsky – you know, the woman who runs the shelter where Faith got Zeus.'

Deacon blew out a disgusted breath. 'Please tell me that she misses the damn shoe-chewer and wants him back.'

Scarlett's lips curved. Deacon was very particular about his shoes, keeping them so shiny that one could see one's face in them. At least until Faith had brought Zeus home. Now Deacon's shoes bore the marks left by tiny pointed puppy teeth. Even though he pretended to be grouchy about the dog, Scarlett knew he was the worst offender when it came to spoiling the ball of orange fur. 'Nope, sorry. But she's putting together a list of high-end groomers who might have given Coco her 'do.'

'Groomers,' Deacon said thoughtfully. 'I hadn't thought of that. Smart.'

'Thanks. But what I don't have yet is the list of the people who made threats to Marcus and the *Ledger*'s reporters. I've emailed and texted and even called Marcus, but he hasn't answered any of my messages.' Which made her both suspicious and disappointed that he hadn't kept his word.

'Do we really need that list now? Especially if Tala knew her killer?'

'Probably not, but Lynda wants to be sure he isn't withholding the list because he's hiding something that can come back to bite us in the ass later, particularly if he's eventually called to be a witness. I was on my way to his office to pick up the list in person when I got the call from Carrie to come here. Ready to go in?'

Deacon grimaced. 'Yeah. Let's get this over with.'

A sentiment Scarlett understood. Bracing herself for the odor she wouldn't get used to if she lived to be a hundred, she pushed open the door to the morgue and grabbed a mask and gloves from the bin just inside, prepared to do her job without complaining.

Carrie looked up from the body on her autopsy table, her eyes magnified by the goggles she wore. 'Detectives.' She pulled a sheet up over the body with a respectful care that always tugged at Scarlett's heart. 'I'm glad you're here. This way, please.' She motioned them to follow her to the wall of refrigerated drawers and pulled one of them halfway out, revealing the top half of Tala's body. 'We ran her prints through AFIS but came up with nothing, so she's got no record.'

Scarlett stared down at Tala's face, remembering the desperation in her eyes seconds before a bullet ripped through her gut, and the agonizing grief in Marcus's voice when he'd seen the bullet hole in her head. Gritting her teeth against the tears that stung her eyes, Scarlett pushed everything from her mind and focused on the body of a young girl who should still be alive. And free.

'I hope the poodle is a decent lead,' she muttered. 'Otherwise we got nothin' to ID her. Cause of death was the head wound, right? Nothing weird or funky we need to know?'

'Lots of funky,' Carrie said, 'but more about her life than her death. She was in very good health. Good dental care, especially in the last few years. Someone had all the cavities in her mouth filled, fairly recently.'

'What is "fairly recently"?' Scarlett asked.

'Longer ago than a year, but no longer than five years, if I had to guess. Her blood tests are within normal levels for all the major vitamins. Her body weight is normal for her height, so she was not nutritionally deprived – but again this is fairly recent. The X-rays show low bone density in her legs and arms.'

Deacon frowned. 'She was malnourished as a child, but her captors have been feeding her well?'

'I can only tell you she ate well,' Carrie said. 'It's your job to figure out where she got the food.'

'Did you find any evidence of drugs in her system?' Scarlett asked.

'Urinalysis came back clean for the usuals, but I've sent blood to the lab for a more detailed screening. I should have that tomorrow.' Gently she drew Tala's hand from beneath the sheet. 'Her hands are rough but her nails and cuticles are well kept. She has calluses on all her fingertips and her knees. She's done manual labor, but someone wanted her hands to look nice. The skin on her face is also smooth. Outwardly – and clothed – she appears the picture of health.'

'But?' Deacon asked.

'But she was beaten. Not enough to break any bones, but enough to leave bruises.' Carrie pulled the sheet to Tala's waist, exposing her torso.

Scarlett sucked in a breath. 'Fucking hell,' she whispered. Nasty dark bruises covered the young woman's entire torso. 'What'd they hit her with?'

'Fists would be my guess, at least for these bruises. Somebody knew what they were doing, hitting her hard enough to cause pain but not enough to require a doctor to set a broken bone or stitch cut flesh.'

'And hitting her where no one would see,' Deacon said quietly. 'Her shirt hid the bruises so that when she walked the dog no one would suspect.

'What did you mean by "cut flesh"?' Scarlett asked, not wanting to hear the answer. Carrie gently turned the body, and Scarlett winced. Beside her, Deacon hissed a curse. Tala's back was a mass of bruises, welts and open cuts.

'It appears to have been done by the buckle end of a belt. Nothing fancy or unique.' Carrie's voice was toneless as she resettled the body and pulled the sheet back over it, her hands briskly capable. But her breath hitched a little as she pulled the drawer out the rest of the way, her swallow audible in the quiet of the morgue.

'You okay, Carrie?' Scarlett asked softly.

Carrie's smile was thin. 'Yeah, sure. It's just that the ones with bruises . . .' She blew out a breath, cleared her throat. 'The welts continue down the backs of her legs, but again, they were hidden by her jeans. Which also hid this.' She pulled the bottom of the sheet up to Tala's knees, revealing a strip of skin worn red and raw, scattered with lesions. A few inches above her ankle, the strip was about an inch high and extended all the way around her leg. 'She was wearing a tracking device, the kind that probationary prisoners wear.'

Scarlett blinked, her thoughts scrambling. 'You cut it off her?' she asked carefully, keeping the *without telling us?* accusation from her voice.

Carrie nodded. 'It was still transmitting when my assistant started processing her. He called CSU, who got here about the same time I did. CSU cut it off and took it with them to the lab. They said they'd contact you about it.'

Scarlett pursed her lips, annoyed. 'They didn't. I would have liked to have known about that.' She glanced up at Deacon. 'Did they contact you?'

He shook his head, clearly equally annoyed. 'Nope. We'll deal with it when we're done here.' Then he turned back to Carrie. 'If they cut it off her and it was still transmitting, it would have sent a tampering alarm to whoever was monitoring it. I might have wanted to time that alarm to our advantage.'

'Depends on the style of tracker they used,' Scarlett said, shoving her annoyance aside for the moment. 'If it detected a pulse or body temp, it would have alarmed the moment she died, or at least as her body cooled. When and where they cut it off her might not have mattered.'

'The lab will tell us what kind of tracker it is, so we'll at least have an indication of when her captors knew she was gone, assuming they weren't the ones who killed her.' Deacon frowned down at the body. 'Either way, the tracker makes no sense. If she knew she was being tracked, why would she arrange to meet Marcus in an alley? She had to have known they'd follow her.'

'She did,' Scarlett murmured, the look in Tala's eyes the split second before she was shot making more sense now. 'She knew who shot her. She knew they'd come after her. Maybe she thought that by leaving in the middle of the night they wouldn't notice for a while.'

'But they watched her at night,' Deacon said. 'She walked the dog at night.'

Scarlett bit at her lip, thinking. Something was off, a detail either missing or perhaps not noticed or understood, but she wasn't sure what it was. 'Not every night. There were a few nights Marcus sat for hours and she didn't show up. Now I'm wondering why that was. It wasn't like they knew she was stopping to listen to him in the park, or they wouldn't have let her return night after night. Why the sporadic schedule?'

'Maybe they had someone else walk the dog those nights, somebody who picked a different path through the park. And maybe they did finally

122

figure out she was stopping to listen to him. Maybe that's what triggered this beating. Didn't Marcus say she was limping the last time he saw her in the park, and that it was at a different time of the day?'

'Yeah, he did. It was what pushed him to leave his card on the bench.' Scarlett turned to the ME. 'Carrie, did you see any evidence of other beatings in the past?'

'No. Her back and legs are too torn up for any scars to be visible to the naked eye, but I might be able to see older subdermal scarring with an ultrasound. How important is it?'

'I don't know. Maybe not at all. I'd just like to know what we're dealing with here.'

'I'll do the test this afternoon.' Carrie pulled the sheet down to cover Tala's legs, gently smoothing it with a light swipe of her gloved hand before pushing the drawer closed. Her gentleness had Scarlett's throat tightening, just as it did every time she'd witnessed it. Apparently reserved for victims of violence, it was motherly in its own way. Almost as if Carrie were tucking a child into bed at night.

I couldn't leave her alone in the dark. The words Marcus had spoken in the alley hit Scarlett's mind with a hard slam. He'd sounded bleak and . . . lost. And Scarlett wondered why. Was it simply the shock of seeing a girl gunned down in front of him? Somehow she didn't think so. He'd served in the military, and as bad as Tala's shooting had been, he'd likely seen things far worse.

'Scarlett? Hello? Yo, Earth to Detective Bishop.' She blinked as Deacon's hand waved in front of her face. He was hunched forward, staring at her with eyes narrowed in concern. 'You okay?'

Cheeks heating in embarrassment, she squared her shoulders. 'Yeah. Sorry. My mind wandered for a second.'

Deacon straightened to his full height. 'Or ten,' he said warily. 'Did you even hear what I just said?'

Scarlett barely resisted the urge to drop her gaze to her shoes. 'No, I didn't. Could you repeat it?'

'I asked Carrie if the victim had been sexually assaulted,' he said, still frowning.

That was a good question, Scarlett thought. *I should have asked it myself.* Instead, she'd been daydreaming about Marcus O'Bannion's emotional state. *Get your brain back in the damn game, Bishop.* 'And was she?' she asked evenly.

'There's no evidence of recent physical trauma per se. No vaginal bruising or fluids present. But she has been sexually active. She has gonorrhea and genital warts, vaginal and anal. They're not visible, so she might not have known she had them. I've sent a culture to the lab to determine what strain is present.'

'Not surprising,' Scarlett said quietly. 'I'm more surprised you didn't find evidence of repeated assault.'

'So was I,' Carrie admitted, 'especially after seeing the bruises and welts. I'll report this to the health department – they'll want to be informed after you've identified her and found her captors. Anyone who's had sexual contact with her is potentially infected.'

'I'd be only too happy if the bastards who raped her got infected too,' Deacon said tightly, 'except that they'll take it home to their wives and girlfriends, who haven't done anything wrong other than believing the lying sonofabitch they had the misfortune to trust in the first place.'

Surprised by the leashed viciousness in his voice, Scarlett turned to study his face. His jaw was clenched, his eyes hard, twin streaks of dark red staining his cheekbones. He was holding on to his temper by a thread. Deacon was a natural protector and she'd seen him get righteously angry on a victim's behalf many times over their ten-month partnership. But this was more than indignant anger. This was fury, and it was personal.

And then Scarlett suddenly understood. She'd known Deacon's sister Dani was HIV positive, but she had never asked when or how she'd contracted the virus. It was simply not her business. But now, looking at Deacon's furious face, she realized that Dani had been one of those innocent girlfriends victimized by a lying sonofabitch.

She placed a careful hand on Deacon's shoulder. 'Easy,' she murmured.

Deacon's chest expanded as he drew a deep breath and slowly, visibly, calmed himself. Closed his eyes. 'I'm sorry.'

'Don't be,' Carrie said. 'I couldn't have said it better myself. So when you report it, it'll be for the innocent wives and girlfriends.'

Carrie's 'when' rather than 'if' seemed to calm Deacon a little further. His eyes opened, and he was back in control. 'You got it, Doc.'

Scarlett gave his arm a squeeze before dropping her hand to her side. 'You'll contact us with anything new?' she asked Carrie.

'Absolutely, but I wasn't finished,' Carrie said.

Scarlett's heart sank. 'There's more?'

Carrie nodded. 'Your victim has given birth at least once. From the pelvic spread, I'd say the birth occurred within the past one to three years and that the child was carried to term.'

Scarlett felt the added weight of new dread settle over her. 'Assuming that the child lived, he's out there somewhere.'

'I'd say her child lived,' Carrie said grimly. 'Your victim was still lactating.'

Deacon's jaw tightened. 'Then we've got a baby out there somewhere who's becoming very hungry.'

Cincinnati, Ohio
Tuesday 4 August, 8.45 A.M.

Marcus stared at the phone on his desk for a long, long moment before forcing himself to pick it up and call his mother. Her maid picked it up on the first ring and Marcus nearly collapsed in relief, like the coward he was. Guilt chased the relief, quickly overwhelming it.

'Yarborough residence. May I help you?'

Della Yarborough had retaken her maiden name when she and Jeremy O'Bannion had divorced almost twenty years ago now. Here in Cincinnati, the Yarborough name had status and his mother had known the power it could wield. But Marcus and Stone had kept Jeremy's name, a gesture of love and support for the stepfather who'd legally adopted them, caring for them like they'd been his own sons.

'Hi, Fiona. It's Marcus. Is she awake?' he asked, even though he knew the answer. The quick pickup of the phone meant that his mother was still asleep. That she was still asleep meant that she'd taken sleeping pills the night before. She'd been going to bed earlier and earlier and sleeping later and later as the weeks went by.

'No, sir,' Fiona said quietly.

'Have you been in to check on her this morning?'

'Yes, sir, three times since dawn. She's sleeping soundly. Can I help you with something?'

'Um, well, yes. When she wakes up, have her call me or Stone, right away.'

'Is something wrong?'

'No, no, we're both fine. But there's a story online that I'd like to talk to her about before she reads it. It will be in the morning papers too, so I need to talk to her before she reads those.'

'All right,' Fiona said hesitantly. 'Should I have her doctor here?'

'No, I just want her to hear my voice and know I'm all right. Thanks, Fi.'

Marcus hung up, torn between anger and pity and fear for his mother. He'd nearly lost her once. He didn't want her to get to that place ever, ever again. Especially by her own hand. But there didn't seem to be much he

125

could do. She'd do what she wanted to do, no matter what he said, no matter how worried he became.

With a slight wince he remembered Cal's almost identical words from morning meeting. *At least I come by my stubbornness honestly.*

He checked his cell phone, knowing he had several calls or texts. He'd felt his phone vibrate at least five times during morning meeting. He sighed when he checked his log. Two of the four calls and two of the texts were from Scarlett Bishop. The others were from his stepfather. Marcus knew what the detective wanted – most likely the same thing she'd wanted before he went into the meeting. The list of threats. But he listened to the new messages anyway, just to hear her voice. And how goddamn pathetic was that?

The first message was another request for a status update, asking if he'd sent the list yet. The second message sounded worried. 'Marcus, it's Scarlett Bishop. I haven't heard from you and I'm . . . well, I just wanted to be sure you were all right. If your back begins to bother you, I hope you'll call for medical attention. I hope you're simply getting some rest. Could you call me when you wake up? I have a few follow-up questions.'

Marcus played the second message twice more and would have played it a third time had his cell not started to ring in that moment. It was his stepfather, Jeremy, which made sense since the last two messages were from him.

He answered, feeling a bit foolish for listening to Scarlett's message several times before playing Jeremy's even once. That Jeremy O'Bannion was his stepfather was a blessing for which he'd be grateful for the rest of his life. The man had come into their lives when he and Stone had been so young, so broken. And so desperate for a good father. Despite being only twenty-one at the time – only eleven years older than Marcus – Jeremy had adopted them, given them his last name and helped drive many of their nightmares away.

Jeremy loved them and Marcus loved him too, even though he and his mother were no longer married. 'Hi, Jeremy. What's up?'

A long sigh. 'God, Marcus, I needed to hear your voice. I've been worried ever since Detective Bishop called me.'

Marcus blinked. Hard. 'Scarlett Bishop called you? Why?'

'She was looking for you. She thought maybe you'd come to my house for some reason, since you weren't answering your home or cell. I made her tell me why she was looking for you because she sounded worried.'

A delicious heat curled around Marcus's heart. 'I'm fine, just busy. I was in morning meeting. I'll call her back.' *When I've finished that damn*

126

list. 'Where are you?' he asked when he heard a familiar bark in the background.

'Home. I went to your apartment to see if you were there, but I only found BB. I . . . brought her home with me for a while. I hope you don't mind. She's . . . I know it sounds silly, but sometimes . . .'

'She's all we have left of Mikhail,' Marcus murmured, his heart breaking for Jeremy's double loss. Jeremy had found out that Mikhail was his son only a short time before Mickey's murder. Jeremy had always loved Mikhail, who'd been conceived after the divorce in what had appeared to be a one-time fling. Marcus understood why his mother had kept the identity of Mikhail's father a secret – she'd been worried that Jeremy's new partner, Keith, would be angry at Jeremy's indiscretion. But the secret had cost both Jeremy and Mikhail dearly. Mikhail had missed out on having the best father on the planet, and poor Jeremy . . . To have found out Mikhail was his son only to lose him so soon thereafter had broken his heart.

'Exactly,' Jeremy said quietly. 'You always seem to understand. Your heart is too big, Marcus. It's going to get you hurt someday.'

'I'm fine,' Marcus assured him. 'Barely a bruise.' That was a goddamn lie, but Marcus told it convincingly. 'Are you all right, Dad?'

He didn't always call Jeremy 'Dad', but sometimes he needed to say it and he thought Jeremy needed to hear it.

'I'm fine,' Jeremy said hoarsely, tears in his voice. 'I tried to call your mother. I didn't want her to read about it online.'

'I know. So did I. But she was still asleep.'

'I'm worried about her, Marcus. She's taking so many pills. Along with her drinking . . .'

One of the things that Marcus loved about Jeremy was that the man loved others so genuinely. He understood why Jeremy hadn't been able to stay married to his mother, but he also knew that the divorce hadn't meant that he had stopped caring about her or her children.

Marcus's mother had explained everything to her sons when she and Jeremy had filed for divorce, because they'd been so angry and hurt with Jeremy for leaving. But Della hadn't been angry or hurt. Jeremy had been honest with her, telling her that he was gay when they'd first met. She'd only asked that he be discreet and not cheat with other women. She'd had enough of that with Marcus and Stone's biological father. Della and Jeremy had nearly a decade of happiness and had produced Audrey together. But then Jeremy had met Sammy.

He'd asked for a divorce, and Della had given her blessing. She'd been so truly happy for them that Marcus and Stone couldn't help but be happy too. They'd all loved Sammy, and when he had been killed in a car accident, they'd all grieved along with Jeremy.

Jeremy's new partner, Keith . . . Well, he was intense. Not a bad guy, but not a super-friendly type. Marcus suspected that he was threatened by the family bonds that Jeremy had been unwilling to sever. Especially Jeremy's bond with Della. Whenever she'd needed him, Jeremy had dropped everything to go to her side.

'I'm worried too,' Marcus said. 'I tried to get her to therapy. I thought Faith might actually have managed it, but Mom backed out at the last minute.'

Jeremy's chuckle was watery. 'That Faith. She's got a big heart too. Promise me you'll be careful, son. Please.'

'I promise. How's Keith?'

'Grumpy, but he's walking again.' Jeremy's husband had had to undergo knee replacements on both legs because his kneecaps had been shot by the same psychopath who'd shot Marcus and stalked and tried to kill his cousin Faith on multiple occasions.

The man had murdered Mikhail in cold blood when he'd found him in the family's cabin in the Kentucky forest. The murderer had been using the cabin to hide the two young women he'd taken hostage, and Mikhail had simply been there at the wrong time. Stone had been the one to find Mikhail's body, sending him spiraling into the dark place where he retreated when his memories became too intense to bear.

Mikhail had been shot in the head. Marcus swallowed hard. *Just like Tala.*

He cleared his throat roughly. Pushed the memory of the hole in Tala's head to the side so that he could focus. 'I'm glad he's doing better. Tell him that we've been missing him at third base.' Keith had been one of the best players on the *Ledger*'s softball team. 'We're six games behind the guys at the country radio station.'

'I'll tell him. I have class this afternoon, so I'll drop BB back at your place around noon. Will you be home by then?'

'God, I hope so,' Marcus muttered. 'If not, it won't be much after that. I'll make sure I walk her this afternoon. Thanks, Jeremy. And if Detective Bishop calls back, tell her I'm fine.'

'That's all you want me to tell her?' Jeremy asked. 'I'm not stupid, son. I heard what she didn't say. She was pretty scared for you this morning too.'

The warmth returned to curl around Marcus's heart. 'That's all I want you to tell her, Dad. And don't tell Audrey. She's a pest about stuff like this.'

'I won't,' Jeremy said, a smile finally in his voice. 'But thank you for confirming it for me. I think Detective Bishop was a little afraid of me. Tell her we're solid. That's a thing, right?'

Marcus chuckled. 'Yes, Dad, it's a thing. Why was she afraid of you?' Jeremy was one of the most non-threatening men on the planet.

'I think she didn't want to make me sad. I like her, Marcus. And she's very pretty.'

'Jeremy, leave him alone,' Keith said in the background. 'Stop playing Cupid.'

'Gotta go, Dad,' Marcus said firmly. 'Later.'

He hung up, hearing Jeremy chuckling as his own lips curved. Until he looked at his computer screen again. It was a mess of cut and pasted names, all from the two threat lists. He had been trying to choose which names he'd give Scarlett for too many hours.

Of course, he could always print it out when it was finished. Then he could take it by the police station and give it to her himself. *First things first, boy*, he told himself. He had to get the damn thing done first.

Nine

Ken Sweeney drummed his fingers on the table in his conference room, waiting impatiently for Demetrius to join them. Ken had called the emergency meeting of his leadership team seconds after Demetrius had informed him that Jason Jackson was not at home.

'Where the hell is Demetrius?' Joel asked, rubbing his eyes. He'd been up all night balancing the real books. What Joel had given Decker was just the tip of their corporate iceberg. 'I'm going to fall asleep here at this table if he doesn't get here soon.'

'You used to be able to pull a week of all-nighters,' Ken said with little sympathy.

'You used to be able to run a six-minute mile,' Joel shot back irritably. 'But neither of us is in college anymore, so shut it.'

Ken calmly lifted his chin and leveled Joel a silent warning. Joel paled slightly, gulped audibly and slid down in his chair. Ken relaxed, satisfied that he'd made his point.

They'd gone to college together – Ken and Joel and Demetrius – becoming three very unlikely friends. Joel had been the nerd, Ken the jock born with a silver spoon in his mouth, and Demetrius the inner-city kid on a football scholarship who'd had more street smarts than actual book learning. Ken and Demetrius had met through the team, Joel joining their group after he'd been assigned to be Demetrius's tutor. Demetrius had been no dummy, though. Of all of them, he might even be the smartest. Ken, of course, was the leader. He always had been. Joel just needed to be reminded of that sometimes.

'Demetrius is on his way in,' Ken said calmly. 'He just texted me from the lobby. But if you're that impatient to sleep, you may leave, of course.'

'No.' Joel's voice was quiet, with the smallest of quivers. 'I'm good.'

130

'I'm so glad,' Ken said, still calm. 'It's not like we have an urgent issue or anything.'

Nervous looks were exchanged between his son, Sean, and Dave Burton, Reuben's second-in-command in Security. Both Sean and Dave were younger than the rest of them by more than a decade. They knew their place in the pecking order and wisely kept silent.

The door opened, then closed quietly behind Demetrius. The man was built like a goddamn tank but still moved with the fluid stealth that had made him a hard man to catch on the football field. He took his seat and cocked a curious brow at Ken. 'Any word from Reuben?'

'None,' Ken said, torn between being furious and worried. 'You?'

Demetrius shook his head. 'Me neither. You planning on making Decker stand outside in the hall for the whole meeting?'

'No,' Ken replied. 'Just until we hash out the full plan. I'm not ready for him to know everything yet. Sean, tell them what you told me.'

Sean cleared his throat, clearly uncomfortable with the tension in the room. 'The tracker,' he began, 'transmitted a tamper alert at 5.45 this morning, while in the vicinity of the morgue. It was moved from the morgue, but the battery died a little later, at the corner of Fourteenth and Race. I'm assuming it was en route to CPD.'

'Shit,' Demetrius muttered. 'Who got killed?'

'The tracker was assigned to Charles Anders,' Ken said, 'one of five workers that we sourced on March fourth, three years ago.'

Demetrius turned on his iPad and, after inputting several passwords, unlocked the spreadsheet where he kept his contracts and sales information. Ken had been averse to Demetrius using the electronic tablet at first, but since it wasn't hooked up to the Internet and couldn't be hacked, he'd finally agreed to it. It could be physically stolen, but then again, Demetrius had pointed out, so could Ken's notebooks, and Demetrius's tablet would be a helluva lot harder for the thief to break into and read.

Each member of Ken's team kept their own records and none was accessible on the Internet. If one of them was caught, whoever had done the catching would not be able to see their entire operation. Joel's data was the most damning, since he kept the actual books, but Ken knew where Joel was at every moment, thanks to the cell phones that each of them carried. Hidden tracking software showed Ken the location of every member of his leadership team. They didn't know he was tracking them. He knew they'd be displeased if they ever found out.

His own phone was the only device that was not tracked. He'd made sure of it.

Reuben's phone had stopped transmitting a few minutes after they'd spoken that morning, but Ken hadn't realized that fact until he'd checked his tracking software after speaking with Demetrius earlier. The last place the phone had been active was on the road that Reuben would have used to get to the office. Either Reuben's battery had gone dead, or the entire phone had been destroyed.

'On that date, we imported eight units from Southeast Asia,' Demetrius said as he flicked through the spreadsheet. 'Most of our acquisitions are placed on the West Coast, but we did bring one shipment here. Ah, yes. On that date we processed a family unit of five recruited from the Philippines – father, mother, two daughters, fourteen and thirteen years old, and a son, nine years old. The father's previous work experience included teaching biology at university level and manual labor on a farm. The mother had been a nurse.'

'Were you able to pinpoint positions on the other four trackers, Sean?' Ken asked.

'Yes. Two of them – the two males – are in what appears to be a factory northwest of Dayton. It's the middle of nowhere. Google Earth shows a large warehouse structure with a parking lot.' Sean turned his laptop around to show Ken and the others. 'Keep in mind that Google also says this image is three years old, so it may not look exactly like this anymore, but this is the location.' He turned his laptop back to face him. 'The other two trackers are located in Anders's main residence in Hyde Park.'

Ken lifted his brows. 'Main residence?'

'Yes, sir,' Sean said. 'I ran a background check as soon as you gave me his name. He's purchased a condo in Vail and a small property in southern France, both as corporate assets.'

Dave Burton, acting head of security until Reuben returned, leaned forward, his elbows on the table. 'The men I sent to sit outside Anders's house say that he is there right now. They've seen him pacing in front of the windows.'

'I'll bet he's pacing,' Ken said grimly. 'He knows he should have contacted me hours ago. Make sure your men don't let him leave.'

'They won't. They're under orders to watch the house, and if they see Anders, his family or any of his assets trying to leave, to pick them up and transport them to our safe house.'

Meaning it was a house safe from scrutiny. Anders, Ken thought, was far from safe. 'Perfect. So the wearer, who is likely still in the morgue, was one of the females.'

Burton frowned. 'Don't you know which tracker was placed on which wearer?' he asked, his disbelief and disapproval apparent.

Everyone tensed. 'No,' Ken said with a tight smile, 'we do not. I'll let your question go this time, since this is your first time dealing with us directly.'

Burton looked around the table, saw the stares and glares, then swallowed hard. 'I'm sorry. I meant no disrespect. It's just that how can I know which live people to chase if I don't know who's missing and presumed dead?'

'We don't keep any more information than we absolutely need to,' Demetrius explained, his deep bass rolling over the table like quiet thunder. 'No trail for our competitors or the authorities to follow.'

'I know which female it was,' Sean said. 'At least I think I do. I had Decker listen to the tracker's audio feed. Most of what he heard at first was just idle chat at the morgue, but then a man started talking about getting her processed and logged in.' He tapped a key on his laptop and an older man's voice came out of the speakers: *Unidentified female, late teens, early twenties, of Asian descent. Multiple gunshot wounds with a large-caliber weapon, one to the abdomen, no exit wound, the other to the left temple, exit wound. Paramedics were called, victim was transported to the hospital, where she was pronounced DOA.*

Sean paused it. 'He goes on to X-ray her torso, where he finds the bullet. Then this.' He hit PLAY again. *No broken bones in the upper thighs, knees and . . . What the . . . What is that? A short pause, then a huge sigh. Hell.*

'After that, he seems to make two phone calls,' Sean explained. 'What we hear next is this.' He hit the PLAY button again. *Vince, I got something here that you need to see . . . Yeah, I mean right now. The gunshot victim from the alley . . . Thanks, man.* Another pause, a second phone call. *Carrie, I need you to come in a little early. We got a homicide in this morning and I just got to processing her. She's wearing an ankle tracker . . . No ID on her, but I'll have her printed by the time you get in here . . . Already called him. He's on his way.*

Sean hit pause again. '"Vince" refers to Vince Tanaka, head of CSU. "Carrie" is Carrie Washington, the head ME. The guy on the tape reports to Dr Washington. What we hear next on the audio is what sounds like him taking the victim's fingerprints, and then CSU arrives and cuts the tracker off the wearer. I checked the CPD dispatch log. They responded to a matching scene this morning at about three A.M., three blocks north of the Meadow homeless shelter.'

Demetrius scowled. 'That's where the dealers and hookers hang.'

And he ought to know, Ken thought. That was where Demetrius had grown up. 'What else did you get from the CPD dispatch log?' Ken asked Sean.

'Initial reports say the wearer of the tracker was with a man when she was shot. The man was also shot, but apparently not injured badly enough to be transported. He was treated at the scene.'

Ken frowned. *Not good at all.* 'Who was the man?'

'He was questioned at the scene and released,' Sean said. 'The log didn't list his name, but I have someone in CPD who owes me a favor and can find out.'

'Do it,' Ken snapped, then looked at Demetrius. 'We need to find Reuben and Jackson. They didn't just disappear into thin air. Someone took them. That Reuben disappeared right after this tracker was cut . . . We can't assume it was a coincidence.'

'When I left Jackson's house,' Demetrius said, 'I drove to Reuben's place, then drove the route he would have taken to work. I saw no evidence of his car. No wrecks. No sign of any struggle.'

Burton shifted uncomfortably in his chair. 'I know where his car is.'

All eyes swung to Reuben's right-hand man. 'Where?' Ken demanded.

A long hesitation. 'In the parking lot of a hotel near the airport,' Burton finally said.

An even longer silence. 'Excuse me?' Demetrius asked. 'He went to the airport?' He turned to Ken, eyes dark with rage. 'And you're only mentioning this to us now?'

Ken held up a hand, stemming Demetrius's fury. 'Burton, how do you know that? And *when* did you know that? And why didn't you tell us immediately?'

Burton blew a frustrated breath straight up his forehead. 'I didn't say anything immediately because I still don't know where Reuben is. I found the car about thirty minutes before coming to this meeting, but I can't see that he actually booked any flights, and he's not checked in at the hotel. Not unless he's done so under another name.'

'You haven't yet covered *how*,' Ken said coldly. 'Define how you found the car.'

Burton blew out another breath, this one through puckered lips. Calming himself. 'Reuben had trackers put on any mode of transportation owned by anyone who worked at this company.'

Demetrius's dark skin grew impossibly darker. 'Anyone? As in *everyone*? As in *me*? And Ken and Joel?'

Burton chanced a nervous glance around the table. 'Yes, sir.'

Ken's fury nearly geysered to the surface. He was barely holding on to his self-control. *I monitor the leadership of this company. Only me.* Reuben could track the employees all he wanted, but the leadership team . . .

134

That had never been included in his job description. 'He dared to do that? To invade our privacy? Who actually put these trackers on? Was it you?'

Burton shook his head hard. 'No, sir. Not on your vehicles. The leadership team's vehicles are maintained by Reuben. I take care of everyone else. But please understand that he put a tracker on his own cars too. He did it so that he would be able to find us in the event of just such a disappearance. He is the head of security, sir. He takes your safety very seriously. And he wasn't spying on you. He would have only used the tracking software if one of you went missing. I didn't have the passwords to see the leadership team's tracker history. I had to find them. That's why it took me so long to locate his car.'

Ken swallowed his rage, mollified only slightly by Burton's explanation. It did make sense for someone to be able to find them should they be attacked or arrested. *But that someone is me.* He had specifically told Reuben that the cars for the leadership team were off limits. His head of security had defied him behind his back.

If they found Reuben alive, Ken was going to fire his ass. After he beat the ever-living shit out of him. 'How did you find the passwords?' he asked Burton.

'Reuben has a safe where he keeps a notebook with passwords and other confidential data. I knew that he keeps the safe combination written on a sheet of paper taped to the underside of his nightstand drawer. He told me about the combination in the event he went missing. The combinations and passwords were all encrypted, of course.'

'Of course,' Demetrius said, looking very much like a bull ready to charge. 'Since you were obviously able to de-encrypt them, you've had access to our whereabouts too.'

To Burton's credit, he didn't flinch. 'Today was the first time that I accessed the tracking software.'

Demetrius shook his head. 'So you say. Even if we believe you, what was to stop you or anyone else from selling the passwords to the highest bidder?'

Which, Ken thought reluctantly, *Reuben might have done.* He was at the airport, after all. At least his car was. *If* they believed Burton. But so far the younger man had given them no reason to disbelieve him.

Ken took out his phone and, making sure that no one could see his screen, sent a text to Alice. *Go to the hotel at the airport. See if Reuben's car is there. ASAP. Keep this to yourself.* A few seconds later, he got Alice's reply. *Give me a moment to shut down my workstation.* It would take her forty-five minutes to get to the airport, but at least Ken would know then whether

Burton spoke truth. And if Reuben's car *was* at the airport hotel? Then they'd have to figure out why.

Meanwhile, he'd been monitoring the brewing confrontation between Demetrius and Burton, who was now shaking his head vehemently.

'No, sir, I have not had access,' he insisted, 'and even if I did look at the passwords, it wouldn't matter. The software has an auto-change feature that resets them. There is no set schedule. It happens every time the program is accessed or at some random frequency if the software goes unchecked. If I had the passwords and sold them, they'd only be good for a short time and then they'd reset. An email goes to Reuben when that happens.'

'So he knows we're looking for him,' Demetrius murmured.

'If he's alive,' Joel added quietly. 'He wouldn't have just run. Not Reuben. He's got as much at stake in this company as any of the rest of us.'

That would have been true of the man Ken thought he'd known, but Reuben's defying him, even allegedly for their own safety, was too startling to ignore.

Burton cleared his throat. 'Assuming he is still alive and can access his email, yes, he will know we are searching for him. But that was the point – that if any of you went mysteriously missing, we would know where to locate you so we could bring you home. One way or the other.'

Ken let out a breath. 'All right,' he said to Burton. 'I want you and Sean to find out where the hell he went. If he left his car at the hotel airport and he's not checked in, then he went somewhere. I know you've checked flights and rental car companies at the airport under his own name, but he could be using an alias, so make sure you check any of the names he's used in the past. Also check the used car dealers in the area, hospitals and the morgue. How are your forensic investigative skills?'

'Like riding a bike,' Burton said grimly. He'd been a cop once. A very long time ago, he'd reported to Reuben when both were with the Knoxville PD. 'It'll come back to me. I'll collect Reuben's car from the airport and we'll go over it with a fine-toothed comb.'

Ken shook his head. 'I'll send a flatbed truck for it. You can go over it when it arrives.'

Burton's eyes narrowed. 'You don't trust me?'

'No. But don't take it personally. I don't trust anyone.' He glanced at Demetrius. 'Do you have anything more?' he asked.

Demetrius shook his head. 'No. Except I want that damn tracker off my damn car right this damn second.'

'That goes double for me,' Joel added.

'Unanimous,' Ken said. 'Sean, can you test our vehicles and make sure they are tracker-free? Good,' he said when Sean nodded. 'Burton, tell the men you have watching Anders's house to bring him in.'

Burton grimaced. 'They aren't very experienced. They don't have finesse. I can't guarantee they'll bring him in without rousing suspicion from the neighbors.'

Demetrius rolled his eyes. 'What the hell kind of ship is Reuben running anyway?'

'We're a bodyguard short with Decker working in Accounting while he's on medical leave,' Burton said tightly. 'And we lost two team members last month. Reuben hasn't found anyone to replace them yet.'

The man and woman who'd been lost had been transporting a shipment from Miami when one of the cargo had charged them with a knife. Both of Reuben's people had been stabbed, the bus they'd been driving smashing into a median strip. Luckily they'd been almost home, which allowed Reuben to reach the wreckage before it had been reported to 911, narrowly averting a major crisis.

Their cargo had been severely dealt with. They'd have punished the bodyguard who had been tasked with searching for weapons in the first place, but he was already dead.

'Fine,' Ken said. 'You go. Take Decker with you. He can't run as fast as he once did, but he can subdue any of the chicken-shit in that family. I want Anders, his wife and daughter delivered to me unharmed. I want to know how his property got free of him and why he didn't think it important enough to inform me.'

'And if he doesn't tell you?' Demetrius asked, a predatory gleam in his dark eyes.

Ken ignored Joel's slight grimace. Their white-collar friend didn't have a taste for wet work. Luckily for Joel, both Ken and Demetrius did.

'He'll tell me,' Ken told him. 'We'll see how badly he wants his wife and daughter to remain unharmed.'

'What about the two women that are still alive and in Anders's house?' Burton asked.

'Bring them back here too. They may have been in on the dead woman's escape.' Ken shot Demetrius an amused look. 'We might have to work overtime.'

'Such a shame,' Demetrius drawled.

Under other circumstances Ken might have smiled. But not today. 'What I want to know is where the hell are Reuben and Jackson? Who was the man in the alley with the dead girl? And how did she escape? I want that damn tracker back. Do whatever you need to do to make that happen. Any questions? Good. Then go.'

Cincinnati, Ohio
Tuesday 4 August, 9.00 A.M.

CSU Specialist Vince Tanaka glanced up when Scarlett and Deacon entered the lab, the magnifying goggles that covered his face making him look like something between a mad scientist and a borg. 'Oh. I was about to call you two.' He flipped one of the magnifying lenses up and glanced at the big clock on the wall, then winced. 'Oh. I was about to call . . . a few hours ago. I got wrapped up in this. Sorry.'

On the worktable before him was the tracking device they'd cut off of Tala's ankle. It was black, sleek and almost . . . petite. Nothing like the clunky models they were used to seeing on parolees and prisoners on house arrest. Then again, most of them weren't built like a seventeen-year-old Filipino girl – only four foot eleven and ninety-two pounds, according to her chart in the morgue. The normal-sized monitors might not have stayed on her leg.

'It's okay,' Scarlett told him. 'It just would have been nice to know sooner. We'd only theorized that Tala was being held as a slave. This takes away all doubt. What can you tell us?'

Deacon had pulled on a pair of gloves and passed a pair to Scarlett. He picked up the device, his mouth bending into a thoughtful frown. 'It's really light.'

'State of the art,' Vince said. 'Weighs less than four ounces. Most courts and correction agencies don't have the budget to buy these new ankle monitors. This particular model isn't supposed to be sold to private individuals, but obviously the victim's captor had access.'

Scarlett studied the device in Deacon's hands. 'Can you trace it back to the manufacturer using the serial number?'

'Already did,' Vince said. 'Kind of, anyway. The manufacturer is Constant Global Surveillance and their head office is in Chicago. This unit was reported to have been damaged during quality control testing. It was supposedly destroyed. CGS was "extremely surprised and upset" to hear I was holding it in my hands. Apparently there will be an internal investigation.'

'I should hope so,' Deacon said as he handed the device to Scarlett. 'Did the manufacturer say how many other units were "damaged during quality control testing"?'

Vince shook his head. 'I asked, but I was told they wouldn't know until they'd conducted their investigation. I'm just glad I didn't call the main office first. If I had, I probably wouldn't even know there was an issue at all.'

'Who *did* you call first?' Deacon asked.

'The customer service number listed on their website. When I told them I wanted to trace one of their units, I was immediately transferred to the shipping department. I got lucky because the person who picked up the phone wasn't the manager – it was a young man who informed me that I was mistaken, that I couldn't have that serial number because it had been destroyed by the quality control lab. I asked to speak to his manager, who immediately asked me to hold. Fifteen minutes later, the company's attorney picked up.'

Scarlett sighed. 'I take it the lawyer denied everything.'

Vince shrugged. 'Well, as much as he could. I was holding the device in question, so unless he wanted to claim it was a counterfeit, he had to tell me something, so he fell back on the whole tried-and-true internal investigation to shut me up.'

'They may be more cooperative once they've had a chance to get their ducks in a row,' Deacon said thoughtfully. 'If they've got someone stealing trackers for black-market resale, they'll want to plug that hole.'

Vince shrugged. 'Or they might insist on a search warrant to give themselves time to cover things up, especially if the scam goes up to the head honchos. Either way, I've already given them a warning by asking my questions. By the time we get there, all the evidence could be shredded.'

'Maybe not,' Deacon said. 'Give me a few minutes.' He walked toward the window, his cell phone to his ear.

'What else about the tracker?' Scarlett asked Vince. 'Is it a positioning device only, or could it detect temperature and pulse?'

'Just a positioning device. Why?'

'Because when you cut it off Tala's body, you probably sent a tamper alert to her captors. They'll know she's in the morgue.'

Tanaka frowned behind the goggles. 'Didn't they put her there? Whoever "they" are.'

'Maybe, maybe not. I think she knew the shooter, but it might not have been her captor. Deacon and I were wondering why she'd chance leaving the house to go to the alley to begin with if she knew she was being tracked. She must have known her captors weren't monitoring her signal, at least for a period of time. By sending the tamper alarm, we informed them she was gone – and dead. And now they know their device is in police custody. Tala was worried that her family would be harmed.' Scarlett sighed. 'We may have pushed that into happening.'

Vince flinched. 'Oh my God.' He looked away for a moment, then looked back, his jaw clenched resolutely. 'Then I'd better help you find them quickly. I can tell you that while her captors could see that she was at least in the vicinity of the morgue, they don't know the device is here at CPD now. The tracker was still sending a weak signal when I took it off, but by the time I got it here, it'd stopped transmitting.'

'Stopped? Why? Did you remove the battery?'

'I didn't have to. It was drained to almost nothing.'

'So her captors would have gotten an alert anyway,' Scarlett murmured.

'Probably within ten minutes of my taking it off her. Half an hour tops. I tested the battery strength before I cut the strap. If it had still been transmitting a strong signal, I would have called you. If I'd known about her family, I would have waited to cut the strap until the battery was completely dead.'

'They've probably figured out we have the tracker, but like you said, if her captors are the ones who shot her, they knew her body would end up in our custody. I suppose it's too much to ask that the tracker had any prints?'

'Just the girl's own fingerprints and a few partials. She didn't pop up on AFIS, but the partials might. Latent will send the partials through the database and get back to us.'

Scarlett bit her lower lip, thinking about the foreign accent in Tala's flawless English. And her last spoken word – *malaya*. Tagalog for freedom. 'It's highly possible that she came into the US from somewhere else.'

'Smuggled in?'

'Maybe – and if that's the case, there won't be any immigration record. But it's also possible she came here legally and was coerced into servitude.'

Vince nodded briskly. 'Then her prints will be on file with Customs and Immigration. I'll check it out ASAP.'

Malaya. 'If they need to narrow the search parameters, have them check immigration records from the Philippines.' Scarlett forced her mind to stop seeing Tala and to remember the crime scene as a whole. 'What about the bullet casing I found in the alley?'

'Latent got a single print, but it's a clear one. It's being processed too, along with this.' Vince stripped the goggles from his face, then brought up a plastic evidence bin from the shelf below his worktable. He was about to pull the lid off when Deacon rejoined them. 'Well?' Vince asked him. 'Can the Feds get the records from the tracker manufacturer without tipping them off?'

'They're planning an unannounced visit as we speak. The Bureau doesn't source from Constant Global Surveillance, but the federal correctional system does. Their contract stipulates that CGS's lab facilities are "open to quality audits conducted by the customer". There's no requirement for advance notice. The Chicago Field Office has agents en route. Hopefully they'll get there before the lab shreds their records.'

'So what are we thinking?' Scarlett asked. 'That someone inside CGS is smuggling working devices out of the factory and selling them on the black market? It doesn't seem like it would be financially worth the risk. These trackers only sell for a few hundred bucks apiece.'

'To legitimate buyers,' Deacon said. 'I imagine that anyone who's purchased a human being through traffickers will pay a good bit more than a few hundred bucks to protect their investment. You can't buy trackers like this on eBay.'

Scarlett shook her head. 'Maybe. It still doesn't seem worth the risk for the guy in the lab to steal them at a rate that would make him any money. If he "destroys" too many during testing, somebody's going to notice. To keep from being caught, it would have to be an every-now-and-then thing. Unless he's not stealing these units for the money. What if he's being forced to provide them?'

Deacon nodded. 'Extortion is a definite possibility. I'll get backgrounds on anyone who had access to the units made around the same time as this one. We'll see if anyone pops, then start with that person and follow the trail. Hopefully to whoever bought this unit.'

'Which was about to give up the ghost when Vince cut it off Tala's leg,' Scarlett said.

'Yeah, I heard. I was on hold when you two were discussing that part, so I listened in. Before we go on to the rest of the evidence,' Deacon said, pointing at the bin Vince held on the worktable, 'I have another question about the tracker. Does it transmit sound or just GPS signal?'

'Well, it depends on who you ask. Constant Global Surveillance's website claims it can be used to buzz the wearer – like a phone in vibrate mode. The buzz is used to remind the wearer of appointments with his parole officer, things like that. But some models can record or transmit live conversations without the wearer knowing it.'

'Holy Big Brother, Batman,' Scarlett muttered. 'Defense attorneys must've had a field day with that.' And of course the mere mention of defense attorneys had her remembering what Bryan had said just hours before. Trent Bracken, a goddamn killer, was going to defend actual people in an actual court. *Not now, Scarlett. Pay attention. For Tala.* 'Can this tracker do that? I mean, could someone have overheard Marcus talking to Tala in the park?'

'Quite possibly,' Vince said. 'I was getting ready to take this one apart to find out what other goodies it's got when you two came in. I'll let you know as soon as I do.'

'Thanks,' she said. 'Marcus was afraid that Tala had been beaten because he'd tried to talk to her. If someone was listening in while she walked the dog, he could be right. We need to know what precipitated the beating – if it was over Marcus or something unrelated.' She pointed to the evidence bin. 'So what's in there?'

'Everything else the victim was wearing or carrying.' Vince lifted the lid, identifying each bagged item as he put it on the worktable. 'Blue jeans, polo shirt, shoes, socks. Crucifix on a necklace chain. Dog treats. And this.' He held up a small plastic evidence bag. 'Ten grams of cocaine. I should have lab results on the purity in a few hours.'

Scarlett frowned. 'The alley where I found her is drug-dealer central, but Carrie didn't find any evidence of drugs in her system.'

Vince made no comment as he put the bag of coke on the table and took three more bags from the bin, silently holding them up for Scarlett and Deacon to see.

'A pacifier, a teething ring and a baggie filled with Cheerios.' Scarlett's heart squeezed painfully in her chest. 'For her baby.'

'The dog treats and the coke were in her left pocket,' Vince said quietly, 'the baby things in her right.'

'The baby's at least eight or nine months old if she was giving him Cheerios,' Scarlett said, hardening her voice so that it didn't waver.

Vince looked surprised. 'I didn't know you knew anything about babies, Scarlett.'

She lifted a shoulder. 'I've got six nieces and nephews. Difficult not to pick up a few things here and there.'

Deacon cleared his throat. 'Can you get DNA off the pacifier, Vince?'

'I already took a sample off the pacifier and the teething ring.'

Deacon nodded once. 'Good. If we don't find the child with her captors, at least we'll be able to show that her child was with her at some point. Was there anything else in her pockets?'

Vince shook his head. 'Nothing. No keys, no money, no ID.'

Scarlett caught Vince's arm as he started to put the baby things back in the bin. 'Wait.' She took the pacifier and held it under the light on the worktable. 'What's this?' she asked, pointing to three black smudges on the pacifier's ring.

'Magic Marker,' Vince said. 'But it's too worn away to see what it used to say.'

She took the pacifier from the bag, then bent closer to the light, squinting at the smudges. 'Can I see your glass?' She held out her hand and Vince dropped the magnifying glass into her palm. 'There are three distinct smudges,' she said, 'about the same space apart. They might have been circles originally. And . . .' She squinted harder, tilting the pacifier one way, then the other, trying to catch the right light on the surface of the plastic ring. 'Colors,' she murmured. 'Tiny leftover pieces of color. Red and blue and . . . yellow? Or maybe green. Each to the left of the black smudged circle.'

'Other magic markers?' Deacon asked.

Absently she nodded. She recognized this pattern, but the memory was hovering on the edge of her mind, just out of reach. And then her brain made the connection. *Holy shit.* Abruptly she straightened, her pulse hammering in her head as she met her partner's curious stare. 'Oh my God. He was wrong.'

Deacon's head was tilted. 'What? Who?'

'Marcus. He was wrong,' she said, her words coming out way too fast. 'Do you ever watch *Wheel of Fortune*?'

Deacon blinked, then nodded warily. 'Yes, quite often recently. Turns out Faith is a closet fan of Pat and Vanna. Why?'

'You know those people who can solve the puzzle with one letter?'

'I hate those people,' Vince muttered. 'They spoil all the fun.'

Scarlett pointed to herself. 'Well *I'm* one of those people. These black smudges could have been lower case a's. The blue, red and yellow – other letters. Blank "a" blank "a" blank "a". *Malaya*. Somebody wrote "Malaya" on this pacifier. What if it doesn't mean "freedom"? What if it's a name?'

Deacon's eyes widened as realization dawned. 'When Tala said "Help Malaya", she wasn't asking Marcus to help free her family.'

Scarlett swallowed hard, Tala's final plea taking on an even deeper meaning. 'She was asking him to save her baby.'

Cincinnati, Ohio
Tuesday 4 August, 9.15 A.M.

Drake snarled when his cell phone's ring tone pulled him out of a sound sleep. He opened one eye and groaned. Stephanie's throwaway phone. 'This better be damn important,' he barked. 'You woke me up.'

'He knows,' Stephanie whispered harshly. 'He came to my room and took my iPhone. Slapped me. Hard. He knows I took Tala out of the house last night. He kept asking me why.'

Drake sat up in bed, rubbing the back of his neck. 'Did you tell him?' he asked softly.

'No!' It was a hissed whisper. 'I didn't. I swore I didn't know what he was talking about, even when he hit me again. But I don't know how long I can hold up.'

'Then get into your fancy car and leave,' Drake said irritably.

'I can't. He took my purse – my wallet, my keys . . . everything. Told me that if he caught me trying to escape, he'd beat me within an inch of my life. I believe him. You have to come. I might be able to sneak out through the servants' door, but I won't get far. You have to come pick me up.'

'In what?'

'I don't know,' Stephanie snapped. 'Figure it out. Just do it fast or it won't matter. If he makes me hurt enough, I might just tell him what he wants to know. Somehow I think that'll hurt you more than me.'

Drake's eyes narrowed at the girl's sudden spine. He hated spine. He thought he'd trained it out of Stephanie, but obviously he'd been wrong. He wanted to tell her to go ahead, tell her father everything. It wasn't like her old man could call the cops or anything. He considered telling her to shove her rich head up her rich ass, that he was going to out her father for the cheating sonofabitch he really was.

But it would be easier just to pick Stephanie up, put a bullet in her head and dump her body in the river. Less fuss all the way around.

'Okay,' he said quietly, going along with her for the moment. 'My sister has a Honda Civic. It's white. Watch for it. I'll text you when I'm two minutes away, okay?'

'Okay.' A shuddering exhale. 'Thank you, Drake.'

'No worries. Just stay out of dear old Dad's sight until I can come get you.'

Cincinnati, Ohio
Tuesday 4 August, 9.15 A.M.

Scarlett pushed through the exit from CPD, dragging in a breath of air that was already hot and humid. She paused on the sidewalk, waiting for Deacon to catch up. Neither of them had said much since leaving Vince's domain, each caught up in their own thoughts.

Malaya is a baby. Tala's baby. And she was out there somewhere, hopefully not alone. Hopefully with someone who would take care of her, make sure she was fed. And safe.

But the reality of the child's situation had hit Scarlett hard as she'd stood staring at that pacifier. Tala had been beaten severely. Held captive. *Owned*. She'd still been nursing, so her baby must have still lived with her. *Help Malaya*.

The panic Tala must have felt became Scarlett's and, chest too tight to breathe, she'd rushed out of CSU, chased by a wave of hot tears that she couldn't let anyone else see.

She gulped more of the humid air, her throat still painfully thick. No wonder Tala had taken such a risk to see Marcus last night. Her baby wasn't safe.

Please God, let that baby be safe.

Scarlett's shoulders stiffened, abruptly aware that she'd whispered a prayer, if only in the privacy of her own mind. She didn't pray. Hadn't prayed in ten years. That she'd just done so meant only that she was exhausted, not that she actually expected the whispered entreaty to do a bit of good. She'd stopped believing in Santa and the Easter Bunny when she was five. She'd stopped believing in prayer ten years ago, when she'd stood over the mutilated body of her best friend.

But at least the shock of hearing herself pray had knocked her out of the thick fog of panic that had seized her chest in a white-knuckled grip. She drew another deep breath, shuddered it out. *What the hell is wrong with you today, Scarlett?* She'd been on an emotional roller coaster since the ringing of her phone had yanked her out of sleep. Since Marcus's voice had rolled over her, waking her up.

Waking up a lot of things, she thought darkly, thinking of the way her body had responded when she'd seen him standing there in that alley. *Too damn many things*.

Of course Bryan's visit hadn't helped, layering regret and guilt on top of her disappointment, then whipping up the fury within her that never seemed to cool. Dredging up the memories that still had the power to trap her in a nightmare, wake her up screaming.

That was why she was so emotional. This roller coaster of feelings had been triggered by remembering Michelle – finding her body, watching her killer go free to live his life. To become a goddamn defense attorney. That would drive anyone crazy. And who wouldn't be upset at the thought of a defenseless baby in the hands of someone capable of administering a beating like Tala had received? To not be moved would make a person a monster. The lump in her throat had almost nothing to do with Marcus O'Bannion. Or his voice, or his face, and especially not his chest without his shirt . . .

145

Yeah, girl, you go on telling yourself that if it makes you feel better. Which it did. It also helped her clear her mind so that she could concentrate on doing her job. On finding that baby before it was too late.

Willing her hands not to tremble, she checked her phone for new messages, emails or voicemails, finding a number of all three. But not one of them from Marcus O'Bannion. He still hadn't returned any of her calls, nor had he sent her the damn list of threats.

You don't need the list, she told herself, knowing that what she really needed was for him to have kept his promise. What was he hiding? Or . . . Her gut tightened as a new worry presented itself. Was it possible that whoever had shot Tala had realized Marcus was still alive and come back to finish the job?

It had been hours since Tala's body had been taken to the morgue. It had to have hit the newsfeeds by now. She did a quick Internet search, and seconds later her phone screen was full of hits. Clicking on the first link, she felt the breath seep from her lungs in the weariest of sighs. It was the *Ledger*'s website, the headline cleverly spinning the tragedy to focus on Marcus. *Local philanthropist shot attempting to save woman's life*, by Stone O'Bannion. The article had been posted online only minutes before.

Now she knew what had kept Marcus so busy that he hadn't been able to send her that damn list. Or return her calls. *Well at least he's not dead*, she thought bitterly.

The story was true. All the facts were there. And even though the byline was Stone's, the voice she heard in her mind as she skimmed the article was Marcus's. It included what she'd told him he could, leaving out what she'd requested he hold back. He hadn't disclosed that he'd seen her in the park or that he'd heard – and recorded – her last words. He made it sound like he'd happened upon her as she lay dying and that he'd been shot while giving first aid. By the end of the article, Marcus had somehow diverted the readers' attention away from the fact that he'd been in the alley to begin with, making it clear that he was nothing but an innocent bystander, a Good Samaritan shot in the back for his efforts.

I make my living digging for news. At least he hadn't lied about that. He'd told her he would print the story. But it didn't change the raw burn of anger in her gut, irrational yet undeniable. Before her, in black and white, was the stark reminder that, no matter how much she wished for him to be different, the real Marcus was not the man she wanted him to be. When all was said and done, he was still a reporter. A man who made his living off the misery of others.

She heard the main door open and close behind her. A few seconds later,

Deacon came to an ambling halt at her side. 'You okay, Scar?'

The concern in his voice sent another wave of emotion crashing into her, the sudden stinging in her eyes making her slam them shut. 'Why wouldn't I be?' she gritted out, her voice harsh and gravelly. Barely recognizable as her own. 'Just because I took off like an insane bat out of hell?' She clenched her jaw to keep the tears at bay. She would not cry. She would not. 'Shit,' she added in a mutter. 'It's just hormones. Ignore me.'

Deacon lightly bumped his shoulder against hers, a silent gesture of support. Then he cleared his throat. 'Well, I've been thinking about the tracker capability.'

She swallowed the lump in her throat, surreptitiously wiping her eyes to clear them before meeting Deacon's gaze. His bi-colored eyes no longer bothered her, but the compassion she saw in them now did. Another wave of emotion threatened to pull her under. She looked away, focused on the traffic crawling by. 'Okay. What about the tracker?'

'It can transmit sound, just like a telephone.'

'I thought Vince had to take it apart to determine that.'

'He did. Didn't take him more than a few minutes to figure it out, but you'd already left.'

Fled. She pressed her fingertips to her temple, trying to think through the headache that invariably came with her tears. Which was one very good reason not to cry. Ever. 'What was the range of the listening part of the device?'

'There isn't one. It's digital, runs off the satellite, same as the GPS. Like a Skype line,' he added when she frowned up at him in confusion.

'Oh.' Now she understood. 'That means there wasn't any place she could go where she couldn't be heard. My God. That poor kid.' And then she really understood and she sucked in a hard breath. 'They wouldn't hear just her voice. They'd hear anyone she talked to. Like Marcus. In the park and in the alley last night.' And if they had heard Tala in the alley? Scarlett's heart began to beat harder. They'd know that Marcus had heard her last words. 'Could they record or would they have had to be listening at that moment?'

'I'm sure they could record if they had the right equipment.'

'I'm sure they had all the bells and whistles,' Scarlett said grimly.

'Not all,' Deacon said softly. 'The device didn't have a camera.'

She frowned. 'So?'

'So, they could hear her in the park and they could see where she was on the map, but they couldn't see her. She walked that dog all by herself, along the paths, through the trees, for at least a few weeks. Maybe longer. Invisible to them.'

147

'You think she left some kind of message in the woods? Something someone might use to rescue her and the baby?'

He shrugged. 'Maybe. It's worth taking a walk through the park to check it out. We don't have our meeting with Agent Troy at the field office for several hours. We have time.'

Scarlett considered it. 'While we're at the park, we can see if the uniforms have made any progress. They've been out since sunup, canvassing the houses in a mile radius of the park with photos of Tala and the dog. Last update I got, nobody had recognized either of them. If they still haven't found anybody who remembers them by the time we get to the park, I'll move on to the list of groomers.' She hesitated, then decided it would be better to check on Marcus and feel like a fool when he was safe and sound than the alternative. 'On the way to the park, let's swing by the *Ledger*'s office.'

Deacon's brow furrowed. 'Why?'

'Because Marcus O'Bannion's called attention to himself as being the last person to see Tala alive.' She held up her phone, showed him the article.

Deacon read it with a groan. 'And I thought I had a flair for drama. He's made himself a damn hero.'

Scarlett rolled her eyes. 'If anyone was listening to Tala's last moments, Marcus has made himself a damn target.'

'The tracker. Shit. They'd know he knew that Tala was a slave. They'd believe he knew about Malaya.'

'And if that tracker was still transmitting when I got there? Whoever was listening got the prologue in the park too. So they'd know this wasn't a chance meeting the way he insinuates in the article.'

'Did you call him?'

Scarlett huffed in frustration. 'I've been calling his cell phone all morning and he hasn't answered. I called his office and the young chickie who answered the phone said that Mr O'Bannion was in conference and could not be disturbed. I called his mother's house, but the maid hadn't seen Mr Marcus for several days and his mother was sleeping and couldn't come to the phone.'

Deacon sighed. 'That means she's either doped herself up or she hit the bottle too hard again. I feel really bad for the woman, losing Mikhail like that, but she's well past the point of concern. She needs help, but no one in the family will admit it.'

Scarlett's heart hurt for Marcus's mother. But her priority right now had to be keeping Marcus alive so that the poor woman didn't lose another son. 'Be that as it may, Marcus wasn't there. I even called Jeremy, but Marcus wasn't there either.' She'd been hesitant to make the call, worried that Marcus's stepfather would hold a grudge against her for what had gone down nine months ago. If he had, he would have had good reason. But he'd been pleasant, helpful even. 'Jeremy called Marcus's apartment for me, but just got voicemail. He even went over there and checked the place out, but Marcus wasn't there and hadn't slept in his bed.'

'Let me try. Maybe he'll pick up if it's my caller ID. What's the number for his cell?'

Scarlett read it out to him. 'That's the disposable he used to call me this morning.' She waited quietly, her worry increasing when Deacon's call got voicemail too. She knew she was being irrational. Marcus was probably simply busy. But she had a nagging feeling in her gut that he wasn't safe, and long ago she'd learned to listen to her gut.

'He's probably working,' Deacon said, 'but if it'll set your mind at ease, we can split up. You go by the *Ledger*, and I'll meet you at the park.'

'Hey,' Scarlett called when he turned to walk away. 'How will you know where to start looking? We don't know which bench Marcus was sitting on, so we don't know which direction Tala came from.'

Deacon looked over his shoulder. 'Ask Marcus when you see him,' he said, then disappeared into the CPD building.

'Yeah,' Scarlett muttered. 'I'll do that.'

Ten

Demetrius closed Ken's office door behind them, having followed him back from the conference room. Ken sank into the chair behind his desk and waited as Demetrius settled into one of the wingback chairs, looking far more comfortable than Decker had a few hours before. Physically comfortable, anyway. There was tension in his friend's face. Ken knew his own face reflected the same tension.

'Did you know that Reuben's wife left him?' Demetrius asked without preamble.

Ken managed to control his blink of surprise, both at the news and that Demetrius would have known it before he did. 'No. When? Why?'

'Yesterday. He didn't tell me, by the way.'

Ken's mind was racing. An angry wife, a sudden trip coinciding with the disappearance of both Reuben and one of his trusted men . . . Ken didn't know how or if it was connected, but none of this boded well. Especially if Reuben's wife had found out what he really did for a living.

'How did you know then?'

'His wife showed up on my doorstep last night, crying. Demanded to know who else he'd been screwing.'

Ken rubbed his forehead. 'Who else? What does that even mean?'

'Remember I told you this morning about the wife of the Brazilian?'

'The one with roving hands who Reuben was supposed to protect you from?' Dread was a sudden vise squeezing his heart. 'Because Reuben liked the attention? Did Miriam find out about the Brazilians?'

'No, but she did find out about the Indians.'

Ken slumped back in his chair. 'Reuben was screwing our Indian supplier too?'

'Not the supplier,' Demetrius hedged. 'Just the guy's daughter.'

'Holy shit.' Ken closed his eyes, wishing he had Reuben in front of

150

him right now. He'd beat the hell out of him. Each one of the four founding members had their proclivities, but they'd all learned to control their baser instincts for the greater good of the business – or at least to not get caught if they indulged elsewhere. Reuben's job was to identify security threats from within the company and without, but it was Demetrius and Ken who dealt with those threats.

If an example was required, Demetrius would beat the hell out of the person and leave his body to be found by others who dared challenge their territory. If information was needed, Ken would carve the person up like a Thanksgiving turkey until they spilled every secret they knew.

Unfortunately, Joel and Reuben's special needs didn't do anything to help the company. Joel had a taste for very young boys, but was smart enough to hunt far from his own backyard. Reuben liked young girls, but he wasn't as discriminating – or as careful – as Joel. Ken thought they'd dealt with Reuben's carelessness years ago, but apparently their intervention hadn't taken.

'At least tell me that the girl's eighteen,' Ken muttered.

'Barely, but yeah, she is. The supplier brought his wife and daughter to New York City last year to visit colleges while he did business with us. We met with him in his hotel suite and the daughter came in at one point. She was in the suite with us for maybe three minutes, just long enough to say hello and get more cash from her father. I don't know how Reuben managed it, but the daughter apparently had a fling with him later that night.' Demetrius rolled his eyes as he shook his head. 'Then believed herself to be "in love".'

'God save me,' Ken muttered. 'How did Miriam find out?'

'She found a note in Reuben's pocket from the girl – on hotel stationery. Miriam managed to persuade someone at the hotel to alert her when the girl checked in again, which happened last week. Then she hired a PI to get pictures of Reuben and the girl together at the hotel.'

Ken ground his teeth. *Reuben, you fucking idiot.* 'Did the PI get pictures?'

'Oh yeah.' Demetrius winced. 'Reuben has tattoos in places I never wanted to see. But that's not the worst part. It was a hotel near the airport, the same one where Reuben's car was found.'

Ken leveled him an annoyed look. 'You knew Reuben went to that hotel this morning?'

'Hell, no.' Demetrius looked offended. 'I would have told you when you called. I didn't put it together until Burton told us where Reuben's car showed up in his tracking program. I didn't want to tell everyone else about the girl, or that Miriam knew about her. We might have to deal with Miriam, and that's not going to be an easy thing for any of us.'

'Shit. I want to kill that sonofabitch Reuben.'

'Stand in line behind Miriam. I'd say you'd be wise not to get in her way right now.'

'Why didn't you tell me last night?'

'I should have. I wanted to talk to Reuben first. Get his side of things. I was worried when you said he'd gone missing, but I didn't want to raise the alarm until I had all the information. Before I got you all riled up, I wanted to make sure he wasn't puking his guts up like Jackson. I didn't put it together until Burton told us that he'd tracked Reuben's car.'

Ken's frown deepened. 'What is Jackson's connection to all this?'

Demetrius sighed. 'Miriam's PI told her that Jackson was the lookout while Reuben was fucking all comers. Miriam may have gotten to both of them.'

'Oh for God's sake.' Ken rubbed his eyes. 'You mean the fact that Jackson passed out on the floor of his office was Miriam's doing?'

'Given that Decker found Jackson passed out in the middle of his shift makes me think that he consumed something just before he left home or when he first got here. It's possible that Miriam drugged them both, especially since she was always sending in cookies and snacks for the guys in Reuben's group. I'll check the security video, see if it shows him eating or drinking.'

'I already checked,' Ken said. 'I wanted to verify what Decker told me. Jackson drank nothing but coffee, but he mixed in his own creamer. He had it in a little silver bottle that he kept in the break-room fridge. Looked like a hip flask, so I can see why Decker thought he might be under the influence.'

'I'll have it analyzed.'

'So where is Jackson? If he's not home, then where is he?'

Demetrius shrugged. 'I don't know. Miriam might have poisoned him, but she isn't strong enough to physically remove him from his home.'

'She could have had a gun. If Jackson was as sick as Decker said, then he wouldn't have been able to fight back.'

'Maybe,' Demetrius said. 'Or Reuben might have stopped by Jackson's house on his way to the airport to pick him up, just to make sure his wife didn't get her hands on him. Miriam was really pissed off. I think she actually would kill them both if she caught them, especially if Jackson was too weak to fight back. I can check with the neighbors again, see if anyone saw either Reuben's or Miriam's car in Jackson's driveway this morning after the cab dropped him off.'

'Hopefully she hasn't killed either of them. Or both,' Ken said grimly.

'But if she hasn't, and if Reuben's got Jackson because he knows his wife is on to him, he might run.'

'They might have already left the country,' Demetrius said with a scowl.

Ken sighed. 'Sean and Burton are looking for him. If anyone can find Reuben, it's Sean. Okay, damage control time. What was in the photos that Miriam got from her PI?'

'Just fucking. But very creative fucking. Reuben is far more limber than I would have expected.'

Ken grimaced. 'Not a picture I want in my head. What else could the PI have?'

'Nothing,' Demetrius said decisively.

Ken sat up straighter. 'You paid him a visit?'

'I sure as hell did. Right after Miriam left my house last night.'

'Is he dead?'

A single nod. 'And disposed of. I have his camera, all of his photo files and his backups. I've got his laptop so that Sean can see if he uploaded the photos anywhere.'

'Smart.'

'I thought so,' Demetrius said mildly.

'What about Miriam?'

Demetrius hesitated. 'I don't think she knows anything else. We'll keep an eye on her. Make sure she doesn't have any meetings of her own. If we need to take her out, we will, but we should wait if we can. It would be too suspicious if she disappeared too close to the PI.'

'This is why I wanted all of us to be single,' Ken growled. 'Damn wives fuck it all up.'

'I know, I know.'

Both Demetrius and Joel were long divorced, and Ken had been dumb enough to marry – twice. He'd had to deal with his own mess when Sean's mother got too curious. Since then he'd played it smart. He liked a woman warming his bed from time to time, but had never let anyone else too close. But Reuben had been married before he'd joined them, and he'd always insisted Miriam had no clue what they really sold. Reuben had been a cop, after all. For him to join forces with drug and sex kingpins was not an option she'd ever even entertained.

'We should have forced Reuben to divorce her before we let him in.' Ken glared at Demetrius. 'Like I told you we should.'

Demetrius's eyes narrowed. 'Are you really going to play "I told you so"?'

Ken considered it, but knew it wouldn't help the current situation. 'What do you know about Burton?'

'Not much more than you do. He was trained by Reuben back in Tennessee. Was his partner for a year when they were Vice. He testified at Reuben's hearing, said he had not taken bribes or stolen coke from the stashes they seized. Then got axed about six months after Reuben did. He's extremely loyal to Reuben, but I think he was a little worried too. Otherwise he would have come and told you that he'd tracked Reuben's car as soon as he found out, instead of trying to find his boss first.'

'I can't believe Reuben's been tracking our cars,' Ken muttered.

'*If* it was the way Burton said it was, with all the password protection and layers of security, then I guess I can't be too mad about it. You did hire him to keep us safe, after all.'

'I should have hired someone to make sure he kept his pants zipped.'

'True that. Have you heard from Alice?'

Ken's brows shot up. 'About what?'

'About whether Reuben's car is parked where Burton said it was.' He rolled his eyes. 'Come on, Kenny. I've known you how long? You were texting in a meeting. You never do that. And when we left the conference room, Alice was gone. She hasn't taken her lunch hour in the four years since she finished law school and came on full time.'

'You know a lot about my secretary,' Ken said coldly.

Demetrius narrowed his eyes again. 'Don't even suggest it, Kenny. She's my goddaughter, for Christsake. And even if she weren't, I don't go for skinny white girls.'

'I'm sorry,' Ken said quietly. And he was, because he knew Demetrius loved Alice like she was his own daughter. 'I'm stressed out about Reuben and took it out on you.'

'It's okay. Just never say it again. What about Decker?' Demetrius asked, and Ken knew that the subject was closed. 'What do you know?'

'Only that he saved my life, risking his own.' Ken's lips curved wryly. 'I can't argue with his priorities.'

'Joel doesn't like him.'

Ken shrugged. 'Joel sees him as a threat. Kid's got wizard accounting skills.'

'Well I don't trust him,' Demetrius said flatly. 'That kid doesn't want Joel's job. He wants yours. Or Reuben's.'

'That might not be such a bad thing. I don't want to do this for the rest of my life. Alice will take over for me, but we're gonna need to hire a replacement for Reuben, ASAP. Even if we do find him, I don't want him here. He's become a liability.' Ken went quiet for a moment, thinking about the ramifications of that statement. They couldn't let Reuben simply walk away, regardless of how this turned out. He knew too much. They'd have to kill him.

Ken pushed that thought away with a shrug. He'd cross that bridge when he got there. 'Regardless of Reuben, we're pushin' fifty, brother. We need to start thinking about retirement.'

Demetrius grimaced. 'You've been listening to Joel again. Are you gonna start talking about 401ks now?'

'Nah. But I don't want to be working my ass off and dodging bullets when I'm sixty.'

Demetrius frowned. 'Then what do you want?'

'My own island, with naked women bringing me drinks in coconuts.'

Demetrius snorted. 'Coconuts? Shit, man. You had me going there for a moment.' He pushed himself out of his chair. 'I gotta requisition a wire transfer from Joel. We're getting a new shipment in from the Brazilians.' He waggled his brows. 'Pretty girls. Very pretty.'

'How old?'

'Oh, they're all eighteen,' Demetrius said with mock seriousness, which told Ken that most of them were far younger.

'You got a buyer?' Ken asked, because Demetrius wasn't into young girls like Reuben. Demetrius looked at their younger acquisitions and saw dollar signs, not sex.

'Better than *a* buyer. I got bidders, buddy. Plural. We're having an online auction. I'm tellin' you, these girls are *pretty*. We are going to be raking it in, hand over fist.'

'What about Gupta?' The Indian was a major supplier of their labor market. He recruited quality stock. Strong backs and quick minds. 'Is he going to cut us off if he finds out about Reuben and his daughter?'

'I hope not.' Demetrius hesitated. 'But Miriam knew the girl's identity. The girl used her credit card to check into the hotel.'

Ken frowned. 'You didn't tell me that. That makes Miriam a huge risk. If she goes directly to Gupta about it, he'll wonder what else she knows. He'll cut us off for sure then, and we won't be able to fulfill our labor customers' orders while we're qualifying someone new.' He paused then. 'You're making a face. Why?'

'Because you're suggesting killing Miriam, but like I said, doing her now will raise suspicions. The PI had a number of clients, mostly jealous wives. That leaves any number of guilty husbands who can be investigated if someone reports the PI missing. But if Miriam goes next, it'll narrow down the possibilities to Reuben, and that leads to us.'

'Not if she commits suicide. It's worked for us in the past.'

Demetrius relaxed. 'Oh. I should have thought of that myself. Reuben's got me rattled, boy. Off my game.'

'Get back on your game then and take care of Miriam before she can tell Gupta that our head of security was banging his daughter.' Ken made a face of his own. 'Oh hell. What if Reuben isn't running from Miriam? What if he's on his way to New York? To be with the girl?'

Demetrius rolled his eyes. 'Fuck. Too bad I took care of the PI,' he muttered. 'I could have hired him to keep tailing Reuben. I'll check with Burton and see who we can send to watch the girl. Maybe one of those new guys he was talking about. We just want to know if Reuben shows up. If he does, I'll zip up to New York and take care of him myself. He can't be allowed to continue down this road. Like you said, he's become a liability.'

Ken sighed. 'I know. Do what you need to—' He was cut off by the sudden ringing of the phone on his desk with Sean's caller ID. 'What do you have?' he answered brusquely and put his son on speaker phone.

'The information you requested.'

Ken realized he was holding his breath. 'You found Reuben.'

'No, sir,' Sean said. 'But I did find the identity of the man who was with the tracker wearer when she was murdered this morning. One of the local papers carried the story online. I—' He was interrupted by a loud squealing klaxon on his end.

'What the hell?' Demetrius barked. 'What is that?'

'Another tampered tracker alert,' Sean said. The klaxon was abruptly silenced, the only sound the clacking of Sean's keyboard. 'After this morning, I had the alerts transferred to my computer. I've got the tracker ID numbers here, and I'm searching for their current location.' A short pause. 'Both are at Chip Anders's house.'

'The other two women Anders purchased,' Ken said grimly.

'Fuck, Sean,' Demetrius hissed. 'Don't tell *us* about the tracker alarm. Tell Burton – he's acting security manager, at least for now. He's got men watching Anders's house, and Burton is on his way there with Decker now to bring in Anders and his family. Burton and Decker can actually *do* something about the alarm.'

'On it,' Sean said. 'I'll call you back when I know something. Oh, and I just sent you a link to the online article about the man who was with the girl in the alley this morning.'

Ken disconnected the speaker phone, brought up the email Sean had sent, clicked on the link . . . then stared at the screen. 'No,' he whispered, all the raging anger he'd felt toward Reuben coalescing into a hard, icy ball, deep in his chest. 'No fucking way.'

'What?' Demetrius demanded.

Ken lifted his eyes. 'Marcus O'Bannion.'

Demetrius's face went flat with shock. 'You are shitting me.'

Ken turned the screen around so that Demetrius could see for himself.

Demetrius's fists clenched on the arms of the wingback chair. 'Fucking hell. *O'Bannion* was the guy with Anders's bitch when she was killed? Motherfucking *hell.*'

Ken wanted to clench his own fists but maintained his calm, turning his laptop back to face him. 'This time, he dies. I do not want a repeat of nine months ago. This is not a democracy. No arguments. If he'd been dealt with properly then, we wouldn't be in this shithole of a mess right now. Are we clear?'

Demetrius nodded stiffly. 'Crystal.'

Cincinnati, Ohio
Tuesday 4 August, 9.30 A.M.

Drake was nearly a mile from Stephanie's house when his phone started buzzing. 'Stephanie,' he muttered when he saw the caller ID. He should have known she would never be able to play it cool in front of her father. If she'd said a goddamn word . . . *I should have killed her this morning.*

He pressed the accelerator a little harder, speeding up as he answered the phone. 'Yeah? What's wrong now?'

'Hurry,' Stephanie hissed on a whispered sob. 'You have to hurry. He's killing her. He's gonna come after me next. You gotta hurry, Drake. *Please.*'

'Killing who? What are you talking about? What the hell is that racket?'

'Another alarm. The other two trackers, they're cut. Daddy is screaming. He's going to think I did it! Hurry!'

Drake slowed down. Dealing directly with her screaming father was more than he'd bargained for. 'Who cut the other two trackers?'

'I don't know. I didn't. Maybe they got knives and did it themselves. They won't get far. He's running outside to look for them, and he's going to kill them,' Stephanie whispered, panic in her voice. 'And then he's going to beat the truth out of me. He said so. He thinks I took the baby. He thinks I'm hiding it.'

'Wait. The baby's gone?'

'Yeah. You have to come, Drake. You have to help me.'

What Drake had to do was make sure he shut her up. He urged the car to go a little faster. 'I'll be there in a few minutes, babe. Get out of the house. Wait for me in our spot.'

'He's locked me in. I don't know if can sneak—' Stephanie screamed as shots rang out at her end of the call. 'Somebody's breaking down the door.'

'Who?' Drake demanded. 'Who's breaking down your door? Who's shooting?'

'Daddy. He's got out his guns. I don't know who's coming. Oh God. They're coming up the stairs. I'll try to make a run for it when they unlock my door. Just be ready to pick me up and get me out of here. Hurry! *Hurry!*'

Then silence. She'd either hung up or had her throwaway cell taken.

Or she'd been shot. Maybe she was already dead and his problem was solved. Either way, he didn't want to get any more involved than he already was. Especially with people waving guns around. Her father was a major prick, but he was a good shot and had a huge gun collection. A fucking arsenal, even. And that he was firing his weapons meant he'd been in his gun safe, which meant he'd have seen by now that one of his guns was missing.

The gun Drake had hidden under the driver's seat. The same one he'd used this morning on Tala and the man she'd been meeting.

He slowed his sister's car, turned around and headed for the interstate. There was no way he was getting caught up in any more Anders craziness. His sister had filled her gas tank last night. That meant he could get to Canada without stopping.

Cincinnati, Ohio
Tuesday 4 August, 9.30 A.M.

'Good morning, Marcus.'

Marcus hadn't been startled at Gayle's greeting, even though his eyes had been glued to his computer screen for the better part of two hours. Her perfume had given her away as soon as she'd come through his office door. It wasn't that she wore too much, or that it was offensive. Not at all. It was the same scent she'd worn every day of his life. It was the scent that had calmed him back into sleep when the nightmares had shaken him awake when he was still a little boy, nightmares filled with the things he'd seen. And the things he'd done.

Because at eight years old, Marcus had stared evil in the face. And then he'd killed it.

Gayle's scent had reminded him of a time when his childhood home had been a safe place. She'd made him feel protected again . . . after. She'd made him believe that he wasn't really a monster. And she'd understood

158

when that belief wasn't enough to wash away his guilt, silently supporting him in whatever he'd done to balance the scales in the years that followed.

But today her scent wasn't calming. Marcus stared at the screen, not looking up to meet her eyes even though he knew she'd stopped on the other side of his desk. He'd showered and shaved and no longer looked like he'd been shot only hours before. He'd known he'd have to confront Gayle about her heart attack and her allowing her niece access to company files. He'd figured he'd know exactly what to say, how to address the issue without revealing that his information had come from Jill. But now that she stood before him, he found himself completely speechless and realized he'd never been angry with her before. He was very angry now. *She should have trusted me.* Like he'd trusted her. *With everything.*

Well, not everything. He hadn't told her about Scarlett Bishop. Aside from Stone's guessing this morning, he hadn't told a soul about Scarlett Bishop and how she'd occupied a corner of his mind from the moment he'd opened his eyes and seen her standing over his hospital bed nine months before. He hadn't needed to tell Gayle, because she'd never met Scarlett. Because Gayle hadn't been with him in the hospital or at Mikhail's funeral. Because she'd had a heart attack and hadn't told him.

A cup of coffee appeared in front of his face and Marcus knew it would be strong and full of enough sugar to make most people grimace. It was one of his only dietary vices and he dared anyone in the office to say a word.

'Marcus? Are you all right? You're scaring me here.'

Finally he looked up. Met her eyes and saw her flinch. 'I'm okay,' he said quietly. 'I hear that you're not.'

'No,' she denied with a smile. 'I'm just fine.'

'Would your cardiologist agree?' he asked, unable – or maybe unwilling – to hide the edge of hurt that sharpened his tone.

Closing her eyes, she sank into the chair in front of his desk. 'Who told you?' she asked, her skin taking on a grayish hue that made Marcus sit up straighter and reach for his phone.

'Do you need a doctor?' he asked.

'No. I'll be okay.' Her eyes opened and in them he saw regret. 'I didn't want to keep this from you, but I didn't want to worry you. I didn't want to worry your mother.'

'And yet you did. She sent someone to look for you, but you'd just disappeared. Without a word. Did you really think that wouldn't worry her?'

She lifted her chin a fraction of an inch, looking up to meet his eyes. 'She was worried enough about you then, and she doesn't even know what you really do every day. I know, and I more than worry. You seem to have this need to punish yourself, Marcus, and it terrifies me.'

He frowned at her. 'No I don't.'

You want to die. You sonofabitch. Marcus winced, Stone's words shoving into his mind before he could stop them. He shoved them back out, narrowing his eyes at Gayle.

'Besides, this isn't about me. This is about you and your heart attack. How do you think it makes me feel knowing you might have died?'

Gayle pulled her body straight, giving him her nanny look. 'About the same as it makes me feel knowing you might have,' she returned evenly. 'Nine months ago or last night.' She held up her tablet, Stone's story front and center. 'I got to enjoy this with my morning coffee. Did you even think about warning your mother and me first?'

'I called Mom. She was still asleep. I told her maid to make sure she called me before she read the story.'

Gayle pursed lips that trembled with anger. 'I guess I should be thankful I made you promise to wear Kevlar.'

He'd told Scarlett it had been his mother who'd made him promise, because it was easier than explaining that Gayle had been the one to mother him when he'd needed it most. She'd want to know why and he wasn't ready to tell her about all that yet. 'Gayle,' he sighed.

'I'm serious. Maybe I should make you promise to wear a combat helmet too.'

Marcus fought the urge to squirm in his chair. He was the publisher of this paper, not a small boy. And certainly not an idiot. But telling himself so was about as successful as telling her. Resolutely he pulled the topic back to her health. 'At least I didn't hide what happened last night. I've never hidden anything from you. You hid a damn heart attack, Gayle.'

'You didn't need to know,' she insisted, raising her voice.

'Didn't need to know?' The lock on his temper popped. 'Goddammit, Gayle!' he thundered. 'You didn't let me take care of you!' He realized he was on his feet, leaning forward, hands propped on his desk, shouting like a lunatic. 'Fuck,' he muttered, easing back into his chair.

'I didn't let you take care of me because you couldn't even take care of yourself,' Gayle said firmly, back at a normal volume.

'That might have been true when it happened. But what about now? Don't you go there,' he warned, jabbing his index finger in her direction when she lifted the tablet to point at Stone's story again, as if to say that Marcus still wasn't taking care of himself. 'This is about *you*.'

Gayle's jaw tightened. 'Don't you point your finger at me, Marcus O'Bannion.'

Marcus drew a breath, slowly let it out. He lowered his hand and calmed his tone. 'I understand why you didn't tell me nine months ago. Even eight months ago. Maybe even six months ago. But I am no longer injured. I am fine. You should have told me.'

Her eyes snapped fire. 'You were shot just a few hours ago,' she whispered fiercely, 'and you can say that you are *fine* with a straight face?'

Marcus looked down at his desk, measuring his words. The personal approach was not cutting it. They were both too angry. He'd stick to business. He lifted his eyes, meeting hers squarely. 'You suffered a heart attack, Gayle. And then you missed a week of work. In a normal situation, HR would have moved you to the disability roster until your doctor cleared you to return, ensuring you received disability pay for that week. But your doctor didn't clear you. You came back prematurely, allowing another employee to fulfill at least some of your responsibilities. You gave that entry-level employee access to confidential company records for which she was not authorized. That is a violation of company policy.' He drew a breath that hurt his chest. 'More than that, it's a violation of my trust.'

Her mouth fell open in shock. 'You think I let Jill see confidential information?'

'She's been screening your emails, Gayle. So no, I don't *think* you let her see confidential information. I *know* you did.'

Gayle paled. 'She's been screening my emails? I didn't tell her she could do that.'

'She's been doing it anyway. She's been tending the threat list.'

Gayle sat back in her chair in shock. 'Oh no.'

'Oh yes. She confronted me with it this morning. Told me that I was expecting too much from you, that my family and I have been taking advantage of you for years. That you would have retired and had your own life if it weren't for us. That the threat list was what caused your heart attack to begin with. Is that true?'

Gayle pressed trembling fingers to her lips. 'No. No one has taken advantage of me. I'm here because you're my family, Marcus. You and Stone and Audrey and your mother. Jeremy, too, even though he doesn't live with us anymore. You're all my family.'

He exhaled abruptly, not even realizing he'd been holding his breath. 'I'm glad. You're our family too. I . . .' The words trailed away under a wave of emotion. 'You've always been there for me. I would never want you to feel like I didn't appreciate what it's cost you. You could have had a husband

and children. A home of your own. Yet you stayed with us.'

Gayle leaned forward in her chair, her expression fierce. 'I *have* a home. I *have* children – you and Stone and Audrey. And Mikhail.' Pain flickered in her eyes. 'And Matty too,' she added in a barely audible whisper. 'God, how I miss them.'

Marcus bowed his head, his chest suddenly too tight to breathe. Matty's name was rarely spoken in his family. And when it was, it was always a whisper, as if speaking his name at a normal volume would . . . wake him up. Because to imagine him sleeping was so much easier than to imagine him dead. Of course, Marcus didn't need to imagine. He'd seen Matty's body close up and very personal. He still saw it in his nightmares and the occasional flash of memory while awake. Now the image of Mikhail's body had become part of the nightmare too. He wondered if Mikhail's name would soon meet the same fate as Matty's. *No*, he thought. *I won't let it.* 'I miss them too,' he answered, his voice cracking. 'Both of them.'

They sat in silence for a long, long moment before Marcus finally looked up to find Gayle hugging herself tight, eyes scrunched shut, her body shaking with silent sobs. If she didn't stop crying, she was going to give herself another heart attack.

He walked around his desk, crouching in front of her chair, a box of tissues in one hand. 'Hey. Don't cry anymore. Please. You're scaring me.'

She glared down at him through her tears. 'I'm scaring you? *I'm* scaring *you*?' She grabbed a handful of tissues and dried her cheeks. 'I could have been *burying* you, Marcus O'Bannion, and you don't even seem to care.'

He'd lost two brothers. She'd lost two boys who'd been sons of her heart. Yet the tears she cried now? *They're because of me.* Because she'd nearly lost him too.

It could have been different. *The shooter could have finished me off with a shot to my head just as easily.* Lying there with the breath knocked out of him, his face scraping the asphalt, he'd been a sitting duck.

Y'think, dumbass? It was Stone's voice in his head, clear as a bell, and Marcus nearly smiled.

Fine. I can be taught. When two people who knew you best told you the exact same thing on the same day . . . Maybe it was time he listened.

He rose from his crouch to sit on the edge of his desk. 'I'm sorry, Gayle. You're right. I didn't mean to upset you. I promise I'll be more careful from now on.'

She sniffed, turning her face away. She was still crying, but the intensity had wound down. At least she wouldn't have another heart attack sitting here in his office.

'I, uh, noticed you didn't include Keith as part of your family,' he said dryly, trying to distract her from her tears. Gayle's dislike of Jeremy's husband was no secret.

Gayle sniffed again, turning back to glare at him. 'I don't like that man. He acts like he owns Jeremy, checking his watch every five seconds when they come over, sighing like a pouting three-year-old so we'll know just how eager he is to leave.'

It was true. No one in the family liked Keith. It had nothing to do with Jeremy's sexual orientation, and everything to do with his choice of partner.

'Keith is the possessive sort, but Jeremy loves him,' Marcus said with a shrug. 'What can you say?'

'Nothing. Not that any of you would listen to anything I say, anyway,' she muttered. She placed her hands on the arms of the chair and started to push herself to her feet. 'Well, I've got to get back to my desk. There's no one at the front.'

'Not so fast.' Leaning forward, Marcus touched two fingers to her shoulder and pushed her back into the chair. 'That you never answered my question hasn't escaped me. What about the list causing your heart attack? Is that true?'

She shook her head, far too calmly. 'No. I had a small arterial blockage just waiting for the right moment to announce itself. It could have happened anywhere I got stressed out. It's actually good it happened here and not when I was in my car doing seventy on the interstate. Jill got me to the hospital quickly. No fuss, no drama. They put me on a beta blocker and that was it. No stent, no surgery. I'm good as new.'

'Hm.' Marcus studied her until her cheeks began to grow pink. 'I never realized how very good you are at dodging my questions. What was the threat you were reading when Jill found you clutching your chest? She said she came back later and you'd hidden it.'

Gayle's chin lifted ever so slightly. 'It doesn't matter. I took care of it.'

Marcus blew out a frustrated breath. 'Could you just answer my god-damn question?'

She glared at him. 'Fine. I'll get you the letter. It's in my safe at home.'

She'd found it credible enough that she'd kept it, he thought. 'Who was it from?'

'Leslie McCord.'

He grimaced. 'Ah, the lovely Mrs McCord,' he said sarcastically. *Lovely* was the last word that described the bitch. 'Wife of Woodrow, aka Woody, aka sex-pervert-slash-high-school-teacher who downloaded kiddie porn to his personal laptop.' It had been the last story he and his team had broken before Mikhail went missing. 'I guess a threat from her isn't such a huge surprise. She was extremely unhappy when her husband's perversion came to light. Went so far as to accuse me of planting those pictures on Woody's hard drive.'

'She never believed he was guilty, but then again, not many loved ones do.'

'Even when the evidence is thrown in their faces,' Marcus said with a nod. 'I'm guessing she blamed us for his suicide.' The bastard had managed to hang himself in jail while awaiting arraignment. 'What was the specific threat?'

Gayle sighed wearily. 'She blamed Stone for writing the story and you for printing it. She blamed everyone at the *Ledger*. Said she hoped you and your reporters would burn in hell for ruining her husband's good name, for ruining his life.'

'That doesn't sound too bad,' he said cautiously. 'We've had a lot worse.'

'She also said she prayed to God that someday someone would show you what it was like to lose someone you loved.' Gayle's gaze locked on to Marcus's face and it was all he could do not to look away. 'She said that a person doesn't know suffering until someone they've loved is tormented, their life snuffed out. She wanted you to go to your grave knowing that your loved one had cried and begged and pleaded, but were shown no mercy, just like her husband was shown none by the *Ledger* and by the police.' She drew a breath, let it out. 'I received the letter the morning after your mother learned that Mikhail was missing.'

'Oh God.' Marcus could only stare. 'You thought Leslie McCord had taken Mikhail.'

'Or that she'd paid someone else to do so. I could only think, *not again*, that it would kill your mother to lose Mikhail the same way she lost Matty.'

Marcus's heart had started to pound, slowly but hard. 'Which she did,' he murmured. 'Just not at the hand of Leslie McCord.' Mikhail had simply run away from home for a few days to get the space to work through some personal problems. He'd gone to the family cabin in the forest of eastern Kentucky, thinking he'd be safe there. Instead he'd surprised a sadistic killer who'd been using the house as a hideout, and was gunned down and tossed into a shallow grave.

Gayle's lips curved bitterly. 'Hell of an irony, isn't it? I got so scared, then the next thing I knew, Jill was screaming at me not to die.'

Marcus dragged the back of his hand across his mouth, trying to think past the memory of that shallow grave and what he'd seen inside. 'Okay, fine, I get why you didn't tell me about the threat when it happened. You ended up in the hospital that day, and so did I.' Gayle because of her heart attack and he because he'd been shot by Mikhail's killer.

Marcus had gone out to the family cabin to search for Stone, who'd already found Mikhail's body. But Mikhail's killer hadn't stopped at murdering their brother. He'd also kidnapped a young woman and a little girl who'd managed to escape their captor's clutches. Marcus had found them, bedraggled and exhausted but alive – only to be discovered by the psychopath, who'd been searching for them. Marcus had acted out of instinct, throwing himself over the woman's body when the killer began shooting. One of the bullets had pierced his lung, landing him in ICU.

So yeah, he hadn't been coherent enough to be told about Gayle's heart attack or the threat that triggered it. Not that day or even that month. Recovery and rehab had taken weeks.

He shook his head. 'But what about later, when you knew Mikhail hadn't been murdered by McCord? After we'd both recovered and come back to work. Why didn't you tell me then?'

'There was no need,' Gayle said.

'How do you know? Leslie could have just waited until we all returned to the office and we'd have been completely unaware. She still might.'

Gayle shook her head. 'Leslie McCord is no longer a threat to anyone.'

Marcus frowned. 'How do you know that?' he insisted.

Gayle opened her mouth, but her voice was drowned out by a clatter in the office outside.

'What the fuck?' It was Stone's voice, and he sounded furious. 'What the mother*fuck* are *you* doing here?'

'I suggest you remove your hand from my arm.' The woman's voice was cool, collected, and very familiar.

She's here. Scarlett Bishop is here.

Eleven

Ken's anger churned as he watched Demetrius pace the floor of his office.

'Why are you still here?' Ken asked coldly.

'I'm trying to figure out what to do.'

Ken lurched to his feet and leaned forward, his hands braced on the glossy wood of his desk. 'I told you what to do. Go and kill that sonofabitch O'Bannion, just like I told you to do nine fucking months ago!'

Demetrius paused his pacing long enough to shoot Ken a glare from the corner of his eye. 'We didn't need to kill him nine fucking months ago! He was out of commission.'

Which they hadn't needed to lift a finger to accomplish. A bona fide serial killer had nearly done their job for them. 'It appears he's no longer out of commission,' Ken said coldly. 'He's out there again – and in our business. Why didn't we know this? I thought we were watching him.'

'We were. According to Reuben's reports, when O'Bannion got out of the hospital, he spent a couple of months recuperating at that mausoleum of his mother's. Since then, he's spent most of his time at the paper.'

Ken straightened, arms crossed over his chest. 'He wasn't at the paper this morning. He was in an alley with one of our assets. God only knows what the little bitch told him.'

Demetrius held up his phone. 'I just read the damn article. Maybe you should too, before you start one of your rants.'

Ken drew a deep breath. 'I am not ranting.'

'Fine. We're having a rational discussion.' Demetrius's eye roll indicated exactly what he thought of that. 'Look, the article says that O'Bannion got there as she was bleeding out. She didn't say anything to him.'

Ken sat back in his chair and scanned the entire article, but he wasn't swayed. O'Bannion was slime. Dangerous slime. 'So he says. The man lies more easily than he breathes.'

'He's the goddamn media,' Demetrius spat. 'Of course he lies. We can listen to more of the recordings from the wearer's ankle tracker. She might not have told O'Bannion anything in that alley, but she told someone something. Enough that he met her there.'

'Why weren't we watching him last night?'

'Because Reuben was short-handed. When he lost his two people in the accident last month, he proposed transferring the person he'd had watching O'Bannion to transporting shipments. We all agreed, including you.'

Ken ground his teeth, remembering now. He had agreed, dammit. 'It was supposed to be temporary. Reuben was supposed to hire someone new.'

'Reuben was supposed to do a lot of things,' Demetrius said evenly. 'It appears he was busy doing *other* things. Like our suppliers' wives and daughters.'

Ken shook his head. 'We've already gone around and around about Reuben. We've got a plan in place for him. Now we're talking about O'Bannion. We should have killed him as soon as he got out of the hospital.'

Demetrius rubbed his palms together. 'Will you stop saying that? We couldn't kill him then. Not without risking the cops connecting him to McCord and his wife. And we couldn't do the suicide thing again. Not so soon after we staged McCord's *and* his wife's suicide.'

They'd arranged for McCord's death in prison – not terribly hard to manage. The man had been about to talk and he would have taken them all down. He'd been hanged in his cell and his jailers had called it suicide. His wife's killing was a necessary snipping of loose ends. They had no way of knowing what she knew, but she'd been vocal in his defense and they'd shut her up as a pre-emptive strike, making it look like she'd OD'd on pills. Two suicides, both fully accepted because the authorities had been expecting it to happen.

The same approach should have been applied to O'Bannion.

'Suicide would have worked after O'Bannion got out of the hospital. He was grieving his brother's death. No one would have blinked.'

Demetrius sighed. 'You're right,' he said quietly. 'I was wrong. We were all wrong except for you. Happy now?'

Ken opened his mouth, a torrent of words at the ready, but he stopped them at the last minute before he could say something he'd truly regret later. 'No, I'm not happy,' he said, forcing himself to find his composure. 'We've made some mistakes. *We*, Demetrius. That includes me too.' Which he didn't truly believe, but it was only important that Demetrius thought he did. 'We need to fix them, starting with O'Bannion.'

Demetrius's mouth curved. 'You are so fulla shit, Kenny,' he said, almost affectionately. 'You don't ever think you're wrong. Why should I believe you're starting now? But you are right in that we do have to fix this. O'Bannion needs to go. But I'm not willing to go to jail, not even for you. So let's figure this thing out.' He sat down in the wingback chair, studying his phone screen with a frown.

Ken reread the article. 'Whoever shot the girl in the alley also shot O'Bannion in the back, but O'Bannion wasn't injured badly enough to go to the hospital. Sean's source says he was treated and released at the scene.' Eyes narrowed, he looked at Demetrius. 'Who shot the girl?'

'Very good question,' Demetrius murmured. 'But a more immediate question might be "With what?" If we can pin down the kind of gun that was used, we can get one and kill O'Bannion. Then – as long as we make sure we get the bullet out of him – nobody will be able to prove that the same shooter didn't come back for him.'

'Will you do that?' Ken asked.

'You're asking this time?' A chuckle. 'Maybe the boy can be taught after all. Yeah, I'll do that. I've got a few favors floatin' around down at CPD. I'll collect some. All I really need to know is the bullet caliber. I'll wait till O'Bannion's alone. But that means you'll have to take care of Reuben's wife. If you're not too rusty.'

Ken raised a brow. 'I'll take care of Miriam. You make sure O'Bannion doesn't cause us any trouble. Any *more* trouble, anyway,' he added bitterly.

'Aye, aye, sir.' Demetrius saluted smartly. 'Since we're back to not asking.'

Ken shot him a dirty look. 'Don't be an asshole, Demetrius.' He rubbed the back of his neck with a sigh. 'Burton should have called by now.'

'I know.'

Sighing again, Ken hit the speaker phone and dialed Burton's cell phone. 'Status?' he snapped when Burton answered, his voice grim.

'We have the Anders family, all three of them. They had to be restrained and . . . muted. None of them were able to get off a phone call for help, so at least we won't have that cleanup.'

'What about the tamper alert?' he asked, already knowing the answer. He'd heard it in Burton's grim tone. Still, Ken held his breath.

'We found the cut trackers in the basement, which apparently had been the women's quarters for the past few years. But both of the women are gone.'

Cincinnati, Ohio
Tuesday 4 August, 9.50 A.M.

Scarlett Bishop. How long had she been standing there? What had she heard? Nothing damaging, Marcus decided. Worst case, she'd heard him rebuking Gayle for giving Jill access to her computer. Best case, she'd heard only Gayle's worry that he'd been shot at. Again. He pushed the panic to the edge of his mind.

The edge of his mind was getting mighty crowded with all the emotions he was shoving over there. The ridiculous thought was enough to make his lips quirk up, so that when he spoke, his voice was only mildly irritated.

'Stone?' he called. 'Escort the detective in, please.'

Stone shoved the door open. His brother looked just like a bar bouncer, his scowl one that would have scared most street thugs. But Scarlett was unaffected, her face serene. And so goddamn beautiful it was all Marcus could do to remember the fact that she'd eavesdropped on a private conversation.

'Detective,' Marcus said evenly. She'd changed her clothes. Gone was the sexy tank top and tight jeans that had hugged her body like a glove, a conservative blouse and slacks in their place. Sadly, a tailored jacket now covered the shoulder holster that he'd found so hot. The black braid that had hung freely down the middle of her back was looped close to her head in a clever spiral, and he wondered how many pins she'd had to use to make it stay that way. The image of his hands pulling those pins out one by one flashed into his mind. She looked good enough to eat.

'She was listening at the door,' Stone snarled.

'There was no one at the desk and I got tired of waiting,' Scarlett said with a shrug of shoulders he now knew were well toned and muscular in a very feminine way.

'You didn't call out for anyone,' Gayle said indignantly. 'I would have come right out.'

'She has a habit of doing that,' Stone said through clenched teeth. 'Showing up and not announcing herself.'

Scarlett and Deacon had tricked Stone the first time they'd met him, walking into his house when he'd called 'Come in', thinking it was Jeremy's husband who'd knocked. They'd announced themselves as police only after they were already through the door. Technically they'd violated Stone's civil rights by barging in unannounced, but technically Stone was with-holding critical evidence about multiple murders at the time, so they'd all let it slide. Now here Scarlett was barging in unannounced again. A repeat

169

offender, as it were. Clearly she didn't mind bending the rules when it suited her. Which shouldn't have made Marcus want her even more, but he had to admit that it did.

Scarlett didn't acknowledge either Gayle or Stone, continuing to regard Marcus with an unflappable calm. *I should be royally pissed off right now*, he thought. But he found himself intrigued instead.

Gayle came to her feet. 'I'll show the detective out.'

Marcus stopped her with a wave of his hand. 'It's all right, Gayle. What can I do for you, Detective?'

'I came by to see if you were all right,' Scarlett said, then arched one black brow. 'Seeing as how you hadn't returned my phone calls.'

He bit back a wince. What could he say? *I ignored your messages because I was busy figuring out which threats would make me the least suspicious to you*? He didn't think so. 'I'm sorry if I worried you. I'm fine, as you can see. Just busy earning a living.'

Scarlett scanned his office, her gaze lingering on the wall covered with the framed newspaper headlines his grandfather had collected over a lifetime. For a moment he thought she'd comment on the front page of the *Malaya*, but then she turned to face him and he frowned. The calm he'd seen when she'd arrived was gone. Now her expression was purposefully blank.

'Earning a living by digging up news,' she said quietly.

The sudden change in her demeanor rubbed him the wrong way. 'We *are* a newspaper, Detective,' he said sharply. 'You've seen that I'm still unharmed, so if there's nothing else?'

The flash of temper in her dark eyes irrationally soothed his irritation. 'You promised me a list of those who'd made threats against you. I expected it hours ago.' She turned her attention to Gayle. 'I assume you're Mr O'Bannion's office manager. He told my partner and me that you keep a list of all the threats to his life made by those unhappy with your newspaper's content. Since he is obviously too busy, can you print me a copy?'

The slight stiffening of Gayle's spine was the only sign that Scarlett's knowledge of the threat list had surprised her. 'I'm afraid you have me at a disadvantage, Detective . . . ?'

'This is Detective Bishop,' Marcus supplied. 'Scarlett Bishop.'

'Homicide,' Scarlett added curtly.

'Detective, this is Gayle Ennis. She manages my office.'

Gayle's eyes widened as Scarlett's name registered. 'You investigated Mikhail's murder,' she said, her voice suddenly rough.

Scarlett's expression changed again, gentling. 'Yes, ma'am,' she said respectfully. 'You knew him?'

Gayle nodded, her throat working as she tried to swallow. 'I was his nanny.'

Startled, Scarlett's mouth opened, then closed. She let out a quiet breath. 'I'm so sorry for your loss,' she murmured. 'I'm working the murder of the young woman who died this morning. She has a family too, and they deserve to know what happened to her. Getting the list would be a major help to my investigation, and every second counts.'

Gayle glanced at Marcus uncertainly.

'I'll take care of this, Gayle.' He squeezed Gayle's shoulder, then crossed his office to where Scarlett still stood in the doorway. He had to fight the urge to lean in closer and sniff her hair. She smelled like wildflowers, just as she had when she'd sat by his hospital bed nine months ago. 'Did you watch the videos?' he asked softly.

She met his eyes. 'Yes. Many times.'

'And you still think you need the list?'

Understanding flickered in her eyes. 'If you're asking if I still think you were the target, the answer is probably no. But I owe it to Tala – and to you – to be sure.'

She'd scored major points with both Stone and Gayle with that answer. *And with me*, he grudgingly admitted. *Shit.*

'All right. If you feel you really need to check it out, I'll get it to you ASAP. Now if there's nothing else, Stone will show you out.'

Stone no longer scowled, his anger having dissipated a little when Scarlett spoke to Gayle with such care. 'Detective? This way, please.'

Scarlett's feet didn't move, her eyes locking with Marcus's. 'I can wait right here while the list is printed,' she said firmly. 'I have a few more things to discuss with you.'

Marcus's eyes narrowed. 'What things?'

'The dog, for one. I may have a lead on identifying the dog and its owner. Since the photos I printed from the video files were rather dark and grainy, I'd like you to accompany me to see if you can identify it from a group of photos in my lead's collection. You're the only one who's seen the dog live and in the flesh,' she added. 'Again, every second counts, so if you can spare the time this morning, I'd appreciate it.'

To spend more time with her or not to spend more time with her? *Duh.* Marcus had already mentally checked his calendar, but he glanced at his cell phone for show. 'I can spare a few hours. Gayle, please clear my—'

'If we get the exclusive,' Stone interrupted.

Scarlett looked over her shoulder at Stone, exasperated. 'Do you *mind*?'

Stone shrugged. 'His time is worth money. Exclusives equal money.

Besides, showing that there was a dog and that its owners are evil can only support Marcus's story. He ran a risk calling you last night. People will assume he was in that alley with an underage girl for nefarious reasons, no matter what we posted this morning. Any chance we can get to reinforce the truth is a good deal for my brother.'

Her brows knit as she considered it. 'Fine. You can have the exclusive, but you have to clear it with me before you print it. Just until we catch Tala's killer,' she added quickly when Stone started to protest. 'I don't want you publishing anything that will tip off the killer and mess up my case.'

'Agreed,' Stone said, as if Marcus weren't even standing there.

'What are the other things?' Marcus wanted her attention off Stone and back on himself.

Scarlett leaned to the left so that she could see Gayle, who still stood next to Marcus's desk. 'What makes you so certain that Leslie McCord is no longer a threat to Mr O'Bannion?'

Marcus glared down at her. 'That has nothing to do with your case.'

She looked up at him, unrepentant. 'I didn't ask you. I asked Ms Ennis.'

'Don't answer her, Gayle,' Stone warned, the thug-scaring scowl reclaiming his face. 'She deliberately eavesdropped on you two. Make her get a goddamn warrant.'

'She doesn't need one,' Gayle said wearily. 'She could find it online in a minute. Leslie McCord is dead. She took a bottle of sleeping pills, so the issue was closed. There was no point in burdening you with it.' She slid past them and around Stone. 'I'll be at my desk.'

'Satisfied, Detective Bishop?' Marcus asked sarcastically.

Scarlett entered his office without asking, taking the chair that Gayle had vacated. 'I will be when I get that list.'

Cincinnati, Ohio
Tuesday 4 August, 9.50 A.M.

Ken focused on maintaining his heart rate. The other women Anders had kept at his house had escaped. Three assets gone in less than twelve hours.

Demetrius sank back into the wingback chair, giving Ken a stunned look.

Things had gone from sugar to shit in a big-time hurry. *If Miriam hasn't killed Reuben,* Ken thought viciously, *he'll wish she had when I'm done with him.*

With an effort, he kept his voice calm. 'What do you mean, both women are gone?' he asked Burton over the speaker phone on his desk.

Demetrius didn't have as good a hold on his own temper. 'Your men were right outside when the tracker alert was activated!' he shouted. 'How fucking hard is it to round up two fucking women?'

A moment of tense, defensive silence on Burton's end. 'I sent the men in as soon as I got the call from Sean. They had to break down a basement door and several interior doors to get in. Anders had armored his house with security doors and windows. They ended up having to shoot their way in. Anders was very well armed.'

'Injuries?' Ken asked.

'One of my men took a bullet in the leg. Through and through. Will probably need stitches. Decker said he can do the stitches if we need him to. He was a medic in Iraq.'

'Mr Decker seems to be multi-talented,' Ken murmured, his calm now icy. If there had been gunfire, someone would have heard it and called 911. 'What about Anders? I want him and his family unharmed.'

'So that *we* can harm them,' Demetrius growled.

'Chip Anders is wounded, but only superficially,' Burton said, then blew out a breath. 'Not that you'd know it by listening to him. He's whining like a stuck pig. His wife has a mark on her face. Decker slapped her after she bit him.'

Ken glared at Demetrius when his lips twitched. 'And the daughter?' Ken asked Burton. Because Miss Anders would likely be the best leverage against her father. 'Did you mark her?'

'Not on her face, but she was slapped as well,' Burton said, grimly satisfied. 'Her ass might be a little red for a few hours. Her fingernails are hard and sharp. She took off the top layer of my face, the bitch. We subdued them, restrained them, gagged them – thank God – then put them in the van, handcuffed to the doors and to each other.'

'What about the authorities?'

'I sent one of the men up ahead to watch for any approaching vehicles. Our guns were silenced, but Anders's weren't. Decker and I searched for the two women whose trackers were cut. We combed the woods behind Anders's house. There was no sign of them. Best we can tell, there was a vehicle waiting. It's been so dry, we won't get any decent prints.'

'A vehicle waiting?' Ken frowned. 'Who orchestrated their release?'

'None of the three Anderses would cop to it. Even before we gagged them.'

'Then bring them to me,' Ken said quietly. 'They *will* tell me.'

'We're about twenty minutes out. We're taking the long way, just in case we were followed.'

'Why would you think that?' Demetrius asked.

'I didn't see anyone. Decker thought he did, but he admitted he might have imagined it. Still, better safe than sorry. Where exactly do you want them? Your house?'

'Yes. Bring them down into the basement. Did you get their computers?'

'Of course. Computers, cell phones, tablets. Wallets and car keys, too. There is a wall safe, but Anders wouldn't divulge the combination, and we couldn't stay there long enough for me to figure it out on my own.'

'The combination will be just one more thing for me to convince Anders to tell me,' Ken said, then disconnected.

'How old is the daughter?' Demetrius asked abruptly.

'Twenty. Goes to Brown.' Ken kept track of his customers. 'Why?'

'Because I have a buyer who'd be very interested in a pretty young Ivy League hellcat.'

Ken hadn't considered that. 'How much?'

'Fifty. Or more. Depends on how pretty she is. I might even get another auction going.'

'Let's wait and see. Perhaps the threat alone will be enough to get one of them talking.'

'Who do you think let the two women go?' Demetrius asked.

'My money's on the daughter. The wife is a piece of work.'

Demetrius rose. 'I'll attend to O'Bannion. Save one of the Anderses for me.'

Twelve

Marcus found his eyes locked on Scarlett's ass as she sauntered past him as if she owned the place. He didn't want to let go of the breath he held, still filled with the scent of her hair. Which was simple foolishness. He should be angry. He should be furious.

Just like Stone is . . . right now. Shit. Marcus registered the change in his brother's breathing almost too late. Shifting, he put himself directly in Stone's path and firmly held his brother's gaze. And tried not to panic.

Because Stone was no longer looking back at him. Instead, Marcus saw nothing but rage and pain. And fear. *Not now. Not in front of Scarlett. Please, Stone. Don't do this now.*

'Stone?' he said under his breath, hoping that Scarlett could not hear.

Stone's eyes flickered wildly, his big chest heaving.

Dammit. I should have anticipated this. Why didn't I anticipate this?

Because he'd been too busy gawking at Scarlett Bishop's ass, that was why. And now there would be hell to pay unless he could calm his brother down fast.

Cops and blatant disrespect were a very bad combo in Stone's world. And coupled with the emotional upheaval he'd been through so far . . . Scarlett had no way of knowing that cops in general were one of the triggers that set him off. But the way she'd practically skipped away from him, dismissing him as if he weren't standing right there? That was the absolute worst thing she could have done.

Now standing with clenched fists, his face hardened with fury, nostrils flaring, Stone resembled a bull preparing to charge. Marcus could easily see his brother throwing Scarlett Bishop over one shoulder and bodily removing her from the office.

Marcus pressed his palm to Stone's chest. 'Easy,' he murmured. 'Take it easy.'

Stone's teeth clenched. 'She has no right to be here. Make her go.'

From the corner of his eye, Marcus could see Scarlett turning in the chair, her expression detached, yet curious. As if Stone were an animal in the zoo. The notion made him angry, but he kept his temper in check. All Stone needed to go nuclear was seeing Marcus upset.

'I'll take care of her.' He moved the hand on Stone's chest to his shoulder and gently gripped it, his other hand patting Stone's cheek, like a coach with a boxer in the ring. 'Breathe, buddy. Just breathe with me. In and out. Nice and slow.'

Stone obeyed, and after a few breaths he closed his eyes, visibly gathering his composure. 'I'm all right, Marcus.'

'I know you are,' Marcus said softly.

Stone swallowed hard, eyes still closed. 'Make her go,' he whispered. 'Please.'

The whisper was like a knife in Marcus's heart, and just like that he was back . . . *there*. In the dark, Stone's broken whisper the only thing he could hear. *Make him go, Marcus. Please. Make him leave so we can go home. I just want to go home.*

I will, he'd whispered back. *Don't worry. It'll be okay. I promise.*

Marcus cleared his throat. 'I will,' he said out loud. Confidently. He hoped. 'Don't worry. It'll be okay.'

'You promise.' It wasn't a question, but a flat statement of fact.

'Yeah,' Marcus said, struggling to keep his voice from breaking. 'I promise. Now breathe with me. In and out. Just a little longer. That's the way.'

Stone breathed along with him for another thirty seconds that felt like thirty minutes, finally shuddering out a harsh breath. When his eyelids lifted, Marcus could see his brother was back in control.

Stone's mouth curved, his half-smile self-deprecating. 'It's okay, Houston. Self-destruct sequence aborted. Genie's back in the bottle.'

Thank God. Marcus let himself relax, his arms dropping to his sides. 'Good enough. Where's Jill?'

'In the back with Diesel. He's watching her.'

'That's good, but you should probably give him a break. She makes him crazy.'

Another slow smile, this one real. 'I know. That's why I asked him to help.'

So relieved that his knees physically wobbled, Marcus laughed. His brother was back. All the way. *For now.* 'You suck.'

'You suck worse.' Sobering, Stone leaned to the left so that he could see around Marcus. 'Detective Bishop,' he said coldly.

'Yes, Mr O'Bannion?' She sounded subdued, surprising Marcus into looking over his shoulder. She looked as subdued as she'd sounded. Subdued and sad. And utterly exhausted.

Marcus knew the feeling.

'This office is private property,' Stone said. 'If we catch you trespassing again, we will report your ass so fast your head will spin. Next time you come, you'd sure as hell better have a warrant in your hands. Do we understand each other?'

Marcus held his breath, hoping Scarlett would just let this go, that she wouldn't make this a pissing match. He was far too tired to play diplomat – or referee.

She nodded. 'Yes, Mr O'Bannion. We do.'

Marcus waited until Stone had turned on his heel and walked away before letting the breath out. He closed his office door and leaned face first against it, his shoulders sagging like cooked pasta, focusing on getting his breathing regulated. Trying to figure out what the hell he was going to say to her. But she surprised him again by speaking first.

'I'm sorry,' she said softly.

He didn't move away from the door. Didn't turn to look at her. He wasn't sure his body would have cooperated if he'd held a gun to his own head. 'For what?'

'For listening in. And for doing whatever I did to instigate . . . whatever that was.'

Suddenly too exhausted to move, Marcus used the last of his energy reserves to flip around so that his back was to the door, then let his knees fold, sinking to the floor. Forearms braced on his bent knees, he bowed his head and closed his eyes.

The creaking of the chair told him she'd stood up. *She's leaving. Dammit.* He should look up. Ask her to stay. He needed to tell her that she hadn't been the cause of Stone's episode. That she'd only been the trigger. But his head felt too heavy to lift, so he stayed as he was.

A rustle of fabric was followed closely by the scent of wildflowers as she approached. He didn't want her to go, but it was probably better for everyone if she did. Except . . .

Dammit. He had to work up at least enough energy to move away from the door.

But she surprised him again, sliding down the door much as he'd done to sit beside him, their bodies separated by mere inches. The door vibrated slightly as she let her head fall back against it. He thought she'd say something, but she didn't, the silence broken only by the ticking of his grandfather's clock and the sound of their breathing.

Her sigh cut through the quiet. 'You've had a busy day,' she murmured. 'Did you sleep?'

'No. Not yet.'

'No wonder you're exhausted.' The words were nearly toneless. 'I was hoping you weren't returning my calls because you were getting some rest.'

He forced his back to straighten so that he leaned against the door beside her, turning his head so that he could see her face. With the exception of her closed eyes, her expression hadn't changed. Subdued, sad. Totally wrung out. And still so goddamn beautiful that his chest ached. 'Why are you here, Scarlett?'

A single weary chuckle. 'I truly did come to make sure you were okay.'

'I'm sorry I didn't answer your calls. Things have been a little . . . hectic around here this morning.'

'Yeah, I got that. But I really do need to talk to you.' Her shoulders remaining slumped against the door, she rolled her head toward him and opened her eyes.

For a moment he could only stare. The eyes he'd thought were black were actually the darkest blue he'd ever seen. *Like the midnight sky.*

Those midnight-blue eyes narrowed. 'Why are you looking at me like that?'

He flushed, embarrassed to have been caught staring. He considered lying, but he was too tired to think of anything convincing. So he told her the truth. 'Your eyes aren't black. I remember them being black. But they're not.' In his fantasies, her eyes had been stark black. Now he'd have to change his fantasies. Because not only were they not black, they weren't stark. They could be soft. Expressive. Vulnerable.

A faint curve of her lips. Kissable lips, he thought. Maybe even biteable. He wanted to lean closer to find out for sure, but was jerked back into common sense mode by the slight wag of her head.

'No, they're not black,' she said. 'But most people think they are.'

He drew a deep breath, letting the scent of wildflowers fill him up. 'I hope most people don't get close enough to see the difference,' he said softly, watching for her reaction, intensely satisfied when those eyes of hers warmed with the same desire he'd glimpsed in the alley when he'd taken off his shirt.

Her throat worked as she swallowed hard, then she broke the spell by rolling her head so that she looked straight ahead. 'I came to be sure that you were okay and to warn you.'

The air between them chilled. 'About?'

She shifted her body, pushing her shoulder away from the door and drawing her long legs up, crossing them so that she sat tailor-style. Her eyes were no longer warm, her expression smoothed to coolly professional, but her hands gave her away, gripping her bent knees so tightly that her knuckles were white. He braced himself for something bad.

'Tala wore a tracker,' she said. 'An ankle tracker.'

His jaw clenched, fury rising, burning him from the inside out. 'Like a common criminal.' *The man. His wife. They own us.* 'Or an asset. Not a person.'

Her nod was steady, but her knuckles were still white. 'Yes. The tracker was sophisticated. We're trying to trace its source. We do know that it could transmit sound. Digitally. I'm no gadget geek, but Deacon is, and he tells me that they could hear anyone around Tala and the range was limited only by the strength of the satellite signal.' She took her cell phone from the pocket of her tailored jacket, tapped the screen and held it out to him, showing him Stone's article.

His hackles rose in self-defense. 'I told you I'd tell the story.'

'I know. But in it you insinuate that you didn't hear Tala's last words.'

He frowned at her. 'I thought that's what you wanted.'

'It was. Until I learned that whoever tracked her could hear every word both of you spoke in that alley.'

He continued to frown, confused. Then . . . he got it. *Fucking hell.* 'They'll know I met her to help her, that she told me about her family.' His tired brain finally kicked back into gear, and new fury bubbled up. 'That's how they knew she'd stopped to listen to me in the park. They hit her for that, so hard that she limped. Didn't they?'

Scarlett's facial expression didn't change, but her eyes flickered with a mixture of pain and compassion, giving him her answer even though she didn't say a word.

'They did,' he said grimly. 'How bad?'

'Bad,' she murmured. 'Really bad.' Her lashes lowered, then lifted in a long blink. The compassion was mostly gone, replaced with the just-the-facts cop.

He found himself leaning closer, bracing his weight on one arm, his palm flat on the floor, inches from her knee. 'How many times do you have to do that each day?'

She blinked again, her smooth brow puckering in a frown. 'Excuse me? Do what?'

She'd been startled by the question, but she hadn't leaned back as he'd expected her to. Instead she leaned forward ever so slightly, closing the gap between them.

'How many times a day do you do that long blink so that you can shove your emotions down? So that you can focus on your job?'

Her chin lifted a fraction and he expected her to tell him to mind his own business. Instead her eyes grew abruptly shiny. 'Too many.' Roughly she cleared her throat, straightening her spine. Putting distance between them. 'The point is that they heard you. They heard you in the park asking her why she was crying, they heard her tell you that she was owned by someone, and because the tracker continued to transmit even after her death, they heard you tell a homicide detective the whole story.'

Marcus stayed where he was, perched halfway on his side. He didn't roll closer, but he wasn't about to back away. 'Okay,' he admitted. 'That sucks. Although you're assuming they were listening at the time of her death. You don't know that for sure.'

She gave him a you-can't-be-that-naive look. 'They were listening when she was at the park, and since it appeared that she knew the shooter, they probably followed her to the alley.'

'Because they suspected she was meeting someone,' he muttered. 'Well at least you agree that she knew her killer.'

'That fact was pretty clear,' she said quietly. 'Thank you for sending me the files. I'll make sure they're viewed only by those who must see them.'

He dropped his gaze to the floor, knowing she was referring to the moment when he'd looked down to see Tala's head, blown apart by the bullet. When he'd cried out, overcome by devastating grief. 'You're welcome,' he said. He hesitated, then sighed. 'And thank you for your discretion. It was a . . . difficult moment for me.'

'I know. It was like you'd discovered Mikhail's body all over again.'

Something in her voice made him jerk his gaze up. The pain was back in her eyes, but this was different from the sorrow she'd shown at Tala's beating. This was personal.

'Who?' he asked simply, and watched her cheeks darken. Once again he thought she'd tell him to mind his own business. Once again she surprised him.

Her swallow was audible. 'My best friend. In college.'

Her hand flexed as she tightened the already punishing grip on her knee. He covered that hand with his own, her skin ice cold against his palm. 'I'm sorry, Scarlett.'

She looked down at his hand but made no attempt to move it, so he left it where it was. 'Thank you. It was a long time ago.'

'Doesn't matter if it was ten years ago or yesterday.' Or nine months ago. Or twenty-seven years. The nightmare never truly went away, hovering in the back of one's mind, waiting to spring when one least expected it.

'True.' She still stared at his hand, her lips opening then closing, as if she was struggling with her next words. When she finally spoke, her whisper was barely audible. 'But when you see or hear something or someone that reminds you, it might as well have been yesterday.'

He frowned, suddenly hearing what she hadn't said. 'Does every homicide you investigate remind you?' *And put that sadness in your eyes?*

'Some,' she murmured distantly. 'Not all. Tala's . . . was rough.'

That, he sensed, was a monumental admission on her part. 'Why do you do it? Why put yourself through that hell every damn day?'

She raised her eyes to his, the intensity of her pain leaving him feeling like he'd been punched in the gut. 'I guess for the same reason you came back to the crime scene this morning. You didn't want to leave Tala alone in the dark. My friend died alone . . . in the dark . . . and her killer was never brought to justice. So for me, she's still there. In the dark. I can't help Michelle, but I can do my damnedest to make sure the victims in my care aren't forgotten.'

Marcus's heart squeezed so hard that he had to draw a breath. He'd known Scarlett Bishop was unique from the moment he'd laid eyes on her nine months ago. The very memory of her face and body made him want her with a ferocity that had left him empty for months. But the more he watched and listened, the more he knew that he had to have *her*. Not the face or the body, although both were unforgettable. He wanted *her*. He wanted to know what it would be like to have her to come home to every night. To wake to every morning.

'I'm glad,' he said when he thought he could speak without his voice breaking. 'I'm glad that they have someone like you.'

Her mouth curved sadly. 'I wish they didn't need someone like me. But evil lives and people suffer, so I do what I can.' She drew a breath, slid her hand out from under his and rose to her feet with the fluid grace of a dancer, somehow smoothing her expression on the way up. She was a cop again, but he was okay with that. 'I need to go.'

He rose more slowly, the muscles in his bruised back shouting at him for sitting on the floor like that for so long. He rolled his shoulders, trying to work out the stiffness as his mind grappled for some way to convince her to stay a little longer. Which was selfish, so he stowed the impulse to beg, but bought a little more time by leaning one shoulder against the door.

'Go where?' he asked, more than gratified when her chin had to jerk up substantially so that she could answer to his face and not his groin.

He swallowed what would have been a grin. She was interested. That was enough for now.

She arched a brow. Tried for cool. He'd let her have it this time. 'To do my job,' she said, sounding affronted that he'd even dare to ask.

'Wonderfully specific,' he said sarcastically.

She didn't rise to the bait. 'The bottom line here is that you are a likely target for Tala's killer as he or she takes care of loose ends. They thought they killed you last night, but you outed yourself as being alive through the story in your paper. Being very honest, I probably can't get you police protection, but I can ask for drive-bys of your house and business during the day.'

'Not necessary,' he said, dropping the sarcasm, because on top of being very honest, she was also very serious. Which was actually pretty cute. But because he valued his life, he kept that thought to himself.

'As you wish,' she said, with a nod toward the door he leaned against. 'If you don't mind, I need to go.'

He did mind, very much, but he pushed away from the door and reached for the knob. Then stopped cold when words came out of his mouth that he had not planned to say. 'What about the list? Isn't that the other reason you dropped by?'

Really, O'Bannion? You shit-for-brains. She'd forgotten all about the damn list and he just had to bring it up again. But he was glad he had, because after a wide-eyed blink, she seemed to relax, her expression looking damn close to relief.

She smiled at him and his heart began to race. 'You can email it to me. At this point it's probably just a formality. It'll allow me to cross the Ts and dot the Is in my report when we arrest Tala's killer.'

She hadn't wanted the damn list, he realized. She just wanted him to follow through on his promises. Now he felt like he had to give her something. *Shit.*

'No, no,' he said lightly. 'I'll plan to email it to you, but then I'll just get pulled into whatever new crisis has been brewing out there while we've been talking. I should do it now, while you're here. It'll just take me a few minutes. Have a seat. Make yourself comfortable.'

She shrugged. 'All right. As long as it's just a few minutes. I've already stayed longer than I planned.' She returned to the chair in front of his desk. 'Thank you, Marcus.'

He eased into his own chair and turned his monitor so that she couldn't see it. 'It's not a problem,' he said, and hoped he wasn't a liar.

Cincinnati, Ohio
Tuesday 4 August, 10.30 A.M.

Ken Sweeney pulled on a pair of gloves as he descended the stairs to his basement at a leisurely stroll, stopping in front of his guests. The three Anderses were tied to chairs, blindfolded and gagged. Their clothes were ripped, their hair disheveled.

Burton and Decker stood behind the trio, looking annoyed.

'Delivered,' Burton said. 'Just as you ordered, sir.' The former cop touched his torn face gingerly. 'Mostly unmarked.'

'Good. Where is the wounded guard?'

'Still in the van,' Decker said. 'Anders shot him with a low-caliber bullet, so it could have been worse. I stopped the blood flow, but I need to get a few supplies to stitch him up. We weren't sure where you'd want him to convalesce. He'll need at least a few days off the leg.'

'Take him to one of the spare rooms on the second floor,' Ken said. 'There are clean towels in the linen closet. You should find all the first aid supplies you need on the top shelf.'

'And then?' Burton asked stiffly.

Ken glanced at his phone. Alice had texted him ten minutes before that she'd found Reuben's car in the airport hotel's parking lot, but so far nothing more. 'The tow service I sent to pick up Reuben's car hasn't yet arrived. When it does, the car will be brought here. You can conduct your forensic examination in the garage. It's quite large, I assure you. You'll have plenty of room. For now, I have another assignment for you.' He handed Burton a sheet of paper. 'Go to this address. Bring the woman of the house to me. Unharmed.' Ken suspected that Miriam would know Burton from his years on the police force and would trust him. 'Ensure that she comes willingly. I'd recommend not telling her where she's going,' he added dryly.

Ken watched recognition flicker in Burton's eyes, followed closely by something that looked like rage. Burton was quiet a long moment, his lips pursed tightly, before giving a single curt nod and turning on his heel.

Yeah, there was some kind of a relationship there, at a minimum. He'd have to watch Burton closely to determine where the man's loyalties lay. *With Reuben or with me?*

Ken pointed to Decker, who stood looking perplexed. 'Treat Burton's face first, then tend to the guard with the gunshot wound. And then come back down here.' Taking the noose he'd fashioned out of coarse twine from the table behind him, he stepped up to Anders's wife, Marlene, and tipped her chin up so that he could slide the noose over her head, making sure he

183

pulled the knot over the hard line of her jaw as he did so. Leaving the noose hanging around her neck, he glanced back at Decker. 'I may need you for some heavy lifting.'

A muted whimper came from Marlene's throat, making him smile. Torture was more effective when the subject was blindfolded, but he wanted to be able to see their eyes while he questioned them. Part of him hoped they'd fold quickly, because he was pressed for time, but another part hoped they'd hold out at least a little while. It had been too long since he'd had a good torture session. He hoped he hadn't become too rusty.

'Go,' he said to Decker. 'Leave us alone. We'll be fine.'

Ken waited until the door at the top of the stairs closed, then clapped his hands briskly.

'All right, Anders,' he said. 'We can do this the easy way or the hard way. It's your call.'

He removed their blindfolds, first Chip's, then Marlene's, then finally the one on the little wildcat who'd raked Burton's face. 'Oh my dear, you are very pretty,' he said quietly, stroking a finger lightly down her cheek, gratified when the girl's eyes widened in terror. A glance to her right – to the noose around Mommy's neck – had her mewling, her terror jacked higher.

He walked over to Chip. 'I want to know what the hell happened in your household. First things first. Tell me why you allowed one of your servants out of the house last night.'

Chip shook his head hard, his grunts sounding like denial.

Ken ripped the duct tape from the man's mouth, causing Chip to cry out in pain. Ken laughed. 'You think that hurt? We haven't even begun.' He pushed the cart covered with tools close enough so that the three Anderses could see its contents – knives of various lengths and sharpness, a selection of scalpels, tweezers, a length of wire with electrodes on one end.

Three pairs of eyes grew large as saucers.

Ken took tweezers from the cart and pulled out the cotton balled up in Chip's mouth. Shaking it out, he saw it was a handkerchief, monogrammed with Chip's initials.

Chip coughed hoarsely. 'Water.'

Ken fed him a small cup from the pitcher that was also on the table. 'Answer my questions. And don't say you don't know. I don't want to hear that.'

Temper flashed in Chip's eyes. 'Too damn bad, because that's the truth. I didn't know she was gone until the alarm went off this morning. We don't know how she got out or what she was doing wherever she was when she got herself shot. Probably turning tricks.' His weak chin lifted defiantly. 'You have no right to drag us here. Let us go now and we won't report you.'

Ken laughed when Marlene's eyes narrowed. 'Somehow I don't think your lovely wife agrees.' He leaned one hip against the cart, sobering. 'You're trying to tell me that you haven't listened to the tapes yet? Because I have.' Well not all, not yet anyway. But enough to know that his property was in the damn morgue in the hands of CPD.

Chip's eyes blazed. 'How did you . . . how did you . . .' he sputtered furiously. 'You can listen, too? *You can listen, too?* That means you've been listening to my family for three years? To my private—'

Ken slapped Chip's face. Hard. So hard the chair teetered for a moment. He waited until the chair had decided to stay upright before answering. 'Yes, Chip.' He popped the 'p', rolling his eyes. *What a ridiculous name for a grown man.* 'I can listen to any private moment that you have in the range of one of the tracking devices I've supplied. However, I don't. I don't care what you do with the property I sell you as long as you follow the rules. You did not follow the rules. When you break my rules, I reserve the right to listen to anything still in my recorded library.' He raised a brow at the look of sheer terror that passed over the face of Anders's pretty daughter.

Bingo, Ken thought. *Someone has been very naughty.* This might have been fun except for the fact that three of his assets had escaped. One was dead, her tracker now in the custody of the cops. The other two . . . Who knew? Ken had a feeling Chip did. A car had been waiting outside when the remaining two females escaped, after all. Either Chip was grossly incompetent or he was a double-crosser. Ken suspected a little of both.

Chip touched his tongue to his now-bleeding lower lip. 'What rule have I broken?' he asked with a sneer, somehow maintaining his fine veneer of contempt.

Ken might have been impressed if Chip hadn't been trembling. 'You didn't inform me the moment she disappeared.'

'Because I didn't know until later,' Chip snapped.

'Later,' Ken said with a nod. 'The alarm went off when?'

Chip exhaled. 'At 5.45 this morning. But you knew that already because you get the tracker alarms too. You can locate any of my property any time you want to.'

'Yes, I can. But, I repeat, I don't. Not unless you break the rules. Which you did. Now, tell me how the girl got out early this morning and how the hell she got into the city. And why you killed her.'

Chip's head reared back. 'I did not kill her. I didn't even know she was gone. She slipped out. Probably to meet a man.'

'You got that last part right at least. She met a man.' Abruptly Ken got into Chip's face and let his full fury show. 'She met a goddamn reporter, you careless sonofabitch!'

That shocked all of them, he saw. The daughter in particular.

Ken strolled over to her. Stroked his fingers down her cheek again. Chuckled when she jerked her head away. He grabbed a handful of her hair, wrapped it around his wrist and yanked, bringing stunned tears to the daughter's eyes. Smiling, he leaned into her upturned face.

'You did it, didn't you?' he asked silkily. He ripped the duct tape from her mouth and shoved the tweezers in her mouth to retrieve the handkerchief used to gag her. Ignoring her choking cough, he yanked her head back again. 'You let her out. Why?'

'I didn't,' the girl stammered. 'I swear.'

'Then who did?'

'I . . . I don't know.'

Ken released her and stepped back. 'The hard way then,' he said, then chuckled when she clenched her eyes shut, obviously bracing for a blow. 'I'm not going to hit you, my dear,' he promised. 'I don't want to mark your face. That would seriously reduce your asking price.'

'Price?' Chip shouted. 'What do you mean, price? My daughter is not for sale!'

'Your daughter is my . . . guest,' Ken said. 'For now. And you, Chip, have nothing to say on the matter, one way or the other.'

The daughter's eyes had grown wide, her skin pale. 'What are you talking about?'

'I'm talking about a beautiful blonde with long legs, a tight ass and creamy skin, when it isn't fright-white, that is. You go to Brown. Good school. Your major?'

'English,' she whispered.

He shrugged. 'You weren't going to do a lot with that anyway. Your name is Stephanie, isn't it? Do you speak any languages?'

Another whisper. 'French.'

Ken nodded. 'Nice. We will add that to your catalog description. Sex talk always sounds better in French. How do you feel about deserts?'

'Deserts?'

'You know – sand. Camels. Guys with towels on their heads. Because we have buyers who love pretty white girls like you.'

She whipped her head around to stare at her father. 'Buyers?'

Her mother had done the same, and now both of them stared at Chip.

'You didn't tell them, did you?' Ken asked, then threw back his head and laughed. 'Oh my. You didn't tell them what kind of man I am? And what kind of man I made you, simply by association?' He turned to the women. 'Ladies, I sell people. Your husband has bought quite a few from me. But you knew that, didn't you, Marlene? Even if your husband never told you, you still knew. If you tell me that you didn't, I'll know you're a liar. The fact that you've never paid your staff and they were forced to wear ankle bracelets to keep them from running away had to have been big clues.'

Marlene stared up at him balefully, but her gag kept her silent.

'So I'll assume you did realize that your husband had procured your staff through illicit channels. Did he tell you that he procured over two dozen more for work in your factories? Ah, I can see that he did. Did he tell you that I also sell to more . . . sensually oriented buyers?'

Marlene's eyes glittered. *Yeah,* he thought. *She'd known.*

'Sex slaves,' Stephanie said, her whisper toneless.

He glanced at the young woman. *Stephanie hadn't known.* 'If that's what you'd like to call it, sure. But I rarely get specimens as nice as you.'

Her swallow was audible. 'If I tell you, will you let me go?'

'Don't say a word,' Chip said from behind clenched teeth. 'He won't let you go. He's lying to you. You've seen his face. He's not letting any of us go.'

Without breaking eye contact with Stephanie, Ken backhanded Chip, sending his chair crashing to the floor. 'You don't give any orders here, Anders,' he said coldly, still looking only at Stephanie. 'Now, my dear, I can make your future home more hospitable or less hospitable, depending on what you tell me.'

Stephanie stared at the crumpled form of her father, confusion warring with the fear in her eyes. But as the seconds ticked by, something new began to flicker around the fear. Understanding and wary calculation replaced the confusion, as if she'd suddenly comprehended her situation and was searching for a way out. 'I . . . don't . . . What was the question?'

Ken saw the reply for what it was – a stall tactic – and had to admit a certain admiration for the girl. But her father couldn't see her face, hadn't realized she'd grasped their reality.

Chip moaned. 'Just . . . hold on, baby. If you tell him what he wants now, he'll kill us all. Or worse. Just wait. She'll . . . tell.'

Ken watched Marlene and Stephanie exchange quick glances. Marlene's was harsh. Commanding. Stephanie's was wide-eyed. But even less terrified.

Ken's eyes narrowed. 'Who will tell . . . *what*?'

Stephanie closed her eyes. Pursed her lips. Her shoulders squared.

Ken's rage exploded. 'Who will tell?' he shouted.

187

'Go to hell,' Chip moaned.

Ken spun on one heel, grabbed a knife from his cart, and pressed the tip to Marlene's carotid. 'I will cut her fucking throat, Chip.' He gripped Stephanie's chin and forced her face toward her mother. 'Open your eyes, Stephanie. Open your eyes or your mother dies. *Now!*'

Stephanie's eyes opened, then filled with fear anew as her gaze locked on the drop of blood slowly rolling down her mother's throat. 'No. No. Don't kill her. *Please* don't kill her. I'll talk. I promise I'll talk.'

'Who is the *she* that's going to tell?' Ken demanded.

'Our servants,' Stephanie spat. 'I let them go. Mila and her daughter Erica. They'll go to the police.'

She's lying. But about exactly what, Ken wasn't sure. 'Why?'

Stephanie frowned. 'Why . . . what?'

Ken had to chuckle. 'Oh, some sheik is going to pay dearly for the privilege of taming you. You've got a quick mind, Stephanie darling.' He dragged the tip of the knife down Marlene's jaw, drawing a new line of crimson. 'But it won't work, sweetheart. So come clean, or I *will* kill her.'

'I'm not lying,' Stephanie insisted hoarsely.

Ken smiled at her. 'All right then. So why did you let the servants go?'

'To create a distraction.' She clenched her teeth. 'I'm sorry, Daddy.'

'I don't understand,' Ken said, feigning bewilderment. He hadn't believed a word she'd said. 'Why would you want to create a distraction?'

'Because my father was angry with me. He was threatening to hurt me because I'd taken Tala out last night. Now please take the knife off my mother's throat.'

'I'll decide when I'll take the knife away, sweetheart.' He pressed it a little harder, just to hear Marlene's panicked whimper. 'Why did you take Tala out?'

Stephanie's throat worked frantically. 'I . . . I'm not . . .' Her eyes scrunched shut. 'You're making me too scared to think.'

'That's the point, Stephanie darling.' He stepped back, deciding to trade the knife for the wired electrodes. He didn't want to get too angry and accidentally kill Marlene too soon. 'That is exactly the point. I have questions, but you're still thinking too much about keeping your lies straight and not enough about giving me the truth.' He twisted the cap off a bottle of water from the cart and poured it liberally over Marlene's head, just smiling when she glared at him. Then he snapped the alligator clips to her ear lobes, squeezing to make sure she felt the maximum pain. 'This device has four settings. This is level one.'

He turned it on, enjoying Marlene's muffled screeching, the arching of her back, her unintelligible begging for the pain to stop. After a minute he turned it off, gratified when Marlene's shoulders sagged. Her eyes wore a glazed look.

'That was level one, Stephanie. Think about it for a few minutes, won't you?'

Ken stepped away and jogged up the stairs to the first-floor foyer. 'Decker!' he called, walking to the base of one of the twin spiral staircases that made his family home unique.

Decker appeared at the top of the stairs, his latex gloves covered in blood. 'Yes, sir?'

'Did you find signs of anyone else at the Anders house?'

Decker frowned. 'No. No one. We swept every room, looking for the missing workers. There was a spare bedroom that appeared to have been used recently, but Mrs Anders swore that's where their dog handler slept when she visited.'

'Dog handler?'

'Yes, sir. Mrs Anders owns a champion poodle. The large size, sir,' Decker clarified when Ken's face twisted in a grimace of contempt. 'Not one of those yappy little ones. There were photos of the dog on the walls in their living room, and lots of ribbons and trophies. The dog was not in the home at the time we were. I checked the closets and under the beds to be sure. I didn't want barking to call attention to the house if someone walked by. I checked Mrs Anders's calendar. The next three weekends were blocked out for dog shows – all in the Midwest, within a day's driving distance. I don't know if the handler keeps the dog for the next three weeks or brings it home in between shows.'

It was possible that this handler was the 'she' Chip had mentioned, but only if the woman was coming back soon. Or if she called in to give updates on the dog and became suspicious about Marlene's absence. Maybe what she was going to tell – to the police, presumably – was that the Anderses were missing.

'Okay,' he said to Decker. 'When you're done stitching up the wounded guard, go back to Anders's house and make sure there is still no one there. Then go to the office and continue listening to the audio files recorded from the trackers. Start with the murdered one, then listen to the two escapees.'

Decker raised a brow. 'You don't want me to come downstairs and help with the heavy lifting?'

'I think I can handle it.'

Ken wandered back to the basement, only to find that Marlene had recovered from her treatment and was glaring at him again. He grabbed the twine still noosed around her neck and pulled it taut until it rubbed raw against the wound he'd made with the knife. 'I have a feeling that you are going to be the key to me getting the answers I want, Mrs Anders. I have absolutely no compunction about putting marks on you, but we can play with the electricity for a little longer.'

He let her go, then turned to Stephanie. 'Let's begin again, shall we?'

Thirteen

Scarlett blinked hard. The chair in Marcus's office felt far too soft and comfortable. It had old-fashioned wings that were slightly padded, perfect for a person to lean their head against for a nap. *But right now you aren't that person.* She gave her head a hard shake. *Stay awake, Scar.*

Fighting a yawn, she abruptly pushed to her feet. *Walk, girl. And look.* Her lieutenant had instructed her to find out if the man was hiding anything, after all. The opportunity to gain a deeper understanding of Marcus through his things might not come again.

'I'm almost done,' Marcus said from behind the wall created by his two huge computer monitors. 'Another few minutes.'

'That's fine,' Scarlett said. 'I just need to stretch my legs.' She crossed the large wood-paneled office, stopping at the far wall.

Covered floor to ceiling with framed newspaper headlines, the wall had caught her attention the moment she'd walked into the room. Some were just the headlines themselves, others the entire front page. Haphazardly arranged, all but one of the frames displayed copies of the *Ledger*. The only other paper represented was the *Malaya*, the Filipino paper Marcus had mentioned that morning. He'd said that his grandfather had been in the Philippines during World War II, but the headline framed on the wall was much more recent, showing the deposition of Ferdinand Marcos in 1986. Scarlett wondered why it had been included. She also knew she was allowing her mind to wander, procrastinating the unpleasant task of telling Marcus about about Tala's baby. The news would undoubtedly upset him, but he needed to know.

But she could hear him still typing on his keyboard. She'd let him finish the list first. Then she'd tell him.

She returned her attention to the *Ledger* headlines – the Wall Street Crash of 1929, the bombing of Pearl Harbor, the ending of World War II in both

191

Europe and Asia. Sputnik and the moon landing. The assassinations of JFK and Martin Luther King. The explosion of *Challenger*. The fall of the Berlin Wall. 9/11. All events that had changed the world.

The local news was mostly sports and weather related. Headlines celebrated back-to-back World Series wins by the Cincinnati Big Red Machine in the seventies, and Pete Rose's breaking of Ty Cobbs's record. Side-by-side headlines recalled the historic Ohio River floods of 1937 and 1997.

'I remember that one,' Scarlett murmured, pointing at the photo under the 1997 headline. 'My uncle lost almost everything he owned. It was the first time in my life a headline affected me personally.'

'I remember it too,' Marcus said from his desk. 'I was with the photographer in the helicopter when he snapped that photo. Seeing what happened from the air . . . it was overwhelming.'

'I can imagine.' Her eyes swept across the wall again as she tried to ignore the tingle that tickled everything feminine inside her body every time the man spoke. 'It's like a history lesson. Right here in black and white.'

'I know.'

With a start she realized he was standing about a foot behind her, having somehow moved away from his desk without a sound. Keeping her gaze locked forward, she drew a quiet breath to slow the sudden tripping of her heart, but couldn't control the shiver that licked across her skin when his scent filled her head.

There should have been nothing extraordinary about his scent. Just soap and a hint of aftershave. She'd smelled the combination on men hundreds, thousands of times. She worked with men, had six brothers, for God's sake. But this . . . This was different. This was Marcus. She'd dreamed of him for months and now she was here with him. Close enough to touch.

Her hands itched to reach out to him, so she shoved them in her pockets. This was not the time or the place. She was on duty and late meeting Deacon at the park. *Time to go, Scarlett. Before you do something you'll regret later*. She'd opened her mouth to tell him she had to leave, with or without the list, when he spoke again, oblivious of her reaction to him.

'I spent some of the best hours of my childhood in this room,' he said quietly. Almost reverently. 'I'd ask my grandfather about each one of these headlines and he'd tell me the story.'

She glanced back over her shoulder, expecting him to be looking at the wall. But his eyes were focused on her face with an intensity that had her swallowing hard. He'd been staring at her, she realized, waiting for her to look at him.

192

With an effort she returned her attention to the wall, knowing her cheeks had to be bright red. 'Did, um, did all of these belong to your grandfather?'

He moved to her side, so close that she could feel the heat of his body. She wanted to lean, just a little, but she kept herself upright.

'Yes, but he didn't collect them all. Some belonged to my great-grandfather – the really old ones, like the Wall Street Crash and Armistice Day in 1918. My grandfather took over the paper in the early fifties, so all the headlines up there after that were his.'

'Except the *Malaya*. Why is it there?'

'He became friends with a Filipino man while he was in the service, and they kept in touch. The man was part of the resistance effort to depose Marcos, and when they succeeded, he sent my grandfather a copy of the paper. Granddad said he was so proud of his friend that he hung the paper here. It's the only non-*Ledger* headline up there.'

'He was a loyal friend.'

'That he was. He was also a hoarder. There are boxes of clippings in my mother's basement. It's a damn fire hazard but I can't bring myself to throw any of it out.'

She heard the wistful affection in his voice. 'You loved him.'

A sigh. 'Yeah. He could be a hard man, but I loved him. He loved us too, in his own way.' A long pause. 'I think some of the things he'd seen, especially during the war, changed him so fundamentally that he couldn't easily open himself up after that. But occasionally we'd see the real him.'

In his own way did not sound promising. 'Was that a good thing?' she asked, not sure she really wanted to hear the answer. 'Seeing the real him, I mean.'

'Sometimes. He could be fun, but more often he'd be moody. Of course, we didn't often see that side of him. Not until we moved in with him.'

'When was that?'

Something indefinable flickered in his eyes. 'When I was eight.'

'Where did you live before?' she asked, trying not to sound like an interrogator.

He lifted a brow. 'Don't even try, Detective,' he said, and her cheeks heated.

'Sorry. I really am just curious, but old habits . . .' She shrugged. 'You know.'

'Yeah, I know,' he said, and for a moment he sounded so . . . incredibly *sad*. 'I was born in Lexington. So was Stone. So we were close enough to visit Granddad often, but we never stayed too long and I think he was able to hide the darker moods. When we moved in, well, pretty quickly we figured out the score. Sometimes he'd be the grandfather we'd known before, happy and funny, throwing a football around with us, giving us rides on his shoulders . . . But other times he'd be so angry. We were never really sure which grandfather we were going to get on any given day.'

She looked up at him with a frown. 'Did he hit you when he was angry?'

He looked down at her, one side of his mouth quirking up. 'Would you have protected me if he had?'

She narrowed her eyes. 'Yeah. I would have.'

The little quirk became a true smile, going all the way to his eyes, and Scarlett found herself momentarily awestruck. His face was a little too rugged to be classically handsome, but when he smiled . . . *My God.* He was beautiful.

'You would have been only about three years old when we moved in with him,' he said. 'But I appreciate the sentiment.'

'I was a damn tough three-year-old,' she said lightly. 'I had to be. I have six brothers.'

He tilted his head, looking intrigued. 'Older or younger?'

'Three of each.'

'Sisters?'

'No, none. I'm the only girl, though not from my parents' lack of trying. My mother finally gave up. And don't think I didn't realize that you failed to answer my question.'

He shook his head. 'I would never underestimate you like that. No. He never hit us. When he got that angry look in his eyes, he'd separate himself from the rest of us. He had a home gym in the basement. Punching bag, boxing ring, free weights. He'd go down there and work off his anger to the point that he could lock it away again.' He paused for a moment, thinking, then shook his head again. 'We always knew that when he came back upstairs from the gym, we wouldn't see the real him for a long while, in any form.'

'He wanted to protect you from himself,' she murmured, understanding more than Marcus knew. 'And himself from you.'

She knew she'd overstepped the moment the words came out of her mouth. Marcus pivoted so that their shoulders no longer nearly touched. It only widened the gap between them a few more inches, but it could have been a football field by the arctic look on his face.

'Excuse me?' Even his voice had grown coldly contemptuous. 'You didn't know him. You didn't know us. We *never* would have hurt him. *Never.*'

'I bet I know him better than you think,' she said quietly, clearly

194

visualizing the tortured man beating the tar out of a punching bag rather than taking out his inescapable fury on small children. 'But you're right. I shouldn't have said that. I didn't mean it the way you took it. I'm sorry.' Still in her pocket, her hand closed over her car keys, gripping them tightly. 'I'll leave now. You don't have to show me out.' She stepped to the side so that she could get by him without brushing against him. 'Please be careful. And don't hesitate to call me if you need me.'

He matched her step, blocking her path. 'Scarlett, I . . .' He shook his head, his expression no longer cold. No longer anything. He'd wiped the emotion from his features. 'I apologize.'

She pulled on her most professional face. 'No need. Now, if you'll let me pass, I need to go. This was supposed to have been a quick stop. I've been keeping Agent Novak waiting.'

His feet didn't budge, but his hand lifted to close gently over her shoulder, the movement slow and careful, as if he was afraid he'd spook her. 'Don't go,' he murmured. 'Not yet. Not like this. Tell me what you did mean.'

She could feel the warmth of his hand through the fabric of her jacket, and this time she gave in to the urge to lean into his touch, just a little. Then shivered when his thumb swept up the side of her neck, just once.

His exhale was ragged, his voice rough as he ran his hand down the length of her arm, lightly but briefly brushing his fingertips against the back of her hand. 'I know he wanted to protect us from himself. I knew that even when I was a kid. But why would he need to protect himself from us? How could we have hurt him?'

She met his eyes, understood the guarded trepidation she saw there because she felt the same way. Now that she had a second to think, she wished she hadn't said anything at all. Marcus O'Bannion was about as far from clueless as a man could get. Her answer would very likely expose her worst vulnerability.

But maybe he needed to see that. *Fair warning and all that shit.*

She thought of the framed copy of the *Malaya* on the wall behind her. 'You said he was in the Philippines. In Bataan. He must have seen, experienced, terrible things.'

'Then and later,' Marcus murmured. 'He was in the press corps in Korea.'

'It changes you, seeing death and dying. People suffering. Knowing you can't stop it or fix it. That you can only do so much. It damages you. Damages your soul. Pieces break off and shrivel up until they're not recognizable as anything that had ever been good. But it sounds like your grandfather still had a fair bit left inside him that was good. That could feel. That cared and, importantly, could maintain reason. He was an adult with strong hands. You were a child and he was afraid he might truly hurt you. That he was able to separate himself before he raised his hand to you is commendable. A lot of people can't do that, and they end up hurting the people they're supposed to love the most. Sometimes physically and sometimes emotionally.'

His eyes were locked on hers, warmer now. Less remote. 'We couldn't have hurt him physically. He was Stone's size and we were children. But we wouldn't have hurt him emotionally either, even when we grew up.'

'I know. I think he probably knew that too. But sometimes it doesn't matter what you know. The fear goes far deeper than that, because that piece of our soul that we keep is the connection to what's left of our humanity. If you allow yourself to open up, even to the people you love the most, and that good part somehow becomes damaged, too? What then?'

'You have nothing,' he murmured.

'Exactly. The need to protect isn't rational. It's instinctive, the way you protect an injured part of your body when you're in a fight. You want to be able to open the gate, to let people in, but only the people you love, who you can trust not to hurt you. Then you close the gate tight when you go back into the world. But sometimes it gets too hard to keep opening and closing the gate. You run out of strength.'

He finally broke eye contact, looking away. 'Or the gate becomes rusty.'

'True,' she said quietly, wondering if either of them was still talking about his grandfather. 'And sometimes you close the gate because you're ashamed to let anyone in. To let anyone see. Because you keep seeing things you can't unsee. And the damage spreads.'

'Like a rot,' he said flatly.

'Yep.' She drew a breath. 'So you close the gate tight. Quarantine the rot. Make sure it doesn't spread to anyone else.'

'So why not quit before the rot consumes you?' he asked, almost as if to himself.

'I suppose only the individual can answer that question for himself.'

He met her eyes once more, his no longer guarded but sharp. 'Or herself?'
She nodded soberly. 'Or herself.'

'So why, Scarlett? Why do you continue seeing things you can't unsee?'

The question took her by surprise. 'Because it's all I know how to do,' she answered honestly.

Anger flashed in those dark brown eyes. 'Let someone else do it.'

She smiled up at him sadly. 'And let the rot spread? That's not the way I'm built.' She cleared her throat. 'And now I'm even later meeting Deacon. I need to go. Just email me the list when it's done.'

'It is done. It's on the printer.' He crossed back to his desk and picked up the single sheet of paper. 'I'll email it to you as well, in case you want to send it to Deacon.'

She took it and scanned the short list of names – only eight. Marcus had added the date of the threat, the exact wording, and a short summary of the article that had incited the person's anger to begin with.

Carefully she folded the paper and slid it into her jacket pocket. 'Thank you. And thank you for calling me this morning. I only wish I had gotten there a little sooner.'

'I wish I had too. I might have gotten her out of there alive.'

Scarlett looked over her shoulder, her eyes drawn to the copy of the *Malaya*, and she realized that she still hadn't told him about the baby. 'I don't think Tala would have left with you. Or with me, for that matter. She was going back to wherever she was being kept.'

He frowned down at her. 'How do you know?'

'*Malaya* wasn't just her way of asking you to free her family. I think Malaya is the name of her child.'

Marcus paled under his tan, just as she'd feared he would. '*Child? She had a child?*'

'Yes.'

'How old?' he asked hoarsely. 'How old is the child?'

'It's hard to say exactly. The ME thought Tala might have given birth anywhere from one to three years ago. If I had to guess, I'd put the baby's age closer to a year. We found a teething ring in Tala's pocket and we know she was still nursing.'

His throat worked hard for a moment. 'She was only seventeen, Scarlett.'

'I know,' she said gently.

'That means she would have gotten pregnant when she was fifteen.'

'I know.'

'She said the man owned her . . .' He looked away without voicing the question they were both asking themselves – was Tala's pregnancy the result of a rape? 'How do you know the baby's name was Malaya?' he asked instead.

'CSU found a pacifier in her pocket that had been labeled at some point. The ink is worn and smudged, but I think it said "Malaya".'

His teeth clenched, a muscle ticking in his jaw. 'Then she's still out there. Unprotected.' Abruptly he turned on his heel and went to his desk, unlocked

197

a drawer and pulled out an older-model Glock and a double shoulder holster.

Scarlett considered asking if that was the gun he'd been carrying that morning while looking for the shooter, but decided the question would keep for a time when he was less . . . volatile.

He met her eyes as he shrugged into the well-worn leather holster, daring her to say a word. When she stared back silently, he broke eye contact to check the Glock's chamber, set the safety and shoved the weapon into the left-hand side of the holster, then loaded the ammo carrier on the right. 'I have a concealed carry permit,' he said through gritted teeth.

'I know,' she said calmly. 'But I would like to know where you think you're going.'

He looked up, his smile a mere baring of his teeth. 'To find the child. Are you coming with me?'

Cincinnati, Ohio
Tuesday 4 August, 11.10 A.M.

Marcus stared at Scarlett across his desk, waiting for the recrimination that would undoubtedly come. Which he undoubtedly deserved. She'd trusted him with details about Tala and her baby that she could have – and probably should have – kept to herself, and he'd reacted by arming himself and acting like a deranged idiot. But . . . *God. A baby.* As soon as Scarlett had told him that Tala had been wearing a tracker, he'd wondered why the girl had taken such a huge risk coming to him. Now he understood.

From across his office, Scarlett studied him with those dark, dark blue eyes. He wondered what she saw. Probably a headstrong, reckless man who tended to get himself shot too often. Not anyone she'd take seriously.

But he wouldn't back down. He couldn't. Tala had come to him for help and he'd failed her. He was not going to fail that innocent child too. Not while he still had breath in his lungs.

'Where will you go?' Scarlett asked him in the same calm voice she'd used when she'd told him about the baby. He wanted to scream when he heard it, but then he remembered the stark pain that had ravaged her eyes when she'd told him how badly Tala had been beaten.

She could only have known that information if she had witnessed it. Which meant she'd viewed Tala's body lying on a slab in the morgue. And it had torn her up inside. Marcus had seen that so very clearly. He'd also seen her wipe that pain from her eyes, hiding it away so that she could function. The calm voice she used now was as much a facade as her expressionless eyes had been.

'Back to the neighborhoods around the park,' he said. 'Someone had to have seen her or that dog.'

'I've had uniforms canvassing the neighborhoods since daybreak. They haven't found anyone who had seen her before – or will admit to it anyway.'

'Because you sent uniforms. They might be more inclined to confide in someone who's not a goddamn cop.'

He thought she'd wince at that, but she didn't. She kept her calm and he wondered how much it cost her to do so. 'Like a reporter?' she asked mildly.

'Yeah. People may not like us and they may not trust us, but there's always one narcissist in the crowd who wants to be on the TV news, even in the nicest of neighborhoods.'

'You're not with the TV news,' she pointed out, her tone logical and emotionless. But he could see her pulse fluttering in the hollow of her throat and knew that while she seemed plasticized on the outside, she was very much alive on the inside.

He pulled a camcorder from the same drawer that had held his gun. 'Fifteen minutes of fame is irresistible to people who crave it, regardless of the medium.'

She lifted one dark eyebrow. 'Are you trying to make me angry with you, Marcus?'

'Maybe. Maybe I just want to see *you*. The real you. I know you're in there somewhere.'

She was quiet for a few pounding beats of his heart. Then she nodded once. 'Yeah, you're right. I'm in here somewhere, but I don't have the luxury of letting the real me out to kick ass and take names just to entertain you. I can't stop you from questioning the neighbors. But understand, if you cross the line, I will arrest you.'

Marcus had to swallow, the mental image of Scarlett kicking ass making his mouth water and his cock grow instantly hard. Which was ridiculous and inappropriate given the gravity of the situation, but completely undeniable. He casually shifted his weight to one foot, trying to relieve the pressure behind the zipper of his jeans.

'Message received, loud and clear,' he managed in a level voice. Then he lifted his brows, unable to resist one last jab at that shell of hers. 'Does this mean that you're not coming with me, Detective?' he asked silkily.

She rolled her eyes. 'Oh for the love of . . .' She huffed an impatient sigh. 'Just try not to get shot again, okay?'

He gave her a sincere nod. 'I'll do my very best.'

199

Shaking her head, she almost marched to the door to his office, then hesitated, her hand on the doorknob. 'Thank you for the list of names. And for the videos.'

'You're welcome,' he said seriously, all posturing shoved aside. 'Thank you for telling me about Tala and her baby. I know you didn't have to.'

She made a face at that. 'And I probably shouldn't have. Do me a favor and keep that out of your paper, even though you make your living digging for news. I'd like to keep my job a little longer.'

'I won't print it or post it. Or blog about it. I promise.'

She nodded once. 'If you do find that one narcissist who craves his fifteen minutes of fame . . .'

'I'll be sure to give you any information I'm able to pick up. Where will you be? Just,' he added when she lifted her eyebrows again, 'so that I know where to find you to tell you.'

She gave him a pitying look. 'Really, Marcus? That's the best you can do? If you want to know where I'm going next with this investigation, just ask.'

He snorted before he thought better of it. 'I did ask earlier. You got that pissy look and said "To do my job."'

Her lips twitched, so slightly that he might have missed it had he not been staring so intently. 'Fair enough,' she murmured. 'Ask again. I'll endeavor to be less pissy.'

He walked around the desk, stopping inches from where she still held the doorknob in an iron grip. He leaned down until their foreheads almost touched, allowing the scent of wildflowers to fill his head. 'Detective Bishop, where are you going next with this investigation?'

That she had to draw a steadying breath before she answered did wonders for his ego.

'I'm meeting Deacon in the park. We figured that if she knew her captors could hear anything she said through the tracker, she might have written something down. He's looking for any message or note she might have hidden under a bush or in the knothole of a tree.'

'He won't find anything.'

She pulled back a few inches, eyes narrowed. 'What makes you so sure?'

'Because I've already looked. I spent hours going over that patch of woods. I didn't need to know about the ankle tracker to know she was desperately afraid of someone or something. I figured she was afraid of being followed, or maybe that she didn't speak English, or maybe even that she was mute. I thought I might find she'd dropped a note on the ground, or hidden one, so I looked . . . and looked. But I found nothing.'

'Did you search at night or in the day?'

'Both.'

She frowned. 'You might have trampled any evidence by searching.'

'Yeah, well I didn't realize she was about to be shot.'

She sighed. 'Good point.' Then she stunned him by poking his chest with her forefinger, hard enough to make him wince. 'If you do go out, make sure you're wearing a vest, and be careful.' And with that she was gone, leaving him staring at the door, listening for any disturbance in the lobby as she made her way to the front door. He turned his gaze to the security monitor on his desk and watched her walk toward the street, immediately checking her phone the moment she was clear of the building.

He realized he'd been staring up at the monitor for more than a minute when his neck started to go stiff. All he could see was Scarlett's back, but still his mouth watered. Which was pretty damn pathetic. The only consolation was that she'd seemed affected by him too.

There would be time to explore the possibilities between them later, once they'd located Tala's baby and the couple who'd owned the girl. To accomplish either of those things, he needed to stay intact. Plus, he kept his promises. Especially promises made to a woman with midnight-blue eyes who had him wishing to hell that he were a better man.

Marcus backed away from the door and stripped out of the shoulder holster, stacking it and its contents on his desk. Once again he opened the drawer that had held his gun and pulled out the old Kevlar vest Stone had retrieved from his apartment that morning. The vest he'd worn in the alley had been a newer, lighter model, one he could wear under a T-shirt without attracting suspicion. But that vest was now in CPD custody, ruined beyond repair anyway. His old vest was bulkier and far more stifling. He'd need to wear a long-sleeved button-up shirt to hide it.

He grimaced. Bulky Kevlar and a long-sleeved shirt. In August. Freaking fantastic. *I'm going to roast to death before any bullet has a chance to do me in*, he thought sourly as he pulled his T-shirt off over his head.

The sharp rap of knuckles was the only warning he had before his door cracked open. 'Marcus?' Gayle said, sounding tense.

He spun, putting his back to the wall behind him. All he needed was for Gayle to see the bruise on his back, which was huge and dark if his current level of discomfort was any indication. 'Not—'

The door pushed all the way open, leaving Gayle holding the outer doorknob and glaring at Scarlett Bishop, who shoved past her and stopped cold.

'She wouldn't take no for an answer,' Gayle said furiously. 'She is the

201

rudest woman I have ever met. Stone isn't here. Should I call 911 and have her removed?'

Scarlett hadn't said a word in her own defense, because she was staring at Marcus. Specifically she was staring at his bare chest, making him want to preen.

But he didn't, of course, keeping his dignity intact – at least on the outside. 'It's okay, Gayle. Leave her alone. And please close the door.'

With a dark glare, Gayle complied, slamming the door with more force than necessary. The sound jerked Scarlett out of her deer-in-the-headlights trance. She turned around quickly, but not before he saw her cheeks turn tomato red.

'I'm sorry,' she said, folding her arms across her chest. 'I . . .' She blew out a breath. 'Are you decent yet?'

'Of course,' he said, grinning when she turned to find him still shirtless. He spread his arms wide, letting her look her fill. 'I am far from indecent. I show a lot more at the beach. Besides, you barged into my office. Again. Would have served you right to find me buck naked.'

The red in her cheeks spread to cover her entire face. 'Do you plan to get dressed anytime soon?' she asked stiffly, making him want to chuckle. 'Because I need your help.'

Instantly he was sober. 'What's happened?' he asked, shoving his arm into the sleeve of the vest. The other sleeve eluded him, though. His back was so sore that reaching behind him had become a problem.

'Nothing bad.' She approached briskly, taking over the task of putting him into the vest. Gently she gripped his forearm and slid it into the sleeve, then pulled the vest snugly around him and snapped all the fasteners in place. 'That bruise on your back has to hurt. Did you ice it?'

'No,' he said tightly, his heart ricocheting inside his chest cavity. Her hands were capable and quick, but they'd been her hands and they'd been all over his torso.

She picked up the T-shirt he'd discarded. 'Were you going to wear this?'

He needed a moment to rein his pulse back to safe levels. 'No. I've got a long-sleeved shirt in my closet. It's in the bathroom. In there.' He pointed vaguely in the right direction.

She'd disappeared into the bathroom when he heard her exclaim, 'Holy shit! This bathroom is bigger than both of mine at home, put together.' She emerged, a dark blue shirt in her hand. 'This one okay?'

'Yeah.' He probably could have dressed himself, but let her do it, breathing in the scent of her hair as she buttoned him up.

'Did you have that bathroom put in or did you inherit it?'

'Inherited. My grandfather liked his creature comforts.'

'I can see that.' She stepped back, all business again. 'I have a task for you, one that I think would be a better use of your time than knocking on doors. You wanna hear it?'

If it allowed him more time with her? *Hell, yeah.* 'Yes,' he said quietly.

'I got a text from a friend who used to have a grooming business.'

'The one who has poodle mug shots for me to ID?'

She blinked, looking startled and a little embarrassed. He wanted to preen even more because he'd thrown the logical, just-the-facts Scarlett Bishop off balance. 'Oh right,' she said. 'I did tell you about her.' She let out a slow breath regaining her composure. 'Anyway, she just texted me to say that she found some old videos she took of standard poodles at a local dog show. She says the picture quality isn't too bad. Since you're the only one who's seen the dog in person, will you go with me to take a look?'

'Of course,' he said, sliding one arm into the shoulder harness, fighting to focus when she reached around him to help with the other side. 'What about meeting Deacon in the park?'

'He hasn't found anything yet and agreed this was a better lead. He's starting to see more people walking their dogs now and he wants to interview them.'

'It's almost lunchtime. The park gets busy then.'

'He's going to show Tala's photo around, see if any of those people remember her, but that's something he can do alone. Talking to the groomer is a better use of my time too. So? Can you spare an hour or so?'

He gestured to the door. 'After you, Detective.'

She shook her head, pointing to the shoulder holster with an arched brow. 'Are you planning to wear that out in public without a jacket? Because if you don't cover it up, you can't come with me. I don't want to look like I'm on a case with Dirty Harry.'

'Shit,' he muttered. 'What's the outside temp?'

'Already in the low nineties, eighty-five percent humidity. Air quality is like pea soup. You wear a jacket over the Kevlar and the shirt and you won't have a chance to shoot any bad guys. You'll be in the ER with heat stroke. Why don't you use the pocket holster you used this morning?'

He narrowed his eyes, studying her. 'Pocket holster?'

'I assumed you wouldn't walk into an alley frequented by drug dealers with a gun holstered at your hip. Not unless you wanted to provoke them. Is that Glock the one you were carrying this morning?'

Hell, he'd known she was observant. He was going to have to be a whole lot more alert. 'If you knew about the other gun, why didn't you confiscate it, like you did my knife? Which I still want back, by the way.'

'I didn't know. I guessed. Didn't seem prudent to run after a shooter with your primary weapon at your ankle. You didn't have any gunshot residue on your hands, so I didn't ask. And you'll get your knife back when CSU is finished with it. They've got more important things to worry about right now.'

Without a word, he changed the holsters and shoved the extra ammo into his shirt pocket. 'My car or yours?'

'Mine,' she said flatly. 'This is an official call, Marcus. Not a date.'

He wanted to grin, but knew better. Opening his office door with a flourish, he waved her through. 'Then after you, Detective.'

Cincinnati, Ohio
Tuesday 4 August, 12.00 P.M.

Scarlett glanced over at the passenger seat, where Marcus slouched, a baseball cap pulled down over his face, snoring softly. He'd fallen asleep about five minutes into the ride.

He'd looked utterly exhausted even as he'd armed himself the first time, planning to go looking for the couple who'd owned Tala. She had no doubt that he would have done just as he'd said, knocking on doors until he found that one narcissist who wanted to be in the news.

And she might still ask him to do that if this lead petered out.

'Marcus.' She nudged his arm gently. 'Marcus, wake up. We're almost there.'

He woke with a jerk, going stiff before he got his bearings and relaxed. He pushed the cap back and turned to look out the window. 'How long was I out?'

'Only about twenty-five minutes. I wanted to prepare you before we descended on Delores.'

He shifted in his seat so that he was staring at her profile. 'Prepare me how?'

'I met Delores nine months ago. She was in the same hospital as you were.' She glanced over to briefly meet his eyes. 'Put there by the same person.'

'Sonofabitch,' he murmured. 'She's the woman who lived.'

'Yep.' Scarlett's lips twitched. 'And she really hates to be referred to like that. She says it makes her feel like Harriet Potter.'

Marcus chuckled. 'Okay, I won't say that to her face.' He sighed, sobering.

'I read about her injuries after I got out of ICU. I wanted to do something to help her, but I wasn't sure what. Jeremy found out that she ran a dog shelter and suggested a donation. He also sent some of his students from the university to take care of the animals until they were placed. Since some of the students were pre-vet, it was a good match. The animals got care and the students got volunteer credits.'

'That was kind of him. Delores's first concern when she came out of her coma was the dogs in her shelter.'

'Jeremy is a very kind man. He always has been. For Stone and me, he was the dad he didn't have to be. He took on someone else's kids and made them his own, even though he was barely grown himself.'

She glanced over again. 'I called him this morning, looking for you when you didn't answer my messages.'

'I know. He called and told me. He was pissed off that I'd worried everyone. Especially you. He said you sounded scared.'

'I was. Not so much for you at that point. I was more concerned. But I was scared to talk to him,' she admitted. 'Afraid that I'd bring back bad memories for him. But if I did, he hid it well. He was the perfect gentleman.'

'I don't think you can bring back bad memories, Scarlett. Not for any of us. We haven't forgotten Mikhail or the pain of losing him, so there's nothing to remember. It's with us every day.' He paused a long moment and she could feel him watching her. 'So if that was stopping you from calling before, put it out of your mind.'

She swallowed, well aware that he was no longer speaking of his uncle, but of himself. 'Good to know,' she murmured. 'But back to Delores.'

'Of course. She who shall not be named "the woman who lived". Does she know I'm coming with you?'

'Yes. She said she was looking forward to meeting you. That you were the only O'Bannion sibling she hadn't yet met.'

Marcus's mouth fell open. 'What? You mean Audrey . . . *and* Stone?'

'Yep.' Scarlett had been completely stunned by the information as well. 'Audrey's visited her several times since she got out of the hospital. Even did a fund-raiser for her shelter. That girl is wicked smart with fund-raising.'

'She learned from my mom, so she learned it from the best.' He shook his head hard. 'Stone too?'

'Stone too. He visited her while she was still in the hospital and here at the shelter. Took her flowers and chocolate and even a stuffed animal dog. She said he was sweet.'

Marcus snorted. 'Sweet? *Stone?*'

Scarlett grinned. 'Yeah, that made me chuckle too.' She sobered abruptly.

'Anyway, she's still recovering. The bullet didn't do as much damage as her hitting her head when she was thrown to the asphalt. And the massive blood loss, of course. She was very nearly dead when she was discovered. Her speech is still a little slurred and she doesn't move as fast as she once did, but she is moving. If you try to help her, she'll snarl at you. She is fiercely independent. She's also a hugger, so if you're not a hugger, you'll need to deal with it.'

'I'm not, but I can make an exception. Anything else?'

Scarlett sighed. 'She still spooks easily, so don't come up behind her. He . . . did that. Came up behind her in that parking lot.'

'So noted,' he said grimly. 'How *did* she survive? I mean, she was shot in the back of the head. People don't normally survive that.'

'She was shot point-blank, which actually was the critical saving factor, believe it or not. It was one of those weird medical marvel things. Deacon's sister was working in the ER at the time. She said even the director of the ER had only seen this happen a half-dozen times in his twenty-five-year career. She must have tilted her head to the side at the last minute, so that the bullet hit her skull at the perfect angle. Rather than penetrating bone, it kind of skimmed over it, traveling in the space between the skin and the skull. Her exit wound was near her temple, but it was truly only a flesh wound.'

She glanced over to see him frowning at her. 'You are bullshitting me,' he said.

She shook her head. 'I swear it's true. You can ask Deacon. Just don't ask Delores. She's not ready to talk about it yet.'

'I will. Ask Deacon, I mean. And I won't ask Delores. So how do you know her? Did you visit her in the hospital too?'

'Only once. I was busy while you all were lounging in hospital beds eating yummy Jell-O.' She let out a quiet sigh. 'There were a lot of bodies to identify when the dust settled.' She cleared her throat brusquely. 'I got to know Delores better once she'd reopened her shelter. Dani and Faith adopted dogs and dragged me along. I got suckered into taking one home with me too.'

'That's nice,' he said quietly. 'Really nice.'

'Not really. Zat gives more to me than he gets, I'm afraid.'

'Yeah, I get that. BB – the dog I've been walking in the park – belonged to Mikhail. I didn't want her at first, but nobody else would take her. Stone *says* he's allergic, and Audrey, while wicked smart with fund-raising, isn't exactly Miss Dependable. She'd forget to feed her or walk her. Jeremy's been busy getting Keith back on his feet.' Marcus shoved his fingers through his hair, suddenly agitated. 'And Mom . . . she couldn't even look at the dog without bursting into tears, even when she was sober.'

'So you took BB,' Scarlett said, trying to soothe the hurt that obviously ran deep. This wasn't the first time he'd mentioned his mother and her sobriety issues.

'Yeah. It's good not to come home to an empty apartment,' he admitted.

'Or an empty house.' Scarlett pulled off the main road and on to a badly paved driveway, wincing when the car hit one of the many potholes in their path. 'Sorry. Delores's driveway is hell on these shocks. I should have brought the Tank.'

'That thing still runs?' he asked, then froze. 'Shit,' he added in a mutter.

Stunned, Scarlett slowed to a stop in front of Delores's house, turning in her seat to stare at him. He averted his face, assiduously staring out the window. 'Marcus? Look at me.'

'I don't think I want to,' he mumbled, startling a laugh from her.

'Well you damn well better, anyway.' She waited until he had, guilty expression on his face. 'How do you know about my Tank?'

'I might have seen it . . . in your driveway.' He winced. 'Once or twice.'

She continued to stare. 'You drove by my *house*? *Twice*?'

'Or so.'

'How did you even know where I live?'

His wince became an annoyed glare. 'Please. Don't insult me. A five-year-old could find your address. I didn't stalk you. Didn't sit outside and watch you. I just . . . drove by.'

She was torn between being appalled and idiotically aroused. 'How many times, Marcus? How many times is "or so"?'

'Four times in nine months. That's all.'

'But . . . why?'

His gaze dropped and he didn't say anything for a long moment. Then he exhaled on a deep sigh. 'I was curious.'

She swallowed, trying to dislodge her heart from her throat. 'About?'

He looked up, met her eyes, and it was like a sucker punch straight to her sternum. 'You.' His mouth curved. Not quite a smile, but so damn sexy that she couldn't tear her eyes away. 'Why? Weren't you curious too? Even just a little?'

Her face grew hot, despite the cool air coming out of the car's vents. 'Maybe a little,' she admitted, then closed her eyes. 'Or maybe a lot.' Her eyes still closed, she flinched when his thumb glided over her cheek, but when his palm cupped her jaw, she leaned into his touch. 'Okay,' she conceded huskily. 'A whole lot.'

His deep chuckle sent a shiver down her spine. 'Good. I was starting to die over here.'

She opened her eyes to find him watching her with a satisfied smile, his eyes grown dark with arousal. 'Don't die,' she whispered. 'Please.'

His smile faded. 'I won't.' His thumb swept over her lips once before he drew his hand away. 'I think your friend knows we're here.'

Scarlett jerked so hard that her back smacked the armrest on the driver's-side door, her face now flaming with embarrassment. She'd completely forgotten where they were and why they'd come. And he was right. Arms folded across her chest, Delores leaned against one of the columns supporting her front porch, a patiently benevolent expression on her face. At her side sat an enormous dog whose head reached past her hip. The dog would have looked big sitting next to anyone, but it dwarfed petite Delores, who couldn't be more than five feet tall.

'Goddammit,' Scarlett hissed. 'This is going to be public knowledge within about five seconds after we leave.'

Marcus sat back in his seat, a frown crunching his brow. 'Did you plan on hiding me?'

'No,' she answered, flustered. 'I just . . . Hell, Marcus. I'm private about things like this. Not like I've had to be very often,' she rolled on, inwardly yelling at herself to shut up.

'How many times is "very often"?' he asked, purposely using her own words against her.

'Two,' she said honestly, then shrugged. 'And a half.' Because Bryan didn't really count as a whole relationship. He'd just been . . . convenient. Which had been wrong for both of them.

Marcus's dark eyebrows shot up, his eyes gleaming. 'A half? What the hell is a half?'

'Don't even go there,' she warned, ripping off her seat belt. 'Come on. We have work to do.'

'Yes, sir, Detective, sir,' he barked, then smiled, causing her to stare stupidly once again. 'As long as you know that we'll finish this conversation once we leave here,' he said silkily, 'seeing as how it'll be public knowledge anyway.'

'Fucking hell,' she muttered. 'Whatever. Let's figure out who owns that damn poodle.'

Fourteen

Cincinnati, Ohio
Tuesday 4 August, 12.00 P.M.

Ken stood at his living room window, watching as Burton gently lowered Reuben's sleeping wife into the front passenger seat of her car. He wasn't certain if Burton's care was due to genuine affection or simply to keep from putting any marks on her body. He wasn't convinced of Burton's loyalty, but he had to admit that the man was a professional in all the ways that counted.

Ken's cell phone rang as Burton drove away, the caller ID belonging to Demetrius. 'I was getting worried,' Ken said tersely.

'Aw, you do care,' Demetrius drawled.

'Where are you?'

'In Loveland, for God's sake. On foot, in the damn woods. You owe me fifteen hundred bucks.'

'What the fuck, Demetrius? Why?'

'Because these Testonis were brand fucking new and now they're ruined.'

Ken gritted his teeth. One of these days he was going to kick Demetrius's fancy shoes up his friend's ass. 'I meant, why are you in Loveland, walking through the woods?'

'Because that's where O'Bannion is. He's with some chick cop.'

'Fanfuckingtastic,' Ken muttered. 'Why are they in the woods?'

'They aren't. I am. I got to O'Bannion's office after she'd gone in, so I don't know when she got there. She came out at 11.20, stood on the sidewalk staring at her phone, then went back in. A few minutes later she came back out with O'Bannion. They got in her car and drove away, her at the wheel. It's a CPD unmarked. They turned into a private drive. If I'd followed, they would have made me, so I parked and hiked through the damn woods. Hold on, I'm sending you a picture of the cop. I think you'll find her . . . interesting.'

Ken's phone buzzed with the new text and, putting Demetrius on speaker, he opened the picture. Then blinked. 'Wow.'

'Yeah,' Demetrius agreed. 'She's a looker, all right.'

Demetrius, as usual, was the master of understatement. The woman was tall, with a thick black braid wound intricately around the back of her head. She was . . . exceptional.

For the first time in a long time, Ken's mouth actually watered. 'Are you thinking what I'm thinking?'

Demetrius chuckled. 'Probably not. You never think as kinked as I do.'

Ken rolled his eyes. 'I'm wondering how much we can get for her. Maybe even pair her up with Stephanie Anders and sell them as a set.'

'You sell all the best toys right out from under us,' Demetrius grumbled. 'I bet she'd be a real fighter in bed. She moves like a coiled spring. I could test her first,' he said slyly.

'We'll see,' Ken said, frowning as he studied the picture more closely. 'She looks familiar. Do I know her?'

'Yeah, you do,' Demetrius said, suddenly all business. 'She looked familiar to me too, so I had DJ dig up some pictures of her for me.'

Demetrius's son DJ had – much like Sean and Alice – proven himself extremely trustworthy over the years.

'She's a homicide detective,' Demetrius went on. 'She's working the murder of the girl in the alley this morning. Detective Scarlett Bishop. She transferred to that CPD/FBI task force a little less than a year ago. MCES or some such shit. She worked the serial killer case last fall.'

Ken put it together. 'She's the woman who came to visit O'Bannion in the hospital. She was also at his kid brother's funeral.'

'Yep. The photos DJ found were ones I took of her at that funeral and outside the hospital back in November.'

'Did DJ run a background?'

'He did. She's squeaky clean.'

'No cop is squeaky clean. I'll have Sean do some deeper checking, see what he can find. Why are Bishop and O'Bannion in Loveland?'

'I have no idea,' Demetrius said, sounding puzzled. 'They came to an animal shelter. It's called Patrick's Place.'

'An animal shelter? O'Bannion's adopting a dog?'

'I don't know. It didn't appear that they were there on any case-related business, though. I think they're . . . involved. O'Bannion woulda had his tongue down her throat in another few seconds if the lady they were visiting hadn't come out on the front porch.'

'Shit,' Ken muttered. 'A cop and a reporter. Together.' It was a bad combination.

'That's what I thought. We take him out and she'll come after us and then it'll be so long to a low profile. Unless we take them together. What do we know about the Anderses? What's O'Bannion's link to them? How did O'Bannion find out about the girl he met in that alley?'

'I'll find out. I've still got the three Anders in the basement.' Ken glanced at the security monitor on the counter. All three of his captives were trying to escape their bonds. Which would accomplish nothing more than marking their skin with rope burn. They would not break free of Ken's knots. 'The mother is the lynchpin holding them together. Chip and little Stephanie will tell me what I want to know once she's incapacitated. Stephanie knows something, but she's holding on to it because Chip believes someone will soon miss them and go to the cops.'

'Someone who?'

'Maybe the poodle's handler – you know, for dog shows – but we're not certain of that. Decker just left here to make sure no one was hiding in Anders's house. He would have gone sooner, but it seems that Chip's bullet did a lot more damage to our guard than he originally thought. Took him quite a while to get the guy stitched up.'

'Do we need to switch places? You can pull in O'Bannion and Bishop. I can get answers out of the Anderses.'

'I think I can manage,' Ken said dryly. 'The Anderses are just a bit more stubborn than most. I hooked Marlene up to my shock box, but none of them broke. I gave them a breather to let them stew while I was taking care of Miriam.'

A short silence, followed by a sigh. 'Reuben's wife knew about us?'

'Oh yeah. She trusted Burton enough to come with him willingly, but when she saw where he'd brought her, she started scratching at him, trying to make him let her go. She screamed that she didn't want to have anything to do with the devil who had corrupted her husband. She ripped up the wounds that Marlene put on his face and cut a few new gouges of her own. So I made her some tea, laced with enough sedative to take out a moose.'

'She drank it? After drugging Jason Jackson, she really drank something you gave her?'

'Not voluntarily, but my knife at her throat convinced her to accept my hospitality. She settled down quickly, told me what I basically wanted to know and fell asleep. Burton's taking her and her car to a cheap motel. He'll dump her in a room and write an appropriately passive-aggressive email to Reuben on her phone, saying she didn't want the kids to come home from school and find her body. Then he'll leave her car at the motel. If Reuben

211

had trackers put on his own vehicles like Burton says he did, and if he's still alive, then he'll find her car and her body soon enough. Fireworks to come, complete with Reuben's wailing and gnashing of teeth.'

'What did she tell you?'

'That I was a perverted bastard who had seduced her husband into my perversions,' Ken said. 'She said that her PI was on to us too. I told her that her PI was already dead. That made her a little more cooperative. Burton pulled her laptop and searched her email. She'd documented what she knew and emailed it to herself. It didn't appear that she'd sent it to anyone else. I suppose she wanted to be able to access it from anywhere in the event that she had to run or we stole her computer. She'd been through Reuben's files that he'd locked away. She'd made a duplicate set of keys. She claimed not to have killed him, though. But she was losing lucidity pretty fast by that point.'

'Has Sean got any leads on where Reuben and Jackson could be?'

'None,' Ken said. 'No credit card usage, no plane or bus tickets purchased or cars rented. He'll keep looking. He's checking all the aliases Reuben's used in the past.'

'And if Reuben's come up with a new alias that we don't know about?'

It was certainly possible. Ken had several that his team didn't know about. Just in case he had to run quickly. 'Then we hope he trusts Burton enough to contact him. I have the only uninjured member of Reuben's team following Burton.'

'To make sure he actually dumps Miriam in a motel room like you told him to?'

'Yes. They have history, Burton and Miriam. I'm not sure if it's because he knew her back when he and Reuben were with Knoxville PD, or if they've gotten cozy recently. But also so that Burton will have a way back. His next task is to search Reuben's car that I had towed.'

'We still sending someone up to New York to follow the girl Reuben was banging?'

'I don't think I will. We're running too thin in the security department. If he's on his way to see the girl, at least he'll be busy for a while and out of our business. If he's left the country, Sean has the best chance of tracking him. And if he's dead, then the problem is solved.'

'Idiot,' Demetrius muttered. 'Couldn't keep his dick zipped. What about the other two trackers that were disabled at the Anderses'?'

'The daughter claims to have done it, but I don't believe her. I'm about to go downstairs and give it another go. I'm not going to waste much more time on them. Especially now that we know that O'Bannion's cozied up to a homicide detective. Dealing with them is going to be the most important thing. Did you get the gun?'

'Yes. Anders's girl was shot with a Ruger P89.'

'I'll have Decker check Anders's gun cabinet while he's there, to see if it looks like anything of that caliber is either missing or has been recently fired.'

'He should look for the ammo. The Ruger was loaded with Black Talons.'

'Huh. You don't see BTs very often anymore except with collectors. Chip did have an extensive armory. Stands to reason he'd collect ammo too. Where did *you* find BTs?'

'In my collection. I bought 'em back in the nineties, when everyone thought they were armor-piercing cop-killers. But it wasn't true,' he added in a dejected tone that made Ken grin.

But Ken sobered abruptly as he was struck by a thought. 'Wait a minute. How did O'Bannion walk away from being shot at that range by hollow-point bullets?'

'He was wearing Kevlar,' Demetrius said.

Ken narrowed his eyes. 'Really? Sonofabitch went in prepared. He knew the girl was trouble. *How* did he know?'

'Does it matter? Once I kill him, he can't tell anyone else whatever it is that he knows.'

'He knew enough to track her to that alley. I told Decker to go into the office and listen to the audio feed from the girl's tracker after he's done checking out the Anders house, but knowing O'Bannion's out there with a cop, I don't want to wait that long. I'll have Sean get started on it right now. O'Bannion may have already told people what he knows.'

'Especially that brother of his,' Demetrius muttered. 'Goddamn trouble-maker.'

'No argument there. But even if he didn't tell his brother, he could have told Bishop.'

'I thought of that when I saw them together. So they both have to go?'

He sounded so hopeful that Ken chuckled. 'Yes, Demetrius. Both O'Bannion and Bishop have to go. The brother too, just in case. But you can't leave any bullets behind in any of the bodies.'

'Got it. So who *did* kill that girl in the alley? Anders?'

'No, I don't think Chip or Marlene knew she'd gotten out. They paid for her. I doubt they'd risk their investment. But the daughter – Stephanie – knows what happened.' Ken glanced at the security monitor. The eyes of all three Anderses were closed, exhaustion lining their faces. 'Looks like they're taking a nap. Time to wake them up and finish this.'

'I'll call you when I've taken care of O'Bannion. After that, his brother.'

'Stone,' Ken murmured, remembering all too well the newspaper headline with Stone O'Bannion's byline – *High school teacher found with kiddie porn stash*. He, Demetrius and Reuben had needed to do some fast cleanup, taking risks they never would have taken had the O'Bannion brothers not come so close. 'Make those O'Bannion boys hurt. A lot.'

'Don't worry,' Demetrius said quietly. 'I will.'

Cincinnati, Ohio
Tuesday 4 August, 12.15 P.M.

Delores Kaminsky was indeed a hugger, Marcus thought as he was dragged down into the petite woman's embrace. And she was far stronger than she looked. He patted her back awkwardly as she held on hard.

Finally she let go and rocked back on her heels to look up at him with a smile that made him smile back. 'It is very nice to meet you, Marcus.'

About thirty-five, she had china-blue eyes, porcelain skin and short blond curls. Standing no more than five feet tall, she resembled one of the antique dolls Audrey had collected as a girl. The enormous dog that had been watching him like a hawk since they'd approached curled up at her feet, apparently welcoming him as well.

'Likewise, Delores. I understand that I'm the last O'Bannion sibling to have the honor of meeting you.'

Her bright blue eyes twinkled. 'Well, we were both busy there for a few months, what with ICU and rehab. I'll forgive you this time. Besides, you're here now and you've brought my favorite homicide detective, so all is forgiven.' She leaned up on her toes to whisper loudly, 'But next time, kiss her, okay? I think it'd sweeten her up.'

From the corner of his eye he saw Scarlett's cheeks darkening from bright pink to an even brighter red. Marcus suspected his own cheeks were a bit red too. 'If I'd known that Stone brought you flowers and candy,' he said, 'I'd have brought you something even better. Purely in the spirit of sibling rivalry, of course.'

'Better than flowers and candy? How is that even possible?' She threw a grin in Scarlett's direction, undeterred when the detective scowled back. 'You're gonna have your hands full with this charmer, Scarlett.'

'I'd rather have my hands filled with evidence,' Scarlett said brusquely.

Delores laughed. 'Oh dear. Detective Bishop is giving us the I've-got-better-things-to-do-with-my-time look, so come on. I've got the video set up on my computer. Angel, with me,' she said, and the enormous dog was instantly at her side. 'Don't worry,' she added as an aside to Marcus as they started walking – very slowly – toward a room off the kitchen. 'Scarlett does that look when she really wants to laugh but doesn't want anyone to know.'

Marcus glanced over his shoulder at Scarlett, who trailed them with her arms folded tight over her chest. 'Is that true, Detective?'

Scarlett glared. 'No.'

Marcus turned back with a snort, following Delores into a room that, underneath all the empty dog cages and bags of kibble, was probably her office. 'Sorry,' she said, flicking her hand dismissively. 'I have enough energy to either take care of my animals or clean. It's obvious which one wins every day.' She pointed to the behemoth of a computer sitting on her desk. 'It's on the screen. All you have to do is push play.'

'Holy crap, Delores,' Scarlett exclaimed. 'How old is this PC?'

'I don't know. Four years, maybe five? I bought it used.'

Scarlett tentatively inspected the CRT monitor with its bulky rear section. 'Do you have some weird sentimental attachment to antiques?'

Delores's lips twitched. 'No, I have a sentimental attachment to my money. I can pay for a new computer or buy food for fifteen dogs for a month. The computer still works and that's the important thing. Now sit in the chair and watch the video.'

Scarlett met Marcus's eyes and pointed to the chair. 'You're the one who's seen the dog. You should watch it.'

He obeyed, dropping into the chair with a wince. The chair was far older than the computer system and very uncomfortable. Delores obviously ran her shelter on a shoestring budget. It made him wonder how much money Audrey had been able to raise and what Delores had done with it. He suspected his answer lay in the bags of dog food stacked floor to ceiling.

He jiggled the mouse, disrupting the dog and cat screen saver and revealing the video Delores had loaded. He hit PLAY, then stiffened when Scarlett leaned in to watch over his shoulder, the scent of wildflowers filling his head once again.

An outdoor ring filled the screen, empty except for a few people wearing ribbons, identifying them as judges. The camera panned the onlookers, gathered in groups around the ring's perimeter.

'Not what I was expecting,' Scarlett murmured. 'I thought they'd be in an arena with chairs, like on TV.'

'Those are national benched dog shows. This is a regular show,' Delores said. 'It was hosted by one of the local clubs in Indiana about two years ago.

215

When the shows are held close by like that, just about all the local show dogs enter. I went because one of my clients entered her standard, but that was a male, so not the dog you're looking for. If the dog you're looking for is local and young, there's a decent possibility that it was entered. It's definitely show quality.'

'You started this midway through the video,' Marcus said. 'Why?'

'Because all the stuff leading up to it is categories you don't care about, puppies and younger dogs. Okay, so here they come. There are twelve dogs in this class. Each one will take a turn around the ring, so you can watch it. You're looking for a white female with a continental clip – that's the most common one, with the rosettes on the hips. But you're lucky because four of the females are either black or cream-colored and three of the dogs are male.'

Marcus blocked Scarlett out of his head, focusing solely on the dogs in the ring. He immediately eliminated two of the females as being too big. The remaining three he watched running around the ring many times before slowly eliminating one of the others, leaving two.

He looked over his shoulder in time to see Scarlett straightening so that they didn't bump noses. 'I can't tell the difference between these two dogs,' he said, 'but they're both close to the dog I saw in the park.'

'Numbers 121 and 130,' Delores said. 'I don't remember them, but we can check their names and owners. Forward the video to twenty-one minutes, ten seconds,' she instructed.

Marcus paused the video on the image of a booklet opened to pages listing all the dogs in the category, with their American Kennel Club names and owners.

'You videoed the entries list,' he said approvingly. 'Very smart.'

'Not so much,' Delores chuckled. 'I was never organized, even before . . . well, you know. I photographed the page after each class was shown because I knew I'd lose the program. But we can get the owners' names from here. Past this, you two are on your own.'

Scarlett placed a hand on his shoulder, leaning closer to the screen. 'Can you blow it up a little, Marcus? I can't read the font.'

Marcus did so, then sighed. 'Number 121's owners live in Chicago.'

On the next page, however, they hit pay dirt, and Scarlett hummed deep in her throat, a satisfied growl. 'But number 130's owner is Ms Marlene Anders, Cincinnati, Ohio, and the dog's name is Coco.'

'Bingo,' Marcus said grimly, then pushed back from the desk. 'Can we take the video file with us, Delores?'

'Sure. We can copy it to a flash drive.' Delores opened a drawer and pawed through the junk inside until she found a drive, then handed it to Marcus. 'Go for it.'

While Marcus copied the file, Scarlett called someone on her team to run a background check on Marlene Anders. When he was finished, Marcus rose from the chair and stooped down to hug Delores before she could hug him first. 'Thank you,' he whispered fiercely.

She hugged him back hard. 'You're welcome.' She let him rise, but didn't let him go, fisting a small hand in the fabric of his shirt. 'I don't know why you need this dog's owner. But you look like you're taking this very personally.'

He felt like he owed her an answer. 'I am.'

'Why?' she pressed.

Marcus glanced at Scarlett and she shook her head.

'You don't need to know that, Delores,' she murmured. 'Trust me?'

Delores turned her head so that she met Scarlett's eyes, her nod nearly imperceptible. Then she looked back up at Marcus, startling the hell out of him with her next words. 'If this is about atonement, you don't have anything to atone for in all that mess nine months ago. You were as much a victim as I was.'

He blinked at her. *What the fuck?* 'Excuse me?'

'You are riddled with guilt, Marcus O'Bannion. It's coming off you in waves.'

Marcus glanced over at Scarlett again, a rebuke on the tip of his tongue until he saw that she was as surprised as he was.

Delores pushed on before either of them could say a word. 'Detective Bishop has shared nothing with me about you. I don't know anything other than that you lost your brother, Mikhail, and that you have a sister and a brother who also feel a helluva lot of survivor guilt.'

He opened his mouth to speak, but she gently patted his shoulder. 'You do realize that they make bulletproof vests lighter than the one you're wearing under this heavy shirt? I could feel it when I hugged you.'

He blinked again at her abrupt subject change. 'Yes, ma'am. But my lighter one got a little . . . used this morning.'

Her smile faded. 'I see. Well it seems you live your life very dangerously, Marcus. I was hoping you'd be a safer kind of guy so that Scarlett could relax when she wasn't on the clock.'

He didn't even have to glance at Scarlett to know her cheeks had flamed again. 'I'll take care of her,' he promised Delores quietly. 'And I'll think about what you said.'

'Thank you,' she replied, then turned to envelop Scarlett in an equally huge hug. 'He's a handsome devil,' she stage-whispered. 'If you decide you don't want him . . .'

'You . . .' Scarlett's mouth worked helplessly much as Marcus's had, but she finally gave up trying to find the words and laughed. 'I have no comebacks. I am zinger-less.'

'I know,' Delores said, a satisfied grin lighting up her face, making her look like a leprechaun who'd found the pot of gold. 'It's my special gift.' She started hustling them to the door. 'I have to start the noon feedings now or I won't be done till dinnertime. Next time you come, you need to bring Zat with you for a visit. Give him a kiss and this from me.' From the pocket of her smock she pulled a plastic bag printed with dog bones and filled with treats.

'Thank you. I will.' Scarlett glanced over her shoulder at Marcus. 'He has a dog too. She might also like some treats.'

'Oh, I knew I liked him for a reason. He's a dog person.' Delores fished another bag of treats from her pocket and gave them to Scarlett. 'You can kiss his dog for me too. But first you should kiss him. I felt really bad about interrupting you two out front earlier. Besides, Faith and Dani will never believe me without a photo. If you kiss him, I'll just snap a fast one. Very discreet.'

Marcus wisely swallowed his snicker, because Scarlett was giving Delores an irritated glare, her face having lost all traces of humor. 'Do you ever stop?' she snapped.

Delores blinked, the picture of wide-eyed innocence. 'No. I'm like a shark.' She bared her teeth, causing Scarlett to roll her eyes.

'Shark, my ass,' Scarlett muttered. 'More like a clownfish.'

Delores's eyes flickered with a hint of hurt. 'You're probably right at that.'

'Delores means,' Marcus said with gentle reproach, 'that if she stops, she dies.'

Delores met his eyes with a small, secret smile, and Scarlett instantly grew remorseful.

'I'm sorry, Delores. I seem to have a case of foot-in-mouth.'

Delores patted Scarlett's arm, then opened the front door. 'Don't worry. It's not fatal. Besides, I know I come on a bit strong. I keep forgetting that even though you hang out with Dani and Faith, you're not them.'

'They are a lot more fun than I am,' Scarlett agreed easily.

Too easily, Marcus thought, and that made him a little angry. He didn't like the way Scarlett seemed to discount herself.

'But,' Scarlett added, 'the thing about sharks dying if they stop swimming isn't entirely true. There are a few sharks that are capable of breathing even while they're still. Nurse sharks for one.' She lifted his brows. 'Bullheads are another. I'd say both are appropriate descriptors for you, Delores.'

Delores stared for a moment, then threw back her head and laughed. 'Well played, Scarlett. Well played. *That* was a comeback.'

Scarlett grinned, pleased. 'Now I'll say goodbye while my foot is still out of my mouth. Thank you, Delores. I appreciate your help.' She leaned forward. 'No one will know where this video came from, so don't worry about any reprisals from the person we're looking for.'

'I won't.' The huge dog at her side, Delores stood on her porch, waving as they turned around and headed back the way they'd come.

Cincinnati, Ohio
Tuesday 4 August, 12.45 P.M.

Ken paused at the foot of the basement stairs when his cell phone rang. He considered ignoring it, eager to get back to his session with the Anderses, but the caller ID said it was Decker.

'Who was in the house?' he asked.

'I don't know, sir. We have a problem. Someone must have called the cops, because there are at least a half-dozen cruisers in front of the house, along with a few unmarked cars and a CSU van. What do you want me to do?'

Ken's exhale was an infuriated hiss. 'Back off. It's all you can do now. I'll contact Sean and have him find out what's going on there. You go to the office and listen to those audio files. I'll get the Anderses to tell me what – or who – they're hiding.'

He slowly put away his cell phone, staring coldly at Chip Anders's overturned chair. The man was asleep. Snoring! That ended abruptly when Ken grabbed him, chair and all, and set him upright, slamming all four legs of the chair to the floor.

'Wh-wh-what?' Chip stammered, his eyes now open and glazed over.

'Don't hurt him!' Stephanie cried, then whimpered when Ken grabbed a handful of her hair and yanked. 'Stop. Please stop.'

'You shut up if you want to stay alive,' Ken warned, then let her go and slapped Chip across the face, hard enough to hurt but not enough to knock him over again. 'You fucking idiot. Your little Rambo act brought the cops to your house.'

Marlene's eyes flew open. Still the only one gagged, she shot daggers with her eyes.

'Cops?' Chip whispered. 'At my house?'

'Yeah. What're they going to find there? Drugs? Porn? Illegal firearms? That person who will tell that you were taken? Will they find any connection to me?'

Chip said nothing, just closed his eyes. New fury bubbled up into Ken's throat. 'Fine. If that's the way you want to play it . . .' He took a short, sharp blade from his cart and moved behind Marlene, grabbing a handful of her hair and yanking her head back against him, exposing the curve of her throat. He removed the noose he'd placed around her neck and tossed it aside before positioning the tip of the blade beneath Marlene's ear. 'Open your eyes, Chip. Time to say bye-bye to your wife.'

Chip's eyes flew open in alarm – just in time to see the blood spurting from his wife's throat. The first spray hit him in the face, the second on his shoulder. Chip screamed like a woman as the third pulse simply flowed down the front of Marlene's no-longer-expensive silk blouse.

'*You freak!*' Chip shouted. 'You *motherfucker!*' A horrified sob rattled his chest. 'You *killed* her! You killed her.' He quickly lost steam, whispering, 'Goddamn you.'

Ignoring him, Ken turned Marlene's chair so that Stephanie could see. Predictably, the girl's eyes were clenched shut. Her face was sheet white, her whole body trembling.

'Come on, Stephanie,' Ken said cajolingly. 'See Mama's big new grin.'

Stephanie turned her head away from her mother and vomited. A tiny bit hit the floor. Most of it hit her shirt, smelling vile. Ken had never been able to stand the smell of vomit.

He left Marlene there, the blood seeping slowly now. Gripping the edges of Stephanie's blouse front with his – thankfully – still gloved hands, he ripped it apart, sending buttons flying. He cut it from her shoulders, leaving her wearing only a tiny lacy bra that covered next to nothing. He dropped the blouse in the trashcan, tied the bag shut, then stripped his gloves off and laid them on top of the tied bag.

He went to the sink behind the bar and washed his hands, returning with a can of air freshener and a chair of his own. He sprayed the air, then turned the chair backwards and straddled it, folding his arms across the back of the chair calmly.

'See, here's the thing, Chip. You fucked with me. You have caused me a lot of trouble today. You have exposed me to the authorities.'

'No,' Chip gasped. 'I didn't. I swear I didn't.'

Ken casually brushed a piece of lint from the lapel of his suit. 'I really don't care who did it. The point remains is that it was done. As the head of your family, you should have kept better track of your wife and daughter.'

Stephanie was hyperventilating and shivering. She still hadn't opened her eyes.

'Now,' Ken continued, 'there is no way you're leaving here alive, Chip. No way. So put the thought out of your mind. You can, however, make your daughter's life a little easier.'

Chip's breaths were fast and shallow, his wife's blood dripping down his face. 'You'll let her go?'

Ken threw back his head and laughed. 'Good one, Chip.' Then he sobered. 'Not a fucking chance. But I won't kill her.'

'You'll sell her. Like one of your whores.'

'You should know. You bought enough of 'em.' Ken shrugged. 'I can make this hard or I can make it easy. Frankly, my business partner wants you to defy me. It means he'll get to test-drive your daughter before I put her on the block. If that's the case, I'll make sure you have a front-row seat. My partner is not a nice man.'

Chip swallowed hard. 'You piece of shit.'

Ken tsked. 'That is inflammatory, pejorative language, Chip. And quite trashy, too. Really, I expected something a little more elegant from you. But I suppose I can see your point of view. What's it gonna be? You talk to me, or I let my partner have your daughter?'

Chip's eyes burned with helpless hate. 'You sick son—'

'Consider your answer carefully,' Ken interrupted. 'I have three men that were injured bringing you in. I'm sure they'd like some kind of compensation too. So tell me what I want to know. How did the girl get out this morning?'

'I don't know,' Chip said through gritted teeth, his face now florid. 'Stephanie said she took her out.'

'Why?'

'*I don't know!*' Chip shouted. '*I don't know!*'

'Stephanie?' Ken prompted. 'You can help yourself here. Why would you take your father's property out to play?'

'Because I needed her,' Stephanie said coldly, her face still turned away.

'Okay, now we're getting somewhere. Say more,' Ken directed pleasantly.

'She bought coke for me.'

Chip's eyes widened. 'You said you weren't using anymore.'

'I lied,' Stephanie spat. 'So punish me, *Daddy*. Bastard,' she added in a mutter. 'You *had* to bring her into our house. You *had* to sleep with her. This is *your* fault. *You* caused this.'

'I did it for you,' Chip tossed back furiously. 'I bought them for you and for your mother.'

'And look where it got *Mother*.' Stephanie's face scrunched up as she squeezed her eyes more tightly shut. 'Fuck you, *Daddy*. Just . . . fuck you.'

'So charming,' Ken said lightly. 'You're finally communicating with each other. Now try communicating with me. I take it, Stephanie, that last night's drug run wasn't an isolated event.'

'No,' Stephanie said shortly.

'Why take the risk?' he asked, genuinely curious.

'Because if I got caught again, I'd get kicked out of school and lose my allowance.'

Ken actually believed that. 'But why take the girl? If she was caught, she'd lead the police back to your house.'

'She never got caught. Not until last night.'

'Who killed her, Stephanie? Did you?'

'No.'

'Then who?'

'I don't know,' the girl said sullenly. 'Some piece of trash that wanted the cash I gave her to buy the coke, I guess. I don't know.'

'Oh I think you do, Stephanie.' Ken stood up, took off his suit coat and hung it on a nearby hook, casually inspecting it for bloodstains, finding a few. Luckily Alice was a wizard at getting blood out of fabric. He folded his shirtsleeves to the middle of his forearms, glancing over to find Stephanie watching him, her expression wildly desperate.

'What are you going to do?' she whispered.

'Well I need answers and you've been uncooperative. I know ways to make you very uncomfortable without leaving a single mark.'

'I've told you the truth.'

'No, dear. You have not.' He started to pull on a pair of latex gloves, but hesitated. 'You don't have a latex allergy, do you?'

'No,' she said numbly. 'What? Why?'

'Because I don't want you to break out in hives. It's really unattractive.' He finished pulling on the gloves, then stood behind her, feeling her shaking with fear. *A good start.*

'Don't kill me,' she whispered hoarsely. 'Please.'

'Get your filthy hands off her,' Chip growled.

Ken smiled at him. 'Sorry, Chip. But you're welcome to watch.' He stood behind her and covered her mouth with one hand, pinching her nose closed with the other. And then he waited until she started to thrash. He waited another twenty seconds, then released her.

Stephanie sucked in air in rasping gulps. 'Oh God, oh God, oh God,' she panted.

He let her get her breath back, then leaned down to murmur in her ear. 'Who shot the girl, Stephanie?'

She said nothing, and he had to admire her spirit. When the bidders saw the video he was recording, at this moment, her price would skyrocket. 'One more time.' He repeated the suffocation, satisfied when she started to whimper against his hand. He released her and let her gulp in a breath before he covered her nose and mouth a third time. 'Tell me, Stephanie. Nod if you plan to tell me. Don't fuck with me, my dear. That will make me angry, and you won't like me angry. Who killed the girl? Was it you?'

She shook her head wildly.

'Are you ready to tell me who it was?' She nodded, and he released her but kept her nose pinched. 'Who, Stephanie?'

'Drake.' She was heaving in air. 'It was Drake.'

Ken was actually surprised. He stepped back and restraddled his chair. 'Drake who?'

'Sonofabitch,' Chip spat. 'I should have known that trailer trash was behind this.'

Ken glanced at Chip, then back at Stephanie, who was shaking like she had the palsy, the after-effect of her near-suffocation. 'Who is Drake?' he asked, enunciating each word.

'My boyfriend,' Stephanie said, still gasping for air. 'Drake Connor. He killed her.'

'Why?'

'Because she was talking to a man.'

'A man, huh? Sounds like Drake came prepared.' Ken glanced at Chip again. 'He shot the girl with a Ruger loaded with BTs.'

Chip's face grew even redder.

'He stole your gun?' Ken guessed.

'I'll kill him,' Chip said quietly, not answering the question. But then he didn't have to. His expression said it all.

'No you won't, but don't worry. I'll kill him for you. Where is he, Stephanie dear?'

'I don't know. I haven't seen him since this morning. Not since we came back from downtown.'

'What does he drive?' Ken asked.

'He doesn't have a car. We always used mine.'

'We'll track him down,' Ken said, hoping that was true. Because he knew that if Drake was smart, he had already hightailed it out of town and had a three-hour head start by now, at least. 'What was Drake's role in all this?'

Stephanie shot a baleful glance at her father, paling when she looked down and saw her mother's body. 'Oh God,' she whimpered. 'Mama.'

'Your mama's worm food,' Ken said flatly. 'If you don't want the same thing to happen to you, you'll talk to me, Stephanie. Why was Drake with you this morning? Why did he bring your father's gun in the first place?'

'It was a bad part of town,' she blurted out. 'We were buying drugs. We did them together. When Tala didn't come right back, he got upset.'

Upset. That was an interesting word choice. 'You said he shot her because she was talking to a man. Who was the man? A cop?'

'He didn't think so. He thought the guy was someone trying to . . . buy Tala. Her services.'

'Your boyfriend thought this mysterious guy was a john?' That was rich. 'But why not just tell the guy to fuck off? Why shoot them both? That doesn't make sense, Stephanie.'

She bit her lip, and Ken could see the wheels turning as she tried to think of an answer to his question.

'You might try the truth,' he suggested mildly. 'Just a thought.'

'He was . . .' Stephanie closed her eyes. 'He was jealous.'

'Really? Still not making sense, Stephanie.'

She blew out a helpless breath. 'He thought she'd been sneaking off to meet the man. He thought they were . . . lovers. Drake got jealous because Tala was . . . his.'

'She was fucking not his,' Chip ground out.

'Tala,' Ken said. 'That was the girl's name? How was she Drake's?'

Stephanie's chin had come up at her father's declaration. 'He'd been fucking her for a while. She was his toy.'

Chip's eyes narrowed and his nostrils flared. 'You ungrateful, spiteful little bitch.'

Ken cocked a brow. *Interesting.* 'Didn't it bother you that he was fucking the servant? He was *your* boyfriend.'

Eyes narrowing, Stephanie gave her father a satisfied sneer. 'I was fucking her too. We did her together.'

'I see,' Ken murmured. And he really was starting to. Chip was breathing hard, fury evident in every charged line of his body. That Stephanie and Drake had fucked his servant was not welcome news. No, not at all. 'Why did you look at your father like that?'

'Like what?' Stephanie asked harshly.

'Like you're thumbing it in his face.'

'Because he wanted to keep her for himself,' Stephanie spat. 'He *loved* her.'

This was getting more interesting by the moment. 'By loved, you mean exactly what?'

'He had a baby with her,' Stephanie said bitterly. 'My daughter this and my daughter that. You'd think it was some kind of rocket scientist instead of a half-breed. Little brat cried all the damn time. I think Tala pinched it to make it cry, just so Mama would hear it.' She kept her chin high, her gaze resolutely away from her mother's body. 'Flaunting the little bastard in Mama's face.'

Ken rose, his heart grown grimly cold. 'We didn't find a baby.'

'Because *she* took it,' Stephanie said.

'You mean Tala?' Ken asked, and Stephanie shook her head with a cold smile. 'The other two escaped women?' he pressed.

Stephanie's smile curled at the edges of her mouth, becoming predatory. 'You wish.'

Cincinnati, Ohio
Tuesday 4 August, 12.45 P.M.

When they were out of sight of the house, both Marcus and Scarlett took their cell phones from their pockets. She placed hers on the dash of her car, put an earbud in her left ear, then used her hands-free to call Deacon Novak.

Marcus logged into the website he used for background searches and inputted *Marlene Anders*. Just in case Scarlett decided not to share everything she learned.

'Hey, Deacon, it's me. Did you get my text?' She listened for a moment, then nodded. 'Got it. Don't wait for me, but don't go in without backup.' She made an impatient sound. 'I know we don't have a warrant. I thought you'd do your thing with the judge. You know, give 'em the eye . . . She is? Good. Lynda can push harder for a warrant than we can. She has more markers to call in, too. I'll meet you there as soon as I can.' She glanced at Marcus. 'Go ahead and send it, but I have Marcus with me. I'm sure he's already run a background on Anders in the time it's taken us to get to the end of Delores's driveway. I'll get the info from him. Suit up, Novak. They've already shot two people today.' She stopped at the end of Delores's long driveway and pulled the earbud out. 'Deacon's sitting out front of the

Anderses' house. Can you hand me the flasher? It's in the glove box.'

Marcus put the blue flashing light in her outstretched hand and watched as she fixed it to the roof of the car. 'Hold on tight,' she said as she floored the accelerator.

'You all need to have turbo engines,' Marcus said, although he was more than a little surprised that the department vehicle had as much pickup as it did.

'We need a lot of things,' she said glumly. 'Like a warrant, for starters.'

'That's what you wanted Deacon to get by giving someone the eye?'

She shot him a quick glare. 'Hey, jack, don't knock it. It's worked before.'

'Really? That's quite a secret weapon.'

'You have no idea.'

'Will he go in without a warrant?'

'Deacon?' She seemed genuinely surprised. 'Probably not. He's a straight shooter.'

Marcus settled into his seat. She was driving faster than he'd anticipated even with the flashing light, but she was in control of the vehicle so he could relax a little. 'Would you?'

'Enter without a warrant?' She made a facial shrug. 'It's possible, I suppose. I've been known to bend the rules from time to time.'

'Like trespassing on private property and listening at closed doors to private conversations?' he asked, only half teasing.

She didn't break a smile. 'I don't know who would do anything that boorish.'

His lips twitched. He didn't care if she wasn't as much fun as her friends. He liked her sarcastic sense of humor. 'So terribly rude.'

One side of her mouth quirked up, then fell again. 'Part of me wishes that Deacon could wait for me,' she confessed, 'but that's not the best thing for the victims.'

Her use of 'for me' was like nails on a chalkboard, but he didn't fight it because he wanted what was best for the victims too. 'Especially the baby. She's gotta be hungry by now.'

'Since her mama's dead in the morgue,' Scarlett said grimly, then cast him a cautious sideways glance. 'You know I can't let you go in with me.'

He shrugged. 'I'll get the story one way or the other.'

She was quiet for a long moment, the only sound that of her tires as they ate up the interstate. 'You're not what I expected, Marcus.'

He turned in his seat to study her profile. 'How so?'

She kept her eyes on the road. 'You say you make your living digging up news. This is a big story. I thought you'd be on your phone to your office, having them send a reporter with a camera to the address that I know you've already looked up.'

'How do you know I didn't contact my office? I could have texted them.'

'But you didn't, did you?'

'No,' he said, and watched her shoulders relax a fraction. She'd been bluffing him, he thought, admiring the effort. But she'd really been hoping that he'd say no.

'Why not?' she asked. 'Some other reporter with a police radio could follow Deacon and his backup to the Anders house and scoop your story.'

'They wouldn't have all the background,' he said, 'so I still have the exclusive. But sometimes it's not about the story. Sometimes it's about doing the right thing.'

A single nod. 'I expected you to say that this morning when I asked you why you came back to the alley, but you didn't. You said that you couldn't leave her alone in the dark. Why?'

He'd known she was perceptive. He should have expected that she'd pick up on that nuance. 'Scarlett,' he drawled, 'sometimes a cigar is just a cigar.'

'Okay,' she said with a shrug. 'Don't tell me. I understand the need to keep some things to yourself. Tell me about Marlene Anders instead.'

Fifteen

Scarlett cleared all thoughts of cigars being cigars from her mind, focusing on the information Marcus was reading to her from the background check he'd run while she'd been coordinating the search of the Anders home with Deacon.

'Marlene Anders is a fifty-two-year-old Caucasian,' Marcus said. 'Married Charles "Chip" Anders when she was twenty-one. She worked as a dental hygienist for ten years, quitting the same year that she gave birth. Her daughter is Stephanie Anders. Marlene has no work history in the years that followed. I see links to about thirty articles, all in the Style section of various newspapers.'

'What about Chip?'

From the corner of her eye she could see him typing on his phone with his finger. 'Chip Anders got an engineering degree from Xavier and went to work in the family-owned snack-food business.' He was quiet for a few minutes. 'The state business database says that the company declared bankruptcy ten years ago. The same year Chip is listed as incorporating a contract manufacturing company. It's privately owned, so we can't see the earnings report, but two years later his and Marlene's address changed from Bridgetown Road to a three-million-dollar place in Hyde Park, less than a quarter-mile from the park where Tala walked their dog.'

Scarlett whistled softly. 'Wow.' Those homes were like something out of a dream. Of course, the fact that Marcus's apartment was in the same neighborhood had not escaped her notice. But then she'd always known he was wealthy. His mother's house was a fricking estate, for God's sake. *My whole house would fit into her foyer*, she thought, then shoved it aside. She loved her house on top of one of the highest hills in the city. And she'd paid for it herself.

None of which was important right now. Finding Tala's baby was

228

critical. She crossed her fingers that the Anderses were the people they were looking for. 'I didn't know the contract manufacturing business was so lucrative.'

'Depends on what they were manufacturing, and for whom. Now this is the interesting part. His business is listed as going from five hundred employees to under a hundred about seven years ago. Seems like it took a downward turn.'

'Lots of businesses did. That's when everything crashed. And poor Chip and Marlene with that new mortgage. Hard times.'

'Exactly. And then,' he said, 'a year later, Chip opened three new facilities, in different parts of the state. None of the locations have more than a hundred employees.'

'But he's churning out enough of whatever it is he's making with a few hundred employees to expand even bigger than he was when he had five hundred. You're thinking he had a little labor help?'

'Yeah.'

Scarlett nodded, considering the picture. 'Me too. But now I've got a few holes to fill.'

Marcus put his phone down, giving her his undivided attention. 'Hit me.'

Her lips curved briefly, but then she was frowning again as the thoughts swirled in her brain. 'Deacon and I wondered how Tala got to the alley. If she lived near the park, which now seems more than likely, it's four and a half miles to the alley. She didn't look hot and sweaty enough in the video to have walked that far in the heat.'

'I wondered the same thing.' His voice hardened. 'I didn't have a chance to ask her.'

'I know,' she said gently, not taking his tone personally. 'At first I thought maybe she lived closer to the alley. That she was transported to the park by a handler. That maybe he or she was watching as she walked the dog. I was thinking that was why her owners felt comfortable enough to allow her the freedom to walk the dog all by herself, because even at night she might meet someone. And then we found out about the tracker. And the baby.'

'The baby was reason enough for her to obey them,' Marcus said. 'Knowing that they could hear her through the tracker was just another layer of intimidation. They didn't need to be watching her so closely. Yeah, I've been thinking the same thing. Now that it's more likely that she lived right near the park, we have to ask the question again – how did she get to the alley? And why did she choose *that* alley?'

Because she was there to buy drugs, Scarlett thought, considering the wisdom of sharing that opinion with him. But she'd told him nearly everything else. 'CSU found a bag of cocaine in her pocket.'

She felt his shock. 'Tala was an addict?' he asked. 'She didn't have any of the signs.'

She wondered how he knew what the signs were, but kept the question to herself. 'The ME found no cocaine in her system and no signs of drug use. No thinning nasal membranes and no track marks.'

'Then maybe she was buying it for someone else. Maybe she was on an errand. Wait a second.' He did another search on his phone. 'Stephanie Anders has an arrest record. One misdemeanor possession of pot, one for coke. No convictions.'

'Money talks.' She glanced at him. 'No offense.'

'None taken. So Miss Stephanie wants some snow, and she sends Tala into the neighborhood with cash. Tala scores, and then ducks into an alley to wait for me.'

'Maybe she used Stephanie Anders's cell phone to text you.' She put her own phone on speaker again and called Deacon. 'Hey, it's me.'

'Hey, you. Lynda doesn't have a warrant yet and nobody's answering the door. The house is fucking huge, so saying we don't hear anything inside is virtually meaningless. At least we haven't attracted too much of a crowd so far, but the SWAT team hasn't arrived yet.'

'Small mercies,' Scarlett murmured. 'Listen, when you do get in, check the daughter's room for drug paraphernalia. Stephanie is . . . Wait. Marcus, how old is she?'

'Twenty. Goes to Brown University.'

'I heard him,' Deacon said. 'So you think the cocaine in Tala's pocket belonged to Stephanie?'

'It's possible.' She told Deacon the rest of the details that Marcus had uncovered. 'I'm about ten minutes out from you. We should get Lynda to use what I just gave you to sweeten the warrant pot.'

'I'll call her,' Deacon said. 'See you soon.'

Cincinnati, Ohio
Tuesday 4 August, 1.25 P.M.

'Dammit,' Scarlett muttered as she turned the car on to the Anderses' street.

Marcus sighed. It seemed like half of CPD had gathered there ahead of them. At the head of the line of cars stood Deacon Novak, arms folded across his chest, jaw taut, his eyes covered by the wraparound shades that had become his trademark. 'Doesn't look like Deacon got the warrant from your boss.'

'He would have called if he had,' she said, stopping the car at the tail end of the line. 'But I was still hoping.' She turned to him, her expression severe. 'Please don't do anything that'll force me to call in favors to bail you out of jail.'

He blinked at her innocently. 'I am a law-abiding citizen, Detective.'

Uncertainty flickered in her eyes. She didn't disbelieve him, he could see. But she wasn't entirely sure of him either. 'Keep it that way,' she murmured. 'Please.'

She hadn't told him to stay in the car. Just not to get caught. So he nodded. 'I'd prefer to call in a few of your favors for something much more pleasurable than bailing me out of jail,' he said quietly. And very, very seriously.

She sucked in a sharp breath, the uncertainty in her eyes flashing to an arousal she immediately shuttered away. 'I'll be back as soon as I can.'

He took a few moments to admire the movement of her long, lean body as she jogged up the line of cars toward her partner. She was . . .

Mine. She's mine.

And she had been from the moment he'd opened his eyes to see her leaning over him as he lay bleeding . . . and dying. He'd been ready to die that day, hadn't truly minded the idea – not until he'd seen her staring down at him. What he'd seen in her dark, dark eyes, which he now knew were the deepest blue he'd ever seen, had called him back. Had filled him with a sudden craving to fight for another day.

It still did. Enough that he should keep his damn ass in her department car and let her do her job. But that wasn't who he was. He owed it to Tala to find her child. He owed it to himself, too, knowing he wouldn't be able to look in the mirror if he sat here and did nothing when he might have an entrée that the cops didn't have.

Sitting here was not the right thing to do, plain and simple.

Taking a plain black ball cap out of his computer bag, he settled it on his head and activated the camera in the bill. He then got out of Scarlett's car quietly, walking in the direction opposite from the Anders house until he reached the line of trees that bordered their property, shielding the house from the road. He made his way through the trees, staying in the shadows.

The basement wall was fully visible at the back of the house, which was built into the valley between two hills. Perfectly centered was a solid, non-windowed door covered by a storm door. Both doors opened level with the ground. There was no cover along the back of the house. No trees or bushes to hide behind. The back yard ran flat for the first hundred feet, before the property sloped back up toward the main road.

He glanced up the hill and saw the unmarked car parked on the other side of the treeline. Of course Deacon would have someone watching the back to prevent the Anderses from making a break for it. Or to aid any of Tala's surviving family who managed to escape. Marcus knew that as soon as he showed himself, the cop in that unmarked would be on his ass, keeping him from trying to gain entry.

Sending up a little prayer, he darted along the basement wall, reaching the back door without interruption, which made him frown and glance over his shoulder at the unmarked car. Nothing. No shouts, no demands for him to stop. Nothing.

Pulling the storm door open, he raised his fist to knock on the entry door, then froze when the storm door literally fell away from the frame. *Shit.* It was now precariously balanced, one corner dug into the dirt, the opposite corner resting against the house, most of its weight supported by Marcus's hold on the handle.

The frame itself was splintered, with both sets of hinges – those of the storm door and the entry door – no longer attached. This was no accident. Someone had broken in and then put the doors back in place so that their forced entry wouldn't be immediately visible.

One little shove and the entry door would be on the floor. Marcus had reached for his phone to text Scarlett to come and see when the detective in question rounded the corner, her annoyance evident in the look on her face and the stiffness of her stride. She was wearing a tactical vest, her service weapon tucked into the built-in holster.

She stopped inches from where he stood. 'What the hell are you doing?' she hissed.

'I was about to knock on the back door,' he said calmly. 'You knew I would.'

'Yeah, but I thought you'd be more discreet about how you did it. Every cop up there saw you come back here.' She narrowed her eyes at the storm door, her attitude abruptly changing as she took in the damage. 'Shit. I need CSU.' She pulled out her phone and dialed. 'Deacon, send Vince down here. The back door's been—'

The door frame exploded, sharp shards of wood showering down on their heads, and Marcus's military training kicked into gear.

Sniper. On the hill behind us. Suddenly the lack of activity from the unmarked car made grim sense. *Shit. No cover here.* They were sitting ducks, standing in the open. Not a single tree they could hide behind. The only cover was inside the house.

He grabbed Scarlett around the waist, hunkered down and shoved his shoulder into the basement door a split second after a second bullet hit the door, inches from where his head had just been.

The hingeless door gave way, and he and Scarlett followed it down, their bodies slamming against it hard as it hit the floor. Marcus rolled them out of the now open doorway as a third bullet hit the floor directly behind them. Concrete shattered, sharp debris pelting his head and back like mini-daggers.

Breathing hard, his body hovering over hers in a protective shell, Marcus lifted his head. The light coming in through the open door had illuminated a section of the basement floor and inner wall. The concrete was a mess, the bullet having hit the floor an inch beyond where the door had come to rest. The shooter had changed his aim as they'd fallen, following their trajectory.

Had Marcus not rolled them out of the way, the bullet would have hit one of them for sure. He looked down at Scarlett's face, relieved to see her alert and aware, her pistol firmly gripped in her right hand. She must have drawn her weapon while they were falling. While a small part of his ego wished she'd trembled and clutched at him just a little, the larger part of him was relieved that she remained cool under fire. She needed that cool to stay alive on a day-to-day basis.

'Are you all right?' he asked quietly.

'Yeah. Just knocked the wind out of me. Are you?'

He nodded once. His head hurt, but it was nothing worse than he'd had before. She twisted in his arms, craning back to study the concrete, then following the trajectory with her eyes. She swallowed hard.

'Damn. We'd have been toast.' She looked up at him, her expression grim even as her eyes filled with approval. 'Fast moves, O'Bannion. Army training?'

'Yeah.' He knew he should get up, but now that they were safe, his adrenaline had plunged, his muscles turning to jelly. His body sagged against her, his hips settling between her thighs. He braced himself on his forearms and lowered his forehead to hers. 'Give me a second.'

She brushed the backs of her fingers against his cheek, a gentle caress. 'We're both okay,' she said softly, making him shudder at the thought of what might have been. 'You did good, Marcus. We're alive.'

He nodded, realizing that he was finally holding her the way he'd been longing to for months, her lips only a breath away. Except he hadn't wanted it like this. Hadn't wanted her in danger. 'You could have been killed.'

She pressed her fingertips to his lips. *'You* could have been killed,' she whispered fiercely. 'He was aiming high. For you, Marcus.' Her eyes roved his face in the semi-darkness, her lips bending in a frown as her fingers lifted to his temple. 'You're bleeding.'

His gaze dropped to her mouth. He wanted nothing more than to kiss the frown off her lips, but knew that once he started, he wouldn't be able to stop. And he didn't want to have to stop, but this was utterly the wrong time and place. 'A chip of concrete, I think. I'm fine.'

'We need to get you checked out,' she said stubbornly, but then her lips trembled. '*I* need to get you checked out. Please,' she added in a whisper.

He wanted to outright refuse, because he hated hospitals, but that slight tremble had gone straight to his gut and the whispered *please* had stripped his defenses bare. 'Later, okay?'

Her throat worked as she tried to swallow. 'Promise me.'

He nodded, not trusting his voice. He no longer trusted his body either, as it had gotten over its scare and was no longer jelly. Far from it. He was growing harder with every second he lay cradled between her thighs. He cleared his throat. 'I need to get up. See if he's still there.'

She shook her head. 'Let me call Deacon first. Get him to check while we both stay clear of the door.' She looked around her, frowning again. 'I dropped my phone when we went through the door. Do you see it?'

'No. Use mine.' He forced his body to stand, ignoring the stiffness in his knees and back. And in his groin. Because this was neither the time nor the place to make all those fantasies reality. That would have to happen later. *But not too much later.*

He offered her a hand, gripping hers harder than he needed to as he tugged her to her feet. Releasing her was one of the hardest things he'd ever done. He gave her his phone. 'Tell him to check out the unmarked car at the top of the hill. The cop inside was too quiet.'

Understanding filled her eyes. 'Shit,' she murmured as she dialed. 'We're okay. We're in the house,' she said without preamble, then proceeded to tell Deacon what had happened.

Marcus blocked out her conversation with Deacon, instead listening intently for the sound of anyone approaching. The shooter had almost gotten them – three times. The guy wasn't likely to give up so easily.

His ears pricked at a faint noise. But it hadn't come from outside. It had come from the basement, to his right. He caught Scarlett's eye and tilted his head in the direction of the sound.

'Gotta go,' she murmured. 'Hurry, Deacon.' She handed Marcus his phone and took a small penlight from the pocket of her vest. 'Where?' she asked, almost soundlessly.

Marcus activated the flashlight app on his phone and pointed it toward the sound. 'There.' He drew the Glock from his pocket holster and crept forward, his head cocked, listening.

There. There it was again. So soft he nearly missed it.

It was a moan. He glanced at Scarlett, saw she'd heard it too.

'Hello?' he called softly. 'We won't hurt you. Please come out.'

Another moan, even fainter than the last one, seconds before all hell broke loose upstairs.

The front door banged twice before he heard it slam open, followed by the thunder of running feet and shouts of 'Police! Hands where we can see them!'

Marcus stopped short when his foot landed on something hard. Aiming his light at his feet, he realized he'd stepped on a cell phone. The phone lay on a carpet, about eight inches from the edge of a twin bed, positioned with its headboard up against the wall. He went down on one knee to examine it.

'Holy shit!' he yelped when bony fingers came into view, appearing disembodied at first glance. Then he realized the hand was connected to an arm, which was attached to a body lying on the floor under the bed.

'Oh God,' he murmured. The phone he'd stepped on was unharmed. But the frail, bony hand that reached for it was not. Bruised, with open wounds, it was covered in dried caked blood.

The hand reached and strained, trying to get the phone. Marcus met Scarlett's eyes, saw that she was as horrified as he was.

'Deacon!' Scarlett shouted into a pocket of quiet. 'We found someone down here. She's hurt but still alive.'

Cincinnati, Ohio
Tuesday 4 August, 1.25 P.M.

Furious, Ken leaned into Stephanie's face, grabbing the back of her head when she would have pulled away. 'Who took the goddamn baby?' he hissed. He didn't give a damn about the baby, but by God, she'd tell him who else had been there when his men had arrived. He left no witnesses. Ever. 'I am tired of your games, Stephanie. Who else was in your house?'

She met his eyes squarely. 'Ask him. She's his too.'

'Shut up, bitch!' Chip snarled. 'You don't know anything. Just shut up.'

Ken spared him a cold glance. 'She seems to know enough, Chip.' Keeping one hand on the back of her head, Ken gripped her chin with the other, digging his fingers into her cheeks so hard he'd definitely leave bruises. Stephanie's eyes flared wide, flickered with shock.

He smiled at her, tightening the grip on her hair. 'You thought you were safe, didn't you?' he asked softly, pleased when she began to tremble again. 'You thought because you're so pretty and I planned to sell you, that I wouldn't hurt you.' He squeezed her face harder, her eyes now shining with tears. 'You thought wrong, dear. Bruises heal in time and I've already shown you that I can hurt you without leaving a mark. But I'm getting too angry for that. You'd better answer me now or I'll get so mad that I won't worry about putting marks on your pretty skin. It won't matter anymore because I will have killed you putting them there.' He kept his voice soft, his smile friendly. He'd learned long ago that the combination scared people far more than a shout.

Stephanie's mouth opened, but no sound came out. No longer was she being coy or feisty. She was truly petrified. *Excellent.*

But then his cell phone picked that moment to ring. Cursing the interruption, he was tempted to ignore it until he realized it was the ringtone he'd set for Demetrius. Keeping his fingers clenched in Stephanie's hair, he released her face to answer the phone. 'Is it done?'

'Not exactly.' A sigh. 'No.'

Maintaining his smile so that his frustration wouldn't show, Ken released Stephanie's hair and patted her cheek. 'You've earned a momentary reprieve, sweetheart. I'll be right back.' Telling Demetrius to hold on, he grabbed the two strips of cloth that had been used to gag Stephanie and her father. He wadded the cloth and shoved one gag into each of their mouths, then went up the stairs to the kitchen, where he could watch his captives on the security monitor.

'All right,' he said calmly to Demetrius. 'What happened? You were supposed to shoot him. That's all.'

'I did shoot him,' Demetrius said, disgruntled. 'I may have missed.'

'You may have missed?' Ken hissed. New rage barreled through him, and he put his speaker phone on mute, letting his furious breath shudder out. *Breathe until you can speak without raising your voice.* He couldn't let his captives hear him losing it. It would give them hope, and he didn't have time to strip new-found hope away. He needed to know who'd witnessed the Anderses' abduction.

'Ken?' Demetrius asked through the speaker a minute later. 'You still there, man?'

Ken unmuted the phone. 'I am here,' he said, calm now that he'd vented off some of the rage. 'What do you mean, you missed?'

'Don't take that tone with me, man,' Demetrius said, his own anger rising. 'And if you're thinking about saying if you want something done right, do it yourself, then I'm out of here.'

It wasn't the first time Demetrius had threatened to close up shop, so Ken let the statement slide. 'I wasn't going to say that,' he said, even though he'd thought it. 'But how could you miss him? We agreed that you'd take a head shot close enough that you'd be able to get the bullet out of him before the cops found it.'

'Things changed,' Demetrius said coldly. 'I followed him and that homicide detective to Anders's house. She got out and went to stand with the white-haired guy. The one in the FBI.'

'Agent Novak,' Ken said. He'd never met the man personally, but he'd read plenty about him, as the agent was a media darling. 'And then?'

'And then O'Bannion got out of the car and slunk around to the back of the house. I doubled back to the main road, which has a view of the back door. Bishop came around to yell at him. I had them both in my sights.'

'And then you shot them.'

'I took care of the plain-clothes cop on watch first.'

Ken groaned. 'You killed a cop?'

'I think he was a Fed.'

'Aw, fuck, Demetrius.'

'I don't know if he's dead. I just didn't want him coming after me when I did O'Bannion and Bishop. They were ready to go into the house. Burton said he and Decker and the guys got fired on by Anders, so I figured there was evidence of a gunfight in the house. If O'Bannion got in and saw that, the cops wouldn't need a warrant. They'd just storm the place. I had a silencer. Nobody was supposed to know they'd been shot.'

'Except you missed.'

'I *may have* missed,' Demetrius said through his teeth. 'The bastard's fast. He moved at the last second. My bullet hit the door exactly where his head had been.'

'Why didn't you shoot him again?'

'I did. Bastard grabbed the woman, shouldered the door open and went through it like it was made of paper.'

'Because Burton's men had already broken the door in.' Ken rubbed his temples. 'O'Bannion will be impossible to catch now. He'll be doubly careful. Plus now we've got CPD and the FBI out for our blood.'

'I may have hit O'Bannion with the second shot,' Demetrius said, completely ignoring the consequences of having shot a Fed. 'I'm monitoring the cops on my police radio. The ones watching the front of the house just called for a second rescue squad. The first one is at the back of the house with the Fed I shot.'

'You think they called the medics because you hit O'Bannion?'

'They're not coming for the detective. I don't think I hit her at all, because he shielded her. It's got to be for O'Bannion. I know I didn't kill him. Probably just grazed him, so they'll just stitch him up and send him home. He still needs to be dealt with. I won't miss him again.'

'Oh my God, Demetrius. Listen to yourself. You shot and may have killed a Fed. O'Bannion aside, the FBI isn't going to let this pass. You're going to have every Fed in the area looking for you.'

'They didn't see me.'

'But they'll find your bullet! Jesus.' Ken's voice had risen, and he sucked in a breath to quiet himself.

'Look,' Demetrius said reasonably. 'They won't know it's us if we deflect. That's why I was going after O'Bannion with my Ruger to begin with – to make it look like whoever shot at him this morning in the alley was just finishing the job. I have to get close enough.'

'How are you planning to do that now?'

'I'm going to his office and I'm going to wait outside for the first person to come out. I will then follow that person and grab them as soon as I can. I'll draw him to me.'

Ken sighed. They were in too deep to turn back now. 'If he escapes again . . .'

'I get it,' Demetrius growled. 'I won't miss again.'

'You'd better not.' He looked up to the security monitor, where he could see both surviving Anderses struggling with their bonds. 'We might have another problem. It seems the Anderses have been holding out on us, buying time because there was either someone still in the house when Burton and Decker got there, or someone who will at least know they've been taken. I think they're hoping for a rescue.'

'Shit. Who was there?'

'The girl was about to tell me when you called. I'm going to put Decker on it. Hopefully he's had a chance to listen to enough of the audio files from the trackers to get an idea of who was in that damn house.'

'I'll take care of O'Bannion quickly, then I'll deal with whoever the Anderses are counting on for rescue.'

'Just sort out O'Bannion. I'll deal with the Anderses and their witnesses myself.'

For a moment Ken thought Demetrius would argue, but his friend finally huffed out a breath. 'Fine. Suit yourself,' he said, his tone hard and angry.

Ken hung up. 'I might just have to,' he murmured. He and Demetrius had been friends for years, but this time the man's cockiness might have caused them irreparable damage.

If CPD and the Feds got one whiff that Demetrius had pulled the trigger on their boy, they'd stop at nothing until he was behind bars or dead. And there was no way that Ken was allowing himself to get pulled down with him. Even if that meant ending Demetrius before the Feds did.

Cincinnati, Ohio
Tuesday 4 August, 1.35 P.M.

Marcus lay on his stomach on the basement floor, shining the light under the bed. An old woman flinched at the glare, moaning again. She looked to be in her seventies, or maybe even older. She'd been beaten severely, her face covered with more cuts and bruises. Her lower lip was split, the blood dried now. The wounds he'd seen on her hands were probably defensive in nature. The thought made him ill. Who would beat an old woman?

Perhaps the same person who'd bought, owned and beaten a young woman so severely that even a seasoned cop like Scarlett had pronounced it 'bad'.

'Ma'am?' Scarlett slid to her stomach, her head touching Marcus's as she squeezed next to him under the bed. 'My name is Detective Bishop. We're going to get you help. Just hold on.'

'Thank you,' the woman whispered.

'Who are you?' Marcus asked her, and had to strain to hear the reply.

'Tabby.'

'Tabby?' he repeated. 'Where's the baby, Tabby?'

A tear rolled down her wrinkled cheek, and Marcus's heart froze. Until he heard Tabby's barely audible words.

'Safe. She's safe.' More tears flowed. 'Not enough. Never enough.' Her bony hand shot out and grabbed Marcus's wrist. 'You're him? The man from the park?'

The basement stairs shook as several people ran down from the first floor. Marcus didn't look over to see who was there. His focus was on the old woman. 'Yes. How did you know about me?'

'Tala . . .' A great gulping breath, followed by a dry hacking cough. 'Told me. I told her to trust you. Make them pay.'

'Who?'

'Nephew. His wife. Their brat. Evil, evil. Please, promise me. Make them pay.'

'Did they do this to you?'

'He did. Chip.'

'Why?'

'Because I took the baby. His baby.'

Marcus's stomach clenched, even though he'd expected the father of Tala's baby to be one of her abusers.

Tabby's lips curved. 'Malaya,' she whispered. 'Free now.'

'That's good,' Scarlett breathed. 'That's very good. Where is she, ma'am?'

'Friend. Annie. Annabelle is her name.'

'Is she a neighbor?' Scarlett asked.

'No.' More of that hacking cough, and then Tabby's eyelids fluttered, her grip on Marcus's wrist weakening. 'Church,' she whispered.

A paramedic moved into their line of vision. 'Detective Bishop, you and the gentleman need to move.'

Marcus and Scarlett rolled to their feet as two uniformed policemen picked up the bed over Tabby's body and moved it to a sterile tarp. The cops' movements were directed by the same man who'd processed the scene of Tala's murder. Meanwhile, two paramedics knelt on either side of Tabby, taking her vitals while getting her medical information. The woman's answers came in fits and spurts.

'I need to ask her more questions,' Scarlett said.

One of the paramedics glanced up and shook his head. 'Her blood pressure is so low it's a wonder she's still breathing.'

'One question,' Scarlett insisted, moving close to the stretcher where the woman had been laid. 'Where are your nephew and his wife and daughter?'

Another smile curved Tabby's lips, this one grimly satisfied. 'They took them. Kicking. Screaming.'

Scarlett crouched beside the stretcher. 'Who is "they"?'

'I don't know.' The words were uttered on an agonized huff of breath, the old woman significantly paler after being moved from the floor to the stretcher. 'Had guns.'

'How did you end up under the bed?' Scarlett asked. Marcus wanted to tug her to her feet to get her to leave the old woman alone. But Tabby waved her closer.

'Chip. Shoved me . . . under the bed.' Another cough racked her. 'When they came.'

The paramedics lifted the stretcher. 'Detective, we have to go. Now.'

'Hey, Bishop,' Deacon called from the other side of the basement. 'Come and see this.'

Marcus didn't ask permission. He simply followed Scarlett. Someone had turned on the lights, illuminating a spartan but clean living space. There was a tiny kitchen, a bath, three beds and three small chests of drawers. For Tala and her family? But then where was the crib?

It was a fair bit nicer than the quarters Marcus had lived in while he was in the army, but if this basement had housed Tala, it was still a prison, no matter how nice and clean it was.

'Oh my,' Scarlett said when she saw the trackers Deacon held. They were identical to the one Tala had worn, and both had also been sliced off their wearers. 'This either just got very good or very bad. If they escaped along with the baby, that's wonderful. But if they were taken by the same people who took Anders and his family by force, then they could be in even more danger than before.'

Marcus bent down to look at the cuts in the tracker straps, taking care not to touch anything. 'I'm guessing they escaped,' he said quietly. 'Look at the jagged edges. They weren't cut. They were sawed by someone without enough strength to cut with a single slice.'

'I was thinking they'd been locked around women's ankles,' Deacon said. 'They aren't big enough to fit on a man's ankle, unless the male was very young. So the baby escaped? That's good news. You got a lead?'

Scarlett nodded. 'Yeah, I do.' She told him about Tabby and her friend from church, Annabelle.

'She said that Chip gave her the bruises for taking the baby,' Marcus added.

'Why did she?' Deacon asked, tilting his head watchfully.

'She didn't say, but she did say it was "not enough".' Marcus pointed at the trackers. 'Maybe this Annabelle person knows where these other two are.'

'Possibly.' Deacon's head tilted a fraction further. 'Why are you here, Marcus?'

Marcus returned Deacon's gaze, not blinking, the man's tone rubbing him the wrong way. 'What?' he drawled. 'You mean existentially?'

Deacon's eyes narrowed. 'Don't. Fuck. With. Me.'

Marcus lifted his chin, maintaining his stare. 'Back atcha. Oh, and I'm all right, by the way. How is that cop in the unmarked car?'

Deacon's mouth tightened to a firm line. 'He's dead,' he said. 'Bullet through the passenger window, through his head.'

Marcus flinched. 'God.' There couldn't have been an exit wound. He'd have seen the cop's blood on the driver's window.

'How did his shooter miss you?' Deacon asked, his tone becoming so mild that it was insulting. 'Far as we can tell from the direction of the bullet that hit Agent Spangler, the shooter would have had a clean, unobstructed shot at you standing at the back door, long before Detective Bishop found you.'

Furious, Marcus leaned forward. 'What are you really asking me, Agent Novak?'

'Deacon,' Scarlett admonished sharply. 'Come on now. And Marcus, back the hell off. God, it's like living at home all over again. Six damn brothers fighting over every damn thing. But at least they were teenagers. *They* had an excuse.' She blew out a breath, then pointed to Marcus's cap. 'That one of your cap-cams?'

'Yes, ma'am,' Marcus said brusquely, mostly embarrassed that she was so right. He was acting like a testosterone-crazed teenager. He took off the cap and put it in her outstretched hand. 'It won't hold much, a minute or so, but you'll be able to see the damage to the door.' He glanced at Deacon. 'As for why I'm here, I came around the back because I figured if someone was home, they might actually talk to a newsman when they wouldn't talk to a cop. I'm not under arrest, there was no crime scene, and I was well within my constitutional right to be exactly where I was.'

'And the shooter didn't miss Marcus,' Scarlett said quietly. 'We both escaped being shot because Marcus acted quickly. Someone had busted that door in before either of us got there. Probably the people who took Anders, his wife and their daughter.'

Deacon nodded stiffly. 'That makes sense. I'm . . . sorry. Spangler – the agent who died – was a friend and I'm . . . not reacting well. I'm glad you're not dead too. Again.'

Marcus exhaled heavily. 'I'm sorry too, Deacon, for your loss. I figured something had to be wrong when nobody stopped me. I figured he'd come down from his car or radio someone else. Then I'd argue loudly enough that whoever was in the house would hear me and let me in, thinking I was on their side.'

'It wasn't the worst plan ever,' Deacon conceded with a scowl. 'So what do we know?'

'Not a hell of a lot,' Scarlett said wearily. 'Somebody named Annabelle – who attended church with Tabby – took the baby. Who knows what happened to the other two women? And who knows who took Chip and his family?'

'And why was Chip's aunt was in the basement under a bed? If he beat her up, why would he hide her under the bed when they came in with guns?' Marcus added. 'Did she come down specifically to get the baby, or did he make her live down here too?'

Scarlett nodded. 'That all this happened hours after Tala's tracker was cut off her can't be a coincidence, so we can assume these events are related. Maybe whoever took the Anderses is the trafficker who sold them Tala and her family.'

Deacon nodded. 'Agreed. But was that person the same person who just shot at Marcus and killed Agent Spangler? And who shot Tala to begin with?'

Marcus looked around with a frown. 'And where is the dog?'

'Coco,' Scarlett murmured. 'The dog's either not here, or it's drugged or dead.'

The Asian man who'd processed the scene this morning joined their little group. Scarlett had called him Sergeant Tanaka, Marcus recalled.

'We'll search the house top to bottom, Deacon.' Tanaka glanced at Marcus with interest. 'You've had a busy day, Mr O'Bannion. I'm glad to hear you're not hurt. Did I also hear you say that the door had been broken in?'

'You did,' Marcus said. 'Someone had pressed the broken wood back together and set the door back into the frame, but it wasn't secure. It fell off its hinges when I shouldered into it. I didn't see any indentations in the door itself, no marks on the paint. I don't think they used anything like a battering ram to force it open.'

'Strong guys,' Deacon said. 'The Anderses didn't leave without a fight. There are bullet holes in the living room walls. The bedroom door was also broken off its hinges.'

'We'll print every surface and search every corner,' Tanaka said. 'And we'll check to see if any of the bullets match the one that Carrie took out of this morning's victim.' He sighed. 'And Agent Spangler.'

Both Scarlett and Deacon went still for a moment. 'He was a new father,' Deacon said quietly. 'His baby's only a few months old.'

Scarlett's eyelids lowered, and when they lifted, Marcus saw the expressionless gaze he'd seen in his office earlier. His heart clenched as he realized that once again she'd shoved her hurt deep down.

'Why was the shooter there?' she asked, her tone sharp and logical. 'Was he waiting for someone to come out of the house? Was he waiting for someone to go into the house? Who? Was he on guard, trying to keep the cops out? If so, why didn't he take any of us out in the front while we were waiting?'

'Maybe it was *because* you were waiting,' Marcus said. 'He knew you didn't have a warrant or you would have gone in. I wonder how long he'd been sitting there. Did the people who took the Anders family leave him on watch duty? Or did he come back for something?'

The three of them moved a few steps back as the paramedics wheeled the stretcher holding a deathly pale Tabby toward the basement stairs. 'Where are you taking her?' Scarlett asked them.

'County,' one of the medics said. 'She's unconscious now. I'll tell them to call you when and if she wakes up.'

Marcus knew County General Hospital well. It was where he and Stone had been taken nine months before. He made a mental note to have Gayle keep in contact with their sources there, so they would also know when Tabby woke up. If she did. Marcus didn't want to consider the fact that the old woman might die, but it seemed she'd done what she felt she needed to do. Even if it wasn't enough, whatever that meant exactly. Although Marcus thought he might know.

The paramedics disappeared up the stairs with Tabby, and Marcus returned his gaze to Deacon, who'd picked up the thread of their conversation.

'If the shooter came back, it might have been because there's evidence here in the house linking Anders to his abductors,' Deacon was saying. 'Which could be good for us if they're the traffickers. He saw us outside and went around the back.'

'When did he shoot Agent Spangler?' Marcus asked.

'I don't know exactly,' Deacon said. 'He hadn't been dead long. The ME will have to give us the time frame.' He closed his eyes tight. 'God. I have to tell his wife.'

Scarlett squeezed Deacon's arm sympathetically. 'I can do it,' she offered.

Deacon shook his head. 'That's okay. You did the last one. Plus I recruited him from the field office into the joint task force with CPD. Zimmerman will go with me.'

Zimmerman, Marcus knew, was the special agent in charge of the FBI's Cincinnati Field Office and Deacon's direct boss. Marcus knew this because Zimmerman had visited him in the hospital. He'd seemed like a decent man.

Scarlett dropped her hand back to her side. 'If you change your mind, let me know.'

'I will.' Deacon turned to Marcus. 'Why did you want to know when he was killed?'

'Because I'm trying to put the pieces together in my mind,' Marcus said, 'to get the timeline straight. If he was killed as soon as he parked back there, then the shooter had to have been here before you arrived, which would mean he was likely left to guard the house. But since he wasn't dead that long, the killer probably came back to find something – or someone.'

'You think he came back for Tabby?' Scarlett asked.

Marcus shrugged. 'Maybe. Whoever broke down the door could have shot Anders and his family and left their bodies here, but they didn't.'

Scarlett nodded. 'They dragged them out kicking and screaming, according to Tabby.'

'Lots of bullet holes in the walls upstairs,' Deacon said. 'There was a definite struggle.'

'They might have killed them when they got them away from the house,' Scarlett continued, 'so that they didn't leave any bodies for us to find. They didn't take Tabby because Chip had shoved her under the bed.'

Deacon frowned. 'It doesn't make sense that he'd try to save her from the thugs that broke in after nearly killing her himself.'

'She was trying to reach for a cell phone when I found her,' Marcus said. 'Chip might have shoved her under the bed not to save her, but so that *she* could save *them* later. Maybe he left the phone so that she could call the police, but she was beaten too badly to crawl out and get it once the intruders were gone.'

'Vince, what can you tell us about the phone?' Deacon asked, motioning the man over.

'It's a throwaway,' Tanaka said. 'The number doesn't match the one that the victim used to text your cell phone, Mr O'Bannion,' he added before Marcus could ask that very question. 'It's bagged and tagged. We'll check it out at the lab, see if we can figure out who it belonged to.'

Scarlett was frowning. 'If the intruders had known Tabby was here, they would have searched until they found her. I don't think they would have left her here to be a witness.'

'So Chip was keeping secrets from his dealer,' Deacon said thoughtfully.

'Secrets they might have since forced out of him,' Marcus said. 'That's why they didn't kill them here – they wanted answers.'

'Like maybe who killed Tala?' Scarlett asked.

Marcus nodded. 'It keeps coming back to her.'

Scarlett retrieved her phone from where it had fallen when she and Marcus barreled through the door. 'I'm calling in for a security detail to stand outside Tabby's door at the hospital. If the shooter did come back to find her here, he might try to get her there. She may be our only witness to what happened here. If she lives.' She made the call, then handed Marcus's cap-cam to Tanaka, who put it in an evidence bag.

'Wait,' she said with a frown when Tanaka opened evidence bags for the trackers Deacon still held. 'Why did they leave the trackers?' she asked.

'What do you mean?' Tanaka asked.

'I'm trying to get the timeline straight in my mind too,' she said. 'If the intruders came in through that door, they would have walked right by these trackers on the floor on their way to the stairs. They kidnapped the Anders family, firing shots in the process. They had to think that the cops might be called at some point. Why leave the trackers here for us to find later? Why not take them?'

'Especially since they're a match for the one you took off Tala,' Deacon added.

Tanaka shrugged. 'I can't venture a guess right now. Did you get the serial numbers from these two?' he asked, holding up the bags with the trackers.

Deacon nodded. 'I did, thanks. I'll check it out ASAP and get back to you. I'm off to pick up Zimmerman.' He glanced at Marcus. 'Lie low for a while, okay? Twice in one day . . . I'd hate to see them get a chance to get lucky on a third try.'

'I'll keep my head down,' Marcus said. It was the most he would promise, because he didn't want to lie to Deacon.

Scarlett's pointed gaze said that she hadn't missed his evasion and that he hadn't heard the end of the matter. 'I'll start tracking down Annabelle,' she said to Deacon.

Deacon sighed wearily. 'Zimmerman and I need to notify Agent Spangler's wife. Don't forget about our meeting at the field office. I'll meet you there.'

When he was gone, Scarlett moved to the open doorway, stepping around the door that lay on the floor. Silently she studied the wreckage, then turned to face Marcus, her expression subdued. 'I'll take you back to your office now.'

Sixteen

Cincinnati, Ohio
Tuesday 4 August, 2.30 P.M.

Scarlett buckled her seat belt, then leaned her head back against the headrest and closed her eyes. She'd been calm through the whole ordeal, but now that they were truly alone, she let herself feel the terror of those moments when bullets were flying far too close to their heads. Or, more accurately, to Marcus's head. Those bullets had not been meant for her. A shooter good enough to follow them as they fell to the ground had aimed several inches above where her own head had been. 'You could have been killed,' she murmured to the man sitting beside her. 'Again.'

'But I wasn't,' Marcus responded calmly, his voice giving her chills despite the fact that the black department car, having been sitting in the August sun, was about five million degrees inside. 'Again,' he added, his voice dipping lower.

A new shiver raced over her skin, tickling between her legs. Swallowing a sigh, she pressed her thighs tighter together, her hands clenching the steering wheel. Words formed in her mind but disappeared before they reached her lips, so she sat there, clenched and . . . wanting.

'Although,' he said after a minute of absolute silence, 'I might die of heat stroke soon if you don't turn on the air.'

The rueful amusement in his voice shook her into action. Starting the car, she kicked on the AC. 'I'm sorry,' she said, looking straight ahead.

'I'm not.'

She twisted her head to stare at him, exhaling when she saw the raw desire in his eyes. 'You can't look at me like that.'

'Why not?' His lips curved, sinfully sexy. 'I'm not a cop. No breaking of police rules there. I'm not a suspect, am I?'

'No.' The word she'd intended to sound businesslike and practical came out husky and breathless.

His jaw clenched and he swallowed hard. 'You can't talk to me that way, then.'

She drew a breath, executed a quick three-point turn, and pulled away from the line of police cars. 'Okay.'

From the corner of her eye, she saw his lips twitch. 'Okay to what?'

'I won't talk to you that way and you won't look at me that way.'

His almost-smile disappeared. 'Where will I, then? And when?'

She didn't pretend not to know what he was asking. She knew what she should say, that they couldn't have a relationship until this case was finished. Or maybe ever, at least until she knew what kind of reporter he was and what kind of threat he represented. But none of that came from her mouth.

'Not at a crime scene. And not in public while this case is still ongoing.' She could feel his gaze, studying her profile.

'Why were you looking at that door in the basement?' he asked.

She blinked, not expecting that response. 'I wanted to see where the bullets hit. He was aiming at you. If you hadn't moved, you'd be dead.'

'But I did move, and the bullets missed us. You're not dead and neither am I. Not by a long shot,' he added in a mutter.

She glanced over at his face, then down at his lap. And had to bite back a whimper. No, he was not dead. Nowhere even close. She clenched her hands around the wheel to keep herself from touching him, from stroking that hard ridge that beckoned her.

'God,' she whispered. 'That's not fair, Marcus.'

'Don't I know it,' he said under his breath, then adjusted himself with a grimace. 'So where, Scarlett, and when?'

'I . . . I don't know. I haven't thought that far.'

'I have,' he said quietly. 'Take me home with you.'

She turned her head with a jerk to stare at him. He was not joking. She'd never seen a man look more serious. Another car tooted its horn, and she abruptly returned her attention to the road just in time to avert an accident. 'You mean now?'

'Yes.'

'I . . . Marcus, we can't do that now. I have to walk my dog and get back to work.'

'Why, Scarlett,' he said, the dry amusement back in his voice. 'I'm only planning to look at you. You know, like *that*. Which I can do while you're walking your dog. Whatever did *you* mean?' He clucked his tongue. 'You naughty woman, you.'

She had to laugh. 'You're . . .' She sobered, then sighed. 'Alive. You're alive.'

'I am,' he said just as soberly, all the humor gone. 'I'm afraid you've seen me at my worst. I'm not normally dodging bullets. This is an unusual day.'

'You wear a bulletproof vest. You get death threats on a regular basis.'

'You're a cop,' he countered evenly. 'People shoot at you all the time.'

'Actually, they don't. I think you're ahead of me in that department.' She tapped the tactical vest she still wore. With a shooter after Marcus, she wasn't taking any chances at being collateral damage. 'This is not my everyday attire.'

'Why don't you want to take me home?'

Unfamiliar panic rose to clog her throat. 'I didn't say that.'

He raked his fingers through the thick dark hair at his temple, then held his bloody hand out far enough for her to see without taking her eyes off the road. 'I need first aid.'

'The concrete chips,' she said. The ones he'd sheltered her from. He'd been hit while she didn't have a scratch on her body.

'You have to take me home with you so that you can clean the wound and bandage me all up.'

She bit her lower lip. 'I meant to have the paramedics look at it.'

'They needed to tend to Tabby.'

'They could have sent another pair of medics and you know it. Dammit, Marcus. I'm taking you to the hospital.'

'No.'

The word sounded almost as panicked as she felt. 'Why not?'

He drew a breath. 'I don't like hospitals.'

'I guess I can understand that, given what happened last year. I don't care much for them myself.' An exit was fast approaching and Scarlett took it.

'Where are we going?' Marcus asked suspiciously.

'I'm going to check you out. If it's worse than I can deal with, I'm taking you to a doctor. Not a hospital,' she added before he could protest.

The first parking lot she saw belonged to a church. At this time of the day, it was largely deserted. Scarlett stopped the car and went around to open Marcus's door. She gave him her hand. 'Stand up. It's too dim in the car and I need more light to see. We're sheltered here. No one can shoot at us unless he comes back here in person.'

And if that happened, she was taking the shooter down.

He cooperated, following her as she led him around the open door, backing him up so that he half sat, half leaned against the hood, his feet planted wide. From this position she'd be able to see a shooter approaching before he saw them. 'Head down,' she said.

'Up, down,' he grumbled, but dropped his chin obediently. 'You're bossy.'

'And you're just figuring that out?' She leaned forward to get a better look at the cut on his head. Then sucked in a breath when he gripped her hips and pulled her closer, tucking her between his spread thighs.

'You said you wanted to look,' he murmured, his voice a low caress that made her shiver from the inside out. 'So look.'

Her hands unsteady, Scarlett ignored the silky invitation, carefully parting the hair around the cut on his head. 'It's not too deep. I think I can fix it.'

'Good.' He pulled her closer, burying his face in the curve of her shoulder and drawing a deep breath. 'You smell so good,' he said, his exhale warm against her skin. 'I could stay here all day. All night.'

The mental image of them writhing between her sheets had her trembling. 'Marcus,' she protested, but it was a weak protest indeed. Every cell in her body was urging her to press closer.

He lifted his head from her shoulder to look into her eyes. He was as serious as she'd ever seen him. 'We're not at a crime scene and nobody is shooting at us. I think we've waited long enough, Scarlett.'

Without further warning, he curled his hand around the back of her neck and pulled her in for a kiss that instantly took her breath away. No gentle introduction, this. His mouth was hard, intense and so . . . proprietary that she could only moan, wrap her arms around his neck, and kiss him back. His hands roved up and down her back impatiently and she cursed the tactical vest she wore for robbing her of his touch. With a frustrated noise deep in his throat, his hands slid down her back, past the vest, to close over her butt, kneading her cheeks.

It felt so good that she almost whimpered. Hell, maybe she did whimper, because he growled and yanked her closer, using his hold on her butt to press her hips into his. She'd felt his erection when he'd lain on top of her in the basement, and it had taken every ounce of her willpower – and the knowledge that a gunman could be coming through the basement door – not to give in to temptation. But now there was no shooter, no situation. Just Marcus, his hands on her ass and the very impressive ridge in his jeans.

All for me. The realization left her heady. And greedy. She rubbed against him, lifting her leg to bracket his hip. *Closer*, was all she could think. She needed to be closer.

His groan vibrated through his chest as he pulled back only far enough to let her breathe, grazing her lips with his. 'I want you,' he said, his voice gone gravelly and rough. 'You know that, don't you?'

'Yes,' she whispered, then smiled against his mouth, a sudden surge of happiness rising up within her. 'I figured that out for myself.'

He squeezed her butt even as he smiled back. 'And?'

Leaning away to see his face, she abruptly sobered as reality came crashing through. *Shit*. They were parked behind a church, going at it like teenagers with no regard for . . . anything.

His smile faded. 'What's wrong?'

'I want you too,' she confessed quietly. 'So much that it scares me.'

His brows crunched together, his body going very still. His hands still covered her ass as if he didn't intend to let her go, and the notion felt way too good. 'Why does it scare you?'

'Because I got so caught up that I forgot to be careful. You're standing out in the open and I wasn't watching. Anything could have happened to you.'

He drew a deep breath, his stiff shoulders relaxing as he exhaled. 'Then you have to take me home with you.' One dark brow lifted. 'We'll be safe there, right?'

Feeling the tension leave his body helped the tension leave hers. 'Yes. But we can't stay there long, and we can't do any more of *this*, no matter how pleasant it's been. I have to find Annabelle and Tala's baby. And the bastards who shot you. Both of them.'

'I'd feel sorry for them if they didn't have it coming. I wouldn't want to be on your shit list.' He pulled away reluctantly. 'So this has been *pleasant*?' he asked, his tone saying he knew full well that it had been so much more.

Scarlett was nearly undone. Willing herself to move away from him, she returned to the driver's seat and buckled up, staring straight ahead. Because if she looked at him, she might not be able to look away. 'Yes,' she said firmly when she heard his seat belt click into place. 'Pleasant. A woman has to make sure you don't get a big head.'

'I think that train's left the station, Detective. It's already pretty big,' he said blandly.

Scarlett whipped her head to stare at him, then snorted a shocked laugh when she saw his innocent expression. 'I'm not sure what to do with you.'

He smiled at her. 'Oh, no worries. I have lots of ideas.'

She put the car in gear and headed toward the highway, feeling breathless in the best of ways. 'I'm sure you do, Mr O'Bannion. I'm sure you do.'

Cincinnati, Ohio
Tuesday 4 August, 2.35 P.M.

Ken strolled down the stairs to his basement, a plate of steaming lasagna in one hand and a glass of iced tea in the other. He'd needed a little extra time to breathe through his temper after his call with Demetrius. To put his thoughts in order. And to make himself lunch.

That cocky, careless sonofabitch. Ken had pulled up the phone-tracking software on his own phone so that he could see Demetrius's actual location while he'd reheated the lasagna from dinner the night before.

Demetrius's phone was where Demetrius had said he'd be – on his way to O'Bannion's newspaper office. Ken had set an alarm so that he'd know if Demetrius veered off course for any reason, then let himself enjoy the aroma of his lunch. He hadn't realized how hungry he'd been until his stomach growled. Holding back from breaking Stephanie Anders's pretty neck had burned a lot of fuel.

The aroma of food served another purpose as well, giving his captives another reminder that they were . . . captives. *At my mercy for food, water. Life itself.* Chip and Stephanie should be hungry and thirsty by now. If the smell of Marlene Anders's blood and the sight of her gaping throat hadn't permanently stolen their appetites.

When he returned to the basement, father and daughter looked up, both their gazes still intense. The break had allowed them to recharge. It would take a little while to wear them back down. Time Ken didn't have. *Stupid fucking Demetrius.* If he'd called thirty seconds later, Ken would have already had the information.

Casually he placed his plate on the cart next to his chair and began to eat and drink, noting the way both Chip and Stephanie followed his every movement. He finished his meal and released a sigh.

'That was really good. Hit the spot. Torture is so very draining, you know.' He stood up, rolling his shoulders. 'Are we ready to begin again, Stephanie?' He removed the gag from her mouth. 'Who took the baby?'

'Tabby,' she said flatly. 'His dear Aunt Tabby. Short for Tabitha. She's seventy-nine years old, five feet six inches tall, about ninety pounds. White hair, wrinkled skin. Mostly blind. She walks with a walker, so she can't have gone far.'

Well, well, well. Looked like little Stephanie was ready to play ball. He'd figured she'd wise up eventually. But the answers she'd given really pissed him off.

Ken thought about the truck tire tracks his men had found out back.

Dear Aunt Tabby could very well have gone far if she'd had someone to pick her up.

'Dad also beat her half to death,' Stephanie added. 'So your boys shouldn't have any problem catching her.'

That's what you think, Ken thought dourly, a few more pieces of the puzzle falling into place. He'd bet good money that dear Aunt Tabby was the reason for the cops summoning the second rescue squad, not because O'Bannion had been injured. Demetrius hadn't touched O'Bannion. *And now the cops have Chip's aunt, a relative Chip never disclosed as living in the household.* Who knew what the old lady knew? *Wonderful.*

He sent a text to Sean, Decker, and Burton with the name and age of Chip's aunt, and the instruction to take care of her. They'd taken care of people inside prison walls. A hospital wouldn't be a cakewalk, but it was definitely doable.

'Thank you, Stephanie. I've just sent my men after her.' He crossed his legs, kept his tone mildly curious. 'So *if* your father beat this aunt half to death, how could she have taken a baby?'

'She took the baby earlier. That's why he beat her. She gave it to someone. I don't know who, and I really mean that I don't know. I didn't know she had friends. He was only keeping her so he could get her social security checks.'

Ken turned to the still-gagged Chip, whose eyes were shooting daggers at his daughter. 'You're kidding me,' Ken said incredulously. 'You're stealing social security from your aunt? That's like, what, five hundred a month? You are one fucked-up piece of work.'

'He did the same to his mother,' Stephanie stated, 'until she threatened to tell. He took care of her so well,' she added sardonically.

'How so?'

'Pillow over her face, probably. I was away at college at the time. That's why he got Mila, you know. Tala's mother. She was a nurse. He got her to take care of his mother.'

Ken studied Stephanie. Hatred glittered in her eyes. 'Wasn't his mother your grandmother?'

'No. I'm not his.'

Chip exhaled, his nostrils flaring in anger, but his eyes revealed his shock. Either he hadn't known, or he hadn't known that she knew.

'Whose are you?' Ken asked.

Stephanie shrugged as best she could, given her bonds. 'His best friend's. Mother got a hoot out of all those dinner parties when Daddy dearest was shooting the breeze with the man screwing his wife. Their affair lasted a long time. Mother almost left Chip when he went broke, but he was able to pull his ass out of the poorhouse.' Her head tilted. 'Probably due to you.'

It was true. Ken had sold Chip his first workers when the guy's business had hit the shitter.

The girl spoke confidently, but Ken noticed that she kept her gaze on his face, sometimes glancing at Chip, making sure she didn't look down at her mother's body between them. She was getting too self-assured, so Ken tossed a verbal grenade into the mix. 'You know, you are either the best actress in the world or the coldest bitch I've ever met. You talk about your mother's affair when she's lying dead next to you?'

Stephanie's eyes closed, a spasm of pain momentarily contorting her pretty face. 'She would want me to get out of here alive. And if giving you what you want is the way to do that, she'd want me to.'

'You're not going free,' he said. 'You do know that, don't you?'

She nodded, her eyes still closed. Her skin paled. 'Yeah. I got that.'

'Just so that we're clear,' he said amiably.

'But you said you could make it easier for me.'

'I did say that, yes. Let's see how this goes, shall we? The more straightforward you are, the more charitable I'll be. So, why did Tabby give the baby to "someone"?' He quirked his fingers in the air.

'I don't know. Maybe she heard Tala was dead and figured there would be no one to feed the brat. Mother and I certainly weren't going to buy it formula, and Tabby wasn't allowed to have any money, so it would have starved because Tala was still nursing it. Or maybe she thought that Mother would get rid of the kid. I don't know.'

The Anders household had been a goddamn nest of vipers. Ken was glad he didn't have to live with them. He almost felt sorry for Aunt Tabby. But not sorry enough to rescind his order to Sean and the others. The old lady had to go. She'd probably find it a mercy.

'Did Tabby let the other two women go too?'

'Probably. I didn't and Mother wouldn't. They were Mother's servants.'

Ken frowned. Stephanie was cooperating, but there was still something off. Something not quite right. She'd given up the aunt so easily, not caring that the woman might be their only hope of rescue.

Drake. Of course, the boyfriend who'd killed Tala. Ken wanted to kick himself. He'd allowed himself to get sidetracked by the baby and the aunt, forgetting about the damn boyfriend, whose last name was . . . He searched his memory. *Ah. Connor. Drake Connor.*

'Stephanie,' he said softly, 'where is Drake?'

The girl blanched.

Bingo, was Ken's first thought, closely followed by, *Shit*. 'Did you call him when my men arrived? Did you tell him you were being taken away?'

'No,' Stephanie said, but her voice cracked.

Ken was on his feet, his palm connecting with her face before she could blink. Her head snapped back, a shrill cry escaping her throat. 'Do not lie to me, girl.'

Shaken, Stephanie stared up at him, and he retook his seat. 'Let's try that again. Did you tell him that you were being taken?'

She looked down, saw her mother's body and dry-heaved. Thankfully, she'd already emptied her stomach the last time she'd puked. 'Yes,' she whispered.

'Where was he when you told him this?'

'On his way to get me.'

'So you think he followed you here?'

An audible swallow. A tiny nod.

Beside her, Chip rolled his eyes. Ken found himself laughing in surprised agreement.

'I think your father is right for once, Stephanie. Drake's not coming to save you. He's halfway to the border by now.' He texted the boy's name to Sean, Decker, and Burton, instructing them to find Drake Connor ASAP. 'Considering he committed murder this morning, it's doubtful he'll be running to the police for assistance. And on the supremely wild chance that he tries to stage a rescue on his own, we'll catch him on his way in. But don't count on that, honey. You're more likely to be struck by lightning or win the Powerball.'

Ken finally saw a flicker of defeat in her eyes. She'd held out for hours, waiting for Drake to save her. It was almost sweet. In a gagging kind of way.

He stood up, dusted his palms on his trouser legs. 'Well, I think I've got what I need from you and dear old Dad here,' he said, perusing the instruments on his cart.

Stephanie made a terrified noise when his intent finally sank in. 'Wait. You said you'd help me if I talked to you.'

'Well that was before you wasted more than half of my day. I do have an actual job, you know, and you've kept me from doing it. I'll probably have to work through dinner to catch up. But don't worry, I won't kill you. I will kill *him*, though,' he said, gesturing at her father. 'He has no value. You set this in motion by taking Tala out without permission. But since he got you into it by buying Tala and her family in the first place, I'll let you pick how he goes. Gun or knife?'

Stephanie's cheeks darkened, fury bending her mouth. 'Which hurts more?'

Ken threw back his head and laughed. 'Oh, I wish I could keep you. But you'd try to get away and I'd eventually have to kill you too.'

Her chin lifted, but he could see the fear in her eyes. 'I'll try to get away from whoever you sell me to,' she said with a bravado that was as fake as a three-dollar bill.

His grin softened to a smile. 'That'll be his problem. But remember, Tala tried to get away. Didn't work out too well for her, did it?' He clapped his hands once. 'So, Stephanie, darling. What's it to be? The knife will hurt more, but it's messy.'

She started to glance down at her mother, but twisted her face away at the last minute. 'Messy works. Just make him scream. And I have a special request.'

Again he was impressed with her guts, and the depth of her anger. 'Depends.'

'I want to tell him something and I want to see his face when I do. But I don't want to see my mother again, not like that. Can you move him?'

He considered it, then nodded. 'That's not unreasonable,' he said. He dragged Chip, chair and all, to where Stephanie could see him without looking at her mother's body.

The stare she directed at Chip was positively glacial. One side of her mouth lifted. 'You might want to ungag him for this. You might enjoy his reaction too.'

One hand firmly gripping his knife – just in case – Ken pulled the wadded cloth from Chip's mouth, anticipating that the man would try to spit at him and easily stepping out of the way when he did. 'Go ahead, Stephanie,' Ken said. 'I'm a busy man.'

'That little bastard baby wasn't yours,' Stephanie told Chip, her tight smile maliciously gleeful. 'It was Drake's.'

Already pale, Chip went white as a sheet. 'You're lying.'

She smiled at him, pure ice and hate. 'No I'm not. When your little bitch whelped, I had a DNA test run, just so I'd know. It was Drake's. Zero chance of error.'

Chip was looking like he wanted to say something but couldn't figure out what. Stephanie turned to Ken. 'You can kill him now. I'm done with him.'

'Wait,' Chip said hoarsely. 'Your mother . . . She would have said something.'

'She didn't know. I didn't tell her.'

Ken stood back, deciding another moment or two wouldn't make a difference, especially when it was getting interesting again. 'Why didn't you tell your mother?' he asked. 'You said that seeing the baby hurt her.'

Stephanie swallowed hard. 'She was mad when I got arrested at school, said if it happened again she'd cut me off and take my car. So I kept the secret as leverage.'

'You would have traded the secret to keep your car?'

'And my credit cards,' she mumbled. 'Doesn't seem important now.'

Ken felt a sting of pity. He sighed heavily. 'Dammit, girl. Now I'm going to have to find you an extra-specially kind buyer. You yanked my heartstrings with that, but now I'm out of time. If you don't want to watch old Chip here bite it, close your eyes.'

But she impressed him once again, coldly watching Ken slit her father's throat. He did it slowly, leaving Chip gurgling at the end.

He cleaned his knife and stripped off his gloves. 'How did you know the baby wasn't Chip's?' he asked her, genuinely curious. 'What made you do a DNA test?'

'I didn't know, exactly,' she said dully, watching the man who'd raised her gasping for his final breaths. 'It had a birthmark on its ass, just like Drake has. I'd found out that Chip wasn't my real father a few years ago, when I got my blood type in school. I thought at first I was adopted and confronted my mother with it. She admitted I wasn't Chip's, that she'd had an affair. Asked me not to make it an issue.' She shook her head. 'I was planning to, of course, but had been saving that for a rainy day. Nothing stops parents from yelling at you like making them yell at each other. I'd been saving the news about Drake being the kid's daddy for a really rainy day, mainly because I knew that Chip wanted more kids.'

'You knew it would hurt him.' Once again Ken was impressed. Not many girls Stephanie's age could hold on to a secret like that for such malicious reasons. *Alice could, but hell, she's my daughter.* And Ken had made sure of that. He'd run paternity tests on both Alice and Sean.

She nodded. 'He was so thrilled to have that little brat. He thought that damn baby was his. That she was nursing it was the only thing keeping Tala alive. Mother would have killed her without batting an eye. She hated how much Chip wanted that kid.' She lifted a shoulder. 'So I guess it worked out that Drake killed her first. Tala's brat wasn't going to nurse forever. Maybe that's why Tala risked double-crossing us.' She looked up at him, meeting his eyes squarely. 'Don't you have an office in Singapore or Bangkok or somewhere outside the country where you need qualified help? Bora Bora, maybe? Or Cameroon? My French is flawless.'

He chuckled. 'Damn, now I wish I did. But I don't, and I have a mess of my own to clean up here. Too many people got involved in this, and Chip there hurt some of my people, so I'm short-handed. And FYI, the cops rescued Aunt Tabby and have sent her to the hospital. I've given the order to have her finished off there.'

Stephanie absorbed this. 'So no one was ever coming to help us, were they?'

'Nope. Sorry.' Bitch of it was, he did feel sorry. And oddly reluctant to leave her tied to the chair, even though he had work to do. He felt oddly reluctant to leave her at all. 'Why did Drake take Chip's gun to the alley?' he asked. 'The truth.'

She lifted a shoulder. 'Tala had been meeting some guy in the park. I was supposed to walk the dog, but I hated to. Stupid dog. I made Tala do it, to get her out of the house when I wanted Drake to myself. I'd send her out at two, three in the morning. A few days ago I caught her humming a tune and got suspicious. Drake and I checked the logs and saw that some nights she stayed in one place for five minutes or more.' Stephanie's smile was reptilian. 'I beat her within an inch of her life. It was a wonder the bitch could walk.'

'How did you know she was meeting a man?' Ken nodded, immediately seeing his own mistake. 'Oh, right. The audio files.'

'Yes. Drake was livid that she was sniffing around the guy in the park. He set her up by telling her we were going into the city that night to buy drugs. He left his jacket in the room with her, with his cell phone in the pocket. He wanted her to use it, and she did. She met the guy in the alley, and . . . you know the rest.'

'Thank you,' he said, and meant it. He carefully locked up his cart with all of his weapons, then left her sitting there. He was halfway up the stairs when she spoke again.

'Excuse me,' she called. 'I don't know your name.'

'You don't need to.'

A frustrated huff. 'How much are you going to ask for me?'

'I don't know. It'll be an auction. But I'll make sure the winner won't beat you.'

'That's not a major comfort,' she said sarcastically. 'How much is the "buy now" option?'

'Like on eBay?' He laughed. 'We're a little more sophisticated than that.' But because she'd intrigued him, he gave her a number that was over-the-moon inflated. 'Two million.'

She considered it. 'I'd like to buy myself, then.'

Startled, he came back down the stairs to stand five feet away, carefully avoiding the pools of Chip's blood. 'What do you propose using for money?'

'I have Chip's bank account passwords.'

'You're lying,' he said, although he appreciated the effort. 'If you had them, you wouldn't have been worried about losing your credit cards.' He went back up the stairs, chuckling at the vile curses she flung at him. 'I'd take you myself, but I'd never sleep a wink,' he said. 'You'd go all Sharon Stone on me the second I closed my eyes, and they'd find me with an ice pick through my heart.'

'What does that even mean?' she demanded, and he laughed again.

'That you are far too young for me, Stephanie. I'll send someone down with some food in a little while.'

He locked the door and texted Alice to come out to the house. He'd send her down to tend to Stephanie, along with Burton. Then he'd have Burton dispose of the bodies.

For a moment – just a moment – he'd been tempted to allow Stephanie to buy herself outright. But that was a crazy thought and Ken Sweeney was not a crazy man. Just once, he'd like to let go with a woman and not worry so much . . . But not with that one. She was trouble with a capital T.

He forced himself to march away from the basement door and into his office, where he planted his ass behind his desk. But rather than working, he opened his phone and checked his tracking program once again. Reuben and his right hand, Jason Jackson, were both still AWOL. Demetrius was still sitting near the *Ledger*'s front door. Burton was on his way back to Ken's house, to do a forensic examination of Reuben's car. Joel was in his home office, no doubt working the books, and Sean and Alice were in the office downtown.

Decker's phone was at County General, which hopefully meant he was taking care of dear Aunt Tabby. The old woman was a loose end they couldn't leave unsnipped.

Everyone was where they should be except for Reuben and Jason Jackson. Ken sent a group text to them all, telling them to come to his house for a mandatory meeting.

His company was spiraling out of control and things had to change. Otherwise Ken would take them all out – every last one of his so-called trusted group – and start all over again on a beach in the Turks and Caicos.

Seventeen

Marcus breathed a quiet sigh of relief when Scarlett turned on to her street. He hadn't been certain that she actually intended to bring him to her house. She'd been totally rattled after that kiss, worried that she'd let go so completely that she'd forgotten her job. Even as the knowledge made him feel ten feet tall, he knew that if she'd turned around mid-route and taken him back to his office, he wouldn't have complained or cajoled. It would have been her choice and he would have honored that. Because that kiss had rattled him too. He wanted her unfettered in her pleasure, wanted to make her forget her own damn name. But she had to want that too.

Now that they were so close to her house, he let himself believe that she did want him enough, that this thing between them had a real chance, whatever 'this thing' was.

He sighed to himself. And now that they were so close to her house – and to her next-door neighbor – he had something he needed to set straight. He hoped what he was about to tell her wouldn't make her change her mind. 'I, um, have a confession to make,' he said, breaking the silence that had filled the car since Scarlett had gotten back on the highway. 'I told you that I drove by your house.'

She downshifted as they started up the enormous hill atop which her house sat as if holding court with the houses gathered around. 'Four times, I think you said.'

'Yeah, well, I did a bit more than just drive by and look. When I saw your big Land Cruiser always parked in the driveway, I wondered whose it was.'

'It's mine,' Scarlett said sharply.

'I know that now. I thought at first it might belong to a . . . significant other.'

'How did you find out it was mine?' she asked.

He braced himself. 'I kind of sort of asked your neighbor.'

Her brows shot up. 'You kind-of-sort-of asked Mrs Pepper?' She huffed in exasperation. 'Oh for God's sake. She's the biggest gossip in the neighborhood.'

'I didn't intend to,' he said defensively. 'And I didn't come straight out and ask her. I have a little more finesse than that.'

'If you managed to get one by Mrs Pepper, then you're a better man than most.'

But he wasn't. He knew that. He was a better man than some, but not most. For months the truth about his mission at the *Ledger* had kept him from pursuing this woman he'd never been able to get out of his mind. No longer, he thought. He still had no intention of dragging her into his bend-the-law world. He wouldn't ask her to look the other way or to betray her integrity by helping him. But he wasn't letting her go. He'd find a way to have it all.

If she hadn't been interested, he wouldn't have pushed her. Hell, he wouldn't even be here right now. But she was. She hadn't pushed him away earlier. Far from it.

He had to touch her again soon or he was going to burn up, from the inside out.

'I'm not sure I managed to get anything by Mrs Pepper. She might remember me.'

'I have no doubt she will,' Scarlett said dryly. 'That woman is old, not dead. She has an appreciation for the male form. She paints, you know. I wouldn't be surprised if you ended up on one of her canvases.'

He grinned at Scarlett's sideways compliment. 'Really? That wouldn't be so bad.'

'She only paints nudes.'

Marcus coughed. 'Well. I'm . . . Thank you, Scarlett. Now I have that image in my mind.'

'Hey, you're the one who tangled with her.'

'I only got out to check the license plates on the Land Cruiser. They were covered in mud.'

She glanced at him from the corner of her eye. 'When was this?'

'Late March.'

'Ah, we'd just had some snow.' She motioned with her hand. 'So, keep going.'

She was enjoying this, he realized. Which was fine with him. 'Well, your neighbor takes her watch responsibilities seriously. She saw me checking out the Land Cruiser and came out to your driveway. "Young man,"' he mimicked in a falsetto, '"do you *mind* telling me why you're on *Detective* Bishop's property? The woman owns *guns*, boy. Lots of *guns*."'

Scarlett laughed. 'She didn't really say that.'

Marcus thought he could watch her laugh all day. *And all night.* 'She totally did, I swear it. I told her that I was interested in buying the Land Cruiser and asked if she knew the name of the owner. She told me that you owned it and always had. I was very relieved.'

'You could have just run my plates,' Scarlett said tartly. 'I'm sure you have the resources to do that.'

'I do, and I did,' he said. 'The search confirmed what she said. Anyway, I did it mainly because I needed to know if I had a chance or if you were already taken. I'm sorry. I should have just asked Deacon. I thought you should know in case your neighbor remembers me.'

'She will. She's almost ninety, but she's still sharp as a tack.'

'I got that. I like your house, by the way,' he said as they pulled into the driveway next to the Land Cruiser. The old Victorian was a charming cacophony of colors. 'It has character.'

Staring up at it, she sighed. 'It looks like a patchwork quilt right now. The old owners painted it willy-nilly with whatever was on sale. Purple, pink, green. Chartreuse, even. Don't get me wrong, I like bright colors, but I want it to be authentic. I've been sanding it, getting it ready to paint it again.'

'What color did you pick?'

'Blue,' she said with a smile. 'A bright robin's-egg blue with butterscotch trim. It was the original color when it was built in 1880. I found an old photo in the historical society's archives with the colors listed on the back. It's slow going, though. I'm nervous about using a power sander, so I've been doing it all by hand.'

'You're sanding it yourself? By hand? I thought you had six brothers.'

'I do. Two of them are married with kids, so they have no free time. Two others are cops and work weird hours, so they're never off when I am. One is a musician. He plays the cello with the Cincinnati Pops.' She wiggled her fingers. 'He can't risk his hands.'

Marcus rolled his eyes, getting out of the car when she did and following her up to the garage door. 'I play an instrument and I do plenty of sanding with my hands.' He wiggled his fingers and she gave him a smile that was half shy and half seduction – and he wasn't even sure she knew she did so.

'I know you play the guitar. I heard it on the videos. I . . . I liked it very much.'

He wanted to grab her and kiss her until she couldn't breathe. 'It's just a hobby. I guess if it were my living, I'd be more careful with my hands.'

'No, you're right. There are plenty of things Nathaniel could do to help me around here, but he's the baby of the family and Mama won't let us put a tool belt on him.' She leaned in a fraction and whispered, 'But he sneaks over here sometimes to help me in my workshop. Don't tell my mother.'

'Your secret is safe with me,' he said, and watched for her reaction.

Her blue eyes flickered with memory, her smile fading. 'I think it just might be,' she murmured, making his heart do a slow roll inside his chest.

They'd had this conversation before, back when he'd been in the hospital. Except their lines had been reversed. She'd remembered – not only the exact words, but she'd heard the nuance in his voice that day and now she reproduced it.

Trust, he thought. They were building trust. It was a damn good start.

Abruptly she bent over and yanked up one of the two garage doors before he could even offer to help. He waited until she'd straightened to say, 'That was only five.'

She blinked. 'What?'

'You said you have six brothers but only mentioned five.'

She moved her shoulders uncomfortably. 'Phin went to Iraq and came back somebody different. He moved down South a while back, but we don't know where. We don't hear from him that often.'

'Oh.' Marcus sighed. 'That happened to a lot of men I knew over there. I'm sorry.'

'Thanks. We're twins, so he was always there until I went to college and he joined up. Now he's gone and I miss him.' She cleared her throat. 'I figured you'd want the nickel tour, so we'll start here.'

'Scar-*lett*!' They turned to find her elderly neighbor standing on the front porch next door, waving to them. 'You forgot to introduce me to your young man.'

'I didn't want to bother you, Mrs Pepper.'

The old woman gave her a stern look. 'Stuff and nonsense. Come here, young man. Closer.' She crooked a finger, and Marcus obeyed, walking across the grass to the old woman's front lawn. 'Closer. My eyes aren't so good anymore.'

'Pfff,' Scarlett said, but followed him as he obeyed, getting right up against her porch railing and looking up to meet a pair of sharp, intelligent eyes. He cocked a brow, wondering if she remembered him. The woman's eyes twinkled, giving him his answer. 'I like this one,' she told Scarlett.

'Much better than that other one. This one's got a pure aura. The other one . . .' She made a face. 'I'm glad you gave him his walking papers.'

Marcus glanced over at Scarlett, his brows nearly leaping off his forehead he raised them so high in question. 'Other one?'

Scarlett's cheeks were flushed. 'I don't mean to be rude, Mrs Pepper, but we're pressed for time. I just came home to walk Zat.'

'Of course.' She sobered abruptly. 'Be careful, Scarlett. I have a bad feeling in my knees. You're overdue for trouble.'

'Yes, ma'am,' Scarlett said dutifully. 'I'll be very careful.'

'You never did tell me your name, young man,' Mrs Pepper said briskly.

'O'Bannion, ma'am. Marcus O'Bannion.'

'It's nice to formally meet you. You come back if you need anything, y'hear?'

'Yes, ma'am,' he said. He gave the old woman a courteous nod, then turned to follow Scarlett into her garage. Once inside, he stood for a moment, looking around, then turned in a circle to see it all. 'Wow.'

Half of the garage was empty, a telltale oil spot on the floor marking it as where she parked her little Audi. But the other half was filled with wood in various stages of production, and with tools – power saws and routers and lathes . . . He sucked in a breath. And with glass.

Stained glass in all colors and shapes sat propped up on shelves. About ten shards in the colors of the rainbow hung from the ceiling, twisting and spinning in the breeze created by the ceiling fan.

'You should have a window,' he said quietly. 'They'd sparkle.'

'They do, when I open both garage doors and let the sunshine in.' She pulled the second door up and stood back, a small smile playing on her lips.

'Did you make them?'

'Yes. These hanging here were the rejects because the glass is all bubbly, but I like them. Sometimes I'll make them bubbly on purpose now.'

'I like them too. All this . . .' He pointed to the woodworking tools. 'All yours?'

'Yep. I inherited it from my grandfather along with the Tank. The Land Cruiser,' she clarified. 'I was the only one of his grandchildren that showed any interest in woodworking. It helps me vent off stress when I have a bad day at work.'

He picked up a finely turned wooden spindle that would eventually end up in a chair. 'You make furniture?'

'Some. I fix a lot. Sometimes people throw away stuff that's still good. It just needs a little TLC. Some sanding, a new leg or some upholstery. A coat of paint or varnish. Then it's good as new. Better, even.'

'What do you do with the furniture you rescue?' he asked.

'Donate it, mostly. I keep some. Give a few pieces as gifts.' She pointed to an old-fashioned roll-top desk that had been stripped and sanded, the drawers freshly stained. 'That's going to be a wedding present for Deacon and Faith. It'll look nice when it's done.'

'Faith will love it,' he said, knowing his cousin's fascination with antiques. She had spent the past nine months inventorying then selling off many of the best pieces she'd inherited from her grandmother, putting the money in a fund for the victims of the killer who'd taken Mikhail's life and the lives of so many others. 'She'll treasure it because you put so much time into it.'

Shrugging self-consciously, Scarlett reached up to pull the string on the overhead light bulb, illuminating the garage before pulling both outer doors down. Marcus considered helping her, but he was enjoying watching the movement of her body as she stretched and turned and flexed. She came to her feet after pulling down the second door and stared at him, clearly seeing the appreciation on his face.

'It's not a crime scene,' he said, looking his fill. He'd seen her shiver before when he'd dropped his voice deeper, so he did that now, shamelessly enticing her with any tool at his disposal. 'And we are definitely not in public.'

'No,' she said huskily, sending every drop of blood from his head to his groin.

He moved toward her, but she sidestepped him. 'Come on,' she said. 'I have to walk the dog.'

Marcus exhaled heavily and followed her from the garage into her laundry room, closing the door behind them. 'You're trying to kill me now,' he muttered, then smiled when he heard her chuckle.

'Maybe just a little, but you can take it.' She dropped to one knee at the sound of pattering of dog claws, their rhythm staccato. 'Hey, boy,' she crooned as a three-legged bulldog came around the corner. Her hands gently cupped the dog's jowly head, her thumbs scratching his ears. 'Fooled you, didn't I? I came in a different door than I left this morning. Made you work to find me.'

The dog looked up lazily and uttered a token growl at Marcus, making her laugh. 'He's not much of a watch dog, but that's okay. Zat, this is Marcus. He's okay.' She looked up at Marcus over her shoulder. 'He won't bite you.'

Marcus hadn't thought he would. He'd been too absorbed in watching Scarlett's face as she talked to the dog to even care if the dog had bitten him. She was softer, gentler than he'd ever seen her. And suddenly he envied the dog, who was the current recipient of that gentle touch. Slowly he eased down on one knee beside her, so close that their hips bumped and her cheeks colored the prettiest pink.

'You adopted him from Delores's shelter, didn't you?' he asked.

'Yes. Not the first time I went out there, or even the second. But he was still around the third time I visited her. I kept thinking that a family with kids would take him and give him a good home, but nobody did. So I did.' Her voice softened to a croon again. 'Idiots didn't know they'd passed over the best dog in the shelter, did they, Zat? So I'm the lucky one.'

Marcus's throat tightened as he wondered if she knew how much she'd just shared with him. This woman fixed broken things. He wondered if she saw him as broken too. He didn't want to think so, even though he knew it was true. 'Why do you call him Zat?' he asked as he scratched behind the dog's ear, for the simple pleasure of brushing against her hand as he did so.

'It's for the movie – *Zatoichi*. He's a blind swordsman.' She shrugged. 'Japanese martial arts movies are a thing with my brothers. Phin especially. I sent him a picture of Zat when I adopted him, hoping it would bring back some good memories of our *Zatoichi* movie marathons, but I haven't heard a word.'

'How long has it been since you sent it?'

'A month.'

'Send it again,' he suggested softly. 'He may want to reconnect but not be able to. Yet. He can always say he didn't get the first text. Or the first twenty. Just don't give up on him.'

'I haven't. I won't.' She met his eyes. 'You haven't given up on Stone.'

'No. I can't. He . . . needs me.'

'Why?'

Marcus hesitated. 'That may be a story for another day.' He waited for her to get angry, but she surprised him again, nodding sagely.

'I get it. Some secrets are yours to tell. Others aren't.' She stood up quickly and walked into her kitchen, done in classic 1970s. But it wasn't retro, it was original, the wallpaper bright enough to make his eyes bleed. 'It's on my list of things to do,' she said apologetically. 'But the stovetop and the microwave both work, so I can eat until I can afford the oven I really want.'

'What do you really want?' he asked, curious now.

She opened a drawer and pulled out a catalog. 'This.'

Marcus whistled at the six-burner, two-oven Viking range. 'That's a monster. Do you cook, too?'

'I was one of seven kids and my mom worked a full-time job. We all can cook.' She paused, lifting her brows. 'But I can *cook*.'

'I have one of these,' he said, pointing to her dream oven. 'In my apartment. It's never been used.'

Her eyes widened. 'That's a crime.' She took the catalog and put it away. 'Speaking of crime, I need to walk Zat, get you back to your job and get back to mine.'

No, not yet. Just a few more minutes. His mind scrambled, then remembered. 'What about my head? You were supposed to fix it.'

She blinked, startled. 'I forgot. I'm sorry. I'll walk him and then tend to you. Come here, Zat. Let's go outside.'

His gaze dropped to her ass when she bent over to fix a leash to the bulldog's collar, and he shoved his hands back in his pockets when they itched to touch her smooth curves.

'Just make yourself at home,' she said. 'But don't sit on anything but the blue couch or the rockers in the living room. Everything else I'm still fixing.'

Marcus followed her to the back door, watching as she patiently waited for the three-legged dog to hop down the steps. Then he watched her pull her cell phone from her pocket as she walked with Zat around her backyard, where the dog proceeded to water every blade of grass he could.

'You're letting out all my AC,' she called over her shoulder, not turning to look at him. 'Close the door or you'll air-condition the whole damn neighborhood. I've got to check my mail. I'll be in soon.'

He complied reluctantly, not wanting to miss a moment of their time together. Which made him sound all touchy-feely, he thought, but he didn't care. Now that he'd decided to go for this relationship, he didn't seem to be able to slow himself down. He wanted her – all of her. And he wanted her now.

She, however, seemed to be wanting to slow things down. He'd have to follow her lead on this one. There was no way he was forcing her to do anything. Even if it killed him. Which it just might.

Reining in his desire, he went into the living room to sit on the blue couch, but stopped short in the doorway. The room resembled a furniture store more than a living room. There were desks and nightstands and even two twin-sized headboards leaning against a wall. Chairs of all shapes and sizes were clustered in groups. Some, like the desk in the corner, were clearly broken, some were works in progress, and others appeared pristine. There were upholstered chairs, desk chairs, dining room chairs ... and three brand-new rocking chairs.

The rockers drew his interest, and he crouched beside one of them, running his hands over the wood, looking it over. The workmanship was flawless, the design sleek yet homey. A carved inscription on one of the curved runners caught his eye. *SAB.*

Scarlett A. Bishop. *She made these.* 'Shit,' he whispered. 'She's really good.'

'Thank you,' she said from behind him.

He looked over his shoulder to see her standing there, her phone in one hand, the wrapped-up leash in the other. She'd shed the tactical vest and her weapons, leaving her in a thin top that showcased every curve. 'What does the A stand for?' he asked.

Her dark brows lifted. 'You mean that didn't come up when you ran my license plates?'

He refused to be embarrassed about that. 'It probably did. I was so relieved that the Land Cruiser belonged to you that I didn't ask for anything else.'

One corner of her mouth quirked up in an almost-smile. 'Anne. The "A" is for Anne.'

'Good Catholic middle name,' he said, and was startled to see her almost-smile fade as her eyes went expressionless.

'The Bishops are a good Catholic family,' she said bitterly, then turned on her heel and disappeared down the hallway, leaving him to wonder what he'd said. Because he'd obviously touched a raw nerve.

He heard water running, and thirty seconds later she reappeared carrying a tackle box with FIRST AID neatly printed on the side. 'Have a seat on the sofa and I'll take care of your head. Then I really need to start working on finding Annabelle. I ran a search of all the churches within a two-mile radius around the Anders house. There are over forty of them, assuming Tabby attended a church nearby. If we expand the search area, we're up in the hundreds.'

Marcus didn't think he should tell her that he'd already tasked Gayle with calling the churches in the area, asking if they had a parishioner named Annabelle. Gayle had found nothing so far. But another thought had occurred to him during the mostly silent drive to Scarlett's house. While she sat the tackle box on a scarred end table, he sat down on the blue couch as she'd directed, then took out his phone and brought up the website he used for background checks. But before he started his search, he noticed that the contents of her first aid kit would put most medics' packs to shame.

'Are you preparing for the apocalypse?' he asked, pointing to the box.

'Close enough,' she said, taking out a pair of latex gloves. 'I'm the babysitter of choice for all my nieces and nephews. They can play rough with each other, so I'm fully certified in CPR – adult and infant – and have taken the basic paramedic's training. No kid's getting hurt on my watch.' She glanced at him as she pulled on the gloves. 'Do you have any latex allergies?'

'Nope. My body is one hundred percent latex tolerant. Especially the retractable parts.' He waggled his brows, which made her laugh.

She looked over his shoulder at his phone. 'What are you doing?'

'I was thinking about Annabelle and Tabby, how their paths might have crossed and how Tabby would get in touch with her.'

'They go to church together and she used that cell phone she was trying to reach when you found her.'

'Maybe. Probably, even. But what if it's simpler than that?'

She sat on the arm of the sofa, so close he could smell her hair. 'What do you mean?'

He forced his mind to clear, a nearly impossible task with her so near. 'Whoever took the Anderses – kicking and screaming – didn't know to look for Tabby, which means Chip kept her a secret. Do you think he'd let her go to church?'

Scarlett bit her lower lip and Marcus swallowed a groan. She shook her head. 'No, you're right. Vince Tanaka had our resident Internet guru do a background on Tabby. I saw the email when I was out walking Zat. The search came back saying that Tabitha Anders's last known address was outside Boston, but the address was obviously a fake. Chip was hiding her for some reason. So if she and Annabelle didn't meet at church . . .'

'Maybe her name is Church.' He typed in Annabelle Church and the Anderses' zip code. Fifteen seconds later, he had a match. Fifteen seconds after that, Google had given him the connection between Tabby and Annabelle. 'Annabelle Church lives three blocks away from the Anderses and is a regular golfer at the country club.' He turned his phone so that she could see the article and photo that Google had provided. 'She won last year's seniors' tournament.'

Scarlett leaned closer to his phone, filling his head with her scent. But she didn't seem to be aware of the effect she had on him, absorbed only in reading the article on Annabelle Church.

'This says that she won the tournament despite suffering from a seizure disorder that's left her unable to drive a car. She drives to the course in this tricked-out golf cart using the bike path.' Taking off the gloves, Scarlett pulled up a map of the Anderses' neighborhood on her phone. 'The bike path runs through the trees behind the Anders house. You're right. I guess I made that harder than it needed to be.'

269

'It was only a guess, Scarlett.'

'A damned good one. Let me get this name to Isenberg. She can send a squad car and someone from Children's Services to get the baby and bring Ms Church in for an interview.' She got up from the arm of the sofa and gave him a hard nod. 'That was good thinking, Marcus. Thank you.'

Her approval warmed him inside even as he cooled on the outside when she stepped away from the sofa to make her call. He sighed heavily, knowing that he'd screwed his chances of getting close to her again as she tended the cut on his head.

Finding Ms Church had been the right thing to do, but too many times the right thing sucked ass.

Eighteen

Cincinnati, Ohio
Tuesday 4 August, 4.15 P.M.

'That was good investigating,' Lynda Isenberg said when Scarlett gave her Annabelle Church's address.

'I can't claim credit,' Scarlett told her. 'Marcus O'Bannion found her.'

'Oh. I see.' A very long pause. 'Anything you need to tell me, Detective Bishop?'

Scarlett winced. Lynda only called her 'Detective Bishop' when Scarlett had done something wrong. Kind of like being called 'Scarlett Anne' by her parents. Both pissed her off. 'No, ma'am.'

'I see. Are you sure? I understand he was there with you at the crime scene.'

'Yes, ma'am, he was. And yes, I'm sure. I have no conflict to report.' Not yet, anyway. All they'd done was kiss a little. *Well, okay, that kiss wasn't exactly little.* But Marcus wasn't a suspect and it wasn't like they'd declared their undying love for each other. Either of those would be a conflict of interest. 'I have to feed and walk my dog but I'll be in the office by the time you have Ms Church brought in to CPD. See you then.' She hung up before Lynda could point-blank ask her if Marcus was with her, only to have her cell phone start chiming with an incoming call.

Scarlett grimaced at the caller ID. When it rained, it poured. She hit *accept* and swallowed her sigh. 'Hi, Dad.'

On the sofa, Marcus's eyes widened with interest.

'Scarlett Anne, are you all right?' he demanded. 'I heard you were shot at.'

Scarlett let the sigh out. Being part of a family of cops meant never having any privacy on the job. Her father had particularly good sources of information – he and Lynda Isenberg were old friends. 'I'm fine, Dad. Not a scratch on me.'

'I heard you were in the line of fire because of a reporter.' Her father's disdain was unmistakable.

'He's a publisher, not a reporter.' It was a fine distinction, but a critical one. A publisher who did the right thing even when it meant losing a scoop. 'And actually I don't have a scratch because of him. He pushed me out of the way. Took all the flying splinters and rock himself, shielding me.'

'Oh,' her father said gruffly. 'Well. I'll thank him when I meet him, then. Your mother wants to see you, to prove to herself that you're not dead.'

Scarlett shook her head. Her mother would never ask her brothers to do the same. 'Tell her I'm not dead,' she said, trying to keep the attitude from her tone. 'I'll drop by when I can, but it won't be today.'

'I should make you tell her yourself,' he grumbled. 'But I know you're busy with this case.' He exhaled heavily. 'Stay safe, okay, baby?'

She forced her lips to curve. 'Okay,' she said with a pleasantness that was equally forced.

A slight hesitation. 'Listen, about this publisher . . . Your lieutenant seems to think he's more than a witness to you.'

Scarlett's teeth clenched. Yet another question her parents wouldn't dream of asking her brothers. 'Is this an official question? Sir?'

A pause, longer than the hesitation. 'And if it is?' her father asked crisply.

'Then I'll tell you the same thing I just told Isenberg. No conflict of interest. Sir. I have things to do. I'll call when I can.' She hung up and drew a deep breath.

Her father always did this to her. Always treated her like she was five years old. She'd thought when she earned her badge that he'd change, but he hadn't. She'd thought when she earned her detective shield that he'd change, but he hadn't then either. He might never change. She'd learn to be okay with that. Someday. At least she knew it was because he cared, but that didn't make it any easier to tolerate.

'I've made things difficult for you, haven't I?' Marcus asked quietly from the sofa.

Yes, you have, but I'm okay with that too. 'No, not really.'

'You lied to your boss. And to your father. Who is also a cop, I take it?'

She frowned at him. 'Yes, he is a cop. I come from a long line of cops. And no, I didn't lie to either of them.'

'You told both of them that you didn't have a conflict.'

'And I don't. You'd be a conflict if you were a suspect.' *Or if I were to fall in love with you.* 'You are not a suspect.'

'And if I were?'

'If I had even an inkling that you were, your ass would be in lockup so fast your head would spin. But you're not a suspect.' She shrugged. 'And sticking with me is the best way to keep it that way. If you're with me, nobody can accuse you of anything.'

His lips curved, making her heart stutter in her chest. 'Protecting me, Scarlett?'

'Maybe. Maybe you need it.' She went back to the table that held her first aid supplies. 'Mr I've-got-concrete-in-my-head.'

'Touché,' he said, sounding pleased. 'You're going to fix me up after all. I thought you'd be racing out of here to interview Annabelle Church.'

'It'll take Lynda a little while to coordinate a pickup with Children's Services, and I'm only fifteen minutes from the precinct, so we've got a little time.' She pulled a headlamp from the box, slipped it over her head and turned it on, then went back to the bathroom to wash her hands again. A minute later she was back, snapping on a new set of gloves. 'Hold still,' she said, sitting on the arm of the sofa again so that she could get close to the cut on his head. Holding a pair of tweezers in one hand, she pushed his hair from the wound with the other and wiped away the dried blood with some soft, dry gauze.

'You look like a coalminer,' he said gruffly.

She frowned again. 'You do realize I'm holding a pair of very pointy tweezers mere millimeters from your head?'

'You do realize you've got your breasts in my face? I have to distract myself somehow, and commenting on your coalminer-ness was the first thing that came to mind.'

She looked down and her cheeks instantly heated, because he was right. She had pressed her breasts almost in his face. She leaned back and dropped her hands, trying to figure out how she could accomplish her task without getting so close to him.

He scowled up at her. 'I'll be quiet. Just get the cut cleaned. I can control my baser instincts that long.'

'I'm sorry. I'm used to patching up little people. The angle is different.' She scooted closer on the arm of the chair so she didn't have to lean over so far. 'I would have had you sit on one of my bar stools,' she said as she finished wiping the dried blood from his head, 'but they're all wobbly. I'll fix one of them so you'll have a stable place to sit while I do this the next time you almost get yourself killed.'

'God, you're snotty when you're being Nurse Nancy.'

She started to laugh, but held it back to keep her hands steady. 'Nurse Nancy?'

'It's a guy thing. Naughty nurse fantasy.'

A single glance at his lap told her he wasn't bluffing. 'Well thank you very much,' she said sarcastically. 'Now I've got that picture in my mind.'

'Are you wearing the naughty nurse uniform in that mental picture?' he asked slyly.

She huffed. 'I am now. I thought you were going to be quiet. I have to make sure you don't have any debris in here before I clean it.' She stole another glance at the very impressive bulge in his lap and had to draw a steadying breath before leaning a little closer to examine the wound. 'I don't see any splinters of wood or shards of concrete.' She reached for a bottle of wound cleaner. 'This should help numb it while I'm cleaning it. Again, no allergies, right?'

'None,' he said, much quieter than he had been before.

She'd leaned in and was squirting cleaner into the wound when he spoke again, his tone very serious. 'What did your neighbor mean about "that other one"? The one you gave walking papers to?'

Damn you, Mrs Pepper. The old woman had said that on purpose. 'Bryan is an ex. Kind of, sort of.'

'Kind of, sort of?' he asked sharply. 'What does that mean?'

'Well, first, I did give him his walking papers, so he is no longer anything other than an old friend. We've been friends since college. Kind of, sort of means that he was off and on. Never anyone steady. We both knew that. He didn't want to take the walking papers at first and kept ignoring them. So I put my foot down and Mrs Pepper heard us.'

His eyebrows shot up. 'She heard you? Was he fighting with you?'

'No, not that time. We were standing in the driveway. I didn't want to let him in the house.'

'Not that time?'

'Like I said, he didn't want to take his walking papers the first several times I handed them to him.'

'When was the first time?'

'Eight months ago.'

His brows shot up. 'Eight?'

She knew what he was asking. 'Like I said, we were off and on, mostly off. "On" was usually at his instigation. He was in a relationship until eight months ago, so that was the first time it came up.'

'And if he'd instigated something nine and a half months ago?'

Right before she'd first met Marcus. She focused on swabbing the cut on his head to keep her hands steady. 'We'd have probably been on. Bryan has always been a friend, Marcus. We always knew that one of us would end this off-and-on thing eventually.'

'Will he remain your friend?'

She hesitated, then nodded. 'Yes,' she said, packing the cut with treated gauze. 'This stuff has antiseptic in it, so you don't need to add anything else. You should probably have a doctor look at the cut. I didn't see any splinters, but sometimes they hide.' She turned back to her kit to trade the wound cleaner for a roll of tape. 'I'm not sure this will keep the gauze in the wound with your hair in the way.'

'Then shave it,' he said curtly. 'I don't want to go to the hospital or see a doctor.'

Scarlett winced, both at the hurt in his tone and at the thought of shaving off any of his beautiful dark hair. She changed the blade on her razor and cleared away just enough hair so that the tape would stick. 'Bryan and I go back a long way, Marcus.'

'Back to your college days. I heard you.'

And it had hurt him. That much was clear. 'He's more like a . . . war buddy than anything else. We went through a rough time together and for a long time only had each other.' She hesitated again, then sighed. 'I don't love him, okay? I never did. Not like that, anyway.'

A moment of silence. 'What did you go through?' he asked carefully.

Her hands stilled as she pressed the tape to his scalp. 'You remember me saying that I'd lost a friend back in college?'

'Of course. Michelle.'

He'd remembered Michelle's name. Scarlett braced herself, willing the words to come. 'I found her body. Thrown behind a dumpster, like she was trash. And there was so much blood.' She gritted her teeth, forcing the images to the side of her mind. 'Bryan was with me. We found her together. It's not something either of us has managed to completely leave behind.'

His sigh was heavy. 'I'm so sorry, Scarlett.'

'It's all right. But there will always be that link between us. I can't make it go away. Trust me, I've tried. I'm sorry.' She'd finished her task, but didn't move away from him. And then a second later she didn't want to move anywhere. He'd leaned into her, closing the distance between them, resting his head against her.

The kiss they'd shared earlier had been intimate. This was much more so.

She peeled off the gloves so that she could stroke his hair. 'I told him that it was over. Today, in fact. When I came home from the alley, he was waiting for me. I'd been avoiding him for the last few weeks because he wouldn't take no for an answer.'

He shuddered in pleasure when she raked her fingers through the hair at the back of his head, so she did it again. 'Do I need to go beat him up for you?' he asked lazily.

Her lips curved. 'Thank you, but no. I can do that on my own, but I don't think that'll be necessary. I . . . told him that there was someone else. He finally got it.'

Marcus pulled back to meet her eyes. 'That someone is me, right?' he asked lightly.

Scarlett chuckled. 'Yes, Marcus.'

He rested his head against her again, his shoulders relaxing. 'Just checking.'

That he could make her smile even as the images of Michelle's broken body continued to flash through her mind was nothing short of a miracle. A gift she didn't intend to squander. She pulled him a little closer, her eyes sliding shut when he wrapped an arm around her waist and simply held her. She felt . . . cocooned. Safe. Wanted.

His arm remained curved around her waist, his hand lightly gripping her hip. He touched her nowhere else, but God, she wanted him to. Her breasts grew heavy, her nipples tight and sensitive, her panties moist. She could smell her own arousal. From the deep breaths he drew, she could tell he could too.

She was going to have to change her clothes before heading back to work. She couldn't go question a woman named Church while smelling like sex.

'I have a confession to make,' he murmured, his breath warm against her breast.

She swallowed hard, her mind no longer on the job. 'More stalking?' she asked, the words coming out husky and thick.

He turned his head so that his lips brushed against her nipple, sending a stream of current straight between her thighs, making her suck in a startled breath. 'No, Detective Smartass,' he muttered. 'Just for that I won't.'

She stroked his hair some more, wondering if he meant that he wouldn't tell her or that he wouldn't touch her. Both were unacceptable. 'Tell me. Please.'

He was quiet for so long that she thought he'd been serious about not confessing, but then he whispered, 'You think I don't like hospitals because of what happened last year.'

One of her hands dropped to his chest, her fingers seeking the place where the bullet had ripped his skin, piercing one of his lungs, but all she felt was his Kevlar vest and she was thankful for it. 'But that's not the reason?'

276

'No. The real reason is that when I was young, my mother spent a lot of time in a hospital. I visited her there and it was not pleasant. The smell of antiseptic makes me . . . Well, it makes me go back to a place I never want to see again.'

There was something here, she thought. Something much deeper. 'Why was your mom in the hospital, Marcus?'

Another, longer, silence. 'She took a lot of pills. I couldn't wake her up, so I called 911. She was almost gone when they got her to the ER.'

'Oh no,' she whispered. 'How old were you?'

'Eight.'

The same age that he'd moved in with his grandfather. 'Why did she take the pills?'

His throat convulsed against her as he fought to swallow. 'It was right around the time my father died. So, uh, no hospitals, okay?'

'Okay.' She kissed the top of his head, wishing she could take the hurt away, but understanding the tentacles those old memories wound into one's brain. And understanding that he'd offered her one of his secrets because she'd given him one of hers. 'If it starts to get infected, I'll call Dani, Deacon's sister. She can check you out here or down at her shelter.'

'All right.' He drew another breath. 'You smell so damn good. I remember that from when you came to see me. When things got too intense, when the smell of antiseptic started to choke me, I'd think about how good you smelled. Like wildflowers.'

'Honeysuckle,' she whispered. 'It's my shampoo. And body wash.'

This time she felt his cheeks crease in a smile. 'Thank you,' he said.

'For what?'

'For replacing the memory of my mom in the hospital with one of you naked and sudsy in the shower. With my hands all over you, getting you very, very clean.'

Everything deep inside her clenched, desperately wanting. 'Oh,' she breathed quietly. 'Unfair, O'Bannion. Really unfair.'

His chuckle was wicked. 'I have another confession,' he said.

She thought she just might like this one better. 'Tell me.'

Abruptly he moved, grabbing her around the waist and yanking her down to the sofa. A second later she was on her back, staring up into his dark eyes. His body was a welcome weight, the bulge in his pants now hard and thick, positioned exactly where it felt the best.

Well, not *exactly* where it felt the best. There wasn't enough time for that. But she wished there was, especially when he began slowly thrusting against her. Her eyes slid closed on a low moan. She really wished there was. 'What is your confession?' she managed, gasping when his thrusts became harder, faster.

His head dipped low, his lips kissing a line of fire up her throat, along her jaw, up to her ear. 'I dream.'

A shudder racked her body. 'So do I. I have for months and months. Since the first day I saw you. Heard you.'

'Why didn't you say anything?' he demanded hoarsely.

She opened her eyes, snaring his gaze. 'Why didn't you?'

His hands kneaded her shoulders fitfully. 'If I did have a reason, for the life of me I can't remember what it was. In my dreams, you're always looking up at me just like this.'

She brushed her fingers against his cheek, already dark with stubble even though he'd shaved only a few hours before. 'In my dreams, it's always your voice.'

'Good to know,' he murmured. His dark eyes flared hot and needy as they slowly traveled from her face to her breasts, lingering there for a heartbeat or two or ten before returning to her face, staring down at her like she was a treat he wanted to devour.

The tight rein she'd kept on her response simply snapped. She slid her hands into his hair, pulling his head down as she lifted hers up, meeting him halfway, kissing him the way she'd done earlier in that parking lot. And in all of her dreams. Their dreams.

He'd been dreaming of her too. *All this time*, she thought. *All this time wasted*.

And then she stopped thinking when he gripped her hips and hauled her into him, his groan vibrating against her lips, her breasts, everywhere he touched her. He took over the kiss, slanting his mouth, teasing her lips with little licks of his tongue, urging her to open for him, then groaning into her mouth when she did.

His hands squeezed her hips, then slid beneath her to flatten at the small of her back, clenching in the fabric of her shirt as he kissed her mindless. He broke away to let them breathe, kissing his way down her throat, then running his tongue back up, and then he was kissing her again like a man starved. She dug her fingers into his muscled shoulders, struggling to get closer to that hard ridge in his jeans.

She heard a low growl of frustration, then realized it had come from her throat. The growl became a moan, his greedy mouth muffling her cry of satisfaction as she thrust back, her release coiling tighter and tighter.

She couldn't remember ever feeling this good while still wearing her clothes. Once again he pulled back to let her breathe, and her head fell against the sofa cushion. She was panting, for God's sake. She could run a seven-minute mile, but he had her so wound up that her lungs felt like they were about to burst. He was panting too, but he didn't seem the least bit deterred, pressing hot, wet kisses down her throat and along the edge of the scoop-neck T-shirt she wore. All while he continued the hard, steady thrusting between her legs.

'Feels so damn good,' she whispered, and he pulled back to meet her eyes, his hunger laid bare.

'I want you,' he said quietly. 'I have dreamed of having you every way imaginable. Woken up so damn hard it hurt. I want to taste you and touch you and stroke you and watch you come for me. Over and over and over. And then I want to come inside you and start all over again until you scream my name.'

Scarlett opened her mouth, but not a single word came out, the images his words evoked winding her even tighter. But her expression must have been sufficient, because his mouth curved with satisfaction.

'Is that a yes?' he asked, dropping his voice a few notes lower.

She swallowed audibly. Nodded. Forced real words out of her mouth. 'That's a yes.'

His eyes closed, his erection becoming even harder when she hadn't thought it possible. Without warning, he palmed her breast and she cried out in stunned pleasure, hardly even aware that he was pushing up her shirt and her bra along with it until she felt his hot, moist mouth close over her bare nipple. A low moan rumbled from her throat as he sucked hard, making everything inside her go taut as a bow. 'Oh God.'

He released her breast and she grasped the back of his neck, urging him back down. 'More. Please. Don't stop.'

'Scarlett.' No longer smooth, his voice sounded raw. Nearly a growl. 'Look at me.'

She did, and instantly felt her inner muscles contract, her body responding to the urgency in his eyes. His hand slid between them, his fingers tugging on the button of her slacks. 'Yes or no?' he whispered hoarsely.

She bucked her hips up against his hand, looking him square in the eye so that there would be no doubt for either of them. 'Yes.'

Lincoln Park, Michigan
Tuesday 4 August, 4.30 P.M.

Drake Connor sat in his sister's car, glaring at the gas gauge and its fucking 'E'. The ads lied. Belle's Civic didn't get nearly the miles per gallon they promised. He should have been able to make it into Detroit. Instead he was sitting on the side of the road with an empty tank, his buddy wasn't answering his cell phone, and his bitch sister had reported her credit card as stolen.

Just because I borrowed it. She didn't have to get her nose all out of joint.

He hadn't been able to get gas a few exits back because the card had been declined. He was lucky he hadn't been caught. He didn't dare try again and he'd already spent the cash he'd taken from her purse on another box of bullets and a greasy burger. The burger had been hours ago and he was starting to get hungry. When he got hungry, he got mean.

So he tried to never get hungry. Thanks to his bitch-face sister, it looked like hunger was going to be unavoidable.

Cursing, he tucked the Ruger he'd stolen from Stephanie's father at his back, in the waistband of his jeans, and untucked his shirt to cover it up. He was going to have to walk.

It was probably for the best. If Belle had reported her credit card stolen, she may have reported the car stolen too. He'd look for food and another car. Then he'd hunt down his buddy and figure out how to sneak over the border.

He set out on foot, wondering where Stephanie was and if she'd given him up to whoever had broken into her house and dragged her family away. If she was even still alive.

He hoped not. If she was dead, she couldn't squeal.

Cincinnati, Ohio
Tuesday 4 August, 4.45 P.M.

Yes. She said yes.

Marcus didn't wait. Couldn't wait. He yanked at the button on her pants then jerked the zipper down, rearing back to kneel on the sofa. She lifted her hips so that he could pull the slacks off her long, long legs while she struggled to get her shirt and bra over her head. The garments he'd so impatiently shoved up her body now joined her pants on the floor, leaving her bare except for the tiny pair of panties cut to show off her legs and hips.

He knelt there for a long moment, staring his fill, rubbing the back of his hand over his mouth. Almost forgetting to breathe. She was all curves and lean muscle, her breasts as perfect as he'd dreamed. The panties were plain white cotton, but the damp spot so clearly visible between her legs made them sexier than the sheerest lace.

He lifted his gaze to her face, saw her watching him with a confidence that stoked him even higher. She was proud of her body, as she should be.

Not breaking her gaze, he unbuttoned his shirt and shrugged out of it. He was working on easing down the zipper of his jeans when she sat up and started pulling on the Velcro straps of the Kevlar vest. His hands froze on his jeans when hers streaked up his bare chest, her fingers raking through the hairs there.

'Do you know how much I wanted to do this in your office?' she murmured huskily.

'As much as I wanted you to?' He closed his eyes and enjoyed the feel of her hands petting him until they abruptly dropped to his jeans, still hanging on his hips. He opened his eyes to see her licking her lips.

'Hurry, Marcus.'

His brain short-circuited and snapped. With his last vestige of sanity, he found the condom he'd stuck in his pocket, then ripped off his jeans and her panties and might still have had the control to lower himself to her gently if she hadn't dug her fingers into his ass and pulled him down against her. He took her mouth without finesse and she kissed him back as wildly, her fingernails raking his ass a sweet hurt.

He slicked his finger between her legs and groaned into her mouth. 'So wet. My God.'

She nipped at his lip. 'Hurry, Marcus,' she whispered.

Somehow he got the condom on, and seconds later plunged into the hottest, tightest, wettest . . . He shuddered violently, his hips rocking up into her of their own volition, hard and fast. He didn't think he could have gone slowly had his life depended on it.

Finally. He slid his arms up under her back, his hands hooking over her shoulders, kissing her mouth, her neck, anything he could reach, all while he rode her hard. She threw her head back, her eyes closed, her mouth open slightly as she met him thrust for thrust.

Suddenly he needed to know she was with him. 'Scarlett. Look at me.'

She struggled to open her eyes, but when she did, his breath froze in his chest. Staring up at him, she was straight from his fantasies, better than any of his dreams. 'I need this,' she said breathlessly. 'Need you.'

He was brutally close to coming, but needed to know he'd gotten her there too. Without slowing his thrusts, he reached between them, found

281

her slick, swollen clit and pressed down with his thumb.

Her body went rigid and her fingers scrabbled for purchase on his ass as she teetered on the edge. He sucked her nipple into his mouth and bit her, shoving her over.

With her scream echoing in his ears, he buried his face in her neck and followed her.

He surfaced to feel her stroking his hair, the hands that had clawed at his skin now gentle. 'Oh my God,' he murmured, and she laughed quietly.

'That about sums it up.'

'I'm crushing you.'

'I don't mind,' she said lazily. 'I think I took a layer of skin off your butt.'

'I don't mind either. It'll grow back.' He exhaled, knowing he had to get up, but not wanting this moment to end. 'Thank you.'

Her hands stilled, her fingers threaded through his hair. 'No thank yous,' she said seriously. 'I needed this too. I don't think I could have concentrated if I hadn't vented off a little of the need.' She kissed his temple, lightening her tone. 'I think the pressure will build up again pretty quickly, though. I got a lot of need saved up for you, mister.'

He smiled against her skin. 'Good. I got the same for you.'

The muted ringing of a cell phone made them both groan. 'That's me,' she said, blindly reaching to the floor, feeling around for her pants, retrieving her phone just as it stopped ringing. 'Shit,' she muttered. 'It was Isenberg. Give me a second.' She redialed, then grimaced when her boss answered. 'It's Scarlett. Sorry, I was walking the dog.'

Marcus lifted his head. 'Lame,' he mouthed, and grinned when she rolled her eyes at him. He dropped his gaze, taking a few moments to admire her breasts again now that his higher brain functions were returning. He'd left a few marks, he noticed, feeling possessively proud of them.

Her nipples were still hard, and he nuzzled one, making sure to pay attention to its mate. Squirming, she grabbed his hair and pulled until he looked back up at her. She was scowling at him. He grinned again.

'Yes, ma'am,' she said to her boss. 'I'll be there as soon as I can. I'll have to pick him up on the way.' She hung up, and he took the phone and tossed it on top of her pile of clothes.

'Who are you going to pick up?' he asked.

'You. You've been summoned to Isenberg's office.'

He lifted his brows. 'Why?'

'I don't know. Let's find out.' She pressed her lips to his chest, and then her tongue darted out, licking his nipple, surprising a gasp out of him.

'At least I didn't do that when you were on the phone with your boss,' she said with a pointed glare.

His smile was smug. 'I *am* the boss.'

Her lips twitched. 'I have to shower up, *boss*. If I do end up interviewing a woman named Annabelle Church, I don't want to do so smelling like sex.' She smacked his ass. 'If you want to shower, there's one in the bathroom down the hall. You'll find towels in the closet, next door down. I'm going upstairs. Do not follow me.'

Her tone was playful, but she was serious. 'Why aren't we conserving water?' he asked, reluctantly pulling out of her body. He rolled to his feet, already missing the wet heat of her.

Halfway to the stairs, she paused and looked over her shoulder. 'Because I haven't had enough of you yet,' she said quietly. 'If I get in a shower with you, I'll be very late.'

Groaning at that mental image, he went in search of the bathroom at the end of the hall, more ridiculously happy than any man had a right to be.

Cincinnati, Ohio
Tuesday 4 August, 5.00 P.M.

Ken nodded his thanks to Alice as she put a cup of tea on the dining room table in front of him. 'Did you feed Stephanie Anders?' he asked her.

Alice made a face. 'Yes. I nearly fed her my finger, because she tried to bite it off. Burton had to put her in the cage. I fed her through the chain links. I feel sorry for the man who buys her. He'll have to muzzle her. And oral? I don't think any sane man would even ask.'

Ken chuckled. 'The man who buys her will do so for the challenge of taming her.'

Alice sat down and sipped her own tea. 'So you say. Make sure they know that there are no refunds on that one. And tell them to get a tetanus booster before they take delivery.'

Decker joined them at the table, his laptop under one arm. 'Surely she can't be that bad.'

'She's worse,' Ken said flatly. 'Pretty, but deadly.' He pointed to the laptop Decker was setting up on the table. 'What's up with that?'

'Sean didn't think he should leave the office,' Decker said. 'Especially with Reuben still AWOL. We're going to hook him up online.'

Burton came in from the attached garage, stripping a pair of latex gloves off his hands. 'Where's Demetrius?'

'Following up on Marcus O'Bannion,' Ken said, not bothering to hide his

283

annoyance. 'O'Bannion has more lives than a damn cat. Demetrius will call in from wherever he is. So will Joel. He says he's too busy with the books to spare the time to come out.'

'Why?' Decker asked with a frown as he finished setting up the video call with Sean.

'Because he has too much work to do himself since I put you back on Security,' Ken told him. 'I need to hire a new accountant to assist him.'

Decker shook his head, looking exasperated. 'No, I mean why is Demetrius spending so much time tailing O'Bannion? Just shoot the fucker in the head.'

'That's what I said,' Burton muttered.

Alice raised her hand. 'I agree. I read the *Ledger*. That man and his reporting team have made more enemies than anyone can count. Just shoot him, for God's sake. Frame one of the people he put in jail a few years ago. They all get out eventually. You could even make it look like O'Bannion killed the guy you're framing in a shootout. Easy peasy.'

Ken smiled at her. She was too cute. 'Easy peasy?'

She folded her arms over her chest, her eyes narrowing. 'Yes. Seriously, Dad, take Demetrius off the job and give it to me. I can shoot as well as any of these guys.'

He patted her hand. 'I know you can. Give Demetrius a little more time. If O'Bannion is still alive by morning, he's all yours.'

'What?' Sean asked from Decker's laptop screen. 'Who's all Alice's?'

'O'Bannion,' Burton said. 'We're tired of Demetrius missing him.'

'Hell, yeah,' Sean grumbled. 'Kill the fucker and let's get back to business.'

'Drop it for now,' Ken ordered. 'Connect Demetrius and Joel on the call.'

Joel looked harried when he answered. Ken frowned at the dark circles under his accountant's eyes. Surely Decker hadn't been carrying that big a load? The kid had only been exposed to the legit business before this morning. 'Joel, when was the last time you slept, man?'

'Two nights ago. I hit a snarl.'

Ken frowned. 'What kind of snarl?'

'One I need to discuss with you privately.'

That didn't sound good. 'When we're done with this call, I'll call you back,' Ken said.

When Demetrius answered, they heard road noise over the speaker. 'I'm following my bait to lure O'Bannion. I got nothing new to report. Call me if anything comes up.'

'No,' Ken said coldly. 'You stay on the line. This is a team meeting. First up, where is Drake Connor?'

'He popped up on a CPD BOLO filed this morning,' Sean said. 'His sister, Belle, reported her car stolen. Later this afternoon, she reported her credit card stolen.'

'I wanted to make sure she wasn't protecting Drake,' Decker said. 'I visited her, searched her home. Her car is missing and there's no sign of Drake. I told her I was a cop, following up on the reports she filed, and asked her why she didn't report her credit card stolen until hours after the car. She said she didn't know that Drake had taken the card until her credit card company called asking if she was in Michigan. Someone tried to use the card to buy gas.'

'Stephanie's boyfriend is headed for Canada, just like I thought,' Ken said. 'Can we track him?'

Decker shook his head. 'His cell phone appears to be a throwaway. Sean's trying to locate the car using its GPS.'

'I just started searching, so it'll be a little while before I come back to you with a location,' Sean said. 'But we know he's near Detroit. How damaging is it if he gets away?'

'He knows that men with guns broke into the Anders house and carted them all away, and he knows that Anders was buying labor from someone. But the cops know both of those things by now, without Drake's help. Considering he killed someone this morning, he's unlikely to go to the cops anyway. It's more that he's a loose end.' And Ken did not like loose ends. 'There isn't anything damaging he can do to us. I just don't like that he's out there as a wild card.'

'When I finish with O'Bannion, I can go after him,' Demetrius offered.

Luckily he couldn't see the rolling eyes of the other members of his team. Even Burton was shaking his head – and Reuben's second-in-command had always welcomed Demetrius's assistance in dealing with security threats. Demetrius had lost the respect of the team. Perhaps it was time to do away with the old guard and bring in a new team. Demetrius had gotten sloppy.

So had Reuben, wherever the hell he was. And Joel looked like he was about to have a heart attack any minute. Whatever snarl he'd found in the books was going to be bad indeed.

'Just focus on O'Bannion,' Ken said to Demetrius. 'He's the biggest threat.'

Alice folded her arms and gave Ken a pointed look. He knew what she was thinking – his biggest threat shouldn't be trusted to someone who kept missing the mark. His girl was right, even though he didn't want to hear it.

'Where is Drake's sister now, Decker?' Ken asked. 'If she can ID you, she's a loose end.'

'Already taken care of,' Decker said. 'I removed her from the house and snipped the loose end.' He drew a quick line across his throat with his forefinger. 'No blood in the house. I took care of her at the disposal site. She's mixed in with the Anderses.'

Ken looked surprised. 'Who told you to do that?'

'I did,' Burton said. 'I've been busy going over Reuben's car.' His jaw tightened, his eyes flashing with bitter anger. 'And taking care of his wife.'

Ken leaned back in his chair, very unhappy. 'Next time, ask me first, Burton. And if your duties upset you that much, perhaps it's time you resigned.' Burton paled, and rightly so. No one resigned. They just stopped breathing. Ken looked Decker up and down. 'You don't seem to be any worse for the experience.'

Decker just shrugged. 'I saw men exploded to bits when their Humvee hit an IED. Body parts strewn all over the goddamn place. I was on the cleanup crew. A woodchipper pointed into an open grave is a lot neater, actually.'

Alice looked horrified. 'Oh my God, Decker. You picked up body parts?'

He didn't blink, his face like hewn stone. 'Somebody had to. We scooped them up, separated them out as best we could, then ID'd them and sent them home in full-size coffins. Waste of a coffin, but I guess it helped the family.' He turned to Ken. 'I didn't mind, sir. Don't blame Burton. I asked what I could do to help. I don't have forensic experience, Burton does. It made sense to us.'

'I decide what makes sense,' Ken said. 'Clear?'

Decker nodded. 'Yes, sir.'

'All right, then. What else do you have to report, Decker?'

Decker hesitated. 'I went to the hospital to eliminate Tabitha Anders, but they have an armed security detail. I figured I needed to wait until we had a plan to get around the guard. For now the old lady isn't saying a word. She's unconscious and isn't expected to live.'

Ken rubbed his forehead. 'You were right to wait, Decker. Alice, you still have that nurse's uniform?'

Alice nodded. 'I'll take care of Aunt Tabby. Not tonight, though. I'll wait until the guards do their shift change in the morning.'

"Thanks. Sean? Have you gone through the computers seized from the Anders house?'

'I have, and I'm glad we got there first. Chip Anders was an idiot who wrote down important and damaging things and thought he could hide the files by encrypting them. A five-year-old could've broken into his files. I have his bank account information and the locations of all his safe deposit boxes. And . . .' Sean sighed, 'a file listing us as his supplier. Specifically Demetrius and you, boss, by name.'

Ken sucked in breath. *Sonofabitch Anders. I'm so glad I killed him, and even happier that Stephanie wanted that puny little prick to hurt.*

Demetrius exploded over the speaker. 'What? What the fuck did you just say?'

'I said,' Sean repeated clearly, 'Chip listed you and Ken as his labor suppliers. If we'd been a little later, that file would be in the hands of the cops.'

'He may have had hard-drive backups,' Decker said. 'We took several sets of keys from his house. One of those keys will hopefully fit the safe deposit box where he hid his backups. If they're hidden in the house, the cops may have found them.'

'Slimy little bastard,' Ken muttered. 'How much money did we get from his accounts?'

'Less than three million,' Sean said. 'He may have offshore accounts. I'll keep looking if you want.'

Ken shook his head. 'I'd rather we concentrate on his safe deposit boxes. I want any backups accounted for and disposed of.'

'I've already identified the backups he made from his operating system logs,' Sean said. 'I'll focus on finding out where he stored them. He probably has an encrypted file on his computer listing the locations for the backups he made. He listed everything else.'

'You may want an alternate story to feed the cops in case they find the backups before we do,' Decker said quietly.

Ken raised his brows. 'Say more.'

'Well, if the cops do find it, you'll claim it's a dirty lie, of course. Then you could have an explanation of why Anders would want to implicate you, a reason he'd hate you that much or how he'd profit by implicating you. Maybe a business deal gone wrong, an affair with his wife, a snub at the country club . . .'

Ken looked at Alice. 'Come up with something good, okay, honey?'

'On it,' Alice said, noting it on a pad of paper.

'What else?' Ken asked.

'I need the trackers you recovered from the Anders house,' Sean said. 'I need to reset them and have them ready for the next shipment.'

Burton frowned. So did Decker. The two men looked at each other with narrowed eyes.

'We gave them to Sean along with the computers,' Decker said.

Sean went still. 'I don't have them.'

Ken's gut did a slow twist and roll. *Not good. Not good at all.* 'Where does the signal say they are?'

'It doesn't. The last place they show up on the tracking software is the Anders basement. They ran out of battery shortly after they were cut from the two women.'

'I saw them in the van when we loaded the Anderses,' Decker said.

Burton nodded. 'So did I.'

'I'm sure they're still in the van,' Decker said. 'They have to be.'

Ken exhaled, unnerved. 'Find them. One ankle tracker falling into the wrong hands was bad enough. Three trackers have the potential of giving away too much information to the police. Demetrius, when's the next shipment due?'

'The Brazilians,' Demetrius said through the speaker phone. 'They're coming in through Miami. I'll be transporting them. If Alice can ride shotgun, I'd appreciate it.'

'Sure,' Alice said with a shrug. 'When are we going to do that?'

'Friday,' Demetrius answered. 'We're getting six, half of which are cherry.'

'That's good,' Joel said, startling Ken, who'd nearly forgotten he was there. 'They should bring a good price. We can use all the income we can get.'

The virgins always brought more. 'Demetrius,' Ken said, 'I want you to set up an auction for the Anders girl. I want her out of here ASAP. She's too much of a pain in the ass. We'll get some photos and a list of her attributes.'

'She does have nice attributes,' Burton allowed.

'And she's fluent in French,' Ken added.

Decker grimaced. 'Plus she knows curse words in at least six other languages. She used every one of them when we were dragging her out of her house.'

'And she bites,' Alice complained loudly.

'She should be sedated for shipment,' Ken said. 'Plan on that.'

'I'll set it up,' Demetrius said. 'I have to go. I've nearly lost my mark twice now because I was distracted by listening to you. I'll call in later.' He disconnected without another word.

So sorry we distracted you, buddy, Ken wanted to say sarcastically, but held his tongue. 'Burton, you haven't given an update on what you've found in Reuben's car.'

'Not much,' Burton admitted. 'A few hairs that belonged to him, a few that belonged to Miriam, but she was his wife. She would have been in his car. I found one hair that's consistent with Jackson's. In the trunk.'

Everyone winced. That the assistant who'd disappeared along with Reuben had been in the trunk was not a good sign. Not good at all.

'Reuben can't just disappear off the face of the earth,' Ken said decisively. 'I've known the man for years and he has expensive tastes. If he falls off the grid and can't get his fancy Belgian beer, he'll have a fit. He's not the kind to rough it in a tent. He's going to surface sooner or later. You are all dismissed. Just keep your phones on.'

Decker and Alice left the room, and Sean and Joel signed off via video. Ken called Joel back on his cell phone. 'So what did you need to tell me that you couldn't say in front of everyone?' he asked.

'I found some money missing from our paycheck account. Five million. I traced half of it to an account that links to Reuben.'

Ken closed his eyes, both surprised and not, all at once. 'Shit. What about the other half?'

'It was harder to trace, but it went into an account that belongs to Demetrius.'

Ken stared at the phone in his hand, disbelieving. 'Are you sure?'

'Very sure. I put a tracer on both accounts. If either Reuben or Demetrius tries to access the money, I'll know. I'm sorry, Kenny.'

'Me too,' Ken sighed. 'Me too.'

Demetrius was his oldest friend, but this was business. He had to go. Demetrius of all people would understand that.

Nineteen

Cincinnati, Ohio
Tuesday 4 August, 5.45 P.M.

'I wish I knew what this was about,' Marcus muttered as he followed Scarlett into the elevator in the lobby of CPD's headquarters. Being summoned by Isenberg was disconcerting. He'd never met the lieutenant, but he knew Scarlett was nervous and that made him edgy.

Scarlett hit the button for the homicide floor, then stepped a foot away from him, her arms crossed over her chest. He didn't mind the distance for now. She'd laid down the rule that there was to be no PDA at crime scenes or in public. He briefly wondered if elevators counted as public, then squelched the thought. Elevators had cameras, and CPD's elevator-cams were probably strong enough to be scoping out his blood cells at this very moment.

'I don't know,' she said glumly. 'Lynda's usually cool, but sometimes she gets a bug up her ass and turns kind of unpredictable. But if she gets on my case for my "involvement" with you, I'm going to go ballistic. She never said a damn word to Deacon when he started shacking up with Faith.'

He smiled at her. 'Are we going to shack up?'

Her cheeks turned red. 'You know what I mean.'

'I don't know if I do or I don't,' he said as the elevator stopped and the doors slid open. 'I may need you to explain it to me.'

'Explain what?' The clipped words came from a woman with short gray hair and steely gray eyes that snapped with temper.

Scarlett tensed. 'Marcus O'Bannion, this is my boss, Lieutenant Isenberg, the CO of the Major Case Enforcement Squad. Lynda, this is Marcus O'Bannion, publisher of the *Ledger*.'

Isenberg glared at him. 'Don't even consider calling me Lynda.' Then she turned to Scarlett. 'Explain what?'

'The hierarchy in MCES,' Scarlett told her. 'You know, how you and

290

SAC Zimmerman share FBI and CPD resources, who gets the final say in any conflict, you know – stuff like that.'

Marcus wasn't sure if he should be impressed or appalled at the ease with which Scarlett lied to her boss. He decided he'd wait to see how he fared with the lieutenant before making a final decision.

'Yeah, well, when you figure it all out, maybe you can tell me,' Isenberg said grumpily. 'Come on. She's waiting.'

Scarlett didn't move, so neither did he. 'Who's waiting?' she asked. 'What's this about?'

Isenberg's smile was a shark-like baring of teeth. 'Miss Annabelle Church. Follow me.'

'Wait,' Marcus said, and Isenberg halted mid-step, turning to face him. 'Did you get the baby from her, Lieutenant? Is the baby safe? And did Annabelle know about the other two escapees? Tala's family?'

Isenberg gave him a hard, indecipherable look. 'Yes, yes, and no,' she said, ticking off her fingers. 'Children's Services is in Interview One with Church and the baby. Church wouldn't relinquish control until she'd talked to her attorney, and to you, Mr O'Bannion.'

Marcus stared at her. 'Me?'

'You. Church said that Tabby Anders told her to keep the baby safe and to contact you if she – Tabby – didn't get in touch with Church by five P.M. today. It seems that after reading your article in the paper today, Tabby Anders trusts you. So, congratulations. You've managed to manipulate public opinion positively.'

Marcus let the sarcastic dig go, shaking his head. 'It wasn't only the article. Tala had told Tabby about me. It was Tabby that encouraged her to trust me.'

'Marcus captured her saying this on the video file that I sent you,' Scarlett said gently. The file he'd captured using his cap-cam.

'I know. I listened to it.'

'Then why are you angry with me?' Marcus asked her bluntly. 'I haven't done anything wrong.'

'No, you haven't.' Isenberg rolled her shoulders as if to loosen them up. 'You're right. But I don't like witnesses dictating the presence of the press. It's a bad precedent to set.'

'I haven't printed anything that I haven't cleared with Detective Bishop first.'

Isenberg shot Scarlett a sharp look of disapproval. 'I know that too. Come along. Both of you. Time's wasting.'

Marcus didn't like the way Isenberg was treating Scarlett, but this wasn't his world, and if his years in the military had taught him anything, it was to respect the chain of command. Biting his tongue, he did as Isenberg requested, following her into a classic interview room with a mirrored wall that undoubtedly hid observers. Those observers had probably muted the volume control, because Tala's baby was wailing at the top of her lungs.

At the table sat an elderly lady with a frail, crêpe-papery look about her. Beside her was a sharply dressed man wearing a two-thousand-dollar suit and shoes that cost at least that much or more, rubbing his temples with a pained look. At the back of the room a woman in her thirties walked back and forth, trying to calm the source of the wailing.

The baby's cries made Marcus's shoulders sag in relief. This was the child that Tala had sacrificed her life to save. He nodded at the elderly woman at the table. 'Ms Church? I'm Marcus O'Bannion.'

'Finally.' Annabelle Church glared at Isenberg. 'I didn't think she was going to let me see you.'

Marcus's lips curved despite his best intentions to keep Isenberg happy. 'Well, I'm here now. But can you give me just a minute?' Without waiting for an answer, he walked to the social worker who was unsuccessfully trying to quiet Tala's child. The baby appeared to be about a year old and – to his relief – very healthy. Physically she seemed no worse for the day's events. Of course the emotional damage was yet to come.

This child has a long row to hoe, he thought, his heart twisting at the big brown eyes that stared up at him, filling with tears. 'Hi, Malaya,' he said softly, pitching his voice in a way that he knew children liked. 'What's wrong, honey?'

Immediately she stopped crying, sniffling a little. Then she stopped his heart by reaching her chubby hands toward him, looking like she was about to cry again.

Marcus glanced at the social worker for permission.

'Just while we're in this room,' the young woman said. 'I have to take her to emergency foster care when we're done here, so please don't get too attached to her.'

'Fair enough,' he said, then gathered the baby in his arms. Hitching her up so that her cheek rested on his pec, he wished he'd taken off the Kevlar so that she had a softer place to rest her head. A few pats to her back and Malaya was asleep, but a glance at Isenberg had his temper rising. The woman was watching him with a resentment she didn't even try to hide.

'I was eighteen when my brother Mikhail was born,' he told the lieutenant, keeping his voice melodic and smooth. 'I spent my senior year of high school getting him to sleep at night to give my mom a break. So if you don't mind,' he continued sweetly, 'please wipe that insulting look off your face or I won't be responsible for the next words that come out of my mouth.'

Isenberg blinked, startled. 'I . . . I apologize.' She shook her head. 'Proceed, Detective Bishop, so we can get that child into emergency foster care before she starts screaming again.'

Scarlett's surprised expression told Marcus that this crass behavior wasn't the lieutenant's norm. Curious, he held his temper and sat at the table, letting Scarlett take the lead.

'Has she been fed?' Scarlett asked quietly.

'Yes,' the social worker answered. 'Ms Church fed her, and I gave her another bottle while we waited for you. I changed her, too. I think she's just scared and tired, but Mr O'Bannion seems to have taken care of that.' The social worker gave him an approving nod.

Scarlett's glance was equally approving. 'That's good.' She took the seat on Marcus's right, across from Annabelle. 'Ms Church,' she started, 'thank you for coming in to talk to us. This has been a trying day for so many people.'

Annabelle took her eyes off the sleeping Malaya long enough to nod at Scarlett. 'I didn't want to come in with the officer and the social worker. I was hoping Tabby would call me. Nobody will tell me what's happened to her.'

'She's at the hospital, getting very good care,' Scarlett said. She'd called for an update on her condition as she and Marcus drove to the police station. 'She was beaten severely.'

Annabelle pressed trembling fingers to lips. 'Oh my Lord. I was afraid of this. She told me to go, not to come back and not to call the police. She didn't want to risk Mila and Erica.'

'Mila and Erica are Tala's family?' Scarlett asked, and Annabelle nodded.

'Mother and younger sister, respectively. Where are they?' Annabelle asked.

'We don't know,' Scarlett said. 'We were hoping they were with you.'

'No, no.' Annabelle shook her head sadly. 'I haven't seen them, not since Tabby gave me the baby.'

'Why did Tabby think she'd be risking Tala's family if she called the police?' Marcus asked, afraid he already knew the answer.

'She was afraid they'd be deported,' Annabelle said, 'or maybe worse. Her nephew told them that the police would put them in jail if they complained. They're here illegally, but Tabby said they're good people. I should have said something this morning, but I was afraid for Tabby too. That nephew of hers . . .' Her eyes narrowed. 'Where is he?'

'We don't know that either,' Scarlett told her. 'Tabby told us that he, his wife and daughter were taken away at gunpoint.'

'Couldn't have happened to a nicer guy,' Annabelle muttered. 'That man is a beast. He's been abusing Tabby for years.'

'Did you know that Tala and her family were being held against their will in the house?' Isenberg asked.

Annabelle shot her another glare. 'No, I did not, not until today. I didn't know about anything other than the fact that Tabby was afraid of her nephew. That I've known for a few weeks. I didn't know there were other people in the house until Tabby called me this morning and asked for my help. She told me that there was a baby in danger and asked me to take the child and ask no questions, just to keep her safe until I heard from her again. And if I didn't hear from her, to contact you, Mr O'Bannion. She told me the baby's mother was the girl that was killed in that alley this morning. The one in your article. She said that you would help us.'

'And I will,' Marcus said, with a side look at Isenberg. 'What about Mila and Erica? How do you know their names?'

'Tabby told me this morning. I came to the house in my golf cart, and she brought the baby to me.' Annabelle smiled sadly at the child in Marcus's arms. 'In a covered basket. Kind of like Moses, I guess. I could see two other women standing in the doorway, holding each other and sobbing. The older woman was clutching a rosary like a lifeline. Tabby said that they were the baby's grandmother and aunt. I asked why they were giving the baby away, and Tabby told me that the baby's mother had been murdered this morning and they were afraid of what would happen to the child. I asked why they didn't come with me, said I'd take them all to the police, but Tabby said they wouldn't leave the house, that they were afraid of being deported.'

She doesn't understand, Marcus thought. *Annabelle doesn't know these women were slaves.* He wondered if Tabby had known, but then he remembered her saying she hadn't done enough. *Never enough.* She had known, he thought, but had probably been too terrified of her nephew to cross him. Considering the severity of the beating Anders had delivered, she had been right to be terrified.

'Tabby asked me not to tell anyone,' Annabelle continued, 'until she could get things sorted out for them. But she said that if something happened to her, she wanted me to call the police anyway. She wanted someone to know their names.' Two fat tears ran down the woman's papery cheeks. 'I didn't understand. I still don't. I do charity fund-raisers and give a lot of my money to the needy, but I don't know this world. I wish I'd followed my instincts and called the police. Those two women might be all right now.'

'They may still be all right,' Scarlett said soothingly. 'Can you give us a description? Maybe sit down with a sketch artist?'

'Like on the television?' Annabelle asked. 'I guess so. I'm not sure how accurate I'll be. But first I want to see Tabby.' She half rose, her large purse looking like a suitcase in her frail hands. 'Which hospital is she in?'

'County,' Scarlett told her, 'but if you'll work with me a little longer, I'd appreciate it. I'll even make sure you get a ride to the hospital.'

'All right.' The woman sat again and folded her hands over the purse in her lap. 'What else do you want to know?'

'I'd like to know how you met Tabby,' Scarlett said. 'And when.'

'It was early in June. I was admiring her hydrangeas,' Annabelle said. 'She was sitting outside in a lawn chair with her face to the sun. I called over to her, saying I wished my hydrangeas looked like hers. At first she got startled, like a little rabbit. She didn't say a word, so I drove away in my cart. The next few days she didn't come out and the lawn chair was nowhere to be seen. But then one day, she was sitting outside again. I called to her and she waved. A little wave like this.' Annabelle wiggled her fingers. 'But she still didn't say anything. It was like she was afraid someone was listening.'

'That sounds familiar,' Marcus muttered, softly patting Malaya's back as she stirred in his arms. 'But eventually she did talk to you.'

'Eventually. We played that little game for a couple of weeks, till one day she got up out of the chair and crossed over to me, using her walker. She introduced herself, gave me a bouquet of the hydrangea blooms, then went back into the house. I thought maybe she was a little . . . you know.' Annabelle tapped her temple. 'Dementia. After another couple of weeks we were having actual conversations. Then one day she had a big bruise on her face. She said she'd fallen down the stairs. I knew better, of course. I told her to come with me, to walk away and she could live with me, but she refused. Said she couldn't leave her girls. I didn't know what she meant then.'

Her gaze fell to Malaya. 'But I do now. I wanted to call the police, but Tabby wouldn't let me. She said everything was fine. She begged me not to call, said she'd send the police away if I did. I should have called. Why didn't I call?'

Amazingly, it was Isenberg who offered comfort. 'Because we're socialized to mind our own business to a certain extent,' she said, laying a hand over Annabelle's. 'Even if you had called, Tabby would have probably told the police that there was no issue, that she had no complaint. You came when she needed you. That counts. That matters. You took that baby and bought her formula and diapers and very likely saved her life. *That* matters, ma'am.'

The tears were streaming down Annabelle's face. 'Thank you, Lieutenant, but I don't think I'll ever forgive myself. What I did today was just a drop in the bucket. What can I do to help Mila and Erica? I have resources. I can offer a reward for their return.'

'I don't think that's a good idea,' the social worker said.

Annabelle bristled. 'Why not?'

'Because,' the social worker said, 'if they're worried about being deported, having their names on the TV with an offered reward is too much like having a price on their heads. They'll bolt and we may never see them again.'

'She's right, ma'am,' Scarlett said gently. 'But I do know someone they might trust. Tala had a crucifix around her neck and you say that Mila had a string of rosary beads?' She looked at her boss. 'Maybe they'll trust a priest.'

Isenberg nodded approvingly. 'I'll get an undercover officer in a collar and robes.'

Marcus opened his mouth to disagree, but Scarlett beat him to it. 'We need to earn their trust,' she protested. 'If they find out that the priest is really a cop, they won't tell us anything.'

'Then I hope you know a priest,' Isenberg said. 'Otherwise I'll have to make some calls to the chaplain's association, because I don't.'

Looking uncomfortable, Scarlett glanced at Marcus. 'Do you know one?'

'We're Episcopalian,' he said apologetically.

Annabelle shrugged. 'I'm a Lutheran. My pastor wears a collar, and he's a very kind man. I can give you his name if you like.'

'Don't look at me,' the social worker said. 'I'm Baptist. No collars.'

Isenberg rolled her eyes. 'I'll get one of the CPD chaplains.'

Scarlett shook her head. 'You don't have to do that, Lieutenant.' Her grimace was so slight that Marcus might have missed it had he not been watching her so closely. 'My uncle is a priest. He's very practical and very kind. He'll do the right thing.'

Marcus wondered why she hadn't brought her uncle up at the beginning. He intended to ask her when they were alone again.

Scarlett squared her shoulders. 'If we don't have any more questions for Ms Church, I'll arrange for her transport to the hospital, and then I'll give my uncle a call.'

Annabelle's attorney spoke up for the first time. 'I'll take my client to the hospital.'

'Your tiny car is too confining,' Annabelle said. 'I've gotten used to my golf cart.'

He smiled at her. 'We can put the top down if you want, Grandma. If we hurry, we can hit the florist on our way there and you can get some nice flowers for your friend.' He handed Marcus his card. 'When Mila and Erica are found, give them this. I don't do immigration law, but I know some people who do. We'll make sure it's pro bono.'

Marcus took the card, taking care not to wake the still sleeping Malaya. 'Thank you,' he said. Annabelle's grandson worked for one of the top firms in the city. Marcus's grandfather had done business with them for years. 'That's very decent of you, Mr Benitez.'

Benitez gave him a nod. 'I was born in this country, as was my father, but his father came over from Cuba on a leaky old fishing boat in the sixties. Not everyone is so lucky as to be born here, and if this situation is what it sounds like, these women were not in that house voluntarily. I want to help if I can. If they want to go home, we can help expedite that. But if they want to stay in this country, they shouldn't have to face deportation on top of everything else they may have suffered.'

Marcus was impressed. This guy had picked up on nuances that many people would not. They had no idea of how and why Tala's family had come to the United States, or if they wanted to go home, but Marcus agreed that after all they'd suffered, the choice shouldn't be taken from them.

Annabelle frowned. 'Are you saying they were kidnapped, Gabriel? And forced to work for that horrible Chip Anders?'

'Not kidnapped, Grandma,' the attorney said, very gently. 'It's called human trafficking, and it happens everywhere. Come on, now. The detectives have to get to work.'

'No.' Annabelle sat unmoving. 'Human trafficking happens in other countries. Like Thailand. Not here, Gabriel. This is Ohio. *Hyde Park*, even. Why would Anders force anyone to work for him? He has plenty of money to pay his employees.'

'Your grandson's right,' Scarlett told her. 'It happens here in Ohio more often than any of us want to believe. Individuals who use forced labor are often rich enough to pay their employees, but they're greedy. They want to cut labor costs so that they can pocket the money they save. They're modern-day slave owners, plain and simple.'

'It's also about power and entitlement,' Marcus added. 'They own people because they can. Until we stop them.'

'I'm sorry, Grandma,' the attorney said soberly.

'I . . .' Visibly shaken, Annabelle pulled a diaper bag from under her chair. 'I had my maid go out and buy baby things,' she said numbly. 'Formula and bottles and diapers. A blanket and a few outfits. But no shoes. She needs shoes.'

'How about a pacifier and a teething ring?' Scarlett asked. 'Tala had them with her, but we had to take them into evidence.'

Annabelle looked in the bag. 'There's a pacifier in here, but it has to be sterilized first. It's still in the package.' Her grandson gently took the bag from her, and handed it to the social worker. Then he led her from the room. She followed him out the door, still looking shocked that human trafficking was happening in upper-crust Hyde Park, right under her nose.

The social worker held out her arms for Malaya. 'I'll take her now, Mr O'Bannion. Thank you. I needed a little break.'

Marcus held Malaya's head close to his chest for a few heartbeats, strangely reluctant to hand her over. 'Will you tell me where she's placed? I'd like to make sure she knows about her mother when she's old enough.'

'She'll go into emergency foster care for now. That's only good for a few days. I can't tell you where she'll be placed after that, but I can give her long-term foster parents your name once she's permanently placed. They'll have to decide whether or not to allow you to see her.'

Marcus wanted to argue, but knew it would be pointless. He knew she was only following the rules. Luckily he knew people in Children's Services who might be able to help him. He put Tala's baby in the social worker's arms. 'Can I have your card?'

The woman gave him one, then turned to Scarlett and gave her one too. 'Detective Bishop, if you need to reach me for any reason, please call.'

Scarlett took the card with a civil nod. 'I'll get an officer to escort you out.' She waved a uniformed officer in, then surprised Marcus by leaning over the baby and lightly kissing her forehead. 'Your mama loved you, little one. I hope you understand that one day.'

When she lifted her head, her eyes were expressionless again and Marcus's throat tightened. She'd been hit as hard in the heart by the baby's safe return as he was. Of course she would be. This was a woman who owned a miner's headlamp and a seriously deluxe first aid kit so that she could keep her nieces and nephews safe.

She looked at him, emotion flaring in her eyes before she did another long blink, restoring her calm. 'At least we know their first names,' she said. 'Mila and Erica. Lynda, I'll call my uncle now if you can wait with Marcus while I do.'

Isenberg inclined her head once. 'Of course. But, Scarlett, wait. I have a question about this uncle-priest of yours.'

Scarlett paused in the doorway. 'Yes?'

'Is he from your father's side or your mother's?'

Scarlett sighed. 'He's my father's youngest brother.'

Isenberg's eyes laughed even though her mouth remained almost grim. 'Then he's Father Bishop?'

Scarlett rolled his eyes. 'If you know what's good for you, you will not laugh at his name. He goes by Father Trace because of that.' Then her mouth curved. 'He says he hasn't sought advancement within the church hierarchy because Father Bishop is bad enough. He doesn't want to be known as Bishop Bishop.'

Isenberg's lips twitched. 'I will be on my best behavior with him.'

Scarlett's brows lifted. 'And with Marcus?'

'Of course,' Isenberg said again, sobering as Scarlett left the room.

Marcus wanted to protest at being left alone with the lieutenant, but he held his tongue for Scarlett's sake. Isenberg had already given her a hard time about spending time with him. He wasn't going to give her any more ammunition.

When the door was closed and they were alone, Isenberg cleared her throat. 'She asked me to stay with you because she knows that I owe you an apology, Mr O'Bannion.'

'You'll have to be more specific, Lieutenant. I'm thinking you owe me more than one.'

One side of her mouth quirked up. 'You might be right,' she said wryly. 'My first exposure to you was nine months ago, when you were shot trying to shield a victim. I thought you had to be a good guy. My opinion has not changed.'

'Then why the hostility?'

Looking down at the table, she exhaled heavily. 'I never met you nine months ago. I only read in Detective Bishop's report about what you'd done. My first personal exposure to you was this morning, when I heard you singing on the video files you took in the park.' She swallowed audibly. 'You were singing the song they sang at the funeral of someone who was close to me. I've been . . . off all day.'

'"Go Rest High On That Mountain",' Marcus murmured. 'It was sung at my brother's funeral too. I couldn't sing it for him myself then because my lung was punctured. I only sang it the first time in the park because I thought I was alone. I sang it the second time because I thought it would draw Tala. It did.'

'I know. Scarlett told me.' Isenberg exhaled again. 'Hearing your voice was a trigger for me as soon as you walked off the elevator, just as I'd known it would be. I knew when you became involved with this case that I would hear your voice again, probably often. Even if you're just talking, it's a trigger. It takes me back to a place and time I'd rather forget. Add to that the loss of one of our team members today, and I'm not myself.'

'Special Agent Spangler.' Marcus felt a stab of guilt that he'd almost forgotten about him. 'I'm sorry for your loss.'

'Thank you. Nevertheless, I took it out on you. I'm sorry. I was wrong.'

It was a pretty apology, he thought. Sincerely delivered. 'It's forgotten,' he said. *As long as it doesn't happen again*, he added silently. 'I'm sorry my singing brought you pain.'

'The pain was already there,' she said with something between a smile and a grimace. 'The pain is *always* there.' She tilted her head, studying him closely. 'Do you intend to pursue my detective?' she asked, abruptly changing the subject.

'Scarlett?' he asked, stunned by her directness. 'I think that's not your business.'

She gave him a hard nod. 'Good. I was hoping you had a spine. You'll need it to deal with Scarlett Bishop. She's a hard nut.'

That long blink thing must fool other people, he thought. Because the woman he wanted with every breath in his body had a soft heart he feared he could smash if he weren't careful. *So be careful*, he told himself. *Be very, very careful.*

He said nothing, just sat staring at her, and Isenberg actually laughed. 'This might be more entertaining than I thought,' she said. 'You might finally be the one to catch her.'

His brows lifted at this. 'Others have tried?'

'Others have tried and failed spectacularly. Others have hit the pavement face first after saying a simple hello. She's got a rep, our Scarlett. Quite the ball-buster.'

He frowned at her phrasing, the lieutenant dropping several notches in his esteem. 'I'm surprised you'd refer to another woman that way. Especially one you claim to respect.'

She smiled at him, a smile so genuine that it nearly knocked him speechless. 'Good enough,' was all she said, and he realized she'd been testing him.

'Did I pass?' he asked dryly.

'With flying colors. For now.' Her smile disappeared like it had never existed. 'Now let's talk about how this case will be covered in your paper. I'd like to keep a few facts back.'

Marcus pulled his phone from his pocket and opened a new file, willing to negotiate. 'Like what?'

Cincinnati, Ohio
Tuesday 4 August, 6.30 P.M.

Scarlett slipped into the now empty observation room to use the phone, hoping she hadn't made a bad decision in leaving Lynda alone with Marcus. Her boss had been off balance since early that morning. Lynda was normally brusque, but not rude. Scarlett wanted to give her an opportunity to talk to Marcus one-on-one, hoping that would bring her around.

Partly for Lynda, partly for Marcus. *But mostly for me*, she thought. There was no telling how long this case would drag on, and she didn't want to keep him a dirty secret. The better Lynda regarded him, the easier doing her job would be.

She watched them for a moment through the glass until she was fairly certain no blood would be shed. Then she picked up the phone and dialed a number firmly engraved into her memory.

'St Ambrose parish, this is Father Trace.'

The sound of her uncle's voice made her heart ache. She hadn't treated him well at all, and had missed him more than she wanted to say. He'd been her favorite uncle. He'd been her confidant – until Michelle's death had stripped the veil from her eyes and she'd seen the truth about prayer. And God. Unfortunately, her uncle had been a constant reminder of that pain, so she'd begun avoiding him. A month had led to a year, then two, then five, and now ten.

'Hello?' he pressed. 'Is anyone there?'

Scarlett cleared her throat. 'Uncle Trace, this is Scarlett.'

A beat of silence. 'I know it is, honey,' he finally said warily. 'I'd know your voice anywhere.'

She deserved his wariness. 'It's been a while. I thought maybe you'd forgotten.'

'Well that's just ridiculous. Just because you haven't spoken more than hello, goodbye and Merry Christmas to me in ten years? You really think I could ever forget your voice? Besides, my caller ID said Cincinnati PD. It's not your father or any of your brothers, unless they've undergone a serious hormonal change, so by process of elimination, it had to be you.'

She laughed unsteadily. 'How are you?'

'The same as the last time you saw and ignored me at Colin's christening,' he said tartly, making her wince. Then his voice softened. 'Why are you calling, Scarlett?'

'I . . . I need your help. I have two women who went missing earlier

301

today. We believe they're victims of human trafficking, so we don't want to put their faces on the news.'

'You'll drive them underground,' he said.

'Exactly. It's a woman and her teenage daughter. The woman's older daughter was murdered this morning in an alley downtown.'

'I read about it. What can I do to help you?'

His voice was as much like a warm blanket as it had been when she was a child. 'The mother carried a rosary and the murdered daughter was wearing a crucifix. I thought if a priest came looking for them, they wouldn't run away. My lieutenant suggested having a cop pose as a priest, but—'

'They wouldn't trust you once they found out,' he interrupted.

'That's what I told her. That's why I'm asking you.'

'Where should I meet you?'

'At the main station.'

'All right.' There was a long, long pause. 'I've missed you, Scarlett.'

Her heart cracked, but she couldn't give him false hope. 'This isn't a return to the fold.'

'That's all right, for now. I've missed *you*. I've waited a long time for you to talk to me again. I'll take a conversation with you however I can get it.'

She let out a breath. 'You still got it, you know that?'

'What, the ability to make you feel guilty even when I'm being nice?'

Her laugh was shaky. 'Yes.'

'Thank you. You've ignored me for ten years,' he said mildly. 'My feelings are hurt. You can take a little guilt.'

'I suppose that's fair. If you could be here five minutes ago, that would be great.'

'If I'm caught speeding, will you make my ticket go away?'

She rolled her eyes. 'How about you get here as soon as legally possible?'

'I think that would be best. How will you go about locating these women?'

She hadn't thought about that yet. Her mind sifted through the possibilities now. 'How are you with dogs?'

'Allergic, just like always. Why?'

'I'd like to pair you up with one of the search-and-rescue handlers. Their dogs can track the women from the house where they were living before they disappeared. They didn't have transportation that we know of. They've had several hours' head start, but if they're still on foot, they can't be that far. Put on your walking shoes. You might be hiking. You might want to take some allergy pills.'

He sighed. 'I take it you want me in a cassock, even though it's seven million degrees outside.'

Her lips twitched. 'Yes please. Look as Catholic as possible.'

'As Catholic as possible, huh? Okay. I haven't worn that cassock in years. I'm not even sure I know where it is, but I'll do my best. I'll see you soon.'

'Actually, give me an hour. I have to get the handlers in position with their dogs.' And she still had to fit the meeting with Deacon and his human trafficking expert in between.

She hung up and stared at the phone in her hand. Somehow this day had developed a life of its own. Saying goodbye to Bryan and hello to Marcus, and now this reunion with Uncle Trace.

She fired off a text to her search-and-rescue contact, grateful when the woman texted right back. *Give me an hour. Romeo and I will be there. Will see if I can get another few pairs to help the search.*

She then dialed Deacon's cell phone, frowning when Faith picked up. 'Scarlett? Deacon's a little b-busy right now. *Ohhh.*' Her moan practically vibrated through the phone. 'Um, yeah, Scarlett. What do you need?' She sounded suspiciously out of breath.

Scarlett rolled her eyes, able to visualize the scenario all too well. Those two were so lovey-dovey it made her want to gag.

'You've *got* to be kidding me. *Really?* You couldn't have waited until tonight? Good God Almighty.'

In the background she heard Deacon's muffled voice. 'Tell her I'll call her back.'

Faith blew out a few short breaths like she was in a Lamaze class. 'Give us a minute. He'll call you right baaa . . . Um, yeah. Right back.'

'Not on my cell. I'm in Interview Room One. No recept—'

Deacon came on the line. 'I will *call* you *back*,' he growled.

The line went dead, and Scarlett turned to face the observation window with an impatient sigh. 'Good God,' she muttered, then went still as she laid eyes on Marcus. He was leaning forward slightly, talking to Lynda, his expression serious and focused. Lynda no longer wore as angry an expression, so she must have patched things up. Her boss looked at the phone on the table between them and pointed to something with a raised eyebrow.

Marcus typed something, then looked up at Lynda who gave him a nod of approval and said something that spread a slow smile over Marcus's face.

Scarlett's heart did a roll in her chest. 'Oh my,' she whispered. He was simply beautiful. And she wanted him. Wanted to be the one to put that slow smile on his face.

He flicked his finger over his phone, scrolling down, and Lynda frowned, saying something that made the smile on his face morph into a frown.

The landline rang and Scarlett answered it, not taking her eyes off the man on the other side of the glass as he and Lynda continued to negotiate whatever it was he was typing.

'Bishop,' Scarlett said.

'It's Faith.' She was whispering. 'I know you need to speak to Deacon, but he's in the shower.'

'I seriously do not need any more information,' Scarlett protested, but with considerably less heat than before. Just watching Marcus O'Bannion made her go all soft inside.

'Yeah, I think you do,' Faith murmured. 'Just listen. I don't have much time. That notification he just did?'

The warmth in Scarlett's chest abruptly chilled. How had she forgotten that so quickly? 'Agent Spangler. What happened?'

'It didn't go well. The wife was angry. She attacked Deacon. Scratched his face badly.'

Scarlett lowered herself into a chair. 'She scratched him? Why? Why didn't he stop her?'

'I think he was too stunned at first.'

'And probably numb,' Scarlett said quietly, putting herself in her partner's place. 'And knowing Deacon, he probably thought on some level that he deserved it.'

Faith sighed. 'I knew you'd understand.'

'Where the hell was SAC Zimmerman?'

'Zimmerman wasn't free, so Deacon went alone.'

The idiot. For a smart man, Deacon could do some seriously stupid things. 'Goddammit, Faith. Why didn't he call me or Lynda? Either of us would have gone with him.'

'I suspect he wishes he had, but doing notifications with Lynda always makes him edgy.'

'She's not the softest bun in the box,' Scarlett agreed.

'Very true. He wanted to call you, but he knew you were looking for some church lady.'

'Annabelle Church. We found her. Is Deacon okay?'

'Physically, yes. Emotionally, no. He's done a lot of notifications to victims' families, but this is the first time he's notified the family of a fellow agent. I was working at home when he got here to change his clothes and clean up—'

'Wait,' Scarlett interrupted. 'Why did he change his clothes?'

'He didn't want to hurt her by restraining her, and she did some damage to his shirt. Ripped it, yanked all the buttons off. She would have dug her nails into his chest if he hadn't been wearing a vest under the shirt.'

Thank God for Kevlar, Scarlett thought, looking at Marcus's bullet-free back. 'It sounds like Spangler's wife was a little unstable before Deacon got there.'

'Possibly. He called her pastor and waited until the man got there. Anyway, I was here when he got home and he was in bad shape. I . . .'

'You tended him,' Scarlett said quietly. 'I get it.'

'He wouldn't want you to know how hard this hit him,' she whispered.

'I get that too. I won't let on I know, although I'll have to tease him a little bit about the interrupted afternoon delight. He'd be suspicious if I didn't.'

Faith's chuckle was a little forced. 'Thanks. He said he'd meet you at the field office, that you have some kind of meeting.'

'We do. I was calling to tell him that we have to make the meeting a fast one because we've had some new developments. I won't be able to wait long if he's late getting there.'

'I'll tell him. Thank you. Oh, and Scarlett? Tell my cousin hi,' she added slyly, drawing out the 'hi' to sound teasingly sultry. 'He's quite a looker, isn't he? If I hadn't found Deacon first, I'd totally be hitting on him. I want details. *All* the details, you understand?'

Scarlett's cheeks heated. 'Good*bye*, Faith.'

She hung up on Faith's wicked laugh and went back into the interview room, where Lynda was glaring at Marcus incredulously. Marcus's eyes were narrowed in challenge.

Scarlett frowned at them both. 'What the hell, people? When I left the observation room, you were working well together. Ten seconds later, you're giving each other the evil eye again. What happened?'

'He was being reasonable,' Lynda said, 'and then all of the sudden he goes literally insane. He wants to be embedded in your investigation. Like in that ridiculous TV show where the writer tags along with the homicide detective.'

Scarlett bit back a grin. 'You mean *Castle*? I like that show. It's cute.'

'This is a homicide investigation,' Lynda said harshly. 'We are not *cute*, Detective.'

'Nor am I a writer of *fiction*,' Marcus said, holding back the temper that flickered in his eyes. 'I'm a journalist and this is a story that needs to be told. How many people out there believe like Annabelle Church, that human trafficking happens only in Thailand? And didn't I do everything you just asked with the story about finding Tabby Anders?'

'Mostly, yes,' Isenberg agreed. 'But that's because I asked you about it directly. You didn't offer anything, O'Bannion, and I've been burned by reporters in the past. You'll give me what I want now, but then later you'll pull a fast one and print whatever satisfies your agenda. And that's how cops and victims die.'

Scarlett had sobered at Lynda's earlier rebuke. Now she tried to smooth the waters, because Marcus's request was not an unreasonable one. At the same time, they'd lost a man today, so she could see Lynda's point of view as well. Lynda was voicing the same fears she herself had harbored before she'd gotten to know Marcus. 'He's been on the up and up so far,' she told her boss rationally. 'That article this morning had nothing in it that I hadn't okayed. And he is right about getting the story out. This is important, Lynda. And I trust him.'

Lynda gave her a hard look. 'He's a loose cannon. He nearly got the two of you killed sneaking into the Anders house, and he may have gotten Agent Spangler killed too.'

Marcus opened his mouth to blurt what would have been an outraged denial. Scarlett held up her hand to stop him, grateful when he restrained himself.

'We have no reason to believe Marcus had anything to do with Agent Spangler's death. And . . .' Scarlett drew a breath, knowing she was about to draw her boss's ire, 'I figured he'd try to get into the house. I didn't tell him not to.'

Lynda sat back, her gray eyes gone stone cold. 'You *knew* he was going back there?'

'I expected him to at least consider it. When I realized he was gone, I followed him.' She sat in the chair between her boss and Marcus. 'Lynda, our hands were tied until we got a warrant. What Marcus did was not illegal – and his actions likely saved Tabby Anders's life. She might have died if she'd had to wait for us to get a warrant to enter the house. Because he found her, we now have Tala's baby safe and sound and we know the names of the other two women. He's been quite useful.'

'Thank you,' Marcus muttered dryly, extremely annoyed. 'I'm so happy to be *useful*.'

Scarlett shot him a be-quiet glare, then turned back to Lynda. 'Let him watch us. We have nothing to hide. He'll let one of us read his reports before he uploads or prints them.' She looked over her shoulder to find him definitely unhappy. 'Right, Marcus?'

Twenty

It was all Marcus could do to keep his temper under control. Let the cops read his reports before he uploaded them? How Scarlett could even think he'd consider that . . .

Meeting her eyes, he shook his head. 'No way,' he said firmly. 'That's censorship. I print the truth, whether it's pleasant for you or not.'

Isenberg's nostrils flared in anger. 'I knew he'd say that. He's a reporter. They're all about their First Amendment rights, but care nothing about the rights of the officers – or victims – they place in danger. They stick their mikes in your face and demand details that could destroy lives, just so they can get their damn story.'

Scarlett had winced at Marcus's words, but she visibly flinched at Isenberg's. Settling herself in her chair, she leaned away from both of them. With a single long blink she'd become grim, and his gut didn't like that at all.

'Scarlett?' he asked. 'What's wrong?'

'Nothing,' she said coolly. 'I'm fine.'

She was not fine. Her eyes had gone beyond expressionless. They were blank. Even Isenberg looked concerned, but Scarlett waved away her boss's questions.

'I said I'm fine.' She turned to Marcus, a determined set to her jaw. 'I'm not telling you not to print the truth. I'm saying that there may be things we'll want to hold back, like this morning. You agreed then. What's different now?'

'Nothing,' he murmured. 'But I don't want anyone thinking they can "approve" my work. You need to trust me that I'll keep my word when we decide what gets kept out.'

He held his breath, waiting for her response, knowing that it was a critical moment for the future of whatever relationship they would have.

She held his gaze for a few heartbeats, then shifted her attention back to her boss without a flicker of emotion. 'You don't trust him,' she said, her tone so coldly logical that Marcus wanted to hit something. 'I understand that. I have a hard time reconciling trust and journalists in the same sentence too. They make their living digging up the news and don't care about the damage they leave behind.'

Fuck, no, he thought viciously. He was not going to take that from anyone, least of all from her. He opened his mouth to protest, but sensing it, she raised her hand just high enough for him to get her message. *Be quiet.*

He bit down on his tongue until he tasted blood, and said nothing.

'But,' Scarlett continued evenly, 'Marcus has never given us a reason to doubt his word. He helped us find the Anderses in the first place by identifying their dog. He had their name a full half-hour before we got to their property, but he didn't print it or upload it. He still hasn't. He's not like most of the other reporters either of us have dealt with. If you don't trust him, then trust me. I'll take responsibility for anything he prints.'

'I don't want or need you to take responsibility for what I do,' he said firmly.

Scarlett met his eyes, hers still cold. 'This is my world, Marcus. This is how it needs to work. If you want me to trust you, then you have to trust me too.'

If he hadn't known how much emotion she was capable of, he would never have guessed at what had to be churning behind that icy stare. The crazy thing was, that made him trust her more. She had more self-control than anyone he'd ever met. More than was healthy, he thought. He, of all people, knew how damaging shoving all one's emotions down deep could be.

'All right,' he said. 'I guess in your place I'd demand the same thing. Especially since you all lost a colleague today.' He watched for any flicker of relief in Scarlett's eyes, but there was none.

'Thank you,' she said, her detachment beginning to make him nervous. 'Is this an acceptable arrangement, Lieutenant?'

'Yes,' Isenberg said. She gave Marcus a sharp look. 'Don't make me regret it.'

It was obvious that nothing he could say was going to change the lieutenant's attitude, so he only sighed and shook his head.

Scarlett stood up. 'I have to meet Deacon at the FBI field office. They haven't agreed to your presence, so it's better if I meet you afterward. I'll broach the topic when I'm with them.'

'What's the meeting about?' he asked.

'We're speaking with the person leading their human trafficking investigation team,' Scarlett said evenly. 'I'm not sure what we'll learn, but I'll share all I can.'

'That's all right. I have some things to take care of at the office.' He pushed to his feet. 'You can escort me out,' he said to Scarlett, then gave Isenberg a nod. 'Lieutenant.'

Marcus was quiet as he followed Scarlett out, trying to figure out what had extinguished the lights in her eyes. Then he remembered, early that morning, the look on her face when he'd said that he made his living digging up the news. Her eyes had gone blank then too. He hadn't understood at the time that that meant she was hiding a very emotional reaction.

He waited until they were in her car before asking, 'What did the reporter do?'

She whipped her head around to stare at him. 'Excuse me?'

'You shut down in there as soon as Isenberg started talking about reporters. Please tell me,' he coaxed. 'It matters to you, obviously. So it matters to me. What did the reporter do? I know it was personal, Scarlett. It's written all over your face.'

She frowned again as she pulled out into traffic. 'I had a poker face before I met you.'

He wanted to smile at that, but couldn't let her distract him from what was at the root of the issue. 'The reporter, Scarlett. What did he do?'

She clenched her jaw, grinding her teeth. 'I told you that my friend was murdered.'

'Yes, back when you were at college. Her name was Michelle. You said her killer never got justice.'

She nodded, seeming to relax a fraction when he remembered the details. 'What I didn't say was that I know exactly who killed her. Trent Bracken. He was Michelle's boyfriend.'

Marcus blinked at the venom in her voice. 'Then why is this Bracken not in prison?'

'Because his daddy hired a high-powered attorney who got him off scot-free,' she said bitterly. 'Now the SOB is a defense attorney himself, right here in town.'

'That has to kill you inside,' Marcus said gently. 'Knowing he's free. But what does that have to do with reporters?'

She sighed wearily. 'When Michelle went missing, we – her friends – told the police that Trent was abusive, that Michelle had been afraid of him. Which was all true. The cops were watching Bracken, but he didn't know it then, because they were keeping it quiet.'

'I take it that he found out.'

She nodded. 'Because some narcissistic, big-mouthed, tiny-dicked *reporter* told everyone in town.' She'd said 'reporter' with an angry sneer, but it was the 'tiny-dicked' adjective that made Marcus cringe. 'At that point Michelle was still alive. But Bracken saw his name in print and went ballistic.' Her throat worked as she tried to swallow. 'I found her body the next day. She was still warm. Her blood was still warm. Still dripping down the wall of the alley where he'd dumped her.'

In an alley? Hell, this day had been a bad one for her. Finding Tala's body in the alley this morning had to have yanked her back in time. He could offer his sympathy, but he didn't think she wanted to hear it right now. Plus, there was more to this reporter issue. He could feel it. 'How did the tiny-dicked reporter find out that Bracken was a suspect?'

Her lips twisted. '*I* told him.'

Marcus blinked again, definitely not expecting that. 'You talked to the reporter? Why?'

'Because I didn't know he was planning to become a reporter. When I told him, he was just my boyfriend.'

'Oh.' Marcus tried to find something to say. 'Tiny-dicked' made a little more sense now, and he couldn't honestly say it bothered him to hear it. 'That's one helluva betrayal.'

'Yeah,' she muttered. 'All the reporters had been bugging me for interviews. Because I was Michelle's best friend, they figured I knew things, and I did, of course. I kept saying "no comment", but the assholes wouldn't leave me alone. As if it wasn't bad enough that my best friend was missing . . . Getting back to my dorm room had become worse than running the gauntlet, so I'd been hiding out in Donny's dorm room.'

'Who was Donny?'

'My boyfriend.'

Marcus frowned. 'I thought Bryan was your college boyfriend.'

Her fingers tightened on the steering wheel. 'No, Bryan and I have always just been friends. I already *told* you that.'

'I'm sorry,' he said quietly, soothing her with his voice, because she was sending out serious touch-me-and-die vibes. 'You did tell me that. So why didn't you just go home? I would think that your six brothers could have scared off any reporters.'

Her chuckle was mirthless. 'Colin and Gil were married and in their own homes, and Phin . . . he was on tour in Iraq. Sawyer and Dorian were still in high school, and they wanted to scare the reporters off but Mom wouldn't let them. Arrest records play havoc with college scholarships. Nate was still in elementary school, still a baby. I did go home, though. After.'

'After you found Michelle's body.'

A sharp nod. 'For a few days. I couldn't stay too long. We were headed into finals week and my parents had sacrificed a lot to send me to college. So I manned up and went back so that I could finish the semester.' One side of her mouth lifted in a bitter half-smile. 'Donny actually had the nerve to come up to me and ask for a follow-up interview.'

'What did you do to him?'

'Made it so that he'd never get a TV job. He was pretty before I bloodied his fucking nose. Afterward, not so much.'

'Good,' Marcus said grimly, then frowned. 'But I jumped ahead. You were saying that you'd been hiding out in his dorm room.'

'Yes, because I was a Class A idiot, trusting the limp-dicked asshole.'

'How old were you, Scarlett?' he asked kindly.

She swallowed hard. 'Twenty,' she whispered, and a single tear streaked down her cheek. 'Twenty and so goddamn stupid. I didn't think he loved me, but I never dreamed he'd use me like that.'

Marcus trailed the backs of his fingers over her damp cheek. 'What did he do, honey?'

'He'd been there for me, listening, letting me cry on his shoulder. I didn't know he'd been taking notes the whole time. He sold his story to one of the network affiliates, with the proviso that he got to be the guest reporter.'

'What news show would have agreed to that?'

'The one that wanted the story the most.'

'So Donny just up and decided he wanted to be a TV reporter one day? Was he taking journalism classes?'

Her mouth tightened, little frown lines spidering into her cheeks. 'No, he was a psychology major. His plan was to use the story to get a job with one of the network shows like *20/20* and become famous using his psycho-know-how to trick people into revealing all.'

Marcus scoffed. 'Was he delusional?'

'As it turns out, yes. I didn't know he wanted to be a reporter. I didn't know he wanted to be famous. I don't think he realized it until Michelle's disappearance became national news.'

'Did he get a job?'

'Yes, but not with the network.'

'Because you broke his fucking nose,' Marcus said with satisfaction, earning him a small smile.

'Exactly. He wrote for a tabloid rag, but never got rich or famous. His writing sucked and his story was a one-hit wonder, so to speak. He never

311

got another big scoop and ended up being fired. He didn't get into grad school for his psych degree either. Now he sells cars.'

'Using his psycho-know-how to get people to buy cars they don't yet know they want.'

'Exactly,' she said again. 'So that's why I don't trust reporters.'

Marcus shook his head. 'He wasn't a real reporter, honey. I think you nailed it when you said he was a narcissist.'

'Once Donny broke the story,' she said far too quietly, 'the *real* reporters were all over me. They would not leave me alone. They followed me from class across campus, sticking their microphones in my face. I'm glad I wasn't carrying back then. I would have shot them.'

He had no doubt that she spoke the truth.

She said nothing for a long, long moment, then sighed heavily. 'I couldn't deal with them at that point, so I hid out in church.'

'Your uncle's church?'

'Yeah. I'd spent a lot of time in the school chapel up until that point, but the reporters followed me in there too. So I called Bryan, because he had a motorbike. He picked me up outside the chapel. Stopped just long enough for me to climb on, and then he was off like a damn rocket. He lost the reporters, then took me to my uncle's church, where he and Uncle Trace waited up with me for most of the night, along with Michelle's family and the rest of mine. She and I had grown up in that church, been confirmed together by the priest before Uncle Trace. We spent the whole night on our knees, praying. Except when we were answering our phones. The damn things buzzed all night. The reporters had gotten our numbers and kept calling. We wanted to turn off the phones but we all kept thinking Michelle might call. That *something* would happen.'

'I understand,' Marcus said softly. *More than you know.*

She glanced at him, guilt in her eyes. 'I know you do. I know how you all worried when Mikhail disappeared. I'm sorry. I know Michelle's family and mine aren't the only families to who have suffered like this.'

'That *was* hell,' he murmured, but at least he'd only found Mikhail's body. He hadn't been there when he died. Marcus closed his eyes. He hadn't had to hear Mikhail's pleas for him to help. He hadn't been so lucky with Matty. And he'd been too young to deal with it.

Mawcus. Matty's screams, the screams of a toddler, permanently etched in Marcus's brain. *Mawcus.* Normally Marcus could block them, pretend that he'd never heard them – when he was awake, anyway. Unlike Stone's anguished cries, which he heard waking or sleeping.

Make him stop, Marcus. I just want to go home.

'Marcus?' she asked, her voice thick with concern. 'Um, Marcus?'

Eyes flipping open, he swallowed a curse. He should have known she'd pick up on his slip. 'How did you find her?' he asked, trying to get her back on to her story and off his.

'I got a text the next morning, from her phone.' Another bitter smile. 'I thought my prayers had been answered. The text just said to meet her behind the dorm, that she didn't want any of the reporters to see her. Asked me not to tell her parents either, because she didn't want them to see her that way.' An audible swallow. 'She texted me a photo of herself. I . . . didn't recognize her right away. Her eye was black, her face bruised. She said that Trent Bracken had done it. I was devastated, but relieved that she was alive.'

'Did you tell her parents?'

'No. Her mother had looked like she'd break any minute. She hadn't slept in days, not since Michelle disappeared. Michelle's dad had finally gotten her to leave the church so that she could go home and sleep. I think he slipped her a sleeping pill, because he had to almost carry her out to the car. I figured I'd get Michelle cleaned up, put ice on her eye and then call her mother. That way her mom could get some rest and Michelle could keep some dignity.'

Marcus frowned. 'That I don't understand.'

'Her parents didn't like Trent. He was rich, they were blue-collar regular folk. They suspected he wasn't . . . gentle with Michelle. But I don't think anyone thought he was beating the shit out of her. Nobody but me. I'd begged her to leave him, and she'd tried. She'd broken up with him the day before she disappeared.'

She'd reached the *Ledger* office and pulled into a parking spot on the street, but Marcus didn't move. 'What happened then?'

'Bryan had left just before dawn. He had a morning paper route, ironically enough. When I got the text, I called him to come get me and he dropped everything. I played it cool with Uncle Trace and the family still at the church, told them I needed to go for a run to clear my head. I met Bryan a few blocks away and he drove like lightning back to the dorm. Most of the reporters were gone. The few that were left were camped out in front of the building, waiting to catch anyone coming out for early classes. Bryan zipped through the alleys behind the dorms and nobody saw us.'

She fell silent, staring straight ahead, her eyes unfocused. Unfortunately Marcus had a good idea of what it was that she was seeing.

'You found her?' he prompted gently.

A nod. 'Yeah. Bryan and I found her together. Trent had finished the job.' A very deep breath. 'I must have screamed, because before I knew it,

313

the alley was crawling with reporters, the guys from the front who'd heard me and run around back. I had cameras flashing in my face and microphones shoved down my throat. I still had her blood on my hands. Literally, I mean. I'm surprised you didn't find pictures in your own archives. If a *Ledger* reporter wasn't personally there, the paper had to have run the story with stock photos.'

He'd find out as soon as he got into the office. 'What happened then?'

'Bryan got me out, called my parents.'

The sudden spurt of jealousy disturbed him. 'He was close with your family?' he asked.

A wan smile. 'Mom always called him her seventh son. She still does. Dad took me home, made sure none of the press bothered me. Dad was already pretty high up in the CPD hierarchy, so nobody fucked with him.' She took another deep breath. 'So that is why I don't like reporters.'

'I wouldn't either, in your place. But I'm not sure that would be my biggest problem.'

Her eyes narrowed dangerously. 'What do you mean?'

'I'd also feel like I'd killed my best friend.'

She glared at him coldly. 'Your psycho-babble is as pathetic as Donny's.'

He didn't take her jab personally. 'But that's what's really at the heart of this, isn't it? You trusted someone who betrayed that trust, and your best friend died as a consequence.'

She was quiet for a long, long moment. 'Yes,' she agreed finally, her voice hoarse. 'You're right. Are you happy? You've dug it out of me. You can leave now.'

He reached over and gently gripped her chin, forcing her to look at him. 'No, I'm not happy, Scarlett. I'm goddamn furious right now – for you. What happened to you was disgusting, and those reporters should have been ashamed. But I'm not going to apologize for something I didn't do. And I wasn't trying to gouge this out of you. We have secrets, all of us do. You're entitled to the secrets you don't want to share – except this one was impacting how you see me.' He gripped her a little tighter, taking care that he didn't hurt her. '*Me*, Scarlett. I am not the man who betrayed you and I am not the reporters who hassled you. I'm not going to sell your story or my soul to sell a few goddamn papers.'

He was breathing hard, his heart beating like a drum in his chest. Until her eyes cleared and her lips curved in a genuine smile.

'I know you're not,' she said. 'I've always known, but I didn't want to trust my gut.'

'Why not?'

'Because I wanted you. Too much. I was willing to believe you weren't what on the surface you should have been. I wanted you to be different, so much that it scared me. It still does.'

'It shouldn't. I'm not always the best man, but everything I've ever done I've believed to be for the best at that moment. Even . . .' He released her abruptly, shaken by what he'd nearly confessed.

Her brows lifted. 'Even what?'

Even murder. 'I really need to go.'

She grabbed a fistful of his shirt and gave it a yank. 'I told you everything, Marcus. *Everything.* Don't you *dare* run away from me now.'

He was still breathing hard, but from panic now, not fury. Closing his eyes, he covered her hand with his, flattening her grip, pressing her palm to his racing heart. He thought she should be able to feel it even through the Kevlar.

'Marcus?' she murmured. When he didn't say anything, she sighed wearily. 'I told you what I did. My best friend is dead because I—'

'You didn't do anything wrong,' he gritted out. He opened his eyes, met hers. '*You* didn't kill anyone.'

She went very still, not breaking eye contact. 'Whatever you did, it can't be as bad as what I did, even inadvertently. Tell me. I trusted you. Please trust me.'

He swallowed hard, fighting to control his pulse. *It's only fair,* he thought. She needed to know exactly who he was before this went any further. Before she gave him even more of her trust. He swallowed again, unsure if the panic was from the memories he'd never truly buried or his fear that she'd walk away once she knew the real him. 'Google Matthias Gargano, Lexington, Kentucky, 1989. I'll tell you the rest later.' He let go of her hand and slid his fingers around the back of her neck, pulling her close for a hard, fast kiss that was all desperate need and no finesse. 'You have a meeting. You'll be late. Call me when you're done.'

He jumped from the car, looking back only once to see her staring after him, her dark blue eyes wide and wondering.

Lincoln Park, Michigan
Tuesday 4 August, 7.25 P.M.

Drake Connor was tired, hot and hungry. He made his feet walk the last twenty yards to the gas station, which was the first place he'd come to that would have cold drinks and air conditioning. He'd walked miles, sticking to back roads. Lots of grass. Tons of countryside.

He'd stayed off the highway because he wasn't sure who was looking for him, and he was becoming more cautious by the moment. *You mean paranoid? No, because it's not paranoia when people are actually looking for you.* Considering his sister had reported her credit card stolen, she'd be sure to have reported her car stolen too. All he needed was for a local lawman to recognize him from a BOLO.

He was thirsty and starving. He still had the issue of no food or money, but he'd already planned how he'd get around that.

Glad that he'd had the presence of mind to go back to Belle's car for his ball cap, he pulled the brim down and leaned against the pole holding the gas station sign a good seventy-five feet in the air. He'd seen the sign long before he'd seen the station. Stood to reason it would have a decent amount of traffic, even though it was getting late. He just had to wait for the right vehicle – with the right driver.

A few minutes later, a possible combination pulled up to one of the pumps. A black SUV with tinted glass. A middle-aged woman got out. She wore a business suit with a skinny black skirt that ended below her knees, which would hamper her ability to run from him or fight him. *That works.* Her shoulders heaved in a weary sigh as she stretched her back. She was tired after her long day. *Excellent.*

Now if she'd only go into the station's convenience store after she finished filling her tank, it would be the perfect setup. Drake slid his hand back under his shirt, making sure the handle of his gun was in the optimal position for a quick draw, pulled the brim of his cap low and waited impatiently.

'Yes,' he whispered when she put the gas pump away, got her purse and started walking inside. If she'd only left her car unlocked, it would have been an A-plus combo, but she pointed the key fob over her shoulder and locked the doors with a beep before slipping the fob in the pocket of her skirt.

Drake followed her into the station and up to the cashier, grabbing her around the neck when she reached the counter. He pressed the barrel of the Ruger against her throat, yanking her back against him when she tried to struggle.

'Hands where I can see them,' he said calmly to the cashier. 'One false move and I'll blow a hole in her neck. Open the cash register and put the money in the nice lady's purse.' He nudged the gun against the woman's neck. 'Open your purse for him, nice lady, and put it on the counter.'

Glaring balefully, the man behind the counter did as he was told, filling the purse with small bills. Drake had timed this well. The lotto numbers were about to be drawn and the Powerball was over fifty million bucks, so everyone had bought tickets on their way home.

'You little punk,' the cashier spat, which was funny considering the man was only five-three or so. He was the little one. *Not me.*

From the corner of his eye, Drake caught a movement in the back hallway where the restrooms were. He didn't think, he just acted, pointing the gun at the cashier and pulling the trigger. He heard a scream as the man went down.

A crazy lady with a shotgun ran from the back toward him. Panic closed Drake's throat when he saw her aiming the shotgun at him. He tightened his hold on the hostage, grabbing her purse and backing out of the store, dragging her with him.

'Put the gun down!' he yelled at the lady with the rifle. 'Don't you fucking move!'

'Please!' his hostage cried. 'Don't shoot! He'll kill me.'

'My husband!' the shotgun lady screamed. She ran behind the counter and dropped from sight, probably to check on the cashier.

'Give me your keys and I won't hurt you,' Drake said to his hostage. 'Unlock your car first, then give me the damn keys.' With any luck it was a smart key and he wouldn't have to put it in the ignition. The woman in the business suit obeyed, and Drake swallowed his panic, dragging his hostage around the SUV to the driver's side. He planned to release her and leave her behind when he got in the car, but she began to struggle.

'No! You're not taking me!' She thrashed her body, leaving Drake with no choice. He pushed her to the ground and put a bullet in her head, then jumped in the SUV. He flung the purse with the money on the passenger seat, then started the engine and—

Shit. His gut turned to liquid when he looked in his rear view. The cashier's wife was running out of the convenience store, aiming the shotgun at the SUV. He floored it, the SUV's tires squealing as he burned rubber, fishtailing as he sped toward the station's exit.

Cincinnati, Ohio
Tuesday 4 August, 7.30 P.M.

Scarlett drove a block away from the *Ledger* building and pulled over again, her heart pounding in her throat. She'd been shaken to the core by her own admission, filled with feelings of guilt and despair as well as grim acceptance of what she'd done, but seeing the panic in Marcus's eyes . . . He'd been experiencing true fear. For a moment there she thought he was going to be sick.

Willing her hands to be steady, she Googled *Matthias Gargano, Lexington,* and *1989*. She frowned when the top result was an article from a Lexington newspaper. About a funeral.

Oh my God. It was a child's funeral. 'Who were you, Matthias Gargano?' she murmured. But she was afraid she already knew.

She kept reading and found her guess had been right on the mark.

Mourners said their final goodbyes to Matthias Gargano, three-year-old son of George Gargano and Della Yarborough-Gargano, at Trinity Episcopal Church. The victim was survived by his parents, grandparents, and his two brothers, Marcus, age 8, and Montgomery, age 6. The tragic victim of a kidnapping gone wrong will be interred in the Yarborough family crypt in Spring Grove Cemetery, Cincinnati, Ohio.

Scarlett had to steady her breathing. *How had she not known about this brother?*

'Oh my God,' she whispered. Mikhail was not the first child Marcus's mother had lost to violence. She'd lost Matthias nearly twenty-five years before. 'That poor woman.'

The next article, from the same Lexington paper, was dated a few days earlier, its headline making her racing heart stop short. 'GARGANO BOYS HOME SAFE'.

'Oh no. No, no, no.' Her stomach twisting into a vicious knot, she read on. The three boys had been kidnapped in a well-orchestrated operation, taken from different places but at the same time. Marcus and Montgomery had been grabbed on their way home from prep school.

Montgomery? That must be Stone, she thought.

The family's chauffeur had been overpowered, drugged, then ejected from the car. The two boys had been drugged and carried to an abandoned warehouse. Three-year-old Matthias had been taken from his bed during his nap by someone posing as one of a construction crew that had been hired to do repairs on the family's penthouse.

A ransom of five million dollars had been demanded. Scarlett's mind spun both at the amount and that Marcus's parents had been able to produce it in less than twenty-four hours. Disaster had struck, though, when the kidnappers realized the FBI and Lexington PD were on to them. The family had been warned not to involve the authorities, but the boys' mother had done so. The furious – and panicked – kidnappers shot at all the boys, hitting two, but their third shot missed the oldest.

Marcus. He'd been kidnapped and shot at. *Shot at. My God. How many times have people tried to kill him?* she wondered, horrified. And he'd only been eight years old.

Eight. That was how old he'd been when his mother was hospitalized after overdosing on pills. Scarlett hated suicide because she was left with the unpleasant task of informing the next of kin and she never had answers for their gut-wrenching questions. But that didn't mean she didn't understand it. She'd even contemplated it herself once or twice after Michelle's death. But Della Yarborough had had two boys left, one of whom had been critically injured. Her boys had needed her. Marcus had needed his mother.

'Oh,' she breathed. That was why Gayle was so special to Marcus. She'd been his nanny during this time. So much made sense now, all the way down to Marcus's protection of Stone.

A car horn blared outside her window and Scarlett suddenly became aware of the time. She was now well and truly late. Pulling back into traffic, she fought to clear her mind.

Whatever Marcus was holding inside had to do with this kidnapping, although nothing she'd read seemed like it would have involved a sin on his part. He'd only been eight, after all. How bad a thing could an eight-year-old do?

None of this had to do with Tala, either, she told herself sternly.

But it had everything to do with Marcus, so while it wasn't the most important thing on her plate, it was important to her. She wanted to understand. Desperately wanted to help. She rolled her eyes at herself. She wanted to fix him.

She'd get that chance if she had to tie him to a chair and make him talk to her.

But for now she had to focus on her job, which was to find Tala's killer.

Twenty-one

Cincinnati, Ohio
Tuesday 4 August, 7.30 P.M.

'You had twenty-eight callers while you were gone,' Gayle informed him archly as he tore past her desk, practically running to his office. 'Marcus!' she snapped. '*Stop.*'

He slowed his pace, stopping with his hand on the handle of his office door. 'I heard you, Gayle. Twenty-eight calls.'

'No. Twenty-eight *callers*. Half of them called more than once. Most were not polite. Most called to comment on the story Stone uploaded this morning. You remember,' she said sarcastically, 'the one where you were unable to save a seventeen-year-old girl you met in an alley. Some of the callers were our advertisers, many of whom wanted to know what the hell you were doing in an alley to begin with. Some threatened to pull their ads. I had to grovel, Marcus.' She sat back, arms folded across her chest. 'You do not pay me enough for this.'

He managed to smile at her. 'You're right. Give yourself a raise.'

'Do not smile at me. Do not try to charm me. You always sucked at it.'

He lost the fake smile, staring at her numbly. 'Then what *do* you want?'

Gayle stood up, frowning. 'What did that woman do to you?'

'Which woman?'

'That damn detective. She drops you off here and drives away with you looking like you saw a ghost. And . . .' Her eyes widened. 'Is that a bandage on your head? What happened?'

He shook his head. 'I'm tired, Gayle. I don't want to go over it again. I've written the story already.' He'd done so while sitting with Isenberg. It wasn't long, and he'd need Stone to punch it up, but it had all the relevant facts. 'I'll email it to you. Where is Stone?'

'Your brother's in his office.' Gayle frowned in disapproval. 'Drinking heavily.'

Marcus wasn't sure if her disapproval was directed at him or at Stone. 'Why?'

'He says you've turned him into a babysitter. He dropped Jill off at the university, then came back here, took a bottle of Lagavulin from your desk drawer and went to his own office.'

'Wonderful,' Marcus muttered. 'First Mom, now Stone.'

Gayle's expression instantly softened. 'Whoa,' she said. 'Your brother and your mother . . . two different things. You don't need to worry about him so much, Marcus.'

'I should save it all for Mom?' he asked darkly, then shook his head. 'I'm sorry. I shouldn't take my bad temper out on you. I'll talk to you later.'

He went into his office and shut his door. A glance at the security monitor showed an empty space where Scarlett's car had been. She was gone, off to the FBI field office to meet with her partner, a good man who'd probably never killed anyone. Outside the line of duty anyway.

His chair groaned when he dropped into it. *What the fuck am I going to tell her?*

The truth. He had to tell her the truth. And hope for the best.

Wearily he picked up the phone and called Stone's office, relieved when his brother didn't sound drunk. 'Can you come see me?' Marcus asked. 'It's important.'

'You're not going to need another Kevlar vest, are you?' Stone asked ominously.

'No. The spare is still good.' He hung up, started his computer and Googled 'Michelle', 'murder' and 'Trent Bracken'.

He sighed as hit after hit was returned. Michelle Schmidt's brutalized body found in an alley behind a dumpster, just as Scarlett had said. Trent Bracken, Michelle's ex-boyfriend, was arrested for the crime when it was shown that the victim had identified him as her abuser in her last text, sent to her best friend.

'Criminal justice major Scarlett Bishop,' Marcus read aloud. There were no photos of Scarlett in the articles he found, although one report described her as 'in shock' at the scene.

'I wonder why,' he muttered. Because it was easier to dwell on Scarlett's trauma than his own, he picked up the phone and dialed Cal. As the editor-in-chief, Cal would know exactly where to find the information in the archives, although most of that information was also tucked away in his brain. 'Who was covering the city's crime beat ten years ago?'

'Jeb was. Why?'

'Shit.' Jeb had died a year ago. 'I wanted to find some articles in the archives.'

'I can search for them, or ask Jill to do it.'

'No,' Marcus said firmly. He didn't want Jill in his business until he was sure she wasn't planning to do something stupid – like turn his team in because of the laws they routinely bent investigating child abusers and wife beaters. He especially didn't want her in Scarlett's business. 'Do you remember a murder that happened at the university, a woman named Michelle Schmidt?'

'I remember that one all too well. I'm surprised you don't – oh, wait. You were over in the Gulf then. What do you want to know, specifically?'

'Everything we've got on the guy who did it. Name was Trent Bracken.'

'Okay,' Cal said slowly. 'Although he was acquitted by a jury, you know.'

Marcus didn't care that he'd been acquitted. He was more concerned about Scarlett at the moment. 'Just get me whatever we have on file. This one is personal.'

'A new case?' Cal asked, unable to hide his excitement.

'No. Like I said this morning, we need to lie low for a little while, until this morning's case is solved. Speaking of which, save room in the printed edition for another article about the possible perpetrators. I was out at the house where this morning's victim was being held. Starting in an hour or so, I'll be embedded in the MCES task force.'

Cal whistled. 'How'd you swing that?'

'Kissed the lieutenant's ass.'

'You're sure you didn't kiss that pretty detective's ass? Because if you didn't, I'll give it the old college try.'

Marcus rolled his eyes. 'You're an old horn dog, Cal.'

Cal chortled. 'And you didn't deny kissing the detective's ass. Anything else I should dig up while I'm in the archives?'

'Yeah. Actually, this is something Jill *can* do. Have her search for anything on human trafficking in the tri-state area – any cases, victim profiles, arrests of perpetrators. I want a wide-net search. If she gets a hit from our archives, I want pictures and any original documentation. She'll likely get a lot of hits, but most will be anecdotal in nature. I want her to separate out anything that includes hard data or an account of trafficker convictions.'

Marcus didn't have the numbers, but he couldn't recall more than a few actual convictions or even trafficker arrests.

Cal was quiet for a second. 'The girl this morning . . . she was being trafficked?'

'It appears so. I'll also need a mobile camera unit.'

'You planning to carry it on your back?'

'I was, yes. Why?'

'Because I saw how you were favoring it this morning. Let me go with you.'

Marcus was stunned. 'You want to go out in the field?' Cal had been manning the archives and the press runs for twenty years.

Cal's answer was gruff. 'Yeah.'

'Mind if I ask why?'

'Yeah, but I'll tell you anyway. One of the women at our synagogue helps out victims of sex trafficking. She did a presentation for the congregation a few months ago. Not a dry eye in the house. Mine included. If the girl in the alley was trafficked, I want to help.'

'It's a scorcher out there, Cal,' Marcus said gently. 'And I've been shot at twice today. I'd feel a lot better if you stayed here and put the intern to work in the archives.'

'Twice?'

'Yeah. Just keep it quiet for a while, okay? Gayle's gonna chew me a new one when she finds out. I'd like to delay that as long as possible.'

'I can't say that I blame you. I'll get to work on the archives. Be careful, Marcus. I only got a few months till retirement and I don't want to have to break in a new boss before then because you got your fool head shot off.'

'Such tender words,' Marcus said, then looked up to see Stone in his doorway. 'Thanks, man.' He hung up, motioned Stone to come in and close the door. 'I'm about to make you a very happy man.'

Stone's eyes lit up. 'You're reassigning Jill to Diesel?'

'Not that happy a man,' Marcus said dryly. 'Diesel would kill me. But I am assigning her to Cal. I need a retrospective on human trafficking. In the meantime, I need your polishing skills.' He quickly emailed Stone the summary he'd written in Isenberg's office. 'This is an account of what happened at the Anders house. They were the people who owned Tala. It's the bare-bones facts. Make it sound good.' Marcus had done some reporting for the *Ledger* when he was younger, but Stone's writing skills had always been superior. 'Take the byline. I'll be sending you regular updates.' He lifted his brows. 'From the front line, as it were. I just got embedded in the CPD/FBI task force.'

Stone ignored Marcus's announcement of his new role. 'You have a bandage on your head,' he said quietly.

Marcus touched it lightly. 'Yes. Scarlett bandaged me up.'

'I'm not going to like what I read in here, am I?' Stone asked through clenched teeth.

'Probably not. But I was wearing Kevlar.'

Stone closed his eyes. 'Hell, Marcus.'

'I'm fine. Really. Now I'm going home to shower and change my clothes. I've been sweating like a damn pig in this torture device. It's heavy as hell. What's the status on you and Jill checking out the threats list?' he asked to change the subject.

Stone's continued glare told him he hadn't been terribly smooth about the topic change. 'We should have done this check a long time ago. A few of the guys we've removed from homes are back to business. A few have new families. A few have new jobs. I sent you a list. It's in your email,' he said tersely, 'but you've been too busy getting shot at to read it.'

Back to business. Abusing their wives and kids. Marcus sank back in his chair, feeling like he'd just been bitch-slapped. 'Well, shit. We got them out of their homes and it didn't do any good at all.'

Stone nodded, his eyes still angry. 'I sent the list to Diesel to see if he could get anything on them quickly. Apparently a number of them learned from the last time, though, and they've password-protected their home computers and are using proxies so damn well that Diesel might not be able to break in.'

'Maybe Scarlett can do something with that list,' Marcus murmured, eyes widening when Stone surged to his feet, jabbing his finger toward his face.

'*No way.* No way in *hell* do you bring that woman into our business. If you want to get yourself arrested, fine, but you let her in and you drag the rest of us down with you.' Stone was furious, his big chest working like a bellows. 'You better choose whose team you're on, Marcus. I don't need this. I had a career. I could go back to it in a heartbeat.'

Marcus blinked at him, startled not by the outburst itself, but by the knowledge that Stone was unhappy that he'd come back to work for the *Ledger*. 'Okay, okay. Settle down. I won't drag you down with me.'

'All right,' Stone grunted. 'I'll get this article polished up. You want to see it before it goes online?'

Marcus nodded. 'Yeah. I need to make sure I didn't forget anything in the heat of the moment.' But that wasn't the real reason. Anything he printed now might as well have Scarlett's byline on it too. She'd put her career on the line when she stood up for his right to tell this story.

'Yeah,' Stone said grimly, and it was as if his brother had read his mind. 'Fine.'

Stone stomped out, passing Cal in Marcus's doorway.

Cal came in. 'The mobile camera unit you asked for isn't here. I remembered that Phillip used it last. He always forgets to return it. It's probably still in the trunk of his car.'

'Tell him to go get it,' Marcus said, annoyed. 'And chew him out for not returning it like he was supposed to. He lives in a fucking hellhole. I'd be surprised if some punk hasn't stolen it out of his trunk by now and sold it on Craigslist.'

'I would tell him, but he's not back yet. Last I saw him, he'd gone to your place to walk BB because you were still out. Maybe he decided to make a stop on his way back here. I called him, but he's not answering his cell.'

Marcus frowned at this. The youngest member of their team, Lisette's brother Phillip was forgetful about equipment, but his cell phone was permanently velcroed to his hand. If it rang, he'd have answered. 'I'm going home now. I'll look for his car on the way. Maybe he got a flat.'

'He'd have called.'

'Maybe his cell's outta juice. He's always playing games on the damn thing. I'll check it out. Don't worry. I'll call you when I find him.'

Cincinnati, Ohio
Tuesday 4 August, 8.15 P.M.

Scarlett found Deacon waiting for her in the lobby of the Cincinnati FBI Field Office. She hoped she wasn't showing her shock at finding out about Marcus's abduction and his brother's death, but she knew she it was written all over her face when Deacon's white brows shot up and his bi-colored eyes narrowed in concern.

'What happened?'

She considered saying nothing, but they didn't lie to each other. Hide shit they didn't want to deal with, sure. But they didn't out-and-out lie, and Scarlett wasn't about to start now.

'I just found out about . . .' Her mouth hung open, no more words coming out. 'I'm sorry, Deacon. I'm just not . . . me at the moment.'

'I can see that,' he said mildly. 'Come with me.'

She followed him into a conference room and lowered herself into a chair, her legs shaky. 'It doesn't have anything to do with this case. I shouldn't even be thinking about it now, but I can't . . . I can't help it.'

'I don't think I've ever seen you this rattled. Talk to me, Scar.'

Tears pricked her eyelids and she sucked in a breath, appalled at herself. A bottle of water appeared on the table in front of her and she used the few seconds it took to chug some down to wrestle her emotions back where they belonged.

She cleared her throat, her gaze locked on the bottle's label. 'Did you know there was a fourth O'Bannion brother?'

Deacon's eyes widened. 'No. I'm sure that Faith doesn't know either.'

'This was long before Jeremy even met Marcus's mother.'

'Della,' Deacon supplied.

'Yes, Della,' she murmured. 'Della was still married to her first husband, so it wouldn't have been O'Bannion gossip at the time. Marcus, Stone and their younger brother Matthias were kidnapped and held for ransom twenty-seven years ago.'

'Oh my God.'

'They lived in Lexington then, and their last name was Gargano. It's not a hard Google if you know the right search terms.'

'How did you get these search terms?' Deacon asked quietly.

'Marcus told me, but only his brother's name, their old last name, Lexington, and the year. He couldn't get any other words out. It was like he'd been electro-shocked or something. But those words were enough. The kidnappers told the parents not to contact the authorities, but Della did and she nearly lost them all. The son who died was only three.'

Deacon dragged his palm down his face. 'Wow. No wonder Della didn't want the FBI in her business when Mikhail was missing. That's gotta be a parent's worst nightmare.'

'Stone was shot, was in a coma for a week. Somehow the bullet meant for Marcus went wide.'

'The lucky bastard's charmed,' Deacon murmured.

'But for how long?' Scarlett sighed. 'Marcus told me not to judge Stone nine months ago. I understand why now.' She also had a new understanding of the episode that she'd witnessed that morning in Marcus's office, and wondered how many times Marcus had talked his brother down over the years.

Deacon squeezed her shoulder. 'You feel better getting it out? Because it's not like I'm rushing you, but I'm rushing you. Our trafficking contacts are waiting for us. Apparently they've got all the info there is on suspected human trafficking rings operating in the tri-state area. We need to go.'

She nodded, pushed to her feet and followed him on unsteady legs. 'I know. I've arranged for a SAR unit to track Tala's mother and sister, so I don't have much time anyway.'

Deacon frowned. 'You think dogs are the best idea?'

'When the dogs are accompanied by a priest, yes.' She gave him the highlights of what they'd learned from Annabelle Church and the agreement Marcus and Lynda had come to.

'Lynda's allowing Marcus to embed with us? How'd you manage that?'

'By reminding her we have nothing to hide. Who are the people we're meeting with?'

'Zimmerman, a senior analyst named Luther Troy, and a new agent who just arrived from DC an hour ago. That's all I know.'

'They brought an agent in just for this?'

'No clue.' He shot her a light-hearted grin. 'Your uncle is really Father Bishop?'

'Yes,' she said with a long-suffering sigh.

'When he grows up, will he become Bishop Bishop?'

She lifted a brow. 'You've met my dad.'

He frowned. 'Yeah.'

'Big guy, right?'

'Yeah,' Deacon said more slowly. 'Why?'

'Uncle Trace is the baby brother, but only in age. He's taller and bigger than my dad. So you go ahead and crack all the Bishop Bishop jokes you want. The good father will crack your head like a walnut.'

Deacon was chuckling as he pushed the conference room door open, but he stopped dead in the doorway. Scarlett barreled into him and leaped back, sputtering. 'What?'

But Deacon wasn't listening. He was too busy staring across the room. Scarlett gave him a little push and slipped around him to see what had caused her partner to freeze in his puppy-chewed shoes.

A woman stood at the far end of a big table, a smile on her face. She was as tall as Scarlett, with dark red hair pulled back in a neat twist. Deacon started walking and she opened her arms, gathering him close for a quick, hard hug.

Scarlett glanced at SAC Zimmerman to find him wearing a small pleased smile.

Deacon was grinning like a lunatic as he pulled out of the embrace. 'What are you doing here?' he asked the woman.

'I work here. Now.'

Deacon's head whipped around to stare at the SAC. '*She's* the new agent?'

Zimmerman nodded. 'She is. She wanted to surprise you.'

'She did,' Deacon said emphatically. 'How, why? When?'

'In a minute.' The woman met Scarlett's gaze directly, her brown eyes assessing. 'You must be Detective Bishop. I've heard a lot about you. I'm—'

Scarlett recognized her now. 'Special Agent Kate Coppola. You were Agent Novak's partner back in Baltimore.' The only photo that Scarlett had

327

seen of the woman had been taken at the wedding of one of Deacon and Coppola's mutual friends, and everyone had been in formal wear, Coppola's hair loose around her shoulders. She looked different in a black suit with minimal makeup. But still gorgeous, Scarlett thought with a tug of envy. But it was the woman's eyes that had sparked Scarlett's recognition. In the photo she'd seemed apart, watchful. Her eyes looked exactly the same today.

Deacon's grimace was embarrassed. 'I'm sorry. Kate, this is my partner, Detective Scarlett Bishop. Scar, this is my *old* partner, Special Agent Katherine Coppola.'

Scarlett's shoulders relaxed, surprising her because she hadn't realized she'd gone so tense. Deacon called her 'Scar' to indicate that they were more than partners. After almost a year on the job together, they'd become friends. Scarlett began to walk toward Kate, but the woman met her halfway, hand extended, a smile on her face.

'Deacon has spoken so highly of you, Detective. I'm glad to finally meet you.'

Scarlett found herself returning the smile without reservation. 'Likewise.' She gestured to the table. 'Have a seat and answer Deacon's questions before he pops a blood vessel.'

Kate laughed, and it was just that simple. Scarlett knew the woman would fit in well with their group.

'I wasn't supposed to start for another few weeks,' she explained. 'I was on leave, wrapping up some personal things back in Baltimore, when SAC Zimmerman called me this morning. He said they might need to bring me in early, that there was a case developing that would be excellent transition training.' She motioned to the man who'd taken the seat beside her. 'This is Special Agent Troy, my new partner.'

'Troy heads our human trafficking task force,' Zimmerman said. 'He was in Cleveland this morning, interviewing some young women rescued from a massage parlor operation. I brought him back when you told me about the young victim of this morning's shooting.'

Troy nodded to all of them. 'The Cleveland operation had ties to organized crime. We know of at least three rings operating in the tri-state area that are similar.' He rolled his eyes. 'Suspected ties. Suspected rings. Suspected organized crime. We don't have any proof.' Then his eyes gleamed. 'But we do have undercover operatives in two of the organizations, one of which is a deep cover op.'

Scarlett sat up straighter, new energy pulsing through her body. 'Can we talk to them?'

Troy shook his head. 'We can't risk it. Even the one that isn't in as deep is too far in for us to grab for a chat. He gets time off in two days. He'll stop in and talk to us then. The one who's fully immersed only communicates with his handler and only when he has something to say. We've sent a message to his handler, but so far we've heard nothing back.'

'I thought so,' Scarlett said with a sigh. 'But I had to ask.'

Troy's look was sympathetic. 'I understand your frustration. I know who these operatives are and where they are, but I'm about as helpless are you are. However, finding the victim in the alley this morning was an amazing break for us.'

Scarlett thought of Marcus, thought he'd be bristling to hear Tala's death referred to in such a way. Scarlett was bristling herself, but understood what Troy meant. 'She broke her leash.'

'To protect her baby, we understand,' Troy said. 'The child is all right?'

Scarlett nodded. 'Yes, she is.' She briefed them on the events of the afternoon, noting the scowls on the Feds' faces when she mentioned Marcus's involvement in finding Tabby and interviewing Annabelle Church. 'We're sending a SAR team out to hopefully retrieve the mother and sister. I don't know if they'll be able to identify the men who took the Anderses or not. The women may have been gone by then.'

Zimmerman nodded. 'I knew about the search for the mother and daughter. Isenberg and I talked right after you all finished questioning Ms Church. I've got resources ready to aid the search if necessary, but for now, I'm leaving it in MCES and CPD's corner.'

Scarlett appreciated Zimmerman's willingness to have Isenberg lead the search. Lynda had allowed FBI resources access to their investigations as well – grudgingly at first, but it got easier each time. That Zimmerman had acquiesced this time surprised Scarlett, though.

'You look surprised, Detective,' Zimmerman said dryly, as if reading her thoughts, and once again she wondered at the disappearance of her legendary poker face. *Marcus*, she thought. It had been slipping since she'd first heard his voice.

'I am,' she admitted. 'I thought you would have yanked the reins from us, considering one of your own was killed today.'

Zimmerman shrugged, his expression abruptly remote. 'These women didn't pull the trigger and Isenberg's cops know the lay of the land better than we do. We've agreed that we will question the women jointly.'

'What about the old woman found at the Anders house?' Kate asked. 'The aunt. Can she be questioned?'

'Not yet. She's still unconscious,' Scarlett said. 'I called on my way over here to check on her. The hospital has my number. The nurse promised they'd text me the instant she wakes up. What about Chip Anders's factories? Did you find any evidence of trafficking there?'

Zimmerman nodded, his smile grimly satisfied. 'Oh yeah. We did simultaneous raids on all three.' He glanced at Deacon, apology written all over his face. 'That's where I was when you called to tell me about Agent Spangler – and why I couldn't go with you to notify his wife.'

Deacon nodded. 'I understand. It's all right. I covered it.'

At a cost, Scarlett thought. But that went with the job. She'd done her share of notifications and it never went well. But at least she'd never been attacked. *Poor Deacon.*

'We pulled out so many illegals,' Zimmerman continued, 'that the factories would have needed to shut down operations even if we hadn't padlocked the doors after clearing out the employees. They didn't have enough labor to maintain even a basic operation. The people we took into custody will take a while to process. We don't have sufficient interpreters to take their statements, so we're still in the identification process.'

'But we have isolated out the other two members of the Bautista family,' Troy said. 'Efren and his son John Paul.'

'Bautista,' Deacon explained when Scarlett frowned in confusion, 'is Tala's last name. Immigration Services contacted me just as I was about to meet you.'

'They got a hit on her fingerprints,' Scarlett murmured.

Deacon nodded. 'I was going to tell you when I first saw you in the lobby, but we ended up discussing the other case. Tala and her family – mother, father, sister and brother – came into the US from the Philippines on an H2B visa. It's since expired. It was only good for a year and they've been here for three.'

'That's the temporary labor visa?' Scarlett asked, and Agent Troy nodded.

'Technically it's supposed to be for temporary seasonal labor,' Troy said. 'Hotels, amusement parks, stuff like that. It's not supposed to be for agricultural jobs, but once they get here, it happens. Over seventy percent of victims of trafficking come into this country *legally*. They don't sneak in. They're lured here by the promise of better jobs.'

Scarlett blinked. That fact she hadn't expected. *Seventy percent?* 'Holy God. Is that what happened to Tala's family?'

'We think so,' Zimmerman said. 'We haven't gotten anything from her father and brother yet. They were afraid to talk to us. Apparently Chip Anders told all his victims that we'd put them in jail if we caught them because their visas were expired.'

'So the rest of Tala's family are now here illegally,' Kate said with a frown. 'I hate when this happens. These victims are tricked into coming to the US by bogus labor recruitment firms operating in their own countries.'

'Like the Philippines?' Deacon asked.

Kate nodded. 'It's one of the top four countries we see victims coming from, second to Mexico. India and Thailand are third and fourth.'

'They're sold out by fellow countrymen trying to make a buck,' Scarlett said quietly.

'Basically,' Troy agreed grimly. 'And not only are they lied to about the jobs they'll get when they arrive, but they often have to pay exorbitant recruitment fees for the privilege.'

'The average is a year's wage in their home country,' Kate added with an angry shake of her head. 'Sometimes it's offered to them as a "loan", but with interest rates so high they'll never pay off their debt. Their wages are gone before they even start working. And that's the ones who even get any wages. So many of those forced into the sex trade get nothing at all.'

'And when they arrive in this country, they find it's all been a lie and they're forced into slavery.' Troy's expression grew weary. 'Sometimes it's slave labor like Chip Anders's factories, and sometimes it's sexual slavery like the raid we did on the massage parlor this morning. Sometimes the victims are held by force or by threat to family members – here or back home. Sometimes they're made to live at the factory, like many of Anders's victims.' He shrugged. 'And sometimes they just don't know how to get free. Their captors take their visas and all their travel documents and then allow the visas to expire.'

'Which is what happened to Tala's family,' Scarlett said, her jaw clenched.

Kate sighed. 'And then their captors tell the victims that they're here illegally now and that Americans hate illegals. They tell the victims to be afraid of the police because we'll arrest them. Most of these people come from countries where law enforcement is corrupt at best, brutal at worst, so they *are* afraid of us.' She sighed again. 'And the truth is, even when they do come to us for help, a lot of the time we have little control over what happens to them next.'

'What does happen to them?' Deacon asked, the look on his face saying he already knew he wouldn't like the answer. Scarlett felt the same apprehension.

'They're kept in this country pending the investigation into their accused traffickers,' Troy said. 'But only about half of the traffickers ever end up being arrested. Most are long gone by the time their victims come forward.' He grimaced in disgust. 'Six percent of the perpetrators were released because they were diplomats. Yeah,' he said when everyone around the table showed their surprise. 'I'm with you all there. But that's another department's focus. My focus has been operations that have organized crime connections. They don't get arrested because they don't usually let their victims escape – another reason why Tala's escape was such a lucky break for us.'

'Still,' Kate said, 'getting free isn't the end of the ordeal for the victims. They're still here illegally.'

'Even though they're victims,' Scarlett said bitterly. She wanted to say it wasn't fair. Because it wasn't. But saying so wouldn't make it any fairer. She'd learned that long ago. Being a victim sucked, and life was rarely fair. 'If they wish to stay, what happens then?'

'Some are granted longer-term visas that can lead to green cards,' Troy said. 'It depends on the individual – and if they want to stay in this country. Many do, because there are more opportunities here than back home, especially for those with higher education. At least a third of labor trafficking victims have attended or graduated from college or a tech school. Some even have graduate degrees. It's easier for these victims to get employment offers, a requirement for them to stay long term. Efren was a teacher back in the Philippines and Mila had some nursing experience. They have skills that make them more, well, desirable, for lack of a better word.'

Scarlett tucked that fact away, wondering what Marcus could do to help the Bautistas find permanent refuge in the United States, assuming they even wanted it after the ordeal they'd suffered. They'd need sponsors and jobs. He could help with that.

'Are Efren, John Paul and the other individuals taken from the factories in good health?' Kate asked, making Scarlett like her even more.

Zimmerman shrugged. 'None of them are starving to death, but they are not in the best of health. Many had been beaten. A lot of malnutrition. They've been grossly overworked and the conditions were deplorable – like something out of a nineteenth-century workhouse. Anders forced the lower-skilled workers to live there, and their dormitories were pretty bleak. Dirty, and hotter than hell. They were prisoners in every sense of the word. Those with more skilled positions, like Tala's father, were allowed to leave the factory at night, but they wore trackers.'

'What were they forced to do?' Scarlett asked.

'Nothing illegal as far as we can see,' Zimmerman replied. 'One factory processed chickens, the other sorted nuts. The third did manual envelope stuffing – coupons and such. It appears that Anders was doing very well. Everyone was busy working when we busted in. Not paying your workers allows you to underbid the competition,' he added, not bothering to hide his disgust.

'How many of the other workers wore the ankle trackers?' Scarlett asked.

'About a third,' Zimmerman said. 'We don't know if that means that Anders got his workers from different sources or not. Hopefully the interviews with the victims will shed some light on this.'

Scarlett thought about Mila and Erica, afraid and on the run. 'If any of the skilled workers happened to not be in the factories at the time of the raids, they might run. They need to know that they won't be prosecuted, that Anders was lying and it's safe to ask for help. You might consider utilizing the media to get the word out.'

Troy looked at Scarlett, his expression unreadable. 'You're talking about bringing in your reporter. He's already written about it in his paper.'

My reporter. Yes. He is. Mine. 'He's the publisher of the *Ledger*,' Scarlett said. 'He's also been embedded with our team while this case remains in motion.'

All three FBI agents turned and frowned at her. 'You're letting a reporter observe your investigation?' Troy asked, sounding appalled.

'He's proven himself trustworthy so far,' Scarlett said evenly, not allowing the defensiveness she felt to come out in her voice. 'This story needs to be told for the sake of the victims and for those who have literally no idea that trafficking is happening in their town, right in front of their eyes. Marcus O'Bannion will tell the story the right way.'

'He's an almost-relative of mine,' Deacon added. 'In a sideways, by-marriage kind of way. From what I've seen, he's a straight arrow.'

'Almost-relative?' Kate asked, looking mildly amused.

'He's my fiancée's step-cousin.' Deacon shrugged. 'Faith adores him. Trusts him too, so that's been good enough for me. I'd recommend using him when you want the media coverage. His paper used to be second in town, but he's built the readership up since he took over five years ago, after returning from Iraq. In a year he'll be ahead of the *Enquirer*.'

'Iraq?' Troy asked, a good deal of his doubt fading with that one word.

'He was army,' Scarlett said. 'A Ranger. Served two tours.'

Troy nodded, looking convinced. 'I want to meet him first.'

'Of course,' Scarlett said. 'He'll be with the SAR team and the priest we've asked to accompany them. Tala's mother was seen with a rosary. We think she'll trust a priest.'

'The priest's okay,' Zimmerman told Troy before the man could utter a protest. 'He's a CPD chaplain.'

Scarlett's brows raised, but she didn't allow her surprise to show. 'He is?'

Zimmerman's lips curved, his eyes twinkling. 'Didn't he tell you when you called him?'

'No,' Scarlett said dryly. 'He did not. He's my uncle,' she explained to the others. 'I shouldn't be surprised. Half of my family are cops. He'll do a good job,' she told Troy.

'Isenberg had him checked out,' Zimmerman added. 'He's got a cool head and experience.'

Scarlett swallowed what would have been a sigh of irritation. Of course Lynda would have her uncle checked out before allowing him access to victims. It might have been nice if Scarlett's word had been enough, though.

'What next?' she asked the group. 'We find Mila and her daughter, reunite them with her husband and son, and find out what they know about the people who brought them into the country?'

'Maybe not in that order,' Troy said. 'But we will reunite them.'

'Soon,' Scarlett murmured. 'They have a daughter to bury.'

'Soon,' Troy promised. 'And I will try to get word to our operatives, see if either of them has heard anything about Anders's capture. Anders is who I want. He knows the names of the traffickers, how much he's paid them, and how he paid them. The victims may be able to describe faces, but it's unlikely they'll know any names. We also need to be aware that there may be other households in this area who've purchased families like the Bautistas. Hopefully those victims won't come to any harm as we investigate.'

'In the meantime, I want you all to be working together,' Zimmerman instructed. 'Troy and Coppola, stay in contact with Novak and Bishop. Trade information.' He met Scarlett's eyes. 'Nothing that comes from us goes to the reporter without my explicit approval.'

'Yes, sir,' Scarlett said. 'I understand.'

'Thank you. Dismissed.' Zimmerman stood up. 'Deacon, I need to talk to you. Privately, please. In my office.'

Twenty-two

Cincinnati, Ohio
Tuesday 4 August, 8.35 P.M.

Marcus parked his Subaru in his assigned slot under the Tower apartment building where he lived, and walked up the flight of stairs to the lobby, his mind on Scarlett. About what she'd told him. And about what he'd told her. He wondered if she'd Googled the kidnapping. If she now understood what he and Stone had been through. What his mother had endured. And what Matty had not survived.

He checked his phone, knowing that she wouldn't have had time to text him yet. She was still in her meeting. *And I have to get moving if I'm going to join the search for Mila and Erica.* He jogged through the lobby, throwing up his hand in a wave to Edgar, who worked the desk.

Then he stopped cold. Because Edgar wasn't at the desk. For the first time since Marcus had moved in five years before, the desk was empty.

'Edgar?' he called, the lobby sounding too empty. The hairs rose on the back of his neck. 'Edgar?'

He rushed around the desk, hoping Edgar had simply taken a bathroom break, but his hope died the moment he saw the old man's body slumped on the floor.

'Oh my God.' Dropping to his haunches, Marcus pressed his fingers to Edgar's throat, trying to find a pulse. 'Edgar. *Edgar.* Talk to me, buddy. Come on.' Marcus's own heart skittered when he found a very faint, feeble pulse. 'Oh God,' he breathed in relief.

But then new dread twisted his gut as he noticed what he had not before – the dark stain on Edgar's uniform in the same place Tala's had been that morning.

Grabbing his cell phone, Marcus called 911. 'My name is Marcus O'Bannion. I've discovered the victim of a shooting in my apartment lobby,' he said, and gave them the address. 'His name is Edgar Kauffman. He's about sixty years old. He's been shot in the abdomen. He's alive, but just barely.'

'Help is on the way,' the operator said. 'Please stay on the line, sir.'

Marcus didn't want to. He wanted to call Scarlett. *Now.* Because his mind was racing. He'd been shot at only hours before, and then the security guard in his apartment building was shot too? He hadn't wanted to believe her when she'd said he'd been the target at the Anders house, but this wasn't a coincidence. *It can't be.*

'Sir?' the operator said sharply. 'Are you still there?'

'Yes.' He put the phone on speaker and laid it on the desk, forcing himself to stay calm as he looked around for something to stem Edgar's bleeding. The older man's gym bag was tucked under the desk, and in it Marcus found a spare shirt. Quickly he balled the shirt up and pressed it to the wound, dragging the bag under Edgar's feet so that they were elevated.

Why? Why shoot an old man? He shoved the questions aside, focusing on Edgar. 'Stay with me, Edgar,' he muttered as he worked to secure the wadded-up shirt to the wound with Edgar's own suspenders. 'Don't you dare die on me too.'

'Sir?' The operator's voice was faint coming through the speaker. Marcus reached for his phone, accidentally jiggling Edgar's computer mouse. The screen flashed to life and Marcus's heart simply stopped.

'Oh my God,' he breathed, horrified, staring at the last entry on the sign-in log. *Phillip.* Edgar had signed Phillip into the building. *Cal said Phillip was coming here to walk BB.* Phillip was *here*, in this building. And so was a killer.

'What is it?' the operator demanded. 'Sir? What's wrong?'

'How long before the paramedics get here?' he demanded.

'Another two minutes,' she said.

Shit. Phillip might not have that long. Phone in hand, Marcus ran to the elevator and pressed the button. 'Come on, you fucker. Come on.'

'Excuse me, sir?'

'Tell the cops to hurry. One of my employees is in my apartment and I think that's where the shooter went too.' The elevator doors opened and Marcus jumped in, swiped his ID card, then jabbed the button for the penthouse. He tossed the ID card on the lobby floor a second before the door closed. 'I'm in the elevator. Tell the cops to come to the penthouse floor. I've left my ID card in the lobby so they can come up. I'm about to lose you.'

Sure enough, his call failed two seconds after the elevator started its climb. The ride was normally quick, but today it felt like he was rising through molasses. When the doors opened, he rushed toward his apartment.

And his racing heart stopped dead in his chest. His front door stood

336

wide open. Where was Phillip? And BB? They'd better be okay. *Please be okay.*

Keeping his phone in one hand, he drew his gun with the other, taking slow, careful steps through the open door. The place had been wrecked, chairs overturned, picture frames pulled from the walls. Marcus's boots crunched as he walked through broken glass, some from the pictures and some from a vase that had been shattered.

The quiet was terrifying. No voices. No barking dog. BB was a barker. She should be barking her fool head off right now. *Be okay. Please be okay.*

'Phillip?' he called softly. 'BB? Come here, girl. It's all right.' He kept his voice soothing and smooth. 'I'm home now. You can come out. It's just me.'

The living room was clear, the den as well. In the kitchen he found the drawers pulled out, silverware strewn all over the floor. And more broken glass.

He crept into the spare bedroom, checking the closet and under the bed, remembering where he had found Tabby Anders.

The room was empty, so he quickly moved to his own bedroom, his heart sinking as he opened the door. 'Oh God,' he whispered. Phillip lay on the floor, covered in blood, BB motionless against the wall a few feet away.

He dropped to his knees next to Phillip, his back to the far wall. No one was going to shoot him in the back a second time today. He laid his gun on the carpet where he could reach it quickly, then searched for Phillip's pulse. *Don't be dead, kid. Please.*

There was no pulse. Rage filled him, pure and lethal, knocking the panic back to where he could think. *Breathe*, he commanded himself. His heart was knocking in his chest so hard that his own pulse was all he could hear, all he could feel. *Control your pulse. Now.*

He dropped his hands to his sides and focused on slowing his own heartbeat until he could think clearly once more, then pressed his fingers against Phillip's throat again. And nearly collapsed in relief. *Thank you.* There was a pulse. It was thready and weak, but it was there.

He grabbed the phone from the nightstand and dialed 911 again, glad he'd kept a landline. He wasn't going to chance losing Phillip because of a dropped call. Putting the phone on speaker, he went for his knife to cut Phillip's shirt away, then remembered he'd given the knife to Scarlett that morning. He pulled his spare from his boot, taking a second to glance at BB as he did so. The dog's chest was moving, but her coat was covered in blood. Her muzzle hung open, her tongue lolling to one side. She was unconscious, but alive.

'This is nine-one-one,' the operator answered. 'What is your emergency?'

Marcus returned his attention to Phillip, who hadn't stirred, his breathing so shallow that his chest didn't appear to be moving at all. He sliced the bloody shirt away, and for the third time that day found himself staring at a massive gut wound. Blood was slowly seeping from the bullet hole, so slowly that Marcus had to fight back his panic once more. He'd seen wounds like this too many times to want to remember, even before Tala's that morning. He'd watched too many soldiers die as medics rushed to save them.

'Gunshot wound to the abdomen. Victim is Phillip Cauldwell, age twenty-seven. Pulse is weak. He is non-responsive. I called a few minutes ago about the victim in the lobby of my building, so first responders should be on the way. Send another team to the penthouse, unit 20B. Both victims have abdominal wounds.'

'Help is on the way. Please stay on the line.'

'I will,' he said, then leaned into Phillip's face. 'You are *not* going to die,' he growled. 'Don't you dare consider it. Stay here. I'll be right back.'

Tucking his gun into its pocket holster, Marcus stood up on legs that shook, rushing to the master bath closet for clean towels and his first aid kit. It was paltry compared to the tackle box Scarlett kept in her house, but it would have to do.

Pressing one of the towels to Phillip's bleeding gut as gently as he could, he pulled his cell from his pocket and dialed Scarlett's number. *Please pick up. I need you.*

Cincinnati, Ohio
Tuesday 4 August, 8.40 P.M.

Deacon followed Zimmerman out, and Agent Troy rose as well, saying he needed to make some calls. Scarlett found herself sitting alone with Kate Coppola, who looked like she had something to say. So did Scarlett, but she waited, letting Kate go first.

'I've heard a lot about you,' Kate said. 'All good.'

'Likewise.' Scarlett looked at the other woman speculatively. 'Can I ask why and how you ended up here?' She was wondering what Faith would think of Deacon's old partner showing up out of the blue.

Kate's smile was rueful. 'I'm not chasing Deacon. And don't deny that that's what you're thinking, because it's written all over your face.'

Scarlett rolled her eyes. *Marcus.* 'Damn that man,' she muttered.

'Deacon?'

'No. A different man.' She regarded the redhead evenly for a moment.

338

'If you're not chasing Deacon, this seems like a big coincidence.'

Kate didn't seem to take offense. 'It's not, really. I was up for a promotion, so I knew I could end up anywhere, and my boss knew I missed working with Deacon.'

Scarlett's brows rose again. 'So Faith has no worries from you, but I should?'

Kate chuckled. 'No. I'm not looking to partner with him again, but I had my choice of a few assignments and . . .' She shrugged self-consciously. 'My old team in Baltimore had become like family. I couldn't stay there and maintain my career path because all the roles I wanted were already filled. But leaving family is hard to do. Especially when you've never really had one before. Seeing the Cincinnati post opening was the biggest relief. I felt like I could keep growing in my job, but be near family too, you know?'

'Because Deacon's like family? Yeah, I get what you mean,' Scarlett said, thinking about the circle of friends he'd pulled her into. 'I understand.'

'But you have your real family here,' Kate said with a small frown. 'Your uncle, at least. Right?'

'I still understand,' Scarlett said. 'The family you make on the job is different than the family you were born into, even when that family loves you.' *So much that it suffocates me.*

Kate's frown disappeared. 'Don't worry that I'm angling to drag Deacon out of MCES. He's happy with you guys and doing what he wants to do. But this job is what *I* want to do.'

'You have experience with traffickers?'

'Unfortunately, yes. Baltimore and Washington don't see as much as some cities, but Baltimore is a port and the Ravens made it into the playoffs last year. Sex trafficking spikes in cities with major league sports.' Her expression had chilled, her eyes remote. 'I got my first case six months ago. Sex trafficking. Some asshole had brought his "stable" in for the big game. We got a tip from a resident that something wasn't right in the house down the street. Boy, was she right. We pulled four young women out of a hellhole that still makes me want to throw up.'

'But you pulled them out,' Scarlett said softly.

Kate swallowed. 'After the fact. We couldn't undo what had happened to them.'

'I know what you mean. All we can do is stop the crime, and catch the criminals. But it's not enough. It'll never be enough. Yet . . . it has to be enough or we crash and burn.'

Kate's eyes opened, her emotions under control. 'I know. I'm sorry. I don't normally whine about it.'

'Neither do I, but when I did, Deacon let me.' Scarlett grinned a little. 'I imagine he helped you too. Which is why you're here?'

A small smile from the other woman. 'He said you were smart.'

'Did you catch the fucker on that first case?'

Kate shook her head, the small smile fading. 'No. He wasn't there when we went in. He got wind of our raid and then he was *in* the wind. No trace. But we got the women out and placed in shelters. All four were under eighteen, two under fifteen. One was an American girl from Iowa, a runaway. The rest entered the country with their families, who'd come in on legal visas, just like Tala's family. Tricked into coming in, then separated. The parents and sons were sold for labor slaves, the daughters into the sex trade. These young girls were threatened that their families would be killed if they didn't comply. So they complied,' she finished grimly. 'Over and over again.'

'So you've made this your calling,' Scarlett murmured.

'Something like that, yes,' Kate said with a nod. 'I'm specializing in it, that's for sure. I'm sorry Tala was killed, but it is a break we never expected. We need to use it to make sure she didn't die in vain. What can you tell me about this reporter she was meeting?'

Scarlett told her everything she knew, except for the part about Marcus's reaction to seeing Tala's bullet-ravaged head. That was private, and she would fall on her sword to keep it that way.

'So they met by coincidence,' Kate mused.

Scarlett shook her head. 'Not entirely. Marcus knew what to look for. He saw the signs that something was wrong.'

'And he got involved. Not many do. I'd like to go with you when you talk with the mother and sister. I'd also like to speak to your reporter.'

'I'll arrange it,' Scarlett said, then glanced at her phone when it buzzed, blinking at the caller ID. 'Speaking of himself. It's Marcus O'Bannion. Excuse me a moment.' She got up from the table and walked to the window, hoping for better reception. 'What's up?' she answered.

'You need to come,' Marcus said quietly, too quietly. 'Now. Please.'

Scarlett's pulse rocketed, but she managed to keep her voice calm. 'Where?'

'My apartment. I'm texting you the address. Bring that CSU guy of yours. Tanaka. He's your best, right?'

'Our very best.'

'Then hurry. Please.'

'Marcus, are you all right?'

But there was no answer. He'd already hung up. A second later

340

her phone buzzed with his text. *7 Hills Twr. Penthouse. 20B.*

Kate ran to her side, her own cell phone in her hand. 'Who should I call?'

'Call nine-one-one. Tell them to get to Seven Hills Tower in Hyde Park, penthouse unit B. Where's Deacon?' She dialed his cell, not waiting for Kate's answer.

Deacon answered on the first ring. 'I'll be another few minutes,' he said.

'I just got a call from Marcus. Something's gone down in his apartment. He asked for Vince and the CSU team.'

'Shit,' Deacon muttered. 'You go. I'll follow as soon as I can.'

'I'm going with you,' Kate told her when she'd hung up.

'Then come. Now.' Scarlett ran toward the entrance, calling Vince while she listened with her other ear to Kate calling 911.

Don't be hurt, Marcus. Don't you dare be hurt.

Cincinnati, Ohio
Tuesday 4 August, 8.45 P.M.

Marcus pocketed his cell phone, knowing that Scarlett would worry and sorry that he'd been so abrupt, but he needed to put all his focus on keeping Phillip alive.

But his friend's blood was pouring from too many places. Marcus couldn't isolate all the wounds. *Not fast enough. I'm not doing this fast enough.* The panic started to climb up his throat, but he shoved it back down and got in Phillip's face again. 'Don't you die on me, Phillip Cauldwell. Don't you dare die on me.'

Phillip's eyelids flickered, but didn't lift. 'Bossy,' he whispered. 'Always so bossy.'

'Damn straight,' Marcus snapped, relief making his body so rubbery that he had trouble keeping himself upright. 'Because I *am* the damn boss and don't you forget it. What happened here?'

'Guy followed me into the lobby. Big guy. Black. Dressed in black, too. Couldn't see his face, had on a ski mask.' Phillip's throat worked, tears leaking from his eyes. 'He killed Edgar. I tried to stop him.'

'No,' Marcus soothed. 'Edgar's not dead. The paramedics should be helping him right now. Tell me about the man. He forced you up here?'

'Yes. Didn't have my knife.'

Phillip lived in a shitty neighborhood and always carried a knife for protection. Lisette had tried a thousand times to get her brother to move away from that hellhole. Marcus had even given him a raise, but Phillip refused to move.

'Left it in your other pants, huh?' Marcus asked, trying to keep his voice light.

'Yep.' A grimace of pain. 'Had to go through a metal detector in Mr Arrogant's building. Sorry.'

Marcus frowned for a moment, then remembered his team's meeting that morning. It had been only twelve hours before, but it seemed like an eternity ago. 'Mr Arrogant' was the corporate vice-president his team had targeted for investigation, the man who'd beaten his wife and child. The man Children's Services couldn't touch because he'd bribed everyone to lie. Phillip had posed as a courier that morning so that he could harvest the names of employees at the abusive vice-president's office, hoping to find someone who'd tell the truth about the man. The shirt Marcus had cut off him was part of his courier uniform.

'Don't say you're sorry. You're alive. How'd you get away?'

'He shot me. Twice.' An agonized grimace twisted his face. 'Dug a slug out with his knife. Hurt . . . like a bitch.'

What the hell? Why would the shooter dig the slug out – and while Phillip was still alive? 'I guess it did,' Marcus said grimly.

'And no, I don't know why he dug the slug out. I can tell you're wondering.' A flicker of a smile, then another grimace of pain. 'Then BB attacked him. Bit his leg. He kicked her off, but it gave me the second I needed.' Phillip drew a breath that rattled frighteningly in his lungs. 'I took his knife and stabbed him. Got him in the bicep. Left side.' Another rattling breath. 'Stuck him like a fucker.'

'Good for you,' Marcus said fiercely.

'But then he shot me again. In the gut. Dropped me like a damn rock. He took a bath towel. Wrapped it around his arm. Didn't even take the knife out.'

'So he didn't leave any blood,' Marcus said grimly.

'No. But BB bit him hard.' A desperate smile bent his lips. 'So get the fucker's DNA from her teeth. Get him for me, boss.'

'You have my word. Did you hear him speak? See anything? The color of his eyes, maybe?' Marcus could hear his own desperation and fought to shove it back.

'I heard him swear when I stabbed him. Deep voice. Eyes, brown. Lashes, black. Curly. Eyelids, dark, a little lighter than the ski mask.' He drew a labored breath. 'He wanted the gut bullet back too. Tried to dig it out.' A grimace. 'With a kitchen knife. He took it with him. The knife. Not the bullet.' Phillip's eyes slid shut. 'God, this really hurts.'

'I know. Hold on a little longer. The ambulance is coming. Stay with me, Phil.'

Another smile, much weaker. 'You're a bossy SOB. You know that, right?'

'Trust me, I know it,' Marcus murmured, then looked up as footsteps thundered across his apartment floor. Medics and a cop appeared in the doorway, and Marcus stood up and stepped back. 'Please help him.'

'We'll do our best,' one of the medics said, gently pushing Marcus further out of the way. 'You need to leave the room, sir. We need space to work.'

Marcus scooped BB up in his arms. She was dead weight, her limbs loose and floppy. 'I'm Marcus O'Bannion,' he said to the cop. 'I've called Detective Bishop of the homicide division. No,' he corrected himself. 'She's MCES, the CPD/FBI task force. She's on her way. This is related to one of her cases. I'll give my statement when she arrives.'

Cincinnati, Ohio
Tuesday 4 August, 8.55 P.M.

Ken sat at the desk in his home office, staring at the tracking software on his phone screen, dreading what he knew he had to do. Demetrius had still not called in, but he wasn't dead. His car was in motion, though driving erratically. After being inside O'Bannion's apartment building for only ten minutes, he'd left and taken a circuitous route to nowhere, it seemed. He hadn't called. Hadn't texted. Had simply driven around in circles.

Which meant he'd missed. Again. If he'd hit O'Bannion, he'd be calling to brag, all cocky and smug. Even if he weren't embezzling funds, Demetrius had to go.

Like . . . permanently.

The prospect might have made Ken annoyed a few months ago. Hell, maybe even a few weeks ago. But Demetrius had fucked up royally. *And if he is stealing money from me, I'll make him sorry he was ever born.*

A cup of tea appeared in front of him and he looked up to see Alice's concerned face. 'You didn't eat any dinner, Dad.'

He switched off his phone before she could ask what he was looking at. He tracked her phone, too. Sean's as well, but he didn't want either of them to know it. Ken trusted both of them, but he wasn't stupid. They were his kids after all. Had his DNA. They'd sell him out if the price was high enough.

'I'm not very hungry, honey. But this tea will hit the spot.'

'You're worrying about Demetrius,' she said, sitting in the chair across from his desk. She'd already dressed for bed, wearing a modest robe and ridiculous Tweety Bird slippers. Above the neck of the robe he could see the bright blue of her University of Kentucky sleep shirt. His girl had graduated *magna cum laude* from Vanderbilt with a law degree from Kentucky. She looked like an innocent child, but he knew that beneath that sweet face was the sharp mind of his heir apparent. Sean was too academic and nerdy, and he'd been coddled by that mother of his. Alice, on the other hand, was a damn shark.

'Of course I'm worried,' he said. 'I haven't heard from him in hours.'

'So he missed O'Bannion again. Dad, this is getting ridiculous. This is a liability situation. He needs to go.'

'We've been friends since we were younger than you. It won't be easy killing him.'

She shook her head. 'Demetrius should have just killed O'Bannion nine months ago when you told him to. Then we wouldn't be in this situation.'

Ken sighed. 'Possibly, but to be fair, we'd still have the Anders situation, which wasn't his fault. Stephanie and her boy toy Drake still would have taken Tala out to play.'

'But if the girl hadn't met O'Bannion in the park, she wouldn't have met him in the alley and gotten herself shot,' Alice countered.

Ken acknowledged her point. 'Yeah, you're right. That was Demetrius's fault too.' He wasn't going to mention the embezzled funds. Not until he knew for sure.

'Let me at him,' Alice said. 'I'll take care of it for you. Then you won't worry that you'll hesitate at the last minute.'

'I might take you up on that, but not yet.'

'This isn't just an inconvenience, Dad,' she said harshly, surprising him with her intensity. 'Demetrius has allowed O'Bannion to operate without any boundaries all day long. O'Bannion runs a newspaper. They investigate stuff. I shouldn't need to draw a diagram here. He nearly brought us down nine months ago when he exposed Woody McCord's kiddie porn collection. If he'd dug a little deeper, he would have realized that he hadn't even touched the tip of the iceberg with McCord. I think he's digging again. He'll have us all in jail the moment his paper hits the stands, and frankly, I don't think you'd like prison, Dad. I know I wouldn't, and I'm not going to allow anyone to put me there. Not even you. So wake up and stop treating this like it's containable.' She leaned forward, her eyes flashing fire. 'It is no longer containable.'

He stared at her, tempted for the first time in a long time to strike her. 'Do not talk to me that way, Alice.'

She blew out an angry breath. 'You won't listen when I talk softly. God knows I've tried. Do you think it was a coincidence that O'Bannion met the girl in that alley this morning? He knows what we're doing and he's building his story. Once he connects Chip Anders to Woody McCord, we are all toast. He may have already. Let me have O'Bannion.'

'O'Bannion or Demetrius?' he asked coolly.

'Both.'

He shook his head. 'Even if I agreed with you, Alice, I can't just let you blow Demetrius away. Not until we get the records of all the business deals he has in place. I need to know his suppliers and existing contracts.'

'Like?' she pressed.

'Like the trackers, for example. We're down three and I don't know how many more we have in inventory nor where he gets them.'

'I do.'

Ken blinked, momentarily distracted. 'You do?'

She leaned back in her chair and sipped her tea, once again the picture of outer restraint. 'Well I don't personally, but DJ knows. He'll tell me.'

'What makes you think Demetrius's son will tell you? He's loyal to a fault.'

'Not as loyal as you think. We talk.' She smiled. 'Sometimes we do more than talk.'

Ken's mouth fell open. 'You and DJ? Since when?'

'Since he grew up, and *how*,' she said bawdily, then sobered. 'But seriously, Demetrius told you that Reuben was screwing around with the suppliers' wives and daughters, but I'll bet he didn't tell you about the money he himself spends, and what he spends it on.'

Ken waited, then gave her an impatient look. 'Don't be melodramatic. Just tell me.'

Alice mimed sniffing a line of coke off the back of her hand.

'Cocaine? Demetrius? No. He's an athlete. He wouldn't do that shit.'

She laughed derisively. 'An athlete? Do you know how many athletes "do that shit"? And don't get me started on the steroids. How do you think he keeps up with those muscles? He's not twenty anymore.'

'How do you know any of this?'

'I found the steroids in his sock drawer.' She shrugged. 'I snooped around Demetrius's house after I let DJ fuck my brains out.'

He put his hands up in surrender. 'Don't.'

'I found Demetrius's stash.' She softened her words with a smile. 'You guys aren't getting any younger, you know. Demetrius is pushing fifty. And so are you.'

Ken winced, knowing she was right. 'Ouch. Should I be worried?'

She sipped her tea demurely. 'Daddy, you won't get a chance to get worried. If you threaten the business with stupid shit, I'll take you out myself.'

'Oof,' he grunted placidly, but took no real offense. He'd expect no less. 'I've been thinking about selling out my share and retiring to my own island.'

'Maybe you should,' she said kindly. 'You've worked every day of your life. Why not enjoy the next forty or fifty years surrounded by half-naked women serving you fruity drinks?'

He laughed at the mental picture, pretty much a dead match for his own daydreams. 'I'm thinking about it. Can you and Sean buy me out?'

'Yes,' she said seriously. 'Unless you plan to charge something exorbitant.'

'I wouldn't dream of it. I have to sleep someti—' The ringing of his cell phone cut him off. 'It's Demetrius.'

'About time,' Alice grumbled. 'Put him on speaker, please.'

He pointed his finger at her. 'Then you have to be as quiet as a church mouse.' She mimed locking her lips while he answered the phone. 'D. Where the hell have you been, man?' he asked, even though he knew exactly where Demetrius had been.

'Uh . . . it's bad, Kenny. I'm hit. And I'm bleedin'. Maybe bleedin' out.'

Alice's eyes grew huge with consternation. 'Idiot,' she mouthed.

'What happened to you?' Ken asked.

'Followed one of O'Bannion's reporters, like we talked.' Demetrius's voice had grown slurred. 'Shot him with the Ruger and was digging out the bullet—'

'So that the wound would match the girl's in the alley,' Ken said impatiently. 'And?'

'O'Bannion's damn dog bit me. Then the damn reporter stabbed me.'

Alice's eyes rolled.

Ken kept his voice calm. He was seeing her point. 'With what?'

'My own goddamn knife,' Demetrius muttered.

Ken rolled his own eyes. *For God's sake.* 'Did you bleed in O'Bannion's apartment?'

A long pause. 'I never said I was in O'Bannion's apartment.'

Alice's brows lifted. 'Busted, Daddy,' she mouthed.

Shit. She knows. She knew that he'd been tracking his leadership team.

Setting her teacup on his desk, Alice took her own phone from her pocket and began typing. She was intent on whatever she was doing, so Ken let her comment go for the moment, keeping his tone level. 'His dog bit you, Demetrius. Unless you shot his employee in the goddamn dog park, his apartment seemed a reasonable assumption.'

Alice looked up from her phone. 'Nice save,' she mouthed, her expression dry.

He jabbed a warning finger at her and she shrugged, dropping her attention back to her phone. She must have found what she was looking for, because her expression abruptly became darkly furious, making him worried.

'Oh.' Demetrius gulped audibly. 'Okay. That makes sense, I guess. No, I didn't bleed anywhere. Not till I got to my car. I kept the knife in my arm till then. Didn't want it to spurt if the little bastard hit an artery.'

If O'Bannion's employee had hit an artery, Demetrius wouldn't have made it to his car, Ken thought sourly. The man was such a hypochondriac. 'Did it spurt?'

'No, just a slow bleed. But it's a mess. I can't go to the hospital. Didn't Decker fix up Reuben's guy that got shot this morning?'

'He did. Where are you, buddy? I'll come get you.'

Alice's mouth opened to protest, and Ken shook his finger at her again while he listened to Demetrius give his address.

'Hold tight, D. I'll be there as soon as I can.' He hung up and glared at Alice. 'Give me a little credit, kid. You're not the only one with a brain, just because you have a damn law degree.'

'What are you going to do?'

'Go get Demetrius and make him tell me his suppliers and contacts.'

'You think he'll just tell you? Really?'

'Really. Demetrius acts like a big stud with all his love of torture and beating people up, but he's a whiny baby when it comes to pain. He acts like a paper cut is a double amputation. I'll get what I need out of him after Decker makes sure he's not going to bleed to death.'

'Nice,' Alice said approvingly.

His finger hovering over Decker's speed dial number, he glanced up at her. 'You knew about the tracking?'

'Yeah,' she said in a *duh* voice. 'For several months now. You stopped asking me where I was when I went on dates. Sean, too.'

'That's why I didn't know about you and DJ.'

She tapped her nose.

'It doesn't . . . bother you?' he asked. 'That I was tracking you?'

347

'Yeah,' she repeated, annoyed. 'But we knew you were worried about your leadership team, so we just left our phones behind when we didn't want you to know where we were.'

'How did you know for sure?' he asked, positive that he was not going to like the answer.

'Sean hacked your phone. Took him a minute and a half. Before you even consider being soft on Demetrius, though, I want you to see this.' She showed him her phone, and he heard himself gasp.

'Fuck.' It was the local TV news website, and the shooting at O'Bannion's apartment building was the top story. Two victims en route to the local hospital with 'grave wounds'. The building was on lockdown. It was good that Demetrius had gotten out when he did.

'Exactly,' she said. 'He didn't mention that he didn't actually kill the employee, or that he shot the security guard, did he?' She let it sink in, then turned to go. 'I'll get the room upstairs ready for him.'

'Alice, wait,' he said, and she paused mid-step. 'You're right. Both of them need to go. I'll take care of Demetrius. O'Bannion is now officially yours.'

She gave him a hard nod. 'Thanks.'

'Two more things.' He waited until she'd turned around to fully face him. 'Are you still monitoring McCord's partner?' The partner who would have been exposed if Marcus O'Bannion and his *Ledger* team had continued to dig for the story nine months ago.

'Yes. He seems to be in control and to have learned from Woody's mistakes.'

'Has he added any assets?'

'A few, but not from us. We're still taking a cut of his profits, though. Not huge profits, but steady, and there's promise for future expansion. McCord's partner welcomed Sean's e-commerce expertise. Locating his server offshore and teaching him about proxies was also . . . appreciated. His appreciation increased the profit trickle to a steady flow. We haven't made personal contact in months. He knows I watch his progress, but as long as the deposits are made every month, I don't bother him.'

It had been an agreement among the team, to take a cut of the business that high school teacher McCord and his more socially prominent partner had successfully started and maintained. But then McCord had thrown his share away when he'd attracted O'Bannion's attention for being a little too friendly with the students in his class.

Wanting to expose McCord's lechery, O'Bannion had somehow hacked his way into McCord's computer and discovered his collection. What

348

O'Bannion had believed to be his collection, anyway. The newsman hadn't realized what he was looking at, because most people didn't have the stomach for those kind of pictures to begin with. To clinically analyze them required a specific kind of individual. Marcus O'Bannion was not that man.

But O'Bannion was a man who didn't give up once he'd gotten the scent of a story. He had published the 'truth', exposing McCord's proclivities to the disgust of the community. Luckily he hadn't published the whole truth. Luckily Sean had been able to remove the more damaging files from McCord's server before the police raided his house, took his computers and tossed his ass in jail.

We had to take a huge risk to ensure that good ole Woody McCord didn't talk. It had been a stroke of fate that O'Bannion had been hospitalized at the same time, his life turned upside down by his own injury and the loss of his brother. Had he kept going, Alice was right. Ken and his entire team would be sitting behind bars.

'And the second thing?' she asked.

'How will you get close to O'Bannion?'

'I don't plan to get close. I don't care if anyone thinks it's related to the girl this morning or not. Like I said earlier today, the man has so many enemies, nobody will know what hit him. I'll make up a room for Demetrius, then I'll focus on the O'Bannion problem.'

Ken dialed Decker as she left the room. 'I need your medical services again,' he said when the younger man answered. 'Meet me in Eden Park near the Conservatory. I'll be waiting next to Demetrius's car. And bring some chloroform or something to knock him out with.' He hung up and dialed Burton. 'I need you to tow Demetrius's vehicle to my garage. I want you to clean out the blood and then get rid of it.'

'Yes, sir.'

Twenty-three

Cincinnati, Ohio
Tuesday 4 August, 9.05 P.M.

Scarlett found Marcus sitting on a sofa in a sleek, opulent living room, cradling a Sheltie in his arms. The dog wasn't moving.

Oh no, she thought, her heart hurting for him even as her body trembled with relief. He was unhurt. Strong, healthy and alive. He looked up, met her eyes, and a new wave of fear passed through her. His looked stark and cold. Empty.

An officer stood behind him, his expression irritated. The man had his hand on his holstered service weapon as if he expected Marcus to bolt and planned to gun him down when he did. 'Are you Bishop?' he asked stiffly.

Scarlett glanced at the man's badge. 'I am Detective Bishop, Officer Towson. Stand down, please.' She could see that there were people in the bedroom and knew from Dispatch that Marcus had made two calls to 911, one for the doorman, Edgar Kauffman, and the other for his employee, Phillip Cauldwell. The second ambulance had still been parked outside, so the medics weren't done with Phillip yet. She looked over her shoulder at Kate, who'd stayed a step behind her the whole way. 'Can you see what's happening in the bedroom?'

Kate nodded and went to the master bedroom. Scarlett carefully sat next to Marcus.

'Are you hurt?' she asked, keeping her voice low and calm. As calm as she could, anyway, with her heart beating a hole in her throat.

'I'm not hurt.' He swallowed hard. 'Phillip Cauldwell's one of my team,' he said, his normally beautiful voice flat and emotionless. 'On the *Ledger*. Good kid. I've known him for years. His sister is Lisette Cauldwell. She's also on my team. She's one of my oldest friends. I need to tell her about Phil. I don't want her to hear it from strangers.' He fixed his gaze on the dog in his arms. 'I also need a vet,' he continued in the same flat voice. 'He hurt her.'

He was in shock, she understood. Not physical shock, but emotional shock. 'The person who attacked Phillip?' she asked softly.

'She bit him. She's evidence, but I don't want her in a cage. I want her taken care of.' Another audible swallow. 'She's all I have left of Mikhail,' he whispered, his voice breaking.

'I understand.' She placed her hand on Marcus's forearm and gave it a light squeeze. 'I called Sergeant Tanaka. He's on his way with a team. I'll ask him to call a forensic vet, okay?' She made the call, then ran her hand gently over the dog's coat. The animal whimpered softly, and Marcus's hold tightened ever so slightly.

Kate came back in and crouched next to the sofa, looking up at Marcus. 'Your friend isn't dead. He's hurt badly, though, but you knew that,' she said honestly. 'You stopped his bleeding, so he'll have a chance.'

'This is Special Agent Coppola,' Scarlett told him. 'She's Deacon's old partner. She's just been transferred here, so she's helping us with this case now. Deacon says you can trust her. Tell us what happened.'

He glanced at Kate before lifting his eyes to Scarlett's again, his still stark and cold. He told them how he'd found the wounded guard in the lobby, how he'd found his apartment trashed. 'He forced Phillip to bring him up here, but I guess he didn't expect the dog to bite him or Phillip to stab him with his own knife.'

'I guess not,' Scarlett said softly. 'I'm glad they took him by surprise.'

'You were right,' Marcus said, his voice as dead as his eyes. 'I was the target this afternoon. They were shooting at me, not you. Maybe this morning in the alley, too. Maybe it's been me all along.'

'Not this morning,' Scarlett murmured. 'Tala's killer tracked her to the alley.'

'And Agent Spangler,' he continued, as if she hadn't said a word. 'Maybe he's dead because of me too. Maybe they've been following me all day.'

Scarlett wanted to sigh. His emotional shock was worse than she'd thought. He was taking responsibility for everything that had gone wrong this day. Although he didn't sound paranoid. He sounded too coldly logical. Her gut had told her to look at Marcus's enemies this morning, but she'd brushed the instinct aside, focusing on Tala as the target.

Because Tala had known her killer. And because Tala's owner had been removed from his home, kicking and screaming. *But then the killer came here. To Marcus's home.* To hell with sighing. Now she wanted to curse in frustration. *I'm missing something important.*

'Who's they?' Kate asked.

'I don't know,' Marcus said, his voice controlled and pulled taut at the same time.

'I think we need to go over that list of yours,' Scarlett said, keeping her voice soft, 'because too many things don't fit together. I need to call my boss. Give me a minute. I'll be right back.' She squeezed his arm as she rose, wishing she could brush a kiss over his lips or take him in her arms, but she knew that comforting him would have to wait.

'Officer Towson,' Scarlett said. 'Bring the building manager up here, please. I want the security tapes for this building. I want to know if the shooter left, from which exit, and when.'

'He's gone,' Officer Towson said. 'I cleared every room.'

Marcus shook his head. 'He's gone from this apartment, but if he's stabbed and bleeding, he may have holed up somewhere else in the building.'

'I'll get the building locked down and handle the door-to-door search,' Kate said. 'Hopefully he hasn't taken anyone hostage, but we might find that someone saw something.'

Scarlett gave her a grateful nod. 'Thanks. I have to give Isenberg an update and find someone else to lead the search for the women.'

'No,' Marcus said, grabbing Scarlett's arm with a speed she hadn't anticipated. He didn't hurt her, but he'd startled her.

'Hands off, buddy,' Towson snapped, grabbing Marcus's wrist and trying to yank it away. Marcus released her, but Scarlett knew that it was only because he didn't want to hurt her.

'I asked you to get the manager, Officer,' Scarlett said, allowing the uniform to feel the sharp end of her tone. 'Please do that. Mr O'Bannion is not a suspect. He is a witness, and we will treat him with respect.'

Towson gave her a dark look. 'Yes, ma'am,' he said mockingly and marched off, leaving Scarlett shaking her head. She could and would deal with Towson later. Now she sat back on the sofa, curling her fingers around Marcus's wrist. 'Why did you tell me no?'

'Because you need to find those women. They can tell you who took Anders.'

'Maybe. But the person who attacked you may *be* the one who took Anders. There's something more going on here than we're seeing. Too many unanswered questions and loose ends left flapping in the wind. I need answers, Marcus. You've been attacked three times today. If you'd been here when this guy forced his way in, you might be the one lying in there.'

He turned to give her a cold glare. 'I should be. Phillip is innocent in all of this.'

'I know Phillip is innocent,' she said, gentling her voice. She still held onto his arm and now brushed her thumb over the fabric of his shirt to try to soothe him. It was all she could do with so many eyes watching. 'But I'm allowed to be glad you're not hurt. Now, we need to think this thing through. If someone's been after you, why did they go after Phillip? Why not just wait for you to get home?'

'Because Phillip stabbed him.'

'I got that, and don't worry. Sergeant Tanaka will do a thorough sweep of your place. If the shooter left anything behind, Tanaka will find it.'

'Phillip said the guy wrapped his arm, left with the knife embedded in it. So no blood.'

'Maybe not. But there's still skin and hair. Tanaka is the best I've ever known. We're going to let him do his job, okay?'

A stiff nod was her answer, and she squeezed his arm lightly again.

'What I meant,' she continued, 'was why did he follow Phillip up? If he wanted you, why not simply wait till you came home?'

His stare never let up. 'Maybe he wanted to force his way in to wait up here for me.'

'Yeah, but . . .' She shook her head. 'He left a victim behind the desk, Marcus. He had to have known the guard would be discovered sooner versus later.' She exhaled, suddenly understanding. 'He was *counting* on the guard being discovered. He wanted you to come home. Wanted to draw you home.'

'That's how I see it,' he said, his voice still cold and expressionless.

'If we look at it that way, I can see how you think you were the target all three times.' She sighed. 'Let's check the security tapes. See what they show. Until then, sit tight with BB. She might be our best lead.'

She stepped toward the door of the master bedroom, watching the medics work on Marcus's friend as she dialed Isenberg. 'It's Scarlett.'

'What's going on at O'Bannion's?' Isenberg asked, foregoing a greeting as she often did.

Scarlett filled her in as Vince Tanaka came through the door with his toolbox filled with gadgets. He put it down and motioned that he was going to have a look around, so Scarlett stayed on the call with Lynda. 'I need to follow this lead,' she told her boss. 'Can you get someone else to accompany my uncle to search for Mila and Erica Bautista? Zimmerman said he told you about finding the father and son, too. Maybe you can have them ready to talk over a speaker phone to Mila and Erica when you get close so that they don't run away.'

'That's a good idea. I'll ask Adam Kimble to accompany the searchers.'

Scarlett winced. 'Is he ready?' Having recently returned from a six-month leave of absence, Adam was looking calmer every day, but every so often Scarlett wondered about how much of his calm was real and how much was for show.

'As ready as he'll ever be,' Lynda said in the tone that dared anyone to disagree.

Scarlett was not planning to take that dare, so she approached from a different angle. 'Erica, the daughter, and John Paul, the son, are both minors. Perhaps it would be a good idea to have a therapist on hand to deal with any immediate issues they might have.'

A pregnant pause, then Lynda snorted. 'Damn, Scarlett, you are good. Sure, let's have a therapist there. If nothing else, it's CYA, but they might be able to help. Who will you call?'

'How about Meredith Fallon? She's proven herself reliable and trustworthy.' And Meredith had also shown an ability to calm Adam Kimble when he'd been agitated.

'I like her. Call her. Is Vince there yet?'

'Yes. He came in a minute ago.'

'Good. Find this guy, Scarlett. Soon.'

The line went dead as Lynda ended the call, and a few moments later the paramedics wheeled Phillip out, an oxygen mask over his face. His eyes were closed, his skin far too gray.

'County,' one of the medics said before Scarlett could ask. 'And yes, we'll have them call you with updates. And yes, we have your cell number.'

'Thank you,' Marcus said, and one of the medics gave him a sympathetic nod before pushing the stretcher into the hall toward the elevator. The cold facade cracked, pain flashing over his face, deep in his eyes. 'I have to tell his sister.'

Scarlett sat back down beside him, wrapping her fingers around his forearm again, wishing she could put her arms around him instead. 'Lisette, right? One of your oldest friends.'

He nodded miserably. 'Lisette works for me too. We've been friends for as long as I can remember. She's like my sister, and Phillip's always been the kid brother who wouldn't leave me the hell alone.' He closed his eyes. 'Dammit to hell.'

'I'm so sorry, Marcus,' she murmured, giving his forearm a hard squeeze. 'Let's catch this sonofabitch.'

Marcus's eyes opened and in them she saw barely bridled rage. 'Yes. Let's.'

alone in the dark

Cincinnati, Ohio
Tuesday 4 August, 9.45 P.M.

Scarlett parked her car in the emergency room lot, switched off the ignition, then turned to look at Marcus with dark eyes that understood his pain. 'You didn't cause this,' she whispered into the quiet.

'You don't know that,' he said, looking at the brightly lit neon sign over the ER entrance. He had. He had caused this. He wasn't sure which person on that damn list he'd pissed off, but whoever shot Phillip was one of them. Of that he was certain.

'I know you didn't cause this,' she said simply. 'But I would like to know why you believe you did.'

He couldn't look at her, even when she reached across the console to stroke the backs of her fingers down his face. 'Some secrets aren't entirely mine to tell,' he said finally, wishing it weren't true. Wishing he hadn't dragged others into the web of deceit and vengeance that had pulled him in so completely that he'd ceased to think about the very real possible consequences.

Like Tala and Agent Spangler being shot, both dying. Like Phillip and Edgar being shot and maybe dying. *Because of me.*

She hooked a finger under his chin and tugged until he looked at her. 'The risks aren't just yours to assume,' she chided gently as she cupped his face in her palm. 'Not anymore.'

She was right. He turned his face into her caress, earning him another. She brushed her thumb over his lips, inexplicably making his eyes sting. 'I'll talk to the others,' he said.

'All right.' A final sweep of fingertips over his stubbled cheek. 'For what it's worth, I don't believe you've done anything wrong.'

'How could you know that?'

'Because that's not how you're built, Marcus. You protect. You don't destroy.'

He swallowed until he'd cleared his throat of the huge lump that had formed there. He didn't deserve her confidence or her comfort. 'I think Lisette will say differently.'

'I don't know her, so I can't say.'

'You don't know me, either.'

'Then let me. Because I want to.' She slid her hand to the back of his neck and drew his head down for a kiss that was relatively chaste, but so sweet it made his eyes sting again. 'Let's go,' she whispered against his lips. 'Your friends need you.'

355

He quickly stowed his gun under the seat. She could wear hers into the hospital, but he couldn't wear his, and he had no desire to have it taken from him. He'd been lucky the snotty officer who'd been the first responder at the apartment hadn't searched him, mostly because he'd held BB on his lap until the forensic vet had arrived. By then the officer was thankfully gone.

Scarlett locked her car and took his hand, holding it as they bypassed the ER, entering through the hospital lobby. Phillip had been taken to surgery, so Lisette and the others had moved to the OR waiting room. Scarlett pulled her hand away only seconds before they joined Marcus's entire team, all of whom were huddled around Lisette. Lisette had been crying, as had Gayle. Cal looked like he was about to. Diesel was huddled in the corner looking like he'd break something given the slightest provocation.

Stone was green around the gills, looking like he was about to throw up. Marcus understood the sentiment. He, Stone and Diesel all hated hospitals for different, but related, reasons.

Jill had joined them also, sitting next to her aunt, her eyes coldly, boldly accusing. Marcus understood. Jill had feared that someone close to Marcus would get hurt if 'they' came after him, trying to finish what they'd begun that morning. No matter how much he hated to admit it, the young woman had been right.

Lisette immediately rose and walked into Marcus's arms, and he tightened them around her, saying nothing as she began to sob again. What could he say, after all? From the corner of his eye he watched Scarlett edge away from the group toward the nurses' desk. She showed them her badge and pointed to their group before returning and taking a seat on the periphery.

Scarlett had isolated herself, keeping her distance from his people and from him. He wished she wouldn't. He wished she'd wrap her arms around his waist and lay her head against his back, but understood why she didn't. Crime scenes and public places, no PDA. This qualified as a very public place.

Rubbing Lisette's back in wide circles, Marcus rested his cheek on top of her head and turned his face so that he could meet Scarlett's eyes. The nod his detective gave him was so slight that he might have missed it had he not been looking. She was still with him, even though she'd put space between them.

'I didn't think you were coming,' Lisette said when her sobs had quieted.

'Don't be ridiculous.' Marcus tipped up her chin and wiped her cheeks with his thumb. 'I got delayed waiting for the vet to come for BB.'

Lisette's eyes widened, but it was Jill who spoke. 'You were more worried about your dog than Phillip?' the girl asked in condescending disbelief.

Marcus hated that this young girl could make him feel so defensive. He ignored her and directed his explanation to Lisette. 'She was a forensic vet,' he said. 'BB bit Phillip's attacker. We might get a DNA sample of the guy from her.'

Lisette's eyes narrowed. 'Good. And in the meantime, I hope he gets gangrene and dies.'

'Not before we catch him,' Marcus said. 'Have you heard anything from the surgeon?'

'Not yet.' She looked up, her face tear-stained. 'What happened?'

Jill's chin came up, her eyes narrowing. She folded her arms across her chest, clearly waiting for an answer. Just like everyone else in the room.

'I don't know, exactly,' Marcus told them. 'Phillip was only able to tell me a little when I found him. He stabbed the shooter once they were in my apartment, but the man didn't say anything. Didn't say why he was there, what he wanted. Nothing.'

'He wanted you,' Jill said flatly. 'And if that had been any one of us, including my aunt, we'd be in surgery now instead of Phillip.'

Every head swung around to look at her, including Scarlett's. The silence was so thick, Marcus could have cut it with a knife. Even Gayle said nothing, her expression too shocked to be admonishing even if she'd wanted to be.

'What?' Jill demanded belligerently. 'You were all thinking it!'

'You little piece of—' Diesel cut himself off with a visible effort. '*You* were thinking it. *I* wasn't.'

'Neither was I,' Stone said coldly.

Cal jumped in to add his two cents, followed by Lisette, who kept one arm squarely around Marcus's waist in support.

Scarlett silenced them all by rising from her chair and walking into the fray. 'Why?' she asked them, and for several seconds they stared at her as if she had three heads.

'Why what?' Gayle finally asked, trying for an innocence she did not achieve.

Scarlett gave her a tight, intolerant smile. 'Why did the shooter want Marcus to begin with? Why would he want to hurt any of you?'

Diesel glanced at Stone, who shook his head mutely. Scarlett saw the exchange but said nothing, simply waiting.

Jill opened her mouth to spout God only knew what, but Gayle grabbed a handful of the young woman's shirt and yanked her niece down until Jill's

357

face was even with hers. 'You've said enough, young lady,' she snapped. 'Shut. Up.'

Shaking her head, Scarlett turned to Lisette. 'Look, I'm sorry for what happened to your brother. But if you all keep playing games, we'll never find the shooter. And I don't mean to make your worry worse, but this killer seems to be tenacious and your brother is a loose end. You're a reporter. I don't have to tell you what happens to loose ends.'

Lisette blanched. 'Oh my God.'

Scarlett turned to the group. 'You might not like me,' she said, 'and that's okay. I don't need you to like me. But I do need you to trust me – with at least enough information to catch this shooter before he harms anyone else. Or comes back to finish what he started. You all seem to care about each other. This is the place where you prove it. Talk to me.'

Lisette opened her mouth, then closed it again, looking helpless and frightened. 'Marcus,' she whispered. 'If that man comes back, he'll kill Phillip.'

Marcus knew it. Deep down, he knew there would be no salvaging their work. If they told Scarlett what she wanted to know, the worst that would probably happen was that they'd be sued by the perpetrators whose privacy they'd invaded by hacking into their personal computer files. The suits would likely go after the *Ledger* as a corporation and the team individually. Especially himself and Stone, since they had the deepest pockets. It was unlikely any of them would see the inside of a jail, but it was possible. It would be safer to keep their mouths shut.

But then Phillip's would-be killer was still out there, and he'd be back.

Marcus knew what he had to do personally, but he wasn't willing to expose his team. 'I'll call Rex,' he said finally. 'He can help us figure out what we can and can't say.' To his relief, his words were met with nods all around. He glanced at Scarlett. 'Rex Clausing is my attorney.'

Scarlett's brows leaped to the top of her forehead. 'You're lawyering up? *Really?*' She folded her arms over her breasts and gave him a death glare. '*Really*, Marcus?'

He accepted her anger without even trying to defend himself. 'I'm sorry. If it were just me, I'd have told you already. But like I said, this is not my secret to share.'

She closed her eyes. Drew a deep breath. Then looked each member of his team in the eye, waiting until they looked away before going on to the next. She ended up with Jill. 'Is there anything you want to tell me, miss?'

'No,' Gayle said forcefully.

'With all due respect, ma'am,' Scarlett said, 'I wasn't speaking to you. Is this young woman a minor?'

'No,' Jill said. 'I'm nineteen, so she can't speak for me. I would love to tell you everything, but I don't know anything. All I know about is the damn list of threats, and you have that already.'

'How do you know I have the list?' Scarlett asked with a frown.

Jill's bravado melted into a frightened wince. 'I overheard my aunt say so.'

Gayle closed her eyes. 'Young lady, I am going to . . . I don't know what. I just don't know. You are seriously disappointing me.'

Scarlett did one of her long blinks, her composure restored. 'How long will it take your attorney to get here?' she asked calmly.

'He's on his way,' Lisette said. 'I called him as soon as Marcus called me.'

Scarlett's appraisal was cool. 'You expected to need an attorney?'

'Rex is also Lisette's ex-husband,' Marcus explained. 'We all grew up together. It was an amicable divorce.'

Scarlett lifted a sarcastic brow. 'I am so glad to hear that.' Rolling her eyes, she held up her phone so that everyone could see the time. 'It has now been an hour since the man you all claim to care for was attacked and left for dead. I have wasted precious minutes listening to you whine and point fingers. If anyone is willing to give me something that will help me catch the SOB who shot your friend' – she turned to Lisette – 'and your brother, just let me know. I'll be in the hallway. Talk amongst yourselves.'

No one said a word as she turned to go, dropping their gazes to the floor while Marcus bit back a frustrated roar. Scarlett was right. One hundred percent. Phillip could die and they were acting like selfish, stupid children.

'They're protecting me,' he told her, cutting off Stone's protest with a look. 'Let's find a private room and I'll tell you.'

She just looked at him over her shoulder. 'Don't waste my time, Marcus.'

He shook his head. 'It doesn't matter who did what. I'm the boss and I did all the dicey stuff. I can walk you through the list and explain why we're being . . . stupid.'

Slowly she pivoted on her heel, those midnight-blue eyes never leaving his. She didn't believe him, but that didn't matter at this point. 'All right. Come with me.'

Diesel lurched to his feet and Scarlett blinked, her eyes growing wider as they followed him up and up. Diesel had that effect on everyone.

'That's bullshit,' he barked, darting a quick glance at Gayle. 'Sorry,' he said meekly.

Gayle shook her head wearily. 'I'm not your mother, Diesel. Thank God for that.'

Scarlett took a step back so that she didn't have to crane her neck to see Diesel's face. 'I don't think we've been formally introduced,' she said.

'Diesel,' Marcus said, 'Detective Scarlett Bishop. Scarlett, this is Diesel Kennedy.'

'Mr Kennedy,' she said. 'Why is this bullshit?'

Diesel jerked his head toward Marcus. 'He's gonna take the fall when I am just as guilty. Probably more so.'

Stone stood up with a sigh. 'And me.'

'Me too,' Lisette whispered.

'And me,' Cal said. 'I'm Calvin Booker, the *Ledger*'s editor-in-chief. Everything goes through me.'

Diesel shrugged, his jaw tight, expression challenging Marcus to disagree. 'Looks like we are Spartacus,' he drawled.

Stone rolled his eyes. 'Shove it, Diesel.'

'Both of you shove it,' Marcus snapped, then pointed to Gayle. 'She's not involved.'

'She knows nothing,' Cal added. 'She just types memos.'

'That's not true,' Gayle protested. 'I know everything *because* I type the memos.'

'You're Spartacus too, ma'am?' Scarlett asked politely, and Marcus felt the insane urge to laugh. It wasn't funny. None of this was funny. These idiot friends of his were going to get themselves in trouble, and they didn't have to. He'd be damned before he dragged Gayle into it.

'*No*,' Marcus, Stone, Diesel, Cal and Lisette said in unison.

Gayle sighed in angry frustration. 'Suit yourselves. You're all crazy, you know that? I'll be bringing you cakes with files in them. How will you like that?'

'Make mine chocolate,' Diesel said, and Gayle dropped her face into her hands.

'I'll still want to talk to you even though you don't know anything, ma'am,' Scarlett said, then turned to Jill. 'And to you.'

'I got nothing to say. I didn't do anything,' Jill said with a shrug.

'Then why don't you and your aunt just wait over here,' Scarlett said, motioning them to a sofa in the corner. 'I need to find us a private room. Don't worry,' she added to Lisette. 'I'll make sure they bring us news of your brother as soon as he's out of surgery.'

Cincinnati, Ohio
Tuesday 4 August, 10.00 P.M.

Scarlett stood back as Marcus's troop found places around the table in the small doctor–patient consulting room. Marcus looked positively grim – and angry with his employees. He'd wanted to take all the blame on his shoulders, which hadn't surprised Scarlett in the least.

That his people had stood with him said more about their loyalty to Marcus than their desire to tell the truth, but it didn't really matter as long as the truth was what she got. She was giving Phillip's attacker more time to escape or plan another attack with every second that ticked away. Part of her wished Deacon were here to help with this, but another part was glad he'd stayed at the crime scene with Agent Coppola. Scarlett wasn't sure if she could stomach any more testosterone. The room was practically reeking with it.

'Are we comfortable?' she asked, and watched Stone O'Bannion roll his eyes.

'No *we* are not,' he muttered. 'But *we* are here, so let's get on with it.'

'Thank you,' Lisette said to her. 'For stationing the policeman outside of the operating room. I feel like Phillip's a little safer, anyway.'

Scarlett's smile was sympathetic. 'It was no trouble.' She'd had to ask for someone to watch Jill and Gayle, anyway. She didn't want them speaking to each other or anyone else without a police witness. She'd positioned it as having a guard keeping an eye on Gayle for her own protection. 'I have brothers,' she added. 'And I do know what you're going through. One of my brothers was shot a few years ago. They operated on him in this hospital, in fact. We all took turns standing guard outside his room until we could bring him home.'

'Is he all right?' Lisette asked, then winced when Scarlett hesitated to answer. 'Oh, I'm so sorry for your loss, Detective. I didn't know.'

'No,' Scarlett said quickly, understanding the woman's confusion. 'He lived. The surgeons here are very good. He just . . . Phin's a vet, and it happened after he came home. We were relieved that he was finally safe, and then he got shot in a bar fight.' She shrugged a shoulder. 'We haven't seen him for a long time, so I'm not sure how to answer your question. I hope he's okay. But we've drifted off topic.'

It had not been unintentional. Nothing she'd shared was a secret. Hell, the *Ledger* had probably carried the story of Phin's debacle, which had started with an argument over a woman. Naturally. Phin had always had a temper, even before the war. The *Ledger* probably had several articles on

361

him. She'd shared Phin's past with Lisette in hopes of creating a bond with the woman who had the most to lose – her brother was not safe until his attacker was behind bars.

Neither was Marcus. *So Lisette Cauldwell isn't the only one with a lot to lose.* Scarlett couldn't let herself think about what might have happened had Marcus arrived at his apartment first. He'd be the one in surgery right now.

She took the empty seat between Marcus and Diesel, the giant who'd been first to share the blame. The man's shoulders took up his space and half of hers, but she didn't budge, forcing him to scoot his chair over a few inches. This caused a ripple effect as everyone moved their chairs, because Stone was on Diesel's right and his shoulders were nearly as wide. She waited until all the chairs had stopped moving and everyone settled.

'I assume this involves the *Ledger* in some way,' she began. From her jacket pocket she pulled the list Marcus had printed up earlier that day. It seemed like a year ago. 'These are the threats I know about.' She looked up at Marcus. 'I also assume this is a . . . truncated list. If you'd sent me the real one, I would have had it minutes after you sent the video files. Yes?'

He nodded, his face flushed with color, making him look like a naughty boy caught with his hand in the cookie jar. 'I thought it would be for the best. I guess I thought wrong.'

'You didn't know,' she murmured. 'I thought Tala was the target too, so let's get past that and figure out who shot your friend.' She put the list on the table, then looked at each person for a few seconds, meeting their eyes before moving to the next. 'What are you doing that makes people want to kill you?'

'We want immunity,' Stone said quietly. 'Especially for Gayle.'

'She only types memos,' Scarlett said dryly. 'And in case you haven't noticed, I haven't Mirandized any of you. Should I be doing so?'

'No.' Marcus drew a breath. 'We target abusers and get them out of their homes. However we have to.'

She blinked slowly, digesting this. She hadn't known exactly what to expect, but hearing this was no shock. She'd told Marcus that he was built to protect, and she'd meant it. She'd figured it had something to do with helping people in distress because he'd reached out to Tala so readily and so naturally. Like it was something he did all the time. That they'd gone to such trouble to cover their tracks was a little more worrying. 'Do you break the law?'

Diesel's massive shoulders shrugged nonchalantly. 'A little hacking. And sometimes we might . . . suggest they should leave town.'

Scarlett's lips twitched. 'If I opened my door and saw you standing there,

Mr Kennedy, you wouldn't have to suggest anything. I'd start running before you opened your mouth.'

Diesel grinned happily. 'Thank you.'

'You're welcome. How do you choose these abusers?' More furtive glances around the table made her huff in annoyance. 'For God's sake, people, spit it out. I don't have all night. And neither does your friend in there. I can't justify a uniformed guard forever, you know.'

'We get referrals, mostly,' Marcus said. 'Some come from people who aren't authorized to share the information. To give their names could jeopardize their jobs, which would mean a lot of needy people wouldn't be helped.'

'So, Social Services,' she said. 'I can understand that. Must be frustrating to see bad people get away with hurting women and kids.'

'You see that every day,' Cal said softly. It was the first time he'd spoken since they'd entered the room.

'Yes,' Scarlett said. 'Every goddamn day. There have been many times I've been tempted to suggest someone leave town.'

'Have you ever done it?' Stone asked, a gleam in his eye.

Ever the reporter, she thought, raising her eyebrows at him. 'Tempted, Stone. That's all I said. For the record.' She eyed the rest of the group. 'So you get referrals. I assume these are referrals about abusers who are too slick to get caught by Children's Services or who have frightened their victims into silence. What do you next? Dig until you find proof of their abuse?'

'Something like that,' Marcus said. 'But sometimes there is no proof of abuse so we have to find something else.'

'Find or fabricate?' she asked him pointedly.

'Mostly find. At times we get a little creative. But it's never a total fabrication.'

Cal cleared his throat. 'I'd call it more entrapment. With cameras set up in advance.'

'Of course.' Scarlett turned to Diesel. 'You're the hacker?'

Pride flickered in his eyes. 'I am. I don't steal. Just . . . rummage.'

Again her lips twitched. It was hard not to like this man. 'Rummage for what?'

'Wrongdoing in general. Sometimes it's obvious.' His lips thinned. 'Like kiddie porn. Sometimes a little less so, like tax evasion or stock fraud.'

Scarlett blinked in surprise. 'Tax evasion or stock fraud?'

'It's a crime,' Lisette said. 'Not as bad, but if it's big enough, it'll land them in federal prison. It gets them away from their families.'

'And,' Cal added, 'even if it's not big enough for the Feds, many times they don't want anyone to know what they've done, so they're more amenable to the suggestion to separate themselves from the household.'

'Extortion,' Scarlett murmured.

'Gentle encouragement,' Cal countered.

'It gets them out of the house,' Scarlett said, trying to keep the approval from her voice but knowing she was only moderately successful. 'But they inevitably return. Then what?'

'They come home to find their families have relocated,' Marcus said. 'We help them start over if that's what they want. New IDs, new jobs. We've helped some of the women go back to school.' He smiled fiercely, proudly. 'One of our cases just graduated with a nursing degree. Another became a pharmacy tech. Another a paralegal. One finished the teaching degree she abandoned when she had too many bruises to show her face on campus. All of these mothers can now support their families on their own. They're making lives for themselves and are no longer isolated and alone. And their kids are no longer afraid.'

Scarlett drew a breath, her chest suddenly tight with emotion that bubbled up, breaking free from where she'd contained it for so long. She'd known Marcus was different the first time she'd heard his voice. She'd known. *No, I'd hoped. Hoped so damn hard.*

'Why do you hide this?' she whispered, meeting his eyes, letting him see everything she felt deep inside. Wishing they were alone so she could show him.

'Because we break the rules,' he whispered back, his stare intensely intimate, despite the fact they were not alone. 'We hack into people's computers, we "gently coerce", and we set people up. We produce fake IDs and print fake birth certificates and passports.'

'The printing press,' she murmured, and a glance at Cal told her she'd guessed right. He lifted his palms to show her fingertips stained black with ink, his narrowed eyes and tilted chin proclaiming unmistakable defiance. 'You're utilizing all of your resources.'

'And skills,' Cal said. 'I learned the craft back before there were computers.'

Beside her, Diesel sighed. 'And if you turn us in, we'll have to stop.'

Scarlett shook her head. Their big concern was being forced to stop their work, more than being prosecuted. Or killed. 'But this is dangerous. Phillip's proof of that.'

'Phillip knew the risks,' Lisette said quietly. 'He accepted them. I want the man who hurt him caught, but none of us want to stop. Phillip wouldn't either, if he were sitting here.'

'But why?' Scarlett asked, looking around the table at each of them. She understood that Marcus and Stone had suffered a childhood trauma, but losing their baby brother to a murdering kidnapper didn't automatically translate to helping abused women and their kids. The rest of them . . . She was perplexed. 'Why do you care so much?'

'We have our reasons,' Diesel said stubbornly, and the rest of them nodded.

It was clear she'd get no further with them, at least not here and now. 'All right. So you break some rules, put some abusers behind bars and "gently coerce" others to step away from the family.' She tapped the paper on the table in front of her. 'Are any of the names on this list viable suspects?'

'No,' Marcus said. 'That's why I chose them.'

Of course you did. Because he hadn't trusted her – then. Of course, she hadn't trusted him, either. In her mind he'd been a reporter, making his living digging up news. How much difference a few hours made. 'Can I get a complete list?'

Marcus pulled a flash drive from the pocket of his pants. 'Here it is.' He put it in her palm and curled her fingers to hold it, covering her hand with his for a long moment before releasing her. 'I'll need to walk you through the names.'

Her skin tingled, missing his warmth as soon as he took his hand away. She had to fight the urge to lean into him. 'We'll figure it out. My next question, I need you to be honest with me, because I don't like surprises that bite me in the ass. How far did your "gentle coercion" go? How physical did you get? Specifically, did any of these names report you for assault?'

A long, long hesitation around the table had her heart sinking. What had they done?

'Report?' Diesel asked, drawing the word out. 'As in, file a police report?'

'Yes.' Her eyes narrowed. 'What kind of report are *you* talking about?'

'No, no,' Diesel said, waving his hands. 'Police report is what you wanted to know. The answer to your question is no. I don't think so.'

'No, or you don't think so?' Scarlett asked.

'Well, any kook can file a police report,' Diesel said with a shrug. 'So anything's possible.'

She sighed. 'What exactly did you all do? I need to know.'

Stone folded his arms over his chest. 'A few assholes might have fallen a few times.'

'Into doors,' Diesel added. 'Or asphalt. Or knuckles.'

'How hard might they have fallen?' Scarlett asked.

'The worst time was when the boys beat some asshole up,' Lisette said.

'Which boys?' Scarlett demanded.

Stone shook his head. 'Not me. I got an alibi. I was covering an election in Colombia.'

Scarlett looked at Marcus. 'You?'

Marcus nodded, unrepentant. 'He was stupid enough to throw the first punch. Look, the SOB had tricked his daughter's best friend into telling him where his wife and kids were hiding, and had gone to their house to drag them back once he got out of jail for molesting his own kids and a few of the neighbors'. The daughter's friend warned them he was coming when she realized she'd been tricked. The man's soon-to-be ex-wife called us.'

'Why didn't she call the cops?' Scarlett asked, and another hush fell over the table.

'He *was* a cop,' Marcus said quietly.

Scarlett exhaled. 'Shit. You beat up a cop?'

'A little,' Diesel said.

'A lot,' Marcus corrected. 'And I'm not sorry. He was not going to be satisfied until they were dead. We threatened to call the cops on him, and he attacked us. So we convinced him to leave and not come back. He did leave – for that day. I worried he'd come back, so we installed a high-tech alarm system in the woman's house and got her a very large dog. He never came back. A few weeks later he died, but not because of anything we did to him.'

Scarlett rubbed her temples, trying to recall the case. Cops going to jail for molesting children didn't happen every day. In a rush, the man's name and face came back to her and she blew out a breath. 'You're right. I knew him. He was a prick who liked to bully anyone weaker than he was. He moved to California and died there. A bar fight or road rage, wasn't it? He was beaten up pretty severely, but I can't remember all the details.' She narrowed her eyes. 'Were you responsible for that?'

'No,' Marcus said. 'We had our run-in with him before that. But none of us cried for him. It happened when I was in the hospital. Stone was recuperating at home. Diesel was with Cal and Lisette, keeping the paper running.'

Scarlett turned to look at Diesel and he met her gaze without flinching. 'I didn't do it,' he said. 'The asshole got drunk and got grabby with a waitress in a bar, which made her steroid-juiced bodybuilder boyfriend very unhappy. Boyfriend is sitting in jail, waiting for his trial.' He smiled nastily. 'I wrote the article about it, though.'

'O-kay,' she murmured, hoping that she never saw Diesel truly angry. That evil smile of his was enough to raise the hairs on the back of her neck. She looked at Marcus. 'Were there any other incidents?'

'A few. Mostly we just had Diesel pay them a visit. He rarely had to do more than raise a finger to convince them to walk away.' He pointed to the flash drive. 'I'll tell you all the details when we go over the list.'

'What about names that aren't on this list?' she asked. 'People you've investigated that haven't made threats? Or the targets of ongoing investigations that haven't been closed, or who you haven't exposed or "gently coerced" yet?'

Lisette drew a sharp breath. 'Mr Arrogant. Phillip was asking questions in his office today.'

'But that doesn't explain the alley or the sniper,' Marcus said.

Lisette's shoulders slumped. 'You're right.'

'Who is Mr Arrogant?' Scarlett asked.

'His real name is Rich McKay,' Lisette said. 'He's a corporate attorney. Works for Wesman Peal, the department store chain. He's a vice-president there.'

'And attorneys know just how to slither around the law,' Scarlett said coldly. 'What was Phillip doing in his office?'

'Trying to find an employee list,' Marcus said. 'We figured if he's beating his wife and kid, he may have been aggressive with his office staff too. Phillip posed as a courier.'

'Then we can use that,' Scarlett said, thinking. 'We can say we're checking out all the places that Phillip's been today as part of our investigation into his attack. Anything else? Any other ongoing cases we need to consider?'

'No,' Stone said. 'Things have been very quiet since the fall.'

Since Mikhail's murder.

'We were just starting to gear back up,' Marcus added.

Scarlett nodded. 'I understand. But you're right,' she said to Marcus. 'I don't think Mr Arrogant is involved in Phillip's attack, because of the shooting this afternoon. If we assume you were the target, the sniper had to either have been waiting at the Anders house or he followed us there.'

Marcus's face suddenly paled. 'Oh shit. Delores.'

Stone stiffened. 'What about Delores?'

The brothers' gazes locked. 'We'd just come from her house,' Marcus said. 'She identified the dog that Tala had been walking in the park. That's how we got the Anderses' address. We drove straight from Delores's shelter to Hyde Park.'

Stone also paled. 'They could have hurt her. Goddammit to hell.' His hands visibly shaking, he pulled out his cell phone and hit a number from his speed dial while the rest of them looked on in stunned surprise. After a moment, he relaxed. 'I was just wondering about your hours,' he said into the phone. 'Thank you.'

Scarlett looked at Marcus, but he appeared equally confused.

'Um . . .' Marcus hesitated. 'Did you have her on speed dial?'

Stone had gone from pale to bright red in a heartbeat. 'Yes.'

'You just asked for her hours,' Diesel said, brows lifted.

Stone's frown was formidable. 'Drop it. I'm serious.' He stared at each person around the table harshly. 'I worry about her being all the way out in Bumfuck. I keep track of her, okay? I just wanted to be sure she was okay.'

'Loveland isn't Bumfuck,' Scarlett said mildly.

He turned his fury on her. 'She lives in the middle of nowhere all alone. Anyone could break in and she couldn't defend herself.'

Scarlett suspected that more was going on, but knew not to push. Stone's feelings were his own. But she could soothe his fears. 'She has a great big dog and I've given her lessons on operating a firearm myself. She's a pretty good shot. You don't need to worry so much.'

The big man drew a deep breath. 'Thank you,' he muttered. 'That's helpful.'

'I'll send an officer out to her place to check on her, and I'll recommend she find somewhere to stay for a few days,' she said, and the glance Stone flashed her was grateful even though he made no further reply.

The brother sitting beside her squeezed her knee. 'Thank you,' Marcus murmured.

She covered his hand with hers. 'It's nothing. She's a good person. And my friend. You should also consider adding security at the *Ledger* building. Maybe even at all of your personal residences. Especially your mother's house, Marcus. Gayle's house too. If they failed luring you with Phillip, they may try again, and your mom and Audrey are alone right now. Gayle's safe here, but she has to go home to sleep at some point.'

Both Marcus and Stone paled. 'We should have thought about that already, dammit,' Stone said, then sent a quick text, talking as he typed. 'I'm contacting the company that does security for Audrey's fund-raisers. I'll post guards at both houses and at the *Ledger*.'

Marcus drew an unsteady breath. 'Mom's driver is retired army and her personal maid is also trained in defense, so she's always covered in the house. They can handle security until the guards get there.'

'I'm texting them too,' Stone said grimly as his fingers continued to fly over his phone's keyboard. 'I don't want them taken by surprise.'

'I already asked for drive-bys on her street when I requested the guard for Phillip,' Scarlett said. 'The department couldn't justify full-time protection, though. You should tell your internal security and the guards you've hired to coordinate with CPD.'

Stone looked stunned. 'Thank you, Detective. That was kind of you.'

'It was a phone call,' Scarlett said simply. 'Your mom's been through a lot. I'd like her to feel safe. To *be* safe.'

Marcus's lips curved ever so slightly at Stone's expression, then he turned his hand palm up to lace his fingers through Scarlett's. 'So what now, Detective?' he asked, his businesslike tone in contrast with the warmth of his hand in hers.

'We start on the list.' She bit her lip. 'But something still doesn't fit. Tala knew her attacker this morning. I'm sure of it.'

Marcus leaned his head back, staring up at the ceiling with a weary sigh. 'You're right. That doesn't f—'

He was cut off by the door opening, revealing a tired surgeon. 'Miss Cauldwell? The duty nurse said I could find you here.'

Everyone at the table came to their feet, including Scarlett. She kept her hold on Marcus's hand, squeezing hard as they waited.

'I'm Lisette Cauldwell,' Lisette said, a quaver in her voice.

Cal slid his arm over Lisette's shoulders, holding her close. 'Is he all right?' he asked.

'He came through the surgery,' the doctor said. 'It was a very serious wound, but he's got a fighting chance. Whoever did first aid did a good job. He might have died had he lost any more blood. We had to give him three pints as it was. He's in recovery and will be moved to ICU. The next twenty-four hours are critical. We'll know something by then, one way or the other.' With a nod, the doctor backed out of the room, closing the door behind him.

Lisette turned into Cal's arms, starting to cry again, her tears a mixture of relief, fear and adrenaline, Scarlett thought. She understood. She'd held her sobbing mother when the surgeon told them Phin would be all right. She'd cried those tears herself when no one was looking.

Marcus sank into his chair, his grip on Scarlett's hand nearly punishing. He dropped his face into his free hand, shuddering as he tried to hold back his own emotion. Scarlett stroked his hair with the hand he wasn't holding, pulling his head to rest his cheek against her stomach, her heart catching when he turned his head to bury his face against her, wrapping his arm around her waist. There was nothing sexual about his embrace. He sought only comfort. From the way he held on, Scarlett wondered how long it had been since anyone had given him comfort. Or, like her, how long since he'd allowed himself to accept it.

At that moment she didn't care who saw them, wouldn't have pushed him away even if Lynda Isenberg had walked in with the commissioner himself. Especially when she felt the front of her thin cotton shirt grow damp. He was crying too and didn't want anyone to see. She'd make sure they didn't.

Her own eyes stinging, she bent so that her lips brushed his ear. 'You heard the doctor,' she murmured thickly. She curled around him, cradling him to her as he clung. 'You probably saved Phillip's life. You didn't cause what happened, nor are you responsible. Whoever broke into your apartment and shot Phillip is responsible.'

His arm around her tightened and his shoulders heaved, the movement nearly imperceptible.

'You listen to me, Marcus O'Bannion,' she whispered fiercely. 'Every person on your team knew the risk. Accepted the risk. Whoever's pissed off enough to kill you could be angry because of something one of the others did to expose him. You are not the sole owner of whatever misplaced guilt you're feeling. You will not shoulder the burden. I won't let you.' She kissed his neck, just below his ear, relieved by the muted chuckle that rumbled in his throat. 'He'll be all right, Marcus. You have to believe that.'

His shoulders sagged on a sigh that warmed her belly through her shirt. 'You play dirty, Detective Bishop,' he said quietly, the muscles in his face tensing as he clenched his eyes shut and rubbed his face against her middle, nuzzling her while he dried his tears.

'Only when I have to,' she said. 'So don't make me.'

One side of his mouth lifted ruefully when he pulled away, releasing her hand to scrub his palms over his face. She surreptitiously buttoned her jacket to hide the dampness on her shirt. She expected he'd be wearing a stoic face when he lowered his hands, but what she saw stole her breath. She'd seen plenty of emotion in his dark eyes – pain and desire, anger and guilt. But now he looked at her with an unmasked need so profound, so . . . *hungry* that it shook her, froze her where she stood. Burned her from the inside out. Made her want to reach for him again, but this time it wouldn't be about comfort.

And she would have done it had Diesel not politely cleared his throat behind her. 'Do you need us anymore?' he asked. 'Cal and I need to get back to the paper. We have an edition to print.'

Scarlett drew a breath, closed her eyes to compose herself. Contain herself. When she opened her eyes, Marcus was still gazing at her like he was a starving wolf. With an effort she pivoted on her heel to look up at Diesel. 'I think I have enough to get started. I may have more questions later.'

Diesel's brows were raised in amusement. 'I take it you're not going to arrest us.'

Scarlett blinked cluelessly. 'For what? I have received no formal complaints against you. Please keep it that way.'

With a grin, Diesel walked around the table and kissed Lisette on the cheek. 'I'll be back, Lissy. They won't let us into ICU for a while anyway. If I don't hear from you, I'll come back and take the night shift so you can sleep.'

'I don't think I'll sleep,' Lisette said, sniffling. 'I think I'll just watch him breathe.'

'Come on, honey.' Cal led Lisette to the door. 'Let's go back and tell Gayle.'

Marcus was right behind Cal, pausing at the door when he realized Scarlett hadn't moved from where she stood. 'Aren't you coming?'

She started to say yes, but realized that Stone still sat at the table, his arms folded across his broad chest, his features bent in a suspicious scowl. 'In a minute,' she said. 'I want to talk to Stone first.'

Because Stone clearly wanted to talk to her. Marcus gave his brother a warning glare before turning to her, that hungry look back in his eyes. 'I'll meet you in the lobby, then we can start working on the list.'

The list was not what she was thinking about when he looked at her that way. But the list was what would keep him alive, so she nodded. 'Stay away from the windows.'

Marcus gave her a quick salute. 'Yes, ma'am.'

Twenty-four

Scarlett sat down across from Stone, and folded her hands in front of her. For a long minute neither of them spoke, Stone glaring at her . . . well, stonily.

Scarlett broke the silence. 'I understand,' she said.

He smiled mockingly. 'Exactly what is it that you understand, Detective Bishop?'

'That you protect him just like he protects you. That you don't trust me.' She hesitated. 'I know what happened twenty-seven years ago.'

Fury roiled behind his eyes. 'You don't know jack shit.'

'I know that you were kidnapped when you were a small child and almost died. I know your baby brother did die. I know that you lost another brother nine months ago and I understand that you nearly lost your only surviving brother three times today.'

A muscle in his cheek twitched as he ground his teeth. 'How did you know about Matty?' he finally asked.

Matty. Matthias's nickname. 'Marcus told me to Google your old last name and Lexington. I did, so I know what the papers covered. No more.' She watched his agitation begin to fade. Marcus had told her that some of the story was Stone's to tell, and she'd suspected that Stone had been worried about personal details Marcus might have shared with her. 'I'm sorry you lost your brother, Stone. Both brothers. I have brothers too. I can't imagine losing any of them, although I came awfully close a time or two. Which I know doesn't mean anything to you, but I want you to know that I understand that you're worried about Marcus.' She sighed. 'Look, I can't promise that everything will be roses, rainbows and happily-ever-after between Marcus and me, but I can promise that I won't hurt him.'

'You won't mean to,' Stone said wearily, all his anger gone. Or at least stowed. 'You should know that I told him to take you out for a spin and then dump your ass.'

She frowned. 'Oh really?'

'But he said he couldn't. Apparently this . . . *thing* he has for you, whatever it is, goes deep.' He leaned forward, looking her squarely in the eye. 'Very deep. Do you understand *that*?'

Scarlett drew a steady breath, unsurprised. 'Very deep' was what she'd seen in Marcus's eyes just minutes before. 'Very deep' was what she'd felt since she'd first heard his voice. It was a connection she'd had with no other man. 'Yes, Stone. I understand. I also understand that you're asking me if I feel the same way.'

Stone didn't budge. 'Do you?'

'Yes.'

Stone shook his head, clearly skeptical. 'You don't know him.'

'Perhaps not. But I know that I want to know more.'

Stone's shoulders slumped. 'My brother deserves to be happy, Detective. Can you promise to make him happy?'

The sadness in his voice, the forlorn hopelessness there, tugged at her heart, making her want to promise that his brother would never be sad or lonely again. But she wouldn't lie.

'I can't,' she said with regret, 'but only because I learned a long time ago that you can't be responsible for someone else's happiness.'

He nodded thoughtfully, surprising her. 'That's true,' he murmured.

'I can promise to take care of him, and if that means protecting him from himself, that's what I'll do.'

Stone studied her for a very long moment, then nodded, still scowling but less so than before. 'Maybe you do know him, after all.' He stood up, looking exhausted and afraid. 'Call me if he decides to go off and be a damn hero,' he said quietly. 'He does that way too often.'

'I've figured that out myself,' she said wryly, wringing a ghost of a smile from his lips that was gone almost before it started. 'And yes, I'll call you.'

A sober nod. 'Thank you, Detective. And please don't forget to arrange for protection for Delores.' He swallowed hard. 'She deserves to be safe and happy too.'

'I'll take care of it as soon as I get to my car. Stone, one question. That young woman back with Gayle, that's her niece?'

His expression instantly hardened. 'Jill.'

'What's her role in all of this?'

'She makes trouble,' he said curtly. 'Marcus gave her a job because Gayle asked him to, but the girl has an attitude that makes me want to—' He bit back the next words.

'I wanted to smack her too,' Scarlett said, and saw his fleeting smile once again. 'She's not part of your team?'

'No. Marcus doesn't trust her.'

'Neither do I. How does the girl know about the threats?'

'She broke into Gayle's computer when her aunt was sick. Claims she was just trying to help, and she may have been, but she's got her sights set on Marcus. She resents him because Gayle mothers him.'

'And you?'

He pushed away from the table. 'She just wants to get in my pants, which Diesel thinks is a real scream. Me, not so much. Spoiled little girls have never been my type.'

Scarlett blinked up at him. 'Um, I meant, does Gayle mother you?'

He blushed, making him look ten years younger. 'Oh. Right. Well, not really. I'm not exactly the type to be mothered by anyone. I need to go now. With Diesel and Cal back at the paper, I'm on Jill-sitting duty.'

'Because she knows about the list,' Scarlett guessed, and he nodded. 'What are you afraid she'll do?'

'I don't know, but I don't trust her not to use it to hurt Marcus, especially after her little outburst in the waiting room. The kid needs to be taken down a notch or two.'

'Then do it,' Scarlett told him.

He shook his head. 'I'm afraid I wouldn't be gentlemanly about it. Marcus is the nice brother. I just . . . am not. Figure this out, please, and find out who's trying to kill my brother.'

'Are you not targeted by any of the threats, Stone?'

He shrugged. 'Some. Most of the more dangerous investigating happened while I was out of the country covering other stories. The really vile assholes are out for Lisette, Phillip and Marcus of course.'

'What about Diesel?'

'Diesel hacks and lends muscle when needed. He's not really a writer, although he pinch-hits from time to time. I wanted to bust his face for keeping this threat list a secret from me. I had no idea that so many people were out for Marcus's blood.'

She came to her feet, fascinated by this side of Stone. 'When did you find out?'

'Right after we lost Mikhail. Marcus was laid up and Cal needed help.'

'So you stepped forward.'

He shrugged uncomfortably. 'I was here. Didn't have anything better to do.'

Scarlett smiled at him kindly. 'You're a fraud, Stone. You want everyone to believe you're a Neanderthal, but there's a good guy in there.'

The look he gave her was witheringly cold. 'I'm no fraud, Detective. I'm not a good guy. I'm not a nice guy. Most of the time I'm not even a very smart guy. But I do love my family and I will do *anything* to keep them safe.' He took a step backward toward the door. 'If you want to help me look like a good guy, then keep Marcus safe. Please.' Then he was gone, leaving Scarlett staring at the empty doorway, her mouth open but with no words to say.

Sadness welled up in her, then helpless rage. At least she'd been old enough to understand when she'd found Michelle's body. Those boys had been traumatized as children so that some bastard kidnapper could get rich quick. Six and eight years old. She couldn't imagine what it must have been like for them.

She gently pushed the thought of a traumatized eight-year-old Marcus aside, replacing it with the memory of the man who'd returned to that alley this morning, risking a scandal. Exposure. Maybe even prosecution, were his team's activities to come to light – to the wrong person, anyway. All because he wouldn't leave Tala Bautista alone in the dark.

This was the man she'd dreamed of for nine months. The man who was waiting for her right now. The man who made everything go tight and hot inside her every time she thought about the way he'd looked at her, like he could never get enough.

The man who wants to have me every way there is until I scream his name.

She was taking him home as soon as she cleared this hospital. She started down the hall, fishing her cell phone out to check her messages as she walked.

'Detective Bishop?'

Scarlett looked over her shoulder to see Phillip's surgeon coming up behind her. Her feet came to a cold stop. 'Oh no,' she whispered. 'Please don't tell me Phillip Cauldwell is dead.'

'No, no. His condition is the same. I'm sorry. I didn't mean to frighten you.' He pulled a small plastic bag from his coat pocket and handed it to her. 'A bullet taken out of Mr Cauldwell's abdominal cavity. I didn't want to give it to you in front of his sister and co-workers.'

Yes. The bullet was mangled, but recognizable as the same type that Carrie Washington had taken from Tala's body that morning. 'Thank you, Doctor. I'll get this to Ballistics ASAP. We may just have a match to this morning's killing.'

Which still didn't fit, she thought. Because Tala knew her attacker.

375

'I thought you might say that, because whoever fired that bullet didn't want it found. There were three gunshot wounds, the first two superficial. The one in Mr Cauldwell's arm was a through and through, the other a shallow wound in his side where it had no danger of hitting anything important. That one had been dug out with a knife. The third bullet was the abdominal wound. There are deep gouges in Mr Cauldwell's tissue, like his attacker had stabbed at the thing. I'm not sure what happened, but it looked like the shooter tried to dig it out and gave up.'

Scarlett smiled, grimly satisfied. 'What happened was Phillip Cauldwell had already stabbed the shooter in the arm. He was bleeding and had to run.'

'Good for Phillip Cauldwell,' the surgeon said coldly. 'Hopefully he took the bastard's arm off.'

Scarlett lifted her brows. 'You sure you're not a cop, Doc?'

'Marine Corps.'

'Ah. Well thank you,' she said, sliding the baggie into her pocket. 'What are his chances, really? Please don't give me the "twenty-four hours will tell" song.'

'Before you told me he'd stabbed the guy, I would have said they were fairly lousy. But it looks like he's a fighter, so better than lousy.'

'Hey, better-than-lousy ain't so bad. Thanks for the bullet.' She gave him a wave and jogged down the hall to where Marcus waited.

Cincinnati, Ohio
Tuesday 4 August, 10.55 P.M.

Marcus was getting impatient, and a little worried. Scarlett had promised she'd only be a few minutes, but it had been much longer than that. He was tempted to go back to the little consultation room and make sure that she and Stone hadn't taken swings at each other.

Instead he called his brother's cell. 'Where are you?' he asked.

'Just getting my car. Gayle said that she's going to keep Jill with her for the night, so I have a temporary reprieve from babysitting. Why? Where are you?'

'Waiting for Scarlett in the lobby. I didn't see you go past.'

'I parked at the ER entrance. Your detective and I didn't have a knock-down-drag-out if that's what you're trying to ask,' he said mildly. 'I don't know where she is.'

The tone of Stone's voice when he mentioned Scarlett had changed, become . . . maybe not friendly, but not hostile either. Perhaps subdued. 'Are you okay? You don't sound like yourself.'

A little pause. 'I'm okay. Listen . . .' He blew out a breath. 'She's not Satan, okay?'

The statement caught Marcus by surprise and he choked on a laugh. 'No, she's not. Look, I'm not trying to get into your business, but after Phillip, I'd like to know where you are. Just in case whoever is trying to get to me tries to hurt you.'

'I'm not Phillip,' Stone said, no longer mild. He'd grown cold and angry again. 'I can take care of myself every bit as well as you can. I don't need you to babysit me.'

'Okay,' Marcus said cautiously. 'Can you at least call in every so often so I know you're okay? You can think about it as babysitting *me*, if you want to. Please, Stone. I need to know you're okay.' *I've always needed to know you're okay.*

'All right,' Stone finally said. 'I'll call in.'

Marcus hung up unhappily and began pacing again, watching for Scarlett. He'd held it together for far longer than he normally would, but he was starting to get antsy, needing to get out of this hospital. Combined with his worry over Stone and the rest of his team . . . And his mother. He couldn't forget about her.

He'd called her before he'd called Stone, to tell her about Phillip so she didn't hear it on the news. Audrey had answered, her tone flat when she'd said Della had turned in early and couldn't be disturbed. That usually meant she had taken a sleeping pill, or two or three. Or she'd had a drink or two. Or a whole fifth.

He and his sister had danced around the topic of an intervention, clashing once again when he'd come out and suggested they try to get their mom into rehab. Audrey still hoped she would pull out of it, and Stone wouldn't even talk about it. *God, we're one fucked-up family.* Marcus almost thought twice about bringing Scarlett into the drama, but he needed her too much to be so charitable.

Marcus was seriously considering going to look for her when she walked into the lobby, talking on her cell phone. Relief washed over him and he felt a smile spread over his face. He probably looked goofy and ridiculous, but he didn't care. She was back and they could finally leave.

She paused mid-step, studying him with concern, but when he smiled, she smiled back. He swore his chest felt lighter, even though his heart had started to pound.

'I'll have it to Ballistics in fifteen minutes,' she said into the phone. 'I'm leaving now.' She hung up and slid her phone into her jacket pocket. 'You ready?' she asked him.

'More than ready. I was about to go AWOL, but I knew you'd worry.'

'I would have,' she said, then shocked Marcus by taking his arm and tugging him out of the lobby double-time.

'What's going to Ballistics?' he asked as she all but dragged him through the parking lot.

'A bullet,' she answered. 'Surgeon dug it out of Phillip.'

Her car was parked beside a tall SUV, and she surprised him again by dragging him to the driver's side of the mammoth vehicle.

'What are you—'

He got no further, because she pushed him against the SUV, wrapped her arms around his neck and pulled him into the hottest kiss he'd ever had. Her fingers tunneled through his hair, and she lifted on her toes as she licked into his mouth, making his already hard cock throb. The groan that rumbled through his chest was met by her frustrated little moan as she rubbed her hips against him, trying to get higher.

Without thinking, he turned them so that her back was against the SUV, and gave her a boost up before trapping her body with his and thrusting between her legs. Her pleasured hum vibrated against his lips, and he put a little swivel into his thrusts as he slid his hands inside her jacket and closed them over her breasts, thumbing nipples that were already so hard he could feel them through her shirt and bra.

She pulled back with a gasp, her head pressed against the SUV. 'Oh God,' she panted. 'You need to stop. I can't . . . Not here in the parking lot. Let me down.'

He ignored her, circling his hips against hers, lowering his head to suck hard on her right breast, the nipple like a pebble against his tongue.

'Marcus,' she groaned. 'Please. Not here. Wait till . . .' She gasped again when he lightly bit her. 'Oh my God. You have to wait until we get home.'

Reluctantly he released her breast, giving it a parting nuzzle before kissing her mouth again. 'You started it,' he murmured against her lips. 'Kissing me like that.'

'You started it,' she said, trying to get her breath. 'I told you not to look at me like that.'

He lowered her feet to the asphalt and rested his forehead against hers. 'Like what?'

'Like you want to eat me alive. I would have jumped you in front of everyone if Diesel hadn't intervened.'

'That was twenty minutes ago.'

She bit his lower lip, then licked it. 'Doesn't matter. Makes me crazy. So crazy that we're standing like this out here in the open.' She pushed his chest lightly, then slipped around him to unlock the car door. 'Get in, please.'

Still wound way too tight, he obeyed. 'How long will it take you to drop off the bullet?'

She slid behind the wheel. 'Ten minutes. I'll go straight to Ballistics and won't talk to anyone else.' She said it like she was promising herself more than him. 'I have to park this car and get mine, so make sure you take everything that belongs to you.'

Like the gun he'd stowed under the passenger seat. He tried to bend down to reach it, but gave up with a grimace. 'Can't yet.'

She shot him a heated glance from beneath her lashes before pulling into traffic. 'Why ever not?' she teased, making him laugh.

'You're evil, Detective Bishop. Get a guy hard as a damn rock, then taunt him about it.'

He choked a second later when her hand shot over to stroke him through his jeans. His head fell back against the headrest on a strangled groan. 'Fuck, Scarlett.'

'That's the plan,' she muttered.

He closed his eyes, thrusting into her hand desperately. Too damn close, he clamped his hand over hers, then forced himself to push her away. 'You're going to make me go off like a damn teenager. I won't last two minutes when I finally get you in your bed. Talking about non-sexual subjects would be helpful.'

She grabbed the steering wheel with both hands and sped through the nearly deserted streets. 'How about we debrief?' she asked, her voice husky and so damn sexy he nearly came just from hearing her. 'I got a voicemail from the forensic vet.'

'Forensic vet' got his attention. 'Is BB okay?'

'Yes. BB is comfortable and resting and you can visit her tomorrow if you like. The vet also said she got a viable sample of skin and blood from her teeth. The samples were delivered to CSU for analysis.'

'That's good,' Marcus said, digging his fingers into his thighs. He still wanted her so much that he was trembling with it. 'Um . . . I checked on Tabby Anders while I was waiting for you. She's still unconscious.' The thought helped deflate him. One more piece of bad news, he thought morosely, and he'd be able to bend over and get his gun from under the seat.

'I checked too,' she murmured. 'When I ID'd myself to the nurse at the OR station when we were waiting with Lisette and the others. The nurse said Tabby was hanging on by her fingernails. She was hurt in so many places.' Her lips thinned. 'That Chip Anders has to be a *real* man to beat an old woman within an inch of her life.'

'What about Mila and Erica?'

She shook her head. 'Nothing yet. They've been searching for hours. The scent trail might be cold, but they haven't found any blood or bodies, so that's hopefully a good sign.'

'We should probably join the search.'

She glanced over at him with a smile that said she understood how much it had pained him to offer to detour the two of them away from the privacy of her house. 'I emailed Isenberg to ask her. She said no, that she'd rather we focus on the list. Can I send it to Isenberg's clerk? She wants him to help us sort through the names, to see who had the opportunity to target you. And Tala and Phillip.' She huffed in frustration, barreling over him as tried to answer her. 'And Delores. Dammit, I forgot about her. I promised Stone I'd get her protection.'

She used the car's hands-free to call in the request, finishing just as she pulled into the CPD parking garage and rolled to a stop next to her aging Audi. She handed him the keys. 'Get in my car and wait for me. I'll return the department car and deliver the bullet.'

'Wait.' He grabbed her wrist gently, rubbing his thumb over her pulse. 'Rewind a second. You asked if you could send the list to the clerk. Not like it is. It's got too much sensitive *Ledger* information on it. I'll use the time you're inside to clean it up, then I'll email it to you. You can forward it to Isenberg's clerk.'

'Thank you.' She leaned toward him, then sighed. 'Cameras,' she muttered.

'Then hurry,' he said, dropping his voice, laughing when she narrowed her eyes. He managed to bend his body enough to get his gun. 'My laptop bag is in the trunk.'

She popped the trunk. 'You should be fine here,' she said, sobering. 'But just in case, be ready to peel rubber.'

His brows went up. 'You're letting me drive this time?'

'This time. Don't get used to it.' She waited until he was safely locked in the Audi before driving away to the parking area reserved for department vehicles.

Cincinnati, Ohio
Tuesday 4 August, 11.15 P.M.

'How bad is it?' Ken asked Decker when the younger man had finished stitching Demetrius up.

Decker peeled off his latex gloves. 'He probably wouldn't have bled to death, but I had to put twenty stitches in that arm. I'm glad you told me to bring something to knock him out with, although it would have been easier for me to get him up here if he'd been awake.'

'You didn't want to have to listen to him bitch,' Ken said. 'How long till he wakes up?'

'The ketamine will wear off in a few hours.' Decker tilted his head, curiosity in his eyes. 'What did you whisper to him as he was going under?'

Luckily Ken knew drugs, and when Decker told him that he'd brought ketamine to knock Demetrius out, he had been thrilled. The person dosed was highly suggestible as the drug was taking effect, his first thoughts when waking influenced by whatever someone had said just as he passed out.

'I told him that every cut I make with my knife will be fatal.'

Decker chuckled. 'Remind me not to fail a mission.'

'Yeah, well . . .' Ken let the thought trail, wishing it hadn't come to this, but not about to back off now. 'Did you find those trackers?'

Decker was sober as he shook his head. 'I know they were in the van, but Burton and I went over every square inch of it and Sean and I checked the box of electronics we brought in.' He hesitated, then shrugged. 'Which means we either dropped them, which is unlikely, or one of the Anderses did something with them, again unlikely as they were bound and blindfolded.'

'Or someone took them,' Ken said grimly. 'Shit.' He narrowed his eyes at Decker. 'How do I know it wasn't you?'

Decker didn't blink. 'I guess you don't. I don't have any reason to do so, though.'

'You want Burton's job,' Ken said, watching Decker's eyes fill with easy agreement. 'You stepped right in and took over when Reuben disappeared this morning.'

'I like to be on the front line. I hate working in Accounting.'

'But you're supposedly good at it.'

A shrug of Decker's massive shoulders. 'I'm good at a lot of things I don't like to do. I signed on to be a bodyguard, not a pencil pusher. I do, however, respect the chain of command.'

'But if a hole opens up in the front line?'

'I step in. That's who I am.' Decker still hadn't broken eye contact, but he made no sudden moves. 'With all due respect, sir, I don't want your job.'

Ken nearly smiled. 'Why not?'

'From what I can see, you sit behind a desk all day. I'd go crazy. I was going crazy sitting in Accounting crunching numbers. I'm not happy Reuben disappeared, but I'll take up the slack and hope I do a good enough job that you don't send me back to pencil-pushing hell.'

'And if I do?'

'I'll die of lead poisoning from stabbing myself in the eye with the damn pencil.'

Ken laughed. 'Well, soldier, let's take it a day at a time. Burton is next in line for Reuben's job. Can you work for him?'

'Yes. He seems like an honest man.'

Ken frowned. 'That's an odd thing to say.' He injected a light note into his tone. 'You do realize this is a criminal enterprise?'

Decker finally smiled. 'Yes, sir. But that's the relationship the organization has to its outside contacts – the suppliers, the customers, the government. Within the organization, relationships need to be transparent and dependable. Like a military. Soldiers kill people. It's their function. Depending on your point of view, that's criminal or patriotic. If you're the enemy, it's very criminal. But within the ranks, you have to know the soldier next to you has your back. I believe I can trust Burton with my back.'

It was an interesting perspective. Ken leaned one shoulder against the wall outside the spare bedroom where Demetrius lay. 'What other skills do you have, Decker?'

A slow, sly grin. 'I'm pretty handy with the woodchipper.'

'O-kay.' Ken wasn't sure if that was Decker's sense of humor or a touch of insanity. He wasn't certain that he cared. 'I've had a long day. I'm going to grab some shut-eye while Sleeping Beauty in there sleeps off the ketamine. Wake me when he comes to.'

'You want me to extract any information from him?' Decker asked quietly.

'No. He's my friend, my responsibility. I'll get what I need.' With that, Ken turned away and walked down the hall to his own bedroom. Once inside, he closed the door, exhausted. He was glad Demetrius would be under for another few hours.

Ken had killed two people today and ordered the deaths of four more. Drake Connor's sister and Reuben's wife had been taken care of. Drake and Marcus O'Bannion were still out there, causing trouble that Ken didn't even want to think about. He'd lost his security chief and found out that Reuben and Demetrius had been stealing from him. Maybe even working together.

He'd been told by his own daughter that he was getting too old for his job. Maybe she was right.

Because he didn't have the energy to extract information from Demetrius at the moment. In the quiet, his heart hurt. He and Demetrius had started out as a couple of grad students selling weed to their peers and together built up a company worth millions, serving customers in more than forty-two countries. Selling them just about any perversion they desired. He wasn't ashamed of that. There would always be buyers for that sort of thing, so there would always be sellers. *Might as well be me.*

He stripped off his shirt and stood in front of his mirror. Yesterday he'd been proud of his reflection. Now . . .

His cell phone began to buzz, and he prayed it wasn't Decker saying Demetrius was awake. Luckily it was Sean. 'What's up?'

Sean sighed. 'Dad, I just heard something on the police radio you need to know about.'

Ken sank down to sit on the edge of his bed, pinching the bridge of his nose. 'What?'

'An unidentified woman was found in a cheap motel about twenty minutes ago. The front desk says they have no record of her having checked in, that she broke into the room, OD'd on a sedative and went to sleep. Description matches Reuben's wife, Miriam.'

'She's dead, right?' Ken had given her the sedative himself and Burton had taken her to the motel to die.

'No. Unconscious, but not dead. The chatter said the police were responding to an anonymous 911. Just thought you should know.'

'Wait a minute.' Ken pinched his nose harder. 'She got picked up twenty minutes ago? But she should have been dead hours ago. I gave her enough sedative to take down Reuben, for God's sake, and she weighs half what he does. If he's still alive,' he muttered. 'If Miriam is alive, somebody pumped her stomach.'

'Or made her throw it all up.' A pause, then a tentative 'Didn't Burton drop her off?'

'Yeah,' Ken said flatly. Burton who hadn't wanted to kill her to begin with. Reuben's second-in-command had history with Reuben's wife. Burton hadn't allowed her to die. He'd arranged for her to be saved, putting them all in jeopardy. *Especially me.* Because Ken had forced Miriam to drink the damn sedative.

'Do you want to buy me out?' he asked Sean abruptly. 'Alice said the two of you did.'

'Maybe. We'd have to clean house.'

Ken huffed bitterly. 'If we keep on losing people, cleaning house won't take too long.'

'Do you want me to find Burton?' Sean asked quietly.

'I know where he is,' Ken said. 'And I know that you're aware of my phone trackers.'

'I wouldn't have been a very good IT person if I hadn't known,' Sean said reasonably. 'I don't hold it against you.'

Ken was quiet for a long moment. 'Can you handle Burton? He's a big guy.'

'No, but Alice can.' It was said with no bitterness or ego. Sean actually sounded proud of his sister, who'd gotten the lion's share of Ken's athletic genes.

'She's not . . . you know . . . *with* Burton too, is she?' Ken asked with a grimace. 'Not like she is with DJ.'

Sean chuckled. 'You really want me to answer that?'

Ken shuddered at the image. 'No. Just get Alice, find Burton and bring him here. I'm not sure where she is. She said she was going to finish off O'Bannion.'

After ending the call, Ken kicked off his shoes and lay on his bed, too weary to take off his pants. The image of Stephanie Anders doing it for him flashed in his mind like unexpected fireworks.

'No thank you,' he whispered to himself. Stephanie Anders was not anyone he would ever take to his bed – and on top of the day he'd had? Ludicrous.

But maybe that was his subconscious trying to tell him it was time to get out. Once he fixed this mess, he'd take his personal bank accounts, along with those of Demetrius, Reuben and Chip Anders and he'd retire.

Once he fixed this mess.

Twenty-five

Cincinnati, Ohio
Tuesday 4 August, 11.30 P.M.

Marcus rubbed his mouth, his lips still tingling from that kiss in the hospital parking lot. Finally, he thought. After nine months of telling himself that he'd only drag her down with him, he'd finally silenced that voice in his head.

There was only one small wrinkle – she hadn't asked him about the kidnapping and Matty. He wondered if she'd had a chance to Google what he'd told her to. She'd been a tad busy, after all. Maybe she hadn't had time. He didn't want to ask. He didn't want to know if she had. Because if she hadn't and if by some chance she had forgotten, he didn't want to bring it up.

Except that she had a right to know. He couldn't keep something like that from her. He'd tell her after all this was over, after he'd had a chance to get to know her completely. After he'd had a full night with her and had woken up with her at least once. He'd have something to take away with him then.

Or maybe he'd tell her and it wouldn't matter. It was possible. She'd taken the *Ledger* activities with a surprisingly open mind. But that was different. His team at the *Ledger* was like a modern-day *Mission: Impossible* team. They'd never actually killed anyone, although he and Diesel had come close a few times.

But what he'd done after Matty died was very, very different. He had killed someone – even if his finger hadn't been on the trigger. He stared down at the gun in his lap. It might have been a murder weapon – *the* murder weapon, even. He simply didn't know. He didn't want to know.

But he did know that every time he carried it, he put himself at risk. When it'd just been himself to worry about, that had been okay. Hell, it might even have been part of the allure. But he didn't just have himself to worry about anymore. Scarlett had put her career on the line for him. She'd stood with him.

He'd have to put the gun away, in his safe where it wouldn't cause her any trouble. He took it from the pocket holster and ran his thumb over the barrel. It was not lost on him that he'd caressed Scarlett's skin the same way a few minutes ago.

The gun had become more than a mere weapon long ago. It was a talisman, just as his knife was, but for very different reasons. Using a different gun would take some getting used to, he thought. But if it uncomplicated even a portion of their lives, it was a small price to pay. Because now that he'd held Scarlett in his arms, now that he'd tasted her lips and watched her face as he made her come . . . and now that he'd felt her hold him so tenderly that he'd thought his heart would club its way right through his chest . . . He knew that he was not letting her go.

He slipped the gun between his seat and the car door, where he could get to it if he needed it, then took his laptop from its case and opened the threat list. He cleaned it up, removing any references to his staff or the more questionable things they'd done, then emailed it to Scarlett.

A noise had his head jerking up and his hand going for the gun next to his seat, but he relaxed when he saw Scarlett knocking on the passenger window. He unlocked the doors, and she slid in, wearing a tactical vest over her T-shirt, her jacket draped over her arm.

'Sorry I took so long.' Her skin was flushed, a light sheen of sweat on her face.

'Were you running?'

She tossed the jacket in the back seat. 'Just a little. Didn't want you to worry about me.'

He poked at the thick, padded bulletproof vest. 'Where were you hiding this?'

'I wasn't. Lynda gave it to me, just in case someone takes a potshot at me too.'

He frowned. 'You should have been wearing this when we went into and out of the hospital. Why weren't you?'

'I left mine at home after we . . .' She shrugged, a blush coloring her cheeks. 'After we had sex on my sofa. I think I was pretty rattled.'

'Don't get that rattled,' he said, angry with himself for not noticing. 'Why don't you wear Kevlar under your clothes like I do?'

'A, because it itches; b, because none of my clothes will hide a vest; c, because they make me roast, and d, because *I* didn't promise my mother I would. I'd rather wear the vests over my clothes. Besides, you're the target, not me.'

'Promise me,' he said fiercely. 'Promise *me* you'll wear one.'

She met his eyes, growing serious. 'I promise. Until this guy is caught, I promise.'

'We'll renegotiate after this guy is caught,' he muttered.

She smiled at him. 'You can start the engine anytime,' she said, pointing at the keys he'd left dangling in the ignition. 'In fact, why didn't you keep the AC going? You could've roasted too.'

'I served two tours in the Gulf,' he reminded her dryly, closing his laptop and laying it on the floorboard behind his seat. He started the car. 'I can take a little heat.'

She rolled her eyes. 'So can I, Mr Macho, but I choose not to.' She cranked up the AC and leaned her face into the air. 'Did you finish with the list?'

'Yes. I emailed it to you.'

'Must have been after I left my desk.' She settled into the seat and checked her phone while he drove them out of the garage and on to the street that led from the city to her house on the hill. 'I got it.' She took a few minutes to scan it, tapped her screen, then put the phone in one of the pockets of the vest. 'I forwarded it to Isenberg. She'll get it to whoever's doing the analysis.'

He glanced at her from the corner of his eye. 'I thought you weren't going to your desk.'

She made a face. 'Isenberg called me while I was in Ballistics. Deacon and Agent Coppola had just come back from your apartment building, and Adam Kimble, the detective who was leading the search for Mila and Erica, had just come back from the field. We did a mini-debrief. I got away as soon as I could.'

'And?'

'And the security tapes showed the killer leaving about five minutes after he entered with Phillip and shot the security guard.'

'What time was that?'

'Forty minutes after eight.'

'Shit. He left only a minute or two before I got there. I may have seen him. Phillip said he was big and African-American.'

'The camera didn't capture his face. He had a ski mask hidden under his cap and pulled it down as he entered the lobby. He was also wearing gloves. The only skin we saw was around the perimeter of the mask's eye holes. His skin was darker than Caucasian, but that's all we can say.'

'We'll ask Phillip more when he wakes up,' Marcus said firmly.

'We will,' she agreed with a hard nod. 'When the shooter came out of your apartment, he went down the stairs, made sure the coast was clear in the lobby and then slipped out the front door. He had a towel wrapped around his arm and the knife still sticking out, just like Phillip told you.'

'He didn't want his blood spurting everywhere.'

'But the towel had already soaked through. Phillip got that blade deep.'

Marcus thought of Edgar and Phillip, both fighting for their lives. 'Good,' he said coldly.

'I agree. Agent Coppola talked to everyone in the building. Nobody saw or heard anything. He must have used a silencer.'

Marcus frowned. 'Silencers for the Ruger are hard to come by. He may have had it custom made.' His frown grew deeper. 'But he didn't use one in the alley. Why?'

'Good question. But he did use a silencer on his rifle when he shot at you and Agent Spangler in back of the Anders house.'

There was a thoughtful quality in her voice that made him look at her. 'What?'

'The surgeon said that the shooter shot Phillip three times. Arm, side and abdomen. Arm was a through and through, but Coppola and Deacon didn't find the bullet, just the casings. The surgeon said the shooter dug the bullet out of Phillip's side and tried to dig the one out of his abdomen but gave up.'

'Because the shooter was bleeding too. He didn't want the bullets found. He left bullets behind at the alley and didn't want the ones in Phillip connected through ballistics. The gun he used on me and Agent Spangler this afternoon was a rifle, so there wouldn't have been a match anyway.' He frowned harder. 'But that doesn't make sense. Why would he go to the trouble of digging the bullets out? He has to know that we know he's the same guy.'

'Do we?' she countered. 'Tala knew her attacker. I saw it in her eyes.'

'So did I,' he murmured. 'When I watched the video later. So you're thinking maybe it's *not* the same shooter? Maybe the two *aren't* related?'

'But someone wants us to think that they are.' She shrugged. 'We'll know soon enough. The ballistics tech was on her way in to do the test. They don't usually work nights, but for something like this they get called in.'

'You mean because a federal agent was killed,' he said flatly.

'No,' she said forcefully. 'Because we have a human trafficking murderer out on the streets. Nobody's complaining about the extra hours.'

'I'm sorry. I shouldn't have said that.'

'It's all right.' She slid her hand over his thigh and squeezed. Comforting him again, he thought. 'Some of the time that's true. But not this time.'

'Why did the search team come back in?'

She sighed. 'They lost the scent. Looks like Mila and Erica hitched a ride. We got their visa pictures and those of the husband and son from

Immigration and have distributed them to all the officers on patrol now, and they'll be passed out at the shift meeting in the morning. Officers are being told to approach the women with care and to show them photos of the husband and son and one that Children's Services took of Malaya. Isenberg had her clerk caption all three photos with "They're alive and safe" in both English and Tagalog.'

'Hopefully that helps. I just hope they don't go under. We might never find them.'

'I know,' she murmured, sounding troubled.

He stopped at a red light and turned to study her profile. 'What's wrong?'

'I just keep thinking about how none of this fits. It doesn't make sense and it's giving me a headache.' She pointed at the traffic light. 'It's green.'

He turned his attention back to the road. 'Wait till the ballistic report comes back,' he suggested. 'At least you'll know if the same gun was used on Tala and Phillip.'

'You're right,' she said quietly, but he could tell she hadn't let it go.

Neither had he. He kept rerunning the events at his apartment building through his mind. 'I'm trying to remember if I saw anyone that matched Phillip's description of his attacker, but I'm coming up empty.'

'Deacon is good at helping people remember things,' she said, surprising him.

'Deacon? How?'

'He's been trained to do hypnotism to calm you down, help you find things your mind's filed in weird places. I watched him do it the first time with Faith nine months ago. Since then he's helped three other victims recall things they either couldn't remember or were afraid to. Don't worry,' she said when he grimaced. 'He won't make you cluck like a chicken. It's just a relaxation technique.'

'I don't think that would work on me. It comes too close to an interrogation, or brainwashing even, and . . . well it probably just wouldn't work.' He left it at that.

'You were trained to resist interrogation and mind control techniques when you were in the military?'

He frowned over at her. 'I never said that.' It was exactly right, though.

'Come on, Marcus. Give me a little credit here. You move like a damn ghost. I'm good at being aware of people coming up from behind me, and you've snuck up on me twice now. Either you've had training or you're secretly Batman.'

He snorted a laugh. 'Okay, fine. You caught me.'

'You mean you really are Batman?' she teased.

He turned onto the road leading to her house and downshifted, making the Audi cough and rattle. 'You may wish I were if this thing dies on us. We may end up scaling the side of the hill with a grappling hook.'

'Big baby,' she chided. 'I run this hill every day when I'm training for a race.'

'Really?' He considered it, grateful for something to think about other than death and bullets and missing, frightened women. A glance over at her showed she'd accepted the momentary reprieve as well. Her eyes were alert and her mouth was curved in a smile that he wanted to see when he opened his eyes in the morning. 'I want to see you run. Especially if I'm running behind you.' The very thought made his mouth water.

'Tomorrow morning,' she challenged. 'Crack of dawn. I triple-dog dare you.'

He shook his head slowly, a very different activity in mind. 'I don't think so.'

'You're refusing a triple-dog dare?'

He pulled into her driveway, turned off the engine and shifted in his seat, resting his forearm on the steering wheel. 'I would never back down from a triple-dog dare. Game on, Bishop.' He reached for her when she grinned, releasing her seat belt with one hand and catching her around the back of her neck with the other, then pulling her close for a kiss that left them both breathless. 'But I think that tomorrow morning I'm not going to want to waste my energy on running that damn hill.'

She caressed his jaw with fingers that trembled. 'Then I think I should give you a rain check on the triple-dog dare.' She kissed him again, then smiled against his lips. 'Mrs Pepper is watching.'

He pulled back far enough to peek around her. 'How do you know?'

'I saw the reflection of her porch light coming on in your window. We should go inside before she comes over to talk to us. She can talk for hours,' she added in a whisper.

He was out of the car and around to her side to open her door in seconds, making her laugh. He tugged her out of the car and put her keys in her hand. 'Unlock the garage door. I'll pull it up so that you can drive the car in.'

'I can open my own garage door, Marcus.'

'I know you can.' He gripped her chin gently, kissing her long and wet and hot, making her sigh when he kissed his way to her ear. His hands itched to run over her curves, but as hot as she looked in the tactical vest, it covered her curves all up. Plus he could see Mrs Pepper peering through the curtains on her living room window. 'Let me open it anyway,' he murmured.

390

'Mrs Pepper will think I'm a gentleman, and I want to get on her good side. She makes great cookies.'

Scarlett shook her head, chuckling while she did as he asked. He waited until she'd parked the car and shut off the engine before pulling the door down, leaving them in semi-darkness. And total privacy. Finally.

He opened the driver's door and pulled her to her feet and into his arms. Then he held her. Just held her. Her arms wrapped around his waist, her head rested on his shoulder.

He was shaking like a teenager, dammit. 'This morning,' he whispered, 'was different.'

'I know.' She lifted on her toes and kissed his mouth softly. 'This morning *we* were different. I didn't know who you really were yet.'

He smiled down at her. 'Batman?'

'No.' She nipped at his lip, then soothed the hurt with the tip of her tongue. 'The man I so desperately hoped you'd be.'

'I'm no hero, Scarlett,' he said soberly.

'Neither am I. I'm just me.'

He kissed her gently, because even though his body craved her, his mind knew this was too important to rush. 'I like "just you".'

'Sometimes I'm not very nice,' she warned.

'I like my roses with a few thorns.'

Her lips twitched, then stilled as she grew very serious. 'I've been alone a long time, Marcus, and I got used to it. But now, with you, I don't feel alone anymore, and that scares the hell out of me. This morning was sex, and that was satisfying and fun. And simple. But this, us right here, right now . . . It isn't simple anymore. This is . . . more.'

He kissed a line down her throat, making her shiver. 'I *want* more.'

Her head fell back, giving him better access. 'Oh good,' she breathed. 'It would suck if I were the only one.'

He unsnapped the vest, lowered his voice. 'What do you want, Scarlett? A husband, children? A picket fence?'

She swallowed, shivering again. 'Yes. I'm greedy. I want it all.'

He nuzzled her neck. 'I can build a fence. And I've always wanted kids. And a wife. So we're starting out on the same page.' He slipped his hand under the vest, cupped her breast, felt the hardness of her nipple against his palm. 'What do you want this minute?'

She laughed breathlessly. 'To drag you off to bed and do all kinds of naughty things.'

His control snapped and he took her mouth roughly, too roughly. But she gave as good as she got, shoving her fingers into his hair and kissing

391

him until he was afraid he'd come right there in her garage.

He reared back, breathing hard. 'What do you need to do first?'

'Walk the dog, take a shower.'

'Then go. I'll get my things and meet you inside. Where's your bedroom?'

'Second floor.' She kissed him hard before pulling out of his arms and walking backward toward the door into the house. 'It's purple.'

He frowned. 'What?'

'My bedroom. It's purple.' She grinned. 'You've been warned. I'll hurry.'

'Okay,' he muttered, somehow managing to bend over far enough to gather up his gun and laptop and her jacket and shoulder holster. 'Purple it is.' He headed into the house and up the stairs, his pulse racing in anticipation even as he felt his shoulders lighten. *Peace*, he realized. *This is peace.*

Cincinnati, Ohio
Tuesday 4 August, 11.55 P.M.

Scarlett normally let Zat struggle up the stairs on his own, but tonight she was impatient. She could hear the shower running, and the thought of Marcus under that spray left her knees weak and her pulse thrumming hard. Everywhere. Scooping Zat into her arms, she ran up the stairs just as the shower shut off.

Holding her breath, she put the dog down gently and walked to the open bathroom door. 'Oh.' It was more a long sigh of appreciation than an actual word. She'd seen him shirtless. She'd seen all the important parts when they'd gone at it like horny weasels on her sofa that afternoon.

But not even her very imaginative daydreams had prepared her for the whole package of deliciousness that was Marcus O'Bannion naked and dripping wet. Broad shoulders bunched and flexed as he toweled the hair on his head, while droplets of water clung to the dark, crisp hair lightly furring across his chest, making her want to lick it all up. And then keep on licking downward. My God, the man was a fantasy in the flesh, and what flesh he had. Long and thick and hard. Remembering how it had felt inside her had her core muscles contracting so hard she shuddered. *Soon.* She'd feel him inside her again soon.

He finished toweling his hair and was dabbing at the bandage on his scalp from his run-in with Chip Anders's splintered door when he saw her standing there, agape. His grin started slow, but spread to his whole face, his cheeks creasing in a way she hadn't yet seen. He looked happy, she realized. And very relaxed. Except for his erection, which grew even larger and harder as she stared, bobbing to its own beat.

'I didn't use too much of your hot water,' he said. 'I didn't know how big your tank was.'

Abruptly she closed her mouth and leaned against the door frame, trying for cool and knowing she was failing utterly. 'It's tankless. It heats the water as you need it. You can run it until you're a giant prune and not run out.'

'Good to know.' He spread his arms wide, making her mouth water. 'So then, come on in. The water's warm.'

'In a minute. I want to look. You are . . .' She sighed again. 'Just as I knew you'd be.'

'You're wearing too many clothes, Detective,' he said lightly. She stepped back into her bedroom to strip, but he wagged his finger. 'No, no. Stand there. It's only fair.'

'Just a minute.' She took off the vest, placing her phone on the nightstand and her gun in the drawer. She considered not checking her messages, but knew she had to. Thankfully there were none. They had a momentary lull and she was taking advantage of it.

She returned to the doorway to peel her shirt over her head, revealing the bra she'd put on after her morning shower. She'd chosen it thinking about the way he'd look at her when he saw it. Pink and lacy, it was one of her very favorites.

His grin faded, his expression becoming the same one that had made her kiss him up against that SUV. 'Come here,' he said quietly, and she walked to the open shower door while her legs shook like jelly. He ran his finger under the scalloped lace edge of the bra, teasing her. Tempting her. 'So damn pretty.' He met her eyes. 'I like it. Take it off before I tear it off.'

It was a front clasp, and he groaned when she popped it open. 'That's all I had to do?'

She laughed and let it fall to the floor, gratified at his sharp intake of breath.

'My God,' he whispered, then stole her breath by taking a breast in each hand reverently, measuring their weight. He kissed the slope of each one, then dropped his hands to his sides, clenching them into fists. 'Keep going, but hurry. You're killing me here.'

She didn't comply, taking her time in pulling out all the pins that held her braid in place. He watched silently, his eyes missing not a single movement as she removed the last pin, her braid falling to the middle of her

393

back as she dumped the pins in a pile on the vanity. She started to loosen the braid, but he stopped her.

'Let me,' he said quietly. He began untangling her hair and running his fingers through it. 'I've wanted to do this since the first time I saw you. I've fantasized about your hair spread all over my pillow.' He smiled. 'Spread all over me.'

Her arousal growing exponentially now, she kicked off her shoes and pushed her slacks to the floor, leaving her clad only in her matching pink lace panties, along with socks and an ankle holster.

His chest expanded as he inhaled. 'Very nice,' he said gruffly. 'The ankle holster is hot. Makes you look very badass.'

'I think the pink lace cancels any badass-itude,' she said, hooking her pinkie in the string that held the front and back triangles together.

'It's a synergistic effect. Trust me on this. Are your panties wet?'

She drew a deep breath. 'If they hadn't been already, they would be now. But they've been wet every time I've been around you today.' She dropped to one knee to take off the ankle holster, then came to her feet. 'I'll be right back.'

'Hurry.'

She obeyed, quickly putting the backup gun next to her service weapon in the nightstand drawer, but when she returned, Marcus was leaning back against the shower wall, slowly stroking himself.

Scarlett couldn't have looked away if someone had threatened to shoot her on the spot. 'You started without me.'

His dark brows lifted, making him look like a smug Greek god. 'I told you to hurry.'

Yanking off the socks, she shimmied out of the panties and kicked them aside. She joined him in the shower, closed the door and turned on the spray.

He pulled her under the water, playing with her hair as it grew soaking wet. He squirted shampoo into his hands and began to wash her hair, strong, long strokes on her scalp. She moaned and leaned her back against his front, letting him drive some of the tension from her shoulders and neck even as he built a sweeter tension between her legs.

'You have a lot of hair, Detective,' he said, his mouth next to her ear. His soapy hand slid down the front of her body, lightly caressing one breast before darting between her thighs, one wicked finger delving deep into the part of her that had already been wet for him. Her gasp made him chuckle. 'This could take a while.'

She wasn't sure if he meant the washing of her hair or the slow stroking he was doing with that finger of his. She didn't care. Didn't think. Just leaned into him and savored the contact after so many months alone. He wasn't rushed, didn't hurry. He just stroked her, languidly working her into a delicious froth until she began thrusting against him, urging him to go faster. Harder.

She protested when he withdrew the finger, using both his hands to rinse the shampoo from her hair, then casually sniffing the various bottles of body wash in the caddy hanging from the shower, as if they had all the time in the world. 'Marcus,' she said, her voice husky. 'Hurry.'

'This is the one I like,' he announced, picking the honeysuckle-scented body wash and pouring it into his hand. He washed her thoroughly, torturing her with touches that were far too light and far too fast, chuckling when she cursed him.

'You're enjoying this,' she accused when he went down on his haunches to soap up her legs, massaging her calves and feet.

He picked up her handheld sprayer and started rinsing her body with warm water, a teasing smile on his face. 'Aren't you?'

'Yes, but— Oh God.' She choked on the words when he abruptly rocked forward to his knees, slid his hands up the backs of her thighs to grab her butt and buried his face between her legs, licking up into her. 'Oh God. Yes. There. Please.'

In seconds he had her whimpering, moaning, her legs threatening to fold beneath her. She clutched his hair, her hips thrusting to get closer, get him deeper. She was close, so close. Then . . . 'No!' she cried when, as abruptly as he'd started, he lurched to his feet, leaving her on the edge and ready to claw his shoulders to make him go back down. Until she saw his face.

He was no longer smiling, his eyes dark and glittering with need. Without looking away from her, he turned the water off, backed her against the wall and kissed her so hard she saw little white lights floating behind her eyelids. He broke off, letting her gulp air into her burning lungs, then lifted her arms around his neck, curved his hands over her butt and shoved the shower door open with his shoulder. He picked her up, and she wound her legs around his hips, wiggling to get his erection up inside her folds, rocking against him as he carried her out of the bathroom. Once in the bedroom, he carefully laid her down on the bed, both of them still soaking wet, the overhead lights blazingly bright.

But she didn't have even another second to think about the wet, because he followed her down, sliding down her body until his mouth was between her legs again. He didn't lick, but went straight for her clit, sucking it into his mouth, making her scream. He didn't stop, sucking her hard, and then his finger was back inside her, then two, stroking her faster and harder and higher.

The orgasm exploded inside her. Hands clawing at the sheets on her bed, her body arched like a bow and she tried to breathe, but the air was stuck in her lungs. And still he didn't stop, sucking and stroking until the wave broke and she collapsed, shuddering and gasping.

And crying. She was crying, tears pouring from her eyes, a sob pushing its way out of her chest. Instantly he was there, hovering over her, brushing the tears away.

'Scarlett,' he whispered hoarsely. 'Did I hurt you?'

'No.' Unable to stop the tears, she let go of the sheets and ran her hands up his chest, feeling the hair tickle the flesh between her fingers. 'It was . . . God, Marcus.' She drew a breath and let it out, feeling her body settle, feeling the tightness in her chest begin to ebb. 'I've never . . . not like that. Never like that. Just . . . intense. Give me a second to come down.'

But he didn't, shoving his hands into her hair and taking her mouth with a fierceness that bordered on pain, but wasn't. She dug her fingers into his shoulders and kissed him back, the taste of herself on his lips making her shiver violently. His hips thrust and rolled, his erection hard as iron against her inner thigh.

Blindly he groped under the pillow and pulled out a foil wrapper. 'When did you put that there?' she asked.

'Before I got in the shower.' He kissed her hard again, then pushed himself to his knees between her legs and ripped the packet with his teeth, almost snarling when she reached to help him. 'Don't,' he warned. 'If you touch me, it'll be all over.'

'No, don't let it be over. Not yet.' Watching as he rolled the condom over himself, she licked her lips, a new thought surprising her. Going down on a man was never something she'd enjoyed, but seeing Marcus so huge and . . . beautiful, she knew she would. Not now, but later. She wanted to make him groan and beg the way he'd done to her.

She looked up and realized he'd been watching her stare at him, and that it had stoked him even higher. 'Later,' he growled, not even a hint of his normally smooth voice remaining. 'I need to be inside you. Now.' Bracing his weight on his arms, he thrust up into her in a single hard stroke, making her moan at the pleasure of being filled. Being taken.

It took her a second to realize that he'd stopped. 'Are you okay? Did I hurt you?' he asked with a frown. He was breathing hard, his arms trembling from the strain of holding himself immobile.

'I'm fine,' she breathed. 'Better than fine. Don't stop. Please.'

'Thank God,' he muttered, and began to move again. 'You feel so good, I'm not sure I could have stopped.'

But he could have, and they both knew it. Because he was still in total control of himself. And her. He knew exactly what to do, how to move. All the right spots to make her moan. He aroused her with his body, but also with the expression he wore as he watched her. It was primal and possessive, proud and lustful, but also . . .

Reverent, she thought, emotion rising to fill her throat once again. He handled her carefully, utterly and completely focused on her every reaction, her every sigh. He made her buck and squirm beneath him, beg and curse and beg again until she wanted to scream from frustration. But still he held back.

He was making sure she felt pleasure even as he took his own, but suddenly that wasn't enough. She wanted to feel him lose control. Wanted to feel the storm she saw in his eyes suck her in and draw her under.

She cupped his face in her hands, caressed his cheekbones with her thumbs. 'Let go,' she whispered. 'Take what you want. I won't break. I promise.'

He shuddered. 'I can't. I want too much. I'll hurt you.'

This was an important moment – she knew it instinctively. One that would set the tone for all the moments to come. She hooked her foot around his calf and, using her other foot as leverage, flipped him to his back so quickly that he lay there, still deep inside her, staring, his eyes wide and stunned. And then darkly aroused. His jaw tightened, his hands gripping her hips so hard it hurt. But it was good hurt, especially when he yanked her hips down on him, driving even deeper up into her.

She leaned over, bit his lip. 'I won't break,' she repeated, enunciating every word, then sat back and rode him hard.

A groan ripped out of his chest and he arched his back, digging his feet into the mattress so that he could push himself higher. Then he rolled them again and drove into her over and over, his thrusts bordering on savage. She met each one, locking his gaze with hers, daring him to slow down.

'Not a chance, Detective,' he muttered, and she laughed.

This, she thought, *this is the way it's supposed to be. The way* we're *supposed to be.*

They said nothing more, gazes locked. Marcus took her hands in his, threading their fingers together, the connection a tender one in stark contrast with the way their bodies were coming together everywhere else.

While the first orgasm had been an explosion, the second hit her like a storm surge, slowly and powerfully pushing every conscious thought out of its way, leaving nothing but pleasure in its wake.

She came down sighing his name, somehow knowing he'd been watching her the whole time, waiting until she could watch him. She squeezed his hands with her own, squeezed his erection with her inner muscles. 'Now,' she whispered. 'Let me see.'

He did, and he was as beautiful as she'd known he'd be. Muscles straining, his erection throbbing and pulsing inside her, his body shuddering as he came. He exhaled once and shuddered as an aftershock kicked in. He released her hands, lowering his body from the push-up position he'd maintained throughout to rest his weight on his forearms. He dropped his forehead to rest gently against hers.

'Scarlett.' It was barely a murmur, but delivered in the velvet voice she'd heard in her dreams for nine long months.

She lifted her hands to stroke his face, her fingers tracing his lips. 'This was more.'

'Yeah. I knew it would be, but I still didn't expect this.' He kissed her then, long and lush, leaving her breathless once again. 'I don't want to move. Ever.'

'Then don't.' She spread her fingers over his chest, sweeping her hands back and forth to feel the hairs tickling her palms. 'Stay here with me, just a little longer.'

Twenty-six

Cincinnati, Ohio
Wednesday 5 August, 12.30 A.M.

Marcus came out of the bathroom and stopped in his tracks. Scarlett was standing next to the bed, bent over the mattress, her shapely butt pointed straight at him. His cock stirred and stood at attention as his mouth watered, and it took him a few seconds to realize that she was stripping the bed.

He crossed the room to cozy up behind her, chuckling when she startled and cursed.

'Dammit, Marcus, stop sneaking up on me.' But she didn't sound angry as she straightened and leaned back into him, resting her forearms on his when he wrapped his arms around her waist. She stiffened in surprise when his cock pressed against her lower back. 'Wow. You're . . . already . . . again. Wow.'

His ego preened. 'It didn't hurt to see you bent over the bed. It gave me ideas.'

'Oh really? I'd like to hear them.'

He brushed his lips over her ear. 'I believe in show, not tell.'

She hummed, interested. 'We need to finish changing the sheets first.'

'I guess we did make them a little wet.'

She looked over her shoulder and laughed up at him. 'More than a little. Do me a favor and go to the hall closet and get another set. The ones on the top shelf fit this bed.'

He kissed her smiling mouth and reluctantly let her go. The king-sized sheets were exactly where she'd said, the closet meticulously arranged. It appeared that his detective was a bit of a neat freak, which was a relief to see. He was a bit of a neat freak himself.

He took the sheets back into her room and stopped cold again. She was kneeling on the floor beside the bare mattress, her head and one arm under the bed. And her butt pointed straight at him once more.

'Woman, are you *trying* to kill me?' he whined.

'Zat's under the bed,' she said, making tsking noises. 'Come here, sweetie. Come out.' She sighed and stood up. 'I think we scared him.' Then she shrugged. 'He'll get used to it.'

Marcus dumped the clean sheets on the bed and helped her put on the fitted one. 'He got used to the purple,' he said blandly.

She laughed. 'Poor Zat. But if you think this is bright, you should see the other rooms. I've been working on fixing the outside first. I'll redo the paint inside later. One task at a time.'

'You could hire someone to do it.'

She frowned at him. 'Unlike you, I'm not rich. Plus, it's more mine if I do it myself.'

'I could do it for you,' he offered slyly. 'I can do all kinds of repairs for you. I don't need the money, so you'd have to find other ways to pay me.'

She tried to decide if he was serious. 'Do you know how to repair stuff?'

He tried not to be offended. 'Who do you think builds the houses we use to relocate the families we told you about tonight? Elves in a hollow tree?'

Her eyes widened. 'You build houses?'

'I help. Diesel does, or did before he got busy at the paper. He's built some low-rent housing in the past. I'm mostly just an investor, but he lets me swing a hammer sometimes.'

She lifted a brow. 'Seems like Diesel has a number of diverse talents. Building, hacking, gentle coercion, philanthropy. Where did you meet him?'

'In the army. He saved my life a few times, I saved his. When we got out, we parted ways, but the next thing I knew I'd inherited the paper and needed someone I could trust to help me with my . . . side business. At that point, Stone was working as a freelancer for other papers and was always on assignment out of the country. I knew I could trust Diesel. He hadn't found a job that interested him yet, so he signed on.'

She'd been changing the pillowcases while he talked and now plumped the pillows invitingly before she sat cross-legged on top of the covers and started braiding her hair. 'He sounds like a good friend. I'm glad you have him.'

He sat beside her and captured her hands in his. 'Don't braid it. Leave it down.'

'It's still wet. It'll be all tangled in the morning.'

'So I'll brush it.' He swept his lips over hers. 'Leave it down. It's my fantasy.'

'Oh,' she breathed, then swallowed hard. 'Okay.'

He'd been all set for another round, but right now he just wanted to hold her. He switched off the lights and climbed under the covers, patting the

400

pillow beside him. 'Come here, Scarlett,' he said, intentionally pitching his voice low. The deep breath she sucked in told him that he'd tickled her fantasy too.

'I thought you had ideas.'

'I do, but they'll keep for a little while. I never got to hold you before.'

'Just a minute. Let me check my messages.' She looked at her phone, her brows furrowing. After a moment's hesitation, she put it back down on the nightstand and climbed under the covers with him, snuggling against his side, her head on his shoulder.

'What was that?'

'What?' Her fingertips idly brushed across his chest, playing with the hairs. Even though it sidetracked his focus, he couldn't make himself tell her to stop.

He rubbed her forehead with one finger. 'The message that made you frown.'

She sighed. 'It's about the guard in your condo.'

Fear squeezed his heart. 'Edgar. What about him? Is he . . . ?'

'No, no,' she assured him. 'Last I heard he was still in recovery. This is about the attack. I saw the security tape while I was in Isenberg's office earlier. Edgar had a gun and pulled it on the shooter, but he hesitated, probably because he didn't want to miss and hit Phillip. The shooter was holding a gun on Phillip using his right hand, but in a very smooth move he whipped his right hand around and pushed the gun up under Phillip's chin, then grabbed the guard's gun and shot him with it – using his left hand.'

Marcus didn't want to visualize it, but his mind wasn't giving him any choice. 'Ambidextrous, with some martial arts experience.'

'I thought either martial arts or military. Or both. Bottom line, he was smooth. Amazing reflexes. Almost like he'd practiced it or at least had it planned.'

'You think he *expected* Edgar to pull his gun?'

'I don't know, but the way he held the gun under Phillip's chin gave the camera a perfect view of the make and model.'

'He wanted us to know what he was carrying.'

'Seems like it. After shooting Edgar, he pocketed Edgar's gun and forced Phillip into the elevator. It would have been more efficient for him to keep his left arm around Phillip's throat and use the gun he came in with to shoot the guard rather than the big switch maneuver.'

'But he didn't want to leave a bullet behind.'

'Right. I wasn't going to tell you about it. Didn't think you needed the images in your mind, but Isenberg wants you to look at the video and see if you can ID the shooter. She sent me a link. You probably have a message from her asking you to call her or me.'

He sat up and turned on the light. 'Why did she wait so long to send it to you? They've had that video for hours.'

'In her email she said that they had to clean it up. The video was poor quality. Truthfully, she was probably debating with herself whether or not she wanted you to see it.' She sat up and found the message on her phone. 'I'm not supposed to forward this to you because it's evidence and we can't let it leak to the press yet. Sorry.'

He rolled his eyes. 'What do I have to do to get your boss to trust me?'

'Be a cop and work for her for a couple years. She didn't trust me right away either.' Scarlett winced. 'Sometimes she still doesn't.'

He sighed. 'Just play it.'

She cued it up and handed him her phone. He hit PLAY quickly before he could manufacture a reason to put it off. He flinched when the clip started, his attention riveted to the fear on Phillip's face.

Scarlett rested her head on his shoulder. 'Start it again,' she murmured. 'I know it's hard, but don't look at Phillip. Look at the man's face.'

He watched the clip from beginning to end, focusing on the shooter's build, his gloved hands, the way he moved, and his eyes, his only visible feature. There was nothing recognizable, so he made himself watch it again and again, his jaw clenching tighter every time the bastard fired at Edgar.

Finally Scarlett pulled the phone from his hands. 'Enough. Your teeth are about to crack. Did you recognize anything about him?'

He clenched his fists helplessly. 'No.'

'Then I'll tell her that.' She slid her hand over his fist, holding him while she called her boss. 'It's Scarlett,' she said when Isenberg picked up. 'Yes, I got it. I showed it to him, but he doesn't recognize the shooter . . . Yes, ma'am, I turned your request around quickly.' She listened for a moment, then closed her eyes, her cheeks turning red. 'Yes, ma'am, he's with me.'

Oh fuck. His outing them to his team was one thing. Her outing herself to her boss was quite another. Part of him wondered if that wasn't the reason Isenberg had waited to send the email. She'd known Scarlett wouldn't delay her response, because a murderer was walking free. *What a fucking bitch.*

He wanted to grab the phone and tell the lieutenant exactly what he thought about her, but he bit his tongue. This was Scarlett's world. Her battle.

'Yes, ma'am,' she said after listening for a full minute. 'Your office, nine sharp. I'll be there.' She hung up and dropped her chin to her chest. 'Well that was fun.'

'What can she do to you?'

'Give me a lecture or put a note in my file. Worst case is I get suspended.' He tugged her to his lap, settled her between his thighs and massaged her scalp, making her sigh quietly. 'But if she really wants to get mean, she'll tell my dad.'

He blinked. 'She's going to tell your father? Why?'

'Because he works in the commissioner's office.'

'Oh. You said he was a cop. You didn't mention he was so high up.'

'You mean you didn't have Diesel check me out?'

'Not really. I did search for your address and run your Land Cruiser's plates, but everything else I wanted to find out myself.' He kissed the curve of her neck. 'I'm sorry she might make trouble for you, but I'm not sorry I'm here.'

'I'm not sorry you're here either. It'll be all right. Why don't you turn out the lights? We should get some sleep.'

He did as she suggested and then pulled her close. To his relief she came easily, resuming her place on his shoulder and her lazy petting of his chest. But she didn't sleep. He could almost hear the wheels turning in her mind.

'What's your brain thinking now?' he asked her.

'That I need to ask you a favor.'

He curled her still-damp hair around his fingers. 'Name it.'

'I need you to lock that gun of yours away. Isenberg knows that Deacon and I suspected you had a second gun in the alley. If she gets annoyed enough at me for sleeping with you, she might find a reason to confiscate your gun.' She hesitated. 'And I'm not sure you'd like that.'

'Why do you think that?' he asked, a little too sharply.

'Because of the way you held BB on your lap when the uniformed officer arrived at your condo tonight so that he wouldn't search you. And . . .' She was silent for a long moment, then drew a breath. 'And because the serial number's filed off.'

She'd shocked him. 'How do you know that?' he asked.

'I saw it this morning when you were loading up that shoulder holster like Rambo.'

'Why didn't you say anything then?'

'Because I wanted to find out why it was filed off and why you continued to carry it.' She lifted her head, propping her chin on his shoulder to look up at him. 'You're not the only one who wants to find things out for yourself.'

'What do you think?'

'I don't know. Maybe you got it in the Gulf, like the knife you're so attached to. Maybe you used it for some gentle coercion and things got out of hand and you don't want to risk a Ballistics match.'

'That didn't happen,' he said flatly, not sure if he was offended or not.

'Which? You didn't get it in the Gulf or you didn't use it for gentle coercion or things didn't get out of hand?'

'All of the above.' He gritted his teeth. 'If you thought I was capable of using it to hurt someone, why am I even here with you? In your bed?'

She continued to regard him calmly. 'Because I didn't really think you did, and even if you did, the other guy probably had it coming.'

He shook his head. 'You confound me, Scarlett.'

'I don't mean to.' She rested her head on his shoulder again. 'Maybe it's just that I understand more than you think. Maybe I've gently coerced once or twice myself.'

She said it so softly he almost didn't hear her. 'Did you get written up?' he asked.

'No. I've never crossed the line. Well, not with both feet. The few times I've toed over it, my partners covered for me. It hasn't happened that often. It gets harder to control it every day, though.'

He remembered what she'd said that morning, when they'd talked about his grandfather. 'Because you see things you can't unsee.'

'Every goddamn day.' She exhaled quietly. 'Tell me why you keep it. Please.'

'I'll put it away,' he promised. 'I'd already planned to.'

'You're evading the subject again.'

He stared at the ceiling, his heart beginning to pound. 'Only because it's hard to talk about. The truth is, I don't know what would happen if it went through Ballistics. Have I ever fired this gun at anyone? Yes. A few times as a warning. Have I ever fired it *into* anyone? No. But I can't promise that my father didn't because I simply don't know.'

'Not Jeremy,' she said softly. 'You mean your real father.'

'Jeremy *is* my real father as far as I'm concerned. I mean my biological father. The man with the sperm. And not much else,' he added in a disgusted mutter.

'He wasn't a good man?'

He laughed bitterly, remembering his father so very clearly. 'No.'

'Yet you carry his gun.'

'No. It's not his. It belonged to my grandfather.'

'Okay,' she said reasonably. 'You loved your grandfather, so it has sentimental value.'

He shook his head. 'No, that's not really it either.' It was hard to talk about because he didn't like to even think about it. 'My grandfather never carried the gun. He kept it in a gun safe. My father . . . took it from time to time, mostly to show off. He probably never killed anyone.'

'"Probably" is not very reassuring,' she said. 'I can test it myself, if you want. Off the books. You'll at least know for sure if it ties to any crimes.'

No way in hell. 'That's okay. I'll put it away and carry one of my other guns.'

'That's fine, but I still want to know why you're so attached to it.'

He sighed. 'I thought you wanted to get some sleep.'

She sat up abruptly, frowning at him. '*Marcus.*'

He stared up at the ceiling, then met her eyes in the light of the moon coming through the window. 'Can you come back down here? It's . . . hard to talk about.'

Her frown changed from angry to concerned. 'That's the second time you've said that,' she said, but slid back down beside him, her head on his chest.

'Because it is.'

She splayed her hand over his heart. 'Your pulse just skyrocketed.'

'Yeah.' He focused on bringing it under control, then gave up when he couldn't concentrate enough to begin. 'Did you Google what I told you to?'

'Yes. I read a few of the articles that came up. I'm sorry, Marcus. You endured what no child should ever go through.'

'Stone had it worse. I only heard it. He saw it.'

'You mean your little brother being killed?'

He nodded, his throat constricting. He was having trouble breathing. Goddammit. 'Yeah.' He forced the word out. Gritted his teeth and beat back the panic. 'Afterward, even after we were safe, I couldn't sleep. Weeks and weeks went by and I still couldn't sleep. I can remember staring at the ceiling for hours on end.'

She was stroking his chest, trying to calm him. 'Understandable.'

'I . . . got my grandfather's gun and I . . . slept with it. Under my pillow.' The stutter he'd suffered for years after the attack tried to come back, shaming him.

'You were only eight years old,' she whispered, pained.

'Old enough to fire a gun if I needed to.'

'Did having the gun keep the nightmares at bay?'

'S-some. Not all.'

'So the gun is a talisman.'

405

'Yes,' he said, relieved. That much was true. Everything else he'd said was also true, just not complete.

'Thank you,' she murmured. 'Thank you for trusting me. I won't betray your trust.'

He winced internally every time she said 'trust', but it wasn't enough to make him say more. *Not now.* Not when she was in his arms. Not when she was believing him. He'd have to tell her. She deserved to know and he knew she would understand. But he wasn't going there tonight.

She leaned up and pressed kisses to his jaw, his chin, his mouth. 'Sleep now.'

If it were only that easy, he thought bitterly. He pulled her a little closer, stroking her hair, and she cuddled up to him. Within minutes she was asleep.

But he wasn't. His heart continued to race as he stared up at the ceiling, wondering how he was going to find the words to tell her the truth.

Cincinnati, Ohio
Wednesday 5 August, 2.30 A.M.

Ken could hear Burton's furious shouts the moment he opened his basement door.

'Sweeney! Goddammit, Sweeney, you little fucker! What the fuck is this? *Sweeney!*'

Ken strolled down the stairs, tugging at the cuffs of his shirt. The nap hadn't been enough to completely recharge him, but it would be enough to get what he needed out of Burton.

His basement was tidy again, no sign of the blood that had pooled on the floor after he'd slit the throats of Chip and Marlene Anders. Stephanie Anders sat on the floor in her cage, her arms hugging the knees she'd pulled to her chest. She wore a plain black shirt now. Pity. She'd been so pretty when he'd ripped off her top. Her eyes were shrewd as she watched him approach Burton, who had been tied to a chair. Hog-tied, actually, in a way that if he struggled, the rope would tighten around his throat like a noose. His jaw was bruised, his eye already black.

The noose and the shiner were both Alice's work, Ken thought, and felt a spurt of pride. His daughter could take care of herself.

He walked up to Burton. Folded his arms across his chest. 'You bellowed, Mr Burton?'

Burton looked up at him, hate in his eyes. 'Why am I here?' he growled.

'Miriam Blackwell is alive.'

Burton blinked in shock, color flooding his face. A very good performance. 'How?'

'That's what I'd like to know. She was found unconscious in her motel room. Anonymous 911 tip. The way I figure it, the only way that would be possible is if someone helped her throw up what I'd just given her.'

'I didn't.'

'Did you care for Reuben's wife, Burton?'

'Yes,' he said levelly. 'But not like you're thinking. I loved her like a sister.'

Again, a good performance. 'What else have you lied about?'

'I haven't.'

Ken backhanded him, sending the chair flying over. The ropes around Burton's neck stopped the chair mid-fall, suspending it at an angle, tightening the noose around Burton's throat. To his credit, Burton held perfectly still. Ken let him hang like that for ten seconds, then twenty, then shoved his foot between the rungs and snapped the chair upright.

Burton drew a ragged, wheezing breath. 'You motherfucker,' he snarled. 'You're insane.'

'We're going to try this again,' Ken said calmly. 'What else have you lied about?'

Burton clenched his teeth. 'Nothing.'

Ken backhanded him again, waited a few seconds longer before righting the chair. 'Where is Reuben?'

'I. Don't. Know.'

Ken hit him again and left him dangling for a full minute while he unlocked the closet where he stored his tool cart. By the time he'd pushed the cart close to Burton, the man had begun to thrash, his skin mottling a dark, ugly red. Ken righted the chair and loosened the rope from behind Burton's back, not intending to become a victim of the man's teeth.

Burton was gasping desperately when Ken returned to his cart and began inspecting his knives. 'You ex-cops are tough, but I've never had one that didn't break. Eventually.'

He chose a scalpel and turned back to see Burton's eyes narrow with promised retaliation. When Burton remained mute, Ken tightened the noose again, leaving only enough slack so that the man could breathe if he was perfectly still.

Then, standing behind him, he briskly sliced away the top of Burton's ear. Burton's shocked cry of pain echoed in the basement. Ken returned to his cart, laying the strip of ear where Burton could see it. 'Where is Reuben, Mr Burton?'

'Go to fucking hell,' Burton hissed, his body trembling, blood running down the side of his neck, soaking the rope. But he didn't move, didn't give the rope a chance to do any more damage.

'Fucking hell actually sounds pleasant,' Ken said with an easy smile. 'Celibate hell would suck. Once again, where is Reuben?'

One half-hour and a full ear later, Ken had to admit he was impressed. Either Burton really didn't know where Reuben was, or he was one tough sonofabitch. He'd sliced away the man's ear a little at a time, recreating it like a puzzle on the tray of his cart, and still Burton admitted to nothing. Not to rescuing Reuben's wife or to knowing Reuben's plan.

It was time to take a break before Burton passed out from blood loss. That would be counterproductive to getting the information Ken really wanted. He'd washed the scalpel and packed his knives into a toolbox so that he could use them upstairs on Demetrius when the door opened at the top of the stairs.

'He's awake, sir,' Decker called down.

'Perfect timing. I was just taking a break here. Can you come down, Decker?' He watched the man's reaction as he came down the stairs and saw Burton tied up in the chair.

Decker took in the blood, the noose, and the reconstructed ear on the cart, all without a flinch or a flicker in his steely eyes. 'Do you want me to bandage him up for you?' he asked.

'Sure, why not. Wouldn't want that cut to get infected.'

A brief twitch of Decker's lips was the only hint of an emotional response. 'No, sir.'

Ken closed the toolbox. 'Is Demetrius restrained?'

'Just like you asked, sir.'

'Good.'

'Why?' Burton growled. 'If Demetrius is a fuckup, just kill him. Quick and clean. What's with the Dr Mengele act?'

'It's not an act. Didn't Reuben ever tell you about my . . . hobbies? Finance and corporate management are only part of my skill set.' Ken smiled. 'Demetrius is an intimidator. Fists like concrete. Reuben is all tactical, planning, keeping people in line. Me? I'm the monster that hides in your closet, the one your mother always told you didn't exist. I'll get out of you what I want to know. One way or the other. Everyone talks eventually.'

With that he left Burton to Decker and climbed the stairs to Demetrius. He found him in one of the extra upstairs bedrooms, the one he kept just for times like this. His oldest friend was awake and completely immobilized. Decker had shackled Demetrius's feet and the wrist of his uninjured arm to the bed frame, while his injured arm and his body were restrained with three leather belts that wrapped under the bed and over his torso, groin and thighs.

Alice had been in here too. Demetrius wore a noose around his neck identical to Burton's. So Ken wouldn't have to worry about him thrashing too much.

Demetrius's nostrils flared when Ken entered the room, his eyes widening at the sight of the toolbox. 'What. The. Fuck?'

Ken sighed. 'I'd say this is going to hurt me more than you, but I'd be lying, obviously. But it will hurt me a lot. Just so you know.'

'You are crazy, man.'

Ken put the toolbox on the nightstand. 'And you're a cokehead who's put my entire company in jeopardy. You could make this easier on all of us by telling me where you've put that iPad you're always using. Decker and I couldn't find it in your car and Sean says you don't appear to have an account on the cloud. Whatever the hell that means. Where are your records?'

Demetrius's body sagged on the bed, the picture of exhaustion. 'Go to hell, *buddy*.'

One benefit of being old friends was knowing your buddy's secret moves. This was Demetrius's. He'd pretend to be too tired to fight and would then lash out with an attack that more often than not took his prey by surprise. Ken wondered what kind of attack he was planning, trussed up like he was.

He wasn't curious enough to let Demetrius try anything. His friend could break his neck while he was choking himself to death and then he wouldn't get anything out of him. Ken chose a pair of pliers and walked around the bed, then – staying well out of Demetrius's reach – latched the pliers onto his pinky finger and twisted.

Demetrius's body jerked, then froze when the noose tightened. 'What are you doing, Kenny?' he whispered.

'Finding out what I need to know so that this company can continue to be profitable after we're both gone. I need your records. Your suppliers. Contacts. Con*tracts*.'

'Where are you going?'

'I'm going to retire. After I get what I need from you, I'm done. Taking my booty and leaving the daily grind to the next generation. Think of this as ensuring that DJ has job security.'

'And if I give you what you need?' His lips twisted bitterly. 'You'll let me go, right?'

'Right.' Ken rolled his eyes. 'Absolutely.'

'I'm not a cokehead. Don't know who told you that.'

'Alice. She says you've been snorting some of the merchandise.'

'Lie.'

'Inventory is missing. And money. Did you and Reuben really think you could embezzle funds that easily?'

Demetrius's brows lowered. 'I have no idea what you're talking about.'

Ken drew a pair of collapsible bolt cutters from the bottom of his toolbox and snapped the arms out to their full length. He eyed Demetrius's body objectively. 'Let's start simply. Where is your iPad?'

'In my car.'

He ran the bolt cutters over one of Demetrius's toes. 'Wrong. We searched the car.'

'It's there.'

He snipped off the top of Demetrius's big toe, waited for the resulting scream to quiet. 'I forgot how high you can scream,' he said. 'Damn, D.' He rubbed his finger in his ear. 'You could break glass with that. Let's try again. Where is the iPad?'

'In the car. Look in the trunk,' Demetrius added, crushing his words together in his haste to get them out. 'Under the carpet.'

'Now we're getting somewhere.' He'd had Burton tow Demetrius's car here so that the bloody seats could be destroyed before they had the vehicle smashed down to scrap. Sean and Alice had been waiting for Burton when he arrived, so the car was still in the garage.

He called Alice, told her to get the iPad and take it to Sean, who'd set up a cot in his office downtown. It would have been easier for Sean to come to the house, but his son was a bit of an eccentric introvert and rarely left his office. Ken had once tried to push him out of his comfort zone, but Sean had a mini-breakdown, and since nobody understood the computer networks he'd set up, Ken now let him stay where he was happiest.

Sean and Alice would have the bulk of Demetrius's knowledge in the iPad, but Ken knew his old friend still kept a lot of information stored in his brain.

He ran the tip of the bolt cutter up the inside of Demetrius's thigh, stopping a fraction of an inch from the family jewels he knew his friend was so proud of.

He smiled down at Demetrius, who was quivering, his nostrils flaring like a bull ready to charge. 'Let's talk passwords.'

Twenty-seven

Cincinnati, Ohio
Wednesday 5 August, 6.00 A.M.

Scarlett smacked the alarm clock on her nightstand, but it kept ringing. 'Fuck,' she muttered, then realized it was her phone. She blinked hard, remembering in an instant.

Marcus. Grabbing the phone, she rolled over to find herself alone in her bed. A frisson of dread raced down her back. She remembered how upset he'd been just before she fell asleep. *I shouldn't have pushed him so hard to tell me about that damn gun.*

Getting out of bed, she threw on shorts and a T-shirt as she answered the phone without looking at the caller ID. This early it could only be Isenberg or Deacon. Or her mother if somebody had died. 'Hello?'

'Scarlett, it's Uncle Trace.'

She stopped short. 'Good morning. I'm sorry I wasn't there for the search last night. I got called to a crime scene.'

'Your lieutenant told me. She said you accompanied the victim to the hospital.'

'We had two, actually. Both are still in ICU. But I don't think you're calling about the two victims, are you?'

'No. I found your missing women.'

She sucked in a startled breath. 'What? Where? When? My boss said the dogs lost the trail, that she thought they'd gotten a ride. She said you'd gone home.'

'That's all true. But then I thought that if they were frightened of deportation – and Catholic – they might ask whoever picked them up to drop them off at a church.'

'For sanctuary,' she murmured. She tossed the shorts aside and went to her closet for trousers, blouse and a jacket. Clearly it was time to start her day. 'Where did you find them?'

'Saint Barbara's. It's just outside of Georgetown, Kentucky.'

411

'Good grief, that's an hour south of here. Somebody took them all the way down there?'

'A trucker. He dropped them off at his old parish.'

'That was nice of him. I wish his parish had been closer.' She'd found clean underwear and one shoe. She wasn't sure where the other had landed when she'd kicked it off last night. 'Are you there now, or did you call them?'

'I'm here. I called first, told the priest to keep them there, then I drove down. I didn't want to call you until I'd confirmed I had the right people, but they are Mila and Erica Bautista.'

She got down on her knees to look under the bed for her errant shoe. No Zat, she thought. Her dog must have overcome his fear of the boisterous sex she and Marcus had had. Unfortunately no shoe either.

'Did you call the local cops?'

'No. They said they'll only talk to Marcus.'

Scarlett pushed herself to her feet. 'How do they know his name?'

'Tabby Anders showed them the newspaper article. She told them that he was the man that Tala had met in the park, who'd offered to help. They said that if I called the police they would run. So don't dress like a cop, okay?'

'Okay. I'll find Marcus and we'll get down there as fast as we can. Tell them he's on his way. Did they say anything?'

'Just that they wanted to see Malaya and Tabby. I assured them that Malaya was safe and being cared for. I called the hospital for an update on Miss Anders. No change.'

'I figured. Nobody's contacted me. Thank you, Uncle Trace. I owe you.'

'Don't say that, Scarlett,' he warned. 'You might not like the marker I call in.'

She sighed. He'd ask her to come back to the Church. She knew it. Right now, she was so grateful to him for finding the women that she felt it was the least she could do. 'I'll get to Saint Barbara's as soon as I can.'

She threw the cop clothes on her bed and picked out a pretty sundress and flats. She got dressed, brushed her teeth, grabbed her hairbrush and went in search of Marcus.

'Marcus?' she called, going down the stairs, but there was no answer. She checked her garage, but her car was there. She'd seen from her bedroom window that the Tank was in the driveway, so unless he'd taken a cab or called someone to get him, he was still here somewhere.

'Zat? Here, boy. Wanna go outside?' But there was no staccato sound of her three-legged dog running to go for a walk. When she got to the kitchen, she saw the remnants of a sandwich, so at least Marcus wasn't hungry, wherever he'd gone.

The only place she hadn't looked was the basement, and sure enough, the hook-and-eye latch was open. She'd installed it the day she'd gotten Zat, worried that she'd accidentally leave the door open and he'd tumble down the steep steps. The house was so old that none of the staircases were built to code, and the staircase to the basement was the worst.

She started down the stairs, relieved to see Zat curled up on the rug at the bottom. She'd started to call Marcus's name, when she heard a sound that silenced her. Hard thuds, interspersed with the vilest curses she'd ever heard, uttered by the most beautiful voice she'd ever known. She got to the bottom of the stairs and watched him, not sure how to approach him.

Marcus was shirtless and shoeless, wearing only a pair of gym shorts that were soaked with sweat and her brother Phin's boxing gloves. Sweat poured off his body as he pounded the ever-living hell out of Phin's old punching bag. He must have found the hook that had come with it, and screwed it into the ceiling beam.

She winced at the sight of his broad back. A big bruise covered a quarter of his skin, the result of the bullet that had been stopped by his Kevlar vest the morning before. He didn't seem to be letting that hold him back, though. She had to admire the athleticism it took to keep the punching bag at a constant angle, but worried that he'd hurt his hands, even while wearing the gloves.

Abruptly he stopped, leaning against the bag, hugging it awkwardly as his shoulders sagged. 'I can smell honeysuckle,' he said quietly, his breaths coming hard and fast.

'I woke up and you were gone.'

'I couldn't sleep. I walked your dog. Fixed the leaking sink in the kitchen. The dripping was driving me fucking nuts.'

'Thank you.' She took a step closer, but he lifted one gloved hand.

'Don't. Don't touch me. Please.' The 'please' sounded shaky, almost like a sob.

'Marcus?' she said gently, respecting his wish for the moment. 'Is it Phillip? Or Edgar?'

'No. They're both still unconscious.'

'Then what are you doing?'

'Had to work it out.'

'Work what out, baby?' she asked, although she thought she knew.

413

I shouldn't have pushed about that damn gun. He told me he was putting it away. That should have been enough.

But even as she said the words in her mind, she knew they weren't true. Marcus needed to confront whatever was haunting him.

He lifted his head, looked around the room without looking at her. 'What is all this stuff? You've got gym-quality equipment here.'

She walked around him, giving him a wide berth, and sat down on the weight bench he'd found in the back room. He'd found the weight set as well. She tallied the sum of the plates at a glance and bit back a frown. He'd been lifting far more weight than a man without a spotter should have been.

'It was all Phin's.'

He still wasn't looking at her. 'Your brother. The one with PTSD that left home.'

'Yes. My twin. When he cleared out, he didn't take anything with him. All this stuff was the contents of his apartment. It was either bring it here or have the landlord haul it to the dumpster. I keep hoping Phin will come home and reclaim it.'

Marcus leaned his forehead against the bag. 'I hope for your sake he does. For his sake too.'

Scarlett needed him ready to roll, physically and emotionally, but she knew that right now, that wasn't a possibility. 'I'm sorry,' she said quietly. 'This is my fault. You weren't ready to answer my questions about that stupid gun and I forced you. I'm sorry, Marcus.'

He shook his head, his forehead a pivot point against the bag. 'No, it's not your fault. It's mine. You had every right to ask. I just didn't know how to tell you.'

'But you did. You were a terrified child and it was your talisman.' She winced. 'I hope it wasn't loaded when you put it under your pillow.'

He pushed off the bag to lean against the wall, sinking to sit on the floor, elbows on his bent knees. Just as he'd done yesterday when he'd talked Stone down from whatever episode his brother had had. And just like yesterday, she joined him there, sliding down the wall to sit beside him. She tucked her knees under the full skirt of the sundress.

'You're pretty in that dress,' he whispered.

'Thank you.' She didn't tell him why she'd dressed this way. Not yet. 'Talk to me, Marcus. Please. I want to help you.'

'To fix me, like all those broken chairs upstairs, or rescue me like your mutt? He's a nice dog, by the way. He likes salami.'

Her lips curved. 'It gives him gas. I'll let him sleep on your side of the bed tonight.'

He huffed a weary chuckle, then bowed his head. 'God, I'm fucked up.'

'Then let me help un-fuck you,' she said, and he laughed, but it sounded forced. Feeling helpless, she stroked his arm and he pulled away.

'I'm sweaty. Your dress is too pretty to be messed up.'

'I have others, and I don't mind sweat.' Tentatively she stroked him again, shoulder all the way down his arm to his glove. She tugged at the Velcro strap and pulled it off, then repeated it with the other. 'Let me see your hands.' She held them to the light. 'Oh Marcus, your knuckles are already starting to swell. Stay here and don't hit anything else.'

She slipped into the basement's utility room and sent a quick text to her uncle saying they'd hit a snag and would be at least an hour later than she'd expected, then lifted the lid of the big chest freezer that had come with the house and rearranged the microwave meals and bags of frozen veggies until she found a couple of gel packs. Her phone buzzed as she closed the freezer lid, a text from her uncle telling her not to worry, that the women had fallen asleep and that he'd watch over them.

Secure in Trace's word, she returned to sit in front of Marcus, putting the ice packs on his knuckles and watching him wince. He said nothing for several minutes, so neither did she. Finally she took the ice packs off and kissed his knuckles, one at a time, and felt him shudder.

'Marcus, I can't help if you don't tell me what's wrong.'

'You can't help me.'

The finality of his statement made her heart ache. 'Then let me hurt with you.'

He lifted his head, unshed tears in his eyes. 'I won't do that to you.'

She got on her knees and took his face in her hands. 'I won't give up.' She kissed him softly. 'I can't give up. I don't know how. My mother always said I was intractable. All those cop genes. But I can wait until you're ready to tell me.'

He pulled free of her touch, but gently, bowing his head again, his hands hanging limply between his knees. 'The kidnapping was an inside job,' he said, startling her.

'That's what the newspapers said, that one of the kidnappers was thought to be part of a handyman crew working in your apartment.'

'My father hired them.'

Her gut did a queasy roll at the tone of his voice, remembering how bitter he'd been when he talked about his father. *Which was the start of the emotional distance that led up to this.* This was not going to be good. 'Hired them how?'

'He hired them to kidnap us. For the ransom.'

415

'Your father wanted the ransom?' She frowned, confused. 'But it was his money.'

'No. It was Mom's money. One hundred percent Yarborough money. My biological father was a gold-digger who lived the high life and had a gambling problem. My mother had bailed him out too many times and they fought about his spending when it got out of hand. I was a quiet kid. A listener. I knew what was going on. I hated him.'

'Did your mother cut him off?'

'Not totally. She finally put him on an allowance and got angry. He hit her.'

'Oh, Marcus, I'm sorry.'

'I wanted to kill him, but he was the size I am now and I was scrawny.'

'You were eight.'

'And so angry. He begged her to forgive him and bought her an expensive bracelet – with her money – as an apology. I wanted her to make him leave, but she forgave him. Turned out it wasn't the first time. He'd run up gambling debts in the past.'

'So he figured he'd stage a kidnapping, get the ransom and pay off his debts.'

He nodded once. 'She didn't know. Doesn't know. Please don't tell her.'

She took his hand, kissed it again. She needed answers, but he needed reassurance even more. 'I won't. I wish I could say I can't imagine a father risking his sons for money, but I can. I've seen it too many times.'

His strong shoulders sagged. 'All those things you can't unsee,' he said. 'And now I just added one more.'

She considered her words carefully. 'If I told you that I'm not visualizing a frightened young boy betrayed by his father, afraid to sleep at night, I'd be lying. If I told you that the image doesn't break my heart, I'd be lying even more. If that hurts your pride, then I'm sorry. But you're mine now, and I will hurt for you if I want to.'

Slowly his head lifted, his eyes intense. Hungry again. 'Say that again,' he whispered.

She didn't pretend to misunderstand. This was too important. 'You're mine, Marcus.'

His eyes slid closed, his swallow audible, his throat working as he fought to contain his emotion. 'God.'

Hoarsely uttered, she couldn't tell if it was plea or prayer. Maybe a little bit of both, she thought, her eyes stinging. Still on her knees, she crawled to his side and drew him into her arms. He turned his head, burying his face in the curve of her shoulder, wrapping his arms around her waist. She held him as the minutes ticked by, rocking him gently, letting him restore his composure.

Finally he drew a deep breath, lifted his head and ran one hand up her back, pulling her down for a hot kiss that left her reeling. 'You're mine, Detective. You have been since that first day I saw you.'

When he'd been shot protecting a woman he'd never even met. She smiled at him. 'I know. But it's nice to hear, isn't it?'

His lips curved, just a little. 'Hell, yeah.' Effortlessly he scooped her into his arms, setting her on his lap, gently pressing her cheek into his chest when she tried to look at him. 'I have something to tell you. It'll be easier if you're not looking at me while I do it.'

She braced herself. *Not gonna be good*, she thought. 'Okay. I'm ready when you are.'

Twenty-eight

'I'm not sure I'll ever be ready to tell anyone, but I need you to know.' He grew still, his only movement the rising and falling of his chest as he breathed. 'You didn't ask me how I knew my father had hired the kidnappers.'

'I wanted to, but I figured you'd tell me when you were ready.'

His arms tightened around her. 'Why am I so lucky?' he murmured, then sighed. 'Mom sent a car to drop us off and pick us up from school every day. Stone and I were taken when our driver was overpowered. He was found a few hours later, wandering the streets in Lexington, drugged and confused. By then, Matty had been taken too.'

'From his bed.'

'Yes. They took us to a warehouse by the river, but we didn't know that. They locked us in an old beef freezer that was no longer used. It smelled bad, but it wasn't cold. Stone and Matty were so scared. I tried to be brave, but I was terrified too. I knew we were rich. I knew my mother worried that something like this might happen one day.' He was quiet for a moment, rubbing a lock of her tangled hair between his thumb and forefinger. 'We weren't tied up at first. I guess they figured three little boys couldn't cause them any trouble.'

'I guess they didn't know the O'Bannion boys,' she said, and he huffed a small laugh.

'The day Jeremy O'Bannion adopted us and gave us his name was the best day of my life, up until that point. I couldn't stand introducing myself as Marcus Gargano. Gargano was *his* name and I hated him.' He'd grown stiff, but he drew a few breaths, his hold on her relaxing. 'The freezer had a single bulb hanging from the ceiling, but the light switch was on the outside wall so we couldn't turn it on.'

'You were trapped, alone in the dark,' she murmured. *His littlest brother had died in the dark. Like Tala.* 'Oh, Marcus.'

Another audible swallow. 'Yeah.' His voice broke and he cleared his throat. 'I'm sorry. I haven't talked about this in twenty-seven years.'

'Your mother didn't get you counseling?' she asked, appalled.

'Sure, but . . . I didn't tell the counselors anything. I couldn't. I wouldn't. I didn't want my mother to know what I'd done and I didn't trust the counselors not to tell her.'

Didn't want his mother to know? *Hell.* 'What did you do?' she asked gently.

'I climbed on a box and unscrewed the light bulb so that they wouldn't have any light when they came in to check on us, then I used a paperclip in my pocket to loosen some of the screws on the metal shelving unit against the wall. I used one of the rods as a club and hit one of the kidnappers with it.'

She jerked in surprise, even as the knowledge registered that he was not answering her question. But this was his story and she'd let him tell it. 'Wow. You were very resourceful.'

'I watched way too much television. It was foolish, actually. I was only eight years old, and even though I hit him with all my might, it didn't hurt him. It just made him mad. He wanted to kill me, but the other kidnapper calmed him down. The two of them brought in a chair and tied me to it, then turned me so that I couldn't see my brothers. They tied Stone and Matty too. Didn't blindfold or gag us.' He shook his head. 'It was winter and we all had colds. The calm one was afraid we'd suffocate if they covered our mouths with duct tape. I couldn't get to my brothers, but I could hear them crying.' He shuddered out a breath. 'Stone kept asking me to make the men go away, saying he just wanted to go home. I kept promising him it would be all right.'

She remembered Stone's near meltdown in Marcus's office the day before. 'He said that yesterday. Said to make me go away. You promised him it would be all right.'

Another shuddering exhale. 'Certain things set him off. One of the kidnappers was the security guard for the warehouse. Told Stone he was a cop and would shoot him if he cried. For a long time he couldn't look at anyone in uniform without unraveling, but he got past that eventually. Jeremy helped a lot. He's a calm man and helped us calm down too.'

'But Stone was in the Army. He wore a uniform.'

'That was a personal challenge to himself. The ultimate "fuck you, world, I'm over that shit". He wore a uniform, served with uniforms, took commands. He served his time and got out. His issue with cops, though . . . It's still there. If he feels threatened by a cop . . .'

'I don't wear a uniform.'

'Doesn't matter. I've always thought that for him to get over his fear of uniforms, he had to transfer it somewhere, so it's generalized to all cops.'

'But . . . He didn't trust me when I met him nine months ago, but he didn't melt down.'

'Not while you were there. He melted down later.'

'That's why you were so fierce that day in the hospital, when I criticized him for lying to us. You told me that when I'd walked a mile in his shoes, then I could judge him. I didn't understand.'

He kissed her temple. 'Of course you didn't. How could you have? I wasn't going to tell you, because it's Stone's secret. But it's mine too.'

She petted his chest, soothing him. 'I won't let him know that I know. I think we've achieved a truce and I don't want to ruin it. Or hurt him any more.'

A shrug of his muscled shoulders. 'Thank you. At this point he doesn't think you're Satan.' His huffed chuckle was sad. 'You made some kind of impression. A good one, I think. It's hard to tell with Stone sometimes.' He straightened his spine against the wall, jostling her a little in his lap, but his arms kept her close.

'There are other things I can't tell you. Things . . . they did to him.' His voice was stark, filled with pain. 'They knew I was listening. Saw how hard I fought to get loose so I could make them stop. I . . .' His chest heaved once. 'That was . . . Oh God. I still hear his voice, crying for me to help him. They didn't touch me. I wish they had. I begged them to, to leave Stone and Matty alone. They just laughed and said I'd get my turn.'

Scarlett was trembling with anger, her fists clenching helplessly. She bit her tongue to keep from saying anything, knowing her fury would spill out into her words.

Marcus stroked her hair. 'More things you can't unsee,' he murmured.

'I hope they're dead.' Because if they weren't, she'd find them and kill them.

'They are very dead.'

The darkly satisfied way he said it made her pull away to try to see his face, but he held her tighter. 'Not yet,' he said harshly. 'Don't look at me yet.'

She ceased her struggling, giving him his privacy. 'Were they caught by the police?'

'No.' He sounded a little amused at that. 'I'm sure they would have preferred the cops.' He resettled her in his lap and continued, his voice surprisingly calm. 'They gave instructions for the ransom, said no police or FBI should be contacted. Gayle told me later that my father wouldn't let my mother contact the authorities, but she snuck away and did it anyway. The Feds followed the pickup man to the warehouse complex. That's how they found us, but they had to do a building-to-building search. When the kidnappers realized the Feds were closing in, they freaked. They grabbed the money and ran, but not before trying to take care of us. We'd seen their faces. I was just a kid. I didn't realize that from the beginning we were dead in their eyes. One of them opened the freezer door and . . . fired.'

His arms tightened around her until she had trouble breathing, but she didn't say a word. He abruptly loosened his hold, his voice trembling now. 'I'm sorry. I didn't mean to hurt you.'

She pressed her fingertips to his lips. 'I'm fine. You don't have to tell me any more.'

'I haven't told you anything yet,' he said wearily.

Her heart sank. What was coming was much worse, then. She kissed the base of his throat, tasting the salt of his sweat. 'Then tell me,' she murmured. 'But you don't have to.'

'I think I do. No, I *know* I do. You need to know. But you need to know why.'

Need to know what? she wanted to demand, but she let him tell it his way. They had time.

'You read the articles so you know that Matty was killed and Stone almost died. They were tied up close to the door, an easy shot. They'd put my chair toward the back. I threw myself down and the chair teetered just enough that the bullet missed my head and grazed my ear. I ended up on the floor and stayed there, waiting for the second shot, but finally realized the bastard thought he'd hit me. He pulled the door shut and left us alone there. In the dark.'

Swallowing the bile that burned her throat, she struggled to hide her horror, but knew that was useless. 'Jesus, Marcus.'

He pressed his lips to her temple and kept them there for a long time. 'I could hear Stone crying, but I couldn't hear Matty at all. Not even breathing. I was thrashing, trying to get free. I'd been thrashing ever since they'd tied me up.'

She cleared her throat. 'How much time, Marcus?'

'We were held for a little more than three days.'

Her chest hurt. 'Three days was an eternity.'

'It was.' A long, long pause. 'When I fell, the wooden back of the chair broke. Between that and the thrashing, I managed to get my hands free. My feet were still tied to the chair's base, but I dragged myself to the door, chair and all. It was locked – the bastards had padlocked it before they ran with the ransom cash, so we were trapped. I got my feet free and tried to use part of the broken chair to get us out. Stone had stopped crying and I thought he was dead too, but I couldn't see to know if he was okay. I guess I became kind of an animal, trying to break the door down. The officers searching our warehouse heard me. When they came in, I saw the uniform and thought they were the kidnappers, come back to finish us off, so I attacked them. I didn't want them near Stone and Matty. It took two officers to pull me away and hold me down.'

'I'm so sorry about Matty.'

He nodded, the stubble on his face catching in her hair. 'He died almost immediately, so he didn't suffer so much. Stone . . . he was hurt bad. I still remember the blood when they carried him out. He was in a coma for a week. In the hospital a lot longer than that. He missed Matty's funeral, which was probably a blessing for him.'

'How did you find out that your father was involved?'

'A few days after we were rescued, the phone rang in our apartment. Gayle was at the hospital sitting with Stone and my mother was asleep. She'd taken a sleeping pill that the doctor had given her. That was the beginning of her addiction. Anyway, I answered the phone before it finished ringing because I didn't want it to wake Mom up. And, um . . .' He swallowed hard. 'I heard him. One of the guys who took us. The one who hurt Stone and Matty. I didn't scream, didn't make a sound. It was like I was frozen with fear because I thought he was coming back. Then I heard my father answer the phone from another extension. It all happened pretty fast. They started talking, and I realized they knew each other. My father was angry. He said, "Nobody was supposed to get hurt. You killed my son and the other might die too." Then the guy told my father that he'd broken the agreement by sending in the FBI. My father blew up, so angry that my mother had involved the law. But he was madder that the other guy hadn't given him his share of the money.'

Scarlett wanted to curse, to hit something. Wanted to kill his father, rip out his withered heart with her bare hands. But she kept her cool. Kept her voice calm and her hand warm on his chest. 'What did you do?'

'I wanted to tell someone, but I didn't know who. Mom was out like a light and Gayle was at the hospital with Stone. My paternal grandfather lived nearby and watched us sometimes, but he was just like my father and I was afraid to tell him. Afraid he wouldn't believe me. I tried to walk out of the apartment to find a beat cop, but my father stopped me from going out, said I could be kidnapped again because they'd gotten away and I'd seen their faces.'

422

'Sonofabitch. He deliberately terrified you.'

'I didn't know what to do. I got paranoid, thinking he was watching me. I was afraid to pick up the phone, afraid that he'd listen to me like I'd listened to him. So I cowered in my room and didn't tell anyone. I didn't know who I could trust.'

'What about your Grandfather Yarborough? You trusted him.'

'I loved him. I loved spending time with him when we visited him, but even back then I never knew who he was going to be, so I was a little scared of him too. He came down to Lexington as soon as we were taken, but he spent all his time at the hospital with my mother and Stone after we were rescued. I never had a moment alone with him when my father wasn't hovering.'

'Your father kept you isolated.'

'Yes. Plus, my grandfather liked my father. Everyone liked my father. He was pleasant and fun and threw a good party. My mother was the moody one, the one everyone said was eccentric. My father was well-loved by everyone who didn't live with us.'

'Gayle lived with you.'

'Gayle got days off. Vacation. My father timed his outbursts very well. And when he couldn't hold back . . . Well, my parents were very good at fighting in private.'

'Dammit, Marcus, I hate the thought of you being so alone in your own home. Surely your mother would have listened when you told her what you'd heard your father say.'

'She would have listened, sure. But she wouldn't have heard. She was in shock. Matty was dead, and Stone almost was. And the bottom line was that she loved my father, even though he'd slap her around sometimes. Nobody knew. I don't even think she knows that I even knew. I kept trying to find the right time to tell her what he did to Stone and Matty, but I never did.'

To Stone and Matty, but not to you. 'How did your father die, Marcus?'

He drew a deep breath and held it.

'Marcus?'

The breath rushed out almost desperately. 'At the funeral, a man came up to my father. Big guy. Really big. Bold, too. Came right up to the casket where we were standing. Asked where his money was. My father said, "It's my son's funeral. Can't you wait?" He asked the man to call him later. So when we got home, I listened and waited. I didn't dare pick up the phone again, but when the call came, I hid nearby and eavesdropped on my father's side of the conversation. He said, "I'll get you the money even if I have to inherit it."'

423

Scarlett's dread amped up. 'He was going to kill your mother?'

'That's what it sounded like to me. And I made my decision then. I remember that night she tucked me in and sang me a lullaby. Kissed me goodnight. I guess I knew she was sad and scared, and I let her treat me like a little boy.'

'You *were* a little boy, Marcus.'

'I sure didn't feel like one anymore, I remember that. I wanted to warn her then, but I didn't know how. I stumbled through it, being all cryptic. It should have been simple. I should have just said, "Your husband paid someone to kidnap your children so he could get some money and now he's trying to kill you." But I couldn't get the words out. I started with "My father" but then stumbled and said "Your husband", and then I just couldn't get the words out. All she got was that I was afraid of my father, and she told me that the psychologists said I might mix up reality with fiction for a while as I processed things.'

'You're right. She listened, but it doesn't sound like she could hear what you were trying to say.'

'I realize that now,' he said with a shrug. 'I hadn't slept in my bed since the police brought me home, and I couldn't sleep that night either. I was worried about my mother, so later that night I went to check on her, but she wouldn't wake up. My father wasn't home and Gayle was still with Stone, so I called 911. They pumped my mother's stomach, but she almost died anyway.'

'Did you tell Gayle about your father that night?'

'No. They took Mom to a different hospital than Stone, and since I'd been home alone with her, the cops took me with them. I heard one of them tell the other to be careful, that I was the kid who'd gone apeshit crazy and clawed up two uniforms a few days before. They even talked about restraining me, and I had a panic attack at the thought.'

'No wonder. Stupid untrained sons of bitches,' she muttered.

'They felt bad when I cried like a baby and begged them not to tie me. They told me if I kept my hands to myself they'd leave me alone, so I made myself small in the backseat of the cruiser and didn't say another word. They called Social Services and a caseworker came to sit with me at the ER. She was pretty and nice and I almost got the courage to tell her, but my father showed up and took me home. I was petrified he was going to kill me too, but he just told me to go to sleep, that my mother would be all right. The next morning I woke up and he was gone. He'd packed a bag and left my mother a note saying that he was going away for a few days, that he needed to clear his head after Matty's funeral and find a way to forgive my mother for endangering his kids by defying him and calling in the FBI.'

'What a prince.'

'Yeah. What had woken me up was a noise in my mother's room. I didn't know I was home alone at that point, so I got up to look. And found the big scary guy from the funeral going through my mother's jewelry box.'

Scarlett blinked. 'Shit.'

'I think that's exactly what I said. He'd found the letter my father had left and was pissed. I was so scared I almost fainted, and the guy actually took pity on me. He told me he didn't hurt little kids, that he only needed to find my father because he owed the guy's boss a lot of money.' Here, Marcus paused, hesitating. 'I knew where my father went when he really wanted to get away.' The words came out in a rush, and she could hear the quickening of his breath.

'Something else you overheard?'

'Of course. Plus, I'd been there. So have you.'

Scarlett frowned, then shook her head when realization dawned. 'No way. The cabin in Kentucky?' Owned by his mother, it was where Mikhail had been murdered nine months ago.

'The very same.' He'd grown quiet, hesitant, and instinctively she knew that this was what he hadn't wanted to tell her.

'You told the scary guy where to find your father?' His silence was answer enough. 'No one can blame you, Marcus. You were just a little boy and scared shitless.'

'It would be so easy to let you believe that, but the truth is, I got really calm all of the sudden, because I believed him when he said he wouldn't hurt me. I thought about Matty dead, Stone almost. My mother not safe. And I made a decision. I asked him if I told him where to find my father, would his boss leave my mother, me and my brother alone, even if he never got paid? He looked me in the eye and said that he wouldn't hurt me but that he couldn't promise what any of the other enforcers might do.'

'Enforcers? This guy was with the mob?'

'Yep. But I didn't know that then. I did know that the two kidnappers had taken the whole ransom. I asked the guy how much my father owed his boss and he said about a million. So I told him the kidnappers had taken five million dollars. I told him if he could find the two kidnappers, he could pay back my father's debt and keep the rest. He said he didn't know where to look for the guys, so I told him he could ask my father about that – and I told him where I thought he could find my dad. He liked that idea because it was more than my father owed.'

'He could pay your father's debt and keep the four million for himself.'

'Which is what I'm sure he ended up doing,' he said quietly with a grim finality that said his story was finished.

'So . . . what happened to your father? Did they find his body in the cabin?'

'That's what I expected to happen, but no. He was found in a hotel room in downtown Lexington three days later. Tied to the bed, shot with a nine mil, right between the eyes. It was set up to look like he'd been robbed by a prostitute – his wallet was empty and there were condoms all over the place.'

'How do you know that?' she asked guardedly.

'I overheard the cops telling my mother at the time, but I also checked out the crime-scene photos years later. Freedom of information, you know,' he added, his tone one of self-hatred. 'My mother was devastated when the cops showed up at our door to deliver the news, and it hit me then exactly what I'd done.'

This was it. 'What exactly *did* you do, Marcus? And I'll tell you up front, if you say you killed your father, I'm not gonna take it.'

'I set him up, Scarlett. I all but paid for his murder.'

'Yes, you set your father up. But you were just trying to protect your family. You knew your mother and brother wouldn't be safe until the debt was paid. So you thought of a way to get it paid. And you wanted to ensure that the plan would work, so you told the guy where he could find your father. You didn't know the guy would kill your father if he found him. You didn't tell him so that he could kill your father. You did it to save your family. Your father was the one who chose to get in touch with the mob in the first place. He deserved what he got.'

'You're bloodthirsty for a cop, you know,' he said lightly.

His minimization pissed her off, so she pushed on his chest until he loosened his hold enough for her to straddle his hips and look him in the eye. The guilt she saw there made her madder.

'I am *not* bloodthirsty. What I am is a cop who's seen more death than I ever want to remember. I've seen too many assholes walk away scot-free. I've seen too many women dead because the system doesn't work for them, because even though they followed the rules and reported their abusive SOB husbands and got restraining orders and *begged for help*, the law couldn't help them until they could prove they were assaulted, and even then the bastards got out by morning and went home to beat them up again.' She poked her finger into his chest. 'You saved your mother's life. Probably Stone's and your own too.' She poked him again. 'You didn't kill your

426

father. You didn't even put out a hit. You were eight years old and simply told the one person who'd listen what had happened to you.' She drew a breath, her body trembling from the anger she was still holding in. 'And if that one person happened to be a mob hit man, well, I consider that to be just a weird, ironically satisfying twist of fate.'

The guilt had disappeared from his eyes, replaced with the hungry look that drove her crazy. 'If I told you that I think I love you, would it be too soon?'

Her heart clenched and twisted at his words, uttered in that smooth voice that made her even crazier. She took his face between her hands and touched her forehead to his. 'Yes, but tell me anyway.'

His lips curved. 'I think I love you, Scarlett Bishop. Or at least I'm well on my way.'

She had to remind herself to breathe. 'Good, because I think I love you too. Even though you have a serious guilt addiction. We have to work on that.'

He kissed her softly, tugged her lower lip gently with his teeth. 'Gonna repair me, Detective?'

She smiled at him as everything fell into place. *I'm happy*, she realized. *And it feels so very nice.* 'No, because you're not broken. Just a little banged up. Just like me.'

He swallowed hard, emotion glittering in his eyes. 'I messed you up. Your pretty dress is all sweaty now.' He ran his hands up her legs, under the hem of her dress and over her bare skin to close on her butt. 'I can help you take it off.'

Disappointment swirled with frustration as she mentally calculated how much time had passed. 'As tempting as that sounds, we have to take a rain check. We have somewhere you need to be. Uncle Trace called. He found Mila and Erica. And they will only talk to you.'

His eyes widened in stunned surprise. 'Why didn't you tell me?'

'Because when I came down here, you were in no frame of mind to be what those women needed.' She kissed him hard and fast. 'Are you now?'

'Yes. Thank you.'

She pushed to her feet, almost whimpering when he removed his hands from her butt. *Later*, she promised herself. *When this is over, we'll have all the time we want.* She stepped back, extended her hand and pulled him up. 'To the shower with you. Hurry.' She kissed his chest, right above his heart. 'You're all sweaty and you smell like a gym.'

He threaded his fingers through hers. 'And you smell like me, so you

427

need to shower too. I'll wash your hair again, and put some conditioner in this time to get those tangles out.'

'How am I supposed to resist an offer like that?' she asked, stopping at the bottom of the stairs to scoop Zat into her arms, but Marcus beat her to it, cradling the dog much like he'd cradled little Malaya yesterday. *And how am I supposed to resist you?*

She couldn't. But now that she'd learned his darkest secret, one that proved he was even more of the man she'd hoped for, she knew that she didn't have to resist him at all.

Cincinnati, Ohio
Wednesday 5 August, 8.20 A.M.

Marcus ended his call and handed his phone to Scarlett to plug into the aging Audi's old-fashioned cigarette lighter. He worried about the old car's rattling engine, but knew better than to suggest Scarlett trade it in for a more reliable model. She fixed things. People too. *And thank God for that.* 'No change on Phillip,' he said with a sigh.

'Tabby Anders is trying to wake up, according to Annabelle Church's grandson, but she's still not coherent.' Scarlett had called Gabriel Benitez to tell him that they were en route to the missing Bautista women. 'Mr Benitez said that he's already called his immigration lawyer friend and they're ready to meet with the family whenever we get them together in a safe place.'

'I've got a place.' Marcus had already reserved the penthouse suite at one of the centrally located hotels downtown. He hadn't done it for the luxury, but for the security. Otherwise Isenberg would want to put the women in protective custody. After being held in slavery for three years, his gut told him the Bautistas would try to run if the police put them in any kind of custody, protective or not.

If they decided to go elsewhere, that would be their right, of course, but he was prepared in the event the Bautista women were willing to come back with them. Hopefully they'd have information about whoever had taken that bastard Anders from his home the day before. Because that person, whoever he was, could be the trafficker they were searching for. Trafficker and murderer and God only knew what else.

'Everything else okay?' Scarlett asked. 'Your conversation with Stone sounded heated.'

'We were arguing about our mother again. I want to push her to go to rehab, and—'

'Stone doesn't want her forced into anything,' she finished sadly.

428

'Exactly.' He tried to smile. 'I think he's really pissed off that he's back to babysitting Jill. We don't know what to do about her. I'd ask Cal to take over when he comes in later, but he's going to be busy doing his job and Phillip's. And Lisette's.' He sighed. 'And mine too, until this shooter's dealt with.'

'I take it that Cal runs the paper when you're not there?' Scarlett asked.

'Cal runs the paper even when I *am* there. He's forgotten more about newspapers than I'll ever learn. He's helped me in so many ways since my grandfather died, both with the day-to-day business of running the paper and in utilizing it to its fullest potential.'

'Delivering justice,' she said.

He winced. 'Delivering justice along with newspapers? Pun not intended, huh.'

She smiled at him. 'No, totally intended.' She tipped her head, studying him, her smile disappearing. 'Will you continue using the paper to its fullest potential when all of this is over?'

Yes was on the tip of his tongue, but he pulled it back to reconsider. 'Will it bother you? Will you be able to look the other way, knowing we're bending the rules?'

'That wasn't what I meant. I was thinking more about the risks. Last night you all agreed that what happened to Phillip was an acceptable risk. I'm wondering if you'll think that in the light of day, especially if Phillip has any long-term physical issues . . . or dies.'

Again he opened his mouth to say *yes*, but again he paused to reconsider. 'I don't know about the others. I imagine they'll still be gung-ho. And I'm still fully committed to what we're doing. But I suppose I'm not making that decision for myself anymore. Yesterday morning I only had me to worry about. Now I have you. I don't want you having to sit in a waiting room wondering if I'm going to wake up. So the risk will have to be evaluated by the situation.'

The smile she gave him made his heart stutter in his chest. 'Thank you. I'm careful on the job, but I'll be doubly so from now on as well.' She worked out a few more tangles, then began to braid her hair. 'You know, you never did tell me about the gun you're so attached to.'

The one he'd hidden in her gun safe. He carried one of hers now.

She hesitated when he didn't answer. 'Is it okay to ask?'

'You can ask me anything you want.' He scratched the back of his neck awkwardly. 'I guess it's easier to talk about now. The day after my father's body was found, the doorbell rang. Gayle was with Stone and Mom was sedated again, so I opened the door and there he was – the scary guy. I

429

thought, "Shit, he was lying after all", and started thinking about where I could run.'

'You're kidding? The enforcer came back?'

'He did. He told me not to worry, that he wasn't there to hurt us. Then he said, "It's done." I told him I'd heard. I told him I felt really guilty, that I shouldn't have told him where to find my father, but that I was glad my mother was safe. Then I asked him why he took him away from the cabin to the hotel and he actually looked embarrassed. Told me I didn't need to know stuff like that. That I was too young. Which, you know, kind of blew my mind. I'd helped him kill my father. I was plenty old enough.'

'You did *not* kill your father,' Scarlett said patiently.

'Yeah, well, the man said the same thing. Then he told me that my father used that hotel to meet "lady friends".'

She winced. 'Oh. So because your father had a history of going there to meet hookers, the police would buy the robbery setup.'

'He told me this like he was giving me a gift. Looking back, I realize that the truth about my father's role in our kidnapping would have whipped the media into a frenzy, and that would have hurt Stone, Mom and me, so it was for the best. There was a minor scandal and heads wagged, but it blew over quickly, mostly because my mother's father stepped in and spread the rumor that she'd already filed for divorce before the kidnapping. He made sure that my mother was described as a divorcee in the *Ledger* articles, rather than a widow. *Ledger* articles were quoted in other papers and soon everyone believed my mother had been divorced. The power of the press,' he added.

'So your mother didn't look like the pathetic cheated-on wife.'

'Exactly. Anyway, I told the hit-man that I still felt guilty for telling him where to find my father, and he said that he would have found the cabin in the public record eventually and gone hunting. Then he said, "When I said it was done, I mean it's *all* done. You don't have to worry about either of the other two guys ever coming back." It was like he really cared, which was strange. I guess in his eyes he'd righted a wrong. Then he said that they'd suffered for what they'd done to my brothers.' He exhaled heavily. 'And I was glad.'

'Me too. What about the money?'

'He said he got all but a few thousand that they'd blown on drugs. That his boss had been paid and the slate was clean.'

'But you still haven't told me about that damn gun.'

'I'm getting to it. After he told me about the kidnappers, he gave me a paper bag with that gun in it.'

'Holy shit. He gave you a *gun*? Why?'

'He said he'd found it with my father's things, saw my grandfather's name engraved on the grip and thought I might want to have it. I wanted to know if it was the gun that he'd used to kill them all, but I was afraid to ask. I wanted it to be and I didn't want it to be, all at once.'

'I think I can understand that. The gun symbolized justice, but also your freedom because they couldn't come back to get you. But I didn't see a name on the grip.'

'I scratched it off.' He gave her a sideways glance. 'At the same time that I scratched off the serial number.'

'*You* scratched them off? Why?'

'Because if it had been used to kill someone, I didn't want my grandfather to get dragged through the mud. He'd already been through enough.'

'You're a kind man. In a twisted sort of way. But I still can't believe he gave a gun to a little kid.'

'I know. I remember gazing up at this terrifying-looking man and saying, "Mister, you realize I'm only eight years old. I'm not even allowed to touch guns."'

Scarlett chuckled. 'What did he say?'

'He patted my head and said, "You won't always be eight, kid." Then he wished me luck and left. I shut the door and thought that was the end of it.' He drew a breath and let it out. 'And then I turned around and there was Gayle, stepping out of the shadows.'

'Shit. Busted big time.'

'She was pale and shaking and holding a rifle I didn't even know she owned. She thought the man was there to kidnap me and she was going to blow his head off. But when she saw I wasn't afraid, she listened to the conversation. She asked me why I'd done it. I told her everything, and she sat down on the floor and cried. Big, huge sobs. I hugged her, told her it would be all right. She said she was crying for me because I'd had to make that decision, because I'd felt so alone and had no one to help me. I thought she'd tell my mother, but she never did. She did take the gun away, though, and gave it to my grandfather when we moved to Ohio once Stone was able to travel. Mom sold the apartment in Lexington and never went back. My grandfather put the gun in his safe, but his combination was easy to guess.'

'The date of the liberation of Bataan?'

'You got it. When we moved to Cincinnati, I was still having nightmares. Stone's were worse, so I took the gun and slept with it under my pillow. My grandfather's house – which now belongs to my mother – has eight bedrooms, but Stone and I shared a room until I joined the Army. When he was really little, my having the gun made him feel better, knowing I could protect him. Later, he got his own guns.' He sighed. 'He has more weapons than a lot of small countries. Knows how to use them, too. He's a helluva shot and he has black belts in three different martial arts.'

She was quiet a long moment. 'Did you ever tell him what your father had done?'

'No. He was so fragile for so long that I didn't dare. But I did tell him that the men who hurt him were dead. I cut out the article from the newspaper and showed it to him.' Marcus swallowed hard. 'He slept with that article under his pillow until the paper disintegrated. I went to the library and downloaded a copy and laminated it at school. I don't know what he did with it after that.'

'You protect him.'

'He's my brother. He knows I carry a lot of guilt, but he thinks my hero complex is because I didn't save him from the men that hurt him. And because I couldn't save Matty. I've considered telling him a thousand times, but I always figure, what's the point? He has enough issues to work through.'

She was quiet for so long that he glanced over at her. 'You don't agree?' he asked.

She shrugged. 'He's your brother. But I suspect he may be stronger than you think. Anyway, back to the gun. Didn't your grandfather ever miss it out of his safe?'

Marcus smiled grimly. 'He knew. Who do you think taught me to shoot?'

She shook her head as if to clear it. 'He let an *eight-year-old* have a *loaded gun*? What kind of man was your grandfather?'

'A man who knew what it was like to fight with demons in your dreams. And he didn't *let* me have it. Not at first. He kept putting it back in the safe and I kept taking it out. He kept changing the combination and I kept figuring it out. Finally we came to an understanding that I wouldn't keep it loaded. He took the clip. He didn't know I'd hidden a loaded clip of my own.'

She frowned. 'That gun could have gone off in the middle of the night!'

'No, because I kept the gun under one pillow and the clip under the other. I practiced until I could load it in seconds. But I was careful. I didn't want Stone to get shot by mistake.'

She shook her head again, harder. 'I was thinking about it going off and shooting *you* in the middle of the night.'

He hesitated, then decided to trust her with the rest of it. 'I don't think I would have cared, Scarlett. There were times I almost hoped it would.'

She turned fully in her seat to face him and it took only a glance to see that all the color had drained from her beautiful face. 'What?' she whispered.

'I still wrestle with what I did that day. I know you think I'm absolved because of my age, but three people are dead who never got their day in court.'

'You think they *deserved* their day in court?'

'No, but my mother deserved to look her husband in the face and know that she wasn't to blame for Matty's death because she called in the FBI. I could never tell her.'

'Because if you'd told her, you'd have had to tell her what you did too. Oh, Marcus.'

'I made my bed. I've had to lie in it all these years. It's hard enough now that I'm old enough to process everything that happened, but then I was just a messed-up kid. The year I was nine, I came damn close to not seeing ten.'

'You wanted to kill yourself?' she asked in a trembling voice. 'When you were *nine*?'

He nodded gravely. 'But I never did. Partly because of Gayle. That she knew and still loved me . . . it made a difference. And partly because Stone still needed me. I couldn't leave him alone. But some days I wished for quiet in my mind because all I heard was *killer, killer, killer.*'

'How did you survive the Army? You had to have killed the enemy.'

'More than my share,' he murmured. 'The Army helped Stone conquer some of his fears. It helped me too. Because by the time I joined up, I was old enough to understand what I was doing and it helped me keep the perspective that the people who kidnapped Matty, Stone and me were the enemy. It helped me square it in my own mind. But it still haunts me. All of my kills do. That's one of the reasons we rarely get physical with the people we target at the *Ledger*. I draw the line at gentle coercion. Although recently . . . especially after Mikhail, it's been hard. I've found myself tempted so ma: $_j$ times to just shoot the damn bastards and be done with it. Then they can't hurt their families again. But I've stayed on my side of the line. Just barely.'

She nodded unsteadily. 'Me too. So we'll prop each other up. But you have to promise me if you ever consider . . . ending yourself again—'

'I haven't,' he interrupted, 'not since I was ten. That's when Mom met Jeremy. We were a real family then. Mom was so happy. She got pregnant with Audrey and then we had a baby in the house again. Mom meeting Jeremy O'Bannion was the best thing to ever happen to us – the dad he didn't have to be. He was only twenty-one when he met Mom. Only eleven years older than me. He could have taken the role of big brother, but he seemed to know how much I needed a father. And he's always been that for me.'

Scarlett wiped her eyes. 'I'm glad,' she said simply, then pointed at the road sign. 'This is the exit for Saint Barbara's. Remember, don't call me Detective.'

'I won't.' He didn't want to lie to the Bautistas, but he didn't want to scare them away either.

She smoothed her dress and checked the visor mirror. 'I look like I've been crying, but it makes me look like less of a cop, so the puffy eyes are okay.'

'You look beautiful.'

'Thank you. So do you. Do you need anything before we talk to Mila and Erica?'

He squeezed her hand. 'Just be with me.'

'Let anyone try to pry me away.'

Twenty-nine

Georgetown, Kentucky
Wednesday 5 August, 8.40 A.M.

Scarlett and Marcus met Trace in the vestibule of Saint Barbara's. Scarlett had been nervous about seeing her uncle again, but Trace obliterated any nerves with a huge bear hug. She held on a few more seconds than she needed to, because for that moment in time he'd made her feel like a child again. Like the past ten years of her life hadn't happened.

Like she wasn't standing in a church of her own free will.

He set her down and tipped her face up, his smile changing to a frown. 'You've been crying.' He turned his frown on Marcus. 'What did you do to her?'

'He's done nothing,' Scarlett said firmly. 'We've been talking and I've been emotional.' She slid her arm around her uncle's waist. 'Uncle Trace, this is Marcus O'Bannion. He tried to help Tala, was with her when she died. Marcus, Father Trace.'

Marcus stuck out his hand. 'Father,' he said politely. 'You're the first member of Scarlett's family that I've had the privilege to meet.'

Trace looked down at Scarlett, his brows lifted. 'Oh, he's good.'

She laughed. 'I know.'

Her uncle shook Marcus's hand. 'They're waiting for you in the choir room. Scarlett, I've told them only that you're my niece.' He hugged her to him again. 'You look very non-coppish. I'll let you decide when to tell them who you are.'

'Are they okay?' Marcus asked. 'Physically?'

'Their feet are pretty cut up. They walked for miles without shoes. I'm so thankful they were picked up by a good person. The trucker recognized that they were afraid and he didn't ask many questions. One of the women in the church washed their feet and bandaged them, but you'll want to have them seen by a doctor. You won't have any trouble communicating from a language standpoint. Their English is impeccable. But they

435

didn't say much. I showed them the pictures of Mr Bautista and young John Paul, but other than crying and giving prayers of thanks that they were safe, they didn't say anything more. They're still very afraid.'

He led them into the church and Scarlett suddenly found it very hard to breathe. She hadn't been lying to Trace. After all the talking she and Marcus had done, her emotions were like a seething cauldron in her gut. Adding to that the memories of Michelle that had been dredged up when she'd found Tala dead in the alley . . .

She swallowed back the lump in her throat and focused on putting one foot in front of the other. But then Marcus took her hand and held it securely in his. Breathing in the scent of his aftershave, she let it calm her.

'You okay?' he whispered.

She tightened her hold. 'Yes.'

They followed her uncle into the choir room and both she and Marcus went abruptly still. Two petite women sat on metal folding chairs, holding hands even more tightly than Scarlett held Marcus's. The older woman was visibly trembling, her eyes bright with tears. The younger was barely sixteen, according to the copies of the visas Immigration had provided, but she looked so much older. Her expression was remote, her dark eyes cold and her shoulders bowed.

'She looks just like Tala,' Marcus murmured, sounding spooked. He released Scarlett's hand and stepped forward, going down on one knee in front of the women so that they could look him in the eye. 'I'm Marcus,' he said quietly. 'And I'm so sorry for your loss.'

Mila Bautista's body began to shake with suppressed sobs, which broke free when Marcus put his arms around them both. Tala's mother leaned into his shoulder and cried, her heart broken.

Beside Scarlett, Trace sighed softly. 'He's for real?'

Scarlett had to blink away her own tears, Mila's grief and Marcus's compassion reaching right into her chest and squeezing her heart until it felt bloodless. She pressed the heel of her hand to her sternum to relieve the ache. 'Yeah. He's very real.'

'I read online that he met Tala Bautista in an alley and tried to help her. Is he in the habit of helping strange young women in the middle of the night?'

She glanced up at Trace who was frowning worriedly. 'Yes, actually, but not like you're thinking.' She quietly explained the situation, adding that Marcus had been shot at a second time and that his friend and the doorman had been shot last night. 'But I still have to wonder who was the target in that alley – Tala or Marcus.'

'It was Tala.' Erica Bautista had pulled out of Marcus's embrace, stroking her mother's hair as Mila continued to cry against Marcus's shoulder. The girl's expression was hard and angry, and Scarlett certainly couldn't blame her for that.

Scarlett pulled another folding chair over so that she could sit facing Mila. 'Why are you so sure?' she asked softly.

'Who are you?' the girl asked, her eyes narrowing shrewdly.

'My name is Scarlett. Father Trace is my uncle. Marcus is my boyfriend and I'm afraid for him, for his safety, so I came along. We want to help you, but nobody really understands what's happening here.'

Erica continued to study her. 'You're with the police,' she said flatly.

Scarlett blinked, startled. Mila pushed Marcus away, lurching to her feet in panic. Scarlett knew that if she stood up she'd tower over the woman, so she remained seated. 'I'm not Immigration. I'm not calling them. I'm here as my uncle's niece. I'm not going to turn you in to anyone. You have my word.'

Mila looked down at Marcus, seeking confirmation, and he nodded. 'She isn't lying,' he said. 'She really is Father Trace's niece and she really is my girlfriend. And she really wants to help you. I called her two nights ago when I knew I was meeting Tala. I wanted a woman there that I could trust.'

'You trust her?' Mila asked, trembling so hard that Scarlett thought she'd fall down.

'With my life,' Marcus said simply, and Mila slowly sat back down.

Scarlett breathed a silent sigh of relief. 'How did you know?'

Erica shrugged. 'He is Father Trace Bishop. You are Scarlett. The article in the newspaper said that Detective Scarlett Bishop was first on the scene.'

Scarlett winced. 'Oh. I didn't mean to deceive you. Well, yes, I did, but only so I wouldn't scare you. I meant what I said. I'm not going to turn you in.'

'Your partner is with the FBI,' Erica said coldly.

Scarlett mentally reviewed the *Ledger* article in her mind, then turned to Marcus, puzzled. 'You didn't mention Deacon in that article, did you?'

Erica's eyes rolled. 'I Googled you, Detective. I used the church's computer. I used to use computers all the time before we came here. It's not that hard. Even for someone like me.'

'Someone like you?' Scarlett said gently. 'You mean a victim of a despicable crime perpetrated by evil people who deserve to be locked up for the rest of their lives?'

Erica looked taken aback. 'No. I meant . . .'

'I know what you meant,' Scarlett said. 'I also know your father was a teacher and your mother a nurse. I know you are educated and smart. I just don't like being tripped up so easily.' She smiled at Erica and watched some of the girl's tension drain away. 'Your sister was incredibly brave and sacrificed everything to try to get her family to safety. I won't let her sacrifice be in vain.'

Erica's lips quivered at the mention of her sister, and both she and her mother began to cry. 'We told her not to go,' Erica sobbed. 'We told her it was too dangerous.'

'She was desperate,' Mila added, wiping her eyes. 'Because of Malaya . . . Tala was determined that her baby wouldn't be raised in that house. So she took the chance.' Her fists clenched. 'I want to kill that man for what he did.'

Marcus covered Mila's fists with his hands, a comforting gesture. 'Chip Anders?'

Fire flashed in the eyes of both women. 'Yes,' Mila hissed. 'And his wife and that daughter they spawned.'

'He's missing,' Scarlett said. 'It appears he and his family were taken away by force. Do you know by whom?'

Mila and Erica looked at each other, satisfaction mixing in with their fury and grief. 'Not by name,' Mila said. 'But he was very scared yesterday when he realized Tala was missing.'

'When did he find out?' Scarlett asked.

Mila opened her mouth to speak, but no words came out. Erica leaned her head on her mother's shoulder and answered for her. 'When the tamper alarm went off,' the young woman said. 'Our trackers were wired into the house alarm. Mama and I weren't allowed to leave.'

'But Tala was,' Marcus said. 'Her job was to walk the dog.'

Mila's lips thinned and she looked away. 'No. Walking the dog was Stephanie's job.'

'The Anderses' daughter,' Scarlett said. 'She's home from college.'

'She's a bitch,' Erica snarled.

Mila looked startled. 'Erica! We are in a church.'

Erica didn't look like she cared. 'She is, Mama. You call her a spawn, I'll call her . . . what I called her.' She looked Scarlett in the eye. 'I hope whoever took her makes her suffer like she made Tala suffer. I hate her.' Her fury disintegrated into a choked sob. 'She killed my sister. Her or that boyfriend of hers.'

Scarlett's ears perked up. 'Boyfriend? We don't know about a boyfriend.'

'Drake Connor,' Erica spat.

Scarlett took the girl's hand long enough to give it a brief, encouraging squeeze. She could barely contain her excitement at this new information,

438

which she sensed might be the link they were looking for. 'What did he do?'

Erica dropped her gaze to her lap, but not before Scarlett saw the shame in the girl's eyes. 'Whatever he wanted,' she said, her tone gone dead.

Scarlett glanced at Marcus. 'Do you want Father Trace and Marcus to leave?' she asked quietly, and Erica nodded.

'We'll be outside,' Marcus said, giving Scarlett's shoulder a stroke as he walked away.

'We're alone,' Scarlett said. 'You can tell me anything you want without shame.'

'Everyone will know,' Erica whispered miserably. 'They will know anyway because why else would *he* buy three women?'

'You're talking about Anders now. He bought you. Not Drake, right?'

Erica scoffed. 'Drake was poor. He didn't have any money. Stephanie dated him just to make her father mad. Her father bought us, all of us. He sent my father and brother away to work in his factory and he made my mother take care of his mother.'

'You mean his aunt?'

'Her too, but when we first came, Mama had to take care of his mother. She was bedridden.' Erica faltered. 'She wasn't mean like him. She wanted to tell someone that we were being forced to work for no money, that he was . . . using us. But then . . . she killed her. Mr Anders's wife put a pillow over her face and suffocated her.'

'Marlene Anders,' Scarlett said, and Erica nodded. 'So Chip's mother was killed by his wife?'

'Because she sympathized with us,' Mila whispered. 'Marlene liked nice things. Liked having servants. She just didn't want to pay for them. She liked having control.'

'What about Aunt Tabby?' Scarlett asked.

Mila's eyes filled anew. 'Is she alive? All Father Trace knew was that she was in the hospital. What happened to her?'

'She's unconscious, but still alive,' Scarlett said. 'I called to check on her on my way down here. She's holding on. She was beaten severely by Chip.'

Both women gasped. 'We left her alone there,' Mila whispered, guilt ravaging her face. 'That beast beat her because she cut our trackers and let us go.'

It was true, and Scarlett wasn't going to insult them by denying it. 'Marcus found her under a bed. She told us about you, said we had to find you and keep you safe.'

Mila bowed her head. 'She is a good woman. We didn't want to leave her there, but she made us. We've prayed for her all night.'

Good luck with that, Scarlett thought, startled to realize that there was more hope than sarcasm in her mental voice. 'Can we get back to Drake?' she asked gently, and watched Erica's shoulders tense and her gaze drop back to her lap. 'He could be important to our investigation. You said he was Stephanie's boyfriend. Did he live close by?'

Erica shrugged. 'Close enough to come by several times a week.'

'You said he did anything he wanted.' She gently took Erica's hand. 'Did he rape you,?'

A very small nod. 'Mostly Tala, but sometimes me when Tala was . . .' She covered her face with her hands. Scarlett very gently tugged her wrists, going down on her knees in front of Erica's chair so that she could see the young woman's face. 'You have nothing to be ashamed of,' she whispered urgently. 'I know this is hard for you.'

'How could you know?' Erica flung back bitterly. 'Have you been raped?'

'No. But I've been a police officer for a long time and I've worked with too many women who have been raped. It's hard for them to tell me what happened, but those that have and that can see their rapists come to justice . . . I think it helps them heal.'

'It's an American court,' Erica said, her bitterness unabated. 'They won't listen to me.'

'I'm an American police officer, and I'm listening to you,' Scarlett said. 'I will do everything in my power to find him and bring him to justice. That's all I can promise. But I need your help. I need to know everything about Drake that you can tell me so that I can find him. I also want to know because someone is trying to hurt Marcus. If Drake knows anything about Tala's murder, he could be the one trying to kill Marcus.'

'Because Marcus is still alive,' Erica said, back to that flat, dead voice. 'Because he had on a Kevlar vest. Why did he? Did he know Tala would be killed?'

'Erica!' Mila exclaimed.

'It's all right,' Scarlett said, knowing that part of Erica's question was simply an attempt to change the subject away from her assault. 'Marcus helps a lot of people who are in abusive relationships. He helps them get out. He thought Tala was being abused and wanted to help her too. He's been shot before, so he wears the vest.'

Erica's nod was grudging. 'Okay.' Her head still down, she looked up from beneath her eyelashes to meet Scarlett's eyes. 'Drake forced Tala to have sex with him every time he could. Every time Mr Anders wasn't home and sometimes when he was. But when she was having her . . . monthly . . .'

'Her period,' Scarlett supplied, and Erica nodded again, miserably, but said nothing. 'Drake would force you when Tala had her period?'

Tears began to roll down Erica's face. A glance up at Mila showed she'd closed her eyes, her heartache so heavy that Scarlett could feel it too. 'Can you tell me what Drake looks like?'

'Tall,' Erica whispered. 'He was six feet. Big shoulders. Strong. Stronger than me. Blond hair, brown eyes.' Her lips curved grimly. 'A broken tooth.'

'Who broke it?'

'Tala. The first time he forced her.'

'Good for Tala.'

Erica's shoulders moved restlessly. 'Not really, because Drake beat her and Stephanie got mad at him. Said her father would see Tala's bruises and be angry. That Tala was his.'

Scarlett squeezed Erica's hands. 'You're doing great, honey. Can you tell me which tooth Tala broke?'

'His front tooth on the bottom.' She tugged one of her hands loose to point to her own mouth. 'This one.'

'Very good. Did you notice any scars or tattoos?'

'One tattoo on his left upper arm.' Erica slipped her hand back into Scarlett's. 'A snake with its mouth open.' She shivered. 'It scared me.'

'It would scare me too,' Scarlett said ruefully. 'Was he dark-skinned, light-skinned?'

'White. But he's tanned now because it's the summer. For a while he worked for the landscapers that cut the grass at the house.'

'That's very helpful. Do you know the name of the landscaping company?'

'Belle's Bluebells,' Mila said stiffly. 'I remember the truck. It's owned by Drake's sister. He quit in June when Stephanie came home from college. She was supplying him with more money than he could make cutting grass.'

'All right, give me a second.' Scarlett took out her phone and typed a text to Deacon.

Locate Drake Connor, sister owns Belle's Bluebells Landscaping. DC is bf of Stephanie Anders. Maybe Tala's killer.

She showed the text to the two women. 'I'm sending this to my partner, Special Agent Deacon Novak. I want you to see that I didn't mention your names, but we need to find Drake.'

'Your partner knows you're here talking to us?' Erica said suspiciously.

'He doesn't know where "here" is.' Scarlett hit SEND. She almost told them about Kate Coppola and the FBI investigation into human trafficking, but she decided to wait. Her instincts told her that the two women were far from being convinced of their safety.

Scarlett moved from the floor back to her seat. 'Anything more you need to tell me about Drake or Stephanie?'

Mila's jaw tightened. 'Stephanie was abusing my Tala as well. Sexually.'

Erica's head whipped around to stare at her mother in new horror. 'Mama, *no*.'

'Yes, Erica,' Mila said heavily. 'They also made her buy their drugs.'

'Because Stephanie got in trouble once before for buying drugs at college,' Scarlett said, and Mila blinked at her in surprise.

'This you knew?'

'I guessed.' She didn't want to tell Mila that Tala had been found with drugs in the pocket of her jeans. 'Your daughter was killed in an area known for its drug dealers. I couldn't figure out why she was there or how she got there until I learned of Stephanie's arrest record. You said that it was Stephanie's job to walk the dog. Why was Tala doing it? And how? If your and Erica's trackers were programmed to alarm if you left the house, why wasn't Tala's?'

'Drake was lazy, but good with computers. He and Stephanie wanted to take Tala with them to buy the drugs, so he got into Mr Anders's computer and figured out how to change the settings. I don't know how. Sometimes Stephanie wanted to have Drake to herself, so she told Tala to walk the dog, and that she'd be following her on the computer. Tala didn't know if she would be, but she was afraid not to believe her.'

'I understand. Especially since they could overhear your conversations with the trackers.'

Mila looked ashamed. 'No privacy, even when they let me see my husband for the last time. We knew they were listening, laughing. Like we were animals in a zoo.'

Scarlett sighed, emotionally drained, and she'd only borne witness to their ordeal. They'd lived it. 'When we find the Anderses, they will be punished. What about the people that brought you into this country?'

Mila shook her head. 'My husband managed all the details. He was tricked.'

'He's being taken care of by the FBI now. They're making sure he has nutrition and medical attention – both Mr Bautista and John Paul.'

Mila went very, very still. 'Then it's true?' she asked, the words no louder than a breath. 'They really are alive?'

Scarlett felt like she'd taken a physical blow. The woman had been sitting there talking to her while still wondering if her husband and son were alive or dead. 'Yes, they're both alive. Father Trace told you this, didn't he? Did you think he was lying?'

New tears rolled down Mila's face as she embraced Erica, who was also crying. 'No,' Mila sobbed, 'but he had pictures that were old, taken before we came here. I thought he might be wrong.'

'Or that the police were lying to him,' Erica added through her tears. 'The Anderses told us that Papa and John Paul were dead.'

But they believe me. The responsibility was immense. 'They are alive. I promise. If you'll allow it, I'll ask my partner to get recent photos. He may have to ask another agent in the FBI. They may guess that you've been found.'

Mila and Erica looked at each other, then both slowly nodded. 'Yes,' Mila said hoarsely. 'I want to see them.'

Scarlett shot the text to Deacon and put her phone down. 'Mila, let's talk bluntly. Pictures will not be enough. You want to see your husband and son in person, don't you? You want your granddaughter back, yes?'

Mila nodded, but said nothing.

Erica started to rise from her chair. 'You promised not to turn us in.'

'And I won't. But this situation may not be as bleak as you believe. You have options. Please, hear me out.'

Erica sat back down. 'What options?' she asked with cold suspicion.

'Do you remember the lady that Tabby called to take Malaya? Her name is Annabelle Church.' They both nodded. 'She took very good care of Malaya, bought her formula and diapers, and when the time came for her to turn Malaya over to Children's Services, she brought her lawyer along so that Malaya's rights were protected.'

'But Malaya is just a baby,' Mila whispered, stunned.

'She's a US citizen,' Scarlett said. 'That fact alone doesn't help you get a green card or citizenship yourselves,' she added when hope filled their eyes, 'but Annabelle's lawyer told us that if we found you, he would make sure an immigration lawyer took your case. For free.'

'Why?' Erica asked, still suspicious.

'First, Annabelle's lawyer is also her grandson. They're nice people. Annabelle went straight to the hospital after meeting with us and she's been at Tabby's bedside ever since. Her grandson stayed with her through the night. Annabelle's grandson doesn't need or want anything from you. His grandfather on his father's side was also an immigrant, so he just wants to help. That means you have legal help from an expert who knows immigration law. I'm not an expert myself, but I do know that because you've been victims of human trafficking, you are eligible to apply for new visas. This one is called a "U visa". It allows you to stay in the country if you're helping law enforcement with an investigation. Mr Bautista will be given the same offer.'

'That's not a green card,' Erica said with a frown. 'Is it?'

'No, but it can lead to one. You'd need an employer to sponsor you. Marcus can help with that. But to get the U visa, you'll need to cooperate with the FBI.'

'Will we go to jail?'

'No. You've done nothing wrong.' Scarlett leaned forward a fraction. 'You are victims of a terrible crime. No one will blame you. Do you understand this?'

Erica lifted her chin, but her lips quivered. 'Americans hate illegal aliens.'

'Not true,' Scarlett said. 'Some do, I'll allow you, but you'll find most Americans will feel compassion for you and anger at the people who tricked you into coming here under false pretenses. The community will want to help. That's not to say everyone will be kind or nice. Illegal immigration is a complicated problem. But you didn't sneak in. You had legal visas when you arrived. I've seen the records.'

'They took them from us,' Mila said in a trembling voice. 'Which doesn't matter now. The visas expired two years ago.'

'You'll get new ones,' Scarlett said with a smile. 'But you'll have to trust me.'

Mila drew a deep breath. 'Where will we have to go?'

'You can come back with us. My partner and some of his fellow FBI agents want to talk to you about the people who brought you here. They'll need your help to catch them.'

Mila twisted her hands together. 'Will you . . . stay with us?'

Scarlett's heart broke and she had to clear her throat. 'As long as I can. Marcus will too. And Father Trace.' She took Mila's hands in hers. 'You have friends here. You're safe.'

'Where will we live?' Erica asked, trying hard to make her question sound forceful, but underneath Scarlett heard a scared little girl.

'We'll find you a place. It might be a safe house at first, just until we figure out who's behind all this. That might mean you'll have a police guard. That doesn't mean you're in jail. It just means we don't want anyone to hurt you.'

'For how long?' Erica persisted.

Scarlett sighed. 'I wish I had an answer for you, Erica. But let me tell you this – Marcus is very, very important to me, and right now his life is in danger every time he walks around in public. Even if I didn't care about you and your family – and I do care – I'd be trying to solve this as fast as possible to keep Marcus safe. That's all I can promise, except that I am *very* good at my job, and so is my partner, Agent Novak.'

Mila was quiet for a long moment while Scarlett held her breath. Then Mila nodded and Scarlett exhaled in relief. 'We'll come with you,' Mila said. 'But no handcuffs.'

Once more Scarlett's heart broke. 'Of course no handcuffs,' she promised gruffly. 'You have my word. I'm going to ask Marcus to come back into the room now and we'll take you to Cincinnati.'

'That's what the other guys said,' Erica muttered as Scarlett turned to go.

Her hand on the doorknob, Scarlett turned back to face the girl. 'Which other guys? Anders and his wife?'

Mila shook her head. 'No. The man and woman who met us at the airport and took us to the Anderses. They said they were married and that they ran the business where we'd be working. We believed them.'

A male/female 'married' pair to meet a family. It made good sense if you were the traffickers. A married couple would inspire confidence, encourage the victims to let their guard down. 'Can you describe them?'

'The man was very big,' Mila said. 'And dark-skinned. Maybe forty years old or a little older. The woman was smaller than the man, but bigger than any of us, including my husband. She had blond hair and was much younger than the man. They pretended to be nice and loving for the first day, but then they stopped for the night and . . .'

'Out came the handcuffs,' Erica said flatly. 'The man was big and strong and fast. Trained in karate, I think. He put Tala in a stranglehold when she tried to get away with me and John Paul. My father tried to fight, but the man switched arms and knocked him unconscious with one punch. And then, um . . .' She looked away. 'He raped Tala. That was our first clue that we were in trouble,' she finished bitterly.

Scarlett released the doorknob without opening the door, slowly walked back to Mila and Erica and knelt in front of the girl. 'Did he rape you too, Erica?'

A hard swallow and a nod.

Scarlett closed her eyes and sighed. 'I'm so sorry.' Then her eyes popped open on a frown as Erica's words sank in. *Big, dark-skinned, fast, with an arm-switching maneuver?* It was a long shot, but worth a try. She took out her phone, pulled up the video of Phillip's attacker that she'd shown Marcus the night before and chose a segment that showcased the man's walk and his eyes through the holes in the ski mask.

Without a word she showed it to the two women and watched them begin to shake.

'That looks like him, like his walk,' Mila whispered. 'I can never forget it. He is in my nightmares all the time.'

'And his eyes,' Erica said flatly. 'He had cold, dead eyes.'

Mila put her arm around Erica. 'It could be him. He's the right size.' Mila's jaw tightened, her shoulders squaring. 'She called him Demetrius. He called her Alice. I don't know if those were their real names or not. Who is the young man with him?'

'Marcus's friend Phillip. He was shot a few minutes later, as was another man.'

Mila's eyes grew wide. 'Did he kill my Tala too?'

'I don't know.' *Tala knew her attacker.* She would have known a man who'd raped her, but apparently both this man, whose name was possibly Demetrius, and Drake Connor had assaulted her. Scarlett should have been relieved that she was finally getting some new pieces to the puzzle, but she wasn't. Her gut told her that something was still missing, and she'd learned to listen to her gut. 'Let's get back to the city so that you can give an artist a description of this Demetrius's face. While we drive, I'll work on getting you reunited with your husband and son.'

Cincinnati, Ohio
Wednesday 5 August, 11.15 A.M.

Deacon Novak was waiting when Marcus and Scarlett arrived at the Netherland Plaza with Mila and Erica. Scarlett was in full cop mode, her eyes darting everywhere, her body positioned to protect the two women who'd been through so much.

Marcus was also keenly aware that Scarlett was positioning herself to protect him, especially when Deacon joined them in the hotel's lobby. The two partners created a wall separating Marcus and the women from anyone who might want to hurt them. He wanted to grab Scarlett by the shoulders and yank her behind him, but he didn't. She was who she was, which was a cop. To deny her the ability to protect him would hurt her deeply, and Marcus couldn't even consider it. Still, he kept his hand on the grip of the gun she'd loaned him out of her own collection, since his old Glock was locked up in her gun safe.

Deacon towered over the two women just like Marcus did, but – just like Marcus had – the Fed hunched his shoulders so that he didn't seem too intimidating. He also wore his trademark wraparound shades inside the hotel so that he didn't startle the women with his odd eyes.

'Mila, Erica,' Scarlett said, 'this is Special Agent Novak, my partner.'

'Mrs Bautista,' Deacon said to Mila, nodding at her. To the scowling Erica he gave an encouraging smile.

Erica still hadn't accepted that she was safe, and Marcus understood that. He knew it would be a long, long time before Erica truly felt safe again.

'And, Miss Bautista,' Deacon said. 'We're very glad we found you. Please come this way.' He ushered them all into the elevator, slid a hotel keycard through the reader, then hit the button for the penthouse, standing in front of the doors until they closed. Only then did he and Scarlett relax. Deacon looked at Scarlett over the petite women's heads. 'Everything is ready. Just as you specified.'

'My dad's here?' Erica asked in a quavering voice. 'And John Paul?'

'Yes,' Deacon said. 'And they're excited to see you. Your dad's a bit thin, just to prepare you.'

Mr Bautista wasn't thin, Marcus thought, having seen the photos Deacon had sent for Scarlett to show the two women. He was emaciated. John Paul appeared well fed, so Marcus assumed the father had been giving his son part of his own food rations.

Tears were running down Mila's face yet again. Marcus wondered that the lady hadn't dehydrated herself with all the tears she'd shed that day. But these tears were happy ones, or at least bittersweet. To be reunited with her husband and son, but to lose her daughter . . .

Marcus cleared his throat. 'Is the attorney here?'

Deacon nodded. 'Both of them are – Gabriel Benitez, Mrs Church's grandson, and Peter Zurich, the immigration attorney.'

'And who's here from the FBI and CPD?' Marcus asked.

'Special Agent Kate Coppola and her partner, Special Agent Luther Troy – they're leading the human trafficking investigation for this region,' Deacon said. 'Isenberg's here too.'

Scarlett winced. 'How is she?'

Deacon's white brows lifted. 'Not as bad as she could be. Not happy that you made so many demands or that you missed your command performance in her office, but she'll survive.'

Scarlett's 'demands' had been designed to make the Bautista family's life simpler. She wanted them to have their reunion in privacy, in a hotel and not the police station. Marcus had been able to help with that, having already reserved the penthouse suite. The hotel had excellent security, and CPD had assigned a uniformed officer to guard the Bautistas' room.

She'd asked that all family interviews be conducted here at the hotel, including the one with the CPD sketch artist. She'd also made it clear that the Bautistas had legal representation, so that no one tried to intimidate them by threatening deportation.

'What command performance?' Erica asked, still suspicious of their motives.

'It's nothing for you to worry about,' Scarlett said with a smile. 'I was supposed to go to my boss's office for a lecture, but I came down to meet you two instead.'

'Will Father Trace be here?' Mila asked.

'He arrived about ten minutes ago,' Deacon told her. Marcus and Scarlett had taken longer to arrive because Scarlett had insisted on driving a circuitous route through the city to make sure they hadn't been followed.

'We also have a counselor available,' Scarlett told Mila as the elevator doors opened. 'Kids and teens are her specialty, but she can help you and your husband as well. She's a friend of mine. She's expecting your call, whenever you'd like to contact her.'

Mila drew in a breath as she stepped out of the elevator. 'Thank you, Detective. For all your help.' She pressed a hand to her heart. 'I'm so nervous.'

'Don't worry, Mama,' Erica said, taking her mother's hand. 'It'll be all right.' Mother and daughter held hands tightly as they walked down the long hall and entered the room.

The emaciated Mr Bautista stood awkwardly, staring at the women as if looking at ghosts. Then John Paul threw himself into his mother's arms, sobbing loudly. A second later, the family was huddled together, crying and rocking each other. Mr Bautista touched his wife's face with a careful reverence, as if not convinced she was real.

Leaving the attorneys in the room with the Bautistas, Marcus followed Scarlett and Deacon into the suite's adjoining room to give the family privacy. He had to wipe his eyes and knew he wasn't the only one. Father Trace and Isenberg were already sitting in the room with two people in black suits – a redhead and a man who was slightly balding.

The lieutenant gave Marcus a brief look before turning her attention to Scarlett. 'We still have to talk about your personal priorities,' she said. 'But this was good work, Scarlett.'

Scarlett shrugged. 'Uncle Trace found them.'

'And you convinced the mother and daughter to trust us.' Isenberg motioned for them to sit at the table. 'We have some debriefing to do.'

'Me too?' Marcus asked Isenburg, letting a little sarcasm into his voice. She scowled.

She scowled. 'Yeah. You didn't print anything I asked you not to, so I'll trust you one more day.'

'Thank you,' he said with exaggerated politeness and took the seat next to Scarlett, who shot him a rueful look before introducing the redhead as Kate Coppola and the balding man as Luther Troy. Scarlett had already told him that Kate had worked with Deacon back in Baltimore and that Deacon trusted her with his life. That was enough for Marcus, because Scarlett trusted Deacon with her life.

Scarlett's uncle excused himself. 'I think I'll see if the Bautistas need me. Once the shock of the reunion passes, they'll be grieving the loss of Tala.' He squeezed Scarlett's shoulder as he passed her chair. 'I heard some of what you said to Mila and Erica back at Saint Barbara's,' he murmured. 'I'm proud of the way you dealt with them.'

He left the room, leaving Scarlett blushing. 'What's new?' she asked Isenberg, her voice a little gruff.

Marcus thought her gruffness was very sweet, and wisely didn't tell her so.

'Number one,' Isenberg said, 'ballistics on the bullet taken out of Phillip Cauldwell shows it was *not* fired from the same gun that killed Tala Bautista.'

'But . . .' Marcus frowned. 'Shit. We thought the shooter at my apartment building yesterday might have been the one who shot Agent Spangler and Tala too. Are we back to square one?'

'Not square one,' Deacon said, 'because the gun used to kill Tala was found – in the possession of Drake Connor.'

Marcus had been listening at the door at Saint Barbara's, so he knew everything the women had shared. He narrowed his eyes at this piece of news. 'So it was Stephanie Anders's boyfriend who killed Tala.'

Deacon nodded. 'So it appears. As soon as you texted me his name, Scarlett, I put out a BOLO and then went to check out his sister at her house. She's not there, but there are signs of a major struggle. There was blood on the kitchen floor and smeared on one of the door frames like she grabbed it when she was being removed. She reported her car stolen yesterday morning. She suspected her brother had taken it. He's been in trouble a few times.'

'He'll be in more trouble when we get our hands on him,' Scarlett

449

said flatly. 'He raped both Tala and her sister and murdered Tala. Now it sounds like he's attacked his own sister. Where is he now?'

Deacon was shaking his head. 'He didn't attack his sister. She was on the phone with her credit card company at three o'clock yesterday afternoon. Drake was nearing Detroit by then.'

'The little prick was headed for Canada,' Marcus said grimly.

'Where is he now?' Scarlett repeated impatiently.

'In a hospital in Detroit,' Deacon said, 'handcuffed to the bed. His name popped up as soon as I ran the BOLO. He held up a gas station, shot the clerk and another customer, then stole the customer's SUV. The customer is dead and the clerk's in critical condition. The clerk's wife, who was doing inventory in the back room, chased after him with a shotgun. Unfortunately for Drake, the wife was a very good shot and she took out his back windshield and a tire as he was driving out of the parking lot. He got out of the SUV and tried to run, so she shot him in the leg and ran back to see to her husband. Fortunately for us, she didn't hit anything vital and left Drake alive for us.'

'Will Detroit PD give him up to us?' Scarlett asked.

'Yes,' Agent Troy said. 'They won't like it, but they won't have a choice. We're charging Drake with conspiracy to human trafficking. Even though he didn't personally buy Tala, he knew her status in the Anders home and took part in it for his own gain. Agents in Detroit are taking custody as we speak. We'll transport him down here as soon as he's able to be moved. In the meantime, we'll get his statement on yesterday's shooting in the alley.'

'I called Detroit PD as soon as Drake's name popped up on the BOLO,' Deacon said. 'They confirmed he'd been found in possession of a Ruger loaded with Black Talons, the same bullet we pulled out of Tala and Phillip. The detective on the case up there expedited the ballistics testing on the Ruger. I got the report as I was leaving the crime scene at Drake's sister's house. Drake's Ruger – which was registered to Chip Anders, by the way – was the same gun that shot Tala and you, Marcus, but not the gun that shot Phillip.'

Scarlett's brow was furrowed in a deep frown. 'So Marcus *wasn't* the target in the alley. Drake must have been gunning after Tala for meeting with Marcus. But that means we still don't know who has been targeting Marcus. If Drake hadn't run, we could say that he realized that Marcus wasn't dead and wanted to finish the job to keep him quiet. But Drake was halfway to Detroit by the time the sniper shot at Marcus and killed Agent Spangler behind the Anders house. And we already know that Drake didn't shoot Phillip and the security guard in Marcus's building because we have the lobby video and Phillip's description.'

'But Drake *is* connected to the guy who invaded my apartment building last night,' Marcus said quietly. 'By Tala.'

Isenberg shook her head. 'You're assuming the man who shot Phillip Cauldwell and the security guard was the same man who transported the Bautistas to Ohio. You can't assume that yet. Not until we have a more positive ID.'

Marcus felt his jaw go taut. 'Mila and Erica identified last night's shooter from the security video.'

Isenberg's expression softened a hair. 'He wore a ski mask, Marcus, and they haven't seen him in three years. Yes, he has the same body type and the same gait. Yes, he does a similar hand-switch maneuver. It very well could be the same man that brought them here, but right now it's supposition. We have to keep our minds open for now.'

Marcus knew she had a valid point, but couldn't bring himself to admit it. Mila and Erica had sounded so certain and he so wanted to believe it was true. That he would track down the bastard who'd put Phillip in ICU was a given in his mind. He desperately wanted to give the Bautistas their justice as well.

'She's right, dammit,' Scarlett muttered under her breath, making Isenberg's lips twitch.

'That happens occasionally,' the lieutenant said dryly.

Scarlett's lips curved. 'Yes, ma'am. It does.' She squared her shoulders. 'The apartment shooter went to a lot of trouble to make it look like Tala's killer was simply finishing the job. He used the same model gun and made sure the building's security camera saw it. He used the same kind of bullets, which he tried not to leave behind, so we wouldn't be able to do ballistics.'

'But how does he connect to me?' Marcus murmured.

'That's the million-dollar question.' Scarlett glanced up at him, understanding in her eyes. 'Hopefully the Bautistas will give us a sketch of his face. Maybe you'll recognize him.'

Agent Coppola cleared her throat. 'There is the possibility that the two aren't connected at all, that someone else wants you dead and is using Tala's murder as a cover.'

'So we're back to the list,' Scarlett murmured. 'Threats made against Marcus's life because of the exposés he's run in the *Ledger*,' she explained to Agents Troy and Coppola, who looked confused. She turned to Isenberg. 'Where are we on the names I sent you last night?'

'My clerk's got last-known addresses for all of them. A few are in jail for other offenses.' Isenberg looked at Marcus shrewdly. 'But you knew that already, didn't you?'

'I knew it was a possibility,' he said honestly. 'I know a few others were in jail and got out and probably should be back in jail.' That he knew from Stone after his brother had checked all the names on the list for status and recent activity. 'Many of those people are child molesters and domestic abusers. A newspaper article and a short stint behind bars aren't going to stop them.'

'No, it won't,' Isenberg said, then turned to Deacon. 'Any update on that ankle tracker?'

'Yes,' Deacon said. 'It got easier after we picked up the other two trackers that Mila and Erica left behind. The serial number on Tala's tracker was recorded as having been destroyed by the quality assurance testers at the plant that makes them,' he explained to Marcus and Agent Troy. 'The federal corrections system buys from that factory and, as the customer, it's authorized to do unannounced quality evaluation. The team from corrections seized copies of the factory's production records for the days on which the three trackers were produced and tested.'

'Sneaky,' Coppola praised.

'Creative,' Deacon corrected.

Coppola grinned. 'Potato, po-tah-to. Glad to see that you haven't lost your touch, Novak.'

Deacon waggled his white brows. 'Thank you. Anyway, they were able to narrow down the list of employees to just two men who worked all three shifts in which the three trackers were tested. They were picked up this morning when they showed up at work and are being transported to Cincinnati for questioning as we speak. One of the men is responsible for the "destructive testing",' he quirked the air with finger quotes, 'of four times as many devices as the other man. I'll pull backgrounds on both of them, but I think we should be looking hardest at the guy with the most devices. He may have been selling to Anders, or, if we're very lucky, he might have been selling to the actual traffickers who brought the victims into the country.'

'Were all the people rescued from Anders's factories wearing trackers?' Marcus asked.

'Not all,' Coppola said. 'Mostly the people who had technical skills, like Efren Bautista. Of those we've gotten to talk to us, about a quarter earned university degrees in the countries where they came from, which is consistent with the data we've gathered on labor trafficking in the past. They wore trackers.'

'How many have you gotten to talk to you?' Marcus asked.

'Not even a third,' Coppola admitted. 'They're afraid of us. I can't blame them.'

'I'd like to talk to them,' Marcus said. 'I may have better luck, especially if the Bautistas vouch for me. These people have a right to have their story told, and I want to do it right. I also plan to ensure they get legal representation as the Bautistas have.'

Troy looked skeptical. 'The attorney Mrs Church's grandson brought here agreed to take the Bautistas' case pro bono. I don't think you can expect him to take on the entire population we extracted yesterday.'

'I'll make sure they get representation if I have to pay for it myself,' Marcus said. 'But I don't think I'll have to. When this story gets out, we'll have a lot of people volunteering to help them. They've been victimized once. I damn well won't see them victimized again.'

He drew a breath when he felt Scarlett's hand on his knee, lightly squeezing. He'd grown angry, he realized, and these two agents didn't deserve that. 'I apologize,' he said. 'I'll get off my soap box now.'

Agent Coppola's smile was sympathetic. 'I don't want to send them all packing, Marcus. My job is to put away the bastards who tricked them into coming into this country under false pretenses. I have to use whatever means necessary in order to do that, but I can be more effective if they're not afraid of me. I don't think I can get clearance to take a reporter in just yet, but when I can, I'll let you talk to them to coax out whatever information you can. If you can get them representation, all the better. As far as I know, these people haven't committed any crimes, or if they have, it was under duress and coercion. I'll propose it to the SAC, see what he says.'

He wanted to scream at the government bureaucracy, but kept his temper checked. 'Thank you.'

A light knock had them all turning toward the door. Scarlett's uncle poked his head in, his expression drawn. 'I think the Bautistas are ready to answer your questions now. But first . . .' He hesitated. 'First they want Marcus to tell them about Tala's last moments. Think of it as closure, son,' he added kindly.

Marcus had told his story to the cops, to his own brother, but telling it to the victim's parents . . . He suddenly felt uncomfortable. But then Scarlett squeezed his knee again, her nod encouraging. He pushed away from the table, gathering his nerve. 'All right,' he said.

Thirty

'We have a problem,' Sean said when Ken answered his cell phone while toweling his hair, still wet from the shower he'd taken to wash off Demetrius's blood. As much as he'd talked up being the monster in the closet to Burton, and as good as he was at it, Ken didn't like doing it. It was draining.

The screams grated on his ears. Harder still was maintaining the balance. *Not enough and they hold back, too much and they die.* He'd left Demetrius alive, but barely. His old friend had more stamina than he'd thought possible. Or maybe his ability to withstand pain was fueled by hatred and a desire for revenge. Or cocaine. Or steroids. Whatever fueled it, Demetrius had held out for so long that Ken had nearly given up.

Now, the words 'We have a problem' were enough to make him twitch.

Ken seriously considered hanging up, driving to the airport and catching the first international flight to anywhere that didn't have an extradition treaty. 'Only one?' he asked sarcastically. 'Today must be Christmas.'

'You know the tracker manufacturer you convinced Demetrius to tell you about?' Sean said, ignoring his sarcasm.

Yeah, Ken knew. He'd had to cut off two of Demetrius's fingers to extract that piece of information. 'Constant Global Surveillance. What about it?'

'The Feds did a raid yesterday, took all the factory's production records. This morning they showed up and took Demetrius's contact and one other individual into custody. Our contact is en route to Cincinnati as we speak.'

'Motherfucking sonofabitch,' Ken growled. 'The cops have traced the trackers back to the source. They have to have more than the first one to be able to identify D's contact.'

'So it would seem,' Sean said calmly. 'What are we going to do?'

Ken rubbed his temples. Breaking Demetrius had tired him out, both physically and mentally. 'I'm assuming the Constant Global Surveillance contact can identify Demetrius, or at least provide the cops with enough information so that they can get a little closer to us. That's what we have to prevent. I'll send Alice to wait outside CPD headquarters. She's no sniper, but she's a decent long-distance shot. Send a photo of the tracker supplier to her phone.'

'She's gonna be mad that you pulled her off O'Bannion. She's been stalking his office all morning, waiting for him to show up.'

'She's going to have to be mad. Just send her the photo. I'll deal with Alice.'

There was a tapping of a keyboard on Sean's end as Ken texted Alice to meet him in his home office. 'Done,' Sean said.

'Good.' Ken quickly dressed and, cell phone in hand, started downstairs to his office, even though he really needed to sleep. 'What I now want to know is how the cops got their hands on those two trackers that were supposedly in the van with the Anders family.'

Sean was quiet for a moment. 'If both Decker and Burton saw them in the van but the cops somehow got them, then somebody either took them back into the Anders house or smuggled them to the cops at some point. I am *positive* that those ankle trackers never entered my office.'

Goddamn you, Demetrius. This whole thing had unraveled because Demetrius hadn't killed that sonofabitch Marcus O'Bannion nine fucking months ago.

He went into his office, closed the door and sank into his chair. 'Either Burton and/or Decker is lying,' he said to Sean, 'or one of the other two guys that Burton sent to retrieve the Anderses turned the trackers over to the cops. The four of them were the only people who had access to the house. One of the guards was bleeding too badly to do any kind of a double-cross. I don't know much about the other except that Reuben hired him. Burton said he was green.'

'His name is Trevino. He was a former cop, just like Burton and Reuben,' Sean said. 'I looked him up. Trevino was fired from the force and prosecuted for helping himself to the cocaine he took from dealers. Did three years in prison. He hasn't been a problem so far.'

Ken digested that as best his tired mind would allow. 'Well, considering that Burton lied about Reuben's wife being dead, he'd be my first guess, but I'll call Trevino in for a chat.'

'Don't forget that Decker went back to the Anders house to search for the aunt,' Sean pointed out. 'He could have taken them back then.'

Ken shook his head. 'But the cops were already at the house by then. Decker left before they could see him.'

'Yeah,' Sean said glumly. 'Has Burton admitted to saving Reuben's wife after you dosed her up and told him to leave her to . . . you know?'

'You know?' Ken asked scornfully.

'Watch what you say on the phone. Just in case we're being recorded. Something is going on here. One of Reuben's people is dicking around with you. Either he's a mole or out for a coup. Maybe it's even Reuben pulling the strings, sitting someplace tropical drinking piña coladas and waiting for you and your team to turn on each other. He strolls back unharmed when the dust settles and takes over.'

Ken blinked, horrified that he hadn't considered that himself already. He really was going soft. *Shit.* And he'd all but said out loud that he was sending Alice to commit a murder. He forced his panicking mind to still, to let him think. 'Burton was steadfast in his denials.' Translated: Ken had tortured the hell out of him and he hadn't admitted a thing. 'I'll need to be more persuasive. Or maybe I'll let Decker do it. Then I'll know if he's as calm and cool as he wants me to believe.' His phone beeped with an incoming call. 'It's Alice,' he said to Sean. 'I'll call you later.' He disconnected and went immediately to the second call.

'Don't argue with me,' he started without saying hello. 'I need you to come here.'

'You told me to focus on O'Bannion, Dad. I can't focus on anything with you changing your mind all the damn time.'

'I told you not to fucking argue with me!' he snapped, and heard her indrawn breath. 'I'm still your boss, and until you either buy me out or bump me off, you listen to me.'

A small silence. 'Yes, *sir*. Where would you like me to focus now, *sir*?'

He almost laughed at the frosty snark in her voice. She was going to make an excellent leader someday. Hopefully soon. 'I'll tell you in a second. First, where are you with your assignment?'

'I thought maybe he'd be at the hospital with his friend, so I waited outside for a while. But he didn't show, so I went to his office. He's not there either, according to his receptionist, but she'd probably lie for him if he told her to. I need to follow him to get his routine.'

'Or lure him. That's what Demetrius was trying to do. Just not too skillfully.'

'I'll consider it,' she said grudgingly. 'What's the new focus?'

'Sean sent you his photo. He'll be delivered to the CPD headquarters for booking sometime in the next hour or two. He's Demetrius's contact for the ankle trackers.'

'And now he's in police custody. Wonderful. I take it you want me to . . .'

'As cleanly as possible. Then back to the primary focus.'

'Got it. I'll call you when I have something.'

'Hurry, honey. I want this over with.' Ken hung up, leaned back in his chair and closed his eyes. He needed to sleep. Just a little.

Cincinnati, Ohio
Wednesday 5 August, 12.30 P.M.

Agents Coppola and Troy had interviewed the family while Scarlett sat with Marcus and her uncle on the sidelines. Deacon had gone into the adjoining room to make all the phone calls required to keep the investigation moving. The two attorneys maintained a steady, fairly silent presence, stopping the Feds only a handful of times to explain a term to the family or to make sure they understood their rights as they answered the questions.

Isenberg stayed in the back of the room with Meredith Fallon, who'd been called by Mrs Bautista for her children, even though both Erica and John Paul insisted they didn't need a therapist. Meredith took no offense, simply smiling as she and Isenberg quietly listened.

Scarlett found her heart breaking again and again, listening to their story, and then to Marcus telling them about Tala's last days. He'd emphasized how brave she'd been and how much she'd loved her family. The Bautistas had cried, holding each other.

Scarlett found herself wiping her eyes, cognizant that she was not the only one of the observers to cry. Marcus's tears ran down his face unchecked. He'd seen Tala die and he hadn't started to deal with the shock. So Scarlett laid her hand on his forearm, lightly stroking his skin with her thumb, just so that he would know she was there.

Efren Bautista dropped his head in shame. 'I feel so stupid,' he said when he'd finished telling them how the family had come to be tricked into human slavery.

'We're educated people,' Mila added, clutching her husband's hand. She hadn't let go since they'd been reunited. Her son sat at her feet, his arms wrapped around her legs. Erica had her arm in her father's and her head on his shoulder. The family was intertwined like a vine.

'We should have known better,' Efren said wearily. 'Now my daughter is dead because I brought us here.'

'Thousands are tricked just like you were, every year,' Kate said softly. 'I know it won't help now, but perhaps someday you can take some comfort in knowing that you're not alone. And certainly not stupid. These traffickers have a very sophisticated operation.'

'And you came to work,' Agent Troy said. 'You were trying to make a better life for your family. There's no shame in that, sir.'

Efren shook his head, completely unconvinced. 'I should have stayed in the Philippines. Tala would still be alive. She would not have been violated, forced to have Anders's baby.'

'She's a beautiful baby,' Marcus said. 'Your granddaughter has Tala's eyes.'

Efren only nodded, his gaze glued to the floor.

'Let me summarize what you've told us so far,' Kate said, 'and then we have a few more questions. Okay?' She waited until Efren nodded, and then went on in a gentle voice. 'You were approached by a neighbor who'd applied with a recruiter and had gotten a job in the United States.' She spelled the neighbor's name and Mila nodded.

'I hope he didn't experience the same nightmare we did,' Mila said. 'We should try to locate him and be sure. He said he was going to work in New York.'

'We will make every attempt to find him,' Kate assured her, 'but you should be aware that many times the neighbor who tells you about the jobs is paid by the recruiter. Many times the neighbor is still in the home village, living very well by betraying his friends. I'm sorry,' she added when Efren and Mila looked stricken. 'I hope I'm wrong.'

'I hope you are too,' Mila whispered. 'The person who told us was Efren's cousin. I don't want to think of him suffering like we have, but . . .' She put her arm around her husband when a strangled cry broke free from his chest.

'He had a new car,' Efren sobbed. 'He said he'd gotten it for his mother to drive when he left. He lied, Mila. He lied and our daughter is gone.'

Scarlett exhaled. To be betrayed by family was another agony they'd have to endure. She met Kate's eyes and could see that she was thinking the same thing.

Once he'd calmed, Kate began again, asking Efren for further details of his recruitment. Efren explained that the recruiter had charged an exorbitant placement fee for his services, so not only had the recruiter been paid by the traffickers, but he'd stolen the Bautistas' savings as well. Efren had taken out a loan at such a high interest rate that it was pretty much assured he would never be able to pay it back. He'd come to the United States hoping for honest work and a living wage, only to find himself in a worse situation than any indentured servant.

The family had been separated almost immediately, Mila and Efren only allowed to see each other only four times during the first year, and not at all in the last two. That had been imposed by Chip Anders, who taunted Efren by telling him he was sleeping with his wife and daughters, then forced his compliance by threatening to do the same to John Paul.

'Do you want to apply for a U visa?' Peter Zurich, the immigration attorney, asked.

Efren shrugged. 'I would be humiliated to go home and be laughed at for being such a fool, but I'll continue to hate myself if we stay, so where we are matters not to me. If Mila and my children want to go back, I'll go back.'

Mila looked panicked. 'I don't know. I . . . I just don't know.'

'When do they have to make a decision, Mr Zurich?' Meredith asked using what Scarlett recognized as her counselor voice. Soothing without being condescending, it had an instant effect on Mila, the poor woman's panic visibly receding.

'Within the next few weeks,' Zurich told them, kindly. 'We need to get a jump on the paperwork, as the others liberated from Anders's factories will also be filing applications and there is a ceiling on how many U visas are issued every year.'

'If they give you permission to start the paperwork and they change their minds,' Meredith asked, 'is that a problem?'

'We can always withdraw an application,' Zurich said.

'Then start it,' Efren said, his eyes remaining downcast. 'Thank you for your kindness.'

Zurich gave all four Bautistas their own cell phones and his business card. 'Call me if you need me.'

Efren didn't take the phone he was offered. 'I can't pay for any of this.'

Zurich placed Efren's phone on the lamp table. 'Right now, don't worry about paying. We're working for you at no charge because we know how many people are in situations just like yours. Five years ago I worked with a family who'd come from India. He was an engineer with a graduate degree and found himself working in a restaurant for no wages. He was embarrassed, much as you are. Today he and his family are US citizens. Their sons are enrolled at the university. And he volunteers his time to help families like his – like yours – get a new start. We call that paying it forward, and someday I'd like to count on your support in the same way.'

Efren looked up then, his eyes red from crying. 'Thank you for trying to restore my dignity. But I fear it is too late.'

'Not too late, sir,' Zurich said. 'Remember, you're not alone in this. We'll talk again soon. For now, rest.' He looked at the two agents. 'You're going to the temporary shelter for the other people pulled from Anders's factories?'

'Yes,' Kate said. 'You'll represent them too?'

'For now. My office is working to get more attorneys on board. Today it's just me.'

'I'll stay for a little while,' Annabelle Church's grandson said. He smiled at Mila. 'My grandmother made me promise to take care of you.'

As the agents and Zurich left, the CPD sketch artist came in. Scarlett rose to give her a hug. 'Lana. Thanks for coming in. I heard it's your day off.'

'I was cleaning house,' Lana D'Amico said with an easy laugh. 'I'm glad to escape it.'

Scarlett led her to where the Bautistas sat, still twined around each other. 'This is Sergeant D'Amico,' she said. 'She's going to create sketches based on your descriptions of the man and woman who brought you to the city. Sergeant D'Amico is one of my friends. She and I were partners many years ago, before I was a detective. Now she's a police artist.'

'I'm very pleased to meet you,' Lana said. Her smile was always so sweet that it put witnesses at ease, and the Bautistas were no exception. All four visibly relaxed when she took the seat that Kate Coppola had occupied.

'Lieutenant Isenberg? Detective Bishop?' Cell phone to his ear, Deacon stood in the doorway to the adjoining room, motioning them to come, his expression unreadable.

Lana settled her sketchbook on her lap. 'Go ahead,' she said to Scarlett, then turned her smile back to the Bautistas. 'We'll be just fine, won't we?'

'You'll want to come too, Marcus,' Deacon said.

The Bautistas might have relaxed, but Marcus had instantly tensed when Deacon appeared, expecting the news to be bad. Scarlett clasped his hand as they walked into the next room.

'It'll be okay,' she murmured so that only he could hear. 'It can't always be bad.'

Deacon ended his call and gave Marcus an encouraging nod. 'This might be hard to watch, but hopefully you'll be glad you did.' He turned his laptop to face them, revealing a lanky young man lying in a hospital bed, his leg wrapped in bandages and mesh. He was handcuffed to the bed rail, trying to look bored but failing utterly. Under the pain was a great deal of fear.

Deacon did a ta-da gesture at the screen. 'Meet Drake Connor.'

Cincinnati, Ohio
Wednesday 5 August, 1.15 P.M.

'Sonofafuckingbitch,' Marcus snarled, and took a step toward the laptop. 'Can that little piece of shit hear me?'

'No,' Deacon said. 'It's a live feed, but he can't see or hear us. The agent

460

and detective have earphones, so we can communicate with them.'

Scarlett tugged on his hand. 'Marcus.'

Marcus drew a steadying breath. 'I'm sorry. Just seeing him . . .' He glanced at Isenberg, surprised that she hadn't thrown him out already. 'I'll control my temper better.'

'I was wondering when I'd really see it,' the lieutenant said. 'I was starting to wonder if you were flesh and blood.'

'Oh, I'd say so,' Scarlett whispered, and Marcus barely swallowed his laugh, grateful for the distraction. He'd needed a moment to shove his temper down and she'd given him that.

'I heard that,' Isenberg said blandly. 'You shouldn't poke the bear through the zoo bars, Detective. Especially since we haven't yet had our chat.'

Marcus's good humor became a scowl, but Scarlett just shook her head and sat down across from her boss, studying the young man on the screen. 'Who are the men in suits?'

'The guy in the black suit is Special Agent McChesney of the Detroit Field Office,' Deacon said. 'The guy in the gray suit is Detective Danhauer, Detroit PD Homicide. They have earpieces, so we can ask them questions. The guy sitting on the other side of the bed is Graham White, public defender.'

'Does Drake know that his sister is missing?' Scarlett asked.

'No, not yet,' Deacon said. 'Detroit hasn't told him. But the really good news is this.' He turned his phone to show them the screen, a photo of a flash drive. 'Found under the SUV he was trying to steal. He'd tossed it there when the cops pulled into the gas station parking lot. It has his thumbprint on it. Detroit PD says it has several encrypted files. They're sharing the files with Tanaka. He and Detroit CSU are working to open them. We've been comparing notes, prepping the agent and the detective. They're waiting for us before they start the interrogation.'

'Tell them to proceed,' Isenberg said.

They started out with the shooting in the gas station, which Drake promptly denied, claiming he'd only tried to steal an SUV. But the detective calmly showed Drake and his lawyer a clip of the security video on his iPad, and Drake became sullen.

'What are you offering?' Drake's lawyer asked.

'Nothing,' the detective said with a tight smile. 'We're not finished.'

'We're barely started,' the agent agreed.

'Where'd you get the gun, Drake?' the detective asked.

'You don't have to answer that,' his lawyer counseled.

461

The detective kept talking. 'It's registered to your girlfriend's daddy. Who is missing, by the way. The whole family is missing. Cinci PD tells us that there were shots fired and the Anders family was removed from their home by force. Did you take them somewhere, Drake? Bury them in a shallow grave, maybe?'

'No. I don't know anything about that.' But his eyes said otherwise. 'I didn't go over there very often. Her father hated me.'

'Drake,' his lawyer cautioned.

'Well he did. I'm just sayin' that I had no cause to go over there.'

'Then how did you get his gun?' the agent asked innocently.

'Stephie gave it to me.' Drake shrugged nonchalantly. 'I live in a rough neighborhood. She was scared for me.'

Deacon leaned into the microphone on his laptop. 'He lives in a low-crime neighborhood,' he murmured to the Detroit agent. 'Not rich, but not rough.'

'When did she give it to you?' the agent was asking.

Drake was quiet for a moment, his eyes calculating before he spoke. 'Last week.'

'So you never visited at night?' the special agent asked.

'I *said* I didn't,' Drake said.

'The punk's fucking pathological,' Marcus muttered. 'He raped Tala and Erica every chance he got.' Scarlett squeezed his hand under the table. He drew another calming breath.

'So you never met up with your girlfriend at night?' the agent pressed.

'He said he didn't,' the lawyer snapped. 'Next question, please.'

The agent ignored him. 'So you and your girlfriend and your Ruger with cop-killing bullets weren't in an alley in Cincinnati two nights ago looking for drugs?'

'No!' He'd been pale from the surgery, but visibly paled further.

'Then how did bullets from your gun – which Stephie gave you last week – get into two victims in that alley early yesterday morning?' The agent tilted his head mockingly. 'We don't understand.'

'It wasn't my gun.'

'Oh it was,' the agent said. 'Ballistics prove it. And your fingerprint was found on one of the casings you left behind.'

The public defender sighed. 'I want copies of the ballistics report and the print match.'

Drake turned on the defender. 'You believe them? You're supposed to be on my side.'

'Are you really that stupid, Drake?' the detective asked, laughter in his voice. 'Your lawyer knows your goose is cooked. They're gonna put a needle in your arm.'

The lawyer shook his head when Drake looked like he wanted to bolt. 'They're lying, Drake, trying to scare you. Michigan hasn't had the death penalty in a hundred and fifty years.'

'Ohio does, though,' the detective said with a cold smile. 'We'll try you here in Michigan for the murder of that woman you shot in the parking lot last night. You'll get life, for sure. But then Ohio will get their turn. You killed that young woman in the alley yesterday. You even went back and shot her in the head to be sure she was dead. You shot the man trying to save her life – in the back. Ohio's gonna be sliding a needle in your arm, boy. I know I'll be there on the other side of the glass, watching.'

'I'll bring popcorn,' the agent deadpanned.

Scarlett snickered, making Marcus's lips twitch, venting off just a smidgeon of his rage, but enough so that he could think.

'I didn't kill anyone,' Drake insisted. 'You have no proof.'

'We have your gun, Drake,' the agent said. 'That's all the proof we need.'

'What do you want?' the defender asked again.

The special agent held up the flash drive, and Drake's eyes narrowed in anger. 'That's not mine,' he exploded.

'Riiiight,' the agent said. 'It's got your thumbprint on it.'

'Because I found it on the ground when that bitch shot me. I must have touched it then.'

The agent shook his head. 'We have your print on the part that plugs into the computer and that was covered up. See, it's right here in the video. There you are getting shot,' he said, speaking slowly as if narrating. 'Oh, and there you are digging it *out of your own pocket* and throwing it under the dead lady's SUV. But at no time did you touch the plug part.'

Drake's jaw clenched and he closed his eyes. 'Fuck you.'

'In your dreams, kid,' the agent said, and the detective laughed.

'We're done here,' the defender said, thin-lipped.

Drake turned to the lawyer, his eyes sly again. 'Tell them I'll decrypt the files on the drive if they let me go.'

The lawyer gave him a stunned look. 'Uh, listen, kid, they are not letting you go.'

Drake shrugged. 'Then they'll never know all of Chip Anders's secrets. And he's got good secrets,' he added conspiratorially.

'Ooh, tell Vince to hurry decoding that thing,' Isenberg said quietly. 'The kid was gonna blackmail Stephie's daddy. We might get information about the traffickers.'

'Don't worry, Drake,' the agent said, pocketing the evidence bag holding the flash drive. 'We've got experts who can decode anything. They should have cracked those files before we leave here.'

'Moving right along,' the detective said, pulling a cell phone out of another bag. 'Your fingerprints are all over it, so don't even try to deny it's yours. This phone was used to text the phone belonging to the man you shot in the back yesterday morning. The text asked him to come to the alley. You in the habit of luring grown men to alleys, Drake?'

'No!' Drake hissed. 'That text didn't come from me.'

'No, it didn't,' the detective said, suddenly sober. 'It was a plea for help from a young woman your girlfriend's daddy bought from human traffickers.'

'Shit,' the defender muttered.

Drake shrugged. 'She probably stole my phone.'

'She had an ankle tracker,' the detective said. 'She was confined to the Anderses' house.'

'Then how'd she get to the alley?' Drake taunted.

'How'd she get to your phone?' the detective threw back. 'It indicates proximity. How close did you get to her, Drake?'

'I never touched her.'

Marcus heard a growl and realized it had come from him.

Squeezing his hand again, Scarlett used her free hand to unmute the microphone. 'Tell him that the rape kit found sperm in the victim,' she said quietly to the cops on the screen, 'and that we'll match it to him.'

'The rape kit found no semen,' Deacon said with a frown.

'I know. I'm interested to see how he denies it. I want him to admit to assaulting Tala so that if Erica decides to press charges, she'll have a foundation.' Scarlett turned back to the microphone. 'Also tell him that he should get checked for genital herpes and gonorrhea while he's in the hospital. That he's a carrier. That is true.'

The Detroit detective gave a tiny nod to show he'd heard. 'You didn't touch her?' he asked Drake. 'Then how did she steal your phone and plead for help? How did the ME find your sperm inside her?'

'That's a lie,' Drake spat. 'I used a condom.'

'Knew it,' Scarlett said with satisfaction. 'Little prick.'

The detective leaned closer, getting into Drake's space. 'You didn't use a condom every time, Drake. The ME found your Cincinnati murder victim had both genital herpes and gonorrhea. On the bright side, you won't have to worry about getting it in prison. You already have it. That'll take some of the pressure off once you get there. Because while we don't have the death penalty, we have far more than our share of gang members who're gonna think you're so pretty.'

Drake's expression was priceless. 'Fuck you,' he gritted out. 'I'm done here. Get out.'

'Tell him about his sister now,' Deacon said quietly.

The detective and the special agent stood up. 'One more thing, Drake,' the agent said, 'and this is very serious. We know you stole your sister's car and her credit card because we found them with your prints all over them.'

'Borrowed,' Drake said with a surly glare.

'Well you should know that you brought trouble to her door. Your sister is gone. Taken. Maybe by the same people who took your girlfriend and her family.'

Drake's lips trembled. 'Nah, she's probably at work. She's always at work.'

The agent shook his head. 'No. Her landscaping van was in the driveway and her purse was on the kitchen table. There was a struggle. She fought hard.'

'You're lying to me. She's fine.'

'I hope you're right. The people who took the Anders family . . . they meant business. You might do better to stay locked up. They were looking for you because they know you messed with their property. The girl who used your phone to text for help was desperate.'

'What are they gonna do when they learn you're in custody?' the detective asked. 'I'm thinking we should take you to Cincinnati and see how well you fare down there.'

Drake blanched. 'It's your job to protect me.'

The detective snorted. 'No, our job is to prove that you shot the cashier and murdered that woman last night. We have it on tape, so I'll admit our job is pretty easy. The creeps that took your sister and your girlfriend are Cincinnati thugs. CPD's job is to find out who killed that young woman in the alley so that they can track it back to the people who forced her to come to this country to begin with – most likely the thugs that went after your sister trying to find you. Nobody's gonna protect you, Drake – not us and not Cinci PD. You help them find out who's after you and you protect yourself.'

'God, he's good,' Scarlett murmured.

'Yeah,' Deacon agreed. 'Don't think it'll be enough, though. Drake's a sociopath.'

The agent pulled out the bag containing the flash drive and let it dangle. 'Last chance to tell us what's on this.'

The lawyer whispered something in Drake's ear. Drake shook his head. 'Unless you offer me something, I'm going to pass. Why should I make your lives easier? Knock yourselves out, guys.'

'Little prick,' Marcus muttered.

The detective retrieved his laptop, and the picture got very bumpy as he and the special agent walked through the white hallways of whatever hospital Drake was in.

Deacon unmuted the microphone. 'I didn't think Drake would break. He didn't care about his sister. He was more worried that they were coming after him.'

'True,' the Detroit detective said through the speaker. 'He's a piece of work.'

'He's right about one thing, though,' Scarlett said. 'We don't have any proof directly tying him to Tala's murder. He can argue that yeah, he screwed her, but he didn't kill her or shoot at Marcus.'

'We need an eyewitness,' Isenberg said. 'Your report mentioned two homeless people who directed you to the body?'

Scarlett nodded. 'Tommy and Edna. I'll find them.'

'We're getting ready to sign off,' the agent said. 'Let us know if you need anything.'

'Popcorn,' Scarlett said grimly, and the two Detroit men laughed, also grimly.

Deacon closed his laptop. 'You okay?' he asked Marcus.

Marcus nodded. 'I feel like writing a story all about Drake,' he said, his voice so harsh that it hurt his throat. 'I'd tell what he did and where he can be found and hope that the traffickers have a subscription to the paper. Little prick.'

'Write it and send it to me,' Isenberg said crisply. 'I may have a thing or two to add.'

He met the woman's normally cold eyes and saw raw fury. 'You'll have it in an hour.'

'What about the suspected employees of the ankle tracker company?' Scarlett asked. 'When will they be in Cincinnati?'

'They should be delivered to CPD any minute.' Deacon looked at Isenberg. 'I assume Marcus can come with us and watch the interview from the observation area?'

'Yeah. I guess he's earned that much,' Isenberg said, stunning them all. She stood up. 'I will still see you back in my office, Detective Bishop. Plan time after the interview with the tracker maker.'

'Yes, ma'am.'

Marcus turned in his seat, watching as the lieutenant walked out the door that led directly into the hallway, bypassing the Bautista family. 'I do not understand that woman.'

'She likes you,' Scarlett said. 'She doesn't like me liking you when I'm working your case. She wants her chance to tell me so, but she's unlikely to suspend me. It's okay, Marcus. She's actually protecting my career for me because she does care.'

Marcus looked at Deacon, who nodded. 'What Scarlett said,' Deacon said. 'Isenberg is complicated, but down deep she's a good boss. Let's pack up, get some lunch. Then we can head over to CPD to talk to the tracker makers.'

There was a knock on the door from the Bautistas' suite, and Lana D'Amico stuck her head in. 'Okay to come in? I have a sketch for you to see. We got a face for the man, but not the woman yet. They . . . Well, they needed a break after describing the man.'

They waved her in, Marcus feeling a tingle of dread on the back of his neck. If he didn't recognize the people who'd hurt Tala and her family, he'd still be in the dark, looking for a connection to explain why someone kept shooting at him.

He held his breath as the sketch artist put her pad on the table in front of him.

'These are based on memories that are three years old,' she said. 'But they all agreed that this was the best likeness of the two people who brought them to Cincinnati.'

'There are some faces you don't forget,' Marcus said quietly. 'That man raped Erica and her sister. The parents had to watch. I think having to see it burns it into your memory.' He didn't realize that he'd clenched his fists until Scarlett's hand covered one of them.

Lana lifted the cover of her sketchbook and Marcus felt all the air seep from his lungs. He stared at the man with the hard, dead eyes.

'I've seen them both. But . . . I don't remember where.' He looked at Scarlett, stunned to feel panic creeping up his chest. That he didn't understand why he was reacting the way he was made the panic worse.

'Yet,' she murmured, cupping the back of his neck, massaging muscles that had grown so stiff that a sharp pain shot up into his skull. 'Relax. It'll come to you.'

Marcus drew a breath, closed his eyes. Tried to relax, but it wasn't coming, and time was not something they had to waste. He met Deacon's steady gaze. 'I hear you can help people remember things.'

Deacon shrugged. 'I help people relax so that they can access the things they've tucked out of reach. You want me do that for you? It's just breathing exercises.'

'I can leave if you want me to,' Scarlett murmured, but Marcus maneuvered his hand so that he held hers instead of the other way around.

'No.' He let go of her hand and slid his arms around her shoulders. Buried his face in her hair. Dragged in a breath so deep it hurt, but he'd filled his head with the scent of honeysuckle and it calmed him. 'Stay,' he whispered, his breath hot on her ear. 'Please. I need you.'

'Well, when you put it like that,' she said with a smile. She turned her head so that his forehead rested on hers. 'It'll be all right. Whatever it is.'

She'd understood. There was something terrifying about that man's face, on a primal level that he couldn't articulate. He had to know what it was, for Edgar and Phillip, for Agent Spangler, for the Bautistas, and for himself.

Thirty-one

Cincinnati, Ohio
Wednesday 5 August, 2.05 P.M.

Deacon Novak was nervous. He'd done this procedure dozens of times and he could count on one hand the number of times he'd been nervous. Because sometimes it worked and sometimes it didn't. It meant more for it to work when he had a connection with the person he was trying to calm. Like he'd had with Faith, of course. And his old boss's wife back in Baltimore.

And now, with Scarlett watching him with such trust, he knew he'd add this to the number of times it meant a lot more. He'd liked Scarlett from the first time he'd met her, had known some of the prickliness was self-protection on her part. He'd seen the real Scarlett Bishop a few times over the almost-year that they'd worked together, but he'd never seen her expression so open.

She was so open because of Marcus O'Bannion. Because this mattered. Marcus wasn't just scared of hypnosis, he was scared about what he was going to remember. That he was one of the bravest men Deacon knew made his fear far more concerning.

Lana D'Amico had taken her sketchbook, leaving the sketch and giving Scarlett a brief hug as she left. Now it was just the three of them in the quiet room.

'It's simple breathing,' Deacon said quietly. 'Nothing more.' He took Marcus through the breathing exercises once, then twice, but the man was too tense.

Scarlett hesitated. 'I'm going to try something, and it's just a little odd.' She took down her braid, working her hair loose so that it lay around her shoulders and halfway down her back. Scarlett was rarely seen with her hair down, and it . . . softened her. She gathered it into a sheaf and lifted it cupped in both hands to Marcus, like an offering.

With a slightly embarrassed glance at Deacon from the corner of his eye,

469

Marcus cradled Scarlett's hands in his and once again buried his face in her hair and drew a deep breath.

Immediately some of the tension left his shoulders.

Deacon met Scarlett's eyes with an indulgent smile. 'It's not the weirdest thing I've ever seen,' he murmured, making her laugh. She covered her mouth, but it was too late. The happy sound wouldn't be contained.

Deacon realized he'd never heard his partner laugh. Not like this, so free and . . . young.

A few seconds later, Marcus's shoulders began to shake and he looked up at her with a grin. 'This is supposed to be serious.'

She cupped his cheek, stroking his skin with her thumb, the caress very . . . intimate. 'Who says?' she murmured. 'It's supposed to be whatever it needs to be for you to be relaxed.'

'I don't think Deacon is *that* understanding,' he murmured back, and Scarlett choked on another laugh, her cheeks growing pink.

All Deacon could think was that Faith better not have any evening appointments. He was getting awfully warm watching Scarlett gentle Marcus O'Bannion.

Deacon cleared his throat and began the exercises again. Marcus followed along, drawing calming breaths from the scent of Scarlett's hair. By the end of the first round, he was very chill.

Not having a date or time to work from, Deacon had to start with Marcus's state of mind at the time of the defining event. 'So how are you, Marcus?'

'A little scared, actually.' It was a hesitant admission.

'Let's back up and do one more round,' Deacon said softly. Once they'd completed another set of breathing exercises, he asked the question again. Marcus's shoulders seemed broader somehow, and Deacon wondered if Marcus's upper body might appear as wide as Stone's if he wasn't so uptight all the time. 'You're seeing this face.' Deacon touched the sketch, watched Marcus recoil, but slowly, like he was moving through honey. Perfect. 'How are you, Marcus?'

'I couldn't breathe.' He made a face. 'Antiseptic.'

'So you were in the hospital?'

'Yeah.'

'As a patient?'

A slight tightening of his jaw. 'Yeah.'

All right. That could mean that this incident had occurred nine months before. He wished he had access to Marcus's medical history, but that would have to be their plan B if this didn't work. Scarlett opened her mouth to speak, but stopped herself before Deacon said anything. He gave her a nod of approval.

'Were you cold, Marcus?' he asked.

'No.'

'Too warm?'

'No.'

'Sad?'

Marcus swallowed hard. 'Yes.'

'Floaty?' Deacon asked, taking a chance that this had occurred while Marcus had been on very strong painkillers. He'd had a collapsed lung, after all.

'Very. You came to me.'

Deacon started to say that he'd been in the hospital at the same time and hadn't visited Marcus, but he realized that he meant Scarlett.

She caressed his cheek again. 'I did,' she murmured in a smooth voice Deacon hadn't known she was capable of.

'You stood guard, but then you left.'

'I put a policeman at your door,' she said quietly, sweetly.

'He left.'

Deacon knew that the guard had been dismissed because they'd caught the man who'd put Marcus in the hospital and killed so many others. They'd thought the danger was past. Apparently they'd been wrong.

'And you were alone,' she whispered. 'In the dark?'

He nodded. 'He came.'

'The man in the sketch?' Deacon asked.

'Yes. Sat in my room.'

Scarlett's mouth opened, her eyes growing frightened. But she kept her voice smooth. 'What happened, baby?'

Marcus's body stiffened, his head snapping up to stare at Scarlett as he caught hold of the memory. 'It was a pillow. He covered my face with it. I couldn't breathe.'

Her eyes had grown wide, her lips firm with anger. Her breathing had become choppy. Frightened. 'He tried to kill you, Marcus.'

Marcus straightened in his chair. 'Why?' he asked, frustrated and bewildered.

Scarlett's gaze drifted to the side, her brows furrowing. 'Nine months ago. What was happening nine months ago? Who was angry with you then?'

'Nobody was mad enough to suffocate me with a pillow,' Marcus said. 'There was the one cop that Diesel and I had to escort away from his family, but he died on his own. He never even put a threat in writing.'

471

Scarlett went still. 'Wait. That one threat. The one that was so bad that it made Gayle have her heart attack. Mc . . . McSomebody.'

'McCord,' Marcus said grimly. 'Woody McCord, high school teacher and collector of kiddie porn. He was the target of our investigation, but Leslie, his wife, wrote the letter. She was dead by then, though, remember? Gayle said she OD'd on sleeping pills.'

'What are you two talking about?' Deacon asked.

Scarlett broke away from Marcus's gaze to look at Deacon. 'Last night I mentioned a list of threats. People who got mad at *Ledger* articles exposing things they'd done. Remember?'

'Usually domestic abuse or child molestation,' Deacon said. 'Are you saying that Woody McCord was one of these threats?'

'Yes,' Scarlett said. 'Well, his wife was. Leslie McCord wrote the letter after her husband committed suicide in jail – he hanged himself. Said she hoped that Marcus lost someone he loved. When Gayle read the letter, they were looking for Mikhail. At that point only Stone knew he was dead. Gayle thought Leslie McCord had something to do with Mikhail's disappearance.'

'It was such a shock, her heart failed,' Marcus said. 'She went into the hospital, and when she got out, she looked up Leslie and found the woman was no longer a threat because she'd OD'd on pills. Her death was ruled a suicide.'

'But that's where it doesn't make sense,' Scarlett said. 'If Woody was dead and Leslie was dead, who is that guy' – she pointed to the sketch – 'and why did he try to kill you in the hospital?'

'It doesn't fit, Scarlett,' Marcus said with a frown. 'It doesn't have to be anybody I pissed off nine months ago. It could have been somebody I pissed off five years ago who was just waiting for me to be a sitting duck in an ICU ward.'

Scarlett sighed. 'You're right.'

'Who actually wrote the article about this McCord guy?' Deacon asked.

'Stone did,' Marcus said.

'That doesn't explain Phillip's attack then, other than trying to lure you,' Scarlett said, disappointed. 'Damn.'

'Phillip wasn't even working that case,' Marcus said. 'That one was Stone and Diesel.'

'Diesel is his IT wizard,' Scarlett explained.

Deacon leaned back in his chair, eyes narrowed. 'How did you find McCord's kiddie porn stash?' he asked, and watched the other two exchange a glance. Then Marcus nodded.

'Diesel has a knack for finding things on people's computers,' Scarlett said.

'He's a hacker,' Deacon said flatly.

'That's such a pejorative term,' Scarlett said. 'He's an . . . explorer.'

Deacon stared her for a long moment, then chuckled. 'Damn, girl. When you fall, you fall hard.' He shook his head. 'I don't care how he got the information. I just wondered why Marcus gets the threat if Stone wrote the article and Diesel the Explorer got the goods.'

Scarlett turned in her chair to look up at Marcus's face. 'Yeah, I wonder that too.'

Marcus drew a deep breath. 'I may have gone to see McCord. In prison.'

'Oh for God's sake.' Scarlett rolled her eyes. 'You gloated, didn't you? Went right in there and said, "Hi, I'm Marcus."' She pitched her voice ridiculously low. '"And I'm the one who just fucked up your life."' She shook her head and her voice was back to normal. 'You didn't want anyone threatening your people. You told everyone on that list that you'd done the investigating, not just the McCords. You gave them all a face to hate. Yours.'

Marcus's eyes had grown wide. 'Damn. You are scary good.'

'I'm just plain scary,' she snapped. 'Especially when people I care about do stupid shit like that. Don't do that anymore. Promise me.'

Marcus grinned. 'I promise. I won't do that anymore.'

'Thank you,' she said, disgruntled. 'So Woody and Leslie hated you, but they were both already dead when you were in the hospital. So who is Mr Pillow and how does he fit into the picture? You had to have crossed paths with him, either physically or during an investigation. And if this Demetrius guy is your Mr Pillow, then you've somehow managed to snag the attention of a ring of human traffickers – nine months *before* you met Tala.'

'Nine months ago, you were dangerous to this guy somehow,' Deacon said, tapping the sketch. 'You still are. You saw something, heard something . . . maybe something you don't even know you saw.'

Marcus rubbed his forehead. 'Fuck,' he muttered. 'Somehow I can't see human traffickers biding their time for five years. Whatever it was, it most likely occurred nine months ago. And the only big story in play then was Woody McCord.'

'So we're back to the kiddie porn collector,' Deacon said thoughtfully. 'Somehow McCord and Demetrius connect and you're the common denominator, Marcus.'

'People started shooting you again when you met Tala,' Scarlett murmured, 'after nine months of nothing. You expose McCord in an article and Demetrius shows up a few days later in the hospital to kill you. You

473

publish a story about saving Tala, and Demetrius shows up to kill you. The connection isn't just between Demetrius and McCord. Tala's in there too somewhere.'

Marcus frowned. 'But the stories are different. Tala was a victim of human trafficking. McCord was a collector of kiddie porn.'

Scarlett stood up and began to pace. 'But they were both the subject of stories published by *you*. Let's assume that this Demetrius character was the one who killed Agent Spangler and took a shot at you at Chip Anders's house, then later came after you at your apartment.'

Marcus still looked unconvinced. 'But Demetrius didn't kill Tala, Drake did.'

Scarlett stopped pacing. 'But her murder put her in the spotlight, bringing Chip Anders into the picture by association. Tala was simply the trigger. Anders is the connection, not Tala.'

'If you're right,' Deacon said, thinking through the various possibilities, 'then Demetrius links to both Anders and McCord. How?'

'I need to check Stone's notes on the McCord story,' Marcus said. 'He's over at the *Ledger* building now. He'll have his notes in his desk. Come on.'

Scarlett held up her hand. 'Wait. First I have to change my clothes.'

'Why are you wearing a dress?' Deacon asked her.

'Because I like her in it,' Marcus said, smiling at her.

She blushed. Deacon didn't think he'd ever seen Scarlett Bishop blush.

'It's because my uncle wanted me to look as non-coppish as possible so we didn't scare Mila and Erica away. Now, we have several places we need to be all at once. Let's figure this out.' Scarlett ticked off a finger. 'First, we have the guys coming from the ankle tracker company. They'll hopefully be able to tell us who was buying the trackers. That should be either Anders or the head traffickers. Hopefully the traffickers.'

'Like Demetrius and Alice,' Marcus said. 'They met the Bautistas at the airport and drove them to Cincinnati.'

Scarlett ticked off a second finger. 'Then we have to find Tommy and Edna to find out if they can put that bastard Drake Connor on the street yesterday when Tala was shot. Third, we want to find out if Demetrius fits into the Woody McCord story.'

Marcus's cell phone buzzed against the table. He grabbed it, read it, then closed his eyes, his shoulders sagging. 'Oh God,' he breathed. 'Thank you.'

Scarlett looked over his shoulder, her smile bright. 'It's a text from Phillip's sister, Lisette. Phillip just woke up and asked for Skyline Chili.'

'You can take him a copy of the sketch,' Deacon said to Scarlett while Marcus immediately called the victim's sister. 'See if he can ID his attacker.'

'I'd rather wait till we have an ID and a photo we can put in an array,' Scarlett said. 'I don't want any lawyers saying later that we led the witness.'

Deacon frowned. 'You're right, but it would be tidy to have IDs for all of yesterday's shootings.'

Scarlett checked the time. 'In another twelve hours or so we'll have DNA on the shooter in Marcus's apartment. The forensic vet got tissue from BB's teeth. It won't give us a name for this guy, but when we find him, it'll give us corroboration.'

Both Deacon and Scarlett's cell phones buzzed at the same time. They grabbed them, then cursed in unison. '*Fuck.*'

Marcus ended his call. 'What? What's happened?'

'Someone took a shot at one of the ankle tracker makers as he was being taken into CPD,' Scarlett told him. 'He wasn't hurt, but the agent next to him took a bullet in the arm when he pushed the tracker guy out of the way. No fatalities.'

Deacon breathed a sigh of relief. He was still shaken by his notification of Agent Spangler's wife yesterday. Then his and Scarlett's phones buzzed with a second text. They read the incoming, then looked at each other with wide grins.

Scarlett caught Marcus around the neck and pulled him down for a loud, smacking kiss on the mouth. 'They caught the shooter who tried to kill the ankle tracker guy,' she said.

Deacon's phone buzzed alone this time. 'From Kate. She and Agent Troy were the ones who caught the shooter.' His grin widened. 'Go, Kate. Pretty good for her second day.'

Deacon dialed Kate's phone and put her on speaker. 'It's me. I'm here with Scarlett and Marcus. I hear congratulations are in order.'

'Hell, yeah,' Kate said. 'Damn, I'm juiced right now. Shooter's a female, blond, mid-twenties. She was on the roof of a building across the street from CPD. We surrounded her as she was squeezing the trigger. That's why she missed the lab tech from Constant Global Surveillance. We yelled "Gun!" into the radio and the agents took the lab tech down. A few seconds different and we'd have been burying the guy. She had a direct bead on him.'

'How did you know to look on the roof?' Marcus asked.

A long pause, then a sigh from Kate. 'We had a tip. That's all I can say, for now anyway. Sorry.'

Scarlett looked at Deacon, her brows raised, and he knew they were both thinking the same thing – the man the Bureau had inside one of the organized crime operations had provided the tip.

'Things are finally coming together,' she told Kate. 'We're getting close to an ID on the shooter who took out Agent Spangler, the guard in Marcus's building, who's still unconscious, and Phillip Cauldwell, who's just woken up.'

'Excellent news about Cauldwell. I'm going to interview the quality tech right away. He's so shaken up from almost getting shot that he should sing like a bird. So if you want to observe, you need to hurry. Deacon, I'd like you to do the interview with me. Like I said, I'm a little juiced.'

Deacon smiled at his phone. 'I'll be there in ten minutes.' He sobered then, thinking of Agent Spangler. 'What about the roof shooter? Was she using the same kind of rifle as the sniper who took out Spangler and almost got Marcus?'

'No,' Kate said. 'Different rifles, different bullets, different range. I have a feeling the chick will be a hard nut to crack. She's got attitude to spare. I may save her for later. She hasn't said a word other than the initial "Fuck!" when we spoiled her shot. She's not giving her name. We printed her and I'd like to give Latent a little time to put 'em through AFIS. I want to know who I'm dealing with when I go into interview with her.'

'Makes sense,' Scarlett said, looking torn. 'I really want to be part of the interview, but we have other priorities.'

'We'll record it,' Deacon promised. 'Go. Wear body armor.'

'I absolutely will,' Scarlett said fervently. 'What with snipers shooting off roofs. Shit. Let's plan on a debrief in Isenberg's conference room at eighteen hundred. I'm going to check on the Bautistas before we head out. Bye, Kate.'

Cincinnati, Ohio
Wednesday 5 August, 2.30 P.M.

Alice was gone. Taken. In custody. Standing in the middle of his living room, Ken stared at the shattered picture window that had been the target of his immediate rage. Now he was numb. Drained. *What now? What do I do now?*

Hearing the crash, Decker ran from the upstairs bedroom, where he'd been tending Demetrius, to peer over the balustrade that ran between the twin spiral staircases.

'Mr Sweeney!' Decker shouted, running down the stairs as Ken stood unmoving. '*Get down.*' He took Ken down in a tackle that was reminiscent of the time the young man had saved him a year ago. Except this time there were no bullets. No danger. Not here. Nothing to see except the destruction Ken had caused himself. Literally and figuratively.

476

After a second of dead silence, Decker lifted his head and frowned. 'Wait. The glass is broken *out*. Not in. Crap.' He leaped to his feet in a graceful movement and held his hand out to pull Ken up. 'I'm so sorry, sir. Did I hurt you?'

Ken rolled to sit up, too spent from his tantrum to stand. He waved Decker's helping hand aside. 'No, Decker. I'm perfectly fine.' *Yep*, he thought sourly, *I'm perfectly fine, perfectly protected, while my daughter sits in jail.*

'I thought someone was shooting at you. What happened here?' Decker checked out the window that Ken had smashed to smithereens. A pedestal that used to hold a five-hundred-year-old Chinese vase was empty, pieces of ceramic strewn on the floor. The antique chair his mother had once loved now lay on the ground outside, covered in glass.

'I threw the chair at the window.'

Decker's expression became wary. 'Why?'

Ken rubbed his eyes wearily. 'Alice was arrested.' He'd just gotten the news from Sean, who'd been equally devastated.

'Oh no,' Decker murmured. 'How, sir?'

'I sent her after the employee of Constant Global Surveillance who'd been taken into custody for supplying our ankle trackers. She was supposed to kill Demetrius's contact before he went into CPD, but they caught her on the roof. Had her surrounded before she could set up her shot. She missed the bastard and got taken into custody.'

'Oh shit,' Decker murmured.

Ken turned narrowed eyes on the young man who could have been a model or a football player or anything else he'd wanted to be, yet had come to work for Ken for a paltry salary. 'It was almost like they knew she would be there ahead of time.'

Decker went still. 'Are you accusing me of something, sir?'

'Maybe. All of this started when you called me yesterday morning. You're new to my company, but you've ingratiated yourself into my service very quickly.'

Decker's jaw was like granite. 'No, sir. I do not agree. May I respectfully remind you that I've worked for you for three years. That I was your bodyguard for all but one month out of those years. That I walked in front of a bullet for you, *sir*. All of this started when your personal leadership team began to fall apart. Joel drinks like a fish. I was always fixing his mistakes on the legit books. I don't even want to think about how he's mucked up the real books. Demetrius snorts coke and generally goofs up anything that doesn't require his fists, and Reuben, wherever the hell he is, is a sex addict. *That's* how all this started.' He was breathing hard, his nostrils flaring. '*Sir.*'

Ken studied the man dispassionately. Decker had just uttered more words at one time than he'd said in the last three years. 'You seem to know quite a bit, Decker.'

Decker bristled. 'I listen at the meetings, sir. I have eyes. I watch what goes on. But I didn't know that Alice had gone after that employee of the tracker company. Had I known, I would have advised strongly against it. It smells of a trap.'

'Really?' Ken said coolly. 'How so?'

'What better way to draw out your opponent than with such an important prisoner?' he said acidly. 'The tracker supplier would know who he was selling to, so the cops knew you'd want him silenced. He was too tempting a prize. Therefore it was a trap.'

And I should have thought of that. 'I have to get her out of there.'

'With all due respect, I don't think that's necessary, sir. Certainly not if you're considering something as drastic as a jailbreak.'

Which is exactly what I was considering. Ken's silence was answer enough.

'She won't break, will she, sir? She won't give your name?'

'No.' Of that Ken was sure. 'Of course not.' Unless they offered her a deal she'd be too smart to refuse. His daughter was not stupid.

'She doesn't have a record, right? No prints in the system? She'll experience a bit of discomfort in lockup, but you'll get her a good lawyer. She'll be out soon.'

'Perhaps.' But he didn't think so. She'd been caught with her finger on the trigger. Someone had known she was there, of that he was certain. But he was running out of people to suspect. Ken rolled to his feet without Decker's help. 'How is Demetrius?'

A quiet exhale. 'He's dead, sir. He lost too much blood. A surgeon might have been able to save him, but . . . I'm sorry. I was coming to tell you when I heard the window smash.'

Ken had felt panic and fury when Sean had told him about Alice's arrest. Now he felt . . . absolutely nothing. Which was preferable.

'Clean up the mess . . . here and upstairs. Thank you.'

'Should I dispo— I mean, what should be done with Demetrius's body?'

'Same place you put Chip and Marlene Anders. Oh, and kill the Anders girl too. Demetrius was supposed to set up an auction and I don't want to do that now.'

'What about the guard who got shot at Anders's house yesterday morning? He's still sedated. And what do you want done with Burton?'

'Whatever you want to do with them. I don't care. I just don't want Burton talking. If the other guard is loyal to Burton, dispose of him, too.' Ken walked to his office and closed the door. He poured himself a stiff drink and dropped into his desk chair. Then he called Sean.

'Dad . . .' Sean sounded as numb as Ken felt. 'What are we going to do now?'

'What I should have done a long time ago.' Ken pushed the glass of bourbon aside and opened his gun safe.

I'm buying a one-way ticket to Bora Bora. I'm going to kill Marcus O'Bannion.

Cincinnati, Ohio
Wednesday 5 August, 3.45 P.M.

Scarlett gave Marcus a sideways glance from the driver's seat of the department unmarked car after leaving her Audi parked in the CPD garage. He was being a little too quiet. 'Do you want to go see Phillip first?' she asked him. 'I understand if you do.'

'No. We need to answer these questions about Demetrius. Lisette's with Phillip now, so he's not alone.' He looked out the car window. 'I've remembered more of what happened when I was in the hospital. It's starting to freak me out a little.'

Ah. 'Tell me.'

'I realized that I'd actually remembered it before, but I thought it was just a bad dream caused by the morphine.' He grimaced. 'That stuff gave me the worst nightmares.'

'What do you remember, Marcus?'

He sighed. 'There was another person there. A woman. I didn't see her face.'

Scarlett had to swallow back her rage. 'Because your face was covered with a pillow.'

'There was that,' he said sarcastically, then paused for a few beats, his forehead furrowed. 'She told him to hurry, that someone was coming. I think that was why he didn't finish with the pillow. They must have left because the charge nurse came in. The machine had been beeping like my IV got pulled.'

'Well it wasn't like you were almost suffocated or anything,' she muttered. 'Thank goodness for the machines.'

'The nurse fixed my IV and I didn't say anything. Couldn't if I'd tried. I think he came back a second time. Had a hypo filled with God knows what and had injected it in the IV bags that were staged to be next in line. I remember needing to tell, but being so out of it that I couldn't. Like that dream where you're screaming in your mind but nothing comes out. I think I wasn't sure if I was dreaming or not. Or even sane,' he added a lot more quietly.

Scarlett hoped she found Demetrius or whatever his real name was because she wanted to kill him with her bare hands. But that wouldn't help Marcus, so she kept her voice mild. 'You were lucid the time I came to see you. He may have found a way to increase your drugs if you were that out of it. Some drugs can make you doubt what you've seen. Some can make you trapped in your own body.'

'I hadn't thought of that.'

She squeezed his hand, relieved to hear his relief. 'Given what we know this man is capable of, drugging you is definitely within the realm of believability. Don't go doubting your sanity yet. So what happened with the IV bags?'

'I don't know. I didn't die, so something obviously happened.'

'Maybe you'll remember more later. Or maybe you could find the nurse who worked your shift that night and ask what she remembers.'

'She wouldn't remember back nine months.'

'Don't be so sure. You were quite the celebrity. You lying there in that bed, so handsome and brave and heroic. A man who jumps in front of bullets to save a stranger is quite a turn-on for a lot of women.' She batted her eyelashes, making him laugh again.

'As long as it is for you,' he said, kissing her hand. 'Where are we going first?'

'To the *Ledger* to see Stone. I want to know about McCord.'

'What about the two people who may have seen Drake?'

'I called the shelter. Tommy and Edna are there, trying to stay out of the heat. Tommy's got a heart condition,' she explained. 'Dani's there and she's going to hold them for me. When we get to the *Ledger*, I want you to go straight in. Same with the shelter.'

'I'm wearing Kevlar.'

'The sniper yesterday was aiming for your head so keep your head down. Don't wait for me and don't be a gentleman. Not when people on roofs might shoot you.'

'What about you?'

'They ain't gunnin' for me. Besides, I'm suited up, too.' She tugged at the collar of the thin Kevlar vest she wore under her shirt. 'Damn thing chafes. Promise me, Marcus. No heroics.'

He made a disgruntled sound. 'All right, fine. I'll tuck and roll.'

He kept his promise, hurrying into the *Ledger*'s lobby when she stopped the car. He grabbed her as soon she came through the door, and before she could protest, his mouth was on hers, his hands moving her head this way and that as he tasted her thoroughly.

'People, people, get a room,' someone called. Sounded like Diesel.

Scarlett smiled against Marcus's mouth before pulling away. 'Very public, Marcus.' Which had likely been the point. There had been a possessiveness to the kiss, as if he wanted his whole world to know.

'I know,' he said, then turned her to face the lobby.

Diesel sat behind the desk, grinning at them. 'Detective.'

'Mr Kennedy,' she said with a nod. She looked around the lobby, noting the presence of the newly hired armed guard in the corner. 'Where is Gayle?'

'I told her to take a coffee break, so I could install extra firewalls on her computer. I shored up the network server already, but Gayle's computer needed extra.'

'Because of Jill,' Scarlett murmured, and beside her Marcus sighed.

Diesel just shrugged. 'So what's up with you two? Other than the need to get a room.'

'We came to see Stone,' Marcus said, serious now. 'You should come too.'

Diesel came to his feet with a frown. 'Okay.'

Marcus led them past his own office and through a door to the back where the rest of the staff worked. Offices with doors lined the walls and the middle was divided into cubicles. He stopped at a closed door with Stone's name on it and knocked.

Stone opened the door right away and gave Scarlett a look that wasn't quite welcoming but was considerably less hostile than before. 'I got your text saying you needed to talk, Marcus, but I didn't expect a party. What's this about?' he asked when he'd shut the door.

Marcus showed them a copy of the sketch of Demetrius, told them what the Bautistas had suffered and what he himself remembered from his hospital stay.

Stone was visibly shaken. 'They tried to kill you in the hospital? Holy shit, Marcus.'

'You attract trouble even when you're unconscious,' Diesel added, stunned and furious on behalf of his friend. 'What the fuck?'

'The obvious threat that week was from Leslie McCord,' Scarlett said, 'but she was dead by the time Marcus was in the hospital. There's a puzzle piece missing. What can you remember about that investigation?'

Both Stone and Diesel winced. 'That was a bad one,' Diesel said softly.

'I . . . I still can't get those pictures out of my head, and I only looked at a few. As soon as I saw what McCord had on his home hard drive, I backed out.'

'I wrote the story,' Stone said, 'then we tipped the Internet Crimes Against Children task force. As soon as they confiscated McCord's computer, we went live with the story.'

'Where are the photos now?' Scarlett asked.

'With the ICAC task force,' Stone said. 'We didn't keep copies.'

'I always keep copies of the hard drives that I hack,' Diesel said, 'except when it's kids. I don't want it and I can't handle it,' he added with brutal honesty.

'Not many can,' Scarlett said. 'What can you give me?'

Stone typed a command, and a minute later his printer was spitting out pages. 'This is the story and all my notes. We got tipped off that McCord was too friendly with some of his students by a few of the boys on the JV football team. Marcus was a volunteer coach.'

'The *Ledger* sponsors youth sports,' Marcus said. 'It's an environment that can make kids vulnerable to predators, but it also fosters a spirit of communication.'

'Not the *Ledger*,' Diesel told Scarlett in a theatric whisper. 'Sponsoring sports was Marcus's idea. And mostly his money.'

She smiled up at the giant of a man who was even larger than Stone. She patted Marcus's thigh as he sat in the chair beside her. 'I'm not surprised.'

Marcus rolled his eyes, embarrassed. 'It's expedient with respect to our team's goal. Kids will talk to a coach or a team sponsor about things they might not tell a teacher – especially when that teacher is the predator. McCord taught freshman science. Some of the boys were creeped out because of how he would get too cozy when he was checking their lab setup. They said the girls felt the same way – uncomfortable. None of the kids would come forward with anything specific, though, so I had Diesel dig.'

Diesel raked his fingers across his shaved head as if he still had hair. 'I . . . I was not expecting what I saw. I mean, I've seen porn collections and I've even seen some kid photos when I poke around people's computers as part of this job, but McCord's collection took it to a whole new level. He had photos, video files . . . big files. Long videos, not just clips.' He swallowed hard. 'Like I said, I backed out as soon as I figured out what I was looking at. I'm no lover of cops, no offense, Detective, but I pitied the ones who had to analyze that vile shit.'

'Okay,' Scarlett said gently, because Diesel was actually trembling. 'You said you turned the entire hard drive over to ICAC. You didn't keep copies of the photos or videos, but what about the rest of the hard drive? Was it all pictures, or were there other file types?'

'Files,' he said on a rough exhale. 'Word files, a few spreadsheets. Hell, I didn't even open them. I ran a check to be sure there were no picture files embedded, then I put them in my safe at home with the drives from all our other investigations.'

Scarlett glanced up at Marcus. 'We need to have a look. I can do it, if you want.'

He nodded grimly. 'I'm gonna accept that offer. I just don't think I can.'

She squeezed his knee, then began skimming the pages Stone had given her. 'So you anonymously tipped ICAC, they got a warrant, found McCord's stash. He's arrested, you publish the story, the community shudders – appropriately – in horror and disgust. McCord loses his job, his pension, goes to jail . . .' She turned the page and frowned. 'He hired an attorney who was going to fight the charges.' She looked up at Stone. 'Fight with what? What did McCord have to bargain with?'

'The attorney wouldn't say,' Stone said. 'I badgered him about it, because I wanted to know too. Finally, after McCord hanged himself, the attorney said that he'd planned to expose his suppliers to get his charges knocked down from possession of child porn to pandering.'

Scarlett blinked. 'Pandering? Really? I mean, it's a lower minimum sentence than for child porn possession so that's why he'd want it, but pandering carries with it an economic element. Was he copping to prostitution? Would a judge even allow that?'

Stone shrugged. 'That's all the attorney would tell me.'

Scarlett found the attorney's name in Stone's story and used her phone to look him up online. 'Shit,' she muttered. 'We won't be following up with him. He's dead.'

Marcus leaned over her shoulder to read along with her. 'Died in an office fire. Arson was suspected.'

'Tidy,' Scarlett said grimly. 'Dammit. McCord said he was going to expose his suppliers, and all of a sudden anyone who can tell us *what* he was going to divulge and against whom is dead.' She put the papers down, spoke aloud the thought that had been circling in her mind since they'd left the hotel. 'Demetrius supplied the Bautistas to Chip Anders for labor. Maybe he supplied children to McCord for—'

'God knows what,' Marcus said from behind clenched teeth.

Scarlett squeezed his knee again, for support. And comfort. Because now she understood his zeal to punish monsters who hurt children. 'Let's take a look at the files you saved, Diesel. You say they're at your house? We can follow you there.'

'I'll go home and get them and bring them to you,' Diesel said.

Scarlett wanted to argue, but there was a sudden undercurrent in the room, a tension that she could feel but that she didn't understand. She squeezed Marcus's knee again, so lightly that no one else would know.

'We don't have that much time,' Marcus said to Diesel, apology in his voice. 'We're headed to the Meadow next. It's a shelter on Race Street.'

'I know it,' Diesel said stiffly. 'I'll meet you there as soon as I can.'

They dispersed, Scarlett holding her question until she and Marcus were alone in his office with the door closed. 'I didn't mean to upset him,' she said. 'What did I say?'

He covered her shoulders with his hands and massaged. 'Nothing wrong. It's just Diesel being fucked in the head. He doesn't like letting people in his house. I've only been there a few times myself.' He leaned in until their foreheads touched. 'I'm afraid to see what he brings us.'

'I know. I couldn't push either of them any further to tell us more. They . . .' She swallowed hard. Thought of what Marcus had told her about Stone, and all the things he hadn't put into words. She'd seen the pain in Stone's eyes, the understanding where there should have been none. Diesel had exhibited that same deer-in-the-headlights panic. 'Diesel too?'

'I don't know. He's never told me. I never asked.' He straightened, kissed the top of her head. 'Let's go, or he'll get to the shelter before we do. He doesn't live far.' He pulled a battered old laptop from a lower desk drawer and slid it into his computer bag.

'What's with the old-style laptop?' she asked.

'It has no internet card. Has no WiFi or even Ethernet cable capability. I use it when I either don't want any chance of someone hacking into my system or when I'm unsure of the file source. I don't want to corrupt the entire *Ledger* server if I open a contaminated file.'

'Diesel taught you that?'

'I knew it myself. I'm moderately skilled with systems, but Diesel is an artist.' He shouldered the bag, then came back to her for a kiss that took her breath away. 'For courage,' he murmured.

'Mine or yours?'

'Ours.'

Thirty-two

Cincinnati, Ohio
Wednesday 5 August, 4.30 P.M.

'I haven't been to the Meadow in years,' Marcus murmured from the passenger seat of Scarlett's department car, his gaze fixed on the roofline as they approached the shelter. This time of day, he might catch a glint of sunlight off the barrel of a rifle, giving them a split-second warning. Sometimes a split second was all a person needed.

Scarlett's gaze was fixed ahead as she drove, searching every shadow and suspicious movement in the ground-floor windows. 'You've been to the shelter?' she asked, and he knew he'd surprised her.

The Lorelle E. Meadows shelter had been around for as long as Marcus could remember. Located in the part of the neighborhood that had not yet been gentrified, it was sandwiched between two buildings with windows that had been boarded up even when he was a kid.

'Many times. Jeremy would bring Stone and me down here on Saturdays to help in the soup kitchen while he worked the clinic. I was twelve or so, Stone ten when we started. We were regular volunteers for years. Of course we were the only volunteers with our own bodyguards,' he added wryly. 'Mom insisted.'

'I understand why.'

'So did Jeremy. He'd bring Sammy with us.'

'Sammy was Jeremy's first partner, right? Stone mentioned him to Deacon and me when we were interviewing him last November. He said that Sammy died in the car wreck that burned Jeremy's hands. And that later Jeremy married Keith, that they'd been friends since high school.'

Marcus nodded, pleased that she'd remembered his family's history, odd as it was. 'Yeah. We didn't know that Sammy and Jeremy were lovers at the time. We just thought they were friends. And that Jeremy trusted him to keep us safe.' His lips curved sadly. 'I don't think Jeremy's been down here since Sammy died. He was so lost, he kind of drifted for a while.'

'That's when Mikhail was conceived?'

'Yeah. That Jeremy was Mikhail's biological father was something only Mom knew until last fall, when Mikhail found out the truth. Even Jeremy hadn't known.' Even though he'd understood her reasons, her actions had made Marcus want to shake his mother for not allowing Jeremy to know his son. And Mikhail to know his father. It was damn sad. His mother had kept it secret because she was afraid of Keith, afraid he would take it out on Mikhail if he found out that Jeremy had . . . taken comfort from her while grieving Sammy.

Too damn sad. 'I often wonder how things would have been different if Jeremy had been allowed to be Mikhail's father from day one. I mean, he always treated him like he treated us when he came to visit – like his own son. Ironic, because Mick was the only one of us brothers who really *was* his.'

'What do you mean? How things would have been different?'

'Jeremy did things with us every day. He was our dad. He made sure we ate our veggies and did our homework and never, ever forgot that having wealth was a privilege. He made sure we knew what it meant to give back to the community. Mikhail didn't get that. I got out of the army when he was twelve and couldn't believe what a brat he'd become. A spoiled brat. So I did with him what Jeremy had done with us.'

Her voice softened. 'You became his father figure. I didn't realize you were so close.'

Marcus nodded, his throat growing thick. 'The last five years, yes. I made him deliver papers for the *Ledger* and made sure he had a curfew, even though he had a bodyguard. I played ball with him and checked his homework. And when Diesel was building affordable housing, I put Mickey's rich ass to work. He whined at first, but he really enjoyed it.' His lips curved on a good memory. 'Especially when he started to see muscle tone, because "the chicks" dug it.' He drew a breath and let it out, the good memory fleeting, a painful one taking its place. 'Mom was smothering him to death with bodyguards. He never got a second to himself. He was like a pacing cat in the zoo. I was the one who convinced Mom to give him some freedom, to get him a car when he turned sixteen.' He closed his eyes, made his mouth utter the words. 'When he ran away, I felt responsible. He picked up his friend and drove to the cabin, then gave his friend the car keys and told him to come back in a week and get him.'

'You know you weren't responsible, Marcus. The monster that shot him was.'

'I knew Mom was scared for him, every day. But I didn't want Mickey growing up scared of shadows, like me and Stone. Too scared to sleep with the light off.' He met her eyes, no smile on his face or in his heart. 'Don't you tell anyone I said that. We both got over it.'

'Your secrets are safe with me,' was all she said, and his heart cracked in two.

'I know.' He shrugged, forced lightness into his tone. 'It's just . . . not very manly to be afraid of the dark.'

She smiled at him. 'Your manliness has never been in question. Nor is your love for your brother. You wanted him to have an easier life, a better life. You wanted him to be a good man and you showed him how.' She swallowed hard, her eyes suddenly bright. 'You're gonna make some lucky kid a good dad, Marcus O'Bannion,' she whispered.

His chest felt like it was going to burst open. 'Thank you.'

Coming to a stop in front of the shelter, she scrubbed the moisture from her eyes, took a long look around them, then up. 'Appears clear. Stay low and don't dawdle.'

'Yes, ma'am,' he said obediently.

They made it through the doors with no issue, immediately running into Diesel, who was waiting just inside. 'I brought the files.' He held out an external hard drive like it was red hot.

Scarlett slid it into her jacket pocket. 'Thank you, Diesel. I appreciate it.'

'*Diesel!*' The delighted cry came from a small boy of about five who was hobbling across the room using crutches. On his leg was a bright green cast.

Diesel looked down in surprise. 'Emilio?' He went down on one knee. 'What are you doing here? What happened to your leg, kid?'

Scarlett looked at Marcus, brows raised in question. 'Pee Wee Soccer,' he murmured. 'Diesel coaches.' The stunned look on her face was priceless.

Emilio gazed up with unadulterated hero worship, because even on one knee, Diesel towered over the boy. 'My brother's got the croup. That's what my grandma said. She took him to see Dr Dani.'

'I don't know who he is,' Diesel said, and the boy giggled.

'*She*,' Emilio said.

'Dr Dani is Deacon Novak's sister,' Scarlett explained. 'She's taking care of Tommy and Edna, the two people Marcus and I came to see.'

Diesel's mouth bent in mild interest. 'Deacon's sister? She got white hair like he does?'

'Only kind of,' Scarlett said. 'Think Rogue from *X-Men* – black hair, white streaks.'

Emilio's smile turned little-boy sly. 'She's real pretty. You should meet her.'

Marcus had first met Dani Novak when she'd visited him in the hospital. She'd accompanied Deacon and Faith to a few of Jeremy's parties in the months since and had endeared herself to his adopted father forever when she'd been able to quote from his most recent article in the *Journal of Medicine*. Dani was kind and funny and it was easy to see that she and Deacon were related. And Emilio was right – she was very pretty, just not as pretty as Marcus's detective.

But if cops were Stone's trigger, doctors in white coats sent Diesel into a PTSD tailspin. Marcus wondered how Diesel was going to get out of meeting Deacon's pretty sister.

Diesel ruffled the boy's hair. 'Not today, kid.' He leaned forward. 'I'm scared of needles, so I don't go around doctors unless I have to,' he said in a low voice. 'Even pretty ones. You gonna tell on me?'

'No,' Emilio said seriously. 'I promise. But she's nice. You'd like her.'

'I'm sure I would,' Diesel said, 'but it still ain't happening.'

Emilio bent his head. 'Who are those people?' he whispered.

'That's Mr Marcus – he's my boss and my friend. And that's . . .' He glanced up at Scarlett. 'Miss Scarlett. She's not my boss. Just my friend.'

Scarlett's smile was a little wobbly as she understood she'd just been accepted. 'It's nice to meet you, Emilio. Your cast is cool. How'd you get it?'

'I tried to slide into home plate,' he said, dejected. 'It didn't work.'

Marcus coughed to hide a chuckle. Scarlett swallowed hers, but Diesel didn't crack a smile.

'That's gotta hurt,' he said. 'I guess it explains why you missed practice last Thursday. But if you want, you can still come to the games and sit on the bench and keep score. You can count, right? And write your numbers?'

'Up to twenty.'

'That should be plenty, since we never score anyway. We can—'

'Emilio! Where are you?' Dani Novak came running from a back room, her white coat flying out behind her.

Scarlett waved her over. 'We've got him, Dani.'

Dani rushed over, her mouth bent in a frown. 'You know you're not supposed to take off like that. Especially not here. Your grandmother nearly had a heart attack.'

Here, Marcus thought, where more than three quarters of the clients were either homeless or addicts or both. With a wary look at Diesel, who was still on one knee, Dani Novak also went down on one knee, putting her body close enough that she could protect the child if she had to. Which was as ridiculous as it was unnecessary. At six-six and almost three hundred pounds of solid muscle, Diesel could toss Dani Novak like a ragdoll.

Not that he ever would. Despite his shaved head and interesting tattoos, the man was shockingly gentle with everyone except the abusers he lived to squash like bugs.

Right now, Diesel was no threat to anyone. Frozen in place, he was staring at Dani's lab coat like it was alive. Marcus considered intervening and finding an excuse to get Dani back behind the clinic door, but he didn't. It was way past time Diesel dealt with his issues.

'But if Grandma had a heart attack,' Emilio said logically, 'you could fix her, right? She says you're a miracle worker.'

Dani pursed her lips, then gave up trying to hold back, and a smile lit up her face. 'You little charmer, you. Maybe I could fix her and maybe I couldn't. Let's just not risk it, okay?' She held out both arms. 'Time to go back to Grandma.'

'Wait.' Emilio tugged her hand. 'Meet my coach, Diesel.'

Dani's brows lifted. 'The coach who encouraged you to slide into home?'

Diesel's shoulders lifted as he sucked in a breath. 'No, ma'am,' he said quietly, making Dani tilt her head the same way Marcus had seen Deacon do.

'That was baseball. Coach Diesel is soccer,' Emilio said proudly.

Dani smiled at Diesel. 'I'm Dr Novak. Everyone calls me Dr Dani.'

Diesel lifted his head and . . . nothing. The silence went on so long that Marcus leaned around to check out Diesel's face and was stunned to see his friend's eyes locked on Dani's, looking dazed. Diesel's mouth seemed to have forgotten how to speak.

'Diesel works with Marcus at the *Ledger*,' Scarlett said, taking pity on him. 'Come on, Emilio. I got things to do and people to see.' She swung the kid up on her hip like she'd done it a million times.

Given that she was the babysitter of choice among her nieces and nephews, she probably had. She'd told Marcus he'd make a great dad. *She'll make a great mom too.* It was a heady thought, having a family of his own. He was so taken by the idea that it took him a moment to realize that Emilio was no longer smiling and had gone completely still. The boy darted an alarmed glance at Dani, then back at the bulge of Scarlett's gun under her jacket. He'd probably felt it when she'd picked him up.

'My gun,' Scarlett murmured to Dani, having gone as still as the boy.

'It's okay, Emilio,' Dani said, rubbing his back. 'She's a cop. My brother's partner.'

Emilio's eyes grew round. 'Oh.'

Dani picked up the boy's crutches. 'Tommy and Edna are in the clinic waiting room, Scarlett.' She looked over her shoulder. 'You coming, Marcus? Coach Diesel?'

'In a minute,' Marcus answered. When the women were back behind the clinic door, he grabbed Diesel's biceps and with a groan yanked him to his feet. 'Lay off the beer, buddy. You're putting on weight.'

Diesel didn't answer, just stood staring at Dani Novak's retreating back. Marcus waved his hand in front of his friend's face. 'Yo. Diesel. You in there?'

A mute nod, then Diesel spun on his heel and walked out of the shelter, not saying a single word. Marcus followed him to the door, watched him take the steps down to the street in one giant stride. 'Diesel? Kennedy, stop!'

Diesel turned and looked up. Expecting to see the dazed, glassy, shaken gaze that came after one of his friend's episodes, Marcus was shocked to find himself staring into the saddest, most defeated eyes he'd ever seen.

'Diesel, wait.' He started walking down the steps until he realized he'd promised Scarlett he'd stay out of bullet range should any shooters be camped on the roofs. 'Talk to me.'

'I'll be all right, Marcus. Stay with your detective. I'll see you later.'

Cincinnati, Ohio
Wednesday 5 August, 4.50 P.M.

'So,' Dani murmured as she and Scarlett went back to the clinic. 'You and Marcus?'

'Oh yeah.' Scarlett chanced a glance at Dani's face and saw that her friend wore a delighted smile. 'It's been him for a long time. I just didn't know he felt the same.'

'I'm really happy for you. I've been grinning ever since Faith called and told me.'

'I didn't think it would be a secret all that long the way you two burn up the phone lines,' Scarlett said wryly. 'Still, less than a day is pretty fast.' She set Emilio down and Dani gave him his crutches. The boy hobbled over to his grandmother, who began to scold him.

Dani looked over her shoulder, her smile dimming. 'Is Marcus's friend okay? I didn't want to embarrass him by asking, but he didn't look so good.'

'I don't know. I only met Diesel last night, but I know there's something going on there. He seems like a decent guy, though. Marcus will tell me if I'm supposed to know. Otherwise . . .' Scarlett shrugged.

'I know. I just can't help but try to fix things.' Dani sighed. 'And people.' She pointed across the room to where the elderly Tommy and Edna sat snoozing in front of the television. 'I've got patients to see, so I'll leave you to your job.'

'Thanks for keeping them here, Dani.' Scarlett took stock of her friend's face, the dark circles under her eyes expertly covered with makeup. 'How are you? Really?'

Dani sighed again. 'Tired. And nauseous. But my counts are back in whack, so I'm healthy. I'm just stressed over not knowing where I'm going next.'

Dani had taken a leave of absence from the hospital where she'd worked in the ER when her HIV status had been exposed. Now she looked around at the waiting room bursting at the seams with people. 'I love my work here, but it doesn't exactly cover the bills, especially since I moved back into my apartment. At least I'm getting some sleep again.' She scrunched up her face. 'Deacon and Faith were keeping me up every night. They weren't exactly quiet while, you know, in the throes. "Oooh, Deacon!"' she cooed.

Scarlett laughed. 'I know. I'm getting to the point where I'm afraid to call him at home. I keep interrupting them.'

Dani tilted her head. 'I haven't heard you laugh like that since . . . maybe never. I'm glad. Marcus is a good influence on you.' Her eyes were wistful for a moment before she forced a smile. 'I have to go. Keep him safe, and yourself too.'

'You always have a room at my place if you need to ditch the apartment.'

Dani walked backward toward her office, shaking her head ruefully. 'Not that I don't appreciate the offer,' she said lightly, 'but then I'd have to hear, "Oooh, Marcus!"' She chuckled when Scarlett blushed, then blew her a kiss. 'Bye now.'

She felt Marcus come up behind her. 'What was that about?' he asked.

'Oh, you know Dani. She and Faith have been giggling over us.' She studied his face, saw his worry over Diesel's abrupt exit. 'I know, I know, some secrets aren't yours to share,' she said gently. 'But you know you can, should you need to.'

'Thanks.' He curled his hand around her neck and pulled her in for a kiss. 'Thanks for that too. I needed it.' He scanned the waiting room. 'That's Tommy and Edna?' he asked.

'Yeah. Let's wake them up.' She took out her phone and brought up her email. 'I had Isenberg's clerk work up a photo array with Drake's picture in it, just in case they did see something. Oh, and don't mind Tommy. He'll propose marriage at least once before we leave.'

'To you or to me?' Marcus asked.

491

She grinned at him. 'Edna might propose to you. We can have a double wedding.'

'How long have you known them?'

'A long, long time. I walked a beat around here when I was right out of the Academy. I've tried to get them housing so many times, but this is the life they know.' She walked over to where they slept, shook them both gently. 'Tommy. Edna. Wake up.'

Edna came awake in a panicked jerk, while Tommy roused slowly. Edna looked around, disoriented. Then she saw Scarlett and relaxed.

'Detective Bishop. Dr Dani said you wanted to talk to us.'

'Miss Scarlett,' Tommy drawled. 'I knew you'd finally come to your senses. Where you taking me for our honeymoon? Better make it the mountains. Cooler this time of year.'

Scarlett went down on her haunches so that they didn't have to look up at her. 'I'm afraid we'll have to put that honeymoon on ice, Tommy. You remember early, early yesterday when I saw you?'

Edna nodded. 'You ran off to that alley where the girl was shot.'

'I came back later to talk to you, but you were gone.'

Edna grimaced. 'Too many cops and flashing lights. Tommy and I took our stuff and found a quieter stoop.' She glanced up. 'Who's he?'

'His name is Marcus. He's the man I was meeting. He was there to help the girl because she was being hurt by the people she lived with. Somebody shot and killed her to keep her from asking Marcus for help. Did you see anything else? Like maybe someone running away?'

'Lots o' people were running away,' Tommy said. 'They hear shots and they scatter, cuz the cops'll think they did it and shoot 'em.' He shrugged. 'Mebbe they did. Don't seem to matter to the cops who they shoot.' He lifted one grizzled gray brow. 'No offense, Miss Scarlett. You're not like them. Is he?'

'Marcus? He's not a cop. He's a reporter.'

Tommy visibly relaxed. 'That's good. Hate to think you'd leave me at the altar for a cop. I saw you kissin' that man.'

Scarlett smiled at him. 'You little sneak. You weren't asleep at all.'

Tommy didn't smile back. 'I sleep with my eyes open, Miss Scarlett,' he said soberly.

'Cops'll sometimes give us a hard time,' Edna said, 'for sleepin' on our stoop. They shake us awake, yell at us.' She dropped her voice, mimicking a cop's command. '"Move along, move along. Can't sleep here."' She shook her head ruefully. 'We've been sleeping on that stoop for years. I don't know why they care. Nobody else is using it.'

Their neighborhood had been the epicenter of racial violence more than a decade before. While things had dramatically improved in the years that followed, many residents still feared and mistrusted the police.

'I'm sorry,' Scarlett said simply. She knew better than to tell them that most of the cops who made them move along were trying to keep them safe. 'Did you see anyone running away who looked like they didn't belong? Someone you didn't know from the neighborhood?'

Edna hesitated. 'I don't want no trouble.' Scarlett waited patiently until Edna sighed, long and heavy. 'Fine,' the old woman said. 'I saw him.' She pointed up at Marcus. 'He was running.'

'I know *he* was there,' Scarlett said mildly. 'One of those shots you heard was fired into his back. Luckily he was wearing a Kevlar vest or he wouldn't be here with me now.'

Edna gave Marcus a thorough looking-over. 'Would be a shame to waste a man like that,' she agreed. 'There was one other. White boy. Blond hair. Ran fast. Cleared an overturned garbage can like one of those guys in the Olympics.'

'You mean like he was running hurdles?' Scarlett asked. The Detroit guys had sent them the background check on Drake. The punk had run track while in high school, so running hurdles fit. 'Did you see his face?'

'Yes,' Edna said. 'He ran right past me.'

'I was too busy lookin' at his gun,' Tommy drawled. 'Kid wavin' it around like some stupid gangbanger.'

Scarlett sighed. 'Why didn't you tell me this yesterday morning?'

'You didn't—'

Scarlett waved her hand. 'I know. I didn't ask.'

'No,' Tommy said. 'I was gonna say that you didn't stick around long enough for me to tell you. You were running toward that alley as fast as he done run away.'

'Oh,' Scarlett said, feeling very foolish. 'Do you think you could pick him out of a lineup?'

Tommy wagged his head side to side. 'All them white boys look the same to me.'

'We're not going into any police station, Detective,' Edna said, folding her arms over her chest. 'Not gonna happen.'

'That's okay. I have a few photos for you to look at.' Holding her phone so that they could see, she flicked through the photos Isenberg's clerk had provided for the array. She'd cajole Edna into the station for a formal identification later if she needed to.

'That's him,' Edna said, identifying Drake on the second pass. 'The third one.'

Yes. We got you, you little fucker. Scarlett kept her expression impassive even as she fiercely fist-pumped the sky on the inside. 'Where did he run after he passed you?'

'To the end of the street. Got into a fancy car. Passenger side.'

'A Mercedes,' Tommy added with gusto. 'Silver. Shone under the street lights. Took off, burnin' rubber.'

Excellent, Scarlett thought. A silver Mercedes had been registered to Stephanie Anders. She quickly typed a text to Vince Tanaka: *Check silver Merc taken from Anders garage for evidence that Drake Connor and Tala Bautista rode in it.*

'Did you see who was driving?' she asked.

'A girl,' Tommy said.

'Figures you'd notice the girl,' Edna grumbled.

'Like you noticed that boy?' Tommy shot back. 'Just cuz there's snow on the roof don't mean the fire's dead.' He licked his lips lasciviously.

'Oh, that fire's dead,' Edna said, annoyed. 'Wasn't more than stick kindlin' anyway.'

'Thank you for that visual,' Scarlett said sarcastically. 'What did she look like?'

'Pretty,' Tommy said. 'Though not nearly as pretty as you.'

'Good to know,' Scarlett said. 'Details? Hair color? Skin color?'

'Blond hair. White skin. Sparkly earrings. Red fingernails. Long, like claws. She held the steering wheel like this.' He positioned his hands with the thumb tucked under and his four fingers sticking straight out. 'That's all I know.'

'That's a lot. Thank you both.'

Edna frowned, troubled. 'Is he gonna come after us? The boy?'

'No. He's in custody two hundred and fifty miles from here.'

'Good.' Edna nodded hard.

'I agree. Now, you two stay cool, okay? It's hot out there.'

Tommy pointed at Marcus. 'Does he talk?'

Scarlett laughed. 'Yes, he does. Why?'

'Tell him to stay here. You run along, Miss Scarlett. I want to talk to him. Alone.'

Scarlett glanced at Marcus with a shrug, then came to her feet and walked to the door, where she texted Isenberg and Deacon with a progress report while watching Tommy, Edna and Marcus from the corner of her eye.

Positive ID for Drake Connor leaving Tala Bautista crime scene yesterday A.M.

494

DC seen with a firearm, getting into silver Merc. Have files from Woody McCord investigation to review. Possible that McCord planned to name his supplier. Product = people/children. Likely for porn. McCord died in jail next day. His attorney died soon after, in a fire, possible arson. Wife died a few days later. All connected to McCord are dead. Possible Demetrius connection is as supplier of people to both Anders and McCord. Headed back into CPD.

Twenty seconds later, Isenberg called her cell phone.

'Good work, Detective.'

Scarlett wanted to sigh. They were still on formal terms. 'Thank you, Lieutenant,' she said, echoing Isenberg's crisp tone. 'I'm not in a place where I can speak freely.'

'Understood. Just listen, then. Agent Coppola finished her interview with the quality tech from Constant Global Surveillance. She was right – he was so shaken from the attempt to kill him that he was happy to give up what he knew in exchange for protection. He named Demetrius Russell as his customer for the ankle trackers. The tech would routinely cull out a few of the trackers for destructive testing, record them as recycled parts, then sell them to Demetrius, who always paid in cash.'

'So he's the link, like we thought.'

'Yes. The quality tech said that he was selling upwards of two hundred units a year.'

Scarlett's mind spun, thinking about all the victims like Tala's family. 'Wow. How did he keep that many destroyed units from being noticed?'

'He's implicated his boss, who was getting a cut of the profit. The Feds are picking up the boss as we speak.'

'Look at the seventh sentence of my text.'

'The one that says McCord died in jail? You think he was murdered in his cell to keep him quiet and didn't commit suicide?'

'Yes. So simple confinement may not be enough protection.'

'Then I'll make sure the Constant Global Surveillance employees have extra guards,' Isenberg said. 'But I also have other news for you. We have information on the sniper on the roof of the building across from CPD. The Feds did some fancy work with their facial recognition software. Her name is Alice Newman. Law degree from the University of Kentucky.'

'And she's a sni—?' Scarlett caught herself. 'Wow.'

'That was our reaction too. She still hasn't said anything besides that she wants a lawyer, but her cell phone had photos of the suspect she tried to shoot today. And of Marcus.'

Scarlett's breath rushed out in a shudder. She cleared her throat, kept her voice level. 'I understand.' She looked at Marcus talking to the two old people and felt a fear so intense that her knees threatened to buckle. Demetrius had tried to kill him nine months ago and then again. yesterday. This woman had obviously taken up the challenge since Demetrius had failed.

There was a woman, she stood in the hall. Told him someone was coming.

Scarlett assumed that the woman who'd warned Demetrius that day in the hospital had been the same woman who'd accompanied him when he'd transported the Bautistas. A woman the Bautistas had called Alice.

'Do you have any recordings of this woman's voice?' she asked her boss. 'Even if it's only saying that she wants a lawyer?'

'Yes. We've been recording her since we brought her in. Why?'

Because even if she refuses to say another word, I can have Marcus listen to her to see if she's the one he remembers being in the hospital when Demetrius came after him. 'Like I said, I can't speak freely here, but I'll tell you as soon as I leave. I'll call back in a few.' Scarlett hung up as Marcus walked away from Tommy and Edna, his expression one of pained amusement that changed to concern as soon as he met her eyes.

'What?'

'Nothing bad, but we need to get back to CPD now.'

Minutes later they were in Scarlett's department car and headed toward CPD. 'What happened?' he asked.

She told him everything Isenberg had shared. 'The woman in your memory, the one who warned Demetrius when he had the pillow on your face . . . Do you think you'd recognize her voice if you heard it again?'

'I don't know,' he said honestly. 'Does it matter? She had my photo on her phone. I was probably going to be her next target.'

'Remembering her voice would allow us to connect her to Demetrius, which involves her in the conspiracy to traffic humans. Otherwise she can claim to be a third party hit-person.'

He lifted his brows. 'Murder for hire is no chump charge.'

'No, but I want justice for Tala. I want every single person who profited from her three years of misery to pay. I want them to die. In the absence of that, I want them to rot in prison forever and know exactly what it means to have someone else control your destiny.' Her eyes stung, her voice trembling. 'I want to be able to look in Malaya's face someday and know that I did everything humanly possible to ensure that her mother's sacrifice was not in vain.'

He let out a slow breath, then reached over and wiped the tears from her cheeks. 'All right. I'll do my best.'

'That's all I can ask,' she whispered.

She drove for a few minutes in silence, gathering her composure. She hadn't intended to get so emotional. She seemed to do that a lot around Marcus O'Bannion. Hell, maybe it was good for her to vent it off. She certainly felt better right now, and he didn't seem to mind.

'You okay now, Miss Scarlett?' he asked lightly, mimicking Tommy's endearment.

'Yeah. I am.' She glanced at him curiously. 'What did Tommy say to you?'

Marcus snorted a laugh. 'All the things that your dad and brothers will say when I finally get to meet them. I'd better not break your heart or he'll break me in half, tear off my arms and beat me with them. That kind of thing.'

'Tommy? Really? Awww, that is so sweet.'

'Sweet? He threatened my life and you call him sweet? You really are bloodthirsty,' he teased.

'Well you don't have to worry. I doubt Tommy's got any follow-through left in him.'

'I don't know about that. The old guy's still got strong hands, and he says he knows how to use them. I'm inclined to believe him. Did you know he has a Purple Heart?'

Scarlett blinked. 'No. I had no idea. Vietnam?'

'Yep. He carries it around in his pocket.'

'He showed you his Purple Heart, just like that? He never showed it to me.'

'He asked me what I'd done with my life. I told him I'd served. That had him backing off just a little to only a partial disemboweling if I hurt you.' He smiled when she laughed, but then he sighed. 'I hate the fact that so many vets are on the streets. Makes me want to fix that.'

'You can't fix everything, Marcus.'

'I know. But I still try. And so do you.' He was quiet for a moment. 'He told me all the things you've done for him and Edna and some of the other street folks.'

Scarlett's cheeks began to heat. 'Tommy exaggerates.'

'I don't think so. He told me about the water you make sure he drinks and the food you just happen to have with you. About how you nag him to go the shelter and make sure he gets appointments at the clinic.'

Scarlett rolled her eyes, her face now hotter than a flame. 'I don't nag. I remind.'

'Hm. He told me about the blankets and the shoes and the gloves you "happened to have with you" last winter when it was so cold. About how you never forget his birthday or Edna's. And he told me that when his sister died, it was you who came to sit with him in the hospital. That was how long ago, Scarlett?'

'Twelve years this fall,' she murmured.

'You were only eighteen then. Not a cop yet.'

'No, not yet, but I knew I'd be one. I miss Tommy's sister. She kept him stable for so long. Tommy didn't use to live on the stoop all the time, you know. He had a shoeshine stand downtown. On Saturday afternoons when my dad was off duty, he'd drive me to dance lessons and take the long way home so he could get Tommy to shine his shoes. This was way out of our way. We lived in Bridgetown and my dance studio was there.'

'Wow. So basically he'd drive all the way from the west side into the city.'

'Exactly. He would park near Tommy's corner and pick me up and carry me on his shoulders, then I'd sit on his lap and listen while he and Tommy talked about nothing at all while Tommy shined his shoes. But it wasn't really nothing. It was my dad getting the pulse of the neighborhood. Creating some trust. I get that now, but I didn't understand when I was a kid. One day when I was a little older, maybe nine or so, I asked Dad why he paid Tommy to shine his shoes when I could do it cheaper, plus he'd save gas money and time. I was a *bargain*.'

Marcus's lips curved. 'Enterprising. What did your dad say?'

'That Tommy needed the money and I didn't. I told him that I did so need it, that I was saving for a girl bicycle with tassels on the handlebars, that I was tired of boy-bike hand-me-downs. That I was his kid and Tommy was some man on the street. Then Dad said he helped Tommy because "but for the grace of God, there go I".'

'Your dad's a vet too?'

'Yeah. He was in Vietnam at the tail end of the war, only for a few months. I didn't understand when I was nine, but hearing that Tommy was a vet, it makes sense now. Anyway, Tommy would go home every few days or so and sleep in a real bed and eat a real meal. Then it became every few weeks, then months, and then when Sondra died, he had no place to go. It was like his only tie to the world snapped. I never really thought about taking care of him. It was just something that you did.'

'*You* do. How many cops do you know who do the same?' Marcus had twisted in his seat and now stared at her profile. She could feel his stare and it was making her uncomfortable.

'I don't know. I don't talk about it.' She frowned. 'Tommy wasn't supposed to either.'

'Because you have a reputation as a ball-buster.'

'Yeah, and I worked damn hard for that reputation,' she said indignantly, making him laugh. 'You think I'm kidding. People like Tommy start breaking radio silence all over the damn place and everyone will start thinking I'm a sap.'

'Your secrets are safe with me, Miss Scarlett.'

She smiled. 'He's called me Miss Scarlett since I was sitting on Dad's knee in a pink tutu eating an ice cream cone. The truth is, I do what I do because I'm selfish. There are times when I am so angry that I want to walk up to some meth-head who's beaten his girlfriend's child to death and put my hands around his neck and squeeze so hard that his head pops like a zit. And there are the times I get rough with a suspect and I have to yank myself back. That's when I drive through the neighborhoods and do something . . .'

'Kind?' Marcus supplied.

'I guess.' She shrugged, feeling awkward. 'It keeps me tethered to the light. So I'm really getting more out of it than Tommy is. Ergo, selfish.'

'You keep on saying that if it makes you feel better,' he said, shaking his head. 'You know, you haven't said much about your father. I assumed he was a . . . distant man.'

Scarlett had to swallow hard. 'No. My dad is pretty wonderful, actually. He worries about me. Mom does too. I used to be their little girl and now I'm this angry, resentful person.'

'You keep saying so. I don't see it.'

She thought about that. 'Maybe when I'm around you I don't feel so angry.'

He smiled. 'I like that explanation.'

'Dad never wanted me to be a cop. He said I had too soft a heart, that I'd be chewed up and spit out. But it's all I ever wanted to be. And when Michelle died and Trent Bracken walked . . . I made a promise to Michelle's memory that I'd be a cop and I wouldn't have a soft heart. That I'd do my job so well that future Trent Brackens wouldn't go free.'

'But your dad is right. You do have a soft heart, and cases like Tala's tear it open. So you do that long-blink thing and shove it all down. How long will you be able to keep that up?'

'For as long as I can. For as long as it takes.'

He sighed. 'I figured you'd say that. I also don't figure I'm in any position to tell you any different.'

'Pot meet kettle,' she said in resignation. She pulled into the CPD parking garage, started to take the keys out and stopped cold as her mind snapped back to the case. 'Wait just a minute. The Feds brought that suspect in from Constant Global Surveillance yesterday. They could have brought him in this way, through a protected parking garage, but they took him in through the front, where he became a target.'

'You're right.' Marcus folded his arms over his chest. 'When we asked how they knew the shooter was on the roof, Coppola said they got a tip.'

'They set it up,' Scarlett said. 'Made the tracker guy bait. Not that I'm complaining, but it was risky.'

'They must have really trusted that tip,' Marcus said, watching her carefully.

Scarlett considered what she was about to say and decided he had a right to know. 'They have a man inside.'

'The Feds?'

'Yeah. I don't know who. Don't know where. Don't know how they contact him. All I know is that I wasn't supposed to tell you that.'

His expression went carefully blank. 'I would have guessed eventually. But thanks for telling me now.'

He said it so stiffly that she was certain 'thank you' was not what he was really thinking. 'I didn't ask you about Diesel.'

'True, but this is different. This impacts my life.'

'I didn't know for sure that it would, not until just now. They were watching more than one trafficking group – which is what they do. They're the human trafficking task force. That's not news to anyone. I didn't know that the undercover Fed was watching the same people who want you dead. I know now. And so do you.'

He relaxed. 'I'm sorry. You're right.'

'Damn straight I'm right. But now you have to act surprised if someone tells you.'

He feigned a shocked look. 'How's this?'

She snickered. 'Don't give up your day job. Come on. Let's go meet Alice Newman.'

Thirty-three

Ken found Decker sweating and shirtless in the bedroom where Demetrius had died. The younger man had a circular saw in his hand and was cutting up the last of the bloody mattress into strips. The room was stifling hot, largely because Decker had opened the window to air the place out. The air conditioning simply wasn't keeping up.

Decker turned the saw off when he saw Ken standing there. 'Almost done, sir,' he said, pulling a hand towel from the back pocket of his jeans and wiping the sweat from his face. 'I'll haul it out and burn it.'

'No. The smoke will attract attention. Just bury it.' Ken was glad to see the mattress go. Killing his oldest friend had been far harder than he'd thought it would be, even though Demetrius had betrayed him.

'Will do.' Decker started to turn the saw back on, but hesitated. 'Anything else?'

'Where are Burton and the Anders girl? I just checked the basement and it's empty.'

'I did what you said. They've been taken care of.'

'Already?'

'Like I said, I like working the woodchipper.' Decker frowned. 'Please don't tell me you changed your mind.'

Ken laughed grimly. 'No. I thought I'd have a last chat with Miss Anders. She was . . .'

'A bitch,' Decker muttered. He turned to show four deep claw marks down his shoulder.

'Wow. I guess that teaches you to wear a shirt.'

Decker glared. 'I *was* wearing a shirt. She grabbed me, up under my sleeve. Those nails of hers were fake. She'd been sharpening them on the concrete foundation of the cage.'

Ken wished he could have seen it. He wished more that he could have gotten to her before Decker had killed her. A good fuck always cleared his head before he went hunting, and thinking of Stephanie Anders clawing at Decker made him even harder than he'd been when he'd gone to the basement looking for her.

'Make sure your tetanus shots are up to date,' he said.

'They are, luckily. Between that bitch and her mother.'

'Oh, that's right. Marlene bit you.'

'Give me a male prisoner any day of the week,' Decker grumbled, then shook off his bad mood. 'When I'm done here, I'm going into the office. With Burton and Reuben gone, the work is piling up. You'll need to hire new security personnel. I thought I'd start compiling a list of ex-military that I know would be interested and trustworthy.'

'Yes, do that,' Ken said, but he was thinking *no* so loudly his teeth ached. He was done, his leadership team decimated. Alice incarcerated. And as much as he wanted to believe she'd be stalwart under questioning, he knew she'd give him up in a heartbeat if she thought it was her best option. He'd be out of the country before she decided on that course of action.

He already had a first-class ticket from Toronto to Papeete, Tahiti, leaving tomorrow night. From Papeete he'd take a charter to Bora Bora, where he'd rented a small bungalow. All under the false ID that he had arranged for himself a long time ago – just in case of an emergency such as this. No one knew about it, not even Alice or Sean.

Ken hadn't yet decided if he'd send for Sean. He'd always had a more hands-off relationship with Sean than he'd had with Alice. Sean had never liked getting his hands dirty. Alice thrived on it. *Damn, I miss her already.* But he wasn't willing to trap himself trying to bust her out of jail. She had access to assets. She was a lawyer, for God's sake. She was better equipped to get herself out of jail than he was.

Decker and the others who were left could do what they pleased. If they wanted to take the contacts Ken and his team had built over the last decade, they were welcome to them. Joel still had the accounting records, after all. Joel might even end up as the leader of the group after Ken was out of the picture. He was welcome to that too. Not that Ken thought Joel would last too much longer. The young pups would either eliminate him or Joel's heart would simply give out. Either way, Joel was a big boy. He'd have to be fine on his own.

Ken had a singular focus – kill Marcus O'Bannion, then get out. O'Bannion was the type to follow him across the world if he put enough of the puzzle together. *I'll snip that loose end so that I don't have to be looking over my shoulder for the next thirty or forty years.*

He'd start hunting at the *Ledger*'s office. Many of O'Bannion's employees had been with him for years. There had to be someone there he'd want to get back were they to be borrowed. And if he didn't find what he was looking for at the *Ledger*, he had a plan B.

He'd found photos on Demetrius's iPad of O'Bannion and that homicide detective sitting in the detective's car outside an animal shelter. Ken had forgotten that Demetrius had tracked them there until he'd seen the photos. It seemed that O'Bannion and the detective were in some kind of very personal relationship. He didn't want to tangle with a cop if he didn't have to, but the pretty homicide detective would make the perfect bait.

'Um . . .' Decker said, and Ken realized he'd been standing there too long. 'Is there anything else you want me to do?'

'No, no. The list of potential hires would be fine. I'll let Sean know to expect you down at the office.' He gave a last, mournful look at the bedroom, falling back on nostalgia to excuse his wool-gathering. 'Demetrius and I had a lot of good times over the years. I'll miss him.'

The look Decker gave him was warily sympathetic. 'I understand, sir.'

No, you really don't. 'Goodnight, Decker. Please lock the front door on your way out.'

Cincinnati, Ohio
Wednesday 5 August, 6.00 P.M.

Marcus had been nervous the last time he'd emerged from the elevator into the MCES squad room, but this time he was doubly so. He knew Scarlett wanted him to identify the woman in Interview Room Four as the one who'd participated in the attempt to kill him nine months ago, and he understood how important it was – both to the case and to Scarlett herself.

Trouble was, he didn't know if he could. He had no compunction fudging a story when the target of their investigation had been guilty of so many, even worse offenses. This woman was definitely a killer – or would have been but for the tip the Feds got from their unnamed source. It should be a no-brainer just to tell Scarlett what she wanted to hear.

But where his conscience had allowed him to fudge facts in the past, this was different. This was for Scarlett, who looked at him like he could do no wrong.

Isenberg was waiting for them at the elevator. 'Mr O'Bannion, Detective Bishop.'

Marcus didn't miss Scarlett's minute wince, and once again he found himself biting back the urge to tell Isenberg to fuck herself. Scarlett had enjoyed an informal, friendly relationship with her boss. *Until I came along,* he thought.

He clenched his teeth and followed the lieutenant to the darkened observation room on the other side of the glass from Interview Room Four. He stepped up to the glass, Scarlett standing at his side, her hands shoved in her pockets. She leaned into him just once, surreptitiously touching his upper arm with her shoulder. Support, he thought.

'If you're not sure, it's okay,' she murmured, so quietly he almost didn't hear. But he did hear, and it was like a weight sliding off his shoulders.

There were a few people sitting along the wall behind them, cops and Feds, including Deacon and Agents Coppola and Troy. The three of them came forward, Deacon taking the spot next to Scarlett. Coppola positioned herself next to Marcus, and Troy hovered in the background.

Marcus was relieved to see that Isenberg had disappeared into the shadows in the back of the room. Scarlett had said that her boss was looking out for her career, but he thought the woman could find a better way to do it.

But he wasn't here for Lieutenant Isenberg. He was here to identify someone who might have tried to kill him if she'd had enough time – the woman on the other side of the glass. *I was her next target.* The realization left him shaken. And pissed.

'That is Alice Newman,' Kate Coppola said. 'She's not happy to be here.'

Alice sat turned away from the glass, her face hidden. She was handcuffed to the chair, her back ramrod straight. Her blond hair was cut in a bob that seemed vaguely familiar.

But he hadn't *seen* her, had he? He'd only *heard* her.

Deacon pointed to the man sitting next to her. 'That's Karl Hohl, the lawyer she called. She asked for the Yellow Pages, since we'd taken her phone, closed her eyes and pointed.'

'I'll have her turned around,' Kate said.

'Not yet,' Marcus said. 'I'd like to hear her voice before I see her face.'

'All right,' Kate said. 'Then I'll try to get her to talk.'

'She hasn't been cooperative,' Deacon said. 'You may have to make your judgment based on the recording.'

'Understand. Try to get her to say "Hurry up".' Or something like that.'

As if sensing she had an audience, Alice Newman turned to look over her shoulder, and Marcus's mouth fell open, dumbstruck. 'Whoa. Holy shit. Holy fucking shit.'

'You know her,' Scarlett murmured, sounding unsurprised. 'Who is she?'

Marcus sure as *hell* was surprised. 'Allison Bassett, the older sister of one of Mikhail's friends from school. Or so she said. I didn't know her brother and I thought I knew all of Mikhail's friends. But after he was gone, people came out of the woodwork to give their condolences. I met a lot of Mickey's friends that I didn't know, so I didn't think anything of it.'

'How did she make contact?' Deacon asked.

'She came to see me in the hospital when I was out of ICU, told me how torn up her brother was. Said that they'd just moved to the area at the beginning of the school year, that her brother was nervous about being the new kid in school, but that Mickey had befriended him. She came to see me several times. We just talked. She never tried to smother me or anything,' he added lightly, but his voice shook a little. The woman had sat three feet away from him. Close enough to kill him in his weakened state had she really wanted to.

'What would you talk about?' Deacon asked.

Scarlett was uncharacteristically silent, watching the woman grimly.

'Mostly me and my family, how my recovery was going, when I was going back to work. She'd read a few of our exposés in the *Ledger* and asked a lot of questions. She even asked about the McCord article, saying how disgusting he was.' He shook his head, still reeling. 'She must have been digging, trying to find out if I planned to pick up the McCord investigation where I left off. Holy God. I had no idea. All those times she was a few feet away from me. God.'

'And after you got out of the hospital?' Kate asked. 'Did she see you again?'

'She stopped by Mom's house a time or two. After I was healthier, I'd see her when I went to the gym and we'd talk while we ran the inside track.'

In the reflection in the glass he saw Kate frown. 'You didn't think it odd?' she asked. 'That maybe she was stalking you?'

Marcus blew out a breath, wondering how Scarlett was going to take what he was about to say. 'No, I didn't think it was odd because, yes, I thought she was stalking me, but not for any reason other than the normal one. I had several women visit me in the hospital. I also got emails, Facebook posts, you name it. When the news story came out about how I got shot . . .'

'Women thought you were a super-stud hero,' Deacon said dryly. 'A savior of damsels in distress.'

Marcus shrugged uncomfortably. 'Something like that. I got a number of interesting propositions, but I knew I was just the flavor of the week. It tapered off quickly enough, except for this one. That she was interested in me was pretty blatant. I flat-out asked her how she'd chosen my gym and she said it was so that she could run into me, that she'd bribed the guy at the counter to tell her when I came in so that she could work out at the same time.'

In the reflection of the window he watched Scarlett do one of her long blinks. He wasn't sure what emotion she was hiding this time – fury that the woman had stalked him, fear that she'd come so close. Hopefully it was not hurt that Marcus had allowed it, because he hadn't.

'I told her I was flattered but not interested,' he said firmly.

'But she kept showing up,' Scarlett said, her tone crisp and professional. Then he felt the fleetest of brushes against his hip – her fingers, still in her pocket, flexing to touch him. All she felt safe doing in the situation.

He let out the breath he was holding. 'She did. I changed my workout time and she'd change hers. I finally told her that there was someone else.' He dropped his voice to a murmur meant only for Scarlett's ears. 'And I meant it.'

Another one of those tiny brushes of her fingers. 'Did she back off?'

'She did, actually. She started working out with another guy and they were all over each over in no time. I was just happy that she wasn't chasing after me anymore. Now I'm wondering who that other guy was, because he'd chat me up too. He just wasn't as obvious about it. The gym – Silver Gym, a block away from the *Ledger* – would have a photo in their system of the guy. She called him DJ. Big guy, African-American, maybe twenty-one. Six-two, had to be two-sixty. Kid could bench three hundred. I can point him out if the gym can pull photos that match.'

Scarlett and Deacon exchanged glances. 'His name was DJ,' she said, 'and he's the right age.'

Marcus got it. 'Demetrius Junior? He could have been. He had the right build.'

'I'll get on it,' Kate said. 'The question is, is she the one who you heard telling Demetrius that someone was coming when he was smothering you?' She handed him an earphone and plugged it into her phone. 'This is what we've got.'

Marcus put the earphone to his ear, hit play on Kate's phone, and heard a harsh, angry voice asking for a lawyer. He listened several times, but shook his head. 'I don't know,' he said honestly. 'It's such a fragmented memory, and this voice doesn't even sound like the one I remember when I was talking to her face to face. Hearing her speak in person didn't make me remember the time she spoke to Demetrius, so I don't think my testimony is that relevant.'

'I figured as much,' Kate said. 'But I had to check anyway.'

'Her being associated with Demetrius's son links her to the traffickers,' Scarlett said.

'Not closely enough,' Kate said with regret. 'Cross your fingers that we get something more useful out of her during interrogation.'

'I can talk to her,' Marcus said. 'Maybe seeing me will startle her into speaking.'

Kate looked to Troy. 'What do you think?'

'You go in first,' Troy said. 'Confront her with what you know and see if you can get her to ID the older man. If she doesn't budge, we can send O'Bannion in to join you.'

'What older man?' Scarlett asked, eyes narrowing suspiciously. 'What do you know that you're not sharing?'

'Chill, Scar,' Deacon murmured, with a light touch to her shoulder. 'Nobody's keeping anything from you. This was hot off the press right before Isenberg brought you in here.'

'I even made copies for you,' Kate said. 'But we didn't want to influence Marcus before he'd had a chance to ID her.' She gave Scarlett a sheet of paper on which several photos were printed. Scarlett held it up to the light coming through the glass, so that Marcus could see too.

He rested his hand against the small of her back and leaned to look over her shoulder. There were three photos. Beside each was an enlargement of a detail in the original. The first was a trio of young women in short shorts and skimpy tank tops, arm in arm, smiling for the camera. The second and third photos were graduation pictures of other people – but which also included Alice Newman in the background. In the third photo, Alice, dressed in her cap and gown, stood with a man old enough to be her father. He was fit and trim, wearing an expensive suit, his arm tight around her shoulders. They weren't posing for the photo and the view of the man's face wasn't complete, but the enlarged detail showed he was smiling with pride.

'We got the name Alice Newman from the DMV database after running her photo through facial recognition software,' Kate explained. 'Then we cross-checked social media and found her tagged in this beach photo. The woman in the middle graduated from Kentucky Law too, so we searched the photos in her social media accounts.'

'You'd think a lawyer would be more careful about her privacy settings,' Marcus said.

'Lucky for us she wasn't,' Scarlett replied.

'We found Alice in the background of two graduation pictures,' Kate went on. 'The man in the third photo has no social media presence that we could find. He's also not in the DMV database. Nor is Demetrius Russell, for

507

that matter.' She rolled her shoulders and cracked her knuckles. 'Wish me luck. Sit tight, Marcus. I'll motion you in when I'm ready.'

Unfortunately, Alice sat mutinously silent, staring at the glass when Kate had the guard turn her chair around. After working it for thirty minutes without a single reaction from Alice, Kate crooked her finger at the glass, motioning Marcus to join her.

Marcus drew a breath and squared his shoulders before walking from the observation room into Interview Four. He didn't say a word at first. Just focused on Alice's reaction when she saw him. He wasn't disappointed, and neither was Kate Coppola.

Alice's eyes narrowed, flashed with pure hate. Had Marcus not been expecting it, he might have taken an actual step back.

'Hello, Allison,' he said quietly. 'Or is it Alice?'

She leaned back in her chair, her lips curving in a bitter smile, full of malice. 'Well, well, well. If it's not Mr Nine Lives himself. I should have killed you when I had the chance.'

Cincinnati, Ohio
Wednesday 5 August, 6.55 P.M.

Scarlett blew out a breath. 'That clarifies things,' she said to Deacon.

'I'd say so,' Deacon murmured. 'The women still get me. They look all sweet, like butter wouldn't melt in their mouths, you know? And then they go all Miz Hyde and freak me the hell out.'

Scarlett smiled at the genuine dismay in his voice. Deacon was the sharpest partner she'd ever had, but he tended to get blindsided by truly evil women. 'It's one of nature's equalizers,' she said, 'like with sea anemones. They look like a pretty flower until their tentacles shoot paralyzing toxin into their unsuspecting prey, and then bada-bing. It's game over.'

'You are blood—'

'You better not be about to say bloodthirsty,' she warned. 'I've got tentacles too.'

'*Pfff*,' Deacon scoffed. 'But I'll tell everyone that you scare me if you want me to.'

'That'll work,' she murmured as Marcus took the chair next to Alice, spun it around and straddled it. 'She was so close to him, so many times, Deacon. Why didn't she kill him when she had the chance?'

'I don't know. She didn't, though,' Deacon said softly, lightly bumping his shoulder into hers. 'Keep telling yourself that. He's alive and she's in custody.'

On the other side of the glass, Marcus broke his silence. 'Why didn't you?' he asked Alice. 'You had a number of opportunities to kill me even after your partner botched the pillow job. Thanks for saving my life, by the way. Demetrius was pretty close to finishing me off when you told him that someone was coming.'

Alice's mouth opened in surprise before she could catch herself. 'He was a useless fool.'

'Bingo,' Deacon murmured.

'I so want her ass to fry,' Scarlett murmured back.

Marcus shrugged at Alice. 'You're here and he's not, so what does that make you?'

'Obedient,' she muttered.

Her lawyer cleared his throat. 'Miss Newman.'

'Don't worry,' she said with a laugh that chilled Scarlett to the bone. 'I'm not going to tell them anything useful. Not unless I get what I want.'

'And what is that, Alice?' Kate asked.

'Immunity. Total and complete.'

Kate choked on a laugh. 'Really? I don't think so.'

Alice smiled smugly. 'Then you're wasting my time. And yours. I walk or you get nothing.'

'Perhaps,' Marcus said quietly. 'Or maybe Agent Coppola doesn't need you. I wonder if DJ will be as stoic when she questions him.'

'DJ's just a boy toy. He knows nothing.'

'Perhaps,' he said again. 'We'll find out soon enough, because he's in the interview room next door,' he lied smoothly. 'I'd love to see his face when he finds out his daddy is dead. Or does he already know? Will he still follow you around like a puppy when he finds out what you've done? I hope not. I'd like to see the kid grow a pair and throw you to the wolves.'

This time Alice's shock was pronounced, her eyes narrowing to mere slits. 'Fuck you, O'Bannion.'

Behind the glass, Deacon tilted his head. 'How did he know that?'

'He guessed,' Scarlett said. 'She said Demetrius *was* a useless fool. Marcus knew that Phillip had stabbed Demetrius. He knew that DJ was younger and Alice had him on a short leash at the gym. He added it up. He's smart like that, you know.'

Deacon rolled his eyes. 'I think I'm going to puke.'

Scarlett's lips twitched. 'Now you know how I've felt all these months.'

Marcus had twisted his face into a grimace. 'I don't think so. I didn't want to fuck you before I found out you wanted to kill me. Desperate women aren't my type.'

'You can go to hell.'

Marcus didn't flinch. Didn't bat an eye as he regarded Alice with contempt. Scarlett's heart swelled with pride. Then collapsed in her chest when he replied.

'Not yet. I haven't used up all of my nine lives.'

'There's still time, Marcus,' Alice said a smile.

'Fucking idiot,' Deacon growled. 'Poking a cornered snake with a stick is not smart.'

'He's got a damn hard head,' Scarlett said, gritting her teeth. 'I'll smack him later.' Her cell phone buzzed, but she ignored it for a moment, not wanting to look away from the viper sitting at the table. *Sitting too damn close to what's mine.*

In the interview room, Marcus raised his brows at Alice. 'Since you're here and Demetrius is dead, someone else will have to take the baton. Who? Not DJ. He's just a puppy. This guy maybe?' He tapped the photo that Kate had enlarged. 'Is he your sugar daddy?'

An almost intangible tightening of Alice's body, then she relaxed with a smile. 'Yes. He was. He paid my tuition and I was his arm candy. Then I graduated and didn't need him anymore. Got a better offer.'

Kate sat next to Marcus. 'Assassin was a better offer?' she asked. 'I wouldn't think you'd need a law degree for that.'

Scarlett's phone buzzed again and she cursed softly, not wanting to miss Alice's answer.

'It's Vince,' Deacon said, looking at his own phone. 'He's decrypted the files from Drake Connor's flash drive. You coming, Scar?'

'In a minute. I want to finish this.' She handed Deacon the external drive that Diesel had given her. 'Can you ask him to scan this for any booby traps? It's got the non-picture files from McCord's computer.'

'Do I want to know how you got these?' Deacon asked.

'No. Tell Vince I'll go through the files. I need to be sure they're safe for my computer.'

'Okay,' Deacon said cautiously. 'I hope you know what you're doing.' He looked over his shoulder. 'You coming, Lynda? Agent Troy?'

Scarlett hadn't forgotten they were back there. Nor had she forgotten that there was one other person sitting in the back row. She waited until Deacon and the others had left before sighing wearily. 'You might as well come closer, Dad.'

Jonas Bishop joined her in front of the glass, crossing his arms over his big chest. 'I didn't know if you knew I was there.'

'Spotted you the minute I walked in, but this wasn't about me or you.

This was about Marcus. I didn't want him distracted. You can talk to him when they're finished.'

'Bossy,' he said, but his hand was gentle when he brushed it over her hair. He put his arm around her shoulders and pulled her close. She went willingly, leaning her head against his chest, but keeping her hands in her pockets.

She didn't want him to find out that he'd been right all along. That she wasn't tough enough to be a cop. That the job had chewed her up and was getting ready to spit her out.

Alice had sat back in her chair again. She'd closed her mouth stubbornly when Kate had joined the conversation and now stared straight ahead.

Kate checked her phone, then gave a quick hand signal to Marcus to stay put. The interview room became quiet as they waited. For what, Scarlett was unsure.

'Why are you here, Dad?'

He squeezed her upper arm. 'I wanted to see you. We don't get to see you enough.'

'I'm sorry.'

'Don't be sorry. Just don't be a stranger.' He hesitated nervously, this big man she'd always thought knew no fear. 'Your uncle said you called him for help.'

'I did. I needed a priest. Trace was an amazing help.'

Another silence as the two of them stood there looking into the interview room. 'So that's him, huh? The man you've chosen.'

There was something in his voice that got her hackles up. 'Yes,' she said, hearing the defensiveness in her own voice. 'Marcus is a damn good man.'

'I wouldn't know,' he said lightly. 'I haven't met him yet.'

'I was going bring him over.' *Eventually*, she thought. 'We've been a little busy.'

'So I hear. I never thought you'd go for a reporter again.'

'Marcus isn't a reporter. He isn't like any media person I've ever met.'

'You mother always thought you'd bring home Bryan someday. Gets herself into a dither worrying about it.'

Scarlett blinked, surprised. 'I thought she liked Bryan.'

'She feels sorry for him because he's essentially motherless. But she never wanted him for you. I kept telling her not to worry about Bryan. That you have more sense than that.'

Scarlett's throat grew tight. 'Thank you.'

'But . . .'

Her back stiffened. 'But?' There was always a *but*.

'Your LT thinks you're risking your career getting too involved with this guy before the case is closed. You know the rules, Scarlett Anne.'

In the past he'd used her full name when he was angry or disappointed in her. This time, there was gentleness and concern.

'I know the rules, Dad.'

'You didn't say you'd follow them.'

'No, I didn't.'

'This . . . thing you have . . . It could destroy your career.'

It wasn't a scolding. It was reality, and Scarlett appreciated the way he said it. 'I know. I hope it doesn't come to that, but if I have to make a choice, I'll choose him. I've waited too long to walk away from him.'

Her father blew out a breath. 'You've known him two days, baby.'

She smiled. 'Longer than that.' Her smile faded when she looked at Alice Newman, sitting with her eyes stubbornly forward. 'Besides, it might be a relief to get off this merry-go-round.' Her voice wobbled, but it felt good to get the words out. 'I'm tired, Dad.'

'How long have you been tired?' he asked, his voice so gentle that her eyes stung.

'When was my first day?' she asked with a teary laugh. 'I take one off the street and two more take his place. Or *her* place.' She blinked to clear her vision, bringing Alice's face into focus. 'She bought and sold people. Children. Families. Like they were animals. She and her group of cohorts tried to kill Marcus, I don't know how many times. Because he's kind and decent and couldn't stand to see a girl suffer. And all I can do is arrest her when what I really want to do is—' She cut herself off abruptly.

'Slice her into pieces?' her father murmured. 'Shove explosives where the sun don't shine? Tie her to a bed, give all her victims a sharp knife, then let them file by her one by one until she looks like a cutlery block?'

Stunned, she reared back, stared up at her father's face. He wore no smile. 'But . . .'

He hooked his forefinger under her chin, lifting it to close her mouth. 'You think you're the only one, Scarlett? Well, you're not.'

'But you've never said anything like that.'

'Not to you. You were a child. That wouldn't have been appropriate. But your mother's heard it all and more. She learned a long time ago that I wouldn't do it. I just needed to say it, to vent off some of the pressure. Your mother understands.'

Scarlett bit her lip, not knowing what he'd do with what she was about to say. 'I think mine is more than a need to vent.'

'How so?'

512

She looked back at the glass. At Marcus waiting patiently while Kate checked her phone. 'I've wanted to kill Trent Bracken so many times,' she whispered.

'Understandable. He killed your best friend and walked away a free man.'

'No, you don't understand. I haven't just wanted to. I've fantasized. I've planned it out, down to giving myself an alibi. There were a few times that I sat outside his house with my service revolver in my hand, hoping he'd come out to take the trash down to the curb. Then one night he did. I pointed the gun and flicked off the safety. I had him in my sight for a good twenty seconds. But I didn't fire and he went back into his house, none the wiser.'

A long, long silence. 'What stopped you?' he asked gruffly.

'I don't know. I think it was pride on some level. When I killed him, I wanted him to know who was taking him out. I wanted to feel the bastard's blood on my hands. Maybe then I wouldn't remember having Michelle's there.'

His hand clenched on her shoulder, an involuntary reflex. 'But you didn't kill him.'

'I just couldn't.' She shrugged. 'I guess you did something right when you raised me.'

'I did a lot of things right, Scarlett Anne.'

'Well.' She filled her lungs. Swallowed hard. 'Regardless, it's not a very good way for a cop to operate. I've caught myself close to the edge too many times to remember. So when Isenberg tells me I'm risking my career, I'm not so upset. I'd rather lose it for Marcus than because I beat a suspect to a pulp because he beat his child to death. Because you were right. I'm not cut out to be a cop. I'm not tough enough.'

He stiffened. 'What the hell, girl? What do you mean, I was right? You're a damn fine cop, Scarlett. I have *never* said otherwise.'

She pulled back to stare at him. 'Yes you did, the day I got into the Academy. I was so excited, but you said my heart was too soft, that the force would chew me up and spit me out.'

He blinked at her in disbelief, but she held his gaze steadily, waiting for him to remember. She saw the moment that he did, because he paled. 'You weren't supposed to hear that,' he said quietly. 'I said that to you mother. In our bedroom.'

'I got up to go to the bathroom and I heard you arguing.'

'No, you heard me venting.' He closed his eyes. 'Dammit, Scarlett. You were still hurting from Michelle. You were like a walking ghost. I was shocked you even passed the psychological. Anyone with eyes could see you were broken.'

'I wasn't broken, Dad.'

'No? What do you call stalking a perp and waiting to shoot him when he takes out the trash?'

She flushed. 'Okay, I guess I deserved that.'

He huffed in frustration. 'Look, you only heard part of that conversation. Your mother told me that you were a lot stronger than I was giving you credit for. That the two of us had raised you to know your own mind. That I needed to trust you. So I did. I didn't say anything to you. I kept my fear to myself. Because I *was* afraid. You did have a soft heart. You still do. But you know what else your mother said that night?'

She shook her head. 'No. What?'

'That you came by that soft heart honestly. That you got it from me. That of all seven of our kids, you were the most like me. She was right. And it's your heart that makes you a damn good cop.' His voice trembled and he cleared his throat. 'And I'll punch the lights out of anyone who says otherwise.'

Scarlett pursed her lips, her eyes filling. 'Don't go punching people,' she whispered hoarsely. 'You'll lose your pension.' She quickly swiped her knuckles under her eyes, wiping away the tears before they could leave streaks on her cheeks.

His chuckle was wet. 'Can't have that. Your mother only stays with me for my retirement package.' He cupped her face in one of his big palms, his eyes glittering with a few tears of his own. 'Why didn't you come to me and talk about this? At least yell at me? Why did you keep this inside you all these years?'

'Because I wanted to prove you wrong. I wanted you to see that I could be a good cop too. That my heart wasn't too soft.'

'Soft, baby. But not too soft. You couldn't have survived all this time otherwise. You would have pulled the trigger on that bastard Bracken and you would have beaten the child abusers. You wouldn't be *Detective* Bishop. You might have cracked, but you didn't break.' He hugged her to him and gave her a little shake. 'And if you'd talked to someone – like your father – then all this anger wouldn't be building up to the level where you're doubting yourself.'

'I didn't want you to see the anger,' she confessed. 'I didn't want you to know how close to the edge I was.'

'So you kept your distance. All this time.' He sighed heavily. 'Dammit, girl. So what are you going to do about it?'

'Stick with Marcus. He said he can't see the anger I'm so afraid of. I think it's because I'm not angry when I'm with him.'

Understanding flickered in his eyes. 'He's your valve.'

'Like Mom is yours.'

'Well then. Bring him to dinner on Sunday. Your brothers will want to meet him. We'll all have a little chat.'

She laughed. 'Don't worry. He got the talk from Tommy this afternoon.'

'Tommy? You mean Shoeshine Tommy?'

'The very same. I keep track of him and some of the others. He's spending time at the Meadow these days. He witnessed one of the perpetrators in my case fleeing the scene yesterday. His and Edna's testimony will ensure that a little prick named Drake Connor gets charged with murder here in Ohio on top of the murders he's done in Michigan. He shot that girl in the alley and tried to kill Marcus too.'

'I didn't know you were keeping track of Tommy too.'

'Too?'

'Sure.' He shrugged. 'I still need my shoes shined and sometimes I don't have time to do it myself.'

Scarlett knew better. Her father had never gone to Tommy for the actual shoeshine. 'But he doesn't have his stand anymore.'

'He still has his shine kit. I seek him out when I have a free minute or two. Not as frequently as I'd like. But he never mentions seeing you.'

'Because I threatened him if he told anyone. He wasn't supposed to tell Marcus.' She scowled. 'I take care of him and the others and they make sure I get informed when they see trouble. Just like you used to all those times we'd go see Tommy for a shoeshine. I was telling Marcus today how you used to take me with you.'

'You looked so cute in your pink tutu,' he said, a smile in his voice. 'You had to have your ice cream too. Black Raspberry Chocolate Chip from Graeter's. Always.'

'Always.' Scarlett's throat thickened again, her chest so tight that it hurt. But it was a good hurt. 'I didn't understand why you went to Tommy for a shoeshine back then, but I do now. I didn't need the Academy, Dad. I learned how to be a cop by watching you.'

His chest expanded on a sudden deep breath that he shuddered out, followed by another harsh exhale. 'Thank you, baby.'

'It's the truth. That's why it hurt so much when I heard what you said. I wanted to be like you.'

He cleared his throat roughly. 'You know I love you, right?'

'Yeah.' She leaned her head on his shoulder. 'You know I love you back, right?'

He hugged her to him, hard. 'Yeah. So are we okay? There are no other misunderstandings we have to deal with?'

'I don't know,' she said cheekily. 'I'll think about it and get back to you.'

He was laughing softly when her cell phone began to buzz with incoming texts. Instantly focused, she read each one, smiling with satisfaction. 'CSU decrypted Drake Connor's flash drive and found all kinds of interesting stuff – including pictures.' She clicked on the first one. 'This is the unidentified man in that graduation photo, except in this photo he's shaking hands with Chip Anders.' She glanced up at her father. 'Anders is the asshole who bought Tala and her family.'

Fury sparked in his eyes. 'Explosives where the sun don't shine.'

'You got that right. The photo is tagged – the man's name is Kenneth Sweeney.' She tilted her phone so that her father could see. 'This next one is Anders and Demetrius Russell. Anders is taking delivery of the Bautistas. That's Anders's living room. I was there yesterday. These are grainy photos, but the decor is recognizable.'

'The photos were taken with a hidden camera,' her father said. 'Anders wanted assurance that he wasn't going to be double-crossed. No honor among criminals.'

'None,' she agreed. 'Drake stole them from Anders's computer to blackmail him later. Now this one . . .' She frowned at the photo for a moment, trying to figure it out. 'That's Chip Anders's hand. See his ring? He's signing a register at a reception desk. This was taken with a camera somewhere on his suit. Probably the pen in his pocket.'

'And there's your sniper, sitting at the receptionist desk.'

Indeed it was. Scarlett clicked to the last photo, another taken with a pen-cam. *Yes.* 'Jackpot. It's Kenneth Sweeney with Demetrius Russell and Alice Newman all together. Marcus didn't have to remember her voice,' Scarlett said, relieved. She'd put too much pressure on him asking him to make the ID.

'I have to say I was impressed with your reporter,' her father said. 'He could have made a positive ID, giving you the arrest and himself a story. But he didn't.'

'No, he didn't. It wouldn't have been the right thing to do. I think you'll like him once you get to know him, Dad.'

'I'm looking forward to it, Scarlett Anne.'

Thirty-four

Cincinnati, Ohio
Wednesday 5 August, 7.15 P.M.

Ken drove around the block three times before choosing a parking place behind the *Ledger* building. There was a back door and a loading dock, although the dock didn't look like it had been used in decades. He didn't have much time to draw O'Bannion out. He needed to be on the road to Toronto by daybreak, ten A.M. at the latest.

He was *not* going to miss his flight tomorrow night. Beaches, palm trees, half-naked women – and freedom – awaited.

He felt the buzz of adrenaline race across his skin as he got his gear ready to go. He had two assault rifles and three handguns and enough ammunition to take out at least a hundred people. Luckily there wouldn't be nearly that many at the main *Ledger* building. More than half of the eighty-five Ledger employees worked at the printing facility on the west side of the city. Most of the staff in the main building would have gone home, but because Ken had done his homework, he knew that at least four of O'Bannion's team were still here. He'd seen their cars parked on the street – Gayle Ennis, the office manager; Cal Booker, the general manager of operations; Stone O'Bannion, reporter and Marcus's brother; and Elvis 'Diesel' Kennedy, chief IT wizard and all-around pain in the ass.

Of all the employees, Stone and Diesel were his prime kill targets. Stone had written the McCord story and someone had hacked into McCord's computer to find evidence of his kiddie collection. That the hacker was the IT wizard was a logical conclusion. He'd shoot Cal Booker if he had to, but the guy was in his sixties and overdue for retirement, so killing him seemed overly cruel. He would take Gayle Ennis with him. He'd seen the way Marcus had behaved around her at Mikhail's funeral.

Marcus would come for Gayle.

Everyone else in the building was fair game if they got in the way of his bullet stream.

Ken had donned body armor from his neck to his balls. He looped the two rifles over his chest, Rambo style, then shoved the handguns into holsters at his waist and ankle. Then he pulled his oversized coveralls up and pushed his arms through the sleeves. The coveralls would hide the guns until he got inside, then he would lower the zipper and go to town.

He hadn't done anything like this in twenty-five years. Not since his and Demetrius's prime income came from the drugs they transported up I-75 from Florida. Those were the days. Joel had still done their books, but Ken and Demetrius had made the rules. And had broken them whenever the hell they wanted.

Shit. When did we get old? Except there was no 'we' anymore. Demetrius was gone. *Dumb bastard. You had to go and make me kill you.*

He pulled on a ski mask, then bunched it up so that it was perched on the top of his head and topped it with a ball cap. He zipped up the coveralls, pulled the cap's bill down to cover his face.

Showtime. He got out of his car feeling a giddy nervousness. Like he was going on his first date. He should have done this all along instead of depending on other people to do it for him. The day he stopped getting his hands dirty was the day he'd started becoming soft. *Old.*

He circled the building and came in through the front. He'd work his way to the back.

He drew a breath as he pushed open the front door, pulled the mask down over his face and the coverall zipper down his chest. He had the rifle cradled in one arm and a handgun in the other hand when the woman at the front desk looked up and Ken smiled.

Excellent. He'd already found Gayle Ennis. He'd grab her and run.

'I'm sorry, we're closed for deliv—' She had a moment of stunned shock, then she started to scream. In seconds he was behind her, his arm slung around her front, the handgun shoved up under her chin.

A burly security guard who'd been standing in the corner rushed forward. He hit the ground running. Literally. His feet were still propelling him forward when Ken's bullets ripped his head open. The guard dropped like a rock. As did the second guard, who rushed Ken from the offices at the rear of the lobby.

Gayle screamed long and loud, warning her fellow office mates.

'Go ahead and scream, Miss Ennis,' Ken murmured in her ear. 'I want them to come. I'm ready for them.'

She clamped her lips shut, trembling so hard he thought she'd faint. He dragged her away from her desk and checked the main office that had 'M. O'Bannion' on the name plate. It was empty. 'Where is he?' Ken asked.

518

'I don't know.'

'Doesn't matter. He'll come for you.' He found the woman's cell phone in her pocket and quickly dropped it into one of his own pockets, just as the first employee ran into the room and went down in a burst of bullets from Ken's gun.

Gayle screamed and Ken approved. 'Very nice,' he murmured in her ear. 'That's how this is going to go down. I shoot, you scream. Your friends come to save you and I shoot some more. Got it?'

He dragged her from the lobby through a door into the newsroom, where a group of cubicles sat in the middle of the room. A third guard fired, then retreated behind a bay of cubicles as the bullet whizzed past Ken's ear. *That was too close.*

'I'll kill Gayle,' Ken called to the guard, pulling her a little closer, completely unashamed to be using a woman as his shield. *Whatever works.* 'Show your face.'

Ken saw a shadow on the newsroom wall, and he aimed for its source. Ken saw the guard's uniform sleeve emerge seconds before the man's full body came into view. Another burst of bullets sent the third guard sliding to the floor.

A door to the left had 'S. O'Bannion' on the name plate. *Stone.*

Ken pushed the door open, but once again found the office empty. *Sonofabitch.* 'Where are they, Gayle?' he asked quietly, but she clamped her lips together and refused to answer.

He dragged her through the cubicles, most of which were empty. The last one had a middle-aged woman huddled under the desk, trying to hide. Ken fired another burst of bullets and Gayle began to sob.

'Stop,' she moaned. 'What do you want? We'll give you what you want.'

'Yes, you will.' Because what he wanted most was Marcus O'Bannion. 'I want Stone and Diesel. Where are they?'

'I'm here.' Stone O'Bannion came through a doorway, his hands out. 'Let her go. You want me, take me.'

'Drop your weapons on the floor and kick them over here and then we'll talk.' Ken waited as Stone took a handgun from his pants pocket and another from an ankle holster and kicked them away.

'Let her go,' Stone demanded. 'Take me instead.'

'I don't want to take you. I want to kill you.' Ken fired another burst, most of the bullets hitting Stone's broad chest. Stone was thrown back, rolling to his side in agony so that the next burst hit his left leg.

Gayle whimpered. 'Stone. Nooo. Please no.'

'Where's Diesel?' Ken demanded.

'I don't know,' Gayle gasped. 'Not here. He left hours ago.'

'I don't believe you. His car is outside.'

'He leaves his car here. No parking on the street where he lives.' Gayle grabbed his wrist and pulled it down, trying to get away from the gun under her chin. Ken just shoved the barrel into her chin harder.

He'd started to drag her toward the back door when he heard the cocking of a rifle. To his right was Cal Booker, holding a shotgun in his hands.

Cal lifted the shotgun to his shoulder. 'Let her g—'

Cursing, Ken shot another spray of bullets into Cal's chest. The older man staggered and fell to the floor and Ken resumed dragging the now-hysterical Gayle out the back door. Opening the door set off an alarm, ironically enough. 'Watch your step, ma'am,' he said as he dragged her down the back stairs to his vehicle. He shoved her through the front passenger door and told her to kneel on the floorboard with her head on the seat. Then he set the child locks so she couldn't escape and cuffed her hands behind her back. He tossed an old blanket over her trembling form and drove away.

Not the best op he'd ever done, but he *had* been out of practice.

As soon as he got his new guest settled in the basement cage, he'd call Marcus. That was a call he was totally looking forward to.

Cincinnati, Ohio
Wednesday 5 August, 7.20 P.M.

Marcus really wanted to get out of the interview room, but Agent Coppola had asked him to stay. He guessed it was because his presence seemed to be keeping Alice Newman on edge and that was what Coppola wanted. The redheaded agent was waiting for something. From the way she kept checking her phone, she wanted Alice to know that.

He hoped Coppola would get whatever she was waiting for soon, because he wanted to get back to Scarlett, who he knew was waiting for him behind the glass. He couldn't see her there, but he knew.

He hadn't even looked at the mirror, actually. There was no way he was taking his eyes off the viper in the chair next to him. Alice was facing dead forward, one hand cuffed to her chair, but her uncuffed hand was curled into a claw and he had not a single doubt that she'd take off a layer of skin or even go for his eyes if she had the chance.

He wasn't going to let her touch him. His skin and eyes belonged to Scarlett.

The thought made him smile despite the seriousness of the situation.

'You think this is funny?' Alice murmured, not looking at him directly. She was staring at his reflection in the mirror.

He sobered abruptly as his blood ran cold for the umpteenth time since he'd walked in the room. 'No, Alice. I don't think this is funny at all. I think it's terrifying that someone as reprehensibly evil as you is walking around among decent people. I think it's terrifying that evil can wear such a pretty face. I think you'll go on deceiving people until you draw your last breath. But you'll have your work cut out for you, because I'm going to make sure people know who you are. Who he is.' Marcus pointed at the photo of Alice with the older man. 'I'm going to make sure that anyone with a TV, a radio, a newspaper or a computer knows exactly how inhuman you are.'

Alice raised her brows. 'Should I start humming "Glory Hallelujah"?'

'I wish you wouldn't,' he said mildly. 'Your voice is like a rusty gate.'

'Oh pardon me, please.' She shot him a smiling look that instantaneously changed her from evil and rotten to the happy, caring young woman who'd visited him in the hospital. She was taunting him, showing him that she could wear her sweet face anytime she wanted to. 'I didn't mean to offend. You singers have such sensitive ears.'

Marcus went still. He'd never told her about his music when she'd visited him in the hospital. He'd been too raw when Mikhail died to think about singing, and he couldn't imagine where else she might have heard him sing. His first thought was that she had been stalking him even in the park, and that was entirely possible. Except that she probably would have gone after Tala earlier had she seen her. Especially if she was the woman who, along with Demetrius, had brought the Bautistas to Chip Anders.

Since Alice hadn't eliminated Tala in the park, it was more likely that she had heard him singing through the girl's ankle tracker. It was another link in the chain connecting her to Demetrius. He owed it to Tala to make that chain as thick and as strong as he could.

Behind him, Agent Coppola's phone buzzed. 'Yes,' she hissed.

She'd finally received what she'd been waiting for. *Thank God.* Marcus rocked back in the chair he straddled, still not taking his eyes off Alice. 'You want her to hum "Glory Hallelujah", Agent Coppola?'

Coppola's chuckle was delightfully happy and confident. 'No, Mr O'Bannion. But she can start practicing the theme song from *Dead Man Walking*.' She walked around to Alice's cuffed side and put her phone on the table. 'Your customer kept records.' She flicked through a series of photos showing Chip Anders with the man in the graduation photo, then with Demetrius. 'Do you remember this day, Alice?' She flicked to the third photo, in which Alice sat at a desk. 'Chip Anders came to visit you.'

521

Alice's 'pretty face' had slid away, leaving her hard and grim.

Coppola flicked to the fourth photo. 'And here you are with Demetrius Russell and Kenneth Sweeney.' A flicker in Alice's eyes was the only reaction she had to Coppola revealing the man's name.

'Are you sure you don't want to start talking to me?' Coppola asked soberly. 'Attempted murder for hire would have gotten you a lengthy sentence on its own. Now I can connect you to a conspiracy to traffic human beings. And successful murder – that of Agent Spangler. You seem like a sharp woman, law degree and all. Think carefully about this.'

'Immunity,' Alice snapped. 'You have nothing that isn't circumstantial.'

'Not yet,' Coppola said quietly. 'We've got records from Woody McCord's computer that we haven't even started going through. Mr O'Bannion, you're free to leave anytime you'd like. I appreciate your help.'

Marcus pushed off the chair, watching Alice as he backed toward the door. 'A lot of circumstantial can add up for a jury. She knew I sang, Agent Coppola. She had to have had access to the audio feed coming through Tala Bautista's ankle tracker. You'll want to make sure you find those recordings when you search her office and residence.'

Coppola's mouth curved, even though she didn't look at him, her gaze also fastened to Alice. 'Again, my thanks, Mr O'Bannion. You've been a big help.'

Marcus paused in the hallway outside the interview room to draw a breath, steadying his nerves. He didn't want to let Scarlett see him so rattled. It would worry her and distract her. Given that they didn't know how many assassins this organization had at its disposal, he couldn't afford for her to be distracted. It was only a matter of time before Alice's colleagues realized that Scarlett was important to him, painting a target on her back.

Once he felt steadier, he entered the observation room, but stopped short. Scarlett stood watching him, her arm around the waist of an older man in a starched uniform. Her father, he thought. Even in the semi-darkness he could see that they had the same eyes – and that her father's eyes were giving him a very thorough study. Marcus wondered how long the man had been watching him, then realized he must have been there since he and Scarlett had arrived.

She slipped away from her father, stopping in front of Marcus, not quite close enough to touch him. But she wanted to. And that was enough for now. 'Are you all right?' she asked.

Marcus forced himself to nod, feeling her father's scrutiny. 'Yes.' There was so much more he wanted to say, but it would have to keep. But he couldn't ignore her puffy eyes. Not caring who was watching, he cupped her face, brushing his thumb over her cheekbone. 'You've been crying. Are you all right?'

She leaned her face into his palm. 'Yes.' Then she smiled at him and he knew she spoke the truth. 'I'm even better now that you're not sitting next to . . . *that*. Come.' She half turned, placing her hand at the small of his back. Just a small touch, but here, in the bowels of CPD headquarters, a big deal. 'Marcus, this is my dad, Lieutenant Jonas Bishop. Dad, Marcus.'

Marcus stretched out his hand. 'Lieutenant. It's good to meet you. Scarlett has told me good things.'

The man didn't hesitate, shaking Marcus's hand with a firm grip that didn't try to intimidate. Marcus appreciated that.

'Likewise,' Bishop said gruffly.

Marcus knew this was an important moment, the first impression that would shape her father's opinion for the years to come. He did not want that impression to be one of a man too weak to hold his own. 'Likewise it's good to meet me or likewise that Scarlett said good things?'

Bishop's lips twitched. 'Yes.'

'All right then.' Marcus released the man's hand. 'What do I call you? Lieutenant? Mr Bishop? Jonas? And please don't say "Yes".'

Bishop shot his daughter an amused look. 'Jonas will do. I think he'll be okay, Scarlett. I have to get home. Your mother has a pot roast in the oven. You're welcome to join us if you'd like. Both of you. I'm sure your mom would like to see you. *Both* of you.'

Scarlett shook her head. 'I've got some files to review. But maybe after I'm done we'll stop by for coffee, if it's not too late. I'll probably need to . . . vent.'

She meant the McCord files, Marcus knew. That wasn't going to be easy. That she'd go to her father for support afterward . . . This was good.

'It's never too late, Scarlett,' Jonas said, his voice gone gruff once again. 'Day or night. You call me.'

'I will.' Without hesitation, she wrapped her arms around her father's neck and hugged him. 'Thank you.'

Jonas's arms locked tightly around her, as if he was afraid she'd run away. 'Don't you dare thank me, Scarlett Anne,' he whispered. 'Don't you dare.'

Marcus didn't know what had passed between the two, but his throat thickened. He stepped back, grateful for the sudden buzzing of his cell phone that gave him an excuse to give them some privacy.

He breathed a small sigh of relief when he saw Diesel's caller ID. No one had heard from him since he'd taken off running from the Meadow a few hours before. 'Hey, man. You okay?' he asked.

'Marcus.' Diesel's voice was shaking. Thick.

He was crying. *Oh God*. Marcus's knees wobbled as all the blood rushed from his face. He sank into a chair. 'What's wrong?'

Scarlett abruptly turned at the panic in his voice. Pulling from her father's embrace, she sank to her knees next to Marcus's chair, her hand gripping his thigh. 'What is it?'

'I don't know.' All he could hear was the rasping sound of Diesel's sobs. 'Diesel, what happened. You gotta talk to me, man. Where are you?'

'At the *Ledger*. They're gone, Marcus. All gone.'

Marcus's heart dropped to his gut like lead. 'I'm going to put you on speaker. Scarlett's here with me. Take a breath. What do you mean, they're gone?'

'They're dead. Cal, Bridget. Oh God. Stone, too.'

Marcus froze. He couldn't breathe. From far away he heard Scarlett telling her father to send help to the *Ledger* building. Then he didn't hear anything at all.

Cincinnati, Ohio
Wednesday 5 August, 7.30 P.M.

'Marcus.' Scarlett took the phone from Marcus's limp grasp, then gripped his hand in hers. 'Breathe.' He was glassy-eyed. In shock. She thumped his chest with her fist, hard. '*Breathe*, goddammit.'

He sucked in a breath, then another. Still unable to speak, he squeezed her hand until she winced, but she didn't let go.

Her father knelt on the other side of Marcus's chair. 'Dispatch has squad cars and ambulances on the way. I've notified Isenberg.'

She acknowledged him with a nod of thanks. 'Diesel,' she said calmly. 'It's Scarlett. Did you hear that? Help is on the way. I need you to stay with me. First of all, are *you* hurt?'

'No. I came in to help Cal with the evening . . .' He choked on another sob, then cleared his throat viciously. 'I found Jerry first. Dead on the floor in the front. Shot. In the back, Bridget. She was under her desk. Hiding. Cal . . . I slipped in his blood.'

She remembered Diesel's reaction to Dani Novak's white coat. He'd obviously had some medical trauma at some point. She kept her voice calm, tried to get him focused. He'd find control if he focused. She hoped. 'Have you checked for pulses?'

524

'No.' He sucked in another breath, sounding calmer already. 'I'm doing that now. Cal's . . . no. Nothing. Stone . . . Oh God. Yes. I got one.'

Scarlett slipped her hand from Marcus's to grip his chin. 'Did you hear that?' she said, making him meet her eyes. 'Stone's alive. He is alive.'

Marcus's lungs emptied in a rush of air, his body trembling. 'What happened, D?'

'I don't know.' Diesel sounded lost. 'Someone came in and shot the place up.'

Marcus surged to his feet, holding on to Scarlett's hands when she tried to push him back into the chair. 'Where were the guards?'

'Here. Dead now.'

'All three of them?' Marcus demanded.

'Yeah.' Sounds of ripping fabric came through the speaker. 'I've got to stop his bleeding. Stone? Hey, Stone. Wake up, buddy. His eyeballs are moving under his lids. Wait. He's trying to talk.'

Marcus stood stiff as a board, waiting. Scarlett rubbed his back, feeling only Kevlar under his shirt, so she cupped his head in her hands and pulled him down so that his forehead rested against hers.

'Breathe, baby,' she whispered. 'Stone's tough. You know this.'

'Fuck.' Diesel's voice had edged back into panic. 'Stone says that he's got Gayle. He shot everyone else, but he took Gayle.'

Marcus sank back into the chair, his face terrifyingly white. 'Who? Where?' He forced the word out. 'Where did he go?'

'I don't know, man. Nobody—' Diesel cut himself off. 'Hold on. I hear something.' They listened to the sound of footsteps, a door opening. 'Holy shit,' Diesel breathed in relief. 'Come on, I need help.'

For several seconds there was nothing but gasps, then screams that faded to whimpers.

'People!' Diesel growled. 'I *said* I need *help*. Jill, find some towels. Liam, stop crying and get a blanket and a pillow for Stone. *Don't* look over there. You look at me. Got that? Go get the cushion off Stone's office chair. *Go.*'

'Diesel's back,' Marcus murmured, then surged to his feet again.

Scarlett grabbed a fistful of his shirt. 'Where are you going?'

'Where do you think?' he snapped.

'You're not thinking, Marcus,' she snapped back. 'Somebody took Gayle. It may have been this Kenneth Sweeney person. Who do they want? *You.* Now settle down so we can figure out what to do. Isenberg's sending people.'

'Novak and Tanaka,' her father murmured.

'You hear that? Deacon is on his way. If there is a whiff of a lead, he'll find it. If there's a hair on the floor, Tanaka will find it. So you stay with me for now.'

'She's right,' Diesel said. 'The ambulance is here,' he added grimly. 'I'm . . . Oh, fucking shit.' He'd started to hyperventilate.

'It's okay,' Marcus said, gritting his teeth. 'Go to my office, and wait for the cops. Who's still standing?'

'No, I'm not leaving. I'm okay. Jill's standing. And Liam. He works for Lisette.'

'I know who the fuck Liam is,' Marcus growled.

'Yeah, but your cop there doesn't. Donna from Accounting and Frank from the warehouse. They all got down to the archive room. They're unhurt. Stone's breathing. The medics are working on him. That's all I know.'

'I'm on my way,' Marcus said, his jaw hard and unyielding.

'No,' Diesel said. 'Go straight to the hospital. Stone's going to need you. So will Audrey and your mother.'

'Is that Marcus on the phone?' It was a young female. 'Marcus, it's Jill.'

Scarlett was surprised. The subdued voice sounded nothing like the young woman who'd been so angry in the OR waiting room the night before.

'Stone's conscious,' Jill said. 'He was wearing Kevlar under his clothes, down past his knees. Liam and I cut his clothes off him so we could try to stop his bleeding. He took a lot of bullets. The Kevlar didn't stop all of them, but the bleeding is slow. Not gushing. Just so you don't worry.'

Scarlett muted Marcus's phone. 'She's too calm. She doesn't know about Gayle.'

Marcus squared his shoulders when she unmuted the phone. 'Jill, where were you?'

'Down in the archive room with Cal.' Her breath hitched, broke. 'Marcus, Cal's—'

'I know,' Marcus interrupted, his face twisting in pain. But he kept his voice level. 'What happened?'

'We heard the shots in the lobby and the next thing we knew Liam, Frank, Donna and me were all being shoved down the stairs by Stone. Cal was already down there. Stone told us all to stay put and he went back up and shut the door. But Cal didn't listen.' Her voice broke again. 'I'm just glad Aunt Gayle had left already.'

They all went silent and Diesel's face must have shown the truth, because Jill began to whimper. 'No. She wasn't here.'

'Jill!' Diesel yelled. 'Wait! Fuck,' he muttered.

Jill's ear-piercing shriek cut through all the background noise.

'Gayle's purse is still on the desk,' Diesel said heavily. 'I gotta go. One of the officers had to pull Jill away from the desk. Do not come here. Go to the hospital. Scarlett? Make him go to the hospital.'

'I'll make sure of it,' Scarlett said grimly. She disconnected and, keeping one hand fisted in Marcus's shirt, found Jeremy's number, dialing it with the other. 'Jeremy, this is Scarlett Bishop. Marcus is all right,' she added quickly when the man gasped. 'But Stone's not.' She quickly filled him in, her gaze locked with Marcus's the entire time. 'Where are you?'

'At home. With Keith.'

Which meant he was at least forty-five minutes away.

'I'm here, Detective,' Keith said. 'I put it on speaker, so I heard it all. Which hospital?'

'I don't know yet. Probably County. They've got the best trauma unit.'

'We're leaving now. Call when you know where they're taking him.'

'Wait,' Jeremy said. 'Does Della know?'

'Not yet. I'll call Audrey. If she's not home, I'll get Mrs Yarborough myself.'

'Thank you, Detective. Marcus?'

Marcus swallowed audibly. 'I'm here, Dad.'

'Okay. I just needed to hear your voice. We're on our way.'

Scarlett disconnected. 'Do you want to call Audrey?'

He nodded, made the call, his voice breaking all the way through. 'They're coming.'

Scarlett slipped his phone into his shirt pocket. 'Your family needs you.'

He shook his head, agony in his eyes. 'Gayle is my family too. God, when I think about what's he doing to her. Sonofabitch. If he hurts her, I'll kill him. I swear it.'

Scarlett drew his head down to hers, touching foreheads again. 'Don't think about that. You can't. We need to focus on finding out where he took her. The "why" is clear. He wants you. And he can't have you. Because you're mine, Marcus. You got that?'

He drew a breath. 'I got it. Let's go. Just stay with me, all right?'

She put her arm around his waist. 'Try to push me away.' She looked up to her father. 'Thanks, Dad.'

'I didn't do anything,' he said. 'You had it.'

The three of them had turned for the door when Marcus froze. Scarlett followed his gaze to the other side of the glass, where Kate Coppola was on the phone, her expression gone grim.

Deacon, Scarlett thought. Deacon had probably called Kate. But Marcus wasn't staring at Kate. He was staring at Alice Newman, who sat smiling. Smirking.

With a roar, Marcus snapped, pulling away before Scarlett could stop him.

'Fuck,' Scarlett muttered, chasing after him into the interview room, grabbing him around the waist and pulling back as hard as she could. But he was six-two and a solid two hundred twenty pounds of muscle. And out of his mind with fury.

He grabbed Alice, chair and all, and shoved her against the wall, reaching his hands for her throat.

'Marcus!' Scarlett yelled. 'Don't! If you kill her, she can't tell us anything.'

It was her father that stopped him, grabbing him by the shoulders and spinning him to the side. Marcus hit the wall hard. The officer standing guard in the room had him in a hold a second later, but Marcus didn't seem to even notice.

'Stop!' Jonas thundered, getting in front of Marcus, right in his face. 'You will not do this.' He jerked his head toward the door. 'Officer, get him out of here and cuff him if you have to. Just until he calms down.'

Scarlett took a minute to cup Marcus's face in her hands. 'She's shit, Marcus. Not worth your freedom. I need you.' She held him until he shuddered out a breath.

'I'm not sorry.' His body still trembled. 'I want her dead.'

'I know,' Scarlett said calmly. 'But if you kill her, they will take you from me. Please,' she added in a whisper. 'Trust me to do my job.'

He stared at her a long time, his breathing slowly calming. Finally he said, 'All right. I'll wait outside.'

Scarlett turned to Alice, who was grinning from ear to ear. Scarlett breathed calmly, letting her lips curve in a smile that no intelligent person would confuse for friendly. She held Alice's gaze until the bitch's grin faded.

'We haven't met, Alice. I'm Detective Bishop.' Dragging Alice's chair back to the table, she briskly cuffed the woman's other hand to the chair, yanking just hard enough to hurt her without the cameras picking up any suspicious movement. Then Scarlett sat down beside her, aware of her father standing at the door. *Protecting me*, she thought. She might not have needed protecting, but it was sure nice to have him watching her back. *Just in case.*

'Are you supposed to impress me?' Alice taunted. 'Scare me?'

'Do you know where you're going, Alice? Of course you do. You're a lawyer. But just in case you graduated at the bottom half of your class, let me explain that you're going to lockup pending your arraignment. Then you'll go to jail, and, sugar, orange is *so* not your color.'

'I'm *so* amused,' Alice said, rolling her eyes. 'Bored now.'

'Then jail's just the thing for you,' Scarlett said, continuing to smile. 'It'll be a *party*. Especially when everyone finds out that you're a pedophile. That you have bought and sold people. Children. For the sex trade.'

Alice shook her head, smiling as if Scarlett were pitiful. 'Pedophile? Really? You can't charge me with that. You're just trying to scare me and it won't work. You're fishing. You have no evidence at all and you know it.'

Scarlett hadn't known for sure, but the calculation in Alice's eyes told her that she'd hit pay dirt. 'I don't have to have evidence and you don't have to be charged. I just have to whisper to whoever's in lockup with you. Pedo was on the table, but you pled down. You're a lawyer. Anyone in jail will believe you're capable of shimmying out of a charge.'

Alice's jaw tightened. 'You've got nothing.'

'We've got pictures of you with Demetrius and Anders and Sweeney.'

'I just got them coffee.'

'It doesn't matter what you actually did, just what the rumor mill *says* you did.' Scarlett leaned forward. 'See, you're gonna be fresh meat to start with. With your pretty hair and soft skin. The others will hate you without knowing anything about you. But then they'll find out. I'll make sure they find out. It'll be fun, Alice. You'll be the belle of the ball. A real live debutante. And you'll stay alive. Your new friends won't want to lose their toy. Just think, Alice. Every day you'll be the center of attention. Everyone will want a piece of you. Every. Day. Every. Night.'

Real fear flickered in Alice's eyes. 'You don't scare me, Detective.'

'That's good, because I haven't touched you, except to cuff you. I do know a few people in the general population who owe me a favor or two. And they'll enjoy paying me back.' She leaned close. 'Because you're so pretty,' she whispered. 'For now.'

Alice glared at her lawyer. 'Are you going to sit there and let her get away with this?'

'Get away with what?' the man asked blandly. 'She's just complimenting you on how pretty you are. She hasn't threatened you at all.'

'I like your attorney, Alice. He's got common sense.' Scarlett stood up, glanced at the doorway to find that Kate Coppola had been silently watching. 'Agent Coppola, I think she's ready to go to lockup. I'll have an officer take her. I'll see you later, Alice. I think you'll enjoy meeting your new friends.'

'I won't tell you anything,' Alice said, but she was very pale. 'You can't bully me.'

'I really didn't think I could. I think I'll get the information I need from DJ.' She made a mental note to make sure he was brought in ASAP. 'My goal, Alice, is to see you get the ultimate prison experience.'

'DJ is in Interview Six,' Kate said. 'For realsies this time. He was brought in a few minutes ago.'

Alice's eyes flashed fury when she realized she'd bought Marcus's earlier lie about DJ having been arrested already. 'You failed him, you know,' she called when Scarlett turned to go.

'Failed who?' Scarlett asked, knowing exactly what Alice was going to say.

'O'Bannion. You told him you'd get me to talk.'

Scarlett smiled at her sweetly. 'No, I told him I'd do my job. One of my jobs is to get justice for the victims. Sometimes justice wears an orange jumpsuit.'

Scarlett left the room before she gave in to the urge to smack the woman senseless, leaning against the wall in the hallway where her father was waiting. 'Where's Marcus?' she asked.

'Right here,' Marcus said as he came out of the observation room. 'I'm calm now. I'm sorry I went after her.'

He looked drawn and exhausted and damn near defeated, worrying her. 'No you're not. I wish I hadn't had to stop you.'

'Are you going to interview DJ now?' he asked.

'Yes, since he's here "for realsies". You need to get to the hospital.' She looked back into the room with a frown. 'Although . . . Shit. The shooting at the *Ledger* was to lure you out. Maybe they'll wait for you at the hospital.'

Marcus opened his mouth to protest, then pursed his lips. 'Kevlar,' he said.

'Head shot,' she countered.

'Tactical helmet,' he returned. 'I wore them all the time in the Gulf. I kept myself alive for years, Scarlett. Trust me. You said it yourself – my family needs me. I'm not hiding here and I'm sure as hell not going to abandon Stone. He needs to know I'm there.'

Scarlett nodded shakily. He was right and she knew it. He'd trusted her to do her job. She had to trust his good sense and the promises he'd made her. 'I trust you to stay alive. I don't trust them to stop trying and maybe hurting a lot of people in the process.'

He blanched. 'Shit. Oh shit.'

'Wait.' She glanced up at her father. 'What can we do to ensure the safety of everyone in that hospital? Because even if Marcus doesn't go—' She held up her hand to quell Marcus's protest. 'I know you're going, but even if you didn't, they may expect you to. If luring you to the hospital is the goal, they'll target it. Dad? What can we do to maximize security for everyone?'

'We'll post officers at every entrance,' her father said, 'and around the ER and OR. Weapons checks for everyone currently on the floor and anyone who gets off the elevator. The hospital itself has security protocols and we'll work with them. It will deter any assault through traditional means, at least.'

'That'll have to be good enough,' she said quietly, her eyes locked to Marcus's. 'I want to talk to DJ. Maybe he'll tell me where to find Kenneth Sweeney. With Demetrius dead and Anders captured, Sweeney may be the one left running the show.'

'I'll take Marcus to the hospital, Scarlett,' her father offered. 'You do your job here.'

Marcus nodded soberly. 'Thank you, Jonas. But if you'll give us a moment first, please?'

'Of course. I'll meet you in the lobby by the elevator.'

Scarlett took Marcus's hand and led him into an unoccupied consultation room, closed the door and gathered him into her arms. He shuddered and held her tighter. 'What will I do?' he whispered. 'Without Stone? And Gayle?'

'For now you believe that you'll get them back. Both of them.'

'And if I don't? It almost killed me to lose Mikhail. If I lost Stone . . .'

Scarlett pulled his head down for a hard kiss. 'Stop. You heard Jill. Stone is conscious. He will live. He's too obstinate not to.'

He nodded, more to convince himself than in agreement. 'So we just need to find Gayle.'

'Exactly.'

He rested his cheek on the top of her head. 'I should have shut the paper down until all this was over,' he said hoarsely. 'Why didn't I do that?'

'Because it would have put a lot of people out of work. You built that paper up, gave your employees financial security. Would any of them have stayed home if you'd given them a choice?'

'I don't know. I'll never know now.' He was quiet for a long moment. 'I've known Cal Booker for as long as I can remember. When I visited my grandfather, before we moved from Lexington, Cal was always here. Never treated me like I was in the way.' He tightened his hold. 'This is my fault, Scarlett. I never expected any of my people to get hurt.'

She thought about him going to the prison, confronting Woody McCord. 'You thought the McCords of the world would only come after you. Maybe you even wanted them to?'

'That's what Stone said, and now . . .'

'Look, Marcus, all I know is that every member of your team looked me in the eye and said it was worth the risk. Cal included.'

'Bridget didn't. Jerry didn't.'

'And for them you hired guards.'

'You're not going to let me feel guilty for this, are you?'

'No. Your family needs you. Your employees need you. They're going to be in shock and grieving. So if you want to do something for Cal, find a way to keep the paper going.'

'You're so calm.'

'But I won't always be. When I'm not, you'll be the calm one. I hear from a reliable source that that's how it's supposed to work.'

'Your dad told you that?'

'Among other things.' She lifted on to her toes to kiss him. 'Now go. I'll be there soon.'

'All right.' Straightening, he blew out a breath. 'I'll see you at the hospital.'

Thirty-five

Cincinnati, Ohio
Wednesday 5 August, 8.45 P.M.

Scarlett found the OR waiting room full of people, including, to her amazement, both of her parents. Jackie Bishop was sitting next to Della, holding her hand. Marcus sat between his mother and Scarlett's father.

Deacon's fiancée, Faith, sat next to her uncle Jeremy, gently holding his hand, which was covered, as always, by the black leather gloves that hid the scars from the burns he'd received years before. Audrey sat on Jeremy's other side, no expression on her face.

Jill occupied the seat next to Audrey, but it was Keith's leg on which she rested her head. Her eyes were closed, but tears were seeping out, wetting the knee of Keith's trousers. Jeremy's husband had an uncharacteristically gentle expression on his face as he stroked the hair off Jill's forehead. Once again Scarlett was reminded of how young the girl was. And how prescient. This was exactly what Jill had feared – her aunt getting hurt because of the risks Marcus and his team had taken.

Lisette and Diesel shared a sofa, looking shell-shocked and numb and alone. Everyone, with the exception of Scarlett's parents, looked shell-shocked.

Everyone, including her parents, wore body armor – heavy vests that looked sadly out of place. Marcus had taken his helmet off once he'd gotten to the safety of the waiting room, but he'd worn it just as he'd promised.

Scarlett went straight to Marcus and kissed his forehead. 'Nothing,' she murmured in his ear. 'I'm sorry. DJ is one of the coolest customers I've seen in years. He wouldn't give me a thing. Even Alice gave us more.'

Marcus's shoulders sagged. 'I didn't think he would, but I'd hoped.'

'I left Kate with him, hoping she'd have better luck. Any news on Stone?'

'In surgery. Deacon came with him in the ambulance but left to go back to the . . .' He swallowed. 'Back to the crime scene. Stone stayed conscious all the way to the hospital. Long enough for us to see him before they took him to the OR.' He opened his mouth, then closed it after looking at his mother.

Scarlett nodded, understanding that they'd debrief more privately. She noted Della Yarborough's curious, yet muted, glance. Marcus's mother wasn't blitzed out, but she had definitely taken something. Maybe a lot of somethings.

Scarlett leaned down and kissed her own mother on the cheek. 'Hi, Mom. I didn't expect to see you here.'

'Your father called to say he wouldn't be home for dinner – and he told me about Marcus. If he's important to you, he's important to us. So we're here.'

Scarlett's heart swelled. 'Thank you.' She turned to Marcus's mother, half kneeling so that the older woman didn't have to look up. 'Mrs Yarborough. I . . . I wish we weren't seeing each other again under these circumstances.'

'Just Della is fine.' Della's mouth curved, but she didn't hold the smile, as if it took too much energy. 'So you and my Marcus . . . ?'

Scarlett's cheeks heated. 'Yes, ma'am. I hope you're okay with that.'

'And if I'm not?'

'I would respectfully keep him anyway.'

Della's smile lasted a little longer this time before dimming. 'You came to Mikhail's funeral. You didn't have to.'

'I did have to.' She hesitated, then shrugged. 'I go to all the funerals. For all of the victims. It seems like the right thing to do.'

A slow-motion nod. 'You'll be perfect for Marcus. So yes, Scarlett, I'm okay with it.'

'Whew.' Scarlett smiled up at her. 'I was worried there for a second or two.' She looked over at her own mother and saw approval. Jackie gave her a nod and it felt good.

Abruptly Della skewered Scarlett with a look. 'Do you know where Gayle is yet?'

'No, ma'am, not yet. But we're looking.' A rustling behind Scarlett had her turning to see Jill coming to her feet, her expression grim, her eyes red from crying.

'Not hard enough,' Jill said coldly. 'You have suspects in custody. You're the super-cop. Make them tell you where that bastard took my aunt.'

Scarlett rose slowly, suddenly bone-tired. 'I'm no super-cop, Jill, and this is real life. The suspects don't always talk. A lot of times they don't. Sometimes – a lot of times – I want to strangle the truth out of them, but I can't do that.'

'Trick them into confessing.'

God, she's young. 'If they're dumb enough to be tricked, they're probably so dumb that I don't need a confession. They leave evidence all over the place. Unfortunately the people who took your aunt aren't dumb.'

Jill wasn't convinced. 'Then make a deal, dammit.'

'That's not going to happen. These people have killed too many people, have bought and sold families and made them slaves. They've trafficked *children*, Jill. Innocent children. We don't even know what the children suffered. Do you think your aunt would really want these criminals walking free, victimizing even more people?'

Jill's face crumpled, her shoulders sagging as she hugged herself, her sobs starting anew. 'They have my aunt. They've killed all those people and they have my aunt.'

Sighing wearily, Scarlett gathered the girl in her arms. For a moment they just stood there, then Jill balled her hands into fists and pounded them into Scarlett's collarbones, so hard that Scarlett found herself knocked back a step and sucking in a lungful of air.

Fury in her eyes, the girls fists came up like she was considering throwing a real punch. 'No,' Jill fumed. 'You don't get to act like you care. Not until you bring her home.'

Scarlett heard both her father and Marcus come to their feet behind her. She lifted her hand, staying them, and took Jill's arm in a firm grip. 'Come on. Let's take a walk.'

'Scarlett?' Faith murmured, looking concerned. 'Remember, she's just a kid.'

Scarlett rolled her eyes. 'Finally somebody sees my mean streak. I thought I'd gone soft.' She heard a few chuckles as the tension in the room went down a notch. Even Jill smiled, and that pissed Scarlett off all over again. 'But you know what? She isn't just a kid. She's nineteen and old enough to take a swing at a cop. So she can damn well listen to what I have to say. Don't worry, Faith. We're just going to take a walk.' She tightened her grip a little when Jill tried to pull free. 'Don't make me worry Faith any more than I already have, *kid*.'

Jill stopped fighting and allowed herself to be led to another, smaller waiting room which was unoccupied. She yanked her arm free, rubbing her wrist. 'You hurt me.'

'That hurt you? Fuck that. You're lucky I didn't break both of your arms.'

The curse got Jill's attention, and the threat made her seethe. 'You wouldn't.'

'You're right. I wouldn't, because *I* can control myself. If I'd let my reflexes rule me, you would have carpet burns on your face right now. I'm going to say this only once. Grow the hell up. You're scared and pissed off. I get that. But you're not the only one who loves Gayle or who's worried about her. You're just the only one throwing a temper tantrum over it. That one hit was your freebie, kid. You touch me again and I will not control myself. Understood?'

'Yes,' Jill said sullenly.

'All right. If you want to be a temperamental brat, stay here alone. If you want to help your aunt, then settle down.'

Jill sat down. 'I'll stay here.'

'Fine.' Scarlett started to leave, but her adrenaline abruptly crashed, along with her blood sugar. Exhaustion hit her almost as hard as Jill had, and the chair next to the kid suddenly looked damn inviting. She dropped into it and let her head fall back.

Jill gave her a snotty look. 'It's only staying here alone if I am *alone*.'

Scarlett threw the look right back. 'Don't you ever shut up, kid?'

'You sound like Stone,' Jill grumbled.

Scarlett snorted. 'Now you're just being mean.'

Jill chuckled, then sighed. 'I'm sorry I hit you. I'm not sure why I did that.'

'I imagine it was because you're scared and upset and I was handy. Don't do it again.'

'Got it. Are you okay?' Jill asked. 'You look a little pale.'

'Long day. I probably should eat. But I don't have the energy to get up and get something. I think I used up the last of my reserves dragging you down here.'

'I have a Snickers bar. I'll split it with you.'

Scarlett wolfed her half down. 'Now I'm only half a monster.'

'You're not *so* bad.'

'High praise.'

Jill sat silent for a whole minute and a half. 'I know what they're doing.'

'Who?'

'Marcus, Gayle, Lisette and the others. They're using the *Ledger* to expose abusers or turning their investigations over to the cops so that the abusers can be arrested.'

'And you know this how?'

'Because a lot of the threats on that list didn't make sense because the stories were never printed in the paper. So why would someone threaten Marcus? But then I cross-checked those threats against arrest records. Almost all of the people making threats had an arrest record for some kind of abuse in the past. I'm not as stupid as Marcus seems to think.'

'He doesn't think you're stupid at all, Jill. That's why you make him nervous. You're smart, but he doesn't know where your loyalties lie.'

'They lie with Gayle. She took me in.'

'And she's all you have left. Don't you think he knows that?'

'I guess.' She mimicked Scarlett's pose, leaning her head back and staring at the ceiling. 'It wasn't really his fault,' she said softly. 'Gayle's heart attack, I mean. She'd been having issues for a while but she wouldn't let me tell anyone.'

'That was stupid of her.'

'She's proud. And she doesn't like to worry Stone and Marcus. She walks on eggshells around them. It's like she's afraid they'll break.'

'Maybe they will.'

It was Jill's turn to snort. 'Those guys are tanks. Nobody bothers them.'

'Not now. Doesn't mean it's always been that way. You got your phone?'

'Duh.' Jill fished it out of her pocket. 'Why?'

'Do me a favor. Google "Matthias Gargano", "Lexington" and "1989".' Scarlett closed her eyes while Jill did so. The girl's gasp told her that she'd found the articles.

'Oh my God. I didn't know. Stone and Marcus . . . they had another brother?'

'Yeah. Matty was killed by the kidnappers and Gayle was the one who kept that family together afterward. She's seen those big tanks as small, scared little boys and that's a hard image to erase. Maybe you understand their relationship a little better now.'

'Yes, I do. And then Mikhail dying too? No wonder Della takes all those sleeping pills. I wouldn't want to be awake either. Poor Aunt Gayle. She grieved Mikhail so much. I kept thinking, *Hello! What about me? Am I chopped liver or something?* I didn't understand.'

'Now you do. Ball's in your court as to what you do with it.'

She blew out a breath. 'I have been a brat, haven't I?'

'Yep.'

Jill huffed a laugh. 'I'll do better.'

'Good.' Eyes still closed, Scarlett kept talking, partly to keep herself awake and partly to keep Jill distracted from the terror that would return once she started thinking about Gayle's current situation. 'I will throw you a bone, though. Gayle's heart attack was indirectly triggered by the team's efforts, so you were right about that. Your concern was well placed. Just not well acted upon.'

'How do you know that, about her heart attack?'

'I was listening at the door yesterday when Gayle told Marcus about the

537

letter she was reading that day. The letter writer threatened to "take away" somebody that Marcus loved just like he'd taken away somebody she loved. Her husband had reportedly committed suicide in prison. Gayle read the letter when Mikhail was missing. Given their past experience with kidnapping . . .'

'Holy shit.' Jill sighed, frustrated. 'That was the worst timing ever. I wish I'd given her the letter when I got it. At least she wouldn't have had to worry about Mikhail.'

Scarlett rolled her head, opening her eyes so that she could see Jill's profile. 'What do you mean? When did you get the letter?'

'The week before. Gayle had missed a few days at work because she was so tired – I guess that was a warning sign for the heart attack. I'd locked the mail up in my desk because she wasn't there. The *Ledger* has a clean desk policy, you know. But I had a big project due for school, so I took a few days off in between. I didn't give her the letters until the day I came back. That was the day she had her heart attack and then later we found out about Mikhail being dead. I know that Mickey was alive when the letter arrived in the mail. If I'd given it to her then, she wouldn't have been so shocked.'

Scarlett frowned. Something wasn't right about that, but her tired brain wasn't sure what. From her pocket she fished out the folded papers that Stone had printed for her earlier that day.

'What's that?' Jill asked.

'Stone's story about Woody McCord, the husband of the woman who wrote the letter.' Getting her second wind, Scarlett rose and paced while she read to herself. She didn't want to share any more with Jill until she knew where she was going with this.

After a minute, she stopped pacing and turned the paper over to write the key dates on the back. 'What day did you actually receive that letter, Jill?'

Puzzled, Jill scooted to sit on the edge of her seat, her brow furrowed. 'Thursday. I remember because Halloween was the next day and I was going to a party with Mikhail and his friends. We went to the party store to pick up our costumes.' She looked away. 'He didn't run away until the weekend, but the party was the last time I saw him alive.'

'I'm sorry to dredge this up, but it's important.'

'Why?' Jill frowned. 'How do you know?'

'I feel it.' Scarlett made a face. 'Too weird, I know, but I've learned to trust my gut. Usually my gut remembers stuff my conscious mind has forgotten.'

Jill gave her a look. 'Maybe you *are* a super-cop,' she said with mild sarcasm.

Scarlett shook her head, ignoring the girl's attitude. 'No. That would be Deacon. The guy remembers *everything*. He kills at *Jeopardy*. I'm just good at *Wheel of Fortune*.' She looked at her page of scribbles. 'If you received that letter on Thursday, it had to have been mailed Monday or Tuesday. Wednesday at the latest.' She wrote that down too.

'Okay,' Jill said. 'So? What does all that mean?'

'So . . . I don't know yet.' Scarlett rearranged her scribbles into a timeline.

Mon. 10/27–Wed. 10/29: letter written/mailed by Leslie McCord
Wed. 10/29: McCord tells his attorney and prosecutor that he will name names
Thurs. 10/30: Letter received at *Ledger* by Jill via USPS
Thurs. 10/30: Woody McCord found hanged in his cell (murder or suicide???)
Mon. 11/3: Leslie McCord ODs on pills (estimated by ME)
Wed. 11/5: Gayle reads letter, has heart attack; Mikhail's body found; Marcus shot
Thurs, 11/6: Leslie's body found in her home per police report

Reviewing the dates, Scarlett saw what she'd been missing. *What it means,* she thought, *is that Leslie McCord wrote a letter referring to her husband's death* before *he died.* She looked up from her notes to meet Jill's curious gaze. 'It means I need to see that letter.'

'Another gut feeling?'

'Yeah. Do you know the combination to your aunt's safe?'

'No. She wouldn't trust me with that. I tried to break in once, to see if I could, but I couldn't.'

Scarlett bet that Diesel could. 'Come with me. You can't stay here alone. It's not safe.'

Jill frowned, but got up. 'Why did you tell me to earlier?'

'Because I was too tired to think. I'm not tired anymore.'

Scarlett jogged back to the main waiting room only to find a full-fledged argument in progress. Marcus and Diesel were nose to nose. Deacon had returned, and he and Scarlett's father were trying to calm the two men down.

'What's going on here?' she demanded. 'Is it Stone?'

Diesel's huge chest was pumping like a bellows. 'No, he's still in surgery.' He shoved a finger into Marcus's chest, a futile gesture considering they all still wore vests. 'Maybe you can make this asshole here see reason. I sure can't.'

Marcus's jaw was tight, his fists clenched much as Jill's had been. Scarlett gently pushed Diesel aside, covered Marcus's fists with her hands, tucked them under her chin, and waited for him to calm down.

Thirty seconds later he'd moved in, trapping their hands between their bodies, dropping his forehead to hers. 'He called.'

'Who?'

'The man who has Gayle,' he murmured.

Oh shit. She had to draw a breath, because her temper was starting to flare hotter than Diesel's. She closed her eyes for four pounding beats of her heart, then opened them, promising herself she'd stay in control. For Marcus. 'Let me guess. He wants a trade.'

'Got it in one,' Diesel said, still furious.

Marcus lifted his head, his nostrils flaring as he tried to control his temper. 'Shut *up*, Diesel. I *mean* it.

'Let me guess,' Scarlett said again, so calmly she stunned herself. 'You want to do it.'

Cincinnati, Ohio
Wednesday 5 August, 9.15 P.M.

'Oh, she's smart, Marcus,' Diesel snapped out. 'Or maybe not, considering she's thrown her lot in with a guy with a goddamn death wish.'

Marcus ground his teeth so hard that a pain spiked up his skull. He couldn't deal with Diesel now. He needed to focus on Scarlett, who'd done the long blink and was now staring up at him with a clinical expression he knew was costing her dearly. 'Diesel, I swear to God, if you don't shut up . . .'

'You'll what?' Diesel said, holding his arms wide. 'You'll hit me? Go ahead. I'll hit back and maybe knock some fucking sense into your head!'

'Um, ex*cuse* me?' A nurse stood in the doorway looking upset. 'Do I need to call Security?'

'No,' Marcus said.

'No, ma'am,' Diesel muttered.

Scarlett still held his fists in her hands. 'All right,' she said quietly. 'Will someone who is sane please tell me what I missed?'

Deacon cleared his throat. 'Well, we're thinking the caller had to be Sweeney because Stone described the shooter's body size as consistent with the man we saw in the photo with Alice. Sweeney said he has Gayle and for

Marcus to meet him at the entrance to Shawnee Lookout Park at midnight. He'll then allow Gayle her freedom, in exchange for Marcus. Marcus wants to do it, with a plan that he hasn't come up with yet. Diesel says he's a fucking fool. I'm somewhere in between the two.' He glanced at Scarlett's father. 'Is that pretty complete, sir?'

'Yeah, I'd say so,' Jonas said.

'And if we had a plan?' Scarlett asked evenly. Too evenly. She was holding herself together so tightly that Marcus thought she'd crack in two.

He knew how she felt. He wanted to . . . hit something. Preferably Diesel.

'Depends on the plan,' her father said. He laid a tentative hand on Marcus's shoulder. 'Have you calmed down enough to think about this, son?'

Marcus shook his head. 'Not yet.'

'At least you're honest,' Jonas muttered.

'What exactly did Sweeney say?' Scarlett asked. 'Exactly.'

Marcus let go of one of her hands to fish his phone out of his pocket. 'I recorded it. It came through as Gayle's caller ID.'

Scarlett pressed her free hand against his chest. 'Jill doesn't need to hear this.'

'I'm staying,' Jill said stubbornly. 'Play it, Marcus.'

'The audio isn't bad,' he murmured in Scarlett's ear. 'I won't show her the video.'

Surprised horror filled her eyes, her manufactured calm gone. 'Holy God.'

'Yeah,' Marcus said grimly. He hit PLAY and squared his shoulders, preparing himself to listen again.

'Hello?' Marcus winced at the sound of his own voice, full of hope. 'Gayle?'

Hearing the twisted chuckle again felt like someone was grabbing his heart right out of his chest.

'No, Marcus, this isn't Gayle. But she's with me. You've caused me a great deal of trouble recently. Let's cut to the chase. I want you to meet me at Shawnee Lookout at midnight. It's a cliché, I realize, but I'm on a tight schedule. Meet me there and I'll put Gayle in your car and she'll be free to leave.'

'Like everyone you butchered at the *Ledger* was free to leave?' Marcus asked coldly.

'That was payback. Like I said, you've caused me trouble. Meet me or don't, but if you don't, Gayle dies. Oh, and don't involve the authorities.'

Marcus clicked it off, not wanting to hurt his mother again with the next line. 'That's pretty much it.'

'Play the rest of it, Marcus,' Della said wearily. 'It doesn't matter anymore.'

Marcus sighed. 'All right.'

Ken Sweeney's voice filled the room once again. 'You know what happened when your mother involved the authorities twenty-seven years ago. Let's not repeat history, shall we?'

'How do I know Gayle's still alive?'

'Ask her yourself,' Sweeney said silkily.

'Marcus.' Gayle sounded frail. 'Don't you dare do this. I—' She was abruptly silenced.

'Midnight,' Sweeney said.

The line went dead.

'What was the video?' Scarlett mouthed.

Marcus leaned in, filled his lungs with the scent of wildflowers. 'He's got Gayle in a cage. She's tied up.' He hesitated. 'He's taken her clothes.'

'Blindfolded?'

He swallowed hard. 'No.'

Scarlett blew out a breath. 'Okay. So I think we can all agree that he's not going to let Gayle go. We need to figure out how to find out where she is. Before midnight.'

Jill covered her mouth with her hand, stifling a whimper.

Lisette got up from the sofa where she'd been numbly sitting since finding out that Cal and the others were dead. She put her arms around Jill and rocked her where they stood. 'You got any ideas, Detective?' Lisette asked brokenly. 'Because I can't think.'

'That's part of his strategy,' Scarlett said. 'Decimate your morale so that your concentration and focus are fractured.' She looked over her shoulder at Deacon. 'You've tried to trace the call?'

Deacon had slumped into the chair next to Faith when it had become clear that Marcus and Diesel weren't going to kill each other. 'Vince is working on it. He's not hopeful. He knows it wasn't really Gayle's phone. If it had been we'd have traced it by now. Sweeney routed it through a spoofing service to make it come up as Gayle's number. The phone is a throwaway.'

That was about what Scarlett had expected. For him to have used Gayle's actual phone would have been far too easy. 'What about that hard drive I gave you? The copy of McCord's files? Did Vince find anything on that?'

Deacon lifted a brow. 'The one you told me to tell him you'd go through yourself?'

She rolled her eyes. 'Hell. Like Vince ever listens to me. What did he find?'

Deacon shook his head wearily. 'Nothing that would lead us to Ken Sweeney.'

Bowing her head, Scarlett rubbed her temples. 'Diesel, can you crack a safe?'

Everyone did a double-take at that. 'Did you say "crack a safe"?' Marcus asked carefully.

'I did. Can you, Diesel? If you can't, we'll get a team over to Gayle's right now, but that might take time we don't have.'

'Why?' Diesel asked helplessly.

'There's a letter in her safe that I want to take a look at.'

Marcus frowned. 'You mean the letter that Leslie McCord wrote? Why?'

'Because she wrote that letter several days *before* her husband was killed. Jill said the letter had arrived a week before Gayle read it.' She took a piece of paper from her pocket and handed it to him. 'It might be nothing, but it's better than sitting here listening to the seconds tick by.'

Marcus read through the timeline, then read it again. 'You're right. Something's off. Can you get the letter, Diesel?'

Diesel glanced at Jonas Bishop and Deacon uneasily. 'Maybe.'

Scarlett's control visibly snapped, and, whirling on Diesel, she jabbed her forefinger up in his face. 'Neither my father nor Deacon will arrest you,' she hissed. 'But I will fucking kill you myself if you don't give me a straight answer. Can you crack the goddamn safe or not? Yes or no?'

Eyes wide, Diesel nodded once. 'Yes.'

She grabbed his arm and shoved him toward the door. 'Then go *do* it,' she cried, exasperated. '*Now.*'

Diesel took off at a fast jog.

'Diesel!' Scarlett yelled. She ran to the doorway, then turned back to the group, rolling her eyes. 'Jill, give Deacon your house keys. Deacon, please go with him, and call me with what the letter says when you get it. I'm going to stay here and try to figure out a damn plan.'

Deacon was instantly on his feet. 'Yes, ma'am.' He dropped a kiss on Faith's mouth, still open in surprise. 'Call you as soon as I can.'

One could have heard a pin drop after Deacon left. Scarlett's mother sat with her mouth open in shock, and her father was biting back a grin. Marcus found himself aroused despite his worry. It was like a balloon had popped inside his chest, so much pressure releasing.

Once again, she'd cleared his mind, allowing him to think.

Scarlett shrugged. 'Sorry, Mom. This is me.'

'Of course it is,' her mother said. 'I'm just . . . Wow. I guess I don't have to worry about you on the job anymore.'

543

'No, ma'am.' Scarlett rubbed her hands together. 'We need a plan, Mr O'Bannion.'

His lips curved with pride. 'Yes, we do, Detective.'

'One that doesn't involve you trading yourself.'

'I'm open to suggestions,' he said mildly.

She scowled at him, then swallowed hard. 'I'm really mad at you, you know. To even consider it.'

He pulled her close and kissed the top of her head. 'I know. But she's Gayle and she's scared. And so am I.'

She pulled away to sit at a table in the corner. 'We need a way to track Sweeney, but we don't even know who he is.'

Lisette sat down across from her. 'I spent the two hours before . . . well, before the shooting searching every database I have for Ken Sweeney. He doesn't exist. Nor does Demetrius Russell.'

'They're using aliases,' Scarlett said, 'which is no shock. Kate said the same. She tried tracking the car Alice was driving. It's stolen. When I left, one of Tanaka's guys was working on breaking into both Alice's and DJ's phones, hoping to find contact information or addresses or anything at all.'

Marcus sat down next to Scarlett. 'Don't be mad, but we need to assume we're not going to find Sweeney in the next two hours.' He pulled up a map of the park on his phone. 'We need a plan that gets me in and out of Shawnee Lookout *alive*.'

She nodded. 'Alive is good.'

Cincinnati, Ohio
Wednesday 5 August, 10.15 P.M.

Ken packed the last of his old photos in a box to go in his suitcase. He was taking only what he couldn't replace. The photos, the first dollar he and Demetrius had made. His MVP trophy he'd earned playing football during his senior year at college. He'd packed his mother's diamond earrings, the tiny ones that had no monetary value. Just sentimental. There was no other jewelry. He'd sold it all years ago. Before he and Demetrius had started the business, of course.

He'd needed the money way back then because he'd wanted to keep his family's home. Which was why he and Demetrius had started the business in the first place.

He'd packed a few changes of clothes, enough cash to get by for a while without raising any flags while going through airport security. He had a bank check he'd use to open an account once he got there. He'd already transferred funds from the other accounts into the offshore account he'd opened years ago under his alias. His rental house was pre-paid for the next six months from that same account.

'I think I'm ready,' he murmured.

'Were you going to say goodbye?'

Ken turned slowly. Sean stood in the doorway, arms loosely crossed over his chest. He didn't look angry, which was good. Ken didn't want to have to kill him too.

'I was going to call when I got there. I didn't know if you'd want to join me or not.'

'Depends on where you're going.'

Ken frowned. 'Why are you here?' Sean so rarely left the downtown office. In fact, the last time he had been out to the family house had been right around the time his mother had disappeared. Of course, Ken knew where Sean's mother was. He'd sent her body through the woodchipper himself. That had been years ago.

'Have you seen the news?' Sean asked.

'No, I've been busy. Why? Is Alice all right?'

'She's fine as far as I know, but someone wearing a ski mask walked into the *Ledger* and starting firing a modified AR-15. It's all over the Internet. Six dead, one wounded. One missing. Four survivors.'

Ken didn't blink. *What the fuck? One wounded? Four survivors?* 'That's terrible,' he said. 'Was one of the dead Marcus O'Bannion?'

'Why hide it?' Sean asked, bemused. 'You've been angling to kill O'Bannion. Why act all innocent now?'

'Habit, maybe.' He zipped up his carry-on. 'Anything else?'

'The cops pulled DJ in, too.'

Ken sat down on the side of his bed, stunned. 'How would they even know?'

'From the gym. Remember? It's how Alice kept an eye on O'Bannion after his accident to make sure he hadn't started digging into the McCord story again. DJ joined the gym too and they spotted each other. Both with weights and with watching O'Bannion. Either Alice talked to the cops or Marcus was called in to ID her and remembered DJ, because they picked him up from the gym this evening.'

'How's he holding up?'

'As far as we know, fine. Why did you feel the need to shoot up the *Ledger*?'

Ken narrowed his eyes. 'I never said I did, but if I did, it's no business of yours.'

'It is my business, because there are cops crawling all over the place. With Alice and DJ in custody, it's only a matter of time before everything comes crashing down. The cops aren't going to let this pass. Neither will Marcus O'Bannion. You murdered his people. He's going to be out for your blood.'

'Let me worry about Marcus.' Ken handed Sean the folder he'd prepared. 'This is everything you need to know. Suppliers, customers, pricing, profits. It's all yours.'

'Such as it is,' Sean said, keeping his arms crossed over his chest. 'After that stunt you pulled tonight, I don't know that our company will be worth diddlyshit. Our customers will go running for the hills if they're smart.'

Ken tossed the folder on the bed. 'Suit yourself. With everyone either in jail or dead, you could rule it all.'

'And I'm telling you that there is nothing left to rule. It's all gone. Including the funds in the company accounts.' Sean lifted his brows. 'I wonder who could have taken that money,' he said mockingly.

'I don't like your tone, son. Talk to Joel. He told me that he'd found missing money and traced it to accounts in Demetrius's and Reuben's names. Maybe that's where the funds went. Reuben's probably sitting in the Caribbean right now, with an underage girl on each knee.'

'Is that where you're going? The Caribbean?'

'No. When I get to where I am going, I'll send for you. It'll be your choice to come.'

'What about Alice?'

'She got caught, Sean. We all know the price of getting caught.' He grabbed his suitcase and carry-on, pushed past his son and went down the stairs.

Sean followed him. 'Who's the woman in the cage?'

'Don't you know?' Ken asked mockingly. 'I thought you knew everything by the way you were talking.'

'You're going to lure O'Bannion here.'

'No. I'm not.'

Sean grabbed his arm. 'Then where? You shot up his office to rile him so that he'd let his guard down when he came after you. You stole his office manager to make sure he came.'

'Looks like you *do* know everything.'

'All alone, Dad? You're going to take O'Bannion on all by yourself?'

Ken smiled condescendingly. 'You're offering to help me? Really?'

Sean's eyes narrowed. 'You can't go alone. That man was an Army Ranger.'

'So? I shot up his office single-handedly. Took out three guards.'

Sean nodded. 'But you left five survivors, not including the woman in the cage. Stone O'Bannion didn't die.'

Ken shrugged. 'Doesn't matter. I covered my face. Now if you don't mind, I have a meeting to prepare for.' He went into the garage to load his luggage in his car, but Sean followed.

'Where's the cash, *Ken*?'

Ken lost his temper. 'I don't know. Now shut up and get out. I don't answer to you, Sean.' He turned his back to load his luggage and realized his mistake too late when the barrel of a gun dug into his kidneys.

'Now you do, *Dad*.'

Cincinnati, Ohio
Wednesday 5 August, 10.15 P.M.

'No,' Isenberg said flatly. She'd arrived at the hospital a short while before to help them develop the plan. Which basically meant that she wanted to tell Marcus what he could and could not do. 'We do not condone the use of civilians as bait in hostage negotiations.'

Scarlett, her father and Deacon's boss Zimmerman had asked Isenberg to join them in their little war room – set up in the same place where Scarlett had interviewed the *Ledger* team the night before – and Marcus had agreed out of respect.

But it didn't mean that he had to agree with Isenberg's opinion.

Marcus shrugged his shoulders and settled his body in the chair he'd deliberately chosen – the chair in which Stone had sat last night. It made him feel a little closer to his brother and at the same time reminded him what was at stake. As if he really needed reminding.

'With all due respect, Lieutenant,' he said, 'it doesn't matter. It's my choice.'

'You're choosing to get killed, then?' Isenberg asked sarcastically, but there was a flicker in her eyes that was genuine concern. The sight helped Marcus get his temper in check. Mostly.

'No, ma'am. But this man has to be stopped. He shot my brother and left him for dead.' Marcus's gaze shifted to the empty chair between Isenberg and Zimmerman, and his hands began to tremble. It was the chair where Cal had been sitting the night before. 'Sweeney killed a man who'd been like family to me for most of my life. Gunned him and too many others down in cold blood. Like they were *nothing*. He sells people – families with children – like they're animals.' He thought of Gayle, how terrified she had to be, and his fury flared. 'He's holding the woman who is a mother to me, and he's got her in a *fucking cage* . . .' His voice faltered and he cleared his throat roughly. 'So forgive me if I don't care what you do or don't condone. This is my family, so it's my business.'

Isenberg bristled. 'It becomes my business when you include my people.'

Marcus stiffened. He hadn't asked for help from anyone but Scarlett. It had been Isenberg, Zimmerman and Jonas Bishop who'd started throwing additional law enforcement bodies into the mix. 'Sweeney needs to be *stopped*. He needs to *pay*. Right now he's fixated on me, so right now I'm the highest-value chip on the table.'

Isenberg narrowed her eyes, but Zimmerman spoke before she could. 'He killed one of my men today too,' he said quietly. 'I want him to pay as much as you do, Mr O'Bannion. I want him stopped. But I want this done right. I want to be smart.'

Marcus started to open his mouth to tell Isenberg and Zimmerman that they could take their people and shove them, but Scarlett shook her head gently, stopping him from messing the whole thing up.

'What would you recommend instead?' she asked, meeting Isenberg's eyes first, then Zimmerman's, then, last, her father's. 'We're putting snipers in the trees around the meeting place – here and here.' She pointed to the map of the park that they'd spread over the table. 'Kate Coppola is an expert marksman and Adam can certainly hold his own.'

They'd tagged Deacon's cousin, Detective Adam Kimble, for the op, and he had agreed right away. Which was nice of the man, because Marcus didn't know Adam from . . . well, from Adam. Marcus understood that Kimble hadn't done it for him. The detective had agreed for Scarlett's sake, as they'd worked together for years, and for Deacon's sake. Faith was about to become Adam's cousin by marriage and since she and Marcus were already cousins, that apparently made Marcus family.

'We've got air support with night IR goggles, plus search-and-rescue dogs on standby,' Scarlett continued levelly. 'We've got an FBI SWAT team gathering on the ground, ready to back us up. Marcus will wear full body armor rather than the Kevlar that Stone was wearing this afternoon.'

Because bullets fired from an assault rifle went through Kevlar like a knife through hot butter. Stone was lucky to be alive. The fifteen bullets hadn't hit anything major. At least that was what they'd been told by the surgeon when he'd come out to speak with them mid-way through the surgery. He'd been "hopeful" that Stone would make it.

Marcus still couldn't let himself relax. Not until he saw Stone and heard his voice.

'What would you recommend instead?' Scarlett asked again.

Zimmerman shook his head. 'Nothing at the moment.'

'I don't know,' Isenberg admitted. 'This feels wrong.'

Scarlett's smile was tight. She was scared too. Marcus could see it in her expression, could feel it in the way she gripped his hand under the table, so hard that his tendons crackled.

'Of course it feels wrong, Lieutenant,' she said. 'It *is* wrong. Sweeney's picked the venue and the time. This could be – and probably is – a trap. If I can find out where he's holding Gayle in the next thirty minutes, we'll punt to our "storm the castle" plan and stage a rescue. Otherwise, Marcus pretends to do a switch, just until we have Gayle in our hands. Then Adam and Kate incapacitate Sweeney and we go in for the arrest. Unless you can think of anything better, *this is the plan.*'

Isenberg turned on Jonas Bishop, her equal in the CPD hierarchy. 'Did you talk to her?'

Jonas nodded. 'I did. She's prepared to turn in her badge if you press her. So, please, think carefully before you press her.'

Isenberg visibly flinched. 'What?'

Marcus's eyes widened as he turned to Scarlett with a combination of shock and dismay. 'You're what?' he demanded. 'No. You are not turning in your badge. Not because of me.'

Scarlett shrugged. 'It's my badge. I can do what I want.'

Marcus met Isenberg's eyes. 'I feel a little sorry for you, Lieutenant.'

Isenberg stared at him for a moment, then shocked him by chuckling. 'Good. You should.' She turned to Scarlett. 'All right, Detective. I can approve your plan without liking it.'

'Yes, ma'am,' Scarlett said mildly.

'And do not think about turning in your badge. It would never have come to that. I would have transferred you first.'

'That's good to know,' Scarlett murmured. 'I believed you were worried for my own good. It's nice to know that for sure.' She checked her phone. 'We should be leaving soon. I don't want to text Deacon again about Diesel and the safe.'

'They'll text us every thirty minutes with progress,' Marcus said. 'Deacon's been good about that.' Deacon was testy because Scarlett kept bugging him between updates.

'I know. I just thought cracking a safe would be faster,' she grumbled. 'It is on TV.'

'I wish he'd done it in five minutes,' Jonas said, 'but I'm actually a little relieved that he isn't so good at it. I might actually have arrested him.' He said it with almost a straight face, but his eyes twinkled at the last minute, defusing some of the tension. 'Except that I wasn't prepared to tangle with you, Scarlett.'

'I called in one of the CPD safe experts,' Isenberg said. 'They were on a call across town, so it may be a little while, but—'

There was a knock on the door of the small conference room and Faith stuck her head in. 'Excuse me, please. Marcus? There's someone here to see you.' She held the door open, and Marcus blinked in surprise at the tiny woman who stood there.

'Delores?'

Scarlett rose to grip the woman's hands. 'Delores, is everything okay?'

'I don't know.' Delores was pale and had been crying. 'That's why I'm here.'

'Delores runs the dog shelter where I got Zat,' Scarlett told her father as she led Delores into the room. 'What brings you here?'

'The hospital wouldn't tell me anything. Where is Stone? Is he all right?'

Surprised, Marcus glanced at Scarlett from the corner of his eye and saw that she was equally perplexed at Delores's sudden arrival and obvious tears. 'He's still in surgery,' he said, 'but the first news was good. He'll make it, but there was a lot of damage.'

Delores sagged. 'But he'll be okay? Oh, thank God.' She sank into the chair Scarlett pulled out and dropped her face into her hands. 'I've been so worried. I finally got in my car and drove out here as soon as I saw the story on the news.' Her china-blue eyes filled with tears. 'I'm so sorry, Marcus.'

'Thank you. Me too.' Marcus proceeded carefully, remembering Stone's reaction when he'd thought Delores might be in danger. There was something going on that they'd missed. 'You only met Stone a few times.'

'More than a few,' she admitted. 'He brings me things for the shelter at least once a week. Stacks heavy bags, helps me clean out cages. He made me promise not to say anything. I think he was worried everyone would think he was a mushy sap. But last night he showed up right at sunset. Told me that you two had been followed yesterday, that a killer could know my name. He stood guard in front of my house last night. All night.'

'Stone?' Marcus said, shocked. 'My brother?'

'My cousin?' Faith asked from the doorway, equally dumbfounded. '*Really?*'

Delores's mouth curved. 'Really. He's very sweet. He never came in, just sat out on my porch working on his computer all night, even though the mosquitoes ate him up. He said he'd come back tonight, but he didn't, and

I got worried. He wasn't answering his cell phone. Then I turned on the news.'

'It got shot up,' Scarlett said. 'We didn't know you were worried or we would have called you. Unfortunately Marcus and I are headed out. We'll be back, but Faith's staying.'

Faith put her arm around Delores's shoulders. 'Come and meet everyone.'

'Oh no, that's all right. I'm not here to intrude. I was just so worried.'

'So is everyone here,' Faith said. 'And you're not intruding.' She gave Scarlett a look that was both hopeful and scared. 'Be careful.'

'Always.' She turned to Marcus. 'You ready?'

Jaw set, he nodded, even though his gut was an absolute mess. 'As I'll ever be.'

Isenberg stood up, her expression severe. 'This is not a suicide mission, Mr O'Bannion. If your lives are in danger, you fall back.'

Marcus said nothing. He wasn't about to give her a reason for canning the op, but he was not leaving Gayle in that cage.

Isenberg rolled her eyes. 'For God's sake.' She stuck her head out the door, looking into the hallway. 'Officer? I'll take it now.' An officer came into view holding a backpack, which Isenberg took, then shoved into Marcus's hands.

It was heavier than he'd expected. He unzipped it with a frown, his chest growing tight as he realized what the lieutenant had done. 'Thermal blanket, first aid kit, water, protein bars, and bolt cutters.' He looked at Scarlett. 'Collapsible, so they're easier to carry.'

Scarlett gave her boss a grateful smile. 'To free Gayle. Thank you, Lynda.'

'Just don't be stupid, Scarlett,' she snapped, but there was no heat behind her words. Only concern. 'One more thing. Agent Coppola is lead on this op. You report to her.'

Scarlett's grateful smile faded. 'Why?'

'Because you are emotionally invested,' Isenberg said. 'I want you both back alive. If Coppola says fall back, you'd sure as hell better say "yes, ma'am". Am I understood?'

Scarlett's nod was curt. 'Yes, ma'am.' She leaned up on her toes and pecked her father's cheek. 'See ya.'

Jonas tilted her chin, locking gazes. 'Your LT made the right call. You are invested.'

'I know,' she murmured. 'I don't have to like it.' She rocked back on her heels. 'Let's move out.'

Cincinnati, Ohio
Wednesday 5 August, 10.28 P.M.

Ken drew a deep breath, keeping his cool despite the gun shoved in his back. His son's gun. He'd been in far tenser situations, but Sean had taken him by surprise and had the upper hand. 'I have to say,' he said mildly, 'that I always thought if either of you staged a coup, it would be your sister.'

'Surprise, surprise,' Sean said coldly, and shoved the barrel harder. 'Start walking. Slowly. Any sudden moves and I'll blow your fucking head off.'

Ken began walking, carefully evaluating his son's stride, his balance, his hold on the weapon. Despite his bravado, Sean had never been in the field, had no experience in these matters. The hand that held the gun trembled, and Sean walked a little too close. Ken had no doubt that he could disarm him easily, but he wanted to know what he was up to first.

He also wanted a clear path away from his son should the disarming not go as planned. So he decided to wait until they were outside before he made his move.

'Why?' Ken asked, putting a tremor in his voice.

'Just walk.'

'If it's the money, we can discuss this.'

Sean laughed. 'It's not the money. I've already taken it all back. Your offshore account has a zero balance.'

Ken stumbled a step, genuinely startled. No one knew about the account in the name of the alias he'd kept secret for years. 'You're lying.'

'Fine,' Sean said easily. 'I'm lying. Mr William J. Bosley.'

Shit, Ken thought, still holding on to his calm. Then Sean rattled off the number of Ken's bank account with a quiet chuckle and his gut turned to water. 'How?' he asked softly, waiting for Sean to make a wrong move or step.

'The same way I found out you were tracking us through our phones. I'm the IT guy. I control all the software, all the devices. Even the ones you believe are private.'

Ken had trusted him completely. Obviously he'd been very wrong. 'Why?'

'Why?' Sean sounded incredulous. 'Really?'

'I rarely ask questions to which I don't want answers,' Ken said sharply. 'Don't play games with me. I asked you *why*.'

'Because my mother did not run off with her yoga instructor,' Sean said, his voice harsh with venom. 'Because she did not abandon me, even though that's what you've told me for years. She didn't leave me voluntarily. You killed her.'

Well, fuck. 'How did you find out?' Ken asked, keeping his voice mildly curious.

'Reuben. He told me that you killed her and . . . disposed of her. That she was in that pit along with all of the others you've had killed over the years.' Sean's voice shook, but his hand clenched on the gun, steadying himself. 'You put my mother through that damn woodchipper.'

Sonofabitch. 'That's a lie,' Ken lied. 'Why would Reuben tell you such a thing?'

'Because I caught him on video with underage girls. More than two dozen times, all different girls,' he added bitterly. 'He was unwilling to go to jail for his perversions so he offered me a trade. The videos I'd taken for the video he'd taken. Of you, killing my mother.'

Shit. Goddamn that Reuben.

They were almost to the garage. He'd overpower Sean and . . . He considered his options. He *would* kill the kid. Once he'd gotten back the money Sean had stolen from him. But he needed Sean physically able to communicate with his voice or a pencil, either would do. Bottom line, he needed Sean to be able to give him passwords and account numbers.

He had a little time before O'Bannion arrived, so he had time to get Sean to spill his secrets. He'd use the same methods against Sean that he'd used against Demetrius.

'Reuben told me that she'd been working with the cops to turn us in,' Ken lied. Sean's mother had hated cops. She'd actually been planning to blackmail Ken and his entire team. 'But now I know you can't trust anything Reuben says. He's stolen money from me. Both he and Demetrius did.'

'No they didn't,' Sean said. '*I* moved that money around. Took Joel forever to find the discrepancy. Joel lied to you too, by the way. There was money in his account too. He moved it elsewhere and is keeping it for himself.'

Ken looked over his shoulder, surprised again. 'You *wanted* me to kill Demetrius.'

Sean gave him a *duh* look. 'I sure as hell didn't want to have to do it myself. Demetrius was insane, especially when he was on the steroids.'

I tortured and killed Demetrius. Because of a lie. Well, no, he corrected himself. He'd killed him because he kept botching up the elimination of Marcus O'Bannion. That part was legit. But he wouldn't have tortured him for that. He would have made it a quick and painless shot to the head. 'Where is Reuben?' he demanded.

'That I don't know. I thought maybe you'd killed him too.'

'I didn't.'

'Too bad. Reuben needed killing. He was a train wreck.'

They were approaching the entrance to the garage. There were two steps down between the laundry room and the garage interior. That would be Ken's chance. If he fucked it up, he believed Sean would be capable of shooting him in the back.

Ken descended the first step, then . . . He whipped around, grabbing Sean's hand and jerking the barrel of the gun toward the concrete floor. At the same time he twisted Sean's wrist hard.

Sean grunted in pain and drove his elbow into Ken's throat. Ken gasped, but used the height difference against his son. Sean was still a step above him, so he grabbed at Sean's elbow as he fell backward, and both men went down.

Ken hit the concrete floor with a back-cracking thud, Sean falling on top of him. But while Ken's back hurt, he'd had far worse pain. Sean had not, and was now a quivering, shaking mess. In a split second, Ken had his son rolled to his back and had wrested the gun from his grip.

Taking no chances, he fired twice, shooting Sean in the knee and in the side. He'd hit none of his important organs, but had robbed him of his mobility. Sean screamed and clutched at empty air, because Ken was already on his feet, the gun pointed at those more vital organs.

'All right, son,' he said coldly. 'Let's talk passwords.'

Thirty-six

Cincinnati, Ohio
Wednesday 5 August, 10.45 P.M.

'Almost there,' Scarlett said quietly. They were less than ten minutes from the site where Marcus would walk into a certain trap. She wanted to talk him out of it, but knew that she couldn't. If he left Gayle with that monster to save his own skin, he'd never forgive himself.

It was who he was and she accepted that.

'Would you have really done it?' he asked. 'Given up your badge?'

'I told my dad that if I were forced to choose, I'd choose you. I never said I'd give up my badge, but that's what it translates to. But you know, if it came down to that, I wouldn't want to stay, anyway. I'm a good cop. I have integrity. If I didn't believe in it, I wouldn't do it. If the department and I came to an impasse, I wouldn't be the one to yield.'

'I'm . . .' He stammered, flustered. 'Thank you.'

She smiled at him. 'If you want to thank me, call Deacon. He's late checking in. If I call, he'll yell at me.'

'Thirty seconds late,' Marcus said, 'but I'll call. For you.' He dialed Deacon's number and put him on speaker.

'Thirty seconds, people,' Deacon growled. 'That's all the late I was. But' – his voice became lighter – 'we have what you asked for. You want me to read it or send it?'

'Both. Send it to my phone,' Scarlett said. 'I'll pull over to look at it.'

'You're welcome, Detective Meanness,' Diesel said.

Scarlett grinned. 'Thank you, Diesel. I'm sorry I threatened you, but you deserved it.'

'I did,' Diesel agreed. 'And I have to admit, it was kind of hot.'

Scarlett started to scold him, then looked over at Marcus. He was nodding vigorously. 'Very hot,' he mouthed, and she swallowed her rebuke, giving Marcus a wink instead. Terrified for Gayle, he was holding on to his composure by a thread. If a little flirtation helped him, Scarlett could flow with it.

'I'm pulling over now,' she said, 'and, Diesel, you are going to forget we ever had this conversation.' By the time she'd stopped the car, the letter had arrived in her email inbox. She and Marcus huddled over her screen, studying the note while Deacon read it aloud.

When they'd finished, Scarlett frowned, completely disappointed. 'It's exactly as Gayle said. Dammit. Thanks anyway, guys,' she said into the phone's speaker. 'I was hoping.'

'Wait a minute,' Marcus said. 'Not so fast.' He expanded her phone's screen and glanced over at her with a smile of satisfaction. 'Look at the return address. That's not where the McCords lived. But it is about five miles from the entrance to the park where we're supposed to meet Sweeney.'

'Oh my God – do you think . . . Could she have put Sweeney's return address on her letter?' Scarlett asked. 'Why would she? How would she even know it?'

'She did it so that we'd check it out,' Diesel said. 'I bet Leslie McCord realized her and her hubby's numbers were up and she wanted someone to know who'd done them in. As for how she knew the address . . . Maybe she'd visited, or even followed Sweeney after a meet. Anders took photos to cover himself. Maybe the McCords wanted a little insurance too.'

'But why not just tell you?' Deacon asked.

Scarlett got it. 'Because she was worried about what would happen to her, but Woody was trying to cut a deal with the prosecution. She didn't want any evidence floating around to indicate that her husband actually was guilty.' She let out a breath of air, 'So, let's rethink our plan. We have a little more than an hour now. It is entirely possible that we're wrong. If so, I want to be able to quickly punt back to plan A – meeting Sweeney where he specified. To that end, we should leave at least Adam in place. We can call Kate to meet us at the address Leslie McCord left us. If we're wrong about Gayle being there, then Kate will be our backup.'

Adam Kimble had camped in that park and knew the layout, so they'd all agreed that he'd go ahead, scout out the area and find a tall tree with a good vantage point of the meeting place. Kate was a sharpshooter, so the base plan had been that she would accompany Adam, finding her own tree.

'Adam and Kate should be at the park by now,' Marcus said. 'Let's tell Kate to meet us at the McCord address.'

Scarlett nodded. 'Kate can be our lookout while we search the place for Gayle.'

'First priority is to get Gayle out, then find Sweeney,' Marcus said. 'I say we give ourselves until 11.30 to find Gayle. If not, I go to the meet as agreed, miked up so that you all can hear. If Kate can safely find a new tree in time, she should. Otherwise, she's Adam's backup on the ground.'

Once they had a visual lock on Gayle, they were to shoot Sweeney to injure, but not to kill. Not unless Sweeney did something stupid, like attempt a double-cross, and then all bets were off and Adam and Kate were to do whatever necessary to bring the bastard down.

Scarlett and Deacon were to remain far enough back so that their presence would go undetected. Unless, again, something went wrong with the trade, or Sweeney simply started shooting. Then they'd sweep in and, like Adam and Kate, do whatever needed to be done to stop him. Not allowing Sweeney to escape was the one thing they'd all agreed on. Either they brought him in alive or they took him down. Permanently.

Marcus gave Scarlett a frighteningly sober look as he added into the speaker phone, 'And, guys, if it comes down to saving only one of us, choose Gayle. Promise me.'

There was silence on the line. Scarlett's lips tightened. She wasn't entertaining that as a possibility. If she did, she'd crack and be utterly useless to everyone.

Finally Deacon sighed. 'All right,' he said quietly. 'But let's pray this McCord address is the right place.'

Scarlett cleared her throat. 'If it is the right place, we storm the castle instead of walking into a slaughter.'

'Not to be too particular,' Deacon commented, 'but what exactly does storming the castle entail?'

Scarlett hesitated. 'Assessing the perimeter first. We can at least check out the house and the property on Google Earth. Then we find a way in, find Gayle and get out.'

'In other words,' Diesel drawled, 'you really have no flippin' idea.'

'Pretty much,' Scarlett admitted. 'We'll play it by ear. It'll be dicey, but at least we're following our plan, not a response to his.'

'I'll contact Kate and Adam,' Deacon said. 'I'll leave Adam in place and have Kate call you to coordinate. I'll meet you at the McCord address in twenty.'

Cincinnati, Ohio
Wednesday 5 August, 11.05 P.M.

'The wall's at least a hundred yards long on each side,' Kate Coppola said as she jogged up to where Scarlett and Marcus stood next to the car they'd parked at the edge of the property to which Leslie McCord had led them. 'Maybe half that widthways. Encloses about an acre.'

Kate had arrived ten minutes earlier and, her rifle strapped to her back, had attempted a perimeter check. Deacon was still ten minutes out. Scarlett checked her phone. They were very quickly running out of time to figure out a way in. Hopefully Sweeney was still in there and they could catch him coming out.

'The wall is eight inches thick and ten feet high,' Kate continued, 'with high-voltage wire on top. There's an iron gate at the end of a long tree-lined driveway. Remote-controlled. I didn't see a guard shack inside, but my angle was bad so there could have been one.'

'Cameras?' Scarlett asked.

'I counted at least sixteen of them on the side of the wall I could see, evenly spaced along the outer perimeter, and they're active. The high-voltage wire is live. I climbed a tree and got a decent view of the interior, but none of the limbs extend over the walls, so there's no entry that way. Good news,' she finished, 'is that with all this security, this is probably Sweeney's place.'

'But bad news,' Scarlett said grimly, 'is that it's a fucking fortress.'

Marcus closed his eyes on a wave of palpable despair, but his voice remained strong. 'Are you sure the wire fence is live?'

'I could hear it humming,' Kate replied briskly, but there was sympathy in her eyes.

He nodded, eyes open and alert once more. 'What else?'

'The wall itself only encloses the house and an attached garage,' Kate said. 'There's a chain-link gate in the back wall that opens to the rest of the property. I didn't run the entire perimeter, so I can't tell you how many acres it covers, only that it's enclosed by a twelve-foot chain-link fence, also high-voltage, also live.'

'If the property database is correct,' Marcus said, 'the entire property is just under forty acres. I ran a quick check as we were driving here. The owner is listed as Kenneth Spiegel, forty-eight years old.'

'Kenneth Spiegel, Kenneth Sweeney,' Kate said. 'At least he did us the courtesy of keeping his first name in his alias.'

'The age is about right too,' Scarlett added, 'assuming Kenneth is the man in the photos with Alice.'

'Did you get a photo of Kenneth Spiegel?' Kate asked.

Marcus said. 'Not yet. Deacon's having Isenberg's clerk search the DMV database. Spiegel still exists – as a name, anyway. He's on record as paying the property taxes every year. He assumed ownership from Martha Spiegel – his mother – twenty-two years ago, when he was twenty-six. It appears this land has been owned by Spiegels for a hundred years. The primary residence is a six-bedroom, three-and-a-half-bath Tudor-style home with a six-car garage, just under four thousand square feet.'

'That's what I saw within the walls,' Kate agreed. 'The back part of the property is mostly forested, but I did see two sheds through the chain-link fence. One is normal-sized – for shovels and stuff – and the other is large, with a high ceiling, almost like a building you'd see at a state fair.'

'Lots of places to hide one small woman,' Scarlett muttered.

'She's likely being kept in the basement,' Marcus said, 'based on the video he sent us. The cage was on a concrete floor and the walls in the background were unfinished.'

'And the sound echoed a little,' Scarlett added. 'I'd start looking there once we get in.'

'Did you see any sign of people?' Marcus asked. 'Guards specifically?'

'Not walking around,' Kate said, 'but there have been people there recently. There's trash in the cans outside and one of the garage doors is up. I took some photos.' She handed over her phone, and Scarlett and Marcus flipped through the pictures, confirming what she had described.

'Any ideas of how we get in?' Scarlett asked.

Marcus shook his head, his shoulders sagging. 'No,' he murmured.

Scarlett curled her hand around his forearm. 'Then we wait for him to come out. If he hasn't left yet, he'll have to come through the front gate. We put Kate up in the tree and she can take him out with a head shot, assuming his vehicle isn't fitted with bullet-resistant glass. If we can't take him out, we disable the car and physically ambush him.'

Marcus lifted his head. Stared at her for a moment, hope in his eyes. 'We have to get him before he knows we're coming. Kate?'

Kate checked the time. 'Deacon will be here soon, but the SWAT guys are still twenty minutes out. I really want the backup.'

'But Sweeney might leave for the meet before they get here,' Marcus protested.

'Kate, let's get as close to the front gate as we can without setting off the security, and find our positions,' Scarlett bargained. 'We won't move in until backup arrives, unless Sweeney's vehicle comes through the gate. Does that work?'

Kate considered it for a split second longer. 'Yeah, that works.'

'Then let's go,' Marcus said, his jaw clenched. 'How do we avoid the cameras?'

'I hid in the tree cover. I assume it worked because nobody shot at me. Follow me.'

Scarlett gave his arm another squeeze. 'You heard the woman, soldier. Fall in.'

Cincinnati, Ohio
Wednesday 5 August, 11.10 P.M.

Ken logged out of his bank account and closed his laptop before turning to look down at his son, who lay on the floor shivering, despite the heat in the garage. Bound hand and foot, Sean boasted fewer fingers and toes than he'd had before they'd started.

It only seemed fair. Ken had taken Demetrius's fingers based on the belief that his old friend had betrayed him, when in reality it had been Sean setting his team up to mistrust each other. Sean fancied himself a grand puppet master, pulling the strings. Sean had been wrong.

'I gotta hand it to you, son,' Ken said. 'You held out far longer than I expected before spilling your secrets.' But he had spilled them. 'You'll be happy to know that I've reclaimed my money – and yours. But not to worry. You won't be needing it anymore.'

Sean stared up at him, hatred and agony glazing his eyes. 'You fucking bastard,' he croaked hoarsely. He'd screamed long and loud, and his voice was mostly gone.

'Watch your tone, boy,' Ken said mildly. Swiping his shirtsleeve over his brow, he wiped away the sweat that dripped into his eyes. He'd opened the garage door to get a little fresh air after finishing with Sean, but the air outside was hot and muggy too. He needed a shower and a change of clothes. *I reek*, he thought. His clothing was smeared with Sean's blood. Now that his money was safe, he needed to clean up and get in position to eliminate O'Bannion.

Ken had no plans to walk up and meet the man. There would be no exchange of pleasantries or threats. No face-to-face final confrontation. He didn't need O'Bannion to know who was killing him. He simply wanted the man dead. He knew the park like the back of his hand. He'd grown up here. He knew where to hide for the best shot that would drop O'Bannion in his tracks and still allow for a speedy and unnoticed escape.

Because he did not want that man following him to the ends of the earth. Ken wanted the freedom to live where and as he pleased.

He reached down to grab Sean's ankles so that he could drag him out of the garage, but hesitated. There were still a few things he needed to know. He met his son's furious – and helpless – gaze. 'So nobody was stealing money, Demetrius was loyal, and you really don't know where Reuben is?'

560

'Go to hell.'

He tapped Sean's shot-out knee with the toe of his boot, making his son moan in pain. 'I'll kick it. You won't like that, I promise. What about Reuben's wife, Miriam? Was she really saved by an anonymous 911 call?' He held his knife poised over the knee wound. 'Don't give me attitude.'

'There was an anonymous 911 call,' Sean gritted. 'But Miriam was already dead. Nobody pumped her stomach or made her vomit. She died because you drugged her.'

Ken clenched his jaw. 'So you lied about Burton double-crossing me, too.'

'No. I didn't lie.' Sean's baring of teeth was a gross parody of a smile. 'You assumed.'

Ken's rage roiled within him. 'I ordered Burton's death. Decker killed him and disposed of him.'

'*You* have a conscience?' Sean scoffed.

'No. But you cost me a man I could have depended on later.' And that pissed him off. Losing a loyal man who'd kill his friend's wife on Ken's command? Burton had been an asset. 'What about your sister?' he asked. 'Was Alice in on this with you?'

Sean pursed his lips like he wasn't going to answer until Ken pushed the blade further into his knee wound. Sean's eyes rolled back and Ken slapped his face hard.

'You will keep it together,' Ken snarled. 'You'll die when I decide it's time. *Was your sister in on this with you?*'

'No!' Sean cried out shrilly. 'She was loyal.' He panted, his face ashen. 'She wanted to buy you out.' His mouth twisted. 'Pay you money.'

'But you didn't,' Ken said quietly. 'You wanted to steal it.'

'I wanted you to die knowing you'd lost it all.' Sean spat the words as tears ran down his face. 'But she *loves* you,' he sneered. 'And I hate her for it.'

Ken blinked, momentarily stunned. 'You would have killed her too?'

'No. No. I couldn't do that.' Sean shook his head, sobs now shaking his body. 'So I got her out of the way.'

Slowly Ken came to his feet, his mind numb, yet racing. Alice *was* out of the way. In custody. *Because I sent her to take care of the tracker supplier*. Because Sean had told him that the supplier was being brought to police headquarters. He grabbed his son by the collar of his blood-soaked shirt. 'You set her up to go to prison?'

'I was going to get her out!' Sean shouted. 'I was going to get her the best lawyer money could buy!'

Ken shook him hard. 'When?'

'After you were dead,' Sean said flatly. 'And I'd put you through the goddamn woodchipper.'

Ken twisted Sean's collar with one hand as he drew his other back and backhanded his son so hard that his head hit the floor with an audible crack. 'You little bastard,' he said quietly. *I want to kill him. Want to break his fucking neck.* But that would be too quick. Too merciful. 'Tell me, Sean,' he continued, still quietly. 'Had you planned to kill me before you put me through the woodchipper?'

Sean blanched, able to see where this was going. The boy was smart that way. 'I hadn't thought about it,' he replied, struggling for bravado.

Ken smiled. 'I have. And I don't.' He had the satisfaction of watching his son's bravado drain away, leaving Sean shaking in a pool of his own blood and tears.

But he couldn't do that right now. He checked the time and cursed. He needed to get clean. O'Bannion was no idiot. He'd most certainly bring all kinds of law enforcement with him. The woods would probably be crawling with cops. And if any of them had called in a canine unit, the dogs would smell him a mile away as he was right now, all covered with blood.

Checking the security of Sean's bonds, he shoved a cloth gag in his son's mouth before cleaning his knives and putting them back in their case. Then he took them and his laptop back into the house. He started the hot water in the master bath as he stripped off his fouled clothing. He'd throw the clothes in the pit with what was left of Sean.

Ken climbed under the hot spray, feeling every one of his forty-seven years. His daughter was in prison and he needed to find a way to get her out. And he had to do it from a long distance away. Because only one thing was crystal clear: he would be on that plane tomorrow when it left for Papeete, no matter what. He'd do what he could for Alice from there.

He considered his options as he lathered off the grime. He could—

Suddenly the lights went out and the AC motor whined as it shut down. No power. The power had gone out. Which it wasn't supposed to do. They had a backup generator. It should have kicked in already, but it hadn't.

Something was wrong.

Ken quickly rinsed himself off and crept from the shower.

Cincinnati, Ohio
Wednesday 5 August, 11.10 P.M.

The wall with its iron gate, evenly spaced cameras and high voltage was exactly as Kate had described, Marcus thought as he and Scarlett followed the agent through the woods. Scarlett lurched forward to tap Kate's shoulder, bringing them all to an abrupt halt.

Scarlett pointed to the mounted camera. 'How did you know they were live?' she whispered.

'The red lights were lit on each of them,' Kate whispered back. But the lights weren't on now. She cocked her head. 'The hum of the high-voltage wire is gone too, and there was more ambient light overhead because of spotlights inside the wall.'

'Someone didn't pay their power bill,' Marcus said. 'If the back fence is also dead, we can go in that way rather than waiting for Sweeney to come through the gate.'

Kate checked the time again, then sent a quick text from her phone. 'To Deacon,' she said quietly. 'I'm telling him that we're going in. We don't know if the power outage is planned or accidental, but it could come back on. Let's cut our way through the chain-link. If the power comes back on, retreat to the forested area until backup arrives. I'll check the two sheds in the back, then I'll find a good vantage point with the garage in view. If he leaves while you're in there, I'll fire as soon as the car clears the garage.'

They set off at a jog through the trees until they reached the point where the wall ended and the chain-link fence began. Marcus plucked a leaf from a tree and dropped it on the fence, relieved when there was no fizzle. He pulled the bolt cutters from the pack and cut a section of fence, three feet wide by five feet tall. The fence curled away, leaving an opening large enough for them to dive through. Even if the power came back on, they had a quick escape route.

Kate disappeared to the left, into the trees in the direction of the two small sheds that she'd seen. Scarlett had already run to the chain-link gate set into the back wall and was cutting away a portion of the gate similar in size to that which Marcus had cut in the fence itself.

She handed him the bolt cutters and he slid them back into the pack. She crawled through the hole she'd cut, fearless but careful. Marcus was right behind her.

Hold on a little longer, Gayle, he thought. *I'm coming for you.*

Cincinnati, Ohio
Wednesday 5 August, 11.15 P.M.

Special Agent Kate Coppola looked over her shoulder to see Marcus and Scarlett disappearing behind the wall of the compound. She silently wished them luck, starkly aware that they'd taken the more dangerous search. Back here in the forested area, there was cover galore should she need to hide, but inside the compound there was a house, its attached garage and a lot of wide-open space.

Marcus O'Bannion was here to save Gayle first and to stop Sweeney second. Scarlett's priorities mirrored his, but Kate's were reversed. Kate was here to arrest the traffickers the Bureau had been following for three years now. Her secondary priority was to make contact with – and to extract, if required – their agent who'd gone deep undercover. They hadn't heard from the agent in weeks. That wasn't too unusual. What was more worrisome was that they hadn't heard from the undercover's handler in several days. The handler was long overdue for his check-in.

She moved through the forest as soundlessly as possible, headed for the larger shed because it was the closer of the two. The structure was about as large as a high-school gymnasium, the walls made of corrugated metal. The roof was a big canopy that rose to a peak in the middle, like that of a circus tent. There was no foundation that she could see and the walls were of the prefabricated type that could be quickly put together and taken apart.

A temporary structure? *Probably.* But what were they using it for?

She heard the loud crack of a twig and ducked back into the trees. A man was approaching from the large shed, but it wasn't Sweeney. Sweeney was in his forties, with dark hair. The man walking toward her was blond and fucking huge. Nearly as big as Marcus's friend Diesel. She didn't want to have to shoot him and alarm anyone in the house, but she also didn't want to have to tangle with him hand-to-hand unless she got the drop on him.

Sliding her rifle over her back, Kate grabbed the limb of the nearest tree, swung herself up onto it, then climbed a few limbs higher until she was certain the man wouldn't see her.

She waited until he'd gotten a few body lengths away from the tree before dropping from the limb to land nearly soundlessly in a crouch. She shoved the barrel of her rifle into his back.

'Hands in the air.' Slowly he complied. 'Higher.' She dug the rifle barrel a bit deeper into his back. '*Higher*, I said. On the ground, face down, Blondie. Do it,' she hissed, and he dropped to his knees, flattening his body on the ground. 'Arms spread, palms down, fingers straight.'

Once again he complied, and she snapped cuffs on while he put up relatively little resistance. 'Where's your boss?' she asked.

'Depends. Who are you?'

She gave the rifle another shove between his shoulder blades. 'I will shoot your fucking head off, make no mistake. Boss. Where?'

'Inside the house, I think. At least he was a few minutes ago. Don't shoot.' He turned his face to the side so that he could look up at her from the corner of his eye. His very blue eye. 'Who are you? Please.'

Her rifle was steady in her hands. 'Special Agent Coppola, FBI. Who are you?'

He let out a breath. 'Finally. You need to send a message to your SAC ASAP. Tell him "Pineapple under the sea".'

'"Pineapple under the sea"?' Startled, Kate went down on one knee to study his face more closely. It could be him under all that grime. Carefully she pushed up his pants leg to his knee and checked for the identifying scar. It was a match. Quickly she unlocked his cuffs. 'Well I'll be damned. Special Agent Davenport, we've been looking for you.'

Cincinnati, Ohio
Wednesday 5 August, 11.15 P.M.

Scarlett and Marcus ran from the back gate toward the garage attached to the house. There were six bay doors, with one open. Hopefully that meant that Sweeney hadn't left yet.

She figured the bastard would bring Gayle to the meet, just to get Marcus to come close enough to be grabbed or shot. Once Sweeney had gotten Marcus, Scarlett had no doubt that he'd kill Gayle next, then anyone who happened to be in his way. He'd already sprayed bullets throughout the *Ledger* building. He was an indiscriminate killer.

But if he hadn't left yet, they still had a chance to grab Gayle and avoid walking into what might be a trap. Although leaving his garage door conveniently open was probably a trap, too. It couldn't matter. Marcus was right. Based on the look of the cage in the video, Gayle was in the basement. They had to go in.

The house itself was simply massive. Built in the Tudor revival style so popular in Cincinnati pre-World War II, it was easily twice the size of Scarlett's house. Partly brick, partly half-timber, it had six windows across the top floor and . . . Scarlett frowned.

There was a large picture window along the back wall whose glass had been shattered. Shards of glass littered the grass, and the opening was now covered with plywood. The window had been broken from the inside out, the broken area visible against the plywood as no one had finished removing the remaining glass. The hole was large. *Body-sized.*

A strangled gasp caught her attention, and she turned to find Marcus staring at the corner of the driveway closest to the open garage door. Blood

565

stained the concrete in a wide swath, as if someone had dragged a body through the open door.

Marcus's face had grown pale in the growing moonlight. 'Not Gayle,' he whispered. 'It can't have been Gayle.'

'No,' she agreed softly. 'They won't kill her until they get you. So let's find her before that happens.' She drew her weapon and started for the door, keeping her back to the wall, but Marcus hadn't moved.

He frowned. 'This feels too damn convenient,' he said, his whisper almost silent. 'The power going off just when we need to get through the fence? Leaving the door open for us?'

She'd thought the same thing. 'He doesn't know we know about this place.'

'Or he didn't. He could have seen Kate doing her perimeter check. Hell, he could have seen us approach on the main road.'

She blew out a breath, trying hard not to be exasperated. 'Entirely possible. This could totally be a trap.'

'I'll go in,' he whispered. 'You stay here.'

Ah. He was protecting her. *I don't think so*. 'No. You go high, I'll go low. Now.'

He closed his eyes for a second, and when he opened them, she saw utter focus and concentration. Gun in his hand, he eased around the garage corner and through the open door.

Soundlessly he crept through the enormous garage, following the bloodstain that stretched from the corner of the driveway to the middle of one of the empty bays. In the bay was a pool of drying blood. Clearly a body had been moved from the garage. The forensic guys would have to determine where it went after being dragged off the driveway.

Scarlett took a photo of the bloody swath, then used her hands to measure the width of the stain. She held them up to show Marcus that whoever had been dragged was much wider than Gayle.

Understanding flickered in his eyes, followed by relief. 'Not Gayle,' he mouthed, then grimly pointed to the van parked in one of the six bays. Scarlett recognized the vehicle from the security video taken outside the *Ledger*'s loading bay. Sweeney had driven it to slaughter the *Ledger*'s employees and to abduct Gayle.

The license plate was different from the one captured in the security video. Someone – likely Sweeney – had changed the plates. Scarlett snapped a photo of the new plate in case things went south. If Sweeney managed to get by them and escape, she'd have to call in a BOLO.

Marcus moved quickly and quietly, opening the van doors to shine his flashlight around the interior. No Gayle. There was a bloodstain on the carpet, but the blood had dried. Had it been Gayle's blood, it would have still been damp. Whoever had bled there had done so fifteen hours or more before.

'Demetrius?' she mouthed, and Marcus shrugged, then reached into the open driver's-side window and brought out a set of keys, pocketing them. Scarlett gave him a nod of approval.

Marcus proceeded to the door that led from the garage into the laundry room. Again he took high, she low. For the first time she was truly seeing the former Army Ranger at work, and she was more than impressed. She'd known he was stealthy and capable, but while she'd had to develop a relationship with her other partners, she and Marcus seemed to flow together like two streams meeting in the woods.

They encountered no resistance, the house having a too-quiet, abandoned feel. With the power out, there wasn't a single sound – not a hum from the fluorescent lights nor the low drone of an AC fan. The silence was oppressive.

Marcus's lips thinned and she knew he was worried that Sweeney had already moved Gayle. She shook her head. 'Think positive,' she mouthed, and he nodded and squared his shoulders.

They moved from the laundry room into a grand foyer. Twin staircases curved upward, where they were connected with a balustrade that provided a bird's-eye view of the lower floor and the front of the property through a large window over the front door. There were bedrooms upstairs. If they didn't find Gayle in the basement, they'd check those rooms next.

They found what they thought was the door to the basement off the foyer, but it turned out to be the kitchen. Marcus went in first, giving her the sign that he'd located the basement door. Scarlett pulled the kitchen door closed behind them, covering Marcus as he opened the door to the basement. Steep stairs disappeared into inky blackness.

This would be the dicey part, walking blind down a flight of stairs, not knowing what they'd find below. *This could be the trap.* Scarlett pointed at Marcus to take the stairs. If Gayle was downstairs and incapacitated, he would be able to carry her. She pointed to herself and the door. She'd stay up top and guard the entrance. It would be too easy for someone to lock them in if they both went downstairs.

She listened intently, not hearing a sound as Marcus navigated the stairs as silently as he did everything else. She drew a breath and prepared to wait.

Cincinnati, Ohio
Wednesday 5 August, 11.20 P.M.

Ken buttoned his shirt, listening for any stray noises downstairs. He'd heard nothing since the power had gone out. He'd jumped from the shower and done a check of the property from the upstairs windows but had seen no one, so he'd gone to his room and quickly picked out clothes in the dark. But he wasn't dismissing the danger.

That the power had gone off now was not coincidental, and he wondered if Sean had made it happen with a timer. Or if his son had a confederate. Except that at this point there wasn't anyone left to be his accomplice.

He let out a breath. Except for Decker and Trevino, the second of Burton's two 'green' guys. Sean was supposed to have checked into Trevino. Ken cursed himself for having underestimated his son. Then he cursed himself for underestimating Reuben.

His jaw tightened. Reuben had probably laughed at Ken, knowing the video he held was a real ace in the hole. Ken thought he might be more pissed off that he hadn't thought to do the same to Reuben.

He finished getting dressed, then checked his tracking program on his cell phone. Decker was at the downtown office, just as he said he'd be. Joel was at his home, as he always was. Looked like those two would be the last men standing after Ken left for his retirement. They could keep the company, or what was left of it. At least until Alice got out of jail.

He didn't have a tracker for Trevino's phone. The guy had been too low on the totem pole to warrant his attention. Ken knew that if he ever got into business again, he wouldn't make the same mistake. Nobody would fall below his radar.

Still hearing nothing downstairs, he grabbed the suitcase he'd just finished packing when Sean had interrupted him earlier, drew his gun and crept down the stairs. He had barely enough time to go to Shawnee Lookout and get into position in the spot he'd chosen in advance. He'd have a perfect view of the park's entrance and a clear line of fire to anyone standing there. He'd do the job, get in the van and drive straight to Toronto.

He wouldn't come back to the house to feed Sean through the wood-chipper while he was still alive, although that would have been immensely satisfying. He also wouldn't take the time – now or later – to put a bullet into poor Gayle. Instead he'd leave word for Decker to come by in a week or so. The woman would be dead by then – her heart wasn't so good. Decker could return the body to the O'Bannions. After losing Marcus and most of the *Ledger*'s staff, having Gayle's body dumped on their doorstep would be one more way to make them suffer.

He slipped down the curved staircase for the last time. He made no sound, his gun at the ready, just in case. But he heard no one. Saw no one.

He paused in the laundry room to ensure the silencer was fixed to his gun. He'd put a bullet through Sean's skull before he drove away. It was far better than the little bastard deserved, but at this point, getting away was all that mattered.

He stepped into the garage and froze.

Sean was gone.

Cincinnati, Ohio
Wednesday 5 August, 11.20 P.M.

'What's in the big shed?' Kate asked Agent Davenport after hauling him to his feet. He rose with a natural grace to brush the dirt and leaves away from his jeans, then his shirt. But some of the leaves stuck to his shirt and he had to peel them off. He dropped them to the ground, each one sticky with blood. 'Shit. Are you hit?'

'No. Not my blood. The shed is their body disposal unit,' he said tersely, and started walking back to the house within the walls. 'Complete with a woodchipper. They dig a big hole, aim the chipper at it, sludge the bodies, add a pinch of composting materials . . .' He wore an expression of disgust. '*Voilà*. No more bodies. When the hole is filled, they take down the shed, dig another hole, move the chipper, and put the shed back up.'

Oh my God. 'Why were you in there?'

'I was hiding someone. Do you have medical backup? Because there's a guy in that shed who will need help.'

'Two ambulances. They'll be waiting at the main road. Where's your handler?'

The large blond stopped abruptly. 'What do you mean? You haven't talked to him?'

'He hasn't checked in for two days. He's overdue.'

'Shit. Then you don't have Reuben Blackwell or Jason Jackson in custody?'

'No,' she said and his jaw went taut. 'Who are those men?'

Agent Davenport grabbed her arm. 'Get someone to 5487 Wharton Court ASAP,' he commanded. 'Agent Symmes is my handler. If he doesn't have ID for whatever reason, he's got a zipper tattoo around his biceps. The other two guys will be Sweeney's men. You don't want them walking free, trust me. If Symmes hasn't called in, something is very, very wrong.'

Kate made the call, then looked up at him. 'What's going on here, Davenport? Who are Reuben Blackwell and Jason Jackson?'

'Reuben Blackwell is Sweeney's head of security and Jackson is one of Reuben's men. If you don't have them, how do you know about Sweeney?'

'Figured it out the hard way, obviously,' she said, starting to walk again. 'If Sweeney's in the house, we need to get there too. Two of my team are in there. Rescue operation. Sweeney took a hostage when he shot up the *Ledger* building.'

'That's why I came back. I heard Sweeney had taken a hostage and I thought I might be able to get her out.'

'Thank you. Tell me about Sweeney's operation.'

'Sweeney's the boss of the trafficking ring. He had three partners – Reuben Blackwell, Demetrius Russell and Joel Whipple.'

'Demetrius we know about,' she said. 'He's dead, isn't he?'

Surprise flashed in Davenport's blue eyes. 'Yeah. How did you know?'

'He was stabbed by the young man he tried to murder last night. Phillip Cauldwell.'

'Oh, that's not how he died,' Davenport said darkly. 'His body is hidden in the big shed along with Sean, Sweeney's son. Sean tried a coup, but Daddy wasn't having it. Sean is the IT guy and he's not quite dead yet. If you can save him, he has access to data you need. He's the guy who needs the ambulance and the medics need to make him a priority.'

'Got it. Have you seen Gayle Ennis, Sweeney's hostage?'

'No, but if she's in the house, he's probably taken her to the basement.'

'Which is where Bishop and O'Bannion were headed.'

'The newspaper guy and the detective? They don't know what they're dealing with.'

Kate shook her head. 'They have a real good idea. Where is everyone else? This place is like a ghost town.'

'Either dead or in jail. They all turned on each other at the end. The accountant, Joel, should be at his house. He's got the books. *All* the books.' He rattled off an address.

Kate called it in. 'Got it. We've got agents on their way. What's in the little shed?'

'It's storage. But the power lines are there.'

'Did you cut the power?'

'Yes. I saw you on the security camera when you climbed the tree to check out the compound. I was hoping you were my backup. Did you find the two ankle trackers I left at the Anders place?'

She nodded. 'That was you too? Where are the three Anderses?'

'Sweeney killed the parents.' He drew a slashing line across his throat. 'Made quite a mess. Did it in front of the daughter.'

'Stephanie,' Kate said. 'What happened to her?'

'She's still alive. Sweeney told me to kill her too, but I hid her in the big shed, behind some packing crates. Stephanie Anders. Piece of work, that one. She's tied and gagged. You can have her. Watch her fingernails,' he added, disgruntled. 'They're lethal.'

Kate bit back a smile. 'Noted. We have her boyfriend in custody, by the way. Detroit Field Office found him. Drake Connor is his name. He had a flash drive on him with files he'd stolen from Stephanie's dad – photos that Anders had taken as insurance against Sweeney. Those photos helped us tie Sweeney to Alice Newman.'

Davenport's smile was vicious. 'Good. She was the heir apparent, you know. She's Sweeney's daughter.'

'Makes sense. We found photos of them at her college graduation in the background of other people's pictures.'

'Facebook?'

Kate nodded. 'Gotta love it.'

'When you take Stephanie in, you'll find a guy named Dave Burton with her – he was Reuben's second-in-command and was acting as Sweeney's security head. His hands are dirty too. Sweeney told me to kill him, so I hid them together. Sweeney thinks they're mush in the pit. As far as I know, he doesn't suspect me. Yet.'

'Got it,' Kate said. 'Let's find Sweeney. I want to end this.'

Cincinnati, Ohio
Wednesday 5 August, 11.20 P.M.

Marcus crept down the stairs, stowing his fear at leaving Scarlett alone at the top. She could take care of herself. The knowledge left him free to focus on listening and watching – for Gayle and for the trap he was sure waited somewhere.

The basement was largely underground, but there must have been a couple of small windows somewhere, because a faint light filtered into the dark space below. Marcus put off using his flashlight, aware that it would make him a target if someone was waiting for him. It had been too easy to get into the property, too easy to get into the house.

He made himself go as still as death, listening for inhales, exhales. He heard a sniffling. Not a sob, but more than a sigh. It was coming from the far corner of the basement, the location consistent with that of the cage in the video that Sweeney had sent.

Gayle. She was alive. Relief had his heart racing and his knees going weak.

He crept up to the cage, barely able to make out the outline of her body in the darkness. 'Gayle,' he whispered. 'It's me.'

He heard a swiftly indrawn breath, then a muffled sob that broke his heart in two. Quickly he pulled the bolt cutters from the backpack and, going by touch, snapped the lock off the cage and carefully set it aside. He pulled the blanket from the pack and opened the cage door, wincing when it squeaked. But no bullets came flying and he heard no other sounds except Gayle's sobs.

Again using touch, he found the places where she'd been bound and quickly cut the ropes, wrapping her in the blanket and pulling her into his arms. 'Sshh,' he whispered, because her sobs had increased in volume. Gently he worked the duct tape from her face, allowing her to drag in a deep breath. 'You have to hold on,' he said in her ear, his words mostly exhaled air rather than spoken. 'Don't cry. We can't let ourselves be heard.'

He felt her body stiffen and shake as she valiantly controlled her tears. Shouldering the backpack, he rose with her in his arms and went for the stairs, making it to the top with barely a sound.

He found Scarlett where he had left her, fiercely guarding his safety. Relief filled her eyes when she saw Gayle, but she didn't say a word. She opened the kitchen door and signaled for him to bring Gayle out. Leading the way, she headed for the exit, pausing in the laundry room to fish the keys to Sweeney's van from his pocket and give him a quick, bright smile.

Marcus couldn't smile back. The hairs on the back of his neck were still raised. This had been too damn easy. The other shoe was poised to fall.

As Scarlett opened the door to the garage, the shoe fell. She had no sooner cleared the two short steps down when she was jerked from his view. A split second later, he heard her agonized cry, followed by the clatter of her gun as it fell to the concrete. The gun slid into view, evidently kicked away.

His mind racing, Marcus took cover behind the open door, pressing his body to the laundry room wall and gathering Gayle closer to his chest.

'Mr O'Bannion.' The voice came from inside the garage, to the left of the open door. It was the man who'd called him, taunting him about Gayle. The man who'd shot his brother and killed Cal. Greasy and smug, the voice sent

Marcus's stomach roiling. 'How lovely of you to visit me. If I'd known you were coming, I'd have planned more of a welcome.'

'Go to fucking hell, Sweeney,' Scarlett said, her breath coming in shallow pants. 'He didn't come with me.'

Sweeney had hurt her. Marcus wasn't sure what the bastard had done, but he could hear the pain in Scarlett's voice.

'Oh please, Detective,' Sweeney said. 'Of course he came with you. I'm surprised you're here. I'll give you that. But whether here or at the designated meeting place, the result will be the same. I won't be leaving any of you alive.'

'You stupid sonofabitch,' Scarlett spat. 'Do you really think I came alone? This place is surrounded by SWAT and Feds who can't wait to get their hands on you. You shot up the *Ledger* office, kidnapped an innocent woman and killed her.'

'I didn't kill the woman,' he said mildly.

'Well she was dead when I found her. Why do think she's not with me?'

'Because O'Bannion has her.'

But Sweeney sounded unsure.

Scarlett laughed bitterly. 'Right. Like he's hiding behind the door. You idiot. I wouldn't bring a damned civilian on a rescue op. Especially one who's emotionally involved.'

'Well if he's not here, then your life means nothing. You hear that, O'Bannion?' he called in a singsong tone. 'I have no reason to keep your girlfriend alive.'

Scarlett scoffed. 'You're not going to kill me. Your life is forfeit as soon as you show your face, no matter what door you leave out of. I'm your ticket out of here.'

No matter what door you leave out of. She was telling Marcus to leave her there and exit through another door. In his arms, Gayle had begun to tremble violently. She bit down on the blanket so that her chattering teeth would make no noise.

He had to get Gayle out of here. To an ambulance. She was going into shock.

'Oh,' Scarlett added to Sweeney, her voice cocky despite the obvious pain she was in, 'I hope you have comfortable shoes, because we'll be walking the whole way.' She grunted a little, then crowed. 'Bye-bye, keys. Hello, SWAT. Through the garage door and into plain sight.'

Marcus grinned, despite his bone-chilling fear. Scarlett had just thrown the keys to the minivan onto the driveway. Hopefully Kate was in a tree, waiting. This was her chance.

573

'Go on now,' Scarlett taunted. 'Go get the keys. I dare you.'

Sweeney just laughed. 'Good try, dear. Throwing your own keys? Clever. Let's go. You can drive. I'll be out of sight, making sure you don't stop.' There were sounds of scuffling as Sweeney dragged her across the concrete floor. Then Sweeney's roar of fury when he realized she really had thrown his keys away.

Marcus knew that this was *his* chance. Trusting Scarlett to take care of herself, he eased away from his hiding place behind the door and slipped out of the laundry room back into the foyer. He took off for the front door, wrestling it open and hurling himself and Gayle into the night.

The moon was just starting to rise in the sky, giving the property a silvery look. It wasn't as bright as spotlights, but if he weren't careful he could be seen. Sticking close to the house, he ran around to the side opposite the garage and through the hole in the chain-link fence in the back wall. A look over his shoulder made his blood grow cold.

Kate Coppola was inching toward the open garage door, a large blond man behind her. He had a gun. Marcus's heart sank. There were no snipers in the trees.

There was no way he was leaving Scarlett to their mercy. *Get Gayle out, then go back.* He ducked through the hole in the gate and sprinted for the hole he'd cut in the fence. He ran through, making a sharp left turn toward the main road.

'Marcus!'

The familiar voice had him stopping in his tracks, turning to see Deacon and Diesel running toward him. Without a second thought, he thrust Gayle into Diesel's arms. 'Get her out of here. Sweeney has Scarlett and one of his goons has Kate.'

'Fucking hell,' Deacon muttered. Phone in one hand, he grabbed Marcus's arm with his other to keep him from running back. 'Just wait a second.'

Marcus pulled free. 'Scarlett doesn't have a second.'

Cincinnati, Ohio
Wednesday 5 August, 11.30 P.M.

Marcus set off at a fast run. He could hear Deacon behind him, calling in for backup. It was about time. He paused at the back chain-link gate, letting Deacon catch up. Together they looked through the fence and Marcus hissed out a furious breath. 'Fuck.'

'Fuck,' Deacon hissed at the same time.

Scarlett was standing in the driveway, dimly visible in the growing moonlight, her hands on the back of her head while Sweeney disarmed her. So far he'd pulled three guns and two knives from her vest and pockets, all while holding his own gun – enhanced with a silencer – at the base of her skull. One of Scarlett's hands was covered in blood. Sweeney had shot her.

Kate Coppola stood in the same position, hands behind her head. The huge blond guy held a pistol to her back, patting her down. He'd slung Kate's rifle on his own back.

Marcus wanted to run through the gate to save Scarlett, but there was no cover. Any fast moves at this point would get her killed. Instead he had to stand there and listen helplessly.

'Thank you, Decker,' Sweeney said. 'I wasn't expecting you, but I'm glad you're here.'

'I would have called, but I forgot my phone. It's still on my desk at the office. I came back because I left my laptop charger on the kitchen counter.'

Marcus frowned, thinking of the spotless kitchen. There hadn't been any charging cords anywhere.

'Well, as I said, I'm glad you're here. You know what to do now.'

'What does he know to do?' Scarlett asked belligerently.

'Kill and dispose,' the big blond said succinctly.

'It's what we do with uninvited guests.' Sweeney gave Kate an appraising look. 'Is this broad your SWAT team and Feds? One redhead with a rifle? Who is she?'

Kate glared at him, but said nothing.

Deftly the man called Decker fished Kate's shield from her jacket pocket. 'Special Agent Kate Coppola,' he said. Pocketing the ID, he cuffed one of Kate's wrists, then pulled her arms behind her back and cuffed the other. Kate looked pissed, and Marcus wondered how the blond had gotten the jump on her.

'Your turn, ma'am,' Decker said to Scarlett, and she laughed bitterly.

'Ma'am? You've got to be kidding.'

'We don't kid, ma'am.' Decker pulled Scarlett away from Sweeney, spun her to face the older man and proceeded to cuff her the same way he'd done to Kate.

'Leave Detective Bishop here for now,' Sweeney said. 'I need her for when O'Bannion returns, because he will. He's just made that way. Take the redhead down to the woodchipper.'

Horrified, Marcus could only stare. *Woodchipper*? He had to fight to control his heart rate. His pulse had just shot into the stratosphere.

'I will, sir,' Decker said politely. 'Oh, I found Sean in the garage when I first arrived. I took the liberty of taking him down to the pit too, so you wouldn't have to.'

Sweeney looked first annoyed, then relieved. 'Thank you, Decker. I appreciate that.'

'Anything else, sir?'

'No, that'll be all for now.'

Marcus and Deacon each drew back, pressing into the wall, waiting for the man named Decker to come through the gate with Kate. They could jump him, freeing Kate.

But noise of a struggle met their ears instead. Kate was fighting like a wildcat, trying to free herself. Sweeney stepped away from Scarlett to help Decker subdue Kate.

Seeing their opening, Marcus and Deacon started running, guns drawn, but came to a dead stop when Scarlett, Kate and the big blond Decker all pulled guns on Sweeney. Both Scarlett and Kate had their cuffs dangling from one wrist.

'Approach slowly,' Decker said to Marcus and Deacon without looking at them. Decker held Kate's rifle pointed at Sweeney's head. 'No sudden moves, please.'

'What the hell, Kate?' Deacon demanded.

Kate jerked her head toward Decker. 'Pineapple under the sea,' she said.

'Oh,' Deacon said. 'You could have told me.'

'I was going to,' Kate snapped. 'I've been busy.'

'What?' Marcus demanded.

'I don't know,' Scarlett said. 'He put a gun in my hand when he pretended to cuff me. I went with it.'

Decker handed Kate's rifle back to her and took another pair of handcuffs from his back pocket as Sweeney watched him with clear malice.

'You had me fooled, Mr Decker.'

'That was the point,' Decker said. 'Sir.'

Abruptly Sweeney twisted and leaped back, rolling toward the pile of weapons he'd taken from Scarlett. Decker stumbled, going down on one knee, shock on his face – and a knife sticking out of his side. Handcuffs dangling from one wrist, Sweeney grabbed two of Scarlett's guns – one in each hand – and began shooting

Stunned, Scarlett staggered backward, falling on her butt. Marcus heard a roar, then realized it had come from his own chest. He began firing, only vaguely aware that Deacon and Kate had lifted their weapons as well. It was mass pandemonium for a brief moment as bullets flew. And then, as quickly as the moment had begun, it was over. The silence that followed was heavy, the air thick with the smell of spent gunpowder.

Sweeney lay on his own driveway, broken, his body riddled with bullets, his eyes staring sightlessly up at the sky.

Just like Tala.

Finally, Marcus thought as he ran to where Scarlett lay on her stomach, arms stretched out in front of her, her weapon still clutched in a classic two-hand hold. She'd rolled into position, he realized, and had fired her share of the bullets into Sweeney. She looked up at him, gave him a hard nod, and his knees buckled with relief.

He grabbed her up into his arms, not caring what anyone else thought. Buried his face in her neck and shuddered out the breath he'd been holding. 'Oh God. I thought he'd got you. I thought you were dead.'

'I'm okay,' she murmured. 'His bullet hit the vest. Just knocked the wind out of me.' She flinched when he hugged her harder. 'Maybe bruised me up some.'

Immediately he loosened his hold, his body starting to tremble. Now that it was all over, he was shaking like a damn leaf. He let himself hold her gently for another long moment, then lifted his head to take stock of the situation.

Deacon was crouched next to Sweeney's body, cuffing his lifeless wrists together before checking his pulse. Kate had slung her rifle over her back and was tending to Decker, who primarily looked annoyed as he pulled the knife out of his side.

'I'm okay, Agent Coppola,' he said with self-disgust. 'I can't believe the little fucker stuck me.' He pushed Kate's hands away, his cheeks flushed with embarrassment. 'I'm okay,' he repeated. 'I got hurt worse on the school playground.' The big man slowly came to his feet. 'There's a first aid kit in the laundry room,' he said. 'I'll plug this with some gauze.'

Marcus opened the backpack Isenberg had given them and pulled out four rolls of gauze. He threw three of them to Decker, keeping one to wrap the grazing wound Sweeney had put on Scarlett's right wrist. 'Is he dead?' he asked as he wrapped Scarlett's arm.

Deacon's odd eyes were filled with warm understanding and cold finality. 'Really most sincerely dead,' he said.

Marcus found his lips twitching at the old movie quote from *The Wizard of Oz.* It was the boost he needed, and he lurched to his feet, helping Scarlett to hers. He walked over to Sweeney's body, gratified to see that most of their shots had hit the man's skull. The top part of his head was simply gone. Sweeney's shirt was peppered with bullet holes, the fabric soaked with blood. But there was one area they'd missed in the frenzied shooting.

Marcus deliberately pointed his gun at Sweeney's chest and pulled the trigger, shooting the man in his non-existent heart. 'That was for Cal,' he said quietly. 'And Tala. And all the others.' He shuddered when Scarlett put her arms around him.

'Sshh. It's over. It's done,' she whispered, rocking him.

It was then he realized he was crying. And so was she.

Cincinnati, Ohio
Wednesday 5 August, 11.55 P.M.

Decker was a stubborn fool, Kate thought as she followed the man into the big shed with its circus-tent ceiling. He'd been stabbed, for God's sake, but acted like it was no more than a mosquito bite, insisting that the paramedics try to save Sweeney's son, Sean, instead of treating him. The two paramedics brought up the rear, lugging their gear through the wooded property.

'They're in here,' Decker said as he slid the door of the large shed open. 'Sean, plus Stephanie Anders and Dave Burton. Burton will also need some attention. Sweeney cut the man's ear off.'

'Wonderful,' Kate muttered.

'The young woman has only minor abrasions and bruises,' Decker went on. 'She gave worse than she got, trust me.'

Kate stopped dead in her tracks when she stepped inside, staring at the industrial-sized chipper, the chute extending over a gaping hole in the ground. The air smelled foul and she had to fight to keep from gagging. She was only moderately successful.

'Sorry about the smell,' Decker murmured. 'I was supposed to dispose of all the bodies this week, but I didn't. Kept them as evidence. Chip and Marlene Anders and Demetrius are all buried in shallow graves here, under this roof. Hopefully the ME's office will get all the evidence they need.'

He walked them to the back corner, where he'd erected a hasty partition out of large pieces of plywood. 'I didn't want Sweeney seeing them. He didn't come out here often, but he'd threatened to put Sean through the shredder himself, so I figured he might come back here eventually.' Decker pulled the partition down.

And froze. 'Shit,' he muttered, running to the chair that held the remains of Stephanie Anders. The girl's throat had been slashed, and blood covered the ground around her.

'That's a bit more than minor abrasions,' Kate said quietly.

Decker stood over another chair, this one empty and turned on its side.

Next to it was an empty wheelbarrow, also on its side. Slashed ropes were strewn over the ground. 'Burton is gone,' he said flatly. 'So is Sean.'

'How? I thought you said Sean was almost dead?'

Decker's lips thinned. 'He looked it. He might have been. Either way, Burton's gone.' He picked up one of the slashed ropes. The edge was jagged. 'Sean must have had a knife stashed. I didn't search him. He was handcuffed. *Dammit.*' He looked pissed with himself. 'Either he or Burton cut their ropes. Whichever one of them did it, the pair of them are free.'

Cincinnati, Ohio
Thursday 6 August, 12.10 A.M.

'Water.' Diesel shoved a bottle in Scarlett's hand and one in Marcus's as they approached him at the front of the property where they'd left their vehicle. The paramedics had arrived and one team had already taken care of Gayle. The other team was with Agent Davenport and Kate. 'Is Sweeney dead?'

'Very much so,' Marcus said. He and Scarlett drained the bottles in very thirsty gulps. 'Damn, I needed that.'

Diesel was ready with more. 'Refill your tear wells,' he told Marcus, giving a pointed look to his eyes, red from crying.

'Fuck off,' Marcus said affectionately. He wasn't ashamed of his tears. It had been cathartic to cry, especially once he'd plugged that final bullet in Sweeney's heart.

Scarlett shook her head. 'Where's Gayle?'

'The ambulance took her to County,' Diesel said. 'They're monitoring her heart. I wanted to go with her, but she insisted I stay to take care of you two. Who's Mr Surfer USA?' he asked, pointing at Decker and Kate, who had just arrived from the back property and were talking to Deacon, their expressions dark and angry.

'I think he's the FBI's undercover agent,' Marcus said.

'None of them look too happy at the moment,' Diesel observed.

'They don't, do they?' Scarlett murmured. 'They went to fetch Sweeney's son, who was injured. Since Sweeney's dead, I think we were hoping Sean could provide details. But from the looks of things, I don't think he made it.'

Diesel gave the Feds a wary look. 'No offense, Scarlett, but there's suddenly too much law enforcement around here.'

Scarlett bit back a smile. 'None taken. I'll give your regrets.'

'I can honestly tell Gayle that I've seen you two with my own eyes, alive and kicking. I'm going back to the hospital to check in on her and Stone.'

Backing away from the growing group of federal agents and SWAT team members, he got into his car and drove away.

'Considering he's terrified of hospitals, that just said a lot,' Marcus said mildly, then sobered abruptly when Deacon, Kate and Agent Davenport approached them. 'What's happened?'

'First things first,' Kate said, pointing at each of them as she introduced them to Davenport.

'You were the man deep under,' Marcus said.

'I was,' Davenport said. 'They knew me as Gene Decker. I'd say my cover's pretty well blown at this point.'

Deacon gave Marcus a look that was half-wince. 'But if the Bureau returns Davenport to undercover status, this might be the biggest story of your life that you can never write.'

'But it's over,' Marcus said, then stilled, apprehension settling over his shoulders. 'Why can't we tell the story? It *is* over, right?'

Davenport shook his head. 'Not yet. At least two of the guys got away – Dave Burton, Sweeney's acting head of security, and Sean Cantrell, who was the IT guy – and Sweeney's son. These guys trafficked all kinds of things. Drugs, porn, people.' His mouth twisted. 'Children.'

'We've started a sweep of the property, but they could have slipped away when we were dealing with Sweeney,' Kate said with a scowl. 'We put out a BOLO.'

'Was Woody McCord one of their customers?' Marcus asked.

Davenport's brows raised. 'Yes. You knew him?'

'We exposed him,' Marcus murmured, 'through the *Ledger*, but we didn't go deep enough. Sweeney was afraid we'd keep digging, so he targeted us.'

'He hated you,' Davenport said. 'They all did. But now they're all dead, in prison or stashed.' His shoulders sagged wearily. 'Except for five – the two that got away, Joel Whipple, who did the books, and the new guy in security, whose name is Trevino.'

'There's a fifth guy stashed under a bed in one of the upstairs rooms. Name's Rod Kinsey. He got shot yesterday morning. I gave him some high-power sedatives and he's been asleep ever since. I doubt he'll know anything. He's a low-level flunky.'

'That's only four,' Marcus said.

'Where are Joel and Trevino?' Scarlett asked. 'And how did the first two get away?'

'We don't know yet,' Kate said grimly. 'Burton and Sean were no longer in the shed when we got there. Someone had cut their bonds and slashed Stephanie Anders's throat. She's dead.'

'Good,' Marcus bit out. 'That the Anders woman is dead, I mean. Not that the others are gone.'

Scarlett laid a hand on his arm, a reminder to calm his temper. 'Let's take it from the beginning,' she said. 'Tell us about Sweeney's organization. We know about Demetrius and Alice, but that's it.'

'All right,' Davenport said. 'Sweeney, Demetrius, Joel and Reuben were the owners of this criminal enterprise. Sweeney and Demetrius started out moving drugs up from Florida back in the eighties. Their legit cover was toys, and still is. They moved a lot of teddy bears stuffed with pills. But then Florida tightened its pill laws. That's when they expanded into trafficking – adults and children, for labor and sex. Sweeney was the CEO and arranged for the sales, Demetrius managed the supply base. As far as I could tell, they were tricking immigrants into coming into the country on a temporary visa. They targeted highly educated individuals because they could get more money for them. They got lower-level laborers too. And they forced people into the sex trade from all over – other countries and this country too. Like I said, Reuben was Security and Joel managed Accounting.'

'What was your role?' Scarlett asked.

'I was hired in as a bodyguard for Sweeney, but I wasn't able to get at any of the good information. My handler arranged a little accident – I got shot and couldn't be a bodyguard any longer. I have a math degree and convinced them I could be an accountant, thinking I could get to the books. But I was only working the legit businesses. I wanted to get back into Security but into tactical, not personal, bodyguard services. I figured with a tactical security job I'd be able to access all kinds of information, but they kept me stuck in Accounting and time was passing and I wasn't gathering the intel I was supposed to.'

'So you created a hole and then filled it?' Kate asked.

'Basically. Reuben was the security chief and Dave Burton's boss. Both of them had been cops together in Tennessee. They had some kind of strong history. I wasn't joining that clique, so I had to bust it up. Jason Jackson worked in the security office of the downtown building. I made friends with Jackson and that gave me the excuse to wander up to Security now and then. I was just waiting for my opportunity to break into the network and find the proof I'd been sent in to discover. I got my chance when Tala's tracker was cut off her. I drugged Jackson – he was the guy on duty that morning – then took him home and made it look like he was too ill to work. I really wanted the top job vacated, so I lured Reuben, the chief of security, to where Jackson was, then I drugged Reuben too and put them both in a safe place. I contacted my handler, in code, and told him where to find the two of them.'

'You wanted Reuben's job?' Scarlett asked.

'Not really. I just wanted him out of the way so that I could get better access to the leadership team. Reuben ran a tight ship, kept all his departments separate. I was Sweeney's bodyguard for a while, but Reuben made sure we bodyguards never got close to the real workings of the business.'

'Where is this place where you stashed Reuben and Jason Jackson?' Deacon asked.

'An apartment near my handler's house. My handler parked Reuben's car at the airport hotel, but he was supposed to go from there to the apartment to take those two into custody. Trouble is, my handler and I lost contact. I was getting ready to make an emergency call to the SAC in the field office when you pulled your rifle on me, Agent Coppola. Everything had gone to shit and I didn't want Sweeney's leadership team to completely kill themselves off.'

'I've sent personnel to the apartment,' Kate told them. 'I haven't heard back yet.'

'Did you get access to the data you needed?' Deacon asked.

'Some of it.' Davenport nodded. 'I copied a lot of it. Some of it's still up here.' He tapped his head. 'Some of it's in the computer in the office, although I think Sean destroyed all that.'

'What about Sean?' Scarlett asked. 'You say he was Sweeney's son?'

'Yes. Sweeney's son and daughter both worked for him. Alice you know.'

'Oh yeah,' Marcus said darkly. 'I know Alice.'

Scarlett rubbed his back comfortingly even as she directed her questions to Davenport. 'What was Alice's role, besides being an evil, conniving bitch?'

Davenport's lips twitched. 'Alice was Sweeney's right hand, his heir apparent. The woman is cold as ice and can think on her feet. Sean is IT. Bookish. Likes to keep to himself. I got the vibe that he didn't like his father, but I never pushed because he would have denied it. The blood in the garage is Sean's. He confronted Sweeney about funds that his old man had taken from company coffers, then taunted him that he'd taken the money back for himself. Then he pulled a gun on him. Sweeney wrestled the gun away from him. Sean was a desk jockey and Sweeney still had a lot of physical strength. Sweeney overpowered Sean, tied him up, then cut off fingers and toes until Sean revealed bank account numbers and passwords.'

'You stood there outside the garage and . . . just listened?' Scarlett said, looking appalled at the thought that Davenport could have witnessed such a thing without stopping it.

'I "just listened" from the small shed,' Davenport corrected icily. 'Once I got access to Sweeney and his house, I planted bugs everywhere that I could. The shed was my listening post. If I'd intervened, my cover would have been blown and three years of work would have gone down the toilet.'

'I apologize,' Scarlett said stiffly, at first annoyed at his response, but then her expression softened. 'That must have been very difficult for you,' she added, her compassion showing.

Davenport acknowledged her words with a half-nod. 'It was,' he said. 'I've known bits and pieces about what's gone on for the past three years. I've saved people where I could. But of course I couldn't do anything for most of the victims. After Sweeney got what he needed from Sean, he threatened to put him through the chipper alive.' He glanced at Marcus. 'He stopped torturing Sean because he had to meet you, so he left him tied up in the garage. I hid Sean away, knowing he was the one with all the real information. That's why I'd been willing to risk calling the field office – to get medical attention for Sean.'

'But Sean is gone,' Marcus said, shaking his head. 'And Burton, who worked for Reuben, is gone too?'

'Yeah. Sean must have had a knife. All the ropes were cut.'

'Why did Sean betray his father?' Scarlett asked.

'Because Sweeney killed his mother.'

'Oh,' Kate said. 'That's pretty powerful motivation.'

Davenport nodded. 'Sean had motivation and brains. We need to find him and Burton.'

'What about Marlene and Chip Anders?' Scarlett asked.

Decker sliced his finger across his throat. 'Sweeney made sure it hurt. I buried them in the big shed. Demetrius is also in one of those graves, but his body is . . . messed up. Sweeney used knives to get information about contracts and suppliers from Demetrius before he died.'

'Good,' Marcus said coldly. 'That bastard shot Phillip and Edgar and killed Agent Spangler. He needed to be put down.'

'Who else did you kill or stash?' Kate asked.

'I didn't kill anybody,' Davenport explained. 'I stashed Reuben, Jason Jackson, Dave Burton, Stephanie Anders and Belle Connor.'

'Drake's sister,' Deacon said. 'Good. I was at that crime scene. I'm glad she's okay. Where is she?'

'I told her that I was a cop and that her life was in danger,' Davenport said. To not go home, but to find a friend and keep her head down for a few days. I hoped she'd call the real cops, actually, to verify my warning. I didn't mean for her to hide from you guys. I messed up her house a little to make it look like a legit abduction, hoping you'd investigate and shine a light on her brother, Drake. Drake would have led you to Stephanie Anders, then to Chip, and then to Sweeney. Although you seem to have found out about Anders on your own.'

'We found Anders through their dog,' Scarlett said. 'Although we never found the dog itself.'

'Marlene claimed it was with its handler. I'm sure the handler's name is written down somewhere in Chip's house. I've got Belle Connor's cell number. We can probably tell her the coast is clear now.'

Deacon tilted his head, studying Davenport. 'You were at Chip Anders' house. You left Mila and Erica's trackers for us to find.'

'Yeah. That nearly got me caught.'

'It was important,' Deacon said. 'Thank you.'

'You also called in the tip about Alice shooting at the suspect from the ankle tracker manufacturer,' Marcus said.

'No, that wasn't me. That was Sean. He wanted to get Alice out of the way.'

'What about Joel?' Kate asked. 'The accountant.'

'He actually may be willing to turn state's evidence. I got the impression that Joel wants out. You should find all the evidence you need in Sweeney's house and office. I for one would be happy if I never went back to either. I'd left for good earlier today, hoping to contact my handler, but then I heard that the *Ledger* had been attacked and that Sweeney had taken Gayle hostage. So I came back.'

'Thank you,' Scarlett said. 'We're all pretty glad you did.'

Marcus rechecked the wound on Scarlett's arm, satisfied when he saw the bleeding had mostly stopped. 'We're going back to the hospital to get this looked at and to be with my family. You know how to find us if you need anything else.'

'And we need to fully brief SAC Zimmerman,' Davenport said meaningfully.

Marcus wondered what else the undercover agent had to share, but didn't even bother asking. They weren't going to tell him any more than they had, and frankly he was stunned that they'd told him that much.

Kate pointed to the paramedics waiting by the ambulance parked at the very end of the entry road. 'Davenport, let them check you out. And if you say you don't need to, then you're a liar,' she snapped when the big man opened his mouth to probably say that very thing. 'You've soaked the gauze you stuck in that wound and now you're leaking out onto your shirt. I don't want you collapsing on me from blood loss while we're debriefing with my boss.'

Davenport touched his side and grimaced when his fingers came away sticky. 'Shit. Fine. But I'm not riding in that damn thing.'

Marcus, Scarlett and Deacon left them to their bickering. 'She's always been a little bossy,' Deacon whispered when they'd gotten a few feet away.

'I heard that, Novak!' Kate called without missing a beat, making Deacon grin.

'And she's got ears like—'

He never finished his sentence. The tail lights on the ambulance suddenly shattered and Davenport staggered, before falling to his knees. He looked down at the blood that already soaked his shirt, his face frozen in shock.

'Everybody down!' Deacon shouted.

Marcus threw himself over Scarlett, hurling them behind the parked ambulance. She gave a little grunt of pain when they hit the ground. Dammit. She'd already been bruised by the bullet that her Kevlar vest had stopped earlier. 'I'm sorry,' he said. 'Are you okay?'

'Yes. Let me up.' She rolled out from under him and onto her hands and knees. Her eyes darted around as she evaluated the scene, then abruptly widened. 'Holy shit. Kate!'

Kate had taken off running down the road toward the main highway, shouldering her rifle as she went. Face contorting in pain, Scarlett pushed herself to her feet and ran after her, drawing her weapon as she ran, pressing her forearm to her ribs.

Marcus followed Scarlett, sparing a backward glance at Deacon who was kneeling next to Davenport, who wasn't moving at all. The paramedics had Davenport's shirt off and . . . *Shit.* It didn't look good. The undercover agent's face was growing paler by the second as the paramedics tried to stop his bleeding.

Suddenly gunfire cracked the air, three rapid shots, followed seconds later by the loud crash of metal and glass. Marcus's heart went into overdrive as he sprinted after Scarlett.

He found her around a bend in the road, staring into the distance, where a black car had just crashed into a clump of trees. Kate stood midway between Scarlett and the wrecked car, her rifle still shouldered and ready to fire at anyone who emerged.

'She shot out their back window and two tires,' Scarlett said, sounding slightly in awe. 'From a half-mile away as they fishtailed.'

Wow, Marcus thought, damn impressed. 'Davenport's down. Deacon's okay.'

She nodded brusquely, her eyes never leaving the black car as she began approaching Kate and the crash scene. Three of the cruisers and two of the Feds' unmarked cars that had been stationed up by the ambulance came roaring past them, surrounding the black car.

'One of the passengers fired at Kate as they tried to get away, but his aim wasn't nearly as good as hers,' Scarlett said, left forearm still braced against her ribs. 'Hopefully she got the little cocksucker who shot Davenport.'

'Are you all right?' Marcus asked, pointing to her side.

'Probably a few bruised ribs. Not likely anything broken. And yes, I'll let the ER look at it,' she added irritably. 'After we get this scene secured.'

When they got close to the black car, Marcus could smell the odor left by the deployed airbags. There were three people inside the car and none of them had been wearing seat belts. None of them appeared to be conscious.

Marcus watched carefully as the officers and Feds checked out the interior of the car, confiscating weapons and ensuring that none of the passengers were still armed before cuffing them. The driver, a young man who appeared to be of Italian heritage, had been faking his unconsciousness and tried to knife one of the cops, but the crash had left him off balance and groggy. The cop was able to easily disarm and cuff him.

The front-seat passenger was genuinely unconscious, as was the man in the backseat, who was missing several fingers and toes. Sweeney's son Sean, Marcus thought. *The SOB.*

Kate had come close to the car, but her eyes were on the trees around the wreck rather than the passengers. She was scanning the scene, still looking for threats, when the ambulance drove by at a careful speed.

Deacon had been following the ambulance in his own vehicle, but pulled over when he got to where they waited. 'They're taking Davenport to the hospital. It's pretty bad, Kate.'

Kate's back stiffened. 'Dammit. Davenport could have ID'd these guys.'

Marcus knew that civilians might hear Kate's words and believe her calloused, but that wasn't true. He'd seen her with the Bautistas that afternoon. She'd been patient and kind. Right now Kate was focused on the job, her adrenaline still pumping from the expert shots she'd just taken. Marcus remembered the focus. It had kept him alive more times than he'd like to recall. When her heart and brain slowed back to normal, Kate would feel fear and sadness, just like everyone else.

'Which is why they targeted him,' Deacon said logically. 'It was a through-and-through. He might have a collapsed lung.'

Marcus winced, remembering his own pierced lung nine months before. 'That won't kill him,' he said to Kate. 'It didn't kill me. Hurt like a bitch, but I'm still standing.'

Kate met his eyes and he could see she was already returning to normal. 'Thank you. He has a lot of information that we need. Obviously Sweeney's holdouts felt the same way.' She took a look at Scarlett. 'Go get yourself checked out. We have this under control. And thank you for backing me up.'

'You didn't need me,' Scarlett said. 'You had it all under control. Keep me apprised?'

Kate gave her a hard nod. 'Absolutely.'

Cincinnati, Ohio
Thursday 6 August, 2.15 A.M.

A cheer rose up when Scarlett followed Marcus back into the OR waiting room. Marcus spread his arms wide and took a bow, rolling his eyes all the while. They'd gotten the call that Stone was awake and asking for them as they were driving back to the hospital, but getting Scarlett's arm stitched up had taken time. Her ribs were bruised but not fractured, just as she'd figured.

Scarlett's father was there to give her a huge bear hug, but she lifted a finger in warning. 'Lightly, Dad. Please,' she said before walking into his arms.

Jonas held her like she was made of spun glass. 'You did something wonderful today, baby girl,' he whispered in her ear. 'Remember this moment, for all of those moments when you want to shove explosives where the sun don't shine.'

Her mother hugged her just as gently, then crushed Marcus in an embrace that surprised him, commanding them both to come to supper the very next day – which was actually that same day. Scarlett wasn't sure she'd be awake, even by supper. She was truly running on fumes and planned to sleep for a week. But she promised her mother, knowing that this was a new start for her and her parents, and for her and Marcus.

Jill threw her arms around Scarlett's neck, thanking her over and over for Gayle's safe return.

Scarlett grasped the girl's shoulders and looked her in the eye. 'You made a difference, telling me about that letter. It's unlikely that any of us would have made it back if Marcus had met Sweeney at the park. It would have been an ambush. So thank you.'

The young woman walked on air for a long time after that.

Marcus and Scarlett gradually made their way back to Stone, who put a finger to his lips when they came in. Delores was curled up in the chair next to him, her hand holding his through the bed rails.

'What is this?' Marcus asked fondly.

'She takes in strays,' Stone said with a shrug.

Marcus's eyes narrowed. 'Never, Stone. I never want to hear you put yourself down like that again. Please.'

Stone shrugged again, his eyes closing, but not before they saw the pain there. 'Cal . . . Bridget. Jerry and those guards. I tried, Marcus.'

'I know. I also know you saved Jill and the other three that you shoved down to the archive room. You're a hero, Stone.'

'Finally,' he murmured. 'Maybe.' He gestured for Scarlett to come close. 'He's in Miami.'

Scarlett frowned in confusion. 'Who?'

'Phineas Bishop, Corporal. Your brother, right?'

Scarlett's throat closed up, her hand flying to cover her mouth as a sob tried to get free. 'You found Phin? How? I've tried for so long.'

'If he doesn't want to be found – or thinks he doesn't – you'd never find him. I spent some time last night sending emails to old Army pals. I know some people who work with vets. On the ground, not in hospitals. Somebody knew somebody who knew Phin. His address is on my computer. I'll send it to you as soon as I can.'

She was having trouble breathing, new tears starting to fall when Marcus slid his arm around her waist, holding her up. 'You . . . Oh my God, Stone,' she whispered. 'Do you know what you've done?'

'Yeah, I do exactly. I gave you your brother back. You gave me mine back too. We're even now.' He looked up, met Marcus's eyes. 'No more death wishes, right?'

Marcus choked out a laugh. 'No, I'm good.'

Stone closed his eyes wearily. 'Really sleepy. Gayle's safe? All the bad guys dead?'

'Yes and yes,' Marcus said. 'We killed the last one ourselves. It was a tie. Me and Scar and Deacon and Kate. And Davenport.'

Stone struggled to open his eyes. 'Who's Davenport?'

Scarlett was still sniffling. 'We'll tell you later. Sleep now. We'll be back.' She kissed his forehead gently. 'Thank you.'

Stone's lips curved. 'You're welcome. Hey, do something for me?'

'Name it,' she whispered.

'Wow. This is power,' he murmured. 'Can you get me all the gear I need to take care of a dog? I think Delores has talked me into adopting one.'

She brushed the hair from his forehead. 'I'll see you tomorrow and you can tell me exactly what you want.'

Marcus led her into the hall. 'Are you going to tell your folks about Phin?'

'I think I'll wait until I get the address. Maybe at dinner tomorrow.'

Marcus let out a long breath. 'Today, you mean. All I want is to go home and fall asleep in your purple room with your dog hiding under the bed. I might never leave.'

They'd made it to the elevator when they heard Kate Coppola calling their names. 'Scarlett, Marcus, wait up.'

They stepped back from the elevator doors. 'What's the news on Davenport?' Scarlett asked.

'Not as bad as we thought. The bullet was a through and through, here.' Kate tapped the left side of her chest. 'He has a cracked rib, pulmonary contusions, and a hemopneumothorax.' She said the words carefully. 'In English, that means he's got a bruised lung and blood in his chest cavity. They gave him a blood transfusion and put in a chest tube.'

Beside her, Marcus grimaced. 'That sounds pretty bad, Kate.'

'Could have been worse. They've got him on a ventilator and put him in a medically induced coma so that he can heal. Apparently the healing part hurts like hell.'

'My injury was a bit different,' Marcus said, 'but the hurting like hell part is the same.'

'What about the three guys in the car? Sweeney's guys?'

'The driver is Danny Trevino and the guy in the front passenger seat was Dave Burton. Both former cops, so their prints were on file. Trevino served time too, so his popped out of AFIS. Trevino ID'd the guy in the backseat as Sean Cantrell, Sweeney's son. Burton died on the way to the ER. My bullet,' she added grimly.

'You kept him from continuing to shoot at us,' Scarlett said levelly. 'Your bullet may have saved our lives.'

'I know. But I wanted him alive to talk. Trevino claims he got a call from Burton – his boss – who needed a pickup. He met them at the main road, presumably while we were confronting Sweeney in the driveway. Burton told Trevino that Sean was bleeding badly but was able to tell Burton about the jackknife stashed in his shoe. Burton flung himself to the ground, chair and all, and managed to get to the knife. He sawed the ropes off Sean, then

Sean got him loose. Burton used the knife to slit Stephanie Anders's throat.'

Scarlett grimaced. 'Even with a sharpened jackknife that wasn't a quick death. She probably suffered. Not that I'm complaining, mind you.'

'I'm not sorry she's dead,' Marcus said tightly. 'But I would have liked Tala's family to have their day in court with her.'

'I know,' Kate said kindly.

'Don't keep me in suspense,' Scarlett said impatiently. 'What about Sean?'

'He's in surgery. The crash hurt him worse than Sweeney did, ironically. Hopefully he'll survive, because he's apparently the one with all the information.' Kate sighed. 'Davenport's handler and the two guys that Davenport stashed are all dead. Looks like a case of a hidden knife again. The crime-scene guys found a ripped hem in Reuben Blackwell's pants. Reuben and Jackson had nearly freed themselves when Agent Symmes came into the apartment. There was a struggle. One of Sweeney's guys stabbed Symmes, but he shot them before they could get away. All three of them died.'

Scarlett sighed. 'Did Agent Symmes have a family?'

'Yeah. Parents only. No wife or kids. Zimmerman and Troy went to do the notification.'

'At least Deacon didn't have to do it,' Scarlett murmured. 'What about Davenport being in a coma? How long does the thorax thing take to heal?'

'Once they bring him out of his coma, a few days to a week. He recorded all the bugged conversations in Sweeney's house, so I have tapes to listen to in the meanwhile.' Kate smiled, and it wasn't pleasant. 'And there's always Alice. I'm going to enjoy that interrogation.'

'She won't tell you anything,' Marcus said wearily.

'Don't be so sure,' Kate said. 'How's Gayle Ennis?'

'Resting comfortably,' Marcus said, his lips curving with a genuine smile that took Scarlett's breath away once again. 'They'll keep her tonight for observation, then let her go home tomorrow. My stepfather, my sister and I will help Gayle's niece take care of her.'

He hadn't included his mother in that caretaker list, Scarlett thought, and now that she'd met Della Yarborough, she understood why. There was a frailty, almost a transparency about the woman, as if one more blow would break her. She thought about how her own mother had sat next to the woman who'd been a stranger to her before tonight. Jackie Bishop had lent Della her strength, and Scarlett felt a surge of pride and love for her mom. And a wave of pity for Marcus for having to be the strong one all the time.

Not anymore. Scarlett would make sure that the man beside her understood that he didn't have to carry all the weight ever again.

'I'm glad Gayle is safe,' Kate said, then hesitated. 'I'm sorry about your friends at the *Ledger*. Please let me know if there's anything you need.'

Scarlett slid her arm around Marcus's waist, gave him a brief but hard hug. 'We will,' she said. 'Now if there's nothing else, we need to get some rest. We have a lot to do tomorrow.'

'Goodnight then,' Kate said. 'And thank you both.'

Scarlett steered Marcus into the nearest elevator, then hit the button for the lobby. 'Together,' she said softly. 'Do you understand, Marcus? You don't have to do any of this alone. You have your family and friends. And you have *my* family and friends.'

His throat worked as he swallowed hard. 'And you?'

'Yes,' she said simply. 'Let's go home.'

Epilogue

Cincinnati, Ohio
Wednesday 12 August, 8.30 P.M.

Scarlett put the last of the dishes in the dishwasher, then wiped down the new stove that had magically appeared in her kitchen two days after they'd killed Sweeney and rescued Gayle. It was the Viking six-burner, two-oven model she'd shown Marcus the first time she'd brought him home. The first time they'd made love.

They'd made a lot of love in the week since, sometimes fast and sometimes slow. Sometimes simply because Marcus had ghosts in his eyes. Scarlett thought that tonight would be one of those times.

'I think that was everything,' her mother said after doing one last check of Scarlett's house for any plates or silverware their open-house guests might have set aside and forgotten. 'I even had your brother check under the beds in case your dogs dragged any bones up there.'

Scarlett smiled at her. 'Thank you, but Zat and BB have been outside all afternoon. If they got a bone, they buried it out back.' Both dogs had been Marcus's shadow today, rarely straying more than a few feet away. Scarlett kissed her mother's cheek. 'Thanks for everything. I've never done an open house after a funeral before. You made this one they'll all remember.'

They'd laid Cal to rest that afternoon and the mood had been somber. Until her mother started to mingle, asking everyone for their favorite memory of Cal. Soon enough, all of Cal's friends were laughing. Some tears, too, but a lot of laughter.

'It's a skill I've picked up over the years,' her mother said, then sighed. 'Unfortunately.'

Because her father and brothers had been to more than their share of funerals too. It was part of being a cop. Or a cop's wife.

'I'm going home now, Scarlett,' she said, patting her daughter's cheek, then looked over her shoulder to where Marcus sat on the back deck, all alone now. 'Take care of him.'

Like she'd seen her mother care for her father all her life. 'I will.'

592

alone in the dark

Locking the front door behind her mom, Scarlett went abruptly still. Music was coming from the deck. Marcus was playing his guitar. She hadn't heard him play in person – only on the tapes he'd made in the park.

He'd sung the Vince Gill ballad for Cal this afternoon as everyone had gathered at the man's graveside. Scarlett had been expecting Marcus to sing, so she was prepared emotionally. What she hadn't expected was the sweetness of Audrey's voice as she'd sung backup in perfect harmony, holding on tight to Marcus's hand. Brother and sister had sung a cappella and not an eye was left dry – except Marcus's own.

Quietly Scarlett joined him on the deck, sitting next to him on the porch swing she'd rescued from a yard sale. From here they had an amazing view of the river. He gave her a quick glance from the corner of his eye and started to put the guitar away, but she stopped him.

'No, I want to hear it. What were you playing?'

He rested his arm atop the guitar's curved side, then propped his chin on his arm. 'That was nice. What your mother did today. Reminding us of why we loved Cal so much.'

He hadn't answered her question, but she let it go. 'I know. Mom's good at that.'

He bent his mouth into a half-frown. 'Cal hated "Go Rest High". Always made him cry.'

Scarlett had been sitting between Marcus and Diesel on the front row of folding chairs at the graveside, and when Marcus had begun to sing, Diesel had lost it. The big man's shoulders had shaken as he'd sobbed his heart out. Scarlett had ended up patting his back through the song and letting him cry on her shoulder.

Marcus hadn't shed a tear until he'd returned to sit next to her, and even then he hadn't made a sound. He'd bowed his head, his shoulders heaving as he'd silently grieved. Scarlett had rubbed his back too, through the dark suit he'd worn.

That he still wore. He hadn't changed after coming back to her house after the graveside service. He still wore the tie, too, although he'd tugged it away from his collar.

Abruptly he thumped his thumb against the guitar's glossy face, his expression annoyed. 'I shouldn't have sung it. I should have sung what Cal liked.'

Scarlett rubbed his back in slow, large circles, just as she'd done at the service. 'I think it helped the attendees,' she murmured. 'It's one of those expected things. Helps people have closure. Funerals are for those we leave behind anyway.' He shrugged, saying nothing. Feeling like she'd answered the test question incorrectly, she scooted closer to him on the swing, sending them rocking. 'What was Cal's favorite song?'

His lips didn't smile. '"What a Wonderful World",' he murmured, and then she recognized the song he'd been strumming. 'I thought of singing it, but it's not a wonderful world. I didn't want to be disrespectful to the families of those we lost in the shooting. For them it won't be a wonderful world for a long, long time. But did I disrespect Cal?'

'I think Cal loved you, Marcus, so much that a little thing like that wouldn't have bothered him at all. You might be right, though, that the other families would have been hurt. My grandpa used to say that if you were in doubt on something like that, don't do it. It's not worth the cost. But you could sing it right now. For him. And for me.'

'All right.' He began to pick the tune, and she realized that she was holding her breath, waiting for him to sing. His voice was the opposite of Louis Armstrong's – smooth where Louis had been growly and gruff – but he made the song just as beautiful.

When he'd finished singing and his guitar had grown quiet, she cradled his face in her hands and kissed him with all the sweetness she could muster. Quickly he took over the kiss, blindly setting the instrument in its stand so that he could pull her onto his lap. When he finally lifted his head, they were both breathing hard.

'I needed that,' he whispered.

'So did I.'

A slow grin spread over his face when he lifted his eyes to the yard next door. 'We have company.'

Mrs Pepper stood on her side of the fence, a look of rapture on her face. She recovered when she saw them looking at her, giving them a little wave. 'I baked you cookies, Marcus,' she called. 'I'll leave them on my front porch. You come get them whenever you like.'

'Thank you, Mrs Pepper,' he called back, smiling when she scurried back into her house. 'She's going to make me fat with those cookies.'

'Nah. I plan to work you hard, painting and fixing stuff. Then I plan to play hard.' She tapped his lips with her finger. 'And no middle school "hard" jokes. You're worse than Stone and Diesel.'

'Who do you think taught Stone everything he knows? Diesel, he came warped.'

She chuckled, content to sit on his lap while he lazily rocked the swing with one foot. 'I always thought it was "dogs say goodnight". The song, I mean. I thought old Louis was singing "bright blessed day, the dogs say goodnight",' not "dark sacred night".'

He laughed out loud for the first time that day, and her heart smiled. 'I kind of like dogs saying goodnight better,' he said, then rocked her for a little while as they watched the sky turn rosy.

'It was nice to see Tabby Anders this afternoon,' Scarlett said. 'She came with Annabelle Church. Tabby's gone to live with her. So have the Bautistas, at least until they get on their feet. Their application for the visa to stay here in the country is going well at this point.'

'I know. They talked to me too today. I know Phillip wished he could be there. Edgar, too.'

'I'm just glad they're both going to be all right,' she said fervently. 'Oh, and I saw Kate.'

'I saw her, but I didn't get a chance to talk to her. Did you?'

'I did. Agent Davenport woke up this morning. Hopefully they'll take him off the ventilator so that he can talk to her. The doctors are saying he'll make a full recovery.'

'That's very good news,' Marcus said, relieved.

Yes, it was, because Sweeney's son Sean hadn't made it. He'd died of his injuries two days after trying to take over his father's business. Scarlett only hoped his pain had been unbearable. But speaking his name aloud seemed wrong at the moment, when they were trying to think of all the lovely things that made the world wonderful.

'Did you see that couple that came up to me after the graveside service?' Marcus asked after another few minutes of silence.

'Which one? The cemetery was super-crowded.'

'The woman who looked like she was twelve months' pregnant.'

'Oh, right. I did see her. Why? Who were they?'

'She was one of the women we helped escape her abusive husband four years ago. She's made a life for herself and her kids. Finished her degree. The man she was with is her new husband of about a year. The baby is due in a few weeks. She said she was having a boy and asked if it would be okay if they named him after Cal.'

'Oh wow.' Scarlett pulled back far enough to see his face. 'That's beautiful.'

'That's what I said. Then I asked the new husband if he was okay with that and didn't he want to name the baby after himself. He said naming it after one of us had been his idea. That if we hadn't gotten her free, he wouldn't have a family today.'

Scarlett's eyes stung. 'That's lovely,' she whispered, not trusting her voice.

Marcus smiled the smile she loved the best, the one that filled his eyes.

'Then the husband said he was grateful we'd said it was okay to choose Cal, because he didn't want a kid named Diesel. He was even more relieved when I told him that Diesel's real name is Elvis.'

Scarlett laughed. 'I guess he would be relieved about that.'

'So it is a wonderful world,' he said quietly. 'For them.'

Scarlett sighed. 'You can't fix everything for everyone, Marcus. You can only do your best, one day at a time. Sometimes bad things happen and we can't change them. Some people are going to get away with murder and some families will be broken. I can't put every killer behind bars and you can't save every abused mother and child.'

'We do what we can,' he murmured. 'But if I'm not doing what I was doing before, what will I do?'

'You mean how can you continue helping people but do it legally so that your girlfriend doesn't have to throw your ass in jail?' she asked dryly.

He kissed the tip of her nose. 'Yes. That.'

She rested her head on his chest. 'I don't know what you should do, but I know you'll figure it out. Whatever you decide to do, you need to remember that you're not alone. Not ever again. Got that, Mr O'Bannion?'

'I think I got it, Detective. I think I should start building a gazebo tomorrow. With screens to keep out the bugs that are eating me alive. And maybe a shade or two for privacy.'

'Mrs Pepper's watching us again?'

He smiled. 'From her upstairs window.'

Scarlett smiled back. 'Then I say we give her a show.'

He kissed her hard. 'I don't think her heart can take what I have in mind.'

She laughed when he stood, carrying her in his arms as if she weighed nothing. 'I bet she's swooning right now,' she said.

'Good for her. Are you swooning?'

'I have been since the moment I first heard your voice. Sing for me and I'm putty in your hands. Play for me and . . . well, hopefully *your* heart can take what happens next.'

He dipped her so that she could grab his guitar. 'I think I'm willing to risk it.'

About Karen Rose

Karen Rose was born in Maryland and was introduced to suspense and horror at the tender age of eight when she accidentally read Poe's *The Pit and the Pendulum*.

After marrying her childhood sweetheart, Karen worked as a chemical engineer (she holds two patents) and a teacher, before taking up a full-time writing career when the characters in her head refused to be silenced. Now Karen is more than happy to share space in her head with her characters and her writing has been rewarded with a series of bestsellers in the UK, the US and beyond.

Karen lives in sunny Florida with her husband and their two children.